The Octopus: A Story of California

and

The Pit: a Story of Chicago

Wilder Publications, Inc.
PO Box 243
Blacksburg, VA 24060-0243

ISBN 13: 978-1-5154-3208-1
First Edition

10 9 8 7 6 5 4 3 2 1

The Octopus: A Story of California

and

The Pit: a Story of Chicago

Frank Norris

The Octopus: A Story of California

BOOK 1

I

Just after passing Caraher's saloon, on the County Road that ran south from Bonneville, and that divided the Broderson ranch from that of Los Muertos, Presley was suddenly aware of the faint and prolonged blowing of a steam whistle that he knew must come from the railroad shops near the depot at Bonneville. In starting out from the ranch house that morning, he had forgotten his watch, and was now perplexed to know whether the whistle was blowing for twelve or for one o'clock. He hoped the former. Early that morning he had decided to make a long excursion through the neighbouring country, partly on foot and partly on his bicycle, and now noon was come already, and as yet he had hardly started. As he was leaving the house after breakfast, Mrs. Derrick had asked him to go for the mail at Bonneville, and he had not been able to refuse.

He took a firmer hold of the cork grips of his handlebars—the road being in a wretched condition after the recent hauling of the crop—and quickened his pace. He told himself that, no matter what the time was, he would not stop for luncheon at the ranch house, but would push on to Guadalajara and have a Spanish dinner at Solotari's, as he had originally planned.

There had not been much of a crop to haul that year. Half of the wheat on the Broderson ranch had failed entirely, and Derrick himself had hardly raised more than enough to supply seed for the winter's sowing. But such little hauling as there had been had reduced the roads thereabouts to a lamentable condition, and, during the dry season of the past few months, the layer of dust had deepened and thickened to such an extent that more than once Presley was obliged to dismount and trudge along on foot, pushing his bicycle in front of him.

It was the last half of September, the very end of the dry season, and all Tulare County, all the vast reaches of the San Joaquin Valley—in fact all South Central California, was bone dry, parched, and baked and crisped after four months of cloudless weather, when the day seemed always at noon, and the sun blazed white hot over the valley from the Coast Range in the west to the foothills of the Sierras in the east.

As Presley drew near to the point where what was known as the Lower Road struck off through the Rancho de Los Muertos, leading on to Guadalajara, he came upon one of the county watering-tanks, a great, iron-hooped tower of wood, straddling clumsily on its four uprights by the roadside. Since the day of its completion, the storekeepers and retailers of Bonneville had painted their advertisements upon it. It was a landmark. In that reach of level fields, the white letters upon it could be read for miles. A watering-trough stood near by, and, as he was very thirsty, Presley resolved to stop for a moment to get a drink.

He drew abreast of the tank and halted there, leaning his bicycle against the fence. A couple of men in white overalls were repainting the surface of the tank, seated on swinging platforms that hung by hooks from the roof. They were painting a sign—an advertisement. It was all but finished and read, "S. Behrman, Real Estate, Mortgages, Main Street, Bonneville, Opposite the Post Office." On the horse-trough that stood in the shadow of the tank was another freshly painted inscription: "S. Behrman Has Something To Say To You."

As Presley straightened up after drinking from the faucet at one end of the horse-trough, the watering-cart itself laboured into view around the turn of the Lower Road. Two mules and two horses, white with dust, strained leisurely in the traces, moving at a snail's pace, their limp ears marking the time; while perched high upon the seat, under a yellow cotton wagon umbrella, Presley recognised Hooven, one of Derrick's tenants, a German, whom every one called "Bismarck," an excitable little man with a perpetual grievance and an endless flow of broken English.

"Hello, Bismarck," said Presley, as Hooven brought his team to a standstill by the tank, preparatory to refilling.

"Yoost der men I look for, Mist'r Praicely," cried the other, twisting the reins around the brake. "Yoost one minute, you wait, hey? I wanta talk mit you."

Presley was impatient to be on his way again. A little more time wasted, and the day would be lost. He had nothing to do with the management of the ranch, and if Hooven wanted any advice from him, it was so much breath wasted. These uncouth brutes of farmhands and petty ranchers, grimed with the soil they worked upon, were odious to him beyond words. Never could he feel in sympathy with them, nor with their lives, their ways, their marriages, deaths, bickerings, and all the monotonous round of their sordid existence.

"Well, you must be quick about it, Bismarck," he answered sharply. "I'm late for dinner, as it is."

"Soh, now. Two minuten, und I be mit you." He drew down the overhanging spout of the tank to the vent in the circumference of the cart and pulled the chain that let out the water. Then he climbed down from the seat, jumping from the tire of the wheel, and taking Presley by the arm led him a few steps down the road.

"Say," he began. "Say, I want to hef some converzations mit you. Yoost der men I want to see. Say, Caraher, he tole me dis morgen—say, he tole me Mist'r Derrick gowun to farm der whole demn rench hisseluf der next yahr. No more tenants. Say,

Caraher, he tole me all der tenants get der sach; Mist'r Derrick gowun to work der whole demn rench hisseluf, hey? ME, I get der sach alzoh, hey? You hef hear about dose ting? Say, me, I hef on der ranch been sieben yahr—seven yahr. Do I alzoh—"

"You'll have to see Derrick himself or Harran about that, Bismarck," interrupted Presley, trying to draw away. "That's something outside of me entirely."

But Hooven was not to be put off. No doubt he had been meditating his speech all the morning, formulating his words, preparing his phrases.

"Say, no, no," he continued. "Me, I wanta stay bei der place; seven yahr I hef stay. Mist'r Derrick, he doand want dot I should be ge-sacked. Who, den, will der ditch ge-tend? Say, you tell 'um Bismarck hef gotta sure stay bei der place. Say, you hef der pull mit der Governor. You speak der gut word for me."

"Harran is the man that has the pull with his father, Bismarck," answered Presley. "You get Harran to speak for you, and you're all right."

"Sieben yahr I hef stay," protested Hooven, "and who will der ditch ge-tend, und alle dem cettles drive?"

"Well, Harran's your man," answered Presley, preparing to mount his bicycle.

"Say, you hef hear about dose ting?"

"I don't hear about anything, Bismarck. I don't know the first thing about how the ranch is run."

"UND DER PIPE-LINE GE-MEND," Hooven burst out, suddenly remembering a forgotten argument. He waved an arm. "Ach, der pipe-line bei der Mission Greek, und der waater-hole for dose cettles. Say, he doand doo ut HIMSELLUF, berhaps, I doand tink."

"Well, talk to Harran about it."

"Say, he doand farm der whole demn rench bei hisseluf. Me, I gotta stay."

But on a sudden the water in the cart gushed over the sides from the vent in the top with a smart sound of splashing. Hooven was forced to turn his attention to it. Presley got his wheel under way.

"I hef some converzations mit Herran," Hooven called after him. "He doand doo ut bei hisseluf, den, Mist'r Derrick; ach, no. I stay bei der rench to drive dose cettles."

He climbed back to his seat under the wagon umbrella, and, as he started his team again with great cracks of his long whip, turned to the painters still at work upon the sign and declared with some defiance:

"Sieben yahr; yais, sir, seiben yahr I hef been on dis rench. Git oop, you mule you, hoop!"

Meanwhile Presley had turned into the Lower Road. He was now on Derrick's land, division No. I, or, as it was called, the Home ranch, of the great Los Muertos Rancho. The road was better here, the dust laid after the passage of Hooven's watering-cart, and, in a few minutes, he had come to the ranch house itself, with its white picket fence, its few flower beds, and grove of eucalyptus trees. On the lawn at the side of the house, he saw Harran in the act of setting out the automatic sprinkler. In the shade of the house, by the porch, were two or three of the greyhounds, part of the pack that were used to hunt down jack-rabbits, and Godfrey, Harran's prize deerhound.

Presley wheeled up the driveway and met Harran by the horse-block. Harran was Magnus Derrick's youngest son, a very well-looking young fellow of twenty-three or twenty-five. He had the fine carriage that marked his father, and still further resembled him in that he had the Derrick nose–hawk-like and prominent, such as one sees in the later portraits of the Duke of Wellington. He was blond, and incessant exposure to the sun had, instead of tanning him brown, merely heightened the colour of his cheeks. His yellow hair had a tendency to curl in a forward direction, just in front of the ears.

Beside him, Presley made the sharpest of contrasts. Presley seemed to have come of a mixed origin; appeared to have a nature more composite, a temperament more complex. Unlike Harran Derrick, he seemed more of a character than a type. The sun had browned his face till it was almost swarthy. His eyes were a dark brown, and his forehead was the forehead of the intellectual, wide and high, with a certain unmistakable lift about it that argued education, not only of himself, but of his people before him. The impression conveyed by his mouth and chin was that of a delicate and highly sensitive nature, the lips thin and loosely shut together, the chin small and rather receding. One guessed that Presley's refinement had been gained only by a certain loss of strength. One expected to find him nervous, introspective, to discover that his mental life was not at all the result of impressions and sensations that came to him from without, but rather of thoughts and reflections germinating from within. Though morbidly sensitive to changes in his physical surroundings, he would be slow to act upon such sensations, would not prove impulsive, not because he was sluggish, but because he was merely irresolute. It could be foreseen that morally he was of that sort who avoid evil through good taste, lack of decision, and want of opportunity. His temperament was that of the poet; when he told himself he had been thinking, he deceived himself. He had, on such occasions, been only brooding.

Some eighteen months before this time, he had been threatened with consumption, and, taking advantage of a standing invitation on the part of Magnus Derrick, had come to stay in the dry, even climate of the San Joaquin for an indefinite length of time. He was thirty years old, and had graduated and post-graduated with high honours from an Eastern college, where he had devoted himself to a passionate study of literature, and, more especially, of poetry.

It was his insatiable ambition to write verse. But up to this time, his work had been fugitive, ephemeral, a note here and there, heard, appreciated, and forgotten. He was in search of a subject; something magnificent, he did not know exactly what; some vast, tremendous theme, heroic, terrible, to be unrolled in all the thundering progression of hexameters.

But whatever he wrote, and in whatever fashion, Presley was determined that his poem should be of the West, that world's frontier of Romance, where a new race, a new people—hardy, brave, and passionate—were building an empire; where the tumultuous life ran like fire from dawn to dark, and from dark to dawn again, primitive, brutal, honest, and without fear. Something (to his idea not much) had been done to catch at that life in passing, but its poet had not yet arisen. The few sporadic attempts, thus he told himself, had only touched the keynote. He strove for the diapason, the great song that should embrace in itself a whole epoch, a complete era, the voice of an entire people, wherein all people should be included—they and their legends, their folk lore, their fightings, their loves and their lusts, their blunt, grim humour, their stoicism under stress, their adventures, their treasures found in a day and gambled in a night, their direct, crude speech, their generosity and cruelty, their heroism and bestiality, their religion and profanity, their self-sacrifice and obscenity—a true and fearless setting forth of a passing phase of history, un-compromising, sincere; each group in its proper environment; the valley, the plain, and the mountain; the ranch, the range, and the mine—all this, all the traits and types of every community from the Dakotas to the Mexicos, from Winnipeg to Guadalupe, gathered together, swept together, welded and riven together in one single, mighty song, the Song of the West. That was what he dreamed, while things without names—thoughts for which no man had yet invented words, terrible formless shapes, vague figures, colossal, monstrous, distorted—whirled at a gallop through his imagination.

As Harran came up, Presley reached down into the pouches of the sun-bleached shooting coat he wore and drew out and handed him the packet of letters and papers.

"Here's the mail. I think I shall go on."

"But dinner is ready," said Harran; "we are just sitting down."

Presley shook his head. "No, I'm in a hurry. Perhaps I shall have something to eat at Guadalajara. I shall be gone all day."

He delayed a few moments longer, tightening a loose nut on his forward wheel, while Harran, recognising his father's handwriting on one of the envelopes, slit it open and cast his eye rapidly over its pages.

"The Governor is coming home," he exclaimed, "to-morrow morning on the early train; wants me to meet him with the team at Guadalajara; AND," he cried between his clenched teeth, as he continued to read, "we've lost the case."

"What case? Oh, in the matter of rates?"

Harran nodded, his eyes flashing, his face growing suddenly scarlet.

"Ulsteen gave his decision yesterday," he continued, reading from his father's letter. "He holds, Ulsteen does, that 'grain rates as low as the new figure would amount to confiscation of property, and that, on such a basis, the railroad could not be operated at a legitimate profit. As he is powerless to legislate in the matter, he can only put the rates back at what they originally were before the commissioners made the cut, and it is so ordered.' That's our friend S. Behrman again," added Harran, grinding his teeth. "He was up in the city the whole of the time the new schedule was being drawn, and he and Ulsteen and the Railroad Commission were as thick as thieves. He has been up there all this last week, too, doing the railroad's dirty work, and backing Ulsteen up. 'Legitimate profit, legitimate profit,'" he broke out. "Can we raise wheat at a legitimate profit with a tariff of four dollars a ton for moving it two hundred miles to tide-water, with wheat at eighty-seven cents? Why not hold us up with a gun in our faces, and say, 'hands up,' and be done with it?"

He dug his boot-heel into the ground and turned away to the house abruptly, cursing beneath his breath.

"By the way," Presley called after him, "Hooven wants to see you. He asked me about this idea of the Governor's of getting along without the tenants this year. Hooven wants to stay to tend the ditch and look after the stock. I told him to see you."

Harran, his mind full of other things, nodded to say he understood. Presley only waited till he had disappeared indoors, so that he might not seem too indifferent to his trouble; then, remounting, struck at once into a brisk pace, and, turning out from the carriage gate, held on swiftly down the Lower Road, going in the direction of Guadalajara. These matters, these eternal fierce bickerings between the farmers of the San Joaquin and the Pacific and Southwestern Railroad irritated him and wearied him. He cared for none of these things. They did not belong to his world. In the picture of that huge romantic West that he saw in his imagination, these dissensions made the one note of harsh colour that refused to enter into the great scheme of harmony. It was material, sordid, deadly commonplace. But, however he strove to shut his eyes to it or his ears to it, the thing persisted and persisted. The romance seemed complete up to that point. There it broke, there it failed, there it became realism, grim, unlovely, unyielding. To be true—and it was the first article of his creed to be unflinchingly true—he could not ignore it. All the noble poetry of the ranch—the valley—seemed in his mind to be marred and disfigured by the presence of certain immovable facts. Just what he wanted, Presley hardly knew. On one hand, it was his ambition to portray life as he saw it—directly, frankly, and through no medium of personality or temperament. But, on the other hand, as well, he wished to see everything through a rose-coloured mist—a mist that dulled all harsh outlines, all crude and violent colours. He told himself that, as a part of the people, he loved the people and sympathised with their hopes and fears, and joys and griefs; and yet Hooven, grimy and perspiring, with his perpetual grievance and his contracted horizon, only revolted him. He had set himself the task of giving true, absolutely true, poetical expression to the life of the ranch, and yet, again and again, he brought up against the railroad, that stubborn iron barrier against which his romance shattered itself to froth and disintegrated, flying spume. His heart went out to the people, and his groping hand met that of a slovenly little Dutchman, whom it was impossible to consider seriously. He searched for the True Romance, and, in the end, found grain rates and unjust freight tariffs.

"But the stuff is HERE," he muttered, as he sent his wheel rumbling across the bridge over Broderson Creek. "The romance, the real romance, is here somewhere. I'll get hold of it yet."

He shot a glance about him as if in search of the inspiration. By now he was not quite half way across the northern and narrowest corner of Los Muertos, at this point some eight miles wide. He was still on the Home ranch. A few miles to the south he could just make out the line of wire fence that separated it from the third division; and to the north, seen faint and blue through the haze and shimmer of the noon sun, a long file of telegraph poles showed the line of the railroad and marked Derrick's northeast boundary. The road over which Presley was travelling ran almost diametrically straight. In front of him, but at a great distance, he could make out the giant live-oak and the red roof of Hooven's barn that stood near it.

All about him the country was flat. In all directions he could see for miles. The harvest was just over. Nothing but stubble remained on the ground. With the one exception of the live-oak by Hooven's place, there was nothing green in sight. The wheat stubble was of a dirty yellow; the ground, parched, cracked, and dry, of a cheerless brown. By the roadside the dust lay thick and grey, and, on either hand, stretching on toward the horizon, losing itself in a mere smudge in the distance, ran the illimitable parallels of the wire fence. And that was all; that and the burnt-out blue of the sky and the steady shimmer of the heat.

The silence was infinite. After the harvest, small though that harvest had been, the ranches seemed asleep. It was as though the earth, after its period of reproduction, its pains of labour, had been delivered of the fruit of its loins, and now slept the sleep of exhaustion.

It was the period between seasons, when nothing was being done, when the natural forces seemed to hang suspended. There was no rain, there was no wind, there was no growth, no life; the very stubble had no force even to rot. The sun alone moved.

Toward two o'clock, Presley reached Hooven's place, two or three grimy frame buildings, infested with a swarm of dogs. A hog or two wandered aimlessly about. Under a shed by the barn, a broken-down seeder lay rusting to its ruin. But overhead, a mammoth live-oak, the largest tree in all the country-side, towered superb and magnificent. Grey bunches of mistletoe and festoons of trailing moss hung from its bark. From its lowest branch hung Hooven's meat-safe, a square box, faced with wire screens.

What gave a special interest to Hooven's was the fact that here was the intersection of the Lower Road and Derrick's main irrigating ditch, a vast trench not yet completed, which he and Annixter, who worked the Quien Sabe ranch, were jointly constructing. It ran directly across the road and at right angles to it, and lay a deep groove in the field between Hooven's and the town of Guadalajara, some three miles farther on. Besides this, the ditch was a natural boundary between two divisions of the Los Muertos ranch, the first and fourth.

Presley now had the choice of two routes. His objective point was the spring at the headwaters of Broderson Creek, in the hills on the eastern side of the Quien Sabe ranch. The trail afforded him a short cut thitherward. As he passed the house, Mrs. Hooven came to the door, her little daughter Hilda, dressed in a boy's overalls and clumsy boots, at her skirts. Minna, her oldest daughter, a very pretty girl, whose love affairs were continually the talk of all Los Muertos, was visible through a window of the house, busy at the week's washing. Mrs. Hooven was a faded, colourless woman, middle-aged and commonplace, and offering not the least characteristic that would distinguish her from a thousand other women of her class and kind. She nodded to Presley, watching him with a stolid gaze from under her arm, which she held across her forehead to shade her eyes.

But now Presley exerted himself in good earnest. His bicycle flew. He resolved that after all he would go to Guadalajara. He crossed the bridge over the irrigating ditch with a brusque spurt of hollow sound, and shot forward down the last stretch of the Lower Road that yet intervened between Hooven's and the town. He was on the fourth division of the ranch now, the only one whereon the wheat had been successful, no doubt because of the Little Mission Creek that ran through it. But he no longer occupied himself with the landscape. His only concern was to get on as fast as possible. He had looked forward to spending nearly the whole day on the crest of the wooded hills in the northern corner of the Quien Sabe ranch, reading, idling, smoking his pipe. But now he would do well if he arrived there by the middle of the afternoon. In a few moments he had reached the line fence that marked the limits of the ranch. Here were the railroad tracks, and just beyond—a huddled mass of roofs, with here and there an adobe house on its outskirts—the little town of Guadalajara. Nearer at hand, and directly in front of Presley, were the freight and passenger depots of the P. and S. W., painted in the grey and white, which seemed to be the official colours of all the buildings owned by the corporation. The station was deserted. No trains passed at this hour. From the direction of the ticket window, Presley heard the unsteady chittering of the telegraph key. In the shadow of one of the baggage trucks upon the platform, the great yellow cat that belonged to the agent dozed complacently, her paws tucked under her body. Three flat cars, loaded with bright-painted farming machines, were on the siding above the station, while, on the switch below, a huge freight engine that lacked its cow-catcher sat back upon its monstrous driving-wheels, motionless, solid, drawing long breaths that were punctuated by the subdued sound of its steam-pump clicking at exact intervals.

But evidently it had been decreed that Presley should be stopped at every point of his ride that day, for, as he was pushing his bicycle across the tracks, he was surprised to hear his name called. "Hello, there, Mr. Presley. What's the good word?"

Presley looked up quickly, and saw Dyke, the engineer, leaning on his folded arms from the cab window of the freight engine. But at the prospect of this further delay, Presley was less troubled. Dyke and he were well acquainted and the best of friends. The picturesqueness of the engineer's life was always attractive to Presley, and more than once he had ridden on Dyke's engine between Guadalajara and Bonneville. Once, even, he had made the entire run between the latter town and San Francisco in the cab.

Dyke's home was in Guadalajara. He lived in one of the remodelled 'dobe cottages, where his mother kept house for him. His wife had died some five years before this time, leaving him a little daughter, Sidney, to bring up as best he could. Dyke himself was a heavy built, well-looking fellow, nearly twice the weight of Presley, with great shoulders and massive, hairy arms, and a tremendous, rumbling voice.

"Hello, old man," answered Presley, coming up to the engine. "What are you doing about here at this time of day? I thought you were on the night service this month."

"We've changed about a bit," answered the other. "Come up here and sit down, and get out of the sun. They've held us here to wait orders," he explained, as Presley, after leaning his bicycle against the tender, climbed to the fireman's seat of worn green leather. "They are changing the run of one of the crack passenger engines down below, and are sending her up to Fresno. There was a smash of some kind on the Bakersfield division, and she's to hell and gone behind her time. I suppose when she comes, she'll come a-humming. It will be stand clear and an open track all the way to Fresno. They have held me here to let her go by."

He took his pipe, an old T. D. clay, but coloured to a beautiful shiny black, from the pocket of his jumper and filled and lit it.

"Well, I don't suppose you object to being held here," observed Presley. "Gives you a chance to visit your mother and the little girl."

"And precisely they choose this day to go up to Sacramento," answered Dyke. "Just my luck. Went up to visit my brother's people. By the way, my brother may come down here—locate here, I mean—and go into the hop-raising business. He's got an option on five hundred acres just back of the town here. He says there is going to be money in hops. I don't know; may be I'll go in with him."

"Why, what's the matter with railroading?"

Dyke drew a couple of puffs on his pipe, and fixed Presley with a glance.

"There's this the matter with it," he said; "I'm fired."

"Fired! You!" exclaimed Presley, turning abruptly toward him. "That's what I'm telling you," returned Dyke grimly.

"You don't mean it. Why, what for, Dyke?"

"Now, YOU tell me what for," growled the other savagely. "Boy and man, I've worked for the P. and S. W. for over ten years, and never one yelp of a complaint did I ever hear from them. They know damn well they've not got a steadier man on the road. And more than that, more than that, I don't belong to the Brotherhood. And when the strike came along, I stood by them—stood by the company. You know that. And you know, and they know, that at Sacramento that time, I ran my train according to schedule, with a gun in each hand, never knowing when I was going over a mined culvert, and there was talk of giving me a gold watch at the time. To hell with their gold watches! I want ordinary justice and fair treatment. And now, when hard times come along, and they are cutting wages, what do they do? Do they make any discrimination in my case? Do they remember the man that stood by them and risked his life in their service? No. They cut my pay down just as off-hand as they do the pay of any dirty little wiper in the yard. Cut me along with—listen to this—cut me along with men that they had BLACK-LISTED; strikers that they took back because they were short of hands." He drew fiercely on his pipe. "I went to them, yes, I did; I went to the General Office, and ate dirt. I told them I was a family man, and that I didn't see how I was going to get along on the new scale, and I reminded them of my service during the strike. The swine told me that it wouldn't be fair to discriminate in favour of one man, and that the cut must apply to all their employees alike. Fair!" he shouted with laughter. "Fair! Hear the P. and S. W. talking about fairness and discrimination. That's good, that is. Well, I got furious. I was a fool, I suppose. I told them that, in justice to myself, I wouldn't do first-class work for third-class pay. And they said, 'Well, Mr. Dyke, you know what you can do.' Well, I did know. I said, 'I'll ask for my time, if you please,' and they gave it to me just as if they were glad to be shut of me. So there you are, Presley. That's the P. & S. W. Railroad Company of California. I am on my last run now."

"Shameful," declared Presley, his sympathies all aroused, now that the trouble concerned a friend of his. "It's shameful, Dyke. But," he added, an idea occurring to him, "that don't shut you out from work. There are other railroads in the State that are not controlled by the P. and S. W."

Dyke smote his knee with his clenched fist.

"NAME ONE."

Presley was silent. Dyke's challenge was unanswerable. There was a lapse in their talk, Presley drumming on the arm of the seat, meditating on this injustice; Dyke looking off over the fields beyond the town, his frown lowering, his teeth rasping upon his pipestem. The station agent came to the door of the depot, stretching and yawning. On ahead of the engine, the empty rails of the track, reaching out toward the horizon, threw off visible layers of heat. The telegraph key clicked incessantly.

"So I'm going to quit," Dyke remarked after a while, his anger somewhat subsided. "My brother and I will take up this hop ranch. I've saved a good deal in the last ten years, and there ought to be money in hops."

Presley went on, remounting his bicycle, wheeling silently through the deserted streets of the decayed and dying Mexican town. It was the hour of the siesta. Nobody was about. There was no business in the town. It was too close to Bonneville for that. Before the railroad came, and in the days when the raising of cattle was the great industry of the country, it had enjoyed a fierce and brilliant life. Now it was moribund. The drug store, the two bar-rooms, the hotel at the corner of the old Plaza, and the shops where Mexican "curios" were sold to those occasional Eastern tourists who came to visit the Mission of San Juan, sufficed for the town's activity.

At Solotari's, the restaurant on the Plaza, diagonally across from the hotel, Presley ate his long-deferred Mexican dinner—an omelette in Spanish-Mexican style, frijoles and tortillas, a salad, and a glass of white wine. In a corner of the room, during the whole course of his dinner, two young Mexicans (one of whom was astonishingly handsome, after the melodramatic fashion of his race) and an old fellow! the centenarian of the town, decrepit beyond belief, sang an interminable love-song to the accompaniment of a guitar and an accordion.

These Spanish-Mexicans, decayed, picturesque, vicious, and romantic, never failed to interest Presley. A few of them still remained in Guadalajara, drifting from the saloon to the restaurant, and from the restaurant to the Plaza, relics of a former generation, standing for a different order of things, absolutely idle, living God knew how, happy with their cigarette, their guitar, their glass of mescal, and their siesta. The centenarian remembered Fremont and Governor Alvarado, and the bandit Jesus Tejeda, and the days when Los Muertos was a Spanish grant, a veritable principality, leagues in extent, and when there was never a fence from Visalia to Fresno. Upon this occasion, Presley offered the old man a drink of mescal, and excited him to talk of the things he remembered. Their talk was in Spanish, a language with which Presley was familiar.

"De La Cuesta held the grant of Los Muertos in those days," the centenarian said; "a grand man. He had the power of life and death over his people, and there was no law but his word. There was no thought of wheat then, you may believe. It was all cattle in those days, sheep, horses—steers, not so many—and if money was scarce, there was always plenty to eat, and clothes enough for all, and wine, ah, yes, by the vat, and oil too; the Mission Fathers had that. Yes, and there was wheat as well, now that I come to think; but a very little—in the field north of the Mission where now it is the Seed ranch; wheat fields were there, and also a vineyard, all on Mission grounds. Wheat, olives, and the vine; the Fathers planted those, to provide the elements of the Holy Sacrament—bread, oil, and wine, you understand. It was like that, those industries began in California—from the Church; and now," he put his chin in the air, "what would Father Ullivari have said to such a crop as Senor Derrick plants these days? Ten thousand acres of wheat! Nothing but wheat from the Sierra to the Coast Range. I remember when De La Cuesta was married. He had never seen the young lady, only her miniature portrait, painted"—he raised a shoulder—"I do not know by whom, small, a little thing to be held in the palm. But he fell in love with that, and marry her he would. The affair was arranged between him and the girl's parents. But when the time came that De La Cuesta was to go to Monterey to meet and marry the girl, behold, Jesus Tejeda broke in upon the small rancheros near Terrabella. It was no time for De La Cuesta to be away, so he sent his brother Esteban to Monterey to marry the girl by proxy for him. I went with Esteban. We were a company, nearly a hundred men. And De La Cuesta sent a horse for the girl to ride, white, pure white; and the saddle was of red leather; the head-stall, the bit, and buckles, all the metal work, of virgin silver. Well, there was a ceremony in the Monterey Mission, and Esteban, in the name of his brother, was married to the girl. On our way back, De La Cuesta rode out to meet us. His company met ours at Agatha dos Palos. Never will I forget De La Cuesta's face as his eyes fell upon the girl. It was a look, a glance, come and gone like THAT," he snapped his fingers. "No one but I saw it, but I was close by. There was no mistaking that look. De La Cuesta was disappointed."

"And the girl?" demanded Presley.

"She never knew. Ah, he was a grand gentleman, De La Cuesta. Always he treated her as a queen. Never was husband more devoted, more respectful, more chivalrous. But love?" The old fellow put his chin in the air, shutting his eyes in a knowing fashion. "It was not there. I could tell. They were married over again at the Mission San Juan de Guadalajara—OUR Mission—and for a week all the town of Guadalajara was in fete. There were bull-fights in the Plaza—this very one—for five days, and to each of his tenants-in-chief, De La Cuesta gave a horse, a barrel of tallow, an ounce of silver, and half an ounce of gold dust. Ah, those were days. That was a gay life. This"—he made a comprehensive gesture with his left hand—"this is stupid."

"You may well say that," observed Presley moodily, discouraged by the other's talk. All his doubts and uncertainty had returned to him. Never would he grasp the subject of his great poem. To-day, the life was colourless. Romance was dead. He had lived too late. To write of the past was not what he desired. Reality was what he longed for, things that he had seen. Yet how to make this compatible with romance. He rose, putting on his hat, offering the old man a cigarette. The centenarian accepted with the air of a grandee, and extended his horn snuff-box. Presley shook his head.

"I was born too late for that," he declared, "for that, and for many other things. Adios."

"You are travelling to-day, senor?"

"A little turn through the country, to get the kinks out of the muscles," Presley answered. "I go up into the Quien Sabe, into the high country beyond the Mission."

"Ah, the Quien Sabe rancho. The sheep are grazing there this week."

Solotari, the keeper of the restaurant, explained:

"Young Annixter sold his wheat stubble on the ground to the sheep raisers off yonder;" he motioned eastward toward the Sierra foothills. "Since Sunday the herd has been down. Very clever, that young Annixter. He gets a price for his stubble, which else he would have to burn, and also manures his land as the sheep move from place to place. A true Yankee, that Annixter, a good gringo."

After his meal, Presley once more mounted his bicycle, and leaving the restaurant and the Plaza behind him, held on through the main street of the drowsing town—the street that farther on developed into the road which turned abruptly northward and led onward through the hop-fields and the Quien Sabe ranch toward the Mission of San Juan.

The Home ranch of the Quien Sabe was in the little triangle bounded on the south by the railroad, on the northwest by Broderson Creek, and on the east by the hop fields and the Mission lands. It was traversed in all directions, now by the trail from Hooven's, now by the irrigating ditch—the same which Presley had crossed earlier in the day—and again by the road upon which Presley then found himself. In its centre were Annixter's ranch house and barns, topped by the skeleton-like tower of the artesian well that was to feed the irrigating ditch. Farther on, the course of Broderson Creek was marked by a curved line of grey-green willows, while on the low hills to the north, as Presley advanced, the ancient Mission of San Juan de Guadalajara, with its belfry tower and red-tiled roof, began to show itself over the crests of the venerable pear trees that clustered in its garden.

When Presley reached Annixter's ranch house, he found young Annixter himself stretched in his hammock behind the mosquito-bar on the front porch, reading "David Copperfield," and gorging himself with dried prunes.

Annixter—after the two had exchanged greetings—complained of terrific colics all the preceding night. His stomach was out of whack, but you bet he knew how to take care of himself; the last spell, he had consulted a doctor at Bonneville, a gibbering busy-face who had filled him up to the neck with a dose of some hogwash stuff that had made him worse—a healthy lot the doctors knew, anyhow. HIS case was peculiar. HE knew; prunes were what he needed, and by the pound.

Annixter, who worked the Quien Sabe ranch—some four thousand acres of rich clay and heavy loams—was a very young man, younger even than Presley, like him a college graduate. He looked never a year older than he was. He was smooth-shaven and lean built. But his youthful appearance was offset by a certain male cast of countenance, the lower lip thrust out, the chin large and deeply cleft. His university course had hardened rather than polished him. He still remained one of the people, rough almost to insolence, direct in speech, intolerant in his opinions, relying upon absolutely no one but himself; yet, with all this, of an astonishing degree of intelligence, and possessed of an executive ability little short of positive genius. He was a ferocious worker, allowing himself no pleasures, and exacting the same degree of energy from all his subordinates. He was widely hated, and as widely trusted. Every one spoke of his crusty temper and bullying disposition, invariably qualifying the statement with a commendation of his resources and capabilities. The devil of a driver, a hard man to get along with, obstinate, contrary, cantankerous; but brains! No doubt of that; brains to his boots. One would like to see the man who could get ahead of him on a deal. Twice he had been shot at, once from ambush on Osterman's ranch, and once by one of his own men whom he had kicked from the sacking platform of his harvester for gross negligence. At college, he had specialised on finance, political economy, and scientific agriculture. After his graduation (he stood almost at the very top of his class) he had returned and obtained the degree of civil engineer. Then suddenly he had taken a notion that a practical knowledge of law was indispensable to a modern farmer. In eight months he did the work of three years, studying for his bar examinations. His method of study was characteristic. He reduced all the material of his text-books to notes. Tearing out the leaves of these note-books, he pasted them upon the walls of his room; then, in his shirt-sleeves, a cheap cigar in his teeth, his hands in his pockets, he walked around and around the room, scowling fiercely at his notes, memorising, devouring, digesting. At intervals, he drank great cupfuls of unsweetened, black coffee. When the bar examinations were held, he was admitted at the very head of all the applicants, and was complimented by the judge. Immediately afterwards, he collapsed with nervous prostration; his stomach "got out of whack," and he all but died in a Sacramento boarding-house, obstinately refusing to have anything to do with doctors, whom he vituperated as a rabble of quacks, dosing himself with a patent medicine and stuffing himself almost to bursting with liver pills and dried prunes.

He had taken a trip to Europe after this sickness to put himself completely to rights. He intended to be gone a year, but returned at the end of six weeks, fulminating abuse of European cooking. Nearly his entire time had been spent in Paris; but of this sojourn he had brought back but two souvenirs, an electro-plated bill-hook and an empty bird cage which had tickled his fancy immensely.

He was wealthy. Only a year previous to this his father—a widower, who had amassed a fortune in land speculation—had died, and Annixter, the only son, had come into the inheritance.

For Presley, Annixter professed a great admiration, holding in deep respect the man who could rhyme words, deferring to him whenever there was question of literature or works of fiction. No doubt, there was not much use in poetry, and as for novels, to his mind, there were only Dickens's works. Everything else was a lot of lies. But just the same, it took brains to grind out a poem. It wasn't every one who could rhyme "brave" and "glaive," and make sense out of it. Sure not.

But Presley's case was a notable exception. On no occasion was Annixter prepared to accept another man's opinion without reserve. In conversation with him, it was almost impossible to make any direct statement, however trivial, that he would accept without either modification or open contradiction. He had a passion for violent discussion. He would argue upon every subject in the range of human knowledge, from astronomy to the tariff, from the doctrine of predestination to the height of a horse. Never would he admit himself to be mistaken; when cornered, he would intrench himself behind the remark, "Yes, that's all very well. In some ways, it is, and then, again, in some ways, it ISN'T."

Singularly enough, he and Presley were the best of friends. More than once, Presley marvelled at this state of affairs, telling himself that he and Annixter had nothing in common. In all his circle of acquaintances, Presley was the one man with whom Annixter had never quarrelled. The two men were diametrically opposed in temperament. Presley was easy-going; Annixter, alert. Presley was a confirmed dreamer, irresolute, inactive, with a strong tendency to melancholy; the young farmer was a man of affairs, decisive, combative, whose only reflection upon his interior economy was a morbid concern in the vagaries of his stomach. Yet the two never met without a mutual pleasure, taking a genuine interest in each other's affairs, and often putting themselves to great inconvenience to be of trifling service to help one another.

As a last characteristic, Annixter pretended to be a woman-hater, for no other reason than that he was a very bull-calf of awkwardness in feminine surroundings. Feemales! Rot! There was a fine way for a man to waste his time and his good money, lally gagging with a lot of feemales. No, thank you; none of it in HIS, if you please. Once only he had an affair—a timid, little creature in a glove-cleaning establishment in Sacramento, whom he had picked up, Heaven knew how. After his return to his ranch, a correspondence had been maintained between the two, Annixter taking the precaution to typewrite his letters, and never affixing his signature, in an excess of prudence. He furthermore made carbon copies of all his letters, filing them away in a compartment of his safe. Ah, it would be a clever feemale who would get him into a mess. Then, suddenly smitten with a panic terror that he had committed himself, that he was involving himself too deeply, he had abruptly sent the little woman about her business. It was his only love affair. After that, he kept himself free. No petticoats should ever have a hold on him. Sure not.

As Presley came up to the edge of the porch, pushing his bicycle in front of him, Annixter excused himself for not getting up, alleging that the cramps returned the moment he was off his back.

"What are you doing up this way?" he demanded.

"Oh, just having a look around," answered Presley. "How's the ranch?"

"Say," observed the other, ignoring his question, "what's this I hear about Derrick giving his tenants the bounce, and working Los Muertos himself—working ALL his land?"

Presley made a sharp movement of impatience with his free hand. "I've heard nothing else myself since morning. I suppose it must be so."

"Huh!" grunted Annixter, spitting out a prune stone. "You give Magnus Derrick my compliments and tell him he's a fool."

"What do you mean?"

"I suppose Derrick thinks he's still running his mine, and that the same principles will apply to getting grain out of the earth as to getting gold. Oh, let him go on and see where he brings up. That's right, there's your Western farmer," he exclaimed contemptuously. "Get the guts out of your land; work it to death; never give it a rest. Never alternate your crop, and then when your soil is exhausted, sit down and roar about hard times."

"I suppose Magnus thinks the land has had rest enough these last two dry seasons," observed Presley. "He has raised no crop to speak of for two years. The land has had a good rest."

"Ah, yes, that sounds well," Annixter contradicted, unwilling to be convinced. "In a way, the land's been rested, and then, again, in a way, it hasn't."

But Presley, scenting an argument, refrained from answering, and bethought himself of moving on.

"I'm going to leave my wheel here for a while, Buck," he said, "if you don't mind. I'm going up to the spring, and the road is rough between here and there."

"Stop in for dinner on your way back," said Annixter. "There'll be a venison steak. One of the boys got a deer over in the foothills last week. Out of season, but never mind that. I can't eat it. This stomach of mine wouldn't digest sweet oil to-day. Get here about six."

"Well, maybe I will, thank you," said Presley, moving off. "By the way," he added, "I see your barn is about done."

"You bet," answered Annixter. "In about a fortnight now she'll be all ready."

"It's a big barn," murmured Presley, glancing around the angle of the house toward where the great structure stood.

"Guess we'll have to have a dance there before we move the stock in," observed Annixter. "That's the custom all around here."

Presley took himself off, but at the gate Annixter called after him, his mouth full of prunes, "Say, take a look at that herd of sheep as you go up. They are right off here to the east of the road, about half a mile from here. I guess that's the biggest lot of sheep YOU ever saw. You might write a poem about 'em. Lamb—ram; sheep graze—sunny days. Catch on?"

Beyond Broderson Creek, as Presley advanced, tramping along on foot now, the land opened out again into the same vast spaces of dull brown earth, sprinkled with stubble, such as had been characteristic of Derrick's ranch. To the east the reach seemed infinite, flat, cheerless, heat-ridden, unrolling like a gigantic scroll toward the faint shimmer of the distant horizons, with here and there an isolated live-oak to break the sombre monotony. But bordering the road to the westward, the surface roughened and raised, clambering up to the higher ground, on the crest of which the old Mission and its surrounding pear trees were now plainly visible.

Just beyond the Mission, the road bent abruptly eastward, striking off across the Seed ranch. But Presley left the road at this point, going on across the open fields. There was no longer any trail. It was toward three o'clock. The sun still spun, a silent, blazing disc, high in the heavens, and tramping through the clods of uneven, broken plough was fatiguing work. The slope of the lowest foothills begun, the surface of the country became rolling, and, suddenly, as he topped a higher ridge, Presley came upon the sheep.

Already he had passed the larger part of the herd—an intervening rise of ground having hidden it from sight. Now, as he turned half way about, looking down into the shallow hollow between him and the curve of the creek, he saw them very plainly. The fringe of the herd was some two hundred yards distant, but its farther side, in that illusive shimmer of hot surface air, seemed miles away. The sheep were spread out roughly in the shape of a figure eight, two larger herds connected by a smaller, and were headed to the southward, moving slowly, grazing on the wheat stubble as they proceeded. But the number seemed incalculable. Hundreds upon hundreds upon hundreds of grey, rounded backs, all exactly alike, huddled, close-packed, alive, hid the earth from sight. It was no longer an aggregate of individuals. It was a mass—a compact, solid, slowly moving mass, huge, without form, like a thick-pressed growth of mushrooms, spreading out in all directions over the earth. From it there arose a vague murmur, confused, inarticulate, like the sound of very distant surf, while all the air in the vicinity was heavy with the warm, ammoniacal odour of the thousands of crowding bodies.

All the colours of the scene were sombre—the brown of the earth, the faded yellow of the dead stubble, the grey of the myriad of undulating backs. Only on the far side of the herd, erect, motionless—a single note of black, a speck, a dot—the shepherd stood, leaning upon an empty water-trough, solitary, grave, impressive.

For a few moments, Presley stood, watching. Then, as he started to move on, a curious thing occurred. At first, he thought he had heard some one call his name. He paused, listening; there was no sound but the vague noise of the moving sheep. Then, as this first impression passed, it seemed to him that he had been beckoned to. Yet nothing stirred; except for the lonely figure beyond the herd there was no one in sight. He started on again, and in half a dozen steps found himself looking over his shoulder. Without knowing why, he looked toward the shepherd; then halted and looked a second time and a third. Had the shepherd called to him? Presley knew that he had heard no voice. Brusquely, all his attention seemed riveted upon this distant figure. He put one forearm over his eyes, to keep off the sun, gazing across the intervening herd. Surely, the shepherd had called him. But at the next instant he started, uttering an exclamation under his breath. The far-away speck of black became animated. Presley remarked a sweeping gesture. Though the man had not beckoned to him before, there was no doubt that he was beckoning now. Without any hesitation, and singularly interested in the incident, Presley turned sharply aside and hurried on toward the shepherd, skirting the herd, wondering all the time that he should answer the call with so little question, so little hesitation.

But the shepherd came forward to meet Presley, followed by one of his dogs. As the two men approached each other, Presley, closely studying the other, began to wonder where he had seen him before. It must have been a very long time ago, upon one of his previous visits to the ranch. Certainly, however, there was something familiar in the shepherd's face and figure. When they came closer to each other, and Presley could see him more distinctly, this sense of a previous acquaintance was increased and sharpened.

The shepherd was a man of about thirty-five. He was very lean and spare. His brown canvas overalls were thrust into laced boots. A cartridge belt without any cartridges encircled his waist. A grey flannel shirt, open at the throat, showed his breast, tanned and ruddy. He wore no hat. His hair was very black and rather long. A pointed beard covered his chin, growing straight and fine from the hollow cheeks. The absence of any covering for his head was, no doubt, habitual with him, for his face was as brown as an Indian's—a ruddy brown quite different from Presley's dark olive. To Presley's morbidly keen observation, the general impression of the shepherd's face was intensely interesting. It was uncommon to an astonishing degree. Presley's vivid imagination chose to see in it the face of an ascetic, of a recluse, almost that of a young seer. So must have appeared the half-inspired shepherds of the Hebraic legends, the younger prophets of Israel, dwellers in the wilderness, beholders of visions, having their existence in a continual dream, talkers with God, gifted with strange powers.

Suddenly, at some twenty paces distant from the approaching shepherd, Presley stopped short, his eyes riveted upon the other.

"Vanamee!" he exclaimed.

The shepherd smiled and came forward, holding out his hands, saying, "I thought it was you. When I saw you come over the hill, I called you."

"But not with your voice," returned Presley. "I knew that some one wanted me. I felt it. I should have remembered that you could do that kind of thing."

"I have never known it to fail. It helps with the sheep."

"With the sheep?"

"In a way. I can't tell exactly how. We don't understand these things yet. There are times when, if I close my eyes and dig my fists into my temples, I can hold the entire herd for perhaps a minute. Perhaps, though, it's imagination, who knows? But it's good to see you again. How long has it been since the last time? Two, three, nearly five years."

It was more than that. It was six years since Presley and Vanamee had met, and then it had been for a short time only, during one of the shepherd's periodical brief returns to that part of the country. During a week he and Presley had been much together, for the two were devoted friends. Then, as abruptly, as mysteriously as he had come, Vanamee disappeared. Presley awoke one morning to find him gone. Thus, it had been with Vanamee for a period of sixteen years. He lived his life in the unknown, one could not tell where—in the desert, in the mountains, throughout all the vast and vague South-west, solitary, strange. Three, four, five years passed. The shepherd would be almost forgotten. Never the most trivial scrap of information as to his whereabouts reached Los Muertos. He had melted off into the surface-shimmer of the desert, into the mirage; he sank below the horizons; he was swallowed up in the waste of sand and sage. Then, without warning, he would reappear, coming in from the wilderness, emerging from the unknown. No one knew him well. In all that countryside he had but three friends, Presley, Magnus Derrick, and the priest at the Mission of San Juan de Guadalajara, Father Sarria. He remained always a mystery, living a life half-real, half-legendary. In all those years he did not seem to have grown older by a single day. At this time, Presley knew him to be thirty-six years of age. But since the first day the two had met, the shepherd's face and bearing had, to his eyes, remained the same. At this moment, Presley was looking into the same face he had first seen many, many years ago. It was a face stamped with an unspeakable sadness, a deathless grief, the permanent imprint of a tragedy long past, but yet a living issue. Presley told himself that it was impossible to look long into Vanamee's eyes without knowing that here was a man whose whole being had been at one time shattered and riven to its lowest depths, whose life had suddenly stopped at a certain moment of its development.

The two friends sat down upon the ledge of the watering-trough, their eyes wandering incessantly toward the slow moving herd, grazing on the wheat stubble, moving southward as they grazed.

"Where have you come from this time?" Presley had asked. "Where have you kept yourself?"

The other swept the horizon to the south and east with a vague gesture.

"Off there, down to the south, very far off. So many places that I can't remember. I went the Long Trail this time; a long, long ways. Arizona, The Mexicos, and, then, afterwards, Utah and Nevada, following the horizon, travelling at hazard. Into Arizona first, going in by Monument Pass, and then on to the south, through the country of the Navajos, down by the Aga Thia Needle—a great blade of red rock jutting from out the desert, like a knife thrust. Then on and on through The Mexicos, all through the Southwest, then back again in a great circle by Chihuahua and Aldama to Laredo, to Torreon, and Albuquerque. From there across the Uncompahgre plateau into the Uintah country; then at last due west through Nevada to California and to the valley of the San Joaquin." His voice lapsed to a monotone, his eyes becoming fixed; he continued to speak as though half awake, his thoughts elsewhere, seeing again in the eye of his mind the reach of desert and red hill, the purple mountain, the level stretch of alkali, leper white, all the savage, gorgeous desolation of the Long Trail.

He ignored Presley for the moment, but, on the other hand, Presley himself gave him but half his attention. The return of Vanamee had stimulated the poet's memory. He recalled the incidents of Vanamee's life, reviewing again that terrible drama which had uprooted his soul, which had driven him forth a wanderer, a shunner of men, a sojourner in waste places. He was, strangely enough, a college graduate and a man of wide reading and great intelligence, but he had chosen to lead his own life, which was that of a recluse.

Of a temperament similar in many ways to Presley's, there were capabilities in Vanamee that were not ordinarily to be found in the rank and file of men. Living close to nature, a poet by instinct, where Presley was but a poet by training, there developed in him a great sensitiveness to beauty and an almost abnormal capacity for great happiness and great sorrow; he felt things intensely, deeply. He never forgot. It was when he was eighteen or nineteen, at the formative and most impressionable period of his life, that he had met Angele Varian. Presley barely remembered her as a girl of sixteen, beautiful almost beyond expression, who lived with an aged aunt on the Seed ranch back of the Mission. At this moment he was trying to recall how she looked, with her hair of gold hanging in two straight plaits on either side of her face, making three-cornered her round, white forehead; her wonderful eyes, violet blue, heavy lidded, with their astonishing upward slant toward the temples, the slant that gave a strange, oriental cast to her face, perplexing, enchanting. He remembered the Egyptian fulness of the lips, the strange balancing movement of her head upon her slender neck, the same movement that one sees in a snake at poise. Never had he seen a girl more radiantly beautiful, never a beauty so strange, so troublous, so out of all accepted standards. It was small wonder that Vanamee had loved her, and less wonder, still, that his love had been so intense, so passionate, so part of himself. Angele had loved him with a love no less than his own. It was one of those legendary passions that sometimes occur, idyllic, untouched by civilisation, spontaneous as the growth of trees, natural as dew-fall, strong as the firm-seated mountains.

At the time of his meeting with Angele, Vanamee was living on the Los Muertos ranch. It was there he had chosen to spend one of his college vacations. But he preferred to pass it in out-of-door work, sometimes herding cattle, sometimes pitching hay, sometimes working with pick and dynamite-stick on the ditches in the fourth division of the ranch, riding the range, mending breaks in the wire fences, making himself generally useful. College bred though he was, the life pleased him. He was, as he desired, close to nature, living the full measure of life, a worker among workers, taking enjoyment in simple pleasures, healthy in mind and body. He believed in an existence passed in this fashion in the country, working hard, eating full, drinking deep, sleeping dreamlessly.

But every night, after supper, he saddled his pony and rode over to the garden of the old Mission. The 'dobe dividing wall on that side, which once had separated the Mission garden and the Seed ranch, had long since crumbled away, and the boundary between the two pieces of ground was marked only by a line of venerable pear trees. Here, under these trees, he found Angele awaiting him, and there the two would sit through the hot, still evening, their arms about each other, watching the moon rise over the foothills, listening to the trickle of the water in the moss-encrusted fountain in the garden, and the steady croak of the great frogs that lived in the damp north corner of the enclosure. Through all one summer the enchantment of that new-found, wonderful love, pure and untainted, filled the lives of each of them with its sweetness. The summer passed, the harvest moon came and went. The nights were very dark. In the deep shade of the pear trees they could no longer see each other. When they met at the rendezvous, Vanamee found her only with his groping hands. They did not speak, mere words were useless between them. Silently as his reaching hands touched her warm body, he took her in his arms, searching for her lips with his. Then one night the tragedy had suddenly leaped from out the shadow with the abruptness of an explosion.

It was impossible afterwards to reconstruct the manner of its occurrence. To Angele's mind—what there was left of it—the matter always remained a hideous blur, a blot, a vague, terrible confusion. No doubt they two had been watched; the plan succeeded too well for any other supposition. One moonless night, Angele, arriving under the black shadow of the pear trees a little earlier than usual, found the apparently familiar figure waiting for her. All unsuspecting she gave herself to the embrace of a strange pair of arms, and Vanamee arriving but a score of moments later, stumbled over her prostrate body, inert and unconscious, in the shadow of the overspiring trees.

Who was the Other? Angele was carried to her home on the Seed ranch, delirious, all but raving, and Vanamee, with knife and revolver ready, ranged the country-side like a wolf. He was not alone. The whole county rose, raging, horror-struck. Posse after posse was formed, sent out, and returned, without so much as a clue. Upon no one could even the shadow of suspicion be thrown. The Other had withdrawn into an impenetrable mystery. There he remained. He never was found; he never was so much as heard of. A legend arose about him, this prowler of the night, this strange, fearful figure, with an unseen face, swooping in there from out the darkness, come and gone in an instant, but leaving behind him a track of terror and death and rage and undying grief. Within the year, in giving birth to the child, Angele had died.

The little babe was taken by Angele's parents, and Angele was buried in the Mission garden near to the aged, grey sun dial. Vanamee stood by during the ceremony, but half conscious of what was going forward. At the last moment he had stepped forward, looked long into the dead face framed in its plaits of gold hair, the hair that made three-cornered the round, white forehead; looked again at the closed eyes, with their perplexing upward slant toward the temples, oriental, bizarre; at the lips with their Egyptian fulness; at the sweet, slender neck; the long, slim hands; then abruptly turned about. The last clods were filling the grave at a time when he was already far away, his horse's head turned toward the desert.

For two years no syllable was heard of him. It was believed that he had killed himself. But Vanamee had no thought of that. For two years he wandered through Arizona, living in the desert, in the wilderness, a recluse, a nomad, an ascetic. But, doubtless, all his heart was in the little coffin in the Mission garden. Once in so often he must come back thither. One day he was seen again in the San Joaquin. The priest, Father Sarria, returning from a visit to the sick at Bonneville, met him on the Upper Road. Eighteen years had passed since Angele had died, but the thread of Vanamee's life had been snapped. Nothing remained now but the tangled ends. He had never forgotten. The long, dull ache, the poignant grief had now become a part of him. Presley knew this to be so.

While Presley had been reflecting upon all this, Vanamee had continued to speak. Presley, however, had not been wholly inattentive. While his memory was busy reconstructing the details of the drama of the shepherd's life, another part of his brain had been swiftly registering picture after picture that Vanamee's monotonous flow of words struck off, as it were, upon a steadily moving scroll. The music of the unfamiliar names that occurred in his recital was a stimulant to the poet's imagination. Presley had the poet's passion for expressive, sonorous names. As these came and went in Vanamee's monotonous undertones, like little notes of harmony in a musical progression, he listened, delighted with their resonance.—Navajo, Quijotoa, Uintah, Sonora, Laredo, Uncompahgre—to him they were so many symbols. It was his West that passed, unrolling there before the eye of his mind: the open, heat-scourged round of desert; the mesa, like a vast altar, shimmering purple in the royal sunset; the still, gigantic mountains, heaving into the sky from out the canyons; the strenuous, fierce life of isolated towns, lost and forgotten, down there, far off, below the horizon. Abruptly his great poem, his Song of the West, leaped up again in his imagination. For the moment, he all but held it. It was there, close at hand. In another instant he would grasp it.

"Yes, yes," he exclaimed, "I can see it all. The desert, the mountains, all wild, primordial, untamed. How I should have loved to have been with you. Then, perhaps, I should have got hold of my idea."

"Your idea?"

"The great poem of the West. It's that which I want to write. Oh, to put it all into hexameters; strike the great iron note; sing the vast, terrible song; the song of the People; the forerunners of empire!"

Vanamee understood him perfectly. He nodded gravely.

"Yes, it is there. It is Life, the primitive, simple, direct Life, passionate, tumultuous. Yes, there is an epic there."

Presley caught at the word. It had never before occurred to him.

"Epic, yes, that's it. It is the epic I'm searching for. And HOW I search for it. You don't know. It is sometimes almost an agony. Often and often I can feel it right there, there, at my finger-tips, but I never quite catch it. It always eludes me. I was born too late. Ah, to get back to that first clear-eyed view of things, to see as Homer saw, as Beowulf saw, as the Nibelungen poets saw. The life is here, the same as then; the Poem is here; my West is here; the primeval, epic life is here, here under our hands, in the desert, in the mountain, on the ranch, all over here, from Winnipeg to Guadalupe. It is the man who is lacking, the poet; we have been educated away from it all. We are out of touch. We are out of tune."

Vanamee heard him to the end, his grave, sad face thoughtful and attentive. Then he rose.

"I am going over to the Mission," he said, "to see Father Sarria. I have not seen him yet."

"How about the sheep?"

"The dogs will keep them in hand, and I shall not be gone long. Besides that, I have a boy here to help. He is over yonder on the other side of the herd. We can't see him from here."

Presley wondered at the heedlessness of leaving the sheep so slightly guarded, but made no comment, and the two started off across the field in the direction of the Mission church.

"Well, yes, it is there—your epic," observed Vanamee, as they went along. "But why write? Why not LIVE in it? Steep oneself in the heat of the desert, the glory of the sunset, the blue haze of the mesa and the canyon."

"As you have done, for instance?"

Vanamee nodded.

"No, I could not do that," declared Presley; "I want to go back, but not so far as you. I feel that I must compromise. I must find expression. I could not lose myself like that in your desert. When its vastness overwhelmed me, or its beauty dazzled me, or its loneliness weighed down upon me, I should have to record my impressions. Otherwise, I should suffocate."

"Each to his own life," observed Vanamee.

The Mission of San Juan, built of brown 'dobe blocks, covered with yellow plaster, that at many points had dropped away from the walls, stood on the crest of a low rise of the ground, facing to the south. A covered colonnade, paved with round, worn bricks, from whence opened the doors of the abandoned cells, once used by the monks, adjoined it on the left. The roof was of tiled half-cylinders, split longitudinally, and laid in alternate rows, now concave, now convex. The main body of the church itself was at right angles to the colonnade, and at the point of intersection rose the belfry tower, an ancient campanile, where swung the three cracked bells, the gift of the King of Spain. Beyond the church was the Mission garden and the graveyard that overlooked the Seed ranch in a little hollow beyond.

Presley and Vanamee went down the long colonnade to the last door next the belfry tower, and Vanamee pulled the leather thong that hung from a hole in the door, setting a little bell jangling somewhere in the interior. The place, but for this noise, was shrouded in a Sunday stillness, an absolute repose. Only at intervals, one heard the trickle of the unseen fountain, and the liquid cooing of doves in the garden.

Father Sarria opened the door. He was a small man, somewhat stout, with a smooth and shiny face. He wore a frock coat that was rather dirty, slippers, and an old yachting cap of blue cloth, with a broken leather vizor. He was smoking a cheap cigar, very fat and black.

But instantly he recognised Vanamee. His face went all alight with pleasure and astonishment. It seemed as if he would never have finished shaking both his hands; and, as it was, he released but one of them, patting him affectionately on the shoulder with the other. He was voluble in his welcome, talking partly in Spanish, partly in English. So he had come back again, this great fellow, tanned as an Indian, lean as an Indian, with an Indian's long, black hair. But he had not changed, not in the very least. His beard had not grown an inch. Aha! The rascal, never to give warning, to drop down, as it were, from out the sky. Such a hermit! To live in the desert! A veritable Saint Jerome. Did a lion feed him down there in Arizona, or was it a raven, like Elijah? The good God had not fattened him, at any rate, and, apropos, he was just about to dine himself. He had made a salad from his own lettuce. The two would dine with him, eh? For this, my son, that was lost is found again.

But Presley excused himself. Instinctively, he felt that Sarria and Vanamee wanted to talk of things concerning which he was an outsider. It was not at all unlikely that Vanamee would spend half the night before the high altar in the church.

He took himself away, his mind still busy with Vanamee's extraordinary life and character. But, as he descended the hill, he was startled by a prolonged and raucous cry, discordant, very harsh, thrice repeated at exact intervals, and, looking up, he saw one of Father Sarria's peacocks balancing himself upon the topmost wire of the fence, his long tail trailing, his neck outstretched, filling the air with his stupid outcry, for no reason than the desire to make a noise.

About an hour later, toward four in the afternoon, Presley reached the spring at the head of the little canyon in the northeast corner of the Quien Sabe ranch, the point toward which he had been travelling since early in the forenoon. The place was not without its charm. Innumerable live-oaks overhung the canyon, and Broderson Creek—there a mere rivulet, running down from the spring—gave a certain coolness to the air. It was one of the few spots thereabouts that had survived the dry season of the last year. Nearly all the other springs had dried completely, while Mission Creek on Derrick's ranch was nothing better than a dusty cutting in the ground, filled with brittle, concave flakes of dried and sun-cracked mud.

Presley climbed to the summit of one of the hills—the highest—that rose out of the canyon, from the crest of which he could see for thirty, fifty, sixty miles down the valley, and, filling his pipe, smoked lazily for upwards of an hour, his head empty of thought, allowing himself to succumb to a pleasant, gentle inanition, a little drowsy comfortable in his place, prone upon the ground, warmed just enough by such sunlight as filtered through the live-oaks, soothed by the good tobacco and the prolonged murmur of the spring and creek. By degrees, the sense of his own personality became blunted, the little wheels and cogs of thought moved slower and slower; consciousness dwindled to a point, the animal in him stretched itself, purring. A delightful numbness invaded his mind and his body. He was not asleep, he was not awake, stupefied merely, lapsing back to the state of the faun, the satyr.

After a while, rousing himself a little, he shifted his position and, drawing from the pocket of his shooting coat his little tree-calf edition of the Odyssey, read far into the twenty-first book, where, after the failure of all the suitors to bend Ulysses's bow, it is finally put, with mockery, into his own hands. Abruptly the drama of the story roused him from all his languor. In an instant he was the poet again, his nerves tingling, alive to every sensation, responsive to every impression. The desire of creation, of composition, grew big within him. Hexameters of his own clamoured, tumultuous, in his brain. Not for a long time had he "felt his poem," as he called this sensation, so poignantly. For an instant he told himself that he actually held it.

It was, no doubt, Vanamee's talk that had stimulated him to this point. The story of the Long Trail, with its desert and mountain, its cliff-dwellers, its Aztec ruins, its colour, movement, and romance, filled his mind with picture after picture. The epic defiled before his vision like a pageant. Once more, he shot a glance about him, as if in search of the inspiration, and this time he all but found it. He rose to his feet, looking out and off below him.

As from a pinnacle, Presley, from where he now stood, dominated the entire country. The sun had begun to set, everything in the range of his vision was overlaid with a sheen of gold.

First, close at hand, it was the Seed ranch, carpeting the little hollow behind the Mission with a spread of greens, some dark, some vivid, some pale almost to yellowness. Beyond that was the Mission itself, its venerable campanile, in whose arches hung the Spanish King's bells, already glowing ruddy in the sunset. Farther on, he could make out Annixter's ranch house, marked by the skeleton-like tower of the artesian well, and, a little farther to the east, the huddled, tiled roofs of Guadalajara. Far to the west and north, he saw Bonneville very plain, and the dome of the courthouse, a purple silhouette against the glare of the sky. Other points detached themselves, swimming in a golden mist, projecting blue shadows far before them; the mammoth live-oak by Hooven's, towering superb and magnificent; the line of eucalyptus trees, behind which he knew was the Los Muertos ranch house—his home; the watering-tank, the great iron-hooped tower of wood that stood at the joining of the Lower Road and the County Road; the long wind-break of poplar trees and the white walls of Caraher's saloon on the County Road.

But all this seemed to be only foreground, a mere array of accessories—a mass of irrelevant details. Beyond Annixter's, beyond Guadalajara, beyond the Lower Road, beyond Broderson Creek, on to the south and west, infinite, illimitable, stretching out there under the sheen of the sunset forever and forever, flat, vast, unbroken, a huge scroll, unrolling between the horizons, spread the great stretches of the ranch of Los Muertos, bare of crops, shaved close in the recent harvest. Near at hand were hills, but on that far southern horizon only the curve of the great earth itself checked the view. Adjoining Los Muertos, and widening to the west, opened the Broderson ranch. The Osterman ranch to the northwest carried on the great sweep of landscape; ranch after ranch. Then, as the imagination itself expanded under the stimulus of that measureless range of vision, even those great ranches resolved themselves into mere foreground, mere accessories, irrelevant details. Beyond the fine line of the horizons, over the curve of the globe, the shoulder of the earth, were other ranches, equally vast, and beyond these, others, and beyond these, still others, the immensities multiplying, lengthening out vaster and vaster. The whole gigantic sweep of the San Joaquin expanded, Titanic, before the eye of the mind, flagellated with heat, quivering and shimmering under the sun's red eye. At long intervals, a faint breath of wind out of the south passed slowly over the levels of the baked and empty earth, accentuating the silence, marking off the stillness. It seemed to exhale from the land itself, a prolonged sigh as of deep fatigue. It was the season after the harvest, and the great earth, the mother, after its period of reproduction, its pains of labour, delivered of the fruit of its loins, slept the sleep of exhaustion, the infinite repose of the colossus, benignant, eternal, strong, the nourisher of nations, the feeder of an entire world. Ha! there it was, his epic, his inspiration, his West, his thundering progression of hexameters. A sudden uplift, a sense of exhilaration, of physical exaltation appeared abruptly to sweep Presley from his feet. As from a point high above the world, he seemed to dominate a universe, a whole order of things. He was dizzied, stunned, stupefied, his morbid supersensitive mind reeling, drunk with the intoxication of mere immensity. Stupendous ideas for which there were no names drove headlong through his brain. Terrible, formless shapes, vague figures, gigantic, monstrous, distorted, whirled at a gallop through his imagination.

He started homeward, still in his dream, descending from the hill, emerging from the canyon, and took the short cut straight across the Quien Sabe ranch, leaving Guadalajara far to his left. He tramped steadily on through the wheat stubble, walking fast, his head in a whirl.

Never had he so nearly grasped his inspiration as at that moment on the hilltop. Even now, though the sunset was fading, though the wide reach of valley was shut from sight, it still kept him company. Now the details came thronging back—the component parts of his poem, the signs and symbols of the West. It was there, close at hand, he had been in touch with it all day. It was in the centenarian's vividly coloured reminiscences—De La Cuesta, holding his grant from the Spanish crown, with his power of life and death; the romance of his marriage; the white horse with its pillion of red leather and silver bridle mountings; the bull-fights in the Plaza; the gifts of gold dust, and horses and tallow. It was in Vanamee's strange history, the tragedy of his love; Angele Varian, with her marvellous loveliness; the Egyptian fulness of her lips, the perplexing upward slant of her violet eyes, bizarre, oriental; her white forehead made three cornered by her plaits of gold hair; the mystery of the Other; her death at the moment of her child's birth. It was in Vanamee's flight into the wilderness; the story of the Long Trail, the sunsets behind the altar-like mesas, the baking desolation of the deserts; the strenuous, fierce life of forgotten towns, down there, far off, lost below the horizons of the southwest; the sonorous music of unfamiliar names—Quijotoa, Uintah, Sonora, Laredo, Uncompahgre. It was in the Mission, with its cracked bells, its decaying walls, its venerable sun dial, its fountain and old garden, and in the Mission Fathers themselves, the priests, the padres, planting the first wheat and oil and wine to produce the elements of the Sacrament—a trinity of great industries, taking their rise in a religious rite.

Abruptly, as if in confirmation, Presley heard the sound of a bell from the direction of the Mission itself. It was the de Profundis, a note of the Old World; of the ancient regime, an echo from the hillsides of mediaeval Europe, sounding there in this new land, unfamiliar and strange at this end-of-the-century time.

By now, however, it was dark. Presley hurried forward. He came to the line fence of the Quien Sabe ranch. Everything was very still. The stars were all out. There was not a sound other than the de Profundis, still sounding from very far away. At long intervals the great earth sighed dreamily in its sleep. All about, the feeling of absolute peace and quiet and security and untroubled happiness and content seemed descending from the stars like a benediction. The beauty of his poem, its idyl, came to him like a caress; that alone had been lacking. It was that, perhaps, which had left it hitherto incomplete. At last he was to grasp his song in all its entity. But suddenly there was an interruption. Presley had climbed the fence at the limit of the Quien Sabe ranch. Beyond was Los Muertos, but between the two ran the railroad. He had only time to jump back upon the embankment when, with a quivering of all the earth, a locomotive, single, unattached, shot by him with a roar, filling the air with the reek of hot oil, vomiting smoke and sparks; its enormous eye, cyclopean, red, throwing a glare far in advance, shooting by in a sudden crash of confused thunder; filling the night with the terrific clamour of its iron hoofs.

Abruptly Presley remembered. This must be the crack passenger engine of which Dyke had told him, the one delayed by the accident on the Bakersfield division and for whose passage the track had been opened all the way to Fresno.

Before Presley could recover from the shock of the irruption, while the earth was still vibrating, the rails still humming, the engine was far away, flinging the echo of its frantic gallop over all the valley. For a brief instant it roared with a hollow diapason on the Long Trestle over Broderson Creek, then plunged into a cutting farther on, the quivering glare of its fires losing itself in the night, its thunder abruptly diminishing to a subdued and distant humming. All at once this ceased. The engine was gone.

But the moment the noise of the engine lapsed, Presley—about to start forward again—was conscious of a confusion of lamentable sounds that rose into the night from out the engine's wake. Prolonged cries of agony, sobbing wails of infinite pain, heart-rending, pitiful.

The noises came from a little distance. He ran down the track, crossing the culvert, over the irrigating ditch, and at the head of the long reach of track—between the culvert and the Long Trestle—paused abruptly, held immovable at the sight of the ground and rails all about him.

In some way, the herd of sheep—Vanamee's herd—had found a breach in the wire fence by the right of way and had wandered out upon the tracks. A band had been crossing just at the moment of the engine's passage. The pathos of it was beyond expression. It was a slaughter, a massacre of innocents. The iron monster had charged full into the midst, merciless, inexorable. To the right and left, all the width of the right of way, the little bodies had been flung; backs were snapped against the fence posts; brains knocked out. Caught in the barbs of the wire, wedged in, the bodies hung suspended. Under foot it was terrible. The black blood, winking in the starlight, seeped down into the clinkers between the ties with a prolonged sucking murmur.

Presley turned away, horror-struck, sick at heart, overwhelmed with a quick burst of irresistible compassion for this brute agony he could not relieve. The sweetness was gone from the evening, the sense of peace, of security, and placid contentment was stricken from the landscape. The hideous ruin in the engine's path drove all thought of his poem from his mind. The inspiration vanished like a mist. The de Profundis had ceased to ring.

He hurried on across the Los Muertos ranch, almost running, even putting his hands over his ears till he was out of hearing distance of that all but human distress. Not until he was beyond ear-shot did he pause, looking back, listening. The night had shut down again. For a moment the silence was profound, unbroken.

Then, faint and prolonged, across the levels of the ranch, he heard the engine whistling for Bonneville. Again and again, at rapid intervals in its flying course, it whistled for road crossings, for sharp curves, for trestles; ominous notes, hoarse, bellowing, ringing with the accents of menace and defiance; and abruptly Presley saw again, in his imagination, the galloping monster, the terror of steel and steam, with its single eye, cyclopean, red, shooting from horizon to horizon; but saw it now as the symbol of a vast power, huge, terrible, flinging the echo of its thunder over all the reaches of the valley, leaving blood and destruction in its path; the leviathan, with tentacles of steel clutching into the soil, the soulless Force, the iron-hearted Power, the monster, the Colossus, the Octopus.

II

On the following morning, Harran Derrick was up and about by a little after six o'clock, and a quarter of an hour later had breakfast in the kitchen of the ranch house, preferring not to wait until the Chinese cook laid the table in the regular dining-room. He scented a hard day's work ahead of him, and was anxious to be at it betimes. He was practically the manager of Los Muertos, and, with the aid of his foreman and three division superintendents, carried forward nearly the entire direction of the ranch, occupying himself with the details of his father's plans, executing his orders, signing contracts, paying bills, and keeping the books.

For the last three weeks little had been done. The crop—such as it was—had been harvested and sold, and there had been a general relaxation of activity for upwards of a month. Now, however, the fall was coming on, the dry season was about at its end; any time after the twentieth of the month the first rains might be expected, softening the ground, putting it into condition for the plough. Two days before this, Harran had notified his superintendents on Three and Four to send in such grain as they had reserved for seed. On Two the wheat had not even shown itself above the ground, while on One, the Home ranch, which was under his own immediate supervision, the seed had already been graded and selected.

It was Harran's intention to commence blue-stoning his seed that day, a delicate and important process which prevented rust and smut appearing in the crop when the wheat should come up. But, furthermore, he wanted to find time to go to Guadalajara to meet the Governor on the morning train. His day promised to be busy.

But as Harran was finishing his last cup of coffee, Phelps, the foreman on the Home ranch, who also looked after the storage barns where the seed was kept, presented himself, cap in hand, on the back porch by the kitchen door.

"I thought I'd speak to you about the seed from Four, sir," he said. "That hasn't been brought in yet."

Harran nodded.

"I'll see about it. You've got all the blue-stone you want, have you, Phelps?" and without waiting for an answer he added, "Tell the stableman I shall want the team about nine o'clock to go to Guadalajara. Put them in the buggy. The bays, you understand." When the other had gone, Harran drank off the rest of his coffee, and, rising, passed through the dining-room and across a stone-paved hallway with a glass roof into the office just beyond.

The office was the nerve-centre of the entire ten thousand acres of Los Muertos, but its appearance and furnishings were not in the least suggestive of a farm. It was divided at about its middle by a wire railing, painted green and gold, and behind this railing were the high desks where the books were kept, the safe, the letter-press and letter-files, and Harran's typewriting machine. A great map of Los Muertos with every water-course, depression, and elevation, together with indications of the varying depths of the clays and loams in the soil, accurately plotted, hung against the wall between the windows, while near at hand by the safe was the telephone.

But, no doubt, the most significant object in the office was the ticker. This was an innovation in the San Joaquin, an idea of shrewd, quick-witted young Annixter, which Harran and Magnus Derrick had been quick to adopt, and after them Broderson and Osterman, and many others of the wheat growers of the county. The offices of the ranches were thus connected by wire with San Francisco, and through that city with Minneapolis, Duluth, Chicago, New York, and at last, and most important of all, with Liverpool. Fluctuations in the price of the world's crop during and after the harvest thrilled straight to the office of Los Muertos, to that of the Quien Sabe, to Osterman's, and to Broderson's. During a flurry in the Chicago wheat pits in the August of that year, which had affected even the San Francisco market, Harran and Magnus had sat up nearly half of one night watching the strip of white tape jerking unsteadily from the reel. At such moments they no longer felt their individuality. The ranch became merely the part of an enormous whole, a unit in the vast agglomeration of wheat land the whole world round, feeling the effects of causes thousands of miles distant–a drought on the prairies of Dakota, a rain on the plains of India, a frost on the Russian steppes, a hot wind on the llanos of the

Argentine.

Harran crossed over to the telephone and rang six bells, the call for the division house on Four. It was the most distant, the most isolated point on all the ranch, situated at its far southeastern extremity, where few people ever went, close to the line fence, a dot, a speck, lost in the immensity of the open country. By the road it was eleven miles distant from the office, and by the trail to Hooven's and the Lower Road all of nine.

"How about that seed?" demanded Harran when he had got Cutter on the line.

The other made excuses for an unavoidable delay, and was adding that he was on the point of starting out, when Harran cut in with:

"You had better go the trail. It will save a little time and I am in a hurry. Put your sacks on the horses' backs. And, Cutter, if you see Hooven when you go by his place, tell him I want him, and, by the way, take a look at the end of the irrigating ditch when you get to it. See how they are getting along there and if Billy wants anything. Tell him we are expecting those new scoops down to-morrow or next day and to get along with what he has until then.... How's everything on Four? ... All right, then. Give your seed to Phelps when you get here if I am not about. I am going to Guadalajara to meet the Governor. He's coming down to-day. And that makes me think; we lost the case, you know. I had a letter from the Governor yesterday.... Yes, hard luck. S. Behrman did us up. Well, good-bye, and don't lose any time with that seed. I want to blue-stone to-day."

After telephoning Cutter, Harran put on his hat, went over to the barns, and found Phelps. Phelps had already cleaned out the vat which was to contain the solution of blue-stone, and was now at work regrading the seed. Against the wall behind him ranged the row of sacks. Harran cut the fastenings of these and examined the contents carefully, taking handfuls of wheat from each and allowing it to run through his fingers, or nipping the grains between his nails, testing their hardness.

The seed was all of the white varieties of wheat and of a very high grade, the berries hard and heavy, rigid and swollen with starch.

"If it was all like that, sir, hey?" observed Phelps.

Harran put his chin in the air.

"Bread would be as good as cake, then," he answered, going from sack to sack, inspecting the contents and consulting the tags affixed to the mouths.

"Hello," he remarked, "here's a red wheat. Where did this come from?"

"That's that red Clawson we sowed to the piece on Four, north the Mission Creek, just to see how it would do here. We didn't get a very good catch."

"We can't do better than to stay by White Sonora and Propo," remarked Harran. "We've got our best results with that, and European millers like it to mix with the Eastern wheats that have more gluten than ours. That is, if we have any wheat at all next year."

A feeling of discouragement for the moment bore down heavily upon him. At intervals this came to him and for the moment it was overpowering. The idea of "what's-the-use" was upon occasion a veritable oppression. Everything seemed to combine to lower the price of wheat. The extension of wheat areas always exceeded increase of population; competition was growing fiercer every year. The farmer's profits were the object of attack from a score of different quarters. It was a flock of vultures descending upon a common prey—the commission merchant, the elevator combine, the mixing-house ring, the banks, the warehouse men, the labouring man, and, above all, the railroad. Steadily the Liverpool buyers cut and cut and cut. Everything, every element of the world's markets, tended to force down the price to the lowest possible figure at which it could be profitably farmed. Now it was down to eighty-seven. It was at that figure the crop had sold that year; and to think that the Governor had seen wheat at two dollars and five cents in the year of the Turko-Russian War!

He turned back to the house after giving Phelps final directions, gloomy, disheartened, his hands deep in his pockets, wondering what was to be the outcome. So narrow had the margin of profit shrunk that a dry season meant bankruptcy to the smaller farmers throughout all the valley. He knew very well how widespread had been the distress the last two years. With their own tenants on Los Muertos, affairs had reached the stage of desperation. Derrick had practically been obliged to "carry" Hooven and some of the others. The Governor himself had made almost nothing during the last season; a third year like the last, with the price steadily sagging, meant nothing else but ruin.

But here he checked himself. Two consecutive dry seasons in California were almost unprecedented; a third would be beyond belief, and the complete rest for nearly all the land was a compensation. They had made no money, that was true; but they had lost none. Thank God, the homestead was free of mortgage; one good season would more than make up the difference.

He was in a better mood by the time he reached the driveway that led up to the ranch house, and as he raised his eyes toward the house itself, he could not but feel that the sight of his home was cheering. The ranch house was set in a great grove of eucalyptus, oak, and cypress, enormous trees growing from out a lawn that was as green, as fresh, and as well-groomed as any in a garden in the city. This lawn flanked all one side of the house, and it was on this side that the family elected to spend most of its time. The other side, looking out upon the Home ranch toward Bonneville and the railroad, was but little used. A deep porch ran the whole length of the house here, and in the lower branches of a live-oak near the steps Harran had built a little summer house for his mother. To the left of the ranch house itself, toward the County Road, was the bunk-house and kitchen for some of the hands.

From the steps of the porch the view to the southward expanded to infinity. There was not so much as a twig to obstruct the view. In one leap the eye reached the fine, delicate line where earth and sky met, miles away. The flat monotony of the land, clean of fencing, was broken by one spot only, the roof of the Division Superintendent's house on Three—a mere speck, just darker than the ground. Cutter's house on Four was not even in sight. That was below the horizon.

As Harran came up he saw his mother at breakfast. The table had been set on the porch and Mrs. Derrick, stirring her coffee with one hand, held open with the other the pages of Walter Pater's "Marius." At her feet, Princess Nathalie, the white Angora cat, sleek, over-fed, self-centred, sat on her haunches, industriously licking at the white fur of her breast, while near at hand, by the railing of the porch, Presley pottered with a new bicycle lamp, filling it with oil, adjusting the wicks.

Harran kissed his mother and sat down in a wicker chair on the porch, removing his hat, running his fingers through his yellow hair.

Magnus Derrick's wife looked hardly old enough to be the mother of two such big fellows as Harran and Lyman Derrick. She was not far into the fifties, and her brown hair still retained much of its brightness. She could yet be called pretty. Her eyes were large and easily assumed a look of inquiry and innocence, such as one might expect to see in a young girl. By disposition she was retiring; she easily obliterated herself. She was not made for the harshness of the world, and yet she had known these harshnesses in her younger days. Magnus had married her when she was twenty-one years old, at a time when she was a graduate of some years' standing from the State Normal School and was teaching literature, music, and penmanship in a seminary in the town of Marysville. She overworked herself here continually, loathing the strain of teaching, yet clinging to it with a tenacity born of the knowledge that it was her only means of support. Both her parents were dead; she was dependent upon herself. Her one ambition was to see Italy and the Bay of Naples. The "Marble Faun," Raphael's "Madonnas" and "Il Trovatore" were her beau ideals of literature and art. She dreamed of Italy, Rome, Naples, and the world's great "art-centres." There was no doubt that her affair with Magnus had been a love-match, but Annie Payne would have loved any man who would have taken her out of the droning, heart-breaking routine of the class and music room. She had followed his fortunes unquestioningly. First at Sacramento, during the turmoil of his political career, later on at Placerville in El Dorado County, after Derrick had interested himself in the Corpus Christi group of mines, and finally at Los Muertos, where, after selling out his fourth interest in Corpus Christi, he had turned rancher and had "come in" on the new tracts of wheat land just thrown open by the railroad. She had lived here now for nearly ten years. But never for one moment since the time her glance first lost itself in the unbroken immensity of the ranches had she known a moment's content. Continually there came into her pretty, wide-open eyes—the eyes of a young doe—a look of uneasiness, of distrust, and aversion. Los Muertos frightened her. She remembered the days of her young girlhood passed on a farm in eastern Ohio—five hundred acres, neatly partitioned into the water lot, the cow pasture, the corn lot, the barley field, and wheat farm; cosey, comfortable, home-like; where the farmers loved their land, caressing it, coaxing it, nourishing it as though it were a thing almost conscious; where the seed was sown by hand, and a single two-horse plough was sufficient for the entire farm; where the scythe sufficed to cut the harvest and the grain was thrashed with flails.

But this new order of things—a ranch bounded only by the horizons, where, as far as one could see, to the north, to the east, to the south and to the west, was all one holding, a principality ruled with iron and steam, bullied into a yield of three hundred and fifty thousand bushels, where even when the land was resting, unploughed, unharrowed, and unsown, the wheat came up—troubled her, and even at times filled her with an undefinable terror. To her mind there was something inordinate about it all; something almost unnatural. The direct brutality of ten thousand acres of wheat, nothing but wheat as far as the eye could see, stunned her a little. The one-time writing-teacher of a young ladies' seminary, with her pretty deer-like eyes and delicate fingers, shrank from it. She did not want to look at so much wheat. There was something vaguely indecent in the sight, this food of the people, this elemental force, this basic energy, weltering here under the sun in all the unconscious nakedness of a sprawling, primordial Titan.

The monotony of the ranch ate into her heart hour by hour, year by year. And with it all, when was she to see Rome, Italy, and the Bay of Naples? It was a different prospect truly. Magnus had given her his promise that once the ranch was well established, they two should travel. But continually he had been obliged to put her off, now for one reason, now for another; the machine would not as yet run of itself, he must still feel his hand upon the lever; next year, perhaps, when wheat should go to ninety, or the rains were good. She did not insist. She obliterated herself, only allowing, from time to time, her pretty, questioning eyes to meet his. In the meantime she retired within herself. She surrounded herself with books. Her taste was of the delicacy of point lace. She knew her Austin Dobson by heart. She read poems, essays, the ideas of the seminary at Marysville persisting in her mind. "Marius the Epicurean," "The Essays of Elia," "Sesame and Lilies," "The Stones of Venice," and the little toy magazines, full of the flaccid banalities of the "Minor Poets," were continually in her hands.

When Presley had appeared on Los Muertos, she had welcomed his arrival with delight. Here at last was a congenial spirit. She looked forward to long conversations with the young man on literature, art, and ethics. But Presley had disappointed her. That he—outside of his few chosen deities—should care little for literature, shocked her beyond words. His indifference to "style," to elegant English, was a positive affront. His savage abuse and open ridicule of the neatly phrased rondeaux and sestinas and chansonettes of the little magazines was to her mind a wanton and uncalled-for cruelty. She found his Homer, with its slaughters and hecatombs and barbaric feastings and headstrong passions, violent and coarse. She could not see with him any romance, any poetry in the life around her; she looked to Italy for that. His "Song of the West," which only once, incoherent and fierce, he had tried to explain to her, its swift, tumultous life, its truth, its nobility and savagery, its heroism and obscenity had revolted her.

"But, Presley," she had murmured, "that is not literature."

"No," he had cried between his teeth, "no, thank God, it is not."

A little later, one of the stablemen brought the buggy with the team of bays up to the steps of the porch, and Harran, putting on a different coat and a black hat, took himself off to Guadalajara. The morning was fine; there was no cloud in the sky, but as Harran's buggy drew away from the grove of trees about the ranch house, emerging into the open country on either side of the Lower Road, he caught himself looking sharply at the sky and the faint line of hills beyond the Quien Sabe ranch. There was a certain indefinite cast to the landscape that to Harran's eye was not to be mistaken. Rain, the first of the season, was not far off.

"That's good," he muttered, touching the bays with the whip, "we can't get our ploughs to hand any too soon."

These ploughs Magnus Derrick had ordered from an Eastern manufacturer some months before, since he was dissatisfied with the results obtained from the ones he had used hitherto, which were of local make. However, there had been exasperating and unexpected delays in their shipment. Magnus and Harran both had counted upon having the ploughs in their implement barns that very week, but a tracer sent after them had only resulted in locating them, still en route, somewhere between The Needles and Bakersfield. Now there was likelihood of rain within the week. Ploughing could be undertaken immediately afterward, so soon as the ground was softened, but there was a fair chance that the ranch would lie idle for want of proper machinery.

It was ten minutes before train time when Harran reached the depot at Guadalajara. The San Francisco papers of the preceding day had arrived on an earlier train. He bought a couple from the station agent and looked them over till a distant and prolonged whistle announced the approach of the down train.

In one of the four passengers that alighted from the train, he recognised his father. He half rose in his seat, whistling shrilly between his teeth, waving his hand, and Magnus Derrick, catching sight of him, came forward quickly.

Magnus—the Governor—was all of six feet tall, and though now well toward his sixtieth year, was as erect as an officer of cavalry. He was broad in proportion, a fine commanding figure, imposing an immediate respect, impressing one with a sense of gravity, of dignity and a certain pride of race. He was smooth-shaven, thin-lipped, with a broad chin, and a prominent hawk-like nose—the characteristic of the family—thin, with a high bridge, such as one sees in the later portraits of the Duke of Wellington. His hair was thick and iron-grey, and had a tendency to curl in a forward direction just in front of his ears. He wore a top-hat of grey, with a wide brim, and a frock coat, and carried a cane with a yellowed ivory head.

As a young man it had been his ambition to represent his native State—North Carolina—in the United States Senate. Calhoun was his "great man," but in two successive campaigns he had been defeated. His career checked in this direction, he had come to California in the fifties. He had known and had been the intimate friend of such men as Terry, Broderick, General Baker, Lick, Alvarado, Emerich, Larkin, and, above all, of the unfortunate and misunderstood Ralston. Once he had been put forward as the Democratic candidate for governor, but failed of election. After this Magnus had definitely abandoned politics and had invested all his money in the Corpus Christi mines. Then he had sold out his interest at a small profit—just in time to miss his chance of becoming a multi-millionaire in the Comstock boom—and was looking for reinvestments in other lines when the news that "wheat had been discovered in California" was passed from mouth to mouth. Practically it amounted to a discovery. Dr. Glenn's first harvest of wheat in Colusa County, quietly undertaken but suddenly realised with dramatic abruptness, gave a new matter for reflection to the thinking men of the New West. California suddenly leaped unheralded into the world's market as a competitor in wheat production. In a few years her output of wheat exceeded the value of her out-put of gold, and when, later on, the Pacific and Southwestern Railroad threw open to settlers the rich lands of Tulare County—conceded to the corporation by the government as a bonus for the construction of the road—Magnus had been quick to seize the opportunity and had taken up the ten thousand acres of Los Muertos. Wherever he had gone, Magnus had taken his family with him. Lyman had been born at Sacramento during the turmoil and excitement of Derrick's campaign for governor, and Harran at Shingle Springs, in El Dorado County, six years later.

But Magnus was in every sense the "prominent man." In whatever circle he moved he was the chief figure. Instinctively other men looked to him as the leader. He himself was proud of this distinction; he assumed the grand manner very easily and carried it well. As a public speaker he was one of the last of the followers of the old school of orators. He even carried the diction and manner of the rostrum into private life. It was said of him that his most colloquial conversation could be taken down in shorthand and read off as an admirable specimen of pure, well-chosen English. He loved to do things upon a grand scale, to preside, to dominate. In his good humour there was something Jovian. When angry, everybody around him trembled. But he had not the genius for detail, was not patient. The certain grandiose lavishness of his disposition occupied itself more with results than with means. He was always ready to take chances, to hazard everything on the hopes of colossal returns. In the mining days at Placerville there was no more redoubtable poker player in the county. He had been as lucky in his mines as in his gambling, sinking shafts and tunnelling in violation of expert theory and finding "pay" in every case. Without knowing it, he allowed himself to work his ranch much as if he was still working his mine. The old-time spirit of '49, hap-hazard, unscientific, persisted in his mind. Everything was a gamble—who took the greatest chances was most apt to be the greatest winner. The idea of manuring Los Muertos, of husbanding his great resources, he would have scouted as niggardly, Hebraic, ungenerous.

Magnus climbed into the buggy, helping himself with Harran's outstretched hand which he still held. The two were immensely fond of each other, proud of each other. They were constantly together and Magnus kept no secrets from his favourite son.

"Well, boy."

"Well, Governor."

"I am very pleased you came yourself, Harran. I feared that you might be too busy and send Phelps. It was thoughtful."

Harran was about to reply, but at that moment Magnus caught sight of the three flat cars loaded with bright-painted farming machines which still remained on the siding above the station. He laid his hands on the reins and Harran checked the team.

"Harran," observed Magnus, fixing the machinery with a judicial frown, "Harran, those look singularly like our ploughs. Drive over, boy."

The train had by this time gone on its way and Harran brought the team up to the siding.

"Ah, I was right," said the Governor. "'Magnus Derrick, Los Muertos, Bonneville, from Ditson & Co., Rochester.' These are ours, boy."

Harran breathed a sigh of relief.

"At last," he answered, "and just in time, too. We'll have rain before the week is out. I think, now that I am here, I will telephone Phelps to send the wagon right down for these. I started blue-stoning to-day."

Magnus nodded a grave approval.

"That was shrewd, boy. As to the rain, I think you are well informed; we will have an early season. The ploughs have arrived at a happy moment."

"It means money to us, Governor," remarked Harran.

But as he turned the horses to allow his father to get into the buggy again, the two were surprised to hear a thick, throaty voice wishing them good-morning, and turning about were aware of S. Behrman, who had come up while they were examining the ploughs. Harran's eyes flashed on the instant and through his nostrils he drew a sharp, quick breath, while a certain rigour of carriage stiffened the set of Magnus Derrick's shoulders and back. Magnus had not yet got into the buggy, but stood with the team between him and S. Behrman, eyeing him calmly across the horses' backs. S. Behrman came around to the other side of the buggy and faced Magnus.

He was a large, fat man, with a great stomach; his cheek and the upper part of his thick neck ran together to form a great tremulous jowl, shaven and blue-grey in colour; a roll of fat, sprinkled with sparse hair, moist with perspiration, protruded over the back of his collar. He wore a heavy black moustache. On his head was a round-topped hat of stiff brown straw, highly varnished. A light-brown linen vest, stamped with innumerable interlocked horseshoes, covered his protuberant stomach, upon which a heavy watch chain of hollow links rose and fell with his difficult breathing, clinking against the vest buttons of imitation mother-of-pearl.

S. Behrman was the banker of Bonneville. But besides this he was many other things. He was a real estate agent. He bought grain; he dealt in mortgages. He was one of the local political bosses, but more important than all this, he was the representative of the Pacific and Southwestern Railroad in that section of Tulare County. The railroad did little business in that part of the country that S. Behrman did not supervise, from the consignment of a shipment of wheat to the management of a damage suit, or even to the repair and maintenance of the right of way. During the time when the ranchers of the county were fighting the grain-rate case, S. Behrman had been much in evidence in and about the San Francisco court rooms and the lobby of the legislature in Sacramento. He had returned to Bonneville only recently, a decision adverse to the ranchers being foreseen. The position he occupied on the salary list of the Pacific and Southwestern could not readily be defined, for he was neither freight agent, passenger agent, attorney, real-estate broker, nor political servant, though his influence in all these offices was undoubted and enormous. But for all that, the ranchers about Bonneville knew whom to look to as a source of trouble. There was no denying the fact that for Osterman, Broderson, Annixter and Derrick, S. Behrman was the railroad.

"Mr. Derrick, good-morning," he cried as he came up. "Good-morning, Harran. Glad to see you back, Mr. Derrick." He held out a thick hand.

Magnus, head and shoulders above the other, tall, thin, erect, looked down upon S. Behrman, inclining his head, failing to see his extended hand.

"Good-morning, sir," he observed, and waited for S. Behrman's further speech.

"Well, Mr. Derrick," continued S. Behrman, wiping the back of his neck with his handkerchief, "I saw in the city papers yesterday that our case had gone against you."

"I guess it wasn't any great news to YOU," commented Harran, his face scarlet. "I guess you knew which way Ulsteen was going to jump after your very first interview with him. You don't like to be surprised in this sort of thing, S. Behrman."

"Now, you know better than that, Harran," remonstrated S. Behrman blandly. "I know what you mean to imply, but I ain't going to let it make me get mad. I wanted to say to your Governor—I wanted to say to you, Mr. Derrick—as one man to another—letting alone for the minute that we were on opposite sides of the case—that I'm sorry you didn't win. Your side made a good fight, but it was in a mistaken cause. That's the whole trouble. Why, you could have figured out before you ever went into the case that such rates are confiscation of property. You must allow us—must allow the railroad—a fair interest on the investment. You don't want us to go into the receiver's hands, do you now, Mr. Derrick?"

"The Board of Railroad Commissioners was bought," remarked Magnus sharply, a keen, brisk flash glinting in his eye.

"It was part of the game," put in Harran, "for the Railroad Commission to cut rates to a ridiculous figure, far below a REASONABLE figure, just so that it WOULD be confiscation. Whether Ulsteen is a tool of yours or not, he had to put the rates back to what they were originally."

"If you enforced those rates, Mr. Harran," returned S. Behrman calmly, "we wouldn't be able to earn sufficient money to meet operating expenses or fixed charges, to say nothing of a surplus left over to pay dividends—"

"Tell me when the P. and S. W. ever paid dividends."

"The lowest rates," continued S. Behrman, "that the legislature can establish must be such as will secure us a fair interest on our investment."

"Well, what's your standard? Come, let's hear it. Who is to say what's a fair rate? The railroad has its own notions of fairness sometimes."

"The laws of the State," returned S. Behrman, "fix the rate of interest at seven per cent. That's a good enough standard for us. There is no reason, Mr. Harran, why a dollar invested in a railroad should not earn as much as a dollar represented by a promissory note—seven per cent. By applying your schedule of rates we would not earn a cent; we would be bankrupt."

"Interest on your investment!" cried Harran, furious. "It's fine to talk about fair interest. I know and you know that the total earnings of the P. and S. W.—their main, branch and leased lines for last year—was between nineteen and twenty millions of dollars. Do you mean to say that twenty million dollars is seven per cent. of the original cost of the road?"

S. Behrman spread out his hands, smiling.

"That was the gross, not the net figure—and how can you tell what was the original cost of the road?"

"Ah, that's just it," shouted Harran, emphasising each word with a blow of his fist upon his knee, his eyes sparkling, "you take cursed good care that we don't know anything about the original cost of the road. But we know you are bonded for treble your value; and we know this: that the road COULD have been built for fifty-four thousand dollars per mile and that you SAY it cost you eighty-seven thousand. It makes a difference, S. Behrman, on which of these two figures you are basing your seven per cent."

"That all may show obstinacy, Harran," observed S. Behrman vaguely, "but it don't show common sense."

"We are threshing out old straw, I believe, gentlemen," remarked Magnus. "The question was thoroughly sifted in the courts."

"Quite right," assented S. Behrman. "The best way is that the railroad and the farmer understand each other and get along peaceably. We are both dependent on each other. Your ploughs, I believe, Mr. Derrick." S. Behrman nodded toward the flat cars.

"They are consigned to me," admitted Magnus.

"It looks a trifle like rain," observed S. Behrman, easing his neck and jowl in his limp collar. "I suppose you will want to begin ploughing next week."

"Possibly," said Magnus.

"I'll see that your ploughs are hurried through for you then, Mr. Derrick. We will route them by fast freight for you and it won't cost you anything extra."

"What do you mean?" demanded Harran. "The ploughs are here. We have nothing more to do with the railroad. I am going to have my wagons down here this afternoon."

"I am sorry," answered S. Behrman, "but the cars are going north, not, as you thought, coming FROM the north. They have not been to San Francisco yet."

Magnus made a slight movement of the head as one who remembers a fact hitherto forgotten. But Harran was as yet unenlightened.

"To San Francisco!" he answered, "we want them here—what are you talking about?"

"Well, you know, of course, the regulations," answered S. Behrman. "Freight of this kind coming from the Eastern points into the State must go first to one of our common points and be reshipped from there."

Harran did remember now, but never before had the matter so struck home. He leaned back in his seat in dumb amazement for the instant. Even Magnus had turned a little pale. Then, abruptly, Harran broke out violent and raging.

"What next? My God, why don't you break into our houses at night? Why don't you steal the watch out of my pocket, steal the horses out of the harness, hold us up with a shot-gun; yes, 'stand and deliver; your money or your life.' Here we bring our ploughs from the East over your lines, but you're not content with your long-haul rate between Eastern points and Bonneville. You want to get us under your ruinous short-haul rate between Bonneville and San Francisco, AND RETURN. Think of it! Here's a load of stuff for Bonneville that can't stop at Bonneville, where it is consigned, but has got to go up to San Francisco first BY WAY OF Bonneville, at forty cents per ton and then be reshipped from San Francisco back to Bonneville again at FIFTY-ONE cents per ton, the short-haul rate. And we have to pay it all or go without. Here are the ploughs right here, in sight of the land they have got to be used on, the season just ready for them, and we can't touch them. Oh," he exclaimed in deep disgust, "isn't it a pretty mess! Isn't it a farce! the whole dirty business!"

S. Behrman listened to him unmoved, his little eyes blinking under his fat forehead, the gold chain of hollow links clicking against the pearl buttons of his waistcoat as he breathed.

"It don't do any good to let loose like that, Harran," he said at length. "I am willing to do what I can for you. I'll hurry the ploughs through, but I can't change the freight regulation of the road."

"What's your blackmail for this?" vociferated Harran. "How much do you want to let us go? How much have we got to pay you to be ALLOWED to use our own ploughs—what's your figure? Come, spit it out."

"I see you are trying to make me angry, Harran," returned S. Behrman, "but you won't succeed. Better give up trying, my boy. As I said, the best way is to have the railroad and the farmer get along amicably. It is the only way we can do business. Well, s'long, Governor, I must trot along. S'long, Harran." He took himself off.

But before leaving Guadalajara Magnus dropped into the town's small grocery store to purchase a box of cigars of a certain Mexican brand, unprocurable elsewhere. Harran remained in the buggy.

While he waited, Dyke appeared at the end of the street, and, seeing Derrick's younger son, came over to shake hands with him. He explained his affair with the P. and S. W., and asked the young man what he thought of the expected rise in the price of hops.

"Hops ought to be a good thing," Harran told him. "The crop in Germany and in New York has been a dead failure for the last three years, and so many people have gone out of the business that there's likely to be a shortage and a stiff advance in the price. They ought to go to a dollar next year. Sure, hops ought to be a good thing. How's the old lady and Sidney, Dyke?"

"Why, fairly well, thank you, Harran. They're up to Sacramento just now to see my brother. I was thinking of going in with my brother into this hop business. But I had a letter from him this morning. He may not be able to meet me on this proposition. He's got other business on hand. If he pulls out—and he probably will—I'll have to go it alone, but I'll have to borrow. I had thought with his money and mine we would have enough to pull off the affair without mortgaging anything. As it is, I guess I'll have to see S. Behrman."

"I'll be cursed if I would!" exclaimed Harran.

"Well, S. Behrman is a screw," admitted the engineer, "and he is 'railroad' to his boots; but business is business, and he would have to stand by a contract in black and white, and this chance in hops is too good to let slide. I guess we'll try it on, Harran. I can get a good foreman that knows all about hops just now, and if the deal pays—well, I want to send Sid to a seminary up in San Francisco."

"Well, mortgage the crops, but don't mortgage the homestead, Dyke," said Harran. "And, by the way, have you looked up the freight rates on hops?"

"No, I haven't yet," answered Dyke, "and I had better be sure of that, hadn't I? I hear that the rate is reasonable, though."

"You be sure to have a clear understanding with the railroad first about the rate," Harran warned him.

When Magnus came out of the grocery store and once more seated himself in the buggy, he said to Harran, "Boy, drive over here to Annixter's before we start home. I want to ask him to dine with us to-night. Osterman and Broderson are to drop in, I believe, and I should like to have Annixter as well."

Magnus was lavishly hospitable. Los Muertos's doors invariably stood open to all the Derricks' neighbours, and once in so often Magnus had a few of his intimates to dinner.

As Harran and his father drove along the road toward Annixter's ranch house, Magnus asked about what had happened during his absence.

He inquired after his wife and the ranch, commenting upon the work on the irrigating ditch. Harran gave him the news of the past week, Dyke's discharge, his resolve to raise a crop of hops; Vanamee's return, the killing of the sheep, and Hooven's petition to remain upon the ranch as Magnus's tenant. It needed only Harran's recommendation that the German should remain to have Magnus consent upon the instant. "You know more about it than I, boy," he said, "and whatever you think is wise shall be done."

Harran touched the bays with the whip, urging them to their briskest pace. They were not yet at Annixter's and he was anxious to get back to the ranch house to supervise the blue-stoning of his seed.

"By the way, Governor," he demanded suddenly, "how is Lyman getting on?"

Lyman, Magnus's eldest son, had never taken kindly toward ranch life. He resembled his mother more than he did Magnus, and had inherited from her a distaste for agriculture and a tendency toward a profession. At a time when Harran was learning the rudiments of farming, Lyman was entering the State University, and, graduating thence, had spent three years in the study of law. But later on, traits that were particularly his father's developed. Politics interested him. He told himself he was a born politician, was diplomatic, approachable, had a talent for intrigue, a gift of making friends easily and, most indispensable of all, a veritable genius for putting influential men under obligations to himself. Already he had succeeded in gaining for himself two important offices in the municipal administration of San Francisco—where he had his home—sheriff's attorney, and, later on, assistant district attorney. But with these small achievements he was by no means satisfied. The largeness of his father's character, modified in Lyman by a counter-influence of selfishness, had produced in him an inordinate ambition. Where his father during his political career had considered himself only as an exponent of principles he strove to apply, Lyman saw but the office, his own personal aggrandisement. He belonged to the new school, wherein objects were attained not by orations before senates and assemblies, but by sessions of committees, caucuses, compromises and expedients. His goal was to be in fact what Magnus was only in name—governor. Lyman, with shut teeth, had resolved that some day he would sit in the gubernatorial chair in Sacramento.

"Lyman is doing well," answered Magnus. "I could wish he was more pronounced in his convictions, less willing to compromise, but I believe him to be earnest and to have a talent for government and civics. His ambition does him credit, and if he occupied himself a little more with means and a little less with ends, he would, I am sure, be the ideal servant of the people. But I am not afraid. The time will come when the State will be proud of him."

As Harran turned the team into the driveway that led up to Annixter's house, Magnus remarked:

"Harran, isn't that young Annixter himself on the porch?"

Harran nodded and remarked:

"By the way, Governor, I wouldn't seem too cordial in your invitation to Annixter. He will be glad to come, I know, but if you seem to want him too much, it is just like his confounded obstinacy to make objections."

"There is something in that," observed Magnus, as Harran drew up at the porch of the house. "He is a queer, cross-grained fellow, but in many ways sterling."

Annixter was lying in the hammock on the porch, precisely as Presley had found him the day before, reading "David Copperfield" and stuffing himself with dried prunes. When he recognised Magnus, however, he got up, though careful to give evidence of the most poignant discomfort. He explained his difficulty at great length, protesting that his stomach was no better than a spongebag. Would Magnus and Harran get down and have a drink? There was whiskey somewhere about.

Magnus, however, declined. He stated his errand, asking Annixter to come over to Los Muertos that evening for seven o'clock dinner. Osterman and Broderson would be there.

At once Annixter, even to Harran's surprise, put his chin in the air, making excuses, fearing to compromise himself if he accepted too readily. No, he did not think he could get around—was sure of it, in fact. There were certain businesses he had on hand that evening. He had practically made an appointment with a man at Bonneville; then, too, he was thinking of going up to San Francisco to-morrow and needed his sleep; would go to bed early; and besides all that, he was a very sick man;

his stomach was out of whack; if he moved about it brought the gripes back. No, they must get along without him.

Magnus, knowing with whom he had to deal, did not urge the point, being convinced that Annixter would argue over the affair the rest of the morning. He re-settled himself in the buggy and Harran gathered up the reins.

"Well," he observed, "you know your business best. Come if you can. We dine at seven."

"I hear you are going to farm the whole of Los Muertos this season," remarked Annixter, with a certain note of challenge in his voice.

"We are thinking of it," replied Magnus.

Annixter grunted scornfully.

"Did you get the message I sent you by Presley?" he began.

Tactless, blunt, and direct, Annixter was quite capable of calling even Magnus a fool to his face. But before he could proceed, S. Behrman in his single buggy turned into the gate, and driving leisurely up to the porch halted on the other side of Magnus's team.

"Good-morning, gentlemen," he remarked, nodding to the two Derricks as though he had not seen them earlier in the day. "Mr. Annixter, how do you do?"

"What in hell do YOU want?" demanded Annixter with a stare.

S. Behrman hiccoughed slightly and passed a fat hand over his waistcoat.

"Why, not very much, Mr. Annixter," he replied, ignoring the belligerency in the young ranchman's voice, "but I will have to lodge a protest against you, Mr. Annixter, in the matter of keeping your line fence in repair. The sheep were all over the track last night, this side the Long Trestle, and I am afraid they have seriously disturbed our ballast along there. We—the railroad—can't fence along our right of way. The farmers have the prescriptive right of that, so we have to look to you to keep your fence in repair. I am sorry, but I shall have to protest—" Annixter returned to the hammock and stretched himself out in it to his full length, remarking tranquilly:

"Go to the devil!"

"It is as much to your interest as to ours that the safety of the public—"

"You heard what I said. Go to the devil!"

"That all may show obstinacy, Mr. Annixter, but—"

Suddenly Annixter jumped up again and came to the edge of the porch; his face flamed scarlet to the roots of his stiff yellow hair. He thrust out his jaw aggressively, clenching his teeth.

"You," he vociferated, "I'll tell you what you are. You're a—a—a PIP!"

To his mind it was the last insult, the most outrageous calumny. He had no worse epithet at his command.

"—may show obstinacy," pursued S. Behrman, bent upon finishing the phrase, "but it don't show common sense."

"I'll mend my fence, and then, again, maybe I won't mend my fence," shouted Annixter. "I know what you mean—that wild engine last night. Well, you've no right to run at that speed in the town limits."

"How the town limits? The sheep were this side the Long Trestle."

"Well, that's in the town limits of Guadalajara."

"Why, Mr. Annixter, the Long Trestle is a good two miles out of Guadalajara."

Annixter squared himself, leaping to the chance of an argument.

"Two miles! It's not a mile and a quarter. No, it's not a mile. I'll leave it to Magnus here."

"Oh, I know nothing about it," declared Magnus, refusing to be involved.

"Yes, you do. Yes, you do, too. Any fool knows how far it is from Guadalajara to the Long Trestle. It's about five-eighths of a mile."

"From the depot of the town," remarked S. Behrman placidly, "to the head of the Long Trestle is about two miles."

"That's a lie and you know it's a lie," shouted the other, furious at S. Behrman's calmness, "and I can prove it's a lie. I've walked that distance on the Upper Road, and I know just how fast I walk, and if I can walk four miles in one hour."

Magnus and Harran drove on, leaving Annixter trying to draw S. Behrman into a wrangle.

When at length S. Behrman as well took himself away, Annixter returned to his hammock, finished the rest of his prunes and read another chapter of "Copperfield." Then he put the book, open, over his face and went to sleep.

An hour later, toward noon, his own terrific snoring woke him up suddenly, and he sat up, rubbing his face and blinking at the sunlight. There was a bad taste in his mouth from sleeping with it wide open, and going into the dining-room of the house, he mixed himself a drink of whiskey and soda and swallowed it in three great gulps. He told himself that he felt not only better but hungry, and pressed an electric button in the wall near the sideboard three times to let the kitchen—situated in a separate building near the ranch house—know that he was ready for his dinner. As he did so, an idea occurred to him. He wondered if Hilma Tree would bring up his dinner and wait on the table while he ate it.

In connection with his ranch, Annixter ran a dairy farm on a very small scale, making just enough butter and cheese for the consumption of the ranch's PERSONNEL. Old man Tree, his wife, and his daughter Hilma looked after the dairy. But there was not always work enough to keep the three of them occupied and Hilma at times made herself useful in other ways. As often as not she lent a hand in the kitchen, and two or three times a week she took her mother's place in looking after Annixter's house, making the beds, putting his room to rights, bringing his meals up from the kitchen. For the last summer she had been away visiting with relatives in one of the towns on the coast. But the week previous to this she had returned and Annixter had come upon her suddenly one day in the dairy, making cheese, the sleeves of her crisp blue shirt waist rolled back to her very shoulders. Annixter had carried away with him a clear-cut recollection of these smooth white arms of hers, bare to the shoulder, very round and cool and fresh. He would not have believed that a girl so young should have had arms so big and perfect. To his surprise he found himself thinking of her after he had gone to bed that night, and in the morning when he woke he was bothered to know whether he had dreamed about Hilma's fine white arms over night. Then abruptly he had lost patience with himself for being so occupied with the subject, raging and furious with all the breed of feemales—a fine way for a man to waste his time. He had had his experience with the timid little creature in the glove-cleaning establishment in Sacramento. That was enough. Feemales! Rot! None of them in HIS, thank you. HE had seen Hilma Tree give him a look in the dairy. Aha, he saw through her! She was trying to get a hold on him, was she? He would show her. Wait till he saw her again. He would send her about her business in a hurry. He resolved upon a terrible demeanour in the presence of the dairy girl—a great show of indifference, a fierce masculine nonchalance; and when, the next morning, she brought him his breakfast, he had been smitten dumb as soon as she entered the room, glueing his eyes upon his plate, his elbows close to his side, awkward, clumsy, overwhelmed with constraint.

While true to his convictions as a woman-hater and genuinely despising Hilma both as a girl and as an inferior, the idea of her worried him. Most of all, he was angry with himself because of his inane sheepishness when she was about. He at first had told himself that he was a fool not to be able to ignore her existence as hitherto, and then that he was a greater fool not to take advantage of his position. Certainly he had not the remotest idea of any affection, but Hilma was a fine looking girl. He imagined an affair with her.

As he reflected upon the matter now, scowling abstractedly at the button of the electric bell, turning the whole business over in his mind, he remembered that to-day was butter-making day and that Mrs. Tree would be occupied in the dairy. That meant that Hilma would take her place. He turned to the mirror of the sideboard, scrutinising his reflection with grim disfavour. After a moment, rubbing the roughened surface of his chin the wrong way, he muttered to his image in the glass:

"That a mug! Good Lord! what a looking mug!" Then, after a moment's silence, "Wonder if that fool feemale will be up here to-day."

He crossed over into his bedroom and peeped around the edge of the lowered curtain. The window looked out upon the skeleton-like tower of the artesian well and the cook-house and dairy-house close beside it. As he watched, he saw Hilma come out from the cook-house and hurry across toward the kitchen. Evidently, she was going to see about his dinner. But as she passed by the artesian well, she met young Delaney, one of Annixter's hands, coming up the trail by the irrigating ditch, leading his horse toward the stables, a great coil of barbed wire in his gloved hands and a pair of nippers thrust into his belt. No doubt, he had been mending the break in the line fence by the Long Trestle. Annixter saw him take off his wide-brimmed hat as he met Hilma, and the two stood there for some moments talking together. Annixter even heard Hilma laughing very gayly at something Delaney was saying. She patted his horse's neck affectionately, and Delaney, drawing the nippers from his belt, made as if to pinch her arm with them. She caught at his wrist and pushed him away, laughing again. To Annixter's mind the pair seemed astonishingly intimate. Brusquely his anger flamed up.

Ah, that was it, was it? Delaney and Hilma had an understanding between themselves. They carried on their affair right out there in the open, under his very eyes. It was absolutely disgusting. Had they no sense of decency, those two? Well, this ended it. He would stop that sort of thing short off; none of that on HIS ranch if he knew it. No, sir. He would pack that girl off before he was a day older. He wouldn't have that kind about the place. Not much! She'd have to get out. He would talk to old man Tree about it this afternoon. Whatever happened, HE insisted upon morality.

"And my dinner!" he suddenly exclaimed. "I've got to wait and go hungry—and maybe get sick again—while they carry on their disgusting love-making."

He turned about on the instant, and striding over to the electric bell, rang it again with all his might.

"When that feemale gets up here," he declared, "I'll just find out why I've got to wait like this. I'll take her down, to the Queen's taste. I'm lenient enough, Lord knows, but I don't propose to be imposed upon ALL the time."

A few moments later, while Annixter was pretending to read the county newspaper by the window in the dining-room, Hilma came in to set the table. At the time Annixter had his feet cocked on the window ledge and was smoking a cigar, but as soon as she entered the room he—without premeditation—brought his feet down to the floor and crushed out the lighted tip of his cigar under the window ledge. Over the top of the paper he glanced at her covertly from time to time.

Though Hilma was only nineteen years old, she was a large girl with all the development of a much older woman. There was a certain generous amplitude to the full, round curves of her hips and shoulders that suggested the precocious maturity of a healthy, vigorous animal life passed under the hot southern sun of a half-tropical country. She was, one knew at a glance, warm-blooded, full-blooded, with an even, comfortable balance of temperament. Her neck was thick, and sloped to her shoulders, with full, beautiful curves, and under her chin and under her ears the flesh was as white and smooth as floss satin, shading exquisitely to a faint delicate brown on her nape at the roots of her hair. Her throat rounded to meet her chin and cheek, with a soft swell of the skin, tinted pale amber in the shadows, but blending by barely perceptible gradations to the sweet, warm flush of her cheek. This colour on her temples was just touched with a certain blueness where the flesh was thin over the fine veining underneath. Her eyes were light brown, and so wide open that on the slightest provocation the full disc of the pupil was disclosed; the lids—just a fraction of a shade darker than the hue of her face—were edged with lashes that were almost black. While these lashes were not long, they were thick and rimmed her eyes with a fine, thin line. Her mouth was rather large, the lips shut tight, and nothing could have been more graceful, more charming than the outline of these full lips of hers, and her round white chin, modulating downward with a certain delicious roundness to her neck, her throat and the sweet feminine amplitude of her breast. The slightest movement of her head and shoulders sent a gentle undulation through all this beauty of soft outlines and smooth surfaces, the delicate amber shadows deepening or fading or losing themselves imperceptibly in the pretty rose-colour of her cheeks, or the dark, warm-tinted shadow of her thick brown hair.

Her hair seemed almost to have a life of its own, almost Medusa-like, thick, glossy and moist, lying in heavy, sweet-smelling masses over her forehead, over her small ears with their pink lobes, and far down upon her nape. Deep in between the coils and braids it was of a bitumen brownness, but in the sunlight it vibrated with a sheen like tarnished gold.

Like most large girls, her movements were not hurried, and this indefinite deliberateness of gesture, this slow grace, this certain ease of attitude, was a charm that was all her own.

But Hilma's greatest charm of all was her simplicity—a simplicity that was not only in the calm regularity of her face, with its statuesque evenness of contour, its broad surface of cheek and forehead and the masses of her straight smooth hair, but was apparent as well in the long line of her carriage, from her foot to her waist and the single deep swell from her waist to her shoulder. Almost unconsciously she dressed in harmony with this note of simplicity, and on this occasion wore a skirt of plain dark blue calico and a white shirt waist crisp from the laundry.

And yet, for all the dignity of this rigourous simplicity, there were about Hilma small contradictory suggestions of feminine daintiness, charming beyond words. Even Annixter could not help noticing that her feet were narrow and slender, and that the little steel buckles of her low shoes were polished bright, and that her fingertips and nails were of a fine rosy pink.

He found himself wondering how it was that a girl in Hilma's position should be able to keep herself so pretty, so trim, so clean and feminine, but he reflected that her work was chiefly in the dairy, and even there of the lightest order. She was on the ranch more for the sake of being with her parents than from any necessity of employment. Vaguely he seemed to understand that, in that great new land of the West, in the open-air, healthy life of the ranches, where the conditions of earning a livelihood were of the easiest, refinement among the younger women was easily to be found—not the refinement of education, nor culture, but the natural, intuitive refinement of the woman, not as yet defiled and crushed out by the sordid, strenuous life-struggle of over-populated districts. It was the original, intended and natural delicacy of an elemental existence, close to nature, close to life, close to the great, kindly earth.

As Hilma laid the table-spread, her arms opened to their widest reach, the white cloth setting a little glisten of reflected light underneath the chin, Annixter stirred in his place uneasily.

"Oh, it's you, is it, Miss Hilma?" he remarked, for the sake of saying something. "Good-morning. How do you do?"

"Good-morning, sir," she answered, looking up, resting for a moment on her outspread palms. "I hope you are better."

Her voice was low in pitch and of a velvety huskiness, seeming to come more from her chest than from her throat.

"Well, I'm some better," growled Annixter. Then suddenly he demanded, "Where's that dog?"

A decrepit Irish setter sometimes made his appearance in and about the ranch house, sleeping under the bed and eating when anyone about the place thought to give him a plate of bread.

Annixter had no particular interest in the dog. For weeks at a time he ignored its existence. It was not his dog. But to-day it seemed as if he could not let the subject rest. For no reason that he could explain even to himself, he recurred to it continually. He questioned Hilma minutely all about the dog. Who owned him? How old did she think he was? Did she imagine the dog was sick? Where had he got to? Maybe he had crawled off to die somewhere. He recurred to the subject all through the meal; apparently, he could talk of nothing else, and as she finally went away after clearing off the table, he went onto the porch and called after her:

"Say, Miss Hilma."

"Yes, sir."

"If that dog turns up again you let me know."

"Very well, sir."

Annixter returned to the dining-room and sat down in the chair he had just vacated. "To hell with the dog!" he muttered, enraged, he could not tell why.

When at length he allowed his attention to wander from Hilma Tree, he found that he had been staring fixedly at a thermometer upon the wall opposite, and this made him think that it had long been his intention to buy a fine barometer, an instrument that could be accurately depended on. But the barometer suggested the present condition of the weather and the likelihood of rain. In such case, much was to be done in the way of getting the seed ready and overhauling his ploughs and drills. He had not been away from the house in two days. It was time to be up and doing. He determined to put in the afternoon "taking a look around," and have a late supper. He would not go to Los Muertos; he would ignore Magnus Derrick's invitation. Possibly, though, it might be well to run over and see what was up.

"If I do," he said to himself, "I'll ride the buckskin." The buckskin was a half-broken broncho that fought like a fiend under the saddle until the quirt and spur brought her to her senses. But Annixter remembered that the Trees' cottage, next the dairy-house, looked out upon the stables, and perhaps Hilma would see him while he was mounting the horse and be impressed with his courage.

"Huh!" grunted Annixter under his breath, "I should like to see that fool Delaney try to bust that bronch. That's what I'D like to see."

However, as Annixter stepped from the porch of the ranch house, he was surprised to notice a grey haze over all the sky; the sunlight was gone; there was a sense of coolness in the air; the weather-vane on the barn—a fine golden trotting horse with flamboyant mane and tail—was veering in a southwest wind. Evidently the expected rain was close at hand.

Annixter crossed over to the stables reflecting that he could ride the buckskin to the Trees' cottage and tell Hilma that he would not be home to supper. The conference at Los Muertos would be an admirable excuse for this, and upon the spot he resolved to go over to the Derrick ranch house, after all.

As he passed the Trees' cottage, he observed with satisfaction that Hilma was going to and fro in the front room. If he busted the buckskin in the yard before the stable she could not help but see. Annixter found the stableman in the back of the barn greasing the axles of the buggy, and ordered him to put the saddle on the buckskin.

"Why, I don't think she's here, sir," answered the stableman, glancing into the stalls. "No, I remember now. Delaney took her out just after dinner. His other horse went lame and he wanted to go down by the Long Trestle to mend the fence. He started out, but had to come back."

"Oh, Delaney got her, did he?"

"Yes, sir. He had a circus with her, but he busted her right enough. When it comes to horse, Delaney can wipe the eye of any cow-puncher in the county, I guess."

"He can, can he?" observed Annixter. Then after a silence, "Well, all right, Billy; put my saddle on whatever you've got here. I'm going over to Los Muertos this afternoon."

"Want to look out for the rain, Mr. Annixter," remarked Billy. "Guess we'll have rain before night."

"I'll take a rubber coat," answered Annixter. "Bring the horse up to the ranch house when you're ready."

Annixter returned to the house to look for his rubber coat in deep disgust, not permitting himself to glance toward the dairy-house and the Trees' cottage. But as he reached the porch he heard the telephone ringing his call. It was Presley, who rang up from Los Muertos. He had heard from Harran that Annixter was, perhaps, coming over that evening. If he came, would he mind bringing over his—Presley's—bicycle. He had left it at the Quien Sabe ranch the day before and had forgotten to come back that way for it.

"Well," objected Annixter, a surly note in his voice, "I WAS going to RIDE over."

"Oh, never mind, then," returned Presley easily. "I was to blame for forgetting it. Don't bother about it. I'll come over some of these days and get it myself."

Annixter hung up the transmitter with a vehement wrench and stamped out of the room, banging the door. He found his rubber coat hanging in the hallway and swung into it with a fierce movement of the shoulders that all but started the seams. Everything seemed to conspire to thwart him. It was just like that absent-minded, crazy poet, Presley, to forget his wheel. Well, he could come after it himself. He, Annixter, would ride SOME horse, anyhow. When he came out upon the porch he saw the wheel leaning against the fence where Presley had left it. If it stayed there much longer the rain would catch it. Annixter ripped out an oath. At every moment his ill-humour was increasing. Yet, for all that, he went back to the stable, pushing the bicycle before him, and countermanded his order, directing the stableman to get the buggy ready. He himself carefully stowed Presley's bicycle under the seat, covering it with a couple of empty sacks and a tarpaulin carriage cover.

While he was doing this, the stableman uttered an exclamation and paused in the act of backing the horse into the shafts, holding up a hand, listening.

From the hollow roof of the barn and from the thick velvet-like padding of dust over the ground outside, and from among the leaves of the few nearby trees and plants there came a vast, monotonous murmur that seemed to issue from all quarters of the horizon at once, a prolonged and subdued rustling sound, steady, even, persistent.

"There's your rain," announced the stableman. "The first of the season."

"And I got to be out in it," fumed Annixter, "and I suppose those swine will quit work on the big barn now."

When the buggy was finally ready, he put on his rubber coat, climbed in, and without waiting for the stableman to raise the top, drove out into the rain, a new-lit cigar in his teeth. As he passed the dairy-house, he saw Hilma standing in the doorway, holding out her hand to the rain, her face turned upward toward the grey sky, amused and interested at this first shower of the wet season. She was so absorbed that she did not see Annixter, and his clumsy nod in her direction passed unnoticed.

"She did it on purpose," Annixter told himself, chewing fiercely on his cigar. "Cuts me now, hey? Well, this DOES settle it. She leaves this ranch before I'm a day older."

He decided that he would put off his tour of inspection till the next day. Travelling in the buggy as he did, he must keep to the road which led to Derrick's, in very roundabout fashion, by way of Guadalajara. This rain would reduce the thick dust of the road to two feet of viscid mud. It would take him quite three hours to reach the ranch house on Los Muertos. He thought of Delaney and the buckskin and ground his teeth. And all this trouble, if you please, because of a fool feemale girl. A fine way for him to waste his time. Well, now he was done with it. His decision was taken now. She should pack.

Steadily the rain increased. There was no wind. The thick veil of wet descended straight from sky to earth, blurring distant outlines, spreading a vast sheen of grey over all the landscape. Its volume became greater, the prolonged murmuring note took on a deeper tone. At the gate to the road which led across Dyke's hop-fields toward Guadalajara, Annixter was obliged to descend and raise the top of the buggy. In doing so he caught the flesh of his hand in the joint of the iron elbow that supported the top and pinched it cruelly. It was the last misery, the culmination of a long train of wretchedness. On the instant he hated Hilma Tree so fiercely that his sharply set teeth all but bit his cigar in two.

While he was grabbing and wrenching at the buggy-top, the water from his hat brim dripping down upon his nose, the horse, restive under the drench of the rain, moved uneasily.

"Yah-h-h you!" he shouted, inarticulate with exasperation. "You—you—Gor-r-r, wait till I get hold of you. WHOA, you!"

But there was an interruption. Delaney, riding the buckskin, came around a bend in the road at a slow trot and Annixter, getting into the buggy again, found himself face to face with him.

"Why, hello, Mr. Annixter," said he, pulling up. "Kind of sort of wet, isn't it?"

Annixter, his face suddenly scarlet, sat back in his place abruptly, exclaiming:

"Oh—oh, there you are, are you?"

"I've been down there," explained Delaney, with a motion of his head toward the railroad, "to mend that break in the fence by the Long Trestle and I thought while I was about it I'd follow down along the fence toward Guadalajara to see if there were any more breaks. But I guess it's all right."

"Oh, you guess it's all right, do you?" observed Annixter through his teeth.

"Why—why—yes," returned the other, bewildered at the truculent ring in Annixter's voice. "I mended that break by the Long Trestle just now and—

"Well, why didn't you mend it a week ago?" shouted Annixter wrathfully. "I've been looking for you all the morning, I have, and who told you you could take that buckskin? And the sheep were all over the right of way last night because of that break, and here that filthy pip, S. Behrman, comes down here this morning and wants to make trouble for me." Suddenly he cried out, "What do I FEED you for? What do I keep you around here for? Think it's just to fatten up your carcass, hey?"

"Why, Mr. Annixter—" began Delaney.

"And don't TALK to me," vociferated the other, exciting himself with his own noise. "Don't you say a word to me even to apologise. If I've spoken to you once about that break, I've spoken fifty times."

"Why, sir," declared Delaney, beginning to get indignant, "the sheep did it themselves last night."

"I told you not to TALK to me," clamoured Annixter.

"But, say, look here—"

"Get off the ranch. You get off the ranch. And taking that buckskin against my express orders. I won't have your kind about the place, not much. I'm easy-going enough, Lord knows, but I don't propose to be imposed on ALL the time. Pack off, you understand and do it lively. Go to the foreman and tell him I told him to pay you off and then clear out. And, you hear me," he concluded, with a menacing outthrust of his lower jaw, "you hear me, if I catch you hanging around the ranch house after this, or if I so much as see you on Quien Sabe, I'll show you the way off of it, my friend, at the toe of my boot. Now, then, get out of the way and let me pass."

Angry beyond the power of retort, Delaney drove the spurs into the buckskin and passed the buggy in a single bound. Annixter gathered up the reins and drove on muttering to himself, and occasionally looking back to observe the buckskin flying toward the ranch house in a spattering shower of mud, Delaney urging her on, his head bent down against the falling rain.

"Huh," grunted Annixter with grim satisfaction, a certain sense of good humour at length returning to him, "that just about takes the saleratus out of YOUR dough, my friend."

A little farther on, Annixter got out of the buggy a second time to open another gate that let him out upon the Upper Road, not far distant from Guadalajara. It was the road that connected that town with Bonneville and that ran parallel with the railroad tracks. On the other side of the track he could see the infinite extension of the brown, bare land of Los Muertos, turning now to a soft, moist welter of fertility under the insistent caressing of the rain. The hard, sun-baked clods were decomposing, the crevices between drinking the wet with an eager, sucking noise. But the prospect was dreary; the distant horizons were blotted under drifting mists of rain; the eternal monotony of the earth lay open to the sombre low sky without a single adornment, without a single variation from its melancholy flatness. Near at hand the wires between the telegraph poles vibrated with a faint humming under the multitudinous fingering of the myriad of falling drops, striking among them and dripping off steadily from one to another. The poles themselves were dark and swollen and glistening with wet, while the little cones of glass on the transverse bars reflected the dull grey light of the end of the afternoon.

As Annixter was about to drive on, a freight train passed, coming from Guadalajara, going northward toward Bonneville, Fresno and San Francisco. It was a long train, moving slowly, methodically, with a measured coughing of its locomotive and a rhythmic cadence of its trucks over the interstices of the rails. On two or three of the flat cars near its end, Annixter plainly saw Magnus Derrick's ploughs, their bright coating of red and green paint setting a single brilliant note in all this array of grey and brown.

Annixter halted, watching the train file past, carrying Derrick's ploughs away from his ranch, at this very time of the first rain, when they would be most needed. He watched it, silent, thoughtful, and without articulate comment. Even after it passed he sat in his place a long time, watching it lose itself slowly in the distance, its prolonged rumble diminishing to a faint murmur. Soon he heard the engine sounding its whistle for the Long Trestle.

But the moving train no longer carried with it that impression of terror and destruction that had so thrilled Presley's imagination the night before. It passed slowly on its way with a mournful roll of wheels, like the passing of a cortege, like a file of artillery-caissons charioting dead bodies; the engine's smoke enveloping it in a mournful veil, leaving a sense of melancholy in its wake, moving past there, lugubrious, lamentable, infinitely sad under the grey sky and under the grey mist of rain which continued to fall with a subdued, rustling sound, steady, persistent, a vast monotonous murmur that seemed to come from all quarters of the horizon at once.

III

When Annixter arrived at the Los Muertos ranch house that same evening, he found a little group already assembled in the dining-room. Magnus Derrick, wearing the frock coat of broadcloth that he had put on for the occasion, stood with his back to the fireplace. Harran sat close at hand, one leg thrown over the arm of his chair. Presley lounged on the sofa, in corduroys and high laced boots, smoking cigarettes. Broderson leaned on his folded arms at one corner of the dining table, and Genslinger, editor and proprietor of the principal newspaper of the county, the "Bonneville Mercury," stood with his hat and driving gloves under his arm, opposite Derrick, a half-emptied glass of whiskey and water in his hand.

As Annixter entered he heard Genslinger observe: "I'll have a leader in the 'Mercury' to-morrow that will interest you people. There's some talk of your ranch lands being graded in value this winter. I suppose you will all buy?"

In an instant the editor's words had riveted upon him the attention of every man in the room. Annixter broke the moment's silence that followed with the remark:

"Well, it's about time they graded these lands of theirs."

The question in issue in Genslinger's remark was of the most vital interest to the ranchers around Bonneville and Guadalajara. Neither Magnus Derrick, Broderson,

Annixter, nor Osterman actually owned all the ranches which they worked. As yet, the vast majority of these wheat lands were the property of the P. and S. W. The explanation of this condition of affairs went back to the early history of the Pacific and Southwestern, when, as a bonus for the construction of the road, the national government had granted to the company the odd numbered sections of land on either side of the proposed line of route for a distance of twenty miles. Indisputably, these sections belonged to the P. and S. W. The even-numbered sections being government property could be and had been taken up by the ranchers, but the railroad sections, or, as they were called, the "alternate sections," would have to be purchased direct from the railroad itself.

But this had not prevented the farmers from "coming in" upon that part of the San Joaquin. Long before this the railroad had thrown open these lands, and, by means of circulars, distributed broadcast throughout the State, had expressly invited settlement thereon. At that time patents had not been issued to the railroad for their odd-numbered sections, but as soon as the land was patented the railroad would grade it in value and offer it for sale, the first occupants having the first chance of purchase. The price of these lands was to be fixed by the price the government put upon its own adjoining lands—about two dollars and a half per acre.

With cultivation and improvement the ranches must inevitably appreciate in value. There was every chance to make fortunes. When the railroad lands about Bonneville had been thrown open, there had been almost a rush in the matter of settlement, and Broderson, Annixter, Derrick, and Osterman, being foremost with their claims, had secured the pick of the country. But the land once settled upon, the P. and S. W. seemed to be in no hurry as to fixing exactly the value of its sections included in the various ranches and offering them for sale. The matter dragged along from year to year, was forgotten for months together, being only brought to mind on such occasions as this, when the rumour spread that the General Office was about to take definite action in the affair.

"As soon as the railroad wants to talk business with me," observed Annixter, "about selling me their interest in Quien Sabe, I'm ready. The land has more than quadrupled in value. I'll bet I could sell it to-morrow for fifteen dollars an acre, and if I buy of the railroad for two and a half an acre, there's boodle in the game."

"For two and a half!" exclaimed Genslinger. "You don't suppose the railroad will let their land go for any such figure as that, do you? Wherever did you get that idea?"

"From the circulars and pamphlets," answered Harran, "that the railroad issued to us when they opened these lands. They are pledged to that. Even the P. and S. W. couldn't break such a pledge as that. You are new in the country, Mr. Genslinger. You don't remember the conditions upon which we took up this land."

"And our improvements," exclaimed Annixter. "Why, Magnus and I have put about five thousand dollars between us into that irrigating ditch already. I guess we are not improving the land just to make it valuable for the railroad people. No matter how much we improve the land, or how much it increases in value, they have got to stick by their agreement on the basis of two-fifty per acre. Here's one case where the P. and S. W. DON'T get everything in sight."

Genslinger frowned, perplexed.

"I AM new in the country, as Harran says," he answered, "but it seems to me that there's no fairness in that proposition. The presence of the railroad has helped increase the value of your ranches quite as much as your improvements. Why should you get all the benefit of the rise in value and the railroad nothing? The fair way would be to share it between you."

"I don't care anything about that," declared Annixter. "They agreed to charge but two-fifty, and they've got to stick to it."

"Well," murmured Genslinger, "from what I know of the affair, I don't believe the P. and S. W. intends to sell for two-fifty an acre, at all. The managers of the road want the best price they can get for everything in these hard times."

"Times aren't ever very hard for the railroad," hazards old Broderson.

Broderson was the oldest man in the room. He was about sixty-five years of age, venerable, with a white beard, his figure bent earthwards with hard work.

He was a narrow-minded man, painfully conscientious in his statements lest he should be unjust to somebody; a slow thinker, unable to let a subject drop when once he had started upon it. He had no sooner uttered his remark about hard times than he was moved to qualify it.

"Hard times," he repeated, a troubled, perplexed note in his voice; "well, yes—yes. I suppose the road DOES have hard times, maybe. Everybody does—of course. I didn't mean that exactly. I believe in being just and fair to everybody. I mean that we've got to use their lines and pay their charges good years AND bad years, the P. and S. W. being the only road in the State. That is—well, when I say the only road—no, I won't say the ONLY road. Of course there are other roads. There's the D. P. and M. and the San Francisco and North Pacific, that runs up to Ukiah. I got a brother-in-law in Ukiah. That's not much of a wheat country round Ukiah though they DO grow SOME wheat there, come to think. But I guess it's too far north. Well, of course there isn't MUCH. Perhaps sixty thousand acres in the whole county—if you include barley and oats. I don't know; maybe it's nearer forty thousand. I don't remember very well. That's a good many years ago. I—"

But Annixter, at the end of all patience, turned to Genslinger, cutting short the old man:

"Oh, rot! Of course the railroad will sell at two-fifty," he cried. "We've got the contracts."

"Look to them, then, Mr. Annixter," retorted Genslinger significantly, "look to them. Be sure that you are protected."

Soon after this Genslinger took himself away, and Derrick's Chinaman came in to set the table.

"What do you suppose he meant?" asked Broderson, when Genslinger was gone.

"About this land business?" said Annixter. "Oh, I don't know. Some tom fool idea. Haven't we got their terms printed in black and white in their circulars? There's their pledge."

"Oh, as to pledges," murmured Broderson, "the railroad is not always TOO much hindered by those."

"Where's Osterman?" demanded Annixter, abruptly changing the subject as if it were not worth discussion. "Isn't that goat Osterman coming down here to-night?"

"You telephoned him, didn't you, Presley?" inquired Magnus.

Presley had taken Princess Nathalie upon his knee stroking her long, sleek hair, and the cat, stupefied with beatitude, had closed her eyes to two fine lines, clawing softly at the corduroy of Presley's trousers with alternate paws.

"Yes, sir," returned Presley. "He said he would be here."

And as he spoke, young Osterman arrived.

He was a young fellow, but singularly inclined to baldness. His ears, very red and large, stuck out at right angles from either side of his head, and his mouth, too, was large—a great horizontal slit beneath his nose. His cheeks were of a brownish red, the cheek bones a little salient. His face was that of a comic actor, a singer of songs, a man never at a loss for an answer, continually striving to make a laugh. But he took no great interest in ranching and left the management of his land to his superintendents and foremen, he, himself, living in Bonneville. He was a poser, a wearer of clothes, forever acting a part, striving to create an impression, to draw attention to himself. He was not without a certain energy, but he devoted it to small ends, to perfecting himself in little accomplishments, continually running after some new thing, incapable of persisting long in any one course. At one moment his mania would be fencing; the next, sleight-of-hand tricks; the next, archery. For upwards of one month he had devoted himself to learning how to play two banjos simultaneously, then abandoning this had developed a sudden passion for stamped leather work and had made a quantity of purses, tennis belts, and hat bands, which he presented to young ladies of his acquaintance. It was his policy never to make an enemy. He was liked far better than he was respected. People spoke of him as "that goat Osterman," or "that fool Osterman kid," and invited him to dinner. He was of the sort who somehow cannot be ignored. If only because of his clamour he made himself important. If he had one abiding trait, it was his desire of astonishing people, and in some way, best known to himself, managed to cause the circulation of the most extraordinary stories wherein he, himself, was the chief actor. He was glib, voluble, dexterous, ubiquitous, a teller of funny stories, a cracker of jokes.

Naturally enough, he was heavily in debt, but carried the burden of it with perfect nonchalance. The year before S. Behrman had held mortgages for fully a third of his crop and had squeezed him viciously for interest. But for all that, Osterman and S. Behrman were continually seen arm-in-arm on the main street of Bonneville. Osterman was accustomed to slap S. Behrman on his fat back, declaring:

"You're a good fellow, old jelly-belly, after all, hey?"

As Osterman entered from the porch, after hanging his cavalry poncho and dripping hat on the rack outside, Mrs. Derrick appeared in the door that opened from the dining-room into the glass-roofed hallway just beyond. Osterman saluted her with effusive cordiality and with ingratiating blandness.

"I am not going to stay," she explained, smiling pleasantly at the group of men, her pretty, wide-open brown eyes, with their look of inquiry and innocence, glancing from face to face, "I only came to see if you wanted anything and to say how do you do."

She began talking to old Broderson, making inquiries as to his wife, who had been sick the last week, and Osterman turned to the company, shaking hands all around, keeping up an incessant stream of conversation.

"Hello, boys and girls. Hello, Governor. Sort of a gathering of the clans to-night. Well, if here isn't that man Annixter. Hello, Buck. What do you know? Kind of dusty out to-night."

At once Annixter began to get red in the face, retiring towards a corner of the room, standing in an awkward position by the case of stuffed birds, shambling and confused, while Mrs. Derrick was present, standing rigidly on both feet, his elbows close to his sides. But he was angry with Osterman, muttering imprecations to himself, horribly vexed that the young fellow should call him "Buck" before Magnus's wife. This goat Osterman! Hadn't he any sense, that fool? Couldn't he ever learn how to behave before a feemale? Calling him "Buck" like that while Mrs. Derrick was there. Why a stable-boy would know better; a hired man would have better manners. All through the dinner that followed Annixter was out of sorts, sulking in his place, refusing to eat by way of vindicating his self-respect, resolving to bring Osterman up with a sharp turn if he called him "Buck" again.

The Chinaman had made a certain kind of plum pudding for dessert, and Annixter, who remembered other dinners at the Derrick's, had been saving himself for this, and had meditated upon it all through the meal. No doubt, it would restore all his good humour, and he believed his stomach was so far recovered as to be able to stand it.

But, unfortunately, the pudding was served with a sauce that he abhorred—a thick, gruel-like, colourless mixture, made from plain water and sugar. Before he could interfere, the Chinaman had poured a quantity of it upon his plate.

"Faugh!" exclaimed Annixter. "It makes me sick. Such—such SLOOP. Take it away. I'll have mine straight, if you don't mind."

"That's good for your stomach, Buck," observed young Osterman; "makes it go down kind of sort of slick; don't you see? Sloop, hey? That's a good name."

"Look here, don't you call me Buck. You don't seem to have any sense, and, besides, it ISN'T good for my stomach. I know better. What do YOU know about my stomach, anyhow? Just looking at sloop like that makes me sick."

A little while after this the Chinaman cleared away the dessert and brought in coffee and cigars. The whiskey bottle and the syphon of soda-water reappeared. The men eased themselves in their places, pushing back from the table, lighting their cigars, talking of the beginning of the rains and the prospects of a rise in wheat. Broderson began an elaborate mental calculation, trying to settle in his mind the exact date of his visit to Ukiah, and Osterman did sleight-of-hand tricks with bread pills. But Princess Nathalie, the cat, was uneasy. Annixter was occupying her own particular chair in which she slept every night. She could not go to sleep, but spied upon him continually, watching his every movement with her lambent, yellow eyes, clear as amber.

Then, at length, Magnus, who was at the head of the table, moved in his place, assuming a certain magisterial attitude. "Well, gentlemen," he observed, "I have lost my case against the railroad, the grain-rate case. Ulsteen decided against me, and now I hear rumours to the effect that rates for the hauling of grain are to be advanced."

When Magnus had finished, there was a moment's silence, each member of the group maintaining his attitude of attention and interest. It was Harran who first spoke.

"S. Behrman manipulated the whole affair. There's a big deal of some kind in the air, and if there is, we all know who is back of it; S. Behrman, of course, but who's back of him? It's Shelgrim."

Shelgrim! The name fell squarely in the midst of the conversation, abrupt, grave, sombre, big with suggestion, pregnant with huge associations. No one in the group who was not familiar with it; no one, for that matter, in the county, the State, the whole reach of the West, the entire Union, that did not entertain convictions as to the man who carried it; a giant figure in the end-of-the-century finance, a product of circumstance, an inevitable result of conditions, characteristic, typical, symbolic of ungovernable forces. In the New Movement, the New Finance, the reorganisation of capital, the amalgamation of powers, the consolidation of enormous enterprises—no one individual was more constantly in the eye of the world; no one was more hated, more dreaded, no one more compelling of unwilling tribute to his commanding genius, to the colossal intellect operating the width of an entire continent than the president and owner of the Pacific and Southwestern.

"I don't think, however, he has moved yet," said Magnus.

"The thing for us, then," exclaimed Osterman, "is to stand from under before he does."

"Moved yet!" snorted Annixter. "He's probably moved so long ago that we've never noticed it."

"In any case," hazarded Magnus, "it is scarcely probable that the deal—whatever it is to be—has been consummated. If we act quickly, there may be a chance."

"Act quickly! How?" demanded Annixter. "Good Lord! what can you do? We're cinched already. It all amounts to just this: YOU CAN'T BUCK AGAINST THE RAILROAD. We've tried it and tried it, and we are stuck every time. You, yourself, Derrick, have just lost your grain-rate case. S. Behrman did you up. Shelgrim owns the courts. He's got men like Ulsteen in his pocket. He's got the Railroad Commission in his pocket. He's got the Governor of the State in his pocket. He keeps a million-dollar lobby at Sacramento every minute of the time the legislature is in session; he's got his own men on the floor of the United States Senate. He has the whole thing organised like an army corps. What ARE you going to do? He sits in his office in San Francisco and pulls the strings and we've got to dance."

"But—well—but," hazarded Broderson, "but there's the Interstate Commerce Commission. At least on long-haul rates they—"

"Hoh, yes, the Interstate Commerce Commission," shouted Annixter, scornfully, "that's great, ain't it? The greatest Punch and Judy; show on earth. It's almost as good as the Railroad Commission. There never was and there never will be a California Railroad Commission not in the pay of the P. and S. W."

"It is to the Railroad Commission, nevertheless," remarked Magnus, "that the people of the State must look for relief. That is our only hope. Once elect Commissioners who would be loyal to the people, and the whole system of excessive rates falls to the ground."

"Well, why not HAVE a Railroad Commission of our own, then?" suddenly declared young Osterman.

"Because it can't be done," retorted Annixter. "YOU CAN'T BUCK AGAINST THE RAILROAD and if you could you can't organise the farmers in the San Joaquin. We tried it once, and it was enough to turn your stomach. The railroad quietly bought delegates through S. Behrman and did us up."

"Well, that's the game to play," said Osterman decisively, "buy delegates."

"It's the only game that seems to win," admitted Harran gloomily. "Or ever will win," exclaimed Osterman, a sudden excitement seeming to take possession of him. His face—the face of a comic actor, with its great slit of mouth and stiff, red ears—went abruptly pink.

"Look here," he cried, "this thing is getting desperate. We've fought and fought in the courts and out and we've tried agitation and—and all the rest of it and S. Behrman sacks us every time. Now comes the time when there's a prospect of a big crop; we've had no rain for two years and the land has had a long rest. If there is any rain at all this winter, we'll have a bonanza year, and just at this very moment when we've got our chance—a chance to pay off our mortgages and get clear of debt and make a strike—here is Shelgrim making a deal to cinch us and put up rates. And now here's the primaries coming off and a new Railroad Commission going in. That's why Shelgrim chose this time to make his deal. If we wait till Shelgrim pulls it off, we're done for, that's flat. I tell you we're in a fix if we don't keep an eye open. Things are getting desperate. Magnus has just said that the key to the whole thing is the Railroad Commission. Well, why not have a Commission of our own? Never mind how we get it, let's get it. If it's got to be bought, let's buy it and put our own men on it and dictate what the rates will be. Suppose it costs a hundred thousand dollars. Well, we'll get back more than that in cheap rates."

"Mr. Osterman," said Magnus, fixing the young man with a swift glance, "Mr. Osterman, you are proposing a scheme of bribery, sir."

"I am proposing," repeated Osterman, "a scheme of bribery. Exactly so."

"And a crazy, wild-eyed scheme at that," said Annixter gruffly. "Even supposing you bought a Railroad Commission and got your schedule of low rates, what happens? The P. and S. W. crowd get out an injunction and tie you up."

"They would tie themselves up, too. Hauling at low rates is better than no hauling at all. The wheat has got to be moved."

"Oh, rot!" cried Annixter. "Aren't you ever going to learn any sense? Don't you know that cheap transportation would benefit the Liverpool buyers and not us? Can't it be FED into you that you can't buck against the railroad? When you try to buy a Board of Commissioners don't you see that you'll have to bid against the railroad, bid against a corporation that can chuck out millions to our thousands? Do you think you can bid against the P. and S. W.?"

"The railroad don't need to know we are in the game against them till we've got our men seated."

"And when you've got them seated, what's to prevent the corporation buying them right over your head?"

"If we've got the right kind of men in they could not be bought that way," interposed Harran. "I don't know but what there's something in what Osterman says. We'd have the naming of the Commission and we'd name honest men."

Annixter struck the table with his fist in exasperation.

"Honest men!" he shouted; "the kind of men you could get to go into such a scheme would have to be DIS-honest to begin with."

Broderson, shifting uneasily in his place, fingering his beard with a vague, uncertain gesture, spoke again:

"It would be the CHANCE of them—our Commissioners—selling out against the certainty of Shelgrim doing us up. That is," he hastened to add, "ALMOST a certainty; pretty near a certainty."

"Of course, it would be a chance," exclaimed Osterman. "But it's come to the point where we've got to take chances, risk a big stake to make a big strike, and risk is better than sure failure."

"I can be no party to a scheme of avowed bribery and corruption, Mr. Osterman," declared Magnus, a ring of severity in his voice. "I am surprised, sir, that you should even broach the subject in my hearing."

"And," cried Annixter, "it can't be done."

"I don't know," muttered Harran, "maybe it just wants a little spark like this to fire the whole train."

Magnus glanced at his son in considerable surprise. He had not expected this of Harran. But so great was his affection for his son, so accustomed had he become to listening to his advice, to respecting his opinions, that, for the moment, after the first shock of surprise and disappointment, he was influenced to give a certain degree of attention to this new proposition. He in no way countenanced it. At any moment he was prepared to rise in his place and denounce it and Osterman both. It was trickery of the most contemptible order, a thing he believed to be unknown to the old school of politics and statesmanship to which he was proud to belong; but since Harran, even for one moment, considered it, he, Magnus, who trusted Harran implicitly, would do likewise—if it was only to oppose and defeat it in its very beginnings.

And abruptly the discussion began. Gradually Osterman, by dint of his clamour, his strident reiteration, the plausibility of his glib, ready assertions, the ease with which he extricated himself when apparently driven to a corner, completely won over old Broderson to his way of thinking. Osterman bewildered him with his volubility, the lightning rapidity with which he leaped from one subject to another, garrulous, witty, flamboyant, terrifying the old man with pictures of the swift approach of ruin, the imminence of danger.

Annixter, who led the argument against him—loving argument though he did—appeared to poor advantage, unable to present his side effectively. He called Osterman a fool, a goat, a senseless, crazy-headed jackass, but was unable to refute his assertions. His debate was the clumsy heaving of brickbats, brutal, direct. He contradicted everything Osterman said as a matter of principle, made conflicting assertions, declarations that were absolutely inconsistent, and when Osterman or Harran used these against him, could only exclaim:

"Well, in a way it's so, and then again in a way it isn't."

But suddenly Osterman discovered a new argument. "If we swing this deal," he cried, "we've got old jelly-belly Behrman right where we want him."

"He's the man that does us every time," cried Harran. "If there is dirty work to be done in which the railroad doesn't wish to appear, it is S. Behrman who does it. If the freight rates are to be 'adjusted' to squeeze us a little harder, it is S. Behrman who regulates what we can stand. If there's a judge to be bought, it is S. Behrman who does the bargaining. If there is a jury to be bribed, it is S. Behrman who handles the money. If there is an election to be jobbed, it is S. Behrman who manipulates it. It's Behrman here and Behrman there. It is Behrman we come against every time we make a move. It is Behrman who has the grip of us and will never let go till he has squeezed us bone dry. Why, when I think of it all sometimes I wonder I keep my hands off the man."

Osterman got on his feet; leaning across the table, gesturing wildly with his right hand, his serio-comic face, with its bald forehead and stiff, red ears, was inflamed with excitement. He took the floor, creating an impression, attracting all attention to himself, playing to the gallery, gesticulating, clamourous, full of noise.

"Well, now is your chance to get even," he vociferated. "It is now or never. You can take it and save the situation for yourselves and all California or you can leave it and rot on your own ranches. Buck, I know you. I know you're not afraid of anything that wears skin. I know you've got sand all through you, and I know if I showed you how we could put our deal through and seat a Commission of our own, you wouldn't hang back. Governor, you're a brave man. You know the advantage of prompt and fearless action. You are not the sort to shrink from taking chances. To play for big stakes is just your game—to stake a fortune on the turn of a card. You didn't get the reputation of being the strongest poker player in El Dorado County for nothing. Now, here's the biggest gamble that ever came your way. If we stand up to it like men with guts in us, we'll win out. If we hesitate, we're lost."

"I don't suppose you can help playing the goat, Osterman," remarked Annixter, "but what's your idea? What do you think we can do? I'm not saying," he hastened to interpose, "that you've anyways convinced me by all this cackling. I know as well as you that we are in a hole. But I knew that before I came here to-night. YOU'VE not done anything to make me change my mind. But just what do you propose? Let's hear it."

"Well, I say the first thing to do is to see Disbrow. He's the political boss of the Denver, Pueblo, and Mojave road. We will have to get in with the machine some way and that's particularly why I want Magnus with us. He knows politics better than any of us and if we don't want to get sold again we will have to have some one that's in the know to steer us."

"The only politics I understand, Mr. Osterman," answered Magnus sternly, "are honest politics. You must look elsewhere for your political manager. I refuse to have any part in this matter. If the Railroad Commission can be nominated legitimately, if your arrangements can be made without bribery, I am with you to the last iota of my ability."

"Well, you can't get what you want without paying for it," contradicted Annixter.

Broderson was about to speak when Osterman kicked his foot under the table. He, himself, held his peace. He was quick to see that if he could involve Magnus and Annixter in an argument, Annixter, for the mere love of contention, would oppose the Governor and, without knowing it, would commit himself to his—Osterman's—scheme.

This was precisely what happened. In a few moments Annixter was declaring at top voice his readiness to mortgage the crop of Quien Sabe, if necessary, for the sake of "busting S. Behrman." He could see no great obstacle in the way of controlling the nominating convention so far as securing the naming of two Railroad Commissioners was concerned. Two was all they needed. Probably it WOULD cost money. You didn't get something for nothing. It would cost them all a good deal more if they sat like lumps on a log and played tiddledy-winks while Shelgrim sold out from under them. Then there was this, too: the P. and S. W. were hard up just then. The shortage on the State's wheat crop for the last two years had affected them, too. They were retrenching in expenditures all along the line. Hadn't they just cut wages in all departments? There was this affair of Dyke's to prove it. The railroad didn't always act as a unit, either. There was always a party in it that opposed spending too much money. He would bet that party was strong just now. He was kind of sick himself of being kicked by S. Behrman. Hadn't that pip turned up on his ranch that very day to bully him about his own line fence? Next he would be telling him what kind of clothes he ought to wear. Harran had the right idea. Somebody had got to be busted mighty soon now and he didn't propose that it should be he.

"Now you are talking something like sense," observed Osterman. "I thought you would see it like that when you got my idea."

"Your idea, YOUR idea!" cried Annixter. "Why, I've had this idea myself for over three years."

"What about Disbrow?" asked Harran, hastening to interrupt. "Why do we want to see Disbrow?"

"Disbrow is the political man for the Denver, Pueblo, and Mojave," answered Osterman, "and you see it's like this: the Mojave road don't run up into the valley at all. Their terminus is way to the south of us, and they don't care anything about grain rates through the San Joaquin. They don't care how anti-railroad the Commission is, because the Commission's rulings can't affect them. But they divide traffic with the P. and S. W. in the southern part of the State and they have a good deal of influence with that road. I want to get the Mojave road, through Disbrow, to recommend a Commissioner of our choosing to the P. and S. W. and have the P. and S. W. adopt him as their own."

"Who, for instance?"

"Darrell, that Los Angeles man—remember?"

"Well, Darrell is no particular friend of Disbrow," said Annixter. "Why should Disbrow take him up?"

"PREE-cisely," cried Osterman. "We make it worth Disbrow's while to do it. We go to him and say, 'Mr. Disbrow, you manage the politics for the Mojave railroad, and what you say goes with your Board of Directors. We want you to adopt our candidate for Railroad Commissioner for the third district. How much do you want for doing it?' I KNOW we can buy Disbrow. That gives us one Commissioner. We need not bother about that any more. In the first district we don't make any move at all. We let the political managers of the P. and S. W. nominate whoever they like. Then we concentrate all our efforts to putting in our man in the second district. There is where the big fight will come."

"I see perfectly well what you mean, Mr. Osterman," observed Magnus, "but make no mistake, sir, as to my attitude in this business. You may count me as out of it entirely."

"Well, suppose we win," put in Annixter truculently, already acknowledging himself as involved in the proposed undertaking; "suppose we win and get low rates for hauling grain. How about you, then? You count yourself IN then, don't you? You get all the benefit of lower rates without sharing any of the risks we take to secure them. No, nor any of the expense, either. No, you won't dirty your fingers with helping us put this deal through, but you won't be so cursed particular when it comes to sharing the profits, will you?"

Magnus rose abruptly to his full height, the nostrils of his thin, hawk-like nose vibrating, his smooth-shaven face paler than ever.

"Stop right where you are, sir," he exclaimed. "You forget yourself, Mr. Annixter. Please understand that I tolerate such words as you have permitted yourself to make use of from no man, not even from my guest. I shall ask you to apologise."

In an instant he dominated the entire group, imposing a respect that was as much fear as admiration. No one made response. For the moment he was the Master again, the Leader. Like so many delinquent school-boys, the others cowered before him, ashamed, put to confusion, unable to find their tongues. In that brief instant of silence following upon Magnus's outburst, and while he held them subdued and over-mastered, the fabric of their scheme of corruption and dishonesty trembled to its base. It was the last protest of the Old School, rising up there in denunciation of the new order of things, the statesman opposed to the politician; honesty, rectitude, uncompromising integrity, prevailing for the last time against the devious manoeuvring, the evil communications, the rotten expediency of a corrupted institution.

For a few seconds no one answered. Then, Annixter, moving abruptly and uneasily in his place, muttered:

"I spoke upon provocation. If you like, we'll consider it unsaid. I don't know what's going to become of us—go out of business, I presume."

"I understand Magnus all right," put in Osterman. "He don't have to go into this thing, if it's against his conscience. That's all right. Magnus can stay out if he wants to, but that won't prevent us going ahead and seeing what we can do. Only there's this about it." He turned again to Magnus, speaking with every degree of earnestness, every appearance of conviction. "I did not deny, Governor, from the very start that this would mean bribery. But you don't suppose that I like the idea either. If there was one legitimate hope that was yet left untried, no matter how forlorn it was, I would try it. But there's not. It is literally and soberly true that every means of help—every honest means—has been attempted. Shelgrim is going to cinch us. Grain rates are increasing, while, on the other hand, the price of wheat is sagging lower and lower all the time. If we don't do something we are ruined."

Osterman paused for a moment, allowing precisely the right number of seconds to elapse, then altering and lowering his voice, added:

"I respect the Governor's principles. I admire them. They do him every degree of credit." Then, turning directly to Magnus, he concluded with, "But I only want you to ask yourself, sir, if, at such a crisis, one ought to think of oneself, to consider purely personal motives in such a desperate situation as this? Now, we want you with us, Governor; perhaps not openly, if you don't wish it, but tacitly, at least. I won't ask you for an answer to-night, but what I do ask of you is to consider this matter seriously and think over the whole business. Will you do it?"

Osterman ceased definitely to speak, leaning forward across the table, his eyes fixed on Magnus's face. There was a silence. Outside, the rain fell continually with an even, monotonous murmur. In the group of men around the table no one stirred nor spoke. They looked steadily at Magnus, who, for the moment, kept his glance fixed thoughtfully upon the table before him. In another moment he raised his head and looked from face to face around the group. After all, these were his neighbours, his friends, men with whom he had been upon the closest terms of association. In a way they represented what now had come to be his world. His single swift glance took in the men, one after another. Annixter, rugged, crude, sitting awkwardly and uncomfortably in his chair, his unhandsome face, with its outthrust lower lip and deeply cleft masculine chin, flushed and eager, his yellow hair disordered, the one tuft on the crown standing stiffly forth like the feather in an Indian's scalp lock; Broderson, vaguely combing at his long beard with a persistent maniacal gesture, distressed, troubled and uneasy; Osterman, with his comedy face, the face of a music-hall singer, his head bald and set off by his great red ears, leaning back in his place, softly cracking the knuckle of a forefinger, and, last of all and close to his elbow, his son, his support, his confidant and companion, Harran, so like himself, with his own erect, fine carriage, his thin, beak-like nose and his blond hair, with its tendency to curl in a forward direction in front of the ears, young, strong, courageous, full of the promise of the future years. His blue eyes looked straight into his father's with what Magnus could fancy a glance of appeal. Magnus could see that expression in the faces of the others very plainly. They looked to him as their natural leader, their chief who was to bring them out from this abominable trouble which was closing in upon them, and in them all he saw many types. They—these men around his table on that night of the first rain of a coming season—seemed to stand in his imagination for many others—all the farmers, ranchers, and wheat growers of the great San Joaquin. Their words were the words of a whole community; their distress, the distress of an entire State, harried beyond the bounds of endurance, driven to the wall, coerced, exploited, harassed to the limits of exasperation. "I will think of it," he said, then hastened to add, "but I can tell you beforehand that you may expect only a refusal."

After Magnus had spoken, there was a prolonged silence. The conference seemed of itself to have come to an end for that evening. Presley lighted another cigarette from the butt of the one he had been smoking, and the cat, Princess Nathalie, disturbed by his movement and by a whiff of drifting smoke, jumped from his knee to the floor and picking her way across the room to Annixter, rubbed gently against his legs, her tail in the air, her back delicately arched. No doubt she thought it time to settle herself for the night, and as Annixter gave no indication of vacating his chair, she chose this way of cajoling him into ceding his place to her. But Annixter was irritated at the Princess's attentions, misunderstanding their motive.

"Get out!" he exclaimed, lifting his feet to the rung of the chair. "Lord love me, but I sure do hate a cat."

"By the way," observed Osterman, "I passed Genslinger by the gate as I came in to-night. Had he been here?"

"Yes, he was here," said Harran, "and—" but Annixter took the words out of his mouth.

"He says there's some talk of the railroad selling us their sections this winter."

"Oh, he did, did he?" exclaimed Osterman, interested at once. "Where did he hear that?"

"Where does a railroad paper get its news? From the General Office, I suppose."

"I hope he didn't get it straight from headquarters that the land was to be graded at twenty dollars an acre," murmured Broderson.

"What's that?" demanded Osterman. "Twenty dollars! Here, put me on, somebody. What's all up? What did Genslinger say?"

"Oh, you needn't get scared," said Annixter. "Genslinger don't know, that's all. He thinks there was no understanding that the price of the land should not be advanced when the P. and S. W. came to sell to us."

"Oh," muttered Osterman relieved. Magnus, who had gone out into the office on the other side of the glass-roofed hallway, returned with a long, yellow envelope in his hand, stuffed with newspaper clippings and thin, closely printed pamphlets.

"Here is the circular," he remarked, drawing out one of the pamphlets. "The conditions of settlement to which the railroad obligated itself are very explicit."

He ran over the pages of the circular, then read aloud:

"'The Company invites settlers to go upon its lands before patents are issued or the road is completed, and intends in such cases to sell to them in preference to any other applicants and at a price based upon the value of the land without improvements,' and on the other page here," he remarked, "they refer to this again. 'In ascertaining the value of the lands, any improvements that a settler or any other person may have on the lands will not be taken into consideration, neither will the price be increased in consequence thereof.... Settlers are thus insured that in addition to being accorded the first privilege of purchase, at the graded price, they will also be protected in their improvements.' And here," he commented, "in Section IX. it reads, 'The lands are not uniform in price, but are offered at various figures from $2.50 upward per acre. Usually land covered with tall timber is held at $5.00 per acre, and that with pine at $10.00. Most is for sale at $2.50 and $5.00.'"

"When you come to read that carefully," hazarded old Broderson, "it—it's not so VERY REASSURING. 'MOST is for sale at two-fifty an acre,' it says. That don't mean 'ALL,' that only means SOME. I wish now that I had secured a more iron-clad agreement from the P. and S. W. when I took up its sections on my ranch, and—and Genslinger is in a position to know the intentions of the railroad. At least, he—he—he is in TOUCH with them. All newspaper men are. Those, I mean, who are subsidised by the General Office. But, perhaps, Genslinger isn't subsidised, I don't know. I—I am not sure. Maybe—perhaps"

"Oh, you don't know and you do know, and maybe and perhaps, and you're not so sure," vociferated Annixter. "How about ignoring the value of our improvements? Nothing hazy about THAT statement, I guess. It says in so many words that any improvements we make will not be considered when the land is appraised and that's the same thing, isn't it? The unimproved land is worth two-fifty an acre; only timber land is worth more and there's none too much timber about here."

"Well, one thing at a time," said Harran. "The thing for us now is to get into this primary election and the convention and see if we can push our men for Railroad Commissioners."

"Right," declared Annixter. He rose, stretching his arms above his head. "I've about talked all the wind out of me," he said. "Think I'll be moving along. It's pretty near midnight."

But when Magnus's guests turned their attention to the matter of returning to their different ranches, they abruptly realised that the downpour had doubled and trebled in its volume since earlier in the evening. The fields and roads were veritable seas of viscid mud, the night absolutely black-dark; assuredly not a night in which to venture out. Magnus insisted that the three ranchers should put up at Los Muertos. Osterman accepted at once, Annixter, after an interminable discussion, allowed himself to be persuaded, in the end accepting as though granting a favour. Broderson protested that his wife, who was not well, would expect him to return that night and would, no doubt, fret if he did not appear. Furthermore, he lived close by, at the junction of the County and Lower Road. He put a sack over his head and shoulders, persistently declining Magnus's offered umbrella and rubber coat, and hurried away, remarking that he had no foreman on his ranch and had to be up and about at five the next morning to put his men to work.

"Fool!" muttered Annixter when the old man had gone. "Imagine farming a ranch the size of his without a foreman."

Harran showed Osterman and Annixter where they were to sleep, in adjoining rooms. Magnus soon afterward retired.

Osterman found an excuse for going to bed, but Annixter and Harran remained in the latter's room, in a haze of blue tobacco smoke, talking, talking. But at length, at the end of all argument, Annixter got up, remarking:

"Well, I'm going to turn in. It's nearly two o'clock."

He went to his room, closing the door, and Harran, opening his window to clear out the tobacco smoke, looked out for a moment across the country toward the south.

The darkness was profound, impenetrable; the rain fell with an uninterrupted roar. Near at hand one could hear the sound of dripping eaves and foliage and the eager, sucking sound of the drinking earth, and abruptly while Harran stood looking out, one hand upon the upraised sash, a great puff of the outside air invaded the room, odourous with the reek of the soaking earth, redolent with fertility, pungent, heavy, tepid. He closed the window again and sat for a few moments on the edge of the bed, one shoe in his hand, thoughtful and absorbed, wondering if his father would involve himself in this new scheme, wondering if, after all, he wanted him to.

But suddenly he was aware of a commotion, issuing from the direction of Annixter's room, and the voice of Annixter himself upraised in expostulation and exasperation. The door of the room to which Annixter had been assigned opened with a violent wrench and an angry voice exclaimed to anybody who would listen:

"Oh, yes, funny, isn't it? In a way, it's funny, and then, again, in a way it isn't."

The door banged to so that all the windows of the house rattled in their frames.

Harran hurried out into the dining-room and there met Presley and his father, who had been aroused as well by Annixter's clamour. Osterman was there, too, his bald head gleaming like a bulb of ivory in the light of the lamp that Magnus carried.

"What's all up?" demanded Osterman. "Whatever in the world is the matter with Buck?"

Confused and terrible sounds came from behind the door of Annixter's room. A prolonged monologue of grievance, broken by explosions of wrath and the vague noise of some one in a furious hurry. All at once and before Harran had a chance to knock on the door, Annixter flung it open. His face was blazing with anger, his outthrust lip more prominent than ever, his wiry, yellow hair in disarray, the tuft on the crown sticking straight into the air like the upraised hackles of an angry hound. Evidently he had been dressing himself with the most headlong rapidity; he had not yet put on his coat and vest, but carried them over his arm, while with his disengaged hand he kept hitching his suspenders over his shoulders with a persistent and hypnotic gesture. Without a moment's pause he gave vent to his indignation in a torrent of words.

"Ah, yes, in my bed, sloop, aha! I know the man who put it there," he went on, glaring at Osterman, "and that man is a PIP. Sloop! Slimy, disgusting stuff; you heard me say I didn't like it when the Chink passed it to me at dinner—and just for that reason you put it in my bed, and I stick my feet into it when I turn in. Funny, isn't it? Oh, yes, too funny for any use. I'd laugh a little louder if I was you."

"Well, Buck," protested Harran, as he noticed the hat in Annixter's hand, "you're not going home just for—"

Annixter turned on him with a shout.

"I'll get plumb out of here," he trumpeted. "I won't stay here another minute."

He swung into his waistcoat and coat, scrabbling at the buttons in the violence of his emotions. "And I don't know but what it will make me sick again to go out in a night like this. NO, I won't stay. Some things are funny, and then, again, there are some things that are not. Ah, yes, sloop! Well, that's all right. I can be funny, too, when you come to that. You don't get a cent of money out of me. You can do your dirty bribery in your own dirty way. I won't come into this scheme at all. I wash my hands of the whole business. It's rotten and it's wild-eyed; it's dirt from start to finish; and you'll all land in State's prison. You can count me out."

"But, Buck, look here, you crazy fool," cried Harran, "I don't know who put that stuff in your bed, but I'm not going; to let you go back to Quien Sabe in a rain like this."

"I know who put it in," clamoured the other, shaking his fists, "and don't call me Buck and I'll do as I please. I WILL go back home. I'll get plumb out of here. Sorry I came. Sorry I ever lent myself to such a disgusting, dishonest, dirty bribery game as this all to-night. I won't put a dime into it, no, not a penny."

He stormed to the door leading out upon the porch, deaf to all reason. Harran and Presley followed him, trying to dissuade him from going home at that time of night and in such a storm, but Annixter was not to be placated. He stamped across to the barn where his horse and buggy had been stabled, splashing through the puddles under foot, going out of his way to drench himself, refusing even to allow Presley and Harran to help him harness the horse.

"What's the use of making a fool of yourself, Annixter?" remonstrated Presley, as Annixter backed the horse from the stall. "You act just like a ten-year-old boy. If Osterman wants to play the goat, why should you help him out?"

"He's a PIP," vociferated Annixter. "You don't understand, Presley. It runs in my family to hate anything sticky. It's—it's—it's heredity. How would you like to get into bed at two in the morning and jam your feet down into a slimy mess like that? Oh, no. It's not so funny then. And you mark my words, Mr. Harran Derrick," he continued, as he climbed into the buggy, shaking the whip toward Harran, "this business we talked over to-night—I'm OUT of it. It's yellow. It's too CURSED dishonest."

He cut the horse across the back with the whip and drove out into the pelting rain. In a few seconds the sound of his buggy wheels was lost in the muffled roar of the downpour.

Harran and Presley closed the barn and returned to the house, sheltering themselves under a tarpaulin carriage cover. Once inside, Harran went to remonstrate with Osterman, who was still up. Magnus had again retired. The house had fallen quiet again.

As Presley crossed the dining-room on the way to his own apartment in the second story of the house, he paused for a moment, looking about him. In the dull light of the lowered lamps, the redwood panelling of the room showed a dark crimson as though stained with blood. On the massive slab of the dining table the half-emptied glasses and bottles stood about in the confusion in which they had been left, reflecting themselves deep into the polished wood; the glass doors of the case of stuffed birds was a subdued shimmer; the many-coloured Navajo blanket over the couch seemed a mere patch of brown.

Around the table the chairs in which the men had sat throughout the evening still ranged themselves in a semi-circle, vaguely suggestive of the conference of the past few hours, with all its possibilities of good and evil, its significance of a future big with portent. The room was still. Only on the cushions of the chair that Annixter had occupied, the cat, Princess Nathalie, at last comfortably settled in her accustomed place, dozed complacently, her paws tucked under her breast, filling the deserted room with the subdued murmur of her contented purr.

IV

On the Quien Sabe ranch, in one of its western divisions, near the line fence that divided it from the Osterman holding, Vanamee was harnessing the horses to the plough to which he had been assigned two days before, a stable-boy from the division barn helping him.

Promptly discharged from the employ of the sheep-raisers after the lamentable accident near the Long Trestle, Vanamee had presented himself to Harran, asking for employment. The season was beginning; on all the ranches work was being resumed. The rain had put the ground into admirable condition for ploughing, and Annixter, Broderson, and Osterman all had their gangs at work. Thus, Vanamee was vastly surprised to find Los Muertos idle, the horses still in the barns, the men gathering in the shade of the bunk-house and eating-house, smoking, dozing, or going aimlessly about, their arms dangling. The ploughs for which Magnus and Harran were waiting in a fury of impatience had not yet arrived, and since the management of Los Muertos had counted upon having these in hand long before this time, no provision had been made for keeping the old stock in repair; many of these old ploughs were useless, broken, and out of order; some had been sold. It could not be said definitely when the new ploughs would arrive. Harran had decided to wait one week longer, and then, in case of their non-appearance, to buy a consignment of the old style of plough from the dealers in Bonneville. He could afford to lose the money better than he could afford to lose the season.

Failing of work on Los Muertos, Vanamee had gone to Quien Sabe. Annixter, whom he had spoken to first, had sent him across the ranch to one of his division superintendents, and this latter, after assuring himself of Vanamee's familiarity with horses and his previous experience—even though somewhat remote—on Los Muertos, had taken him on as a driver of one of the gang ploughs, then at work on his division.

The evening before, when the foreman had blown his whistle at six o'clock, the long line of ploughs had halted upon the instant, and the drivers, unharnessing their teams, had taken them back to the division barns—leaving the ploughs as they were in the furrows. But an hour after daylight the next morning the work was resumed. After breakfast, Vanamee, riding one horse and leading the others, had returned to the line of ploughs together with the other drivers. Now he was busy harnessing the team. At the division blacksmith shop—temporarily put up—he had been obliged to wait while one of his lead horses was shod, and he had thus been delayed quite five minutes. Nearly all the other teams were harnessed, the drivers on their seats, waiting for the foreman's signal.

"All ready here?" inquired the foreman, driving up to Vanamee's team in his buggy.

"All ready, sir," answered Vanamee, buckling the last strap.

He climbed to his seat, shaking out the reins, and turning about, looked back along the line, then all around him at the landscape inundated with the brilliant glow of the early morning.

The day was fine. Since the first rain of the season, there had been no other. Now the sky was without a cloud, pale blue, delicate, luminous, scintillating with morning. The great brown earth turned a huge flank to it, exhaling the moisture of the early dew. The atmosphere, washed clean of dust and mist, was translucent as crystal. Far off to the east, the hills on the other side of Broderson Creek stood out against the pallid saffron of the horizon as flat and as sharply outlined as if pasted on the sky. The campanile of the ancient Mission of San Juan seemed as fine as frost work. All about between the horizons, the carpet of the land unrolled itself to infinity. But now it was no longer parched with heat, cracked and warped by a merciless sun, powdered with dust. The rain had done its work; not a clod that was not swollen with fertility, not a fissure that did not exhale the sense of fecundity. One could not take a dozen steps upon the ranches without the brusque sensation that underfoot the land was alive; roused at last from its sleep, palpitating with the desire of reproduction. Deep down there in the recesses of the soil, the great heart throbbed once more, thrilling with passion, vibrating with desire, offering itself to the caress of the plough, insistent, eager, imperious. Dimly one felt the deep-seated trouble of the earth, the uneasy agitation of its members, the hidden tumult of its womb, demanding to be made fruitful, to reproduce, to disengage the eternal renascent germ of Life that stirred and struggled in its loins.

The ploughs, thirty-five in number, each drawn by its team of ten, stretched in an interminable line, nearly a quarter of a mile in length, behind and ahead of Vanamee. They were arranged, as it were, en echelon, not in file—not one directly behind the other, but each succeeding plough its own width farther in the field than the one in front of it. Each of these ploughs held five shears, so that when the entire company was in motion, one hundred and seventy-five furrows were made at the same instant. At a distance, the ploughs resembled a great column of field artillery. Each driver was in his place, his glance alternating between his horses and the foreman nearest at hand. Other foremen, in their buggies or buckboards, were at intervals along the line, like battery lieutenants. Annixter himself, on horseback, in boots and campaign hat, a cigar in his teeth, overlooked the scene.

The division superintendent, on the opposite side of the line, galloped past to a position at the head. For a long moment there was a silence. A sense of preparedness ran from end to end of the column. All things were ready, each man in his place. The day's work was about to begin.

Suddenly, from a distance at the head of the line came the shrill trilling of a whistle. At once the foreman nearest Vanamee repeated it, at the same time turning down the line, and waving one arm. The signal was repeated, whistle answering whistle, till the sounds lost themselves in the distance. At once the line of ploughs lost its immobility, moving forward, getting slowly under way, the horses straining in the traces. A prolonged movement rippled from team to team, disengaging in its passage a multitude of sounds—the click of buckles, the creak of straining leather, the subdued clash of machinery, the cracking of whips, the deep breathing of nearly four hundred horses, the abrupt commands and cries of the drivers, and, last of all, the prolonged, soothing murmur of the thick brown earth turning steadily from the multitude of advancing shears.

The ploughing thus commenced, continued. The sun rose higher. Steadily the hundred iron hands kneaded and furrowed and stroked the brown, humid earth, the hundred iron teeth bit deep into the Titan's flesh. Perched on his seat, the moist living reins slipping and tugging in his hands, Vanamee, in the midst of this steady confusion of constantly varying sensation, sight interrupted by sound, sound mingling with sight, on this swaying, vibrating seat, quivering with the prolonged thrill of the earth, lapsed to a sort of pleasing numbness, in a sense, hypnotised by the weaving maze of things in which he found himself involved. To keep his team at an even, regular gait, maintaining the precise interval, to run his furrows as closely as possible to those already made by the plough in front—this for the moment was the entire sum of his duties. But while one part of his brain, alert and watchful, took cognisance of these matters, all the greater part was lulled and stupefied with the long monotony of the affair.

The ploughing, now in full swing, enveloped him in a vague, slow-moving whirl of things. Underneath him was the jarring, jolting, trembling machine; not a clod was turned, not an obstacle encountered, that he did not receive the swift impression of it through all his body, the very friction of the damp soil, sliding incessantly from the shiny surface of the shears, seemed to reproduce itself in his finger-tips and along the back of his head. He heard the horse-hoofs by the myriads crushing down easily, deeply, into the loam, the prolonged clinking of trace-chains, the working of the smooth brown flanks in the harness, the clatter of wooden hames, the champing of bits, the click of iron shoes against pebbles, the brittle stubble of the surface ground crackling and snapping as the furrows turned, the sonorous, steady breaths wrenched from the deep, labouring chests, strap-bound, shining with sweat, and all along the line the voices of the men talking to the horses. Everywhere there were visions of glossy brown backs, straining, heaving, swollen with muscle; harness streaked with specks of froth, broad, cup-shaped hoofs, heavy with brown loam, men's faces red with tan, blue overalls spotted with axle-grease; muscled hands, the knuckles whitened in their grip on the reins, and through it all the ammoniacal smell of the horses, the bitter reek of perspiration of beasts and men, the aroma of warm leather, the scent of dead stubble—and stronger and more penetrating than everything else, the heavy, enervating odour of the upturned, living earth.

At intervals, from the tops of one of the rare, low swells of the land, Vanamee overlooked a wider horizon. On the other divisions of Quien Sabe the same work was in progress. Occasionally he could see another column of ploughs in the adjoining division—sometimes so close at hand that the subdued murmur of its movements reached his ear; sometimes so distant that it resolved itself into a long, brown streak upon the grey of the ground. Farther off to the west on the Osterman ranch other columns came and went, and, once, from the crest of the highest swell on his division, Vanamee caught a distant glimpse of the Broderson ranch. There, too, moving specks indicated that the ploughing was under way. And farther away still, far off there beyond the fine line of the horizons, over the curve of the globe, the shoulder of the earth, he knew were other ranches, and beyond these others, and beyond these still others, the immensities multiplying to infinity.

Everywhere throughout the great San Joaquin, unseen and unheard, a thousand ploughs up-stirred the land, tens of thousands of shears clutched deep into the warm, moist soil.

It was the long stroking caress, vigorous, male, powerful, for which the Earth seemed panting. The heroic embrace of a multitude of iron hands, gripping deep into the brown, warm flesh of the land that quivered responsive and passionate under this rude advance, so robust as to be almost an assault, so violent as to be veritably brutal. There, under the sun and under the speckless sheen of the sky, the wooing of the Titan began, the vast primal passion, the two world-forces, the elemental Male and Female, locked in a colossal embrace, at grapples in the throes of an infinite desire, at once terrible and divine, knowing no law, untamed, savage, natural, sublime.

From time to time the gang in which Vanamee worked halted on the signal from foreman or overseer. The horses came to a standstill, the vague clamour of the work lapsed away. Then the minutes passed. The whole work hung suspended. All up and down the line one demanded what had happened. The division superintendent galloped past, perplexed and anxious. For the moment, one of the ploughs was out of order, a bolt had slipped, a lever refused to work, or a machine had become immobilised in heavy ground, or a horse had lamed himself. Once, even, toward noon, an entire plough was taken out of the line, so out of gear that a messenger had to be sent to the division forge to summon the machinist.

Annixter had disappeared. He had ridden farther on to the other divisions of his ranch, to watch the work in progress there. At twelve o'clock, according to his orders, all the division superintendents put themselves in communication with him by means of the telephone wires that connected each of the division houses, reporting the condition of the work, the number of acres covered, the prospects of each plough traversing its daily average of twenty miles.

At half-past twelve, Vanamee and the rest of the drivers ate their lunch in the field, the tin buckets having been distributed to them that morning after breakfast. But in the evening, the routine of the previous day was repeated, and Vanamee, unharnessing his team, riding one horse and leading the others, returned to the division barns and bunk-house.

It was between six and seven o'clock. The half hundred men of the gang threw themselves upon the supper the Chinese cooks had set out in the shed of the eating-house, long as a bowling alley, unpainted, crude, the seats benches, the table covered with oil cloth. Overhead a half-dozen kerosene lamps flared and smoked.

The table was taken as if by assault; the clatter of iron knives upon the tin plates was as the reverberation of hail upon a metal roof. The ploughmen rinsed their throats with great draughts of wine, and, their elbows wide, their foreheads flushed, resumed the attack upon the beef and bread, eating as though they would never have enough. All up and down the long table, where the kerosene lamps reflected themselves deep in the oil-cloth cover, one heard the incessant sounds of mastication, and saw the uninterrupted movement of great jaws. At every moment one or another of the men demanded a fresh portion of beef, another pint of wine, another half-loaf of bread. For upwards of an hour the gang ate. It was no longer a supper. It was a veritable barbecue, a crude and primitive feasting, barbaric, homeric.

But in all this scene Vanamee saw nothing repulsive. Presley would have abhorred it—this feeding of the People, this gorging of the human animal, eager for its meat. Vanamee, simple, uncomplicated, living so close to nature and the rudimentary life, understood its significance. He knew very well that within a short half-hour after this meal the men would throw themselves down in their bunks to sleep without moving, inert and stupefied with fatigue, till the morning. Work, food, and sleep, all life reduced to its bare essentials, uncomplex, honest, healthy. They were strong, these men, with the strength of the soil they worked, in touch with the essential things, back again to the starting point of civilisation, coarse, vital, real, and sane.

For a brief moment immediately after the meal, pipes were lit, and the air grew thick with fragrant tobacco smoke. On a corner of the dining-room table, a game of poker was begun. One of the drivers, a Swede, produced an accordion; a group on the steps of the bunk-house listened, with alternate gravity and shouts of laughter, to the acknowledged story-teller of the gang. But soon the men began to turn in, stretching themselves at full length on the horse blankets in the racklike bunks. The sounds of heavy breathing increased steadily, lights were put out, and before the afterglow had faded from the sky, the gang was asleep.

Vanamee, however, remained awake. The night was fine, warm; the sky silver-grey with starlight. By and by there would be a moon. In the first watch after the twilight, a faint puff of breeze came up out of the south. From all around, the heavy penetrating smell of the new-turned earth exhaled steadily into the darkness. After a while, when the moon came up, he could see the vast brown breast of the earth turn toward it. Far off, distant objects came into view: The giant oak tree at Hooven's ranch house near the irrigating ditch on Los Muertos, the skeleton-like tower of the windmill on Annixter's Home ranch, the clump of willows along Broderson Creek close to the Long Trestle, and, last of all, the venerable tower of the Mission of San Juan on the high ground beyond the creek.

Thitherward, like homing pigeons, Vanamee's thoughts turned irresistibly. Near to that tower, just beyond, in the little hollow, hidden now from his sight, was the Seed ranch where Angele Varian had lived. Straining his eyes, peering across the intervening levels, Vanamee fancied he could almost see the line of venerable pear trees in whose shadow she had been accustomed to wait for him. On many such a night as this he had crossed the ranches to find her there. His mind went back to that wonderful time of his life sixteen years before this, when Angele was alive, when they two were involved in the sweet intricacies of a love so fine, so pure, so marvellous that it seemed to them a miracle, a manifestation, a thing veritably divine, put into the life of them and the hearts of them by God Himself. To that they had been born. For this love's sake they had come into the world, and the mingling of their lives was to be the Perfect Life, the intended, ordained union of the soul of man with the soul of woman, indissoluble, harmonious as music, beautiful beyond all thought, a foretaste of Heaven, a hostage of immortality.

No, he, Vanamee, could never, never forget, never was the edge of his grief to lose its sharpness, never would the lapse of time blunt the tooth of his pain. Once more, as he sat there, looking off across the ranches, his eyes fixed on the ancient campanile of the Mission church, the anguish that would not die leaped at his throat, tearing at his heart, shaking him and rending him with a violence as fierce and as profound as if it all had been but yesterday. The ache returned to his heart a physical keen pain; his hands gripped tight together, twisting, interlocked, his eyes filled with tears, his whole body shaken and riven from head to heel.

He had lost her. God had not meant it, after all. The whole matter had been a mistake. That vast, wonderful love that had come upon them had been only the flimsiest mockery. Abruptly Vanamee rose. He knew the night that was before him. At intervals throughout the course of his prolonged wanderings, in the desert, on the mesa, deep in the canon, lost and forgotten on the flanks of unnamed mountains, alone under the stars and under the moon's white eye, these hours came to him, his grief recoiling upon him like the recoil of a vast and terrible engine. Then he must fight out the night, wrestling with his sorrow, praying sometimes, incoherent, hardly conscious, asking "Why" of the night and of the stars.

Such another night had come to him now. Until dawn he knew he must struggle with his grief, torn with memories, his imagination assaulted with visions of a vanished happiness. If this paroxysm of sorrow was to assail him again that night, there was but one place for him to be. He would go to the Mission—he would see Father Sarria; he would pass the night in the deep shadow of the aged pear trees in the Mission garden.

He struck out across Quien Sabe, his face, the face of an ascetic, lean, brown, infinitely sad, set toward the Mission church. In about an hour he reached and crossed the road that led northward from Guadalajara toward the Seed ranch, and, a little farther on, forded Broderson Creek where it ran through one corner of the Mission land. He climbed the hill and halted, out of breath from his brisk wall, at the end of the colonnade of the Mission itself.

Until this moment Vanamee had not trusted himself to see the Mission at night. On the occasion of his first daytime visit with Presley, he had hurried away even before the twilight had set in, not daring for the moment to face the crowding phantoms that in his imagination filled the Mission garden after dark. In the daylight, the place had seemed strange to him. None of his associations with the old building and its surroundings were those of sunlight and brightness. Whenever, during his long sojourns in the wilderness of the Southwest, he had called up the picture in the eye of his mind, it had always appeared to him in the dim mystery of moonless nights, the venerable pear trees black with shadow, the fountain a thing to be heard rather than seen.

But as yet he had not entered the garden. That lay on the other side of the Mission. Vanamee passed down the colonnade, with its uneven pavement of worn red bricks, to the last door by the belfry tower, and rang the little bell by pulling the leather thong that hung from a hole in the door above the knob.

But the maid-servant, who, after a long interval opened the door, blinking and confused at being roused from her sleep, told Vanamee that Sarria was not in his room. Vanamee, however, was known to her as the priest's protege and great friend, and she allowed him to enter, telling him that, no doubt, he would find Sarria in the church itself. The servant led the way down the cool adobe passage to a larger room that occupied the entire width of the bottom of the belfry tower, and whence a flight of aged steps led upward into the dark. At the foot of the stairs was a door opening into the church. The servant admitted Vanamee, closing the door behind her.

The interior of the Mission, a great oblong of white-washed adobe with a flat ceiling, was lighted dimly by the sanctuary lamp that hung from three long chains just over the chancel rail at the far end of the church, and by two or three cheap kerosene lamps in brackets of imitation bronze. All around the walls was the inevitable series of pictures representing the Stations of the Cross. They were of a hideous crudity of design and composition, yet were wrought out with an innocent, unquestioning sincerity that was not without its charm. Each picture framed alike in gilt, bore its suitable inscription in staring black letters. "Simon, The Cyrenean, Helps Jesus to Carry His Cross."

"Saint Veronica Wipes the Face of Jesus."

"Jesus Falls for the Fourth Time," and so on. Half-way up the length of the church the pews began, coffin-like boxes of blackened oak, shining from years of friction, each with its door; while over them, and built out from the wall, was the pulpit, with its tarnished gilt sounding-board above it, like the raised cover of a great hat-box. Between the pews, in the aisle, the violent vermilion of a strip of ingrain carpet assaulted the eye. Farther on were the steps to the altar, the chancel rail of worm-riddled oak, the high altar, with its napery from the bargain counters of a San Francisco store, the massive silver candlesticks, each as much as one man could lift, the gift of a dead Spanish queen, and, last, the pictures of the chancel, the Virgin in a glory, a Christ in agony on the cross, and St. John the Baptist, the patron saint of the Mission, the San Juan Bautista, of the early days, a gaunt grey figure, in skins, two fingers upraised in the gesture of benediction.

The air of the place was cool and damp, and heavy with the flat, sweet scent of stale incense smoke. It was of a vault-like stillness, and the closing of the door behind Vanamee reechoed from corner to corner with a prolonged reverberation of thunder.

However, Father Sarria was not in the church. Vanamee took a couple of turns the length of the aisle, looking about into the chapels on either side of the chancel. But the building was deserted. The priest had been there recently, nevertheless, for the altar furniture was in disarray, as though he had been rearranging it but a moment before. On both sides of the church and half-way up their length, the walls were pierced by low archways, in which were massive wooden doors, clamped with iron bolts. One of these doors, on the pulpit side of the church, stood ajar, and stepping to it and pushing it wide open, Vanamee looked diagonally across a little patch of vegetables—beets, radishes, and lettuce—to the rear of the building that had once contained the cloisters, and through an open window saw Father Sarria diligently polishing the silver crucifix that usually stood on the high altar. Vanamee did not call to the priest. Putting a finger to either temple, he fixed his eyes steadily upon him for a moment as he moved about at his work. In a few seconds he closed his eyes, but only part way. The pupils contracted; his forehead lowered to an expression of poignant intensity. Soon afterward he saw the priest pause abruptly in the act of drawing the cover over the crucifix, looking about him from side to side. He turned again to his work, and again came to a stop, perplexed, curious. With uncertain steps, and evidently wondering why he did so, he came to the door of the room and opened it, looking out into the night. Vanamee, hidden in the deep shadow of the archway, did not move, but his eyes closed, and the intense expression deepened on his face. The priest hesitated, moved forward a step, turned back, paused again, then came straight across the garden patch, brusquely colliding with Vanamee, still motionless in the recess of the archway.

Sarria gave a great start, catching his breath.

"Oh—oh, it's you. Was it you I heard calling? No, I could not have heard—I remember now. What a strange power! I am not sure that it is right to do this thing, Vanamee. I—I HAD to come. I do not know why. It is a great force—a power—I don't like it. Vanamee, sometimes it frightens me."

Vanamee put his chin in the air.

"If I had wanted to, sir, I could have made you come to me from back there in the Quien Sabe ranch."

The priest shook his head.

"It troubles me," he said, "to think that my own will can count for so little. Just now I could not resist. If a deep river had been between us, I must have crossed it.

Suppose I had been asleep now?"

"It would have been all the easier," answered Vanamee. "I understand as little of these things as you. But I think if you had been asleep, your power of resistance would have been so much the more weakened."

"Perhaps I should not have waked. Perhaps I should have come to you in my sleep."

"Perhaps."

Sarria crossed himself. "It is occult," he hazarded. "No; I do not like it. Dear fellow," he put his hand on Vanamee's shoulder, "don't—call me that way again; promise. See," he held out his hand, "I am all of a tremble. There, we won't speak of it further. Wait for me a moment. I have only to put the cross in its place, and a fresh altar cloth, and then I am done. To-morrow is the feast of The Holy Cross, and I am preparing against it. The night is fine. We will smoke a cigar in the cloister garden."

A few moments later the two passed out of the door on the other side of the church, opposite the pulpit, Sarria adjusting a silk skull cap on his tonsured head. He wore his cassock now, and was far more the churchman in appearance than when Vanamee and Presley had seen him on a former occasion.

They were now in the cloister garden. The place was charming. Everywhere grew clumps of palms and magnolia trees. A grapevine, over a century old, occupied a trellis in one angle of the walls which surrounded the garden on two sides. Along the third side was the church itself, while the fourth was open, the wall having crumbled away, its site marked only by a line of eight great pear trees, older even than the grapevine, gnarled, twisted, bearing no fruit. Directly opposite the pear trees, in the south wall of the garden, was a round, arched portal, whose gate giving upon the esplanade in front of the Mission was always closed. Small gravelled walks, well kept, bordered with mignonette, twisted about among the flower beds, and underneath the magnolia trees. In the centre was a little fountain in a stone basin green with moss, while just beyond, between the fountain and the pear trees, stood what was left of a sun dial, the bronze gnomon, green with the beatings of the weather, the figures on the half-circle of the dial worn away, illegible.

But on the other side of the fountain, and directly opposite the door of the Mission, ranged against the wall, were nine graves—three with headstones, the rest with slabs. Two of Sarria's predecessors were buried here; three of the graves were those of Mission Indians. One was thought to contain a former alcalde of Guadalajara; two more held the bodies of De La Cuesta and his young wife (taking with her to the grave the illusion of her husband's love), and the last one, the ninth, at the end of the line, nearest the pear trees, was marked by a little headstone, the smallest of any, on which, together with the proper dates—only sixteen years apart—was cut the name "Angele Varian."

But the quiet, the repose, the isolation of the little cloister garden was infinitely delicious. It was a tiny corner of the great valley that stretched in all directions around it—shut off, discreet, romantic, a garden of dreams, of enchantments, of illusions. Outside there, far off, the great grim world went clashing through its grooves, but in here never an echo of the grinding of its wheels entered to jar upon the subdued modulation of the fountain's uninterrupted murmur.

Sarria and Vanamee found their way to a stone bench against the side wall of the Mission, near the door from which they had just issued, and sat down, Sarria lighting a cigar, Vanamee rolling and smoking cigarettes in Mexican fashion.

All about them widened the vast calm night. All the stars were out. The moon was coming up. There was no wind, no sound. The insistent flowing of the fountain seemed only as the symbol of the passing of time, a thing that was understood rather than heard, inevitable, prolonged. At long intervals, a faint breeze, hardly more than a breath, found its way into the garden over the enclosing walls, and passed overhead, spreading everywhere the delicious, mingled perfume of magnolia blossoms, of mignonette, of moss, of grass, and all the calm green life silently teeming within the enclosure of the walls.

From where he sat, Vanamee, turning his head, could look out underneath the pear trees to the north. Close at hand, a little valley lay between the high ground on which the Mission was built, and the line of low hills just beyond Broderson Creek on the Quien Sabe. In here was the Seed ranch, which Angele's people had cultivated, a unique and beautiful stretch of five hundred acres, planted thick with roses, violets, lilies, tulips, iris, carnations, tube-roses, poppies, heliotrope—all manner and description of flowers, five hundred acres of them, solid, thick, exuberant; blooming and fading, and leaving their seed or slips to be marketed broadcast all over the United States. This had been the vocation of Angele's parents—raising flowers for their seeds. All over the country the Seed ranch was known. Now it was arid, almost dry, but when in full flower, toward the middle of summer, the sight of these half-thousand acres royal with colour—vermilion, azure, flaming yellow—was a marvel. When an east wind blew, men on the streets of Bonneville, nearly twelve miles away, could catch the scent of this valley of flowers, this chaos of perfume.

And into this life of flowers, this world of colour, this atmosphere oppressive and clogged and cloyed and thickened with sweet odour, Angele had been born. There she had lived her sixteen years. There she had died. It was not surprising that Vanamee, with his intense, delicate sensitiveness to beauty, his almost abnormal capacity for great happiness, had been drawn to her, had loved her so deeply.

She came to him from out of the flowers, the smell of the roses in her hair of gold, that hung in two straight plaits on either side of her face; the reflection of the violets in the profound dark blue of her eyes, perplexing, heavy-lidded, almond-shaped, oriental; the aroma and the imperial red of the carnations in her lips, with their almost Egyptian fulness; the whiteness of the lilies, the perfume of the lilies, and the lilies' slender balancing grace in her neck. Her hands disengaged the odour of the heliotropes. The folds of her dress gave off the enervating scent of poppies. Her feet were redolent of hyacinths.

For a long time after sitting down upon the bench, neither the priest nor Vanamee spoke. But after a while Sarria took his cigar from his lips, saying:

"How still it is! This is a beautiful old garden, peaceful, very quiet. Some day I shall be buried here. I like to remember that; and you, too, Vanamee."

"Quien sabe?"

"Yes, you, too. Where else? No, it is better here, yonder, by the side of the little girl."

"I am not able to look forward yet, sir. The things that are to be are somehow nothing to me at all. For me they amount to nothing."

"They amount to everything, my boy."

"Yes, to one part of me, but not to the part of me that belonged to Angele–the best part. Oh, you don't know," he exclaimed with a sudden movement, "no one can understand. What is it to me when you tell me that sometime after I shall die too, somewhere, in a vague place you call Heaven, I shall see her again? Do you think that the idea of that ever made any one's sorrow easier to bear? Ever took the edge from any one's grief?"

"But you believe that–"

"Oh, believe, believe!" echoed the other. "What do I believe? I don't know. I believe, or I don't believe. I can remember what she WAS, but I cannot hope what she will be. Hope, after all, is only memory seen reversed. When I try to see her in another life–whatever you call it–in Heaven–beyond the grave–this vague place of yours; when I try to see her there, she comes to my imagination only as what she was, material, earthly, as I loved her. Imperfect, you say; but that is as I saw her, and as I saw her, I loved her; and as she WAS, material, earthly, imperfect, she loved me. It's that, that I want," he exclaimed. "I don't want her changed. I don't want her spiritualised, exalted, glorified, celestial. I want HER. I think it is only this feeling that has kept me from killing myself. I would rather be unhappy in the memory of what she actually was, than be happy in the realisation of her transformed, changed, made celestial. I am only human. Her soul! That was beautiful, no doubt. But, again, it was something very vague, intangible, hardly more than a phrase. But the touch of her hand was real, the sound of her voice was real, the clasp of her arms about my neck was real. Oh," he cried, shaken with a sudden wrench of passion, "give those back to me. Tell your God to give those back to me–the sound of her voice, the touch of her hand, the clasp of her dear arms, REAL, REAL, and then you may talk to me of Heaven."

Sarria shook his head. "But when you meet her again," he observed, "in Heaven, you, too, will be changed. You will see her spiritualised, with spiritual eyes. As she is now, she does not appeal to you. I understand that. It is because, as you say, you are only human, while she is divine. But when you come to be like her, as she is now, you will know her as she really is, not as she seemed to be, because her voice was sweet, because her hair was pretty, because her hand was warm in yours. Vanamee, your talk is that of a foolish child. You are like one of the Corinthians to whom Paul wrote. Do you remember? Listen now. I can recall the words, and such words, beautiful and terrible at the same time, such a majesty. They march like soldiers with trumpets. 'But some man will say'—as you have said just now—'How are the dead raised up? And with what body do they come? Thou fool! That which thou sowest is not quickened except it die, and that which thou sowest, thou sowest not that body that shall be, but bare grain. It may chance of wheat, or of some other grain. But God giveth it a body as it hath pleased him, and to every seed his own body.... It is sown a natural body; it is raised a spiritual body.' It is because you are a natural body that you cannot understand her, nor wish for her as a spiritual body, but when you are both spiritual, then you shall know each other as you are—know as you never knew before. Your grain of wheat is your symbol of immortality. You bury it in the earth. It dies, and rises again a thousand times more beautiful. Vanamee, your dear girl was only a grain of humanity that we have buried here, and the end is not yet. But all this is so old, so old. The world learned it a thousand years ago, and yet each man that has ever stood by the open grave of any one he loved must learn it all over again from the beginning."

Vanamee was silent for a moment, looking off with unseeing eyes between the trunks of the pear trees, over the little valley.

"That may all be as you say," he answered after a while. "I have not learned it yet, in any case. Now, I only know that I love her—oh, as if it all were yesterday—and that I am suffering, suffering, always."

He leaned forward, his head supported on his clenched fists, the infinite sadness of his face deepening like a shadow, the tears brimming in his deep-set eyes. A question that he must ask, which involved the thing that was scarcely to be thought of, occurred to him at this moment. After hesitating for a long moment, he said:

"I have been away a long time, and I have had no news of this place since I left. Is there anything to tell, Father? Has any discovery been made, any suspicion developed, as to—the Other?"

The priest shook his head.

"Not a word, not a whisper. It is a mystery. It always will be."

Vanamee clasped his head between his clenched fists, rocking himself to and fro.

"Oh, the terror of it," he murmured. "The horror of it. And she—think of it, Sarria, only sixteen, a little girl; so innocent, that she never knew what wrong meant, pure as a little child is pure, who believed that all things were good; mature only in her love. And to be struck down like that, while your God looked down from Heaven and would not take her part." All at once he seemed to lose control of himself. One of those furies of impotent grief and wrath that assailed him from time to time, blind, insensate, incoherent, suddenly took possession of him. A torrent of words issued from his lips, and he flung out an arm, the fist clenched, in a fierce, quick gesture, partly of despair, partly of defiance, partly of supplication. "No, your God would not take her part. Where was God's mercy in that? Where was Heaven's protection in that? Where was the loving kindness you preach about? Why did God give her life if it was to be stamped out? Why did God give her the power of love if it was to come to nothing? Sarria, listen to me. Why did God make her so divinely pure if He permitted that abomination? Ha!" he exclaimed bitterly, "your God! Why, an Apache buck would have been more merciful. Your God! There is no God. There is only the Devil. The Heaven you pray to is only a joke, a wretched trick, a delusion. It is only Hell that is real."

Sarria caught him by the arm.

"You are a fool and a child," he exclaimed, "and it is blasphemy that you are saying. I forbid it. You understand? I forbid it."

Vanamee turned on him with a sudden cry. "Then, tell your God to give her back to me!"

Sarria started away from him, his eyes widening in astonishment, surprised out of all composure by the other's outburst. Vanamee's swarthy face was pale, the sunken cheeks and deep-set eyes were marked with great black shadows. The priest no longer recognised him. The face, that face of the ascetic, lean, framed in its long black hair and pointed beard, was quivering with the excitement of hallucination. It was the face of the inspired shepherds of the Hebraic legends, living close to nature, the younger prophets of Israel, dwellers in the wilderness, solitary, imaginative, believing in the Vision, having strange delusions, gifted with strange powers. In a brief second of thought, Sarria understood. Out into the wilderness, the vast arid desert of the Southwest, Vanamee had carried his grief. For days, for weeks, months even, he had been alone, a solitary speck lost in the immensity of the horizons; continually he was brooding, haunted with his sorrow, thinking, thinking, often hard put to it for food. The body was ill-nourished, and the mind, concentrated forever upon one subject, had recoiled upon itself, had preyed upon the naturally nervous temperament, till the imagination had become exalted, morbidly active, diseased, beset with hallucinations, forever in search of the manifestation, of the miracle. It was small wonder that, bringing a fancy so distorted back to the scene of a vanished happiness, Vanamee should be racked with the most violent illusions, beset in the throes of a veritable hysteria.

"Tell your God to give her back to me," he repeated with fierce insistence.

It was the pitch of mysticism, the imagination harassed and goaded beyond the normal round, suddenly flipping from the circumference, spinning off at a tangent, out into the void, where all things seemed possible, hurtling through the dark there, groping for the supernatural, clamouring for the miracle. And it was also the human, natural protest against the inevitable, the irrevocable; the spasm of revolt under the sting of death, the rebellion of the soul at the victory of the grave.

"He can give her back to me if He only will," Vanamee cried. "Sarria, you must help me. I tell you—I warn you, sir, I can't last much longer under it. My head is all wrong with it—I've no more hold on my mind. Something must happen or I shall lose my senses. I am breaking down under it all, my body and my mind alike. Bring her to me; make God show her to me. If all tales are true, it would not be the first time. If I cannot have her, at least let me see her as she was, real, earthly, not her spirit, her ghost. I want her real self, undefiled again. If this is dementia, then let me be demented. But help me, you and your God; create the delusion, do the miracle."

"Stop!" cried the priest again, shaking him roughly by the shoulder. "Stop. Be yourself. This is dementia; but I shall NOT let you be demented. Think of what you are saying. Bring her back to you! Is that the way of God? I thought you were a man; this is the talk of a weak-minded girl."

Vanamee stirred abruptly in his place, drawing a long breath and looking about him vaguely, as if he came to himself.

"You are right," he muttered. "I hardly know what I am saying at times. But there are moments when my whole mind and soul seem to rise up in rebellion against what has happened; when it seems to me that I am stronger than death, and that if I only knew how to use the strength of my will, concentrate my power of thought—volition—that I could—I don't know—not call her back—but—something—"

"A diseased and distorted mind is capable of hallucinations, if that is what you mean," observed Sarria.

"Perhaps that is what I mean. Perhaps I want only the delusion, after all."

Sarria did not reply, and there was a long silence. In the damp south corners of the walls a frog began to croak at exact intervals. The little fountain rippled monotonously, and a magnolia flower dropped from one of the trees, falling straight as a plummet through the motionless air, and settling upon the gravelled walk with a faint rustling sound. Otherwise the stillness was profound.

A little later, the priest's cigar, long since out, slipped from his fingers to the ground. He began to nod gently. Vanamee touched his arm.

"Asleep, sir?"

The other started, rubbing his eyes.

"Upon my word, I believe I was."

"Better go to bed, sir. I am not tired. I think I shall sit out here a little longer."

"Well, perhaps I would be better off in bed. YOUR bed is always ready for you here whenever you want to use it."

"No—I shall go back to Quien Sabe—later. Good-night, sir."

"Good-night, my boy."

Vanamee was left alone. For a long time he sat motionless in his place, his elbows on his knees, his chin propped in his hands. The minutes passed—then the hours. The moon climbed steadily higher among the stars. Vanamee rolled and smoked cigarette after cigarette, the blue haze of smoke hanging motionless above his head, or drifting in slowly weaving filaments across the open spaces of the garden.

But the influence of the old enclosure, this corner of romance and mystery, this isolated garden of dreams, savouring of the past, with its legends, its graves, its crumbling sun dial, its fountain with its rime of moss, was not to be resisted. Now that the priest had left him, the same exaltation of spirit that had seized upon Vanamee earlier in the evening, by degrees grew big again in his mind and imagination. His sorrow assaulted him like the flagellations of a fine whiplash, and his love for Angele rose again in his heart, it seemed to him never so deep, so tender, so infinitely strong. No doubt, it was his familiarity with the Mission garden, his clear-cut remembrance of it, as it was in the days when he had met Angele there, tallying now so exactly with the reality there under his eyes, that brought her to his imagination so vividly. As yet he dared not trust himself near her grave, but, for the moment, he rose and, his hands clasped behind him, walked slowly from point to point amid the tiny gravelled walks, recalling the incidents of eighteen years ago. On the bench he had quitted he and Angele had often sat. Here by the crumbling sun dial, he recalled the night when he had kissed her for the first time. Here, again, by the rim of the fountain, with its fringe of green, she once had paused, and, baring her arm to the shoulder, had thrust it deep into the water, and then withdrawing it, had given it to him to kiss, all wet and cool; and here, at last, under the shadow of the pear trees they had sat, evening after evening, looking off over the little valley below them, watching the night build itself, dome-like, from horizon to zenith.

Brusquely Vanamee turned away from the prospect. The Seed ranch was dark at this time of the year, and flowerless. Far off toward its centre, he had caught a brief glimpse of the house where Angele had lived, and a faint light burning in its window. But he turned from it sharply. The deep-seated travail of his grief abruptly reached the paroxysm. With long strides he crossed the garden and reentered the Mission church itself, plunging into the coolness of its atmosphere as into a bath. What he searched for he did not know, or, rather, did not define. He knew only that he was suffering, that a longing for Angele, for some object around which his great love could enfold itself, was tearing at his heart with iron teeth. He was ready to be deluded; craved the hallucination; begged pitifully for the illusion; anything rather than the empty, tenantless night, the voiceless silence, the vast loneliness of the overspanning arc of the heavens.

Before the chancel rail of the altar, under the sanctuary lamp, Vanamee sank upon his knees, his arms folded upon the rail, his head bowed down upon them. He prayed, with what words he could not say for what he did not understand—for help, merely, for relief, for an Answer to his cry.

It was upon that, at length, that his disordered mind concentrated itself, an Answer—he demanded, he implored an Answer. Not a vague visitation of Grace, not a formless sense of Peace; but an Answer, something real, even if the reality were fancied, a voice out of the night, responding to his, a hand in the dark clasping his groping fingers, a breath, human, warm, fragrant, familiar, like a soft, sweet caress on his shrunken cheeks. Alone there in the dim half-light of the decaying Mission, with its crumbling plaster, its naive crudity of ornament and picture, he wrestled fiercely with his desires—words, fragments of sentences, inarticulate, incoherent, wrenched from his tight-shut teeth.

But the Answer was not in the church. Above him, over the high altar, the Virgin in a glory, with downcast eyes and folded hands, grew vague and indistinct in the shadow, the colours fading, tarnished by centuries of incense smoke. The Christ in agony on the Cross was but a lamentable vision of tormented anatomy, grey flesh, spotted with crimson. The St. John, the San Juan Bautista, patron saint of the Mission, the gaunt figure in skins, two fingers upraised in the gesture of benediction, gazed stolidly out into the half-gloom under the ceiling, ignoring the human distress that beat itself in vain against the altar rail below, and Angele remained as before—only a memory, far distant, intangible, lost.

Vanamee rose, turning his back upon the altar with a vague gesture of despair. He crossed the church, and issuing from the low-arched door opposite the pulpit, once more stepped out into the garden. Here, at least, was reality. The warm, still air descended upon him like a cloak, grateful, comforting, dispelling the chill that lurked in the damp mould of plaster and crumbling adobe.

But now he found his way across the garden on the other side of the fountain, where, ranged against the eastern wall, were nine graves. Here Angele was buried, in the smallest grave of them all, marked by the little headstone, with its two dates, only sixteen years apart. To this spot, at last, he had returned, after the years spent in the desert, the wilderness—after all the wanderings of the Long Trail. Here, if ever, he must have a sense of her nearness. Close at hand, a short four feet under that mound of grass, was the form he had so often held in the embrace of his arms; the face, the very face he had kissed, that face with the hair of gold making three-cornered the round white forehead, the violet-blue eyes, heavy-lidded, with their strange oriental slant upward toward the temples; the sweet full lips, almost Egyptian in their fulness—all that strange, perplexing, wonderful beauty, so troublous, so enchanting, so out of all accepted standards.

He bent down, dropping upon one knee, a hand upon the headstone, and read again the inscription. Then instinctively his hand left the stone and rested upon the low mound of turf, touching it with the softness of a caress; and then, before he was aware of it, he was stretched at full length upon the earth, beside the grave, his arms about the low mound, his lips pressed against the grass with which it was covered. The pent-up grief of nearly twenty years rose again within his heart, and overflowed, irresistible, violent, passionate. There was no one to see, no one to hear. Vanamee had no thought of restraint. He no longer wrestled with his pain—strove against it. There was even a sense of relief in permitting himself to be overcome. But the reaction from this outburst was equally violent. His revolt against the inevitable, his protest against the grave, shook him from head to foot, goaded him beyond all bounds of reason, hounded him on and into the domain of hysteria, dementia. Vanamee was no longer master of himself—no longer knew what he was doing.

At first, he had been content with merely a wild, unreasoned cry to Heaven that Angele should be restored to him, but the vast egotism that seems to run through all forms of disordered intelligence gave his fancy another turn. He forgot God. He no longer reckoned with Heaven. He arrogated their powers to himself—struggled to be, of his own unaided might, stronger than death, more powerful than the grave. He had demanded of Sarria that God should restore Angele to him, but now he appealed directly to Angele herself. As he lay there, his arms clasped about her grave, she seemed so near to him that he fancied she MUST hear. And suddenly, at this moment, his recollection of his strange compelling power—the same power by which he had called Presley to him half-way across the Quien Sabe ranch, the same power which had brought Sarria to his side that very evening—recurred to him. Concentrating his mind upon the one object with which it had so long been filled, Vanamee, his eyes closed, his face buried in his arms, exclaimed:

"Come to me—Angele—don't you hear? Come to me."

But the Answer was not in the Grave. Below him the voiceless Earth lay silent, moveless, withholding the secret, jealous of that which it held so close in its grip, refusing to give up that which had been confided to its keeping, untouched by the human anguish that above there, on its surface, clutched with despairing hands at a grave long made. The Earth that only that morning had been so eager, so responsive to the lightest summons, so vibrant with Life, now at night, holding death within its embrace, guarding inviolate the secret of the Grave, was deaf to all entreaty, refused the Answer, and Angele remained as before, only a memory, far distant, intangible, lost.

Vanamee lifted his head, looking about him with unseeing eyes, trembling with the exertion of his vain effort. But he could not as yet allow himself to despair. Never before had that curious power of attraction failed him. He felt himself to be so strong in this respect that he was persuaded if he exerted himself to the limit of his capacity, something—he could not say what—must come of it. If it was only a self-delusion, an hallucination, he told himself that he would be content.

Almost of its own accord, his distorted mind concentrated itself again, every thought, all the power of his will riveting themselves upon Angele. As if she were alive, he summoned her to him. His eyes, fixed upon the name cut into the headstone, contracted, the pupils growing small, his fists shut tight, his nerves braced rigid.

For a few seconds he stood thus, breathless, expectant, awaiting the manifestation, the Miracle. Then, without knowing why, hardly conscious of what was transpiring, he found that his glance was leaving the headstone, was turning from the grave. Not only this, but his whole body was following the direction of his eyes. Before he knew it, he was standing with his back to Angele's grave, was facing the north, facing the line of pear trees and the little valley where the Seed ranch lay. At first, he thought this was because he had allowed his will to weaken, the concentrated power of his mind to grow slack. And once more turning toward the grave, he banded all his thoughts together in a consummate effort, his teeth grinding together, his hands pressed to his forehead. He forced himself to the notion that Angele was alive, and to this creature of his imagination he addressed himself:

"Angele!" he cried in a low voice; "Angele, I am calling you—do you hear? Come to me—come to me now, now."

Instead of the Answer he demanded, that inexplicable counter-influence cut across the current of his thought. Strive as he would against it, he must veer to the north, toward the pear trees. Obeying it, he turned, and, still wondering, took a step in that direction, then another and another. The next moment he came abruptly to himself, in the black shadow of the pear trees themselves, and, opening his eyes, found himself looking off over the Seed ranch, toward the little house in the centre where Angele had once lived.

Perplexed, he returned to the grave, once more calling upon the resources of his will, and abruptly, so soon as these reached a certain point, the same cross-current set in. He could no longer keep his eyes upon the headstone, could no longer think of the grave and what it held. He must face the north; he must be drawn toward the pear trees, and there left standing in their shadow, looking out aimlessly over the Seed ranch, wondering, bewildered. Farther than this the influence never drew him, but up to this point—the line of pear trees—it was not to be resisted.

For a time the peculiarity of the affair was of more interest to Vanamee than even his own distress of spirit, and once or twice he repeated the attempt, almost experimentally, and invariably with the same result: so soon as he seemed to hold Angele in the grip of his mind, he was moved to turn about toward the north, and hurry toward the pear trees on the crest of the hill that over-looked the little valley.

But Vanamee's unhappiness was too keen this night for him to dwell long upon the vagaries of his mind. Submitting at length, and abandoning the grave, he flung himself down in the black shade of the pear trees, his chin in his hands, and resigned himself finally and definitely to the inrush of recollection and the exquisite grief of an infinite regret.

To his fancy, she came to him again. He put himself back many years. He remembered the warm nights of July and August, profoundly still, the sky encrusted with stars, the little Mission garden exhaling the mingled perfumes that all through the scorching day had been distilled under the steady blaze of a summer's sun. He saw himself as another person, arriving at this, their rendezvous. All day long she had been in his mind. All day long he had looked forward to this quiet hour that belonged to her. It was dark. He could see nothing, but, by and by, he heard a step, a gentle rustle of the grass on the slope of the hill pressed under an advancing foot. Then he saw the faint gleam of pallid gold of her hair, a barely visible glow in the starlight, and heard the murmur of her breath in the lapse of the over-passing breeze. And then, in the midst of the gentle perfumes of the garden, the perfumes of the magnolia flowers, of the mignonette borders, of the crumbling walls, there expanded a new odour, or the faint mingling of many odours, the smell of the roses that lingered in her hair, of the lilies that exhaled from her neck, of the heliotrope that disengaged itself from her hands and arms, and of the hyacinths with which her little feet were redolent, And then, suddenly, it was herself—her eyes, heavy-lidded, violet blue, full of the love of him; her sweet full lips speaking his name; her hands clasping his hands, his shoulders, his neck—her whole dear body giving itself into his embrace; her lips against his; her hands holding his head, drawing his face down to hers.

Vanamee, as he remembered all this, flung out an arm with a cry of pain, his eyes searching the gloom, all his mind in strenuous mutiny against the triumph of Death. His glance shot swiftly out across the night, unconsciously following the direction from which Angele used to come to him.

"Come to me now," he exclaimed under his breath, tense and rigid with the vast futile effort of his will. "Come to me now, now. Don't you hear me, Angele? You must, you must come."

Suddenly Vanamee returned to himself with the abruptness of a blow. His eyes opened. He half raised himself from the ground. Swiftly his scattered wits readjusted themselves. Never more sane, never more himself, he rose to his feet and stood looking off into the night across the Seed ranch.

"What was it?" he murmured, bewildered.

He looked around him from side to side, as if to get in touch with reality once more. He looked at his hands, at the rough bark of the pear tree next which he stood, at the streaked and rain-eroded walls of the Mission and garden. The exaltation of his mind calmed itself; the unnatural strain under which he laboured slackened. He became thoroughly master of himself again, matter-of-fact, practical, keen.

But just so sure as his hands were his own, just so sure as the bark of the pear tree was rough, the mouldering adobe of the Mission walls damp—just so sure had Something occurred. It was vague, intangible, appealing only to some strange, nameless sixth sense, but none the less perceptible. His mind, his imagination, sent out from him across the night, across the little valley below him, speeding hither and thither through the dark, lost, confused, had suddenly paused, hovering, had found Something. It had not returned to him empty-handed. It had come back, but now there was a change—mysterious, illusive. There were no words for this that had transpired. But for the moment, one thing only was certain. The night was no longer voiceless, the dark was no longer empty. Far off there, beyond the reach of vision, unlocalised, strange, a ripple had formed on the still black pool of the night, had formed, flashed one instant to the stars, then swiftly faded again. The night shut down once more. There was no sound—nothing stirred.

For the moment, Vanamee stood transfixed, struck rigid in his place, stupefied, his eyes staring, breathless with utter amazement. Then, step by step, he shrank back into the deeper shadow, treading with the infinite precaution of a prowling leopard. A qualm of something very much like fear seized upon him. But immediately on the heels of this first impression came the doubt of his own senses. Whatever had happened had been so ephemeral, so faint, so intangible, that now he wondered if he had not deceived himself, after all. But the reaction followed. Surely, there had been Something. And from that moment began for him the most poignant uncertainty of mind. Gradually he drew back into the garden, holding his breath, listening to every faintest sound, walking upon tiptoe. He reached the fountain, and wetting his hands, passed them across his forehead and eyes. Once more he stood listening. The silence was profound.

Troubled, disturbed, Vanamee went away, passing out of the garden, descending the hill. He forded Broderson Creek where it intersected the road to Guadalajara, and went on across Quien Sabe, walking slowly, his head bent down, his hands clasped behind his back, thoughtful, perplexed.

V

At seven o'clock, in the bedroom of his ranch house, in the white-painted iron bedstead with its blue-grey army blankets and red counterpane, Annixter was still asleep, his face red, his mouth open, his stiff yellow hair in wild disorder. On the wooden chair at the bed-head, stood the kerosene lamp, by the light of which he had been reading the previous evening. Beside it was a paper bag of dried prunes, and the limp volume of "Copperfield," the place marked by a slip of paper torn from the edge of the bag.

Annixter slept soundly, making great work of the business, unable to take even his rest gracefully. His eyes were shut so tight that the skin at their angles was drawn into puckers. Under his pillow, his two hands were doubled up into fists. At intervals, he gritted his teeth ferociously, while, from time to time, the abrupt sound of his snoring dominated the brisk ticking of the alarm clock that hung from the brass knob of the bed-post, within six inches of his ear.

But immediately after seven, this clock sprung its alarm with the abruptness of an explosion, and within the second, Annixter had hurled the bed-clothes from him and flung himself up to a sitting posture on the edge of the bed, panting and gasping, blinking at the light, rubbing his head, dazed and bewildered, stupefied at the hideous suddenness with which he had been wrenched from his sleep.

His first act was to take down the alarm clock and stifle its prolonged whirring under the pillows and blankets. But when this had been done, he continued to sit stupidly on the edge of the bed, curling his toes away from the cold of the floor; his half-shut eyes, heavy with sleep, fixed and vacant, closing and opening by turns. For upwards of three minutes he alternately dozed and woke, his head and the whole upper half of his body sagging abruptly sideways from moment to moment. But at length, coming more to himself, he straightened up, ran his fingers through his hair, and with a prodigious yawn, murmured vaguely:

"Oh, Lord! Oh-h, LORD!"

He stretched three or four times, twisting about in his place, curling and uncurling his toes, muttering from time to time between two yawns:

"Oh, Lord! Oh, Lord!"

He stared about the room, collecting his thoughts, readjusting himself for the day's work.

The room was barren, the walls of tongue-and-groove sheathing—alternate brown and yellow boards—like the walls of a stable, were adorned with two or three unframed lithographs, the Christmas "souvenirs" of weekly periodicals, fastened with great wire nails; a bunch of herbs or flowers, lamentably withered and grey with dust, was affixed to the mirror over the black walnut washstand by the window, and a yellowed photograph of Annixter's combined harvester—himself and his men in a group before it—hung close at hand. On the floor, at the bedside and before the bureau, were two oval rag-carpet rugs. In the corners of the room were muddy boots, a McClellan saddle, a surveyor's transit, an empty coal-hod and a box of iron bolts and nuts. On the wall over the bed, in a gilt frame, was Annixter's college diploma, while on the bureau, amid a litter of hair-brushes, dirty collars, driving gloves, cigars and the like, stood a broken machine for loading shells.

It was essentially a man's room, rugged, uncouth, virile, full of the odours of tobacco, of leather, of rusty iron; the bare floor hollowed by the grind of hob-nailed boots, the walls marred by the friction of heavy things of metal. Strangely enough, Annixter's clothes were disposed of on the single chair with the precision of an old maid. Thus he had placed them the night before; the boots set carefully side by side, the trousers, with the overalls still upon them, neatly folded upon the seat of the chair, the coat hanging from its back.

The Quien Sabe ranch house was a six-room affair, all on one floor. By no excess of charity could it have been called a home. Annixter was a wealthy man; he could have furnished his dwelling with quite as much elegance as that of Magnus Derrick. As it was, however, he considered his house merely as a place to eat, to sleep, to change his clothes in; as a shelter from the rain, an office where business was transacted—nothing more.

When he was sufficiently awake, Annixter thrust his feet into a pair of wicker slippers, and shuffled across the office adjoining his bedroom, to the bathroom just beyond, and stood under the icy shower a few minutes, his teeth chattering, fulminating oaths at the coldness of the water. Still shivering, he hurried into his clothes, and, having pushed the button of the electric bell to announce that he was ready for breakfast, immediately plunged into the business of the day. While he was thus occupied, the butcher's cart from Bonneville drove into the yard with the day's supply of meat. This cart also brought the Bonneville paper and the mail of the previous night. In the bundle of correspondence that the butcher handed to Annixter that morning, was a telegram from Osterman, at that time on his second trip to Los Angeles. It read:

"Flotation of company in this district assured. Have secured services of desirable party. Am now in position to sell you your share stock, as per original plan."

Annixter grunted as he tore the despatch into strips. "Well," he muttered, "that part is settled, then."

He made a little pile of the torn strips on the top of the unlighted stove, and burned them carefully, scowling down into the flicker of fire, thoughtful and preoccupied.

He knew very well what Osterman referred to by "Flotation of company," and also who was the "desirable party" he spoke of.

Under protest, as he was particular to declare, and after interminable argument, Annixter had allowed himself to be reconciled with Osterman, and to be persuaded to reenter the proposed political "deal." A committee had been formed to finance the affair—Osterman, old Broderson, Annixter himself, and, with reservations, hardly more than a looker-on, Harran Derrick. Of this committee, Osterman was considered chairman. Magnus Derrick had formally and definitely refused his adherence to the scheme. He was trying to steer a middle course. His position was difficult, anomalous. If freight rates were cut through the efforts of the members of the committee, he could not very well avoid taking advantage of the new schedule. He would be the gainer, though sharing neither the risk nor the expense. But, meanwhile, the days were passing; the primary elections were drawing nearer. The committee could not afford to wait, and by way of a beginning, Osterman had gone to Los Angeles, fortified by a large sum of money—a purse to which Annixter,

Broderson and himself had contributed. He had put himself in touch with Disbrow, the political man of the Denver, Pueblo and Mojave road, and had had two interviews with him. The telegram that Annixter received that morning was to say that Disbrow had been bought over, and would adopt Parrell as the D., P. and M. candidate for Railroad Commissioner from the third district.

One of the cooks brought up Annixter's breakfast that morning, and he went through it hastily, reading his mail at the same time and glancing over the pages of the "Mercury," Genslinger's paper. The "Mercury," Annixter was persuaded, received a subsidy from the Pacific and Southwestern Railroad, and was hardly better than the mouthpiece by which Shelgrim and the General Office spoke to ranchers about Bonneville.

An editorial in that morning's issue said:

"It would not be surprising to the well-informed, if the long-deferred re-grade of the value of the railroad sections included in the Los Muertos, Quien Sabe, Osterman and Broderson properties was made before the first of the year. Naturally, the tenants of these lands feel an interest in the price which the railroad will put upon its holdings, and it is rumoured they expect the land will be offered to them for two dollars and fifty cents per acre. It needs no seventh daughter of a seventh daughter to foresee that these gentlemen will be disappointed."

"Rot!" vociferated Annixter to himself as he finished. He rolled the paper into a wad and hurled it from him.

"Rot! rot! What does Genslinger know about it? I stand on my agreement with the P. and S. W.—from two fifty to five dollars an acre—there it is in black and white. The road IS obligated. And my improvements! I made the land valuable by improving it, irrigating it, draining it, and cultivating it. Talk to ME. I know better."

The most abiding impression that Genslinger's editorial made upon him was, that possibly the "Mercury" was not subsidised by the corporation after all. If it was; Genslinger would not have been led into making his mistake as to the value of the land. He would have known that the railroad was under contract to sell at two dollars and a half an acre, and not only this, but that when the land was put upon the market, it was to be offered to the present holders first of all. Annixter called to mind the explicit terms of the agreement between himself and the railroad, and dismissed the matter from his mind. He lit a cigar, put on his hat and went out.

The morning was fine, the air nimble, brisk. On the summit of the skeleton-like tower of the artesian well, the windmill was turning steadily in a breeze from the southwest. The water in the irrigating ditch was well up. There was no cloud in the sky. Far off to the east and west, the bulwarks of the valley, the Coast Range and the foothills of the Sierras stood out, pale amethyst against the delicate pink and white sheen of the horizon. The sunlight was a veritable flood, crystal, limpid, sparkling, setting a feeling of gayety in the air, stirring up an effervescence in the blood, a tumult of exuberance in the veins.

But on his way to the barns, Annixter was obliged to pass by the open door of the dairy-house. Hilma Tree was inside, singing at her work; her voice of a velvety huskiness, more of the chest than of the throat, mingling with the liquid dashing of the milk in the vats and churns, and the clear, sonorous clinking of the cans and pans. Annixter turned into the dairy-house, pausing on the threshold, looking about him. Hilma stood bathed from head to foot in the torrent of sunlight that poured in upon her from the three wide-open windows. She was charming, delicious, radiant of youth, of health, of well-being. Into her eyes, wide open, brown, rimmed with their fine, thin line of intense black lashes, the sun set a diamond flash; the same golden light glowed all around her thick, moist hair, lambent, beautiful, a sheen of almost metallic lustre, and reflected itself upon her wet lips, moving with the words of her singing. The whiteness of her skin under the caress of this hale, vigorous morning light was dazzling, pure, of a fineness beyond words. Beneath the sweet modulation of her chin, the reflected light from the burnished copper vessel she was carrying set a vibration of pale gold. Overlaying the flush of rose in her cheeks, seen only when she stood against the sunlight, was a faint sheen of down, a lustrous floss, delicate as the pollen of a flower, or the impalpable powder of a moth's wing. She was moving to and fro about her work, alert, joyous, robust; and from all the fine, full amplitude of her figure, from her thick white neck, sloping downward to her shoulders, from the deep, feminine swell of her breast, the vigorous maturity of her hips, there was disengaged a vibrant note of gayety, of exuberant animal life, sane, honest, strong. She wore a skirt of plain blue calico and a shirtwaist of pink linen, clean, trim; while her sleeves turned back to her shoulders, showed her large, white arms, wet with milk, redolent and fragrant with milk, glowing and resplendent in the early morning light.

On the threshold, Annixter took off his hat.

"Good morning, Miss Hilma."

Hilma, who had set down the copper can on top of the vat, turned about quickly.

"Oh, GOOD morning, sir;" and, unconsciously, she made a little gesture of salutation with her hand, raising it part way toward her head, as a man would have done.

"Well," began Annixter vaguely, "how are you getting along down here?"

"Oh, very fine. To-day, there is not so much to do. We drew the whey hours ago, and now we are just done putting the curd to press. I have been cleaning. See my pans. Wouldn't they do for mirrors, sir? And the copper things. I have scrubbed and scrubbed. Oh, you can look into the tiniest corners, everywhere, you won't find so much as the littlest speck of dirt or grease. I love CLEAN things, and this room is my own particular place. Here I can do just as I please, and that is, to keep the cement floor, and the vats, and the churns and the separators, and especially the cans and coppers, clean; clean, and to see that the milk is pure, oh, so that a little baby could drink it; and to have the air always sweet, and the sun—oh, lots and lots of sun, morning, noon and afternoon, so that everything shines. You know, I never see the sun set that it don't make me a little sad; yes, always, just a little. Isn't it funny? I should want it to be day all the time. And when the day is gloomy and dark, I am just as sad as if a very good friend of mine had left me. Would you believe it? Just until within a few years, when I was a big girl, sixteen and over, mamma had to sit by my bed every night before I could go to sleep. I was afraid in the dark. Sometimes I am now. Just imagine, and now I am nineteen—a young lady."

"You were, hey?" observed Annixter, for the sake of saying something. "Afraid in the dark? What of—ghosts?"

"N-no; I don't know what. I wanted the light, I wanted—" She drew a deep breath, turning towards the window and spreading her pink finger-tips to the light. "Oh, the SUN. I love the sun. See, put your hand there—here on the top of the vat—like that. Isn't it warm? Isn't it fine? And don't you love to see it coming in like that through the windows, floods of it; and all the little dust in it shining? Where there is lots of sunlight, I think the people must be very good. It's only wicked people that love the dark. And the wicked things are always done and planned in the dark, I think. Perhaps, too, that's why I hate things that are mysterious—things that I can't see, that happen in the dark." She wrinkled her nose with a little expression of aversion. "I hate a mystery. Maybe that's why I am afraid in the dark—or was. I shouldn't like to think that anything could happen around me that I couldn't see or understand or explain."

She ran on from subject to subject, positively garrulous, talking in her low-pitched voice of velvety huskiness for the mere enjoyment of putting her ideas into speech, innocently assuming that they were quite as interesting to others as to herself. She was yet a great child, ignoring the fact that she had ever grown up, taking a child's interest in her immediate surroundings, direct, straightforward, plain. While speaking, she continued about her work, rinsing out the cans with a mixture of hot water and soda, scouring them bright, and piling them in the sunlight on top of the vat.

Obliquely, and from between his narrowed lids, Annixter scrutinised her from time to time, more and more won over by her adorable freshness, her clean, fine youth. The clumsiness that he usually experienced in the presence of women was wearing off. Hilma Tree's direct simplicity put him at his ease. He began to wonder if he dared to kiss Hilma, and if he did dare, how she would take it. A spark of suspicion flickered up in his mind. Did not her manner imply, vaguely, an invitation? One never could tell with feemales. That was why she was talking so much, no doubt, holding him there, affording the opportunity. Aha! She had best look out, or he would take her at her word.

"Oh, I had forgotten," suddenly exclaimed Hilma, "the very thing I wanted to show you—the new press. You remember I asked for one last month? This is it. See, this is how it works. Here is where the curds go; look. And this cover is screwed down like this, and then you work the lever this way." She grasped the lever in both hands, throwing her weight upon it, her smooth, bare arm swelling round and firm with the effort, one slim foot, in its low shoe set off with the bright, steel buckle, braced against the wall.

"My, but that takes strength," she panted, looking up at him and smiling. "But isn't it a fine press? Just what we needed."

"And," Annixter cleared his throat, "and where do you keep the cheeses and the butter?" He thought it very likely that these were in the cellar of the dairy.

"In the cellar," answered Hilma. "Down here, see?" She raised the flap of the cellar door at the end of the room. "Would you like to see? Come down; I'll show you."

She went before him down into the cool obscurity underneath, redolent of new cheese and fresh butter. Annixter followed, a certain excitement beginning to gain upon him. He was almost sure now that Hilma wanted him to kiss her. At all events, one could but try. But, as yet, he was not absolutely sure. Suppose he had been mistaken in her; suppose she should consider herself insulted and freeze him with an icy stare. Annixter winced at the very thought of it. Better let the whole business go, and get to work. He was wasting half the morning. Yet, if she DID want to give him the opportunity of kissing her, and he failed to take advantage of it, what a ninny she would think him; she would despise him for being afraid. He afraid! He, Annixter, afraid of a fool, feemale girl. Why, he owed it to himself as a man to go as far as he could. He told himself that that goat Osterman would have kissed Hilma Tree weeks ago. To test his state of mind, he imagined himself as having decided to kiss her, after all, and at once was surprised to experience a poignant qualm of excitement, his heart beating heavily, his breath coming short. At the same time, his courage remained with him. He was not afraid to try. He felt a greater respect for himself because of this. His self-assurance hardened within him, and as Hilma turned to him, asking him to taste a cut from one of the ripe cheeses, he suddenly stepped close to her, throwing an arm about her shoulders, advancing his head.

But at the last second, he bungled, hesitated; Hilma shrank from him, supple as a young reed; Annixter clutched harshly at her arm, and trod his full weight upon one of her slender feet, his cheek and chin barely touching the delicate pink lobe of one of her ears, his lips brushing merely a fold of her shirt waist between neck and shoulder. The thing was a failure, and at once he realised that nothing had been further from Hilma's mind than the idea of his kissing her.

She started back from him abruptly, her hands nervously clasped against her breast, drawing in her breath sharply and holding it with a little, tremulous catch of the throat that sent a quivering vibration the length of her smooth, white neck. Her eyes opened wide with a childlike look, more of astonishment than anger. She was surprised, out of all measure, discountenanced, taken all aback, and when she found her breath, gave voice to a great "Oh" of dismay and distress.

For an instant, Annixter stood awkwardly in his place, ridiculous, clumsy, murmuring over and over again:

"Well—well—that's all right—who's going to hurt you? You needn't be afraid—who's going to hurt you—that's all right."

Then, suddenly, with a quick, indefinite gesture of one arm, he exclaimed:

"Good-bye, I—I'm sorry."

He turned away, striding up the stairs, crossing the dairy-room, and regained the open air, raging and furious. He turned toward the barns, clapping his hat upon his head, muttering the while under his breath:

"Oh, you goat! You beastly fool PIP. Good LORD, what an ass you've made of yourself now!"

Suddenly he resolved to put Hilma Tree out of his thoughts. The matter was interfering with his work. This kind of thing was sure not earning any money. He shook himself as though freeing his shoulders of an irksome burden, and turned his entire attention to the work nearest at hand.

The prolonged rattle of the shinglers' hammers upon the roof of the big barn attracted him, and, crossing over between the ranch house and the artesian well, he stood for some time absorbed in the contemplation of the vast building, amused and interested with the confusion of sounds—the clatter of hammers, the cadenced scrape of saws, and the rhythmic shuffle of planes—that issued from the gang of carpenters who were at that moment putting the finishing touches upon the roof and rows of stalls. A boy and two men were busy hanging the great sliding door at the south end, while the painters—come down from Bonneville early that morning—were engaged in adjusting the spray and force engine, by means of which Annixter had insisted upon painting the vast surfaces of the barn, condemning the use of brushes and pots for such work as old-fashioned and out-of-date.

He called to one of the foremen, to ask when the barn would be entirely finished, and was told that at the end of the week the hay and stock could be installed.

"And a precious long time you've been at it, too," Annixter declared.

"Well, you know the rain—"

"Oh, rot the rain! I work in the rain. You and your unions make me sick."

"But, Mr. Annixter, we couldn't have begun painting in the rain. The job would have been spoiled."

"Hoh, yes, spoiled. That's all very well. Maybe it would, and then, again, maybe it wouldn't."

But when the foreman had left him, Annixter could not forbear a growl of satisfaction. It could not be denied that the barn was superb, monumental even.

Almost any one of the other barns in the county could be swung, bird-cage fashion, inside of it, with room to spare. In every sense, the barn was precisely what Annixter had hoped of it. In his pleasure over the success of his idea, even Hilma for the moment was forgotten.

"And, now," murmured Annixter, "I'll give that dance in it. I'll make 'em sit up."

It occurred to him that he had better set about sending out the invitations for the affair. He was puzzled to decide just how the thing should be managed, and resolved that it might be as well to consult Magnus and Mrs. Derrick.

"I want to talk of this telegram of the goat's with Magnus, anyhow," he said to himself reflectively, "and there's things I got to do in Bonneville before the first of the month."

He turned about on his heel with a last look at the barn, and set off toward the stable. He had decided to have his horse saddled and ride over to Bonneville by way of Los Muertos. He would make a day of it, would see Magnus, Harran, old Broderson and some of the business men of Bonneville.

A few moments later, he rode out of the barn and the stable-yard, a fresh cigar between his teeth, his hat slanted over his face against the rays of the sun, as yet low in the east. He crossed the irrigating ditch and gained the trail—the short cut over into Los Muertos, by way of Hooven's. It led south and west into the low ground overgrown by grey-green willows by Broderson Creek, at this time of the rainy season a stream of considerable volume, farther on dipping sharply to pass underneath the Long Trestle of the railroad. On the other side of the right of way, Annixter was obliged to open the gate in Derrick's line fence. He managed this without dismounting, swearing at the horse the while, and spurring him continually. But once inside the gate he cantered forward briskly.

This part of Los Muertos was Hooven's holding, some five hundred acres enclosed between the irrigating ditch and Broderson Creek, and half the way across, Annixter came up with Hooven himself, busily at work replacing a broken washer in his seeder. Upon one of the horses hitched to the machine, her hands gripped tightly upon the harness of the collar, Hilda, his little daughter, with her small, hob-nailed boots and boy's canvas overalls, sat, exalted and petrified with ecstasy and excitement, her eyes wide opened, her hair in a tangle.

"Hello, Bismarck," said Annixter, drawing up beside him. "What are YOU doing here? I thought the Governor was going to manage without his tenants this year."

"Ach, Meest'r Ennixter," cried the other, straightening up. "Ach, dat's you, eh? Ach, you bedt he doand menege mitout me. Me, I gotta stay. I talk der straighd talk mit der Governor. I fix 'em. Ach, you bedt. Sieben yahr I hef bei der rench ge-stopped; yais, sir. Efery oder sohn-of-a-guhn bei der plaice ged der sach bud me. Eh? Wat you tink von dose ting?"

"I think that's a crazy-looking monkey-wrench you've got there," observed Annixter, glancing at the instrument in Hooven's hand.

"Ach, dot wrainch," returned Hooven. "Soh! Wail, I tell you dose ting now whair I got 'em. Say, you see dot wrainch. Dat's not Emericen wrainch at alle. I got 'em at Gravelotte der day we licked der stuffun oudt der Frainch, ach, you bedt. Me, I pelong to der Wurtemberg redgimend, dot dey use to suppord der batterie von der Brince von Hohenlohe. Alle der day we lay down bei der stomach in der feildt behindt der batterie, und der schells von der Frainch cennon hef eggsblode–ach, donnerwetter!–I tink efery schell eggsblode bei der beckside my neck. Und dat go on der whole day, noddun else, noddun aber der Frainch schell, b-r-r, b-r-r b-r-r, b-r-AM, und der smoag, und unzer batterie, dat go off slow, steady, yoost like der glock, eins, zwei, boom! eins, zwei, boom! yoost like der glock, ofer und ofer again, alle der day. Den vhen der night come dey say we hev der great victorie made. I doand know. Vhat do I see von der bettle? Noddun. Den we gedt oop und maerch und maerch alle night, und in der morgen we hear dose cennon egain, hell oaf der way, far-off, I doand know vhair. Budt, nef'r mindt. Bretty qnick, ach, Gott–" his face flamed scarlet, "Ach, du lieber Gott! Bretty zoon, dere wass der Kaiser, glose bei, und Fritz, Unzer Fritz. Bei Gott, den I go grazy, und yell, ach, you bedt, der whole redgimend: 'Hoch der Kaiser! Hoch der Vaterland!' Und der dears come to der eyes, I doand know because vhy, und der mens gry und shaike der hend, und der whole redgimend maerch off like dat, fairy broudt, bei Gott, der head oop high, und sing 'Die Wacht am Rhein.' Dot wass Gravelotte."

"And the monkey-wrench?"

"Ach, I pick 'um oop vhen der batterie go. Der cennoniers hef forgedt und leaf 'um. I carry 'um in der sack. I tink I use 'um vhen I gedt home in der business. I was maker von vagons in Carlsruhe, und I nef'r gedt home again. Vhen der war hef godt over, I go beck to Ulm und gedt marriet, und den I gedt demn sick von der armie. Vhen I gedt der release, I clair oudt, you bedt. I come to Emerica. First, New Yor-ruk; den Milwaukee; den Sbringfieldt-Illinoy; den Galifornie, und heir I stay."

"And the Fatherland? Ever want to go back?"

"Wail, I tell you dose ting, Meest'r Ennixter. Alle-ways, I tink a lot oaf Shairmany, und der Kaiser, und nef'r I forgedt Gravelotte. Budt, say, I tell you dose ting. Vhair der wife is, und der kinder–der leedle girl Hilda–DERE IS DER VATERLAND. Eh? Emerica, dat's my gountry now, und dere," he pointed behind him to the house under the mammoth oak tree on the Lower Road, "dat's my home. Dat's goot enough Vaterland for me."

Annixter gathered up the reins, about to go on.

"So you like America, do you, Bismarck?" he said. "Who do you vote for?"

"Emerica? I doand know," returned the other, insistently. "Dat's my home yonder. Dat's my Vaterland. Alle von we Shairmens yoost like dot. Shairmany, dot's hell oaf some fine plaice, sure. Budt der Vaterland iss vhair der home und der wife und kinder iss. Eh? Yes? Voad? Ach, no. Me, I nef'r voad. I doand bodder der haid mit dose ting. I maig der wheat grow, und ged der braid fur der wife und Hilda, dot's all. Dot's me; dot's Bismarck."

"Good-bye," commented Annixter, moving off.

Hooven, the washer replaced, turned to his work again, starting up the horses. The seeder advanced, whirring.

"Ach, Hilda, leedle girl," he cried, "hold tight bei der shdrap on. Hey MULE! Hoop! Gedt oop, you."

Annixter cantered on. In a few moments, he had crossed Broderson Creek and had entered upon the Home ranch of Los Muertos. Ahead of him, but so far off that the greater portion of its bulk was below the horizon, he could see the Derricks' home, a roof or two between the dull green of cypress and eucalyptus. Nothing else was in sight. The brown earth, smooth, unbroken, was as a limitless, mud-coloured ocean. The silence was profound.

Then, at length, Annixter's searching eye made out a blur on the horizon to the northward; the blur concentrated itself to a speck; the speck grew by steady degrees to a spot, slowly moving, a note of dull colour, barely darker than the land, but an inky black silhouette as it topped a low rise of ground and stood for a moment outlined against the pale blue of the sky. Annixter turned his horse from the road and rode across the ranch land to meet this new object of interest. As the spot grew larger, it resolved itself into constituents, a collection of units; its shape grew irregular, fragmentary. A disintegrated, nebulous confusion advanced toward Annixter, preceded, as he discovered on nearer approach, by a medley of faint sounds. Now it was no longer a spot, but a column, a column that moved, accompanied by spots. As Annixter lessened the distance, these spots resolved themselves into buggies or men on horseback that kept pace with the advancing column. There were horses in the column itself. At first glance, it appeared as if there were nothing else, a riderless squadron tramping steadily over the upturned plough land of the ranch. But it drew nearer. The horses were in lines, six abreast, harnessed to machines. The noise increased, defined itself. There was a shout or two; occasionally a horse blew through his nostrils with a prolonged, vibrating snort. The click and clink of metal work was incessant, the machines throwing off a continual rattle of wheels and cogs and clashing springs. The column approached nearer; was close at hand. The noises mingled to a subdued uproar, a bewildering confusion; the impact of innumerable hoofs was a veritable rumble. Machine after machine appeared; and Annixter, drawing to one side, remained for nearly ten minutes watching and interested, while, like an array of chariots—clattering, jostling, creaking, clashing, an interminable procession, machine succeeding machine, six-horse team succeeding six-horse team—bustling, hurried—Magnus Derrick's thirty-three grain drills, each with its eight hoes, went clamouring past, like an advance of military, seeding the ten thousand acres of the great ranch; fecundating the living soil; implanting deep in the dark womb of the Earth the germ of life, the sustenance of a whole world, the food of an entire People.

When the drills had passed, Annixter turned and rode back to the Lower Road, over the land now thick with seed. He did not wonder that the seeding on Los Muertos seemed to be hastily conducted. Magnus and Harran Derrick had not yet been able to make up the time lost at the beginning of the season, when they had waited so long for the ploughs to arrive. They had been behindhand all the time. On Annixter's ranch, the land had not only been harrowed, as well as seeded, but in some cases, cross-harrowed as well. The labour of putting in the vast crop was over. Now there was nothing to do but wait, while the seed silently germinated; nothing to do but watch for the wheat to come up.

When Annixter reached the ranch house of Los Muertos, under the shade of the cypress and eucalyptus trees, he found Mrs. Derrick on the porch, seated in a long wicker chair. She had been washing her hair, and the light brown locks that yet retained so much of their brightness, were carefully spread in the sun over the back of her chair. Annixter could not but remark that, spite of her more than fifty years, Annie Derrick was yet rather pretty. Her eyes were still those of a young girl, just touched with an uncertain expression of innocence and inquiry, but as her glance fell upon him, he found that that expression changed to one of uneasiness, of distrust, almost of aversion.

The night before this, after Magnus and his wife had gone to bed, they had lain awake for hours, staring up into the dark, talking, talking. Magnus had not long been able to keep from his wife the news of the coalition that was forming against the railroad, nor the fact that this coalition was determined to gain its ends by any means at its command. He had told her of Osterman's scheme of a fraudulent election to seat a Board of Railroad Commissioners, who should be nominees of the farming interests. Magnus and his wife had talked this matter over and over again; and the same discussion, begun immediately after supper the evening before, had lasted till far into the night.

At once, Annie Derrick had been seized with a sudden terror lest Magnus, after all, should allow himself to be persuaded; should yield to the pressure that was every day growing stronger. None better than she knew the iron integrity of her husband's character. None better than she remembered how his dearest ambition, that of political preferment, had been thwarted by his refusal to truckle, to connive, to compromise with his ideas of right. Now, at last, there seemed to be a change. Long continued oppression, petty tyranny, injustice and extortion had driven him to exasperation. S. Behrman's insults still rankled. He seemed nearly ready to countenance Osterman's scheme. The very fact that he was willing to talk of it to her so often and at such great length, was proof positive that it occupied his mind. The pity of it, the tragedy of it! He, Magnus, the "Governor," who had been so staunch, so rigidly upright, so loyal to his convictions, so bitter in his denunciation of the New Politics, so scathing in his attacks on bribery and corruption in high places; was it possible that now, at last, he could be brought to withhold his condemnation of the devious intrigues of the unscrupulous, going on there under his very eyes? That Magnus should not command Harran to refrain from all intercourse with the conspirators, had been a matter of vast surprise to Mrs. Derrick. Time was when Magnus would have forbidden his son to so much as recognise a dishonourable man.

But besides all this, Derrick's wife trembled at the thought of her husband and son engaging in so desperate a grapple with the railroad—that great monster, iron-hearted, relentless, infinitely powerful. Always it had issued triumphant from the fight; always S. Behrman, the Corporation's champion, remained upon the field as victor, placid, unperturbed, unassailable. But now a more terrible struggle than any hitherto loomed menacing over the rim of the future; money was to be spent like water; personal reputations were to be hazarded in the issue; failure meant ruin in all directions, financial ruin, moral ruin, ruin of prestige, ruin of character. Success, to her mind, was almost impossible. Annie Derrick feared the railroad. At night, when everything else was still, the distant roar of passing trains echoed across Los Muertos, from Guadalajara, from Bonneville, or from the Long Trestle, straight into her heart. At such moments she saw very plainly the galloping terror of steam and steel, with its single eye, cyclopean, red, shooting from horizon to horizon, symbol of a vast power, huge and terrible; the leviathan with tentacles of steel, to oppose which meant to be ground to instant destruction beneath the clashing wheels. No, it was better to submit, to resign oneself to the inevitable. She obliterated herself, shrinking from the harshness of the world, striving, with vain hands, to draw her husband back with her.

Just before Annixter's arrival, she had been sitting, thoughtful, in her long chair, an open volume of poems turned down upon her lap, her glance losing itself in the immensity of Los Muertos that, from the edge of the lawn close by, unrolled itself, gigantic, toward the far, southern horizon, wrinkled and serrated after the season's ploughing. The earth, hitherto grey with dust, was now upturned and brown. As far as the eye could reach, it was empty of all life, bare, mournful, absolutely still; and, as she looked, there seemed to her morbid imagination—diseased and disturbed with long brooding, sick with the monotony of repeated sensation—to be disengaged from all this immensity, a sense of a vast oppression, formless, disquieting. The terror of sheer bigness grew slowly in her mind; loneliness beyond words gradually enveloped her. She was lost in all these limitless reaches of space. Had she been abandoned in mid-ocean, in an open boat, her terror could hardly have been greater. She felt vividly that certain uncongeniality which, when all is said, forever remains between humanity and the earth which supports it. She recognised the colossal indifference of nature, not hostile, even kindly and friendly, so long as the human ant-swarm was submissive, working with it, hurrying along at its side in the mysterious march of the centuries. Let, however, the insect rebel, strive to make head against the power of this nature, and at once it became relentless, a gigantic engine, a vast power, huge, terrible; a leviathan with a heart of steel, knowing no compunction, no forgiveness, no tolerance; crushing out the human atom with sound less calm, the agony of destruction sending never a jar, never the faintest tremour through all that prodigious mechanism of wheels and cogs.

Such thoughts as these did not take shape distinctly in her mind. She could not have told herself exactly what it was that disquieted her. She only received the vague sensation of these things, as it were a breath of wind upon her face, confused, troublous, an indefinite sense of hostility in the air.

The sound of hoofs grinding upon the gravel of the driveway brought her to herself again, and, withdrawing her gaze from the empty plain of Los Muertos, she saw young Annixter stopping his horse by the carriage steps. But the sight of him only diverted her mind to the other trouble. She could not but regard him with aversion. He was one of the conspirators, was one of the leaders in the battle that impended; no doubt, he had come to make a fresh attempt to win over Magnus to the unholy alliance.

However, there was little trace of enmity in her greeting. Her hair was still spread, like a broad patch of back, and she made that her excuse for not getting up. In answer to Annixter's embarrassed inquiry after Magnus, she sent the Chinese cook to call him from the office; and Annixter, after tying his horse to the ring driven into the trunk of one of the eucalyptus trees, came up to the porch, and, taking off his hat, sat down upon the steps.

"Is Harran anywhere about?" he asked. "I'd like to see Harran, too."

"No," said Mrs. Derrick, "Harran went to Bonneville early this morning."

She glanced toward Annixter nervously, without turning her head, lest she should disturb her outspread hair.

"What is it you want to see Mr. Derrick about?" she inquired hastily. "Is it about this plan to elect a Railroad Commission? Magnus does not approve of it," she declared with energy. "He told me so last night."

Annixter moved about awkwardly where he sat, smoothing down with his hand the one stiff lock of yellow hair that persistently stood up from his crown like an Indian's scalp-lock. At once his suspicions were all aroused. Ah! this feemale woman was trying to get a hold on him, trying to involve him in a petticoat mess, trying to cajole him. Upon the instant, he became very crafty; an excess of prudence promptly congealed his natural impulses. In an actual spasm of caution, he scarcely trusted himself to speak, terrified lest he should commit himself to something. He glanced about apprehensively, praying that Magnus might join them speedily, relieving the tension.

"I came to see about giving a dance in my new barn," he answered, scowling into the depths of his hat, as though reading from notes he had concealed there. "I wanted to ask how I should send out the invites. I thought of just putting an ad. in the 'Mercury.'"

But as he spoke, Presley had come up behind Annixter in time to get the drift of the conversation, and now observed:

"That's nonsense, Buck. You're not giving a public ball. You MUST send out invitations."

"Hello, Presley, you there?" exclaimed Annixter, turning round. The two shook hands.

"Send out invitations?" repeated Annixter uneasily. "Why must I?"

"Because that's the only way to do."

"It is, is it?" answered Annixter, perplexed and troubled. No other man of his acquaintance could have so contradicted Annixter without provoking a quarrel upon the instant. Why the young rancher, irascible, obstinate, belligerent, should invariably defer to the poet, was an inconsistency never to be explained. It was with great surprise that Mrs. Derrick heard him continue:

"Well, I suppose you know what you're talking about, Pres. Must have written invites, hey?"

"Of course."

"Typewritten?"

"Why, what an ass you are, Buck," observed Presley calmly. "Before you get through with it, you will probably insult three-fourths of the people you intend to invite, and have about a hundred quarrels on your hands, and a lawsuit or two."

However, before Annixter could reply, Magnus came out on the porch, erect, grave, freshly shaven. Without realising what he was doing, Annixter instinctively rose to his feet. It was as though Magnus was a commander-in-chief of an unseen army, and he a subaltern. There was some little conversation as to the proposed dance, and then Annixter found an excuse for drawing the Governor aside. Mrs. Derrick watched the two with eyes full of poignant anxiety, as they slowly paced the length of the gravel driveway to the road gate, and stood there, leaning upon it, talking earnestly; Magnus tall, thin-lipped, impassive, one hand in the breast of his frock coat, his head bare, his keen, blue eyes fixed upon Annixter's face. Annixter came at once to the main point.

"I got a wire from Osterman this morning, Governor, and, well—we've got Disbrow. That means that the Denver, Pueblo and Mojave is back of us. There's half the fight won, first off."

"Osterman bribed him, I suppose," observed Magnus.

Annixter raised a shoulder vexatiously.

"You've got to pay for what you get," he returned. "You don't get something for nothing, I guess. Governor," he went on, "I don't see how you can stay out of this business much longer. You see how it will be. We're going to win, and I don't see how you can feel that it's right of you to let us do all the work and stand all the expense. There's never been a movement of any importance that went on around you that you weren't the leader in it. All Tulare County, all the San Joaquin, for that matter, knows you. They want a leader, and they are looking to you. I know how you feel about politics nowadays. But, Governor, standards have changed since your time; everybody plays the game now as we are playing it–the most honourable men. You can't play it any other way, and, pshaw! if the right wins out in the end, that's the main thing. We want you in this thing, and we want you bad. You've been chewing on this affair now a long time. Have you made up your mind? Do you come in? I tell you what, you've got to look at these things in a large way. You've got to judge by results. Well, now, what do you think? Do you come in?"

Magnus's glance left Annixter's face, and for an instant sought the ground. His frown lowered, but now it was in perplexity, rather than in anger. His mind was troubled, harassed with a thousand dissensions.

But one of Magnus's strongest instincts, one of his keenest desires, was to be, if only for a short time, the master. To control men had ever been his ambition; submission of any kind, his greatest horror. His energy stirred within him, goaded by the lash of his anger, his sense of indignity, of insult. Oh for one moment to be able to strike back, to crush his enemy, to defeat the railroad, hold the Corporation in the grip of his fist, put down S. Behrman, rehabilitate himself, regain his self-respect. To be once more powerful, to command, to dominate. His thin lips pressed themselves together; the nostrils of his prominent hawk-like nose dilated, his erect, commanding figure stiffened unconsciously. For a moment, he saw himself controlling the situation, the foremost figure in his State, feared, respected, thousands of men beneath him, his ambition at length gratified; his career, once apparently brought to naught, completed; success a palpable achievement. What if this were his chance, after all, come at last after all these years. His chance! The instincts of the old-time gambler, the most redoubtable poker player of El Dorado County, stirred at the word. Chance! To know it when it came, to recognise it as it passed fleet as a wind-flurry, grip at it, catch at it, blind, reckless, staking all upon the hazard of the issue, that was genius. Was this his Chance? All of a sudden, it seemed to him that it was. But his honour! His cherished, lifelong integrity, the unstained purity of his principles? At this late date, were they to be sacrificed? Could he now go counter to all the firm built fabric of his character? How, afterward, could he bear to look Harran and Lyman in the face? And, yet–and, yet–back swung the pendulum–to neglect his Chance meant failure; a life begun in promise, and ended in obscurity, perhaps in financial ruin, poverty even. To seize it meant achievement, fame, influence, prestige, possibly great wealth.

"I am so sorry to interrupt," said Mrs. Derrick, as she came up. "I hope Mr. Annixter will excuse me, but I want Magnus to open the safe for me. I have lost the combination, and I must have some money. Phelps is going into town, and I want him to pay some bills for me. Can't you come right away, Magnus? Phelps is ready and waiting."

Annixter struck his heel into the ground with a suppressed oath. Always these fool feemale women came between him and his plans, mixing themselves up in his affairs. Magnus had been on the very point of saying something, perhaps committing himself to some course of action, and, at precisely the wrong moment, his wife had cut in. The opportunity was lost. The three returned toward the ranch house; but before saying good-bye, Annixter had secured from Magnus a promise to the effect that, before coming to a definite decision in the matter under discussion, he would talk further with him.

Presley met him at the porch. He was going into town with Phelps, and proposed to Annixter that he should accompany them.

"I want to go over and see old Broderson," Annixter objected.

But Presley informed him that Broderson had gone to Bonneville earlier in the morning. He had seen him go past in his buckboard. The three men set off, Phelps and Annixter on horseback, Presley on his bicycle.

When they had gone, Mrs. Derrick sought out her husband in the office of the ranch house. She was at her prettiest that morning, her cheeks flushed with excitement, her innocent, wide-open eyes almost girlish. She had fastened her hair, still moist, with a black ribbon tied at the back of her head, and the soft mass of light brown reached to below her waist, making her look very young.

"What was it he was saying to you just now," she exclaimed, as she came through the gate in the green-painted wire railing of the office. "What was Mr. Annixter saying? I know. He was trying to get you to join him, trying to persuade you to be dishonest, wasn't that it? Tell me, Magnus, wasn't that it?"

Magnus nodded.

His wife drew close to him, putting a hand on his shoulder.

"But you won't, will you? You won't listen to him again; you won't so much as allow him—anybody—to even suppose you would lend yourself to bribery? Oh, Magnus, I don't know what has come over you these last few weeks. Why, before this, you would have been insulted if any one thought you would even consider anything like dishonesty. Magnus, it would break my heart if you joined Mr. Annixter and Mr. Osterman. Why, you couldn't be the same man to me afterward; you, who have kept yourself so clean till now. And the boys; what would Lyman say, and Harran, and every one who knows you and respects you, if you lowered yourself to be just a political adventurer!"

For a moment, Derrick leaned his head upon his hand, avoiding her gaze. At length, he said, drawing a deep breath: "I am troubled, Annie. These are the evil days. I have much upon my mind."

"Evil days or not," she insisted, "promise me this one thing, that you will not join Mr. Annixter's scheme." She had taken his hand in both of hers and was looking into his face, her pretty eyes full of pleading.

"Promise me," she repeated; "give me your word. Whatever happens, let me always be able to be proud of you, as I always have been. Give me your word. I know you never seriously thought of joining Mr. Annixter, but I am so nervous and frightened sometimes. Just to relieve my mind, Magnus, give me your word."

"Why—you are right," he answered. "No, I never thought seriously of it. Only for a moment, I was ambitious to be—I don't know what—what I had hoped to be once—well, that is over now. Annie, your husband is a disappointed man."

"Give me your word," she insisted. "We can talk about other things afterward."

Again Magnus wavered, about to yield to his better instincts and to the entreaties of his wife. He began to see how perilously far he had gone in this business. He was drifting closer to it every hour. Already he was entangled, already his foot was caught in the mesh that was being spun. Sharply he recoiled. Again all his instincts of honesty revolted. No, whatever happened, he would preserve his integrity. His wife was right. Always she had influenced his better side. At that moment, Magnus's repugnance of the proposed political campaign was at its pitch of intensity. He wondered how he had ever allowed himself to so much as entertain the idea of joining with the others. Now, he would wrench free, would, in a single instant of power, clear himself of all compromising relations. He turned to his wife. Upon his lips trembled the promise she implored. But suddenly there came to his mind the recollection of his new-made pledge to Annixter. He had given his word that before arriving at a decision he would have a last interview with him. To Magnus, his given word was sacred. Though now he wanted to, he could not as yet draw back, could not promise his wife that he would decide to do right. The matter must be delayed a few days longer.

Lamely, he explained this to her. Annie Derrick made but little response when he had done. She kissed his forehead and went out of the room, uneasy, depressed, her mind thronging with vague fears, leaving Magnus before his office desk, his head in his hands, thoughtful, gloomy, assaulted by forebodings.

Meanwhile, Annixter, Phelps, and Presley continued on their way toward Bonneville. In a short time they had turned into the County Road by the great watering-tank, and proceeded onward in the shade of the interminable line of poplar trees, the wind-break that stretched along the roadside bordering the Broderson ranch. But as they drew near to Caraher's saloon and grocery, about half a mile outside of Bonneville, they recognised Harran's horse tied to the railing in front of it. Annixter left the others and went in to see Harran.

"Harran," he said, when the two had sat down on either side of one of the small tables, "you've got to make up your mind one way or another pretty soon. What are you going to do? Are you going to stand by and see the rest of the Committee spending money by the bucketful in this thing and keep your hands in your pockets? If we win, you'll benefit just as much as the rest of us. I suppose you've got some money of your own—you have, haven't you? You are your father's manager, aren't you?"

Disconcerted at Annixter's directness, Harran stammered an affirmative, adding:

"It's hard to know just what to do. It's a mean position for me, Buck. I want to help you others, but I do want to play fair. I don't know how to play any other way. I should like to have a line from the Governor as to how to act, but there's no getting a word out of him these days. He seems to want to let me decide for myself."

"Well, look here," put in Annixter. "Suppose you keep out of the thing till it's all over, and then share and share alike with the Committee on campaign expenses."

Harran fell thoughtful, his hands in his pockets, frowning moodily at the toe of his boot. There was a silence. Then:

"I don't like to go it blind," he hazarded. "I'm sort of sharing the responsibility of what you do, then. I'm a silent partner. And, then—I don't want to have any difficulties with the Governor. We've always got along well together. He wouldn't like it, you know, if I did anything like that."

"Say," exclaimed Annixter abruptly, "if the Governor says he will keep his hands off, and that you can do as you please, will you come in? For God's sake, let us ranchers act together for once. Let's stand in with each other in ONE fight."

Without knowing it, Annixter had touched the right spring.

"I don't know but what you're right," Harran murmured vaguely. His sense of discouragement, that feeling of what's-the-use, was never more oppressive. All fair means had been tried. The wheat grower was at last with his back to the wall. If he chose his own means of fighting, the responsibility must rest upon his enemies, not on himself.

"It's the only way to accomplish anything," he continued, "standing in with each other... well,... go ahead and see what you can do. If the Governor is willing, I'll come in for my share of the campaign fund."

"That's some sense," exclaimed Annixter, shaking him by the hand. "Half the fight is over already. We've got Disbrow you know; and the next thing is to get hold of some of those rotten San Francisco bosses. Osterman will—" But Harran interrupted him, making a quick gesture with his hand.

"Don't tell me about it," he said. "I don't want to know what you and Osterman are going to do. If I did, I shouldn't come in."

Yet, for all this, before they said good-bye Annixter had obtained Harran's promise that he would attend the next meeting of the Committee, when Osterman should return from Los Angeles and make his report. Harran went on toward Los Muertos. Annixter mounted and rode into Bonneville.

Bonneville was very lively at all times. It was a little city of some twenty or thirty thousand inhabitants, where, as yet, the city hall, the high school building, and the opera house were objects of civic pride. It was well governed, beautifully clean, full of the energy and strenuous young life of a new city. An air of the briskest activity pervaded its streets and sidewalks. The business portion of the town, centring about Main Street, was always crowded. Annixter, arriving at the Post Office, found himself involved in a scene of swiftly shifting sights and sounds. Saddle horses, farm wagons—the inevitable Studebakers—buggies grey with the dust of country roads, buckboards with squashes and grocery packages stowed under the seat, two-wheeled sulkies and training carts, were hitched to the gnawed railings and zinc-sheathed telegraph poles along the curb. Here and there, on the edge of the sidewalk, were bicycles, wedged into bicycle racks painted with cigar advertisements. Upon the asphalt sidewalk itself, soft and sticky with the morning's heat, was a continuous movement. Men with large stomachs, wearing linen coats but no vests, laboured ponderously up and down. Girls in lawn skirts, shirt waists, and garden hats, went to and fro, invariably in couples, coming in and out of the drug store, the grocery store, and haberdasher's, or lingering in front of the Post Office, which was on a corner under the I.O.O.F. hall. Young men, in shirt sleeves, with brown, wicker cuff-protectors over their forearms, and pencils behind their ears, bustled in front of the grocery store, anxious and preoccupied. A very old man, a Mexican, in ragged white trousers and bare feet, sat on a horse-block in front of the barber shop, holding a horse by a rope around its neck. A Chinaman went by, teetering under the weight of his market baskets slung on a pole across his shoulders. In the neighbourhood of the hotel, the Yosemite House, travelling salesmen, drummers for jewelry firms of San Francisco, commercial agents, insurance men, well-dressed, metropolitan, debonair, stood about cracking jokes, or hurried in and out of the flapping white doors of the Yosemite barroom. The Yosemite 'bus and City 'bus passed up the street, on the way from the morning train, each with its two or three passengers. A very narrow wagon, belonging to the Cole & Colemore Harvester Works, went by, loaded with long strips of iron that made a horrible din as they jarred over the unevenness of the pavement. The electric car line, the city's boast, did a brisk business, its cars whirring from end to end of the street, with a jangling of bells and a moaning plaint of gearing. On the stone bulkheads of the grass plat around the new City Hall, the usual loafers sat, chewing tobacco, swapping stories. In the park were the inevitable array of nursemaids, skylarking couples, and ragged little boys. A single policeman, in grey coat and helmet, friend and acquaintance of every man and woman in the town, stood by the park entrance, leaning an elbow on the fence post, twirling his club.

But in the centre of the best business block of the street was a three-story building of rough brown stone, set off with plate glass windows and gold-lettered signs. One of these latter read, "Pacific and Southwestern Railroad, Freight and Passenger Office," while another much smaller, beneath the windows of the second story bore the inscription, "P. and S. W. Land Office."

Annixter hitched his horse to the iron post in front of this building, and tramped up to the second floor, letting himself into an office where a couple of clerks and bookkeepers sat at work behind a high wire screen. One of these latter recognised him and came forward.

"Hello," said Annixter abruptly, scowling the while. "Is your boss in? Is Ruggles in?"

The bookkeeper led Annixter to the private office in an adjoining room, ushering him through a door, on the frosted glass of which was painted the name, "Cyrus Blakelee Ruggles." Inside, a man in a frock coat, shoestring necktie, and Stetson hat, sat writing at a roller-top desk. Over this desk was a vast map of the railroad holdings in the country about Bonneville and Guadalajara, the alternate sections belonging to the Corporation accurately plotted. Ruggles was cordial in his welcome of Annixter. He had a way of fiddling with his pencil continually while he talked, scribbling vague lines and fragments of words and names on stray bits of paper, and no sooner had Annixter sat down than he had begun to write, in full-bellied script, ANN ANN all over his blotting pad.

"I want to see about those lands of mine—I mean of yours—of the railroad's," Annixter commenced at once. "I want to know when I can buy. I'm sick of fooling along like this."

"Well, Mr. Annixter," observed Ruggles, writing a great L before the ANN, and finishing it off with a flourishing D. "The lands"—he crossed out one of the N's and noted the effect with a hasty glance—"the lands are practically yours. You have an option on them indefinitely, and, as it is, you don't have to pay the taxes."

"Rot your option! I want to own them," Annixter declared. "What have you people got to gain by putting off selling them to us. Here this thing has dragged along for over eight years. When I came in on Quien Sabe, the understanding was that the lands—your alternate sections—were to be conveyed to me within a few months."

"The land had not been patented to us then," answered Ruggles.

"Well, it has been now, I guess," retorted Annixter.

"I'm sure I couldn't tell you, Mr. Annixter."

Annixter crossed his legs weariedly.

"Oh, what's the good of lying, Ruggles? You know better than to talk that way to me."

Ruggles's face flushed on the instant, but he checked his answer and laughed instead.

"Oh, if you know so much about it—" he observed.

"Well, when are you going to sell to me?"

"I'm only acting for the General Office, Mr. Annixter," returned Ruggles. "Whenever the Directors are ready to take that matter up, I'll be only too glad to put it through for you."

"As if you didn't know. Look here, you're not talking to old Broderson. Wake up, Ruggles. What's all this talk in Genslinger's rag about the grading of the value of our lands this winter and an advance in the price?"

Ruggles spread out his hands with a deprecatory gesture.

"I don't own the 'Mercury,'" he said.

"Well, your company does."

"If it does, I don't know anything about it."

"Oh, rot! As if you and Genslinger and S. Behrman didn't run the whole show down here. Come on, let's have it, Ruggles. What does S. Behrman pay Genslinger for inserting that three-inch ad. of the P. and S. W. in his paper? Ten thousand a year, hey?"

"Oh, why not a hundred thousand and be done with it?" returned the other, willing to take it as a joke.

Instead of replying, Annixter drew his check-book from his inside pocket.

"Let me take that fountain pen of yours," he said. Holding the book on his knee he wrote out a check, tore it carefully from the stub, and laid it on the desk in front of Ruggles.

"What's this?" asked Ruggles.

"Three-fourths payment for the sections of railroad land included in my ranch, based on a valuation of two dollars and a half per acre. You can have the balance in sixty-day notes."

Ruggles shook his head, drawing hastily back from the check as though it carried contamination.

"I can't touch it," he declared. "I've no authority to sell to you yet."

"I don't understand you people," exclaimed Annixter. "I offered to buy of you the same way four years ago and you sang the same song. Why, it isn't business. You lose the interest on your money. Seven per cent. of that capital for four years—you can figure it out. It's big money."

"Well, then, I don't see why you're so keen on parting with it. You can get seven per cent. the same as us."

"I want to own my own land," returned Annixter. "I want to feel that every lump of dirt inside my fence is my personal property. Why, the very house I live in now—the ranch house—stands on railroad ground."

"But, you've an option"

"I tell you I don't want your cursed option. I want ownership; and it's the same with Magnus Derrick and old Broderson and Osterman and all the ranchers of the county. We want to own our land, want to feel we can do as we blame please with it. Suppose I should want to sell Quien Sabe. I can't sell it as a whole till I've bought of you. I can't give anybody a clear title. The land has doubled in value ten times over again since I came in on it and improved it. It's worth easily twenty an acre now. But I can't take advantage of that rise in value so long as you won't sell, so long as I don't own it. You're blocking me."

"But, according to you, the railroad can't take advantage of the rise in any case. According to you, you can sell for twenty dollars, but we can only get two and a half."

"Who made it worth twenty?" cried Annixter. "I've improved it up to that figure. Genslinger seems to have that idea in his nut, too. Do you people think you can hold that land, untaxed, for speculative purposes until it goes up to thirty dollars and then sell out to some one else—sell it over our heads? You and Genslinger weren't in office when those contracts were drawn. You ask your boss, you ask S. Behrman, he knows. The General Office is pledged to sell to us in preference to any one else, for two and a half."

"Well," observed Ruggles decidedly, tapping the end of his pencil on his desk and leaning forward to emphasise his words, "we're not selling NOW. That's said and signed, Mr. Annixter."

"Why not? Come, spit it out. What's the bunco game this time?"

"Because we're not ready. Here's your check."

"You won't take it?"

"No."

"I'll make it a cash payment, money down—the whole of it—payable to Cyrus Blakelee Ruggles, for the P. and S. W."

"No."

"Third and last time."

"No."

"Oh, go to the devil!"

"I don't like your tone, Mr. Annixter," returned Ruggles, flushing angrily. "I don't give a curse whether you like it or not," retorted Annixter, rising and thrusting the check into his pocket, "but never you mind, Mr. Ruggles, you and S. Behrman and Genslinger and Shelgrim and the whole gang of thieves of you—you'll wake this State of California up some of these days by going just one little bit too far, and there'll be an election of Railroad Commissioners of, by, and for the people, that'll get a twist of you, my bunco-steering friend—you and your backers and cappers and swindlers and thimble-riggers, and smash you, lock, stock, and barrel. That's my tip to you and be damned to you, Mr. Cyrus Blackleg Ruggles."

Annixter stormed out of the room, slamming the door behind him, and Ruggles, trembling with anger, turned to his desk and to the blotting pad written all over with the words LANDS, TWENTY DOLLARS, TWO AND A HALF, OPTION, and, over and over again, with great swelling curves and flourishes, RAILROAD, RAILROAD, RAILROAD.

But as Annixter passed into the outside office, on the other side of the wire partition he noted the figure of a man at the counter in conversation with one of the clerks. There was something familiar to Annixter's eye about the man's heavy built frame, his great shoulders and massive back, and as he spoke to the clerk in a tremendous, rumbling voice, Annixter promptly recognised Dyke.

There was a meeting. Annixter liked Dyke, as did every one else in and about Bonneville. He paused now to shake hands with the discharged engineer and to ask about his little daughter, Sidney, to whom he knew Dyke was devotedly attached.

"Smartest little tad in Tulare County," asserted Dyke. "She's getting prettier every day, Mr. Annixter. THERE'S a little tad that was just born to be a lady. Can recite the whole of 'Snow Bound' without ever stopping. You don't believe that, maybe, hey? Well, it's true. She'll be just old enough to enter the Seminary up at Marysville next winter, and if my hop business pays two per cent. on the investment, there's where she's going to go."

"How's it coming on?" inquired Annixter.

"The hop ranch? Prime. I've about got the land in shape, and I've engaged a foreman who knows all about hops. I've been in luck. Everybody will go into the business next year when they see hops go to a dollar, and they'll overstock the market and bust the price. But I'm going to get the cream of it now. I say two per cent. Why, Lord love you, it will pay a good deal more than that. It's got to. It's cost more than I figured to start the thing, so, perhaps, I may have to borrow somewheres; but then on such a sure game as this—and I do want to make something out of that little tad of mine."

"Through here?" inquired Annixter, making ready to move off.

"In just a minute," answered Dyke. "Wait for me and I'll walk down the street with you."

Annixter grumbled that he was in a hurry, but waited, nevertheless, while Dyke again approached the clerk.

"I shall want some empty cars of you people this fall," he explained. "I'm a hop-raiser now, and I just want to make sure what your rates on hops are. I've been told, but I want to make sure. Savvy?" There was a long delay while the clerk consulted the tariff schedules, and Annixter fretted impatiently. Dyke, growing uneasy, leaned heavily on his elbows, watching the clerk anxiously. If the tariff was exorbitant, he saw his plans brought to naught, his money jeopardised, the little tad, Sidney, deprived of her education. He began to blame himself that he had not long before determined definitely what the railroad would charge for moving his hops. He told himself he was not much of a business man; that he managed carelessly.

"Two cents," suddenly announced the clerk with a certain surly indifference.

"Two cents a pound?"

"Yes, two cents a pound—that's in car-load lots, of course. I won't give you that rate on smaller consignments."

"Yes, car-load lots, of course... two cents. Well, all right."

He turned away with a great sigh of relief.

"He sure did have me scared for a minute," he said to Annixter, as the two went down to the street, "fiddling and fussing so long. Two cents is all right, though. Seems fair to me. That fiddling of his was all put on. I know 'em, these railroad heelers. He knew I was a discharged employee first off, and he played the game just to make me seem small because I had to ask favours of him. I don't suppose the General Office tips its slavees off to act like swine, but there's the feeling through the whole herd of them. 'Ye got to come to us. We let ye live only so long as we choose, and what are ye going to do about it? If ye don't like it, git out.'"

Annixter and the engineer descended to the street and had a drink at the Yosemite bar, and Annixter went into the General Store while Dyke bought a little pair of red slippers for Sidney. Before the salesman had wrapped them up, Dyke slipped a dime into the toe of each with a wink at Annixter.

"Let the little tad find 'em there," he said behind his hand in a hoarse whisper. "That'll be one on Sid."

"Where to now?" demanded Annixter as they regained the street. "I'm going down to the Post Office and then pull out for the ranch. Going my way?"

Dyke hesitated in some confusion, tugging at the ends of his fine blonde beard.

"No, no. I guess I'll leave you here. I've got—got other things to do up the street. So long."

The two separated, and Annixter hurried through the crowd to the Post Office, but the mail that had come in on that morning's train was unusually heavy. It was nearly half an hour before it was distributed. Naturally enough, Annixter placed all the blame of the delay upon the railroad, and delivered himself of some pointed remarks in the midst of the waiting crowd. He was irritated to the last degree when he finally emerged upon the sidewalk again, cramming his mail into his pockets. One cause of his bad temper was the fact that in the bundle of Quien Sabe letters was one to Hilma Tree in a man's handwriting.

"Huh!" Annixter had growled to himself, "that pip Delaney. Seems now that I'm to act as go-between for 'em. Well, maybe that feemale girl gets this letter, and then, again, maybe she don't."

But suddenly his attention was diverted. Directly opposite the Post Office, upon the corner of the street, stood quite the best business building of which Bonneville could boast. It was built of Colusa granite, very solid, ornate, imposing. Upon the heavy plate of the window of its main floor, in gold and red letters, one read the words: "Loan and Savings Bank of Tulare County." It was of this bank that S. Behrman was president. At the street entrance of the building was a curved sign of polished brass, fixed upon the angle of the masonry; this sign bore the name, "S. Behrman," and under it in smaller letters were the words, "Real Estate, Mortgages."

As Annixter's glance fell upon this building, he was surprised to see Dyke standing upon the curb in front of it, apparently reading from a newspaper that he held in his hand. But Annixter promptly discovered that he was not reading at all. From time to time the former engineer shot a swift glance out of the corner of his eye up and down the street. Annixter jumped at a conclusion. An idea suddenly occurred to him. Dyke was watching to see if he was observed—was waiting an opportunity when no one who knew him should be in sight. Annixter stepped back a little, getting a telegraph pole somewhat between him and the other. Very interested, he watched what was going on. Pretty soon Dyke thrust the paper into his pocket and sauntered slowly to the windows of a stationery store, next the street entrance of S. Behrman's offices. For a few seconds he stood there, his back turned, seemingly absorbed in the display, but eyeing the street narrowly nevertheless; then he turned around, gave a last look about and stepped swiftly into the doorway by the great brass sign. He disappeared. Annixter came from behind the telegraph pole with a flush of actual shame upon his face. There had been something so slinking, so mean, in the movements and manner of this great, burly honest fellow of an engineer, that he could not help but feel ashamed for him. Circumstances were such that a simple business transaction was to Dyke almost culpable, a degradation, a thing to be concealed.

"Borrowing money of S. Behrman," commented Annixter, "mortgaging your little homestead to the railroad, putting your neck in the halter. Poor fool! The pity of it. Good Lord, your hops must pay you big, now, old man."

Annixter lunched at the Yosemite Hotel, and then later on, toward the middle of the afternoon, rode out of the town at a canter by the way of the Upper Road that paralleled the railroad tracks and that ran diametrically straight between Bonneville and Guadalajara. About half-way between the two places he overtook Father Sarria trudging back to San Juan, his long cassock powdered with dust. He had a wicker crate in one hand, and in the other, in a small square valise, the materials for the Holy Sacrament. Since early morning the priest had covered nearly fifteen miles on foot, in order to administer Extreme Unction to a moribund good-for-nothing, a greaser, half Indian, half Portuguese, who lived in a remote corner of Osterman's stock range, at the head of a canon there. But he had returned by way of Bonneville to get a crate that had come for him from San Diego. He had been notified of its arrival the day before.

Annixter pulled up and passed the time of day with the priest.

"I don't often get up your way," he said, slowing down his horse to accommodate Sarria's deliberate plodding. Sarria wiped the perspiration from his smooth, shiny face.

"You? Well, with you it is different," he answered. "But there are a great many Catholics in the county—some on your ranch. And so few come to the Mission. At High Mass on Sundays, there are a few—Mexicans and Spaniards from Guadalajara mostly; but weekdays, for matins, vespers, and the like, I often say the offices to an empty church—'the voice of one crying in the wilderness.' You Americans are not good churchmen. Sundays you sleep—you read the newspapers."

"Well, there's Vanamee," observed Annixter. "I suppose he's there early and late."

Sarria made a sharp movement of interest.

"Ah, Vanamee—a strange lad; a wonderful character, for all that. If there were only more like him. I am troubled about him. You know I am a very owl at night. I come and go about the Mission at all hours. Within the week, three times I have seen Vanamee in the little garden by the Mission, and at the dead of night. He had come without asking for me. He did not see me. It was strange. Once, when I had got up at dawn to ring for early matins, I saw him stealing away out of the garden. He must have been there all the night. He is acting queerly. He is pale; his cheeks are more sunken than ever. There is something wrong with him. I can't make it out. It is a mystery. Suppose you ask him?"

"Not I. I've enough to bother myself about. Vanamee is crazy in the head. Some morning he will turn up missing again, and drop out of sight for another three years. Best let him alone, Sarria. He's a crank. How is that greaser of yours up on Osterman's stock range?"

"Ah, the poor fellow—the poor fellow," returned the other, the tears coming to his eyes. "He died this morning—as you might say, in my arms, painfully, but in the faith, in the faith. A good fellow."

"A lazy, cattle-stealing, knife-in-his-boot Dago."

"You misjudge him. A really good fellow on better acquaintance."

Annixter grunted scornfully. Sarria's kindness and good-will toward the most outrageous reprobates of the ranches was proverbial. He practically supported some half-dozen families that lived in forgotten cabins, lost and all but inaccessible, in the far corners of stock range and canyon. This particular greaser was the laziest, the dirtiest, the most worthless of the lot. But in Sarria's mind, the lout was an object of affection, sincere, unquestioning. Thrice a week the priest, with a basket of provisions—cold ham, a bottle of wine, olives, loaves of bread, even a chicken or two—toiled over the interminable stretch of country between the Mission and his cabin. Of late, during the rascal's sickness, these visits had been almost daily. Hardly once did the priest leave the bedside that he did not slip a half-dollar into the palm of his wife or oldest daughter. And this was but one case out of many.

His kindliness toward animals was the same. A horde of mange-corroded curs lived off his bounty, wolfish, ungrateful, often marking him with their teeth, yet never knowing the meaning of a harsh word. A burro, over-fed, lazy, incorrigible, browsed on the hill back of the Mission, obstinately refusing to be harnessed to Sarria's little cart, squealing and biting whenever the attempt was made; and the priest suffered him, submitting to his humour, inventing excuses for him, alleging that the burro was foundered, or was in need of shoes, or was feeble from extreme age. The two peacocks, magnificent, proud, cold-hearted, resenting all familiarity, he served with the timorous, apologetic affection of a queen's lady-in-waiting, resigned to their disdain, happy if only they condescended to enjoy the grain he spread for them.

At the Long Trestle, Annixter and the priest left the road and took the trail that crossed Broderson Creek by the clumps of grey-green willows and led across Quien Sabe to the ranch house, and to the Mission farther on. They were obliged to proceed in single file here, and Annixter, who had allowed the priest to go in front, promptly took notice of the wicker basket he carried. Upon his inquiry, Sarria became confused. "It was a basket that he had had sent down to him from the city."

"Well, I know—but what's in it?"

"Why—I'm sure—ah, poultry—a chicken or two."

"Fancy breed?"

"Yes, yes, that's it, a fancy breed." At the ranch house, where they arrived toward five o'clock, Annixter insisted that the priest should stop long enough for a glass of sherry. Sarria left the basket and his small black valise at the foot of the porch steps, and sat down in a rocker on the porch itself, fanning himself with his broad-brimmed hat, and shaking the dust from his cassock. Annixter brought out the decanter of sherry and glasses, and the two drank to each other's health.

But as the priest set down his glass, wiping his lips with a murmur of satisfaction, the decrepit Irish setter that had attached himself to Annixter's house came out from underneath the porch, and nosed vigorously about the wicker basket. He upset it. The little peg holding down the cover slipped, the basket fell sideways, opening as it fell, and a cock, his head enclosed in a little chamois bag such as are used for gold watches, struggled blindly out into the open air. A second, similarly hooded, followed. The pair, stupefied in their headgear, stood rigid and bewildered in their tracks, clucking uneasily. Their tails were closely sheared. Their legs, thickly muscled, and extraordinarily long, were furnished with enormous cruel-looking spurs. The breed was unmistakable. Annixter looked once at the pair, then shouted with laughter.

"'Poultry'—'a chicken or two'—'fancy breed'—ho! yes, I should think so. Game cocks! Fighting cocks! Oh, you old rat! You'll be a dry nurse to a burro, and keep a hospital for infirm puppies, but you will fight game cocks. Oh, Lord! Why, Sarria, this is as good a grind as I ever heard. There's the Spanish cropping out, after all."

Speechless with chagrin, the priest bundled the cocks into the basket and catching up the valise, took himself abruptly away, almost running till he had put himself out of hearing of Annixter's raillery. And even ten minutes later, when Annixter, still chuckling, stood upon the porch steps, he saw the priest, far in the distance, climbing the slope of the high ground, in the direction of the Mission, still hurrying on at a great pace, his cassock flapping behind him, his head bent; to Annixter's notion the very picture of discomfiture and confusion.

As Annixter turned about to reenter the house, he found himself almost face to face with Hilma Tree. She was just going in at the doorway, and a great flame of the sunset, shooting in under the eaves of the porch, enveloped her from her head, with its thick, moist hair that hung low over her neck, to her slim feet, setting a golden flash in the little steel buckles of her low shoes. She had come to set the table for Annixter's supper. Taken all aback by the suddenness of the encounter, Annixter ejaculated an abrupt and senseless, "Excuse me." But Hilma, without raising her eyes, passed on unmoved into the dining-room, leaving Annixter trying to find his breath, and fumbling with the brim of his hat, that he was surprised to find he had taken from his head. Resolutely, and taking a quick advantage of his opportunity, he followed her into the dining-room.

"I see that dog has turned up," he announced with brisk cheerfulness. "That Irish setter I was asking about."

Hilma, a swift, pink flush deepening the delicate rose of her cheeks, did not reply, except by nodding her head. She flung the table-cloth out from under her arms across the table, spreading it smooth, with quick little caresses of her hands. There was a moment's silence. Then Annixter said:

"Here's a letter for you." He laid it down on the table near her, and Hilma picked it up. "And see here, Miss Hilma," Annixter continued, "about that—this morning—I suppose you think I am a first-class mucker. If it will do any good to apologise, why, I will. I want to be friends with you. I made a bad mistake, and started in the wrong way. I don't know much about women people. I want you to forget about that—this morning, and not think I am a galoot and a mucker. Will you do it? Will you be friends with me?"

Hilma set the plate and coffee cup by Annixter's place before answering, and Annixter repeated his question. Then she drew a deep, quick breath, the flush in her cheeks returning.

"I think it was—it was so wrong of you," she murmured. "Oh! you don't know how it hurt me. I cried—oh, for an hour."

"Well, that's just it," returned Annixter vaguely, moving his head uneasily. "I didn't know what kind of a girl you were—I mean, I made a mistake. I thought it didn't make much difference. I thought all feemales were about alike."

"I hope you know now," murmured Hilma ruefully. "I've paid enough to have you find out. I cried—you don't know. Why, it hurt me worse than anything I can remember. I hope you know now."

"Well, I do know now," he exclaimed.

"It wasn't so much that you tried to do—what you did," answered Hilma, the single deep swell from her waist to her throat rising and falling in her emotion. "It was that you thought that you could—that anybody could that wanted to—that I held myself so cheap. Oh!" she cried, with a sudden sobbing catch in her throat, "I never can forget it, and you don't know what it means to a girl."

"Well, that's just what I do want," he repeated. "I want you to forget it and have us be good friends."

In his embarrassment, Annixter could think of no other words. He kept reiterating again and again during the pauses of the conversation:

"I want you to forget it. Will you? Will you forget it—that—this morning, and have us be good friends?"

He could see that her trouble was keen. He was astonished that the matter should be so grave in her estimation. After all, what was it that a girl should be kissed? But he wanted to regain his lost ground.

"Will you forget it, Miss Hilma? I want you to like me."

She took a clean napkin from the sideboard drawer and laid it down by the plate.

"I—I do want you to like me," persisted Annixter. "I want you to forget all about this business and like me."

Hilma was silent. Annixter saw the tears in her eyes.

"How about that? Will you forget it? Will you—will—will you LIKE me?"

She shook her head.

"No," she said.

"No what? You won't like me? Is that it?"

Hilma, blinking at the napkin through her tears, nodded to say, Yes, that was it. Annixter hesitated a moment, frowning, harassed and perplexed.

"You don't like me at all, hey?"

At length Hilma found her speech. In her low voice, lower and more velvety than ever, she said:

"No—I don't like you at all."

Then, as the tears suddenly overpowered her, she dashed a hand across her eyes, and ran from the room and out of doors.

Annixter stood for a moment thoughtful, his protruding lower lip thrust out, his hands in his pocket.

"I suppose she'll quit now," he muttered. "Suppose she'll leave the ranch—if she hates me like that. Well, she can go—that's all—she can go. Fool feemale girl," he muttered between his teeth, "petticoat mess." He was about to sit down to his supper when his eye fell upon the Irish setter, on his haunches in the doorway. There was an expectant, ingratiating look on the dog's face. No doubt, he suspected it was time for eating.

"Get out—YOU!" roared Annixter in a tempest of wrath.

The dog slunk back, his tail shut down close, his ears drooping, but instead of running away, he lay down and rolled supinely upon his back, the very image of submission, tame, abject, disgusting. It was the one thing to drive Annixter to a fury. He kicked the dog off the porch in a rolling explosion of oaths, and flung himself down to his seat before the table, fuming and panting.

"Damn the dog and the girl and the whole rotten business—and now," he exclaimed, as a sudden fancied qualm arose in his stomach, "now, it's all made me sick. Might have known it. Oh, it only lacked that to wind up the whole day. Let her go, I don't care, and the sooner the better."

He countermanded the supper and went to bed before it was dark, lighting his lamp, on the chair near the head of the bed, and opening his "Copperfield" at the place marked by the strip of paper torn from the bag of prunes. For upward of an hour he read the novel, methodically swallowing one prune every time he reached the bottom of a page. About nine o'clock he blew out the lamp and, punching up his pillow, settled himself for the night.

Then, as his mind relaxed in that strange, hypnotic condition that comes just before sleep, a series of pictures of the day's doings passed before his imagination like the roll of a kinetoscope.

First, it was Hilma Tree, as he had seen her in the dairy-house—charming, delicious, radiant of youth, her thick, white neck with its pale amber shadows under the chin; her wide, open eyes rimmed with fine, black lashes; the deep swell of her breast and hips, the delicate, lustrous floss on her cheek, impalpable as the pollen of a flower. He saw her standing there in the scintillating light of the morning, her smooth arms wet with milk, redolent and fragrant of milk, her whole, desirable figure moving in the golden glory of the sun, steeped in a lambent flame, saturated with it, glowing with it, joyous as the dawn itself.

Then it was Los Muertos and Hooven, the sordid little Dutchman, grimed with the soil he worked in, yet vividly remembering a period of military glory, exciting himself with recollections of Gravelotte and the Kaiser, but contented now in the country of his adoption, defining the Fatherland as the place where wife and children lived. Then came the ranch house of Los Muertos, under the grove of cypress and eucalyptus, with its smooth, gravelled driveway and well-groomed lawns; Mrs. Derrick with her wide-opened eyes, that so easily took on a look of uneasiness, of innocence, of anxious inquiry, her face still pretty, her brown hair that still retained so much of its brightness spread over her chair back, drying in the sun; Magnus, erect as an officer of cavalry, smooth-shaven, grey, thin-lipped, imposing, with his hawk-like nose and forward-curling grey hair; Presley with his dark face, delicate mouth and sensitive, loose lips, in corduroys and laced boots, smoking cigarettes—an interesting figure, suggestive of a mixed origin, morbid, excitable, melancholy, brooding upon things that had no names. Then it was Bonneville, with the gayety and confusion of Main Street, the whirring electric cars, the zinc-sheathed telegraph poles, the buckboards with squashes stowed under the seats; Ruggles in frock coat, Stetson hat and shoe-string necktie, writing abstractedly upon his blotting pad; Dyke, the engineer, big-boned. Powerful, deep-voiced, good-natured, with his fine blonde beard and massive arms, rehearsing the praises of his little daughter Sidney, guided only by the one ambition that she should be educated at a seminary, slipping a dime into the toe of her diminutive slipper, then, later, overwhelmed with shame, slinking into S. Behrman's office to mortgage his homestead to the heeler of the corporation that had discharged him. By suggestion, Annixter saw S. Behrman, too, fat, with a vast stomach, the check and neck meeting to form a great, tremulous jowl, the roll of fat over his collar, sprinkled with sparse, stiff hairs; saw his brown, round-topped hat of varnished straw, the linen vest stamped with innumerable interlocked horseshoes, the heavy watch chain, clinking against the pearl vest buttons; invariably placid, unruffled, never losing his temper, serene, unassailable, enthroned.

Then, at the end of all, it was the ranch again, seen in a last brief glance before he had gone to bed; the fecundated earth, calm at last, nursing the emplanted germ of life, ruddy with the sunset, the horizons purple, the small clamour of the day lapsing into quiet, the great, still twilight, building itself, dome-like, toward the zenith. The barn fowls were roosting in the trees near the stable, the horses crunching their fodder in the stalls, the day's work ceasing by slow degrees; and the priest, the Spanish churchman, Father Sarria, relic of a departed regime, kindly, benign, believing in all goodness, a lover of his fellows and of dumb animals, yet, for all that, hurrying away in confusion and discomfiture, carrying in one hand the vessels of the Holy Communion and in the other a basket of game cocks.

VI

It was high noon, and the rays of the sun, that hung poised directly overhead in an intolerable white glory, fell straight as plummets upon the roofs and streets of Guadalajara. The adobe walls and sparse brick sidewalks of the drowsing town radiated the heat in an oily, quivering shimmer. The leaves of the eucalyptus trees around the Plaza drooped motionless, limp and relaxed under the scorching, searching blaze. The shadows of these trees had shrunk to their smallest circumference, contracting close about the trunks. The shade had dwindled to the breadth of a mere line. The sun was everywhere. The heat exhaling from brick and plaster and metal met the heat that steadily descended blanketwise and smothering, from the pale, scorched sky. Only the lizards—they lived in chinks of the crumbling adobe and in interstices of the sidewalk—remained without, motionless, as if stuffed, their eyes closed to mere slits, basking, stupefied with heat. At long intervals the prolonged drone of an insect developed out of the silence, vibrated a moment in a soothing, somnolent, long note, then trailed slowly into the quiet again. Somewhere in the interior of one of the 'dobe houses a guitar snored and hummed sleepily. On the roof of the hotel a group of pigeons cooed incessantly with subdued, liquid murmurs, very plaintive; a cat, perfectly white, with a pink nose and thin, pink lips, dozed complacently on a fence rail, full in the sun. In a corner of the Plaza three hens wallowed in the baking hot dust their wings fluttering, clucking comfortably.

And this was all. A Sunday repose prevailed the whole moribund town, peaceful, profound. A certain pleasing numbness, a sense of grateful enervation exhaled from the scorching plaster. There was no movement, no sound of human business. The faint hum of the insect, the intermittent murmur of the guitar, the mellow complainings of the pigeons, the prolonged purr of the white cat, the contented clucking of the hens—all these noises mingled together to form a faint, drowsy bourdon, prolonged, stupefying, suggestive of an infinite quiet, of a calm, complacent life, centuries old, lapsing gradually to its end under the gorgeous loneliness of a cloudless, pale blue sky and the steady fire of an interminable sun.

In Solotari's Spanish-Mexican restaurant, Vanamee and Presley sat opposite each other at one of the tables near the door, a bottle of white wine, tortillas, and an earthen pot of frijoles between them. They were the sole occupants of the place. It was the day that Annixter had chosen for his barn-dance and, in consequence, Quien Sabe was in fete and work suspended. Presley and Vanamee had arranged to spend the day in each other's company, lunching at Solotari's and taking a long tramp in the afternoon. For the moment they sat back in their chairs, their meal all but finished. Solotari brought black coffee and a small carafe of mescal, and retiring to a corner of the room, went to sleep.

All through the meal Presley had been wondering over a certain change he observed in his friend. He looked at him again.

Vanamee's lean, spare face was of an olive pallor. His long, black hair, such as one sees in the saints and evangelists of the pre-Raphaelite artists, hung over his ears. Presley again remarked his pointed beard, black and fine, growing from the hollow cheeks. He looked at his face, a face like that of a young seer, like a half-inspired shepherd of the Hebraic legends, a dweller in the wilderness, gifted with strange powers. He was dressed as when Presley had first met him, herding his sheep, in brown canvas overalls, thrust into top boots; grey flannel shirt, open at the throat, showing the breast ruddy with tan; the waist encircled with a cartridge belt, empty of cartridges.

But now, as Presley took more careful note of him, he was surprised to observe a certain new look in Vanamee's deep-set eyes. He remembered now that all through the morning Vanamee had been singularly reserved. He was continually drifting into reveries, abstracted, distrait. Indubitably, something of moment had happened.

At length Vanamee spoke. Leaning back in his chair, his thumbs in his belt, his bearded chin upon his breast, his voice was the even monotone of one speaking in his sleep.

He told Presley in a few words what had happened during the first night he had spent in the garden of the old Mission, of the Answer, half-fancied, half-real, that had come to him.

"To no other person but you would I speak of this," he said, "but you, I think, will understand—will be sympathetic, at least, and I feel the need of unburdening myself of it to some one. At first I would not trust my own senses. I was sure I had deceived myself, but on a second night it happened again. Then I was afraid—or no, not afraid, but disturbed—oh, shaken to my very heart's core. I resolved to go no further in the matter, never again to put it to test. For a long time I stayed away from the Mission, occupying myself with my work, keeping it out of my mind. But the temptation was too strong. One night I found myself there again, under the black shadow of the pear trees calling for Angele, summoning her from out the dark, from out the night. This time the Answer was prompt, unmistakable. I cannot explain to you what it was, nor how it came to me, for there was no sound. I saw absolutely nothing but the empty night. There was no moon. But somewhere off there over the little valley, far off, the darkness was troubled; that ME that went out upon my thought—out from the Mission garden, out over the valley, calling for her, searching for her, found, I don't know what, but found a resting place—a companion. Three times since then I have gone to the Mission garden at night. Last night was the third time."

He paused, his eyes shining with excitement. Presley leaned forward toward him, motionless with intense absorption.

"Well—and last night," he prompted.

Vanamee stirred in his seat, his glance fell, he drummed an instant upon the table.

"Last night," he answered, "there was—there was a change. The Answer was—" he drew a deep breath—"nearer."

"You are sure?"

The other smiled with absolute certainty.

"It was not that I found the Answer sooner, easier. I could not be mistaken. No, that which has troubled the darkness, that which has entered into the empty night—is coming nearer to me—physically nearer, actually nearer."

His voice sank again. His face like the face of younger prophets, the seers, took on a half-inspired expression. He looked vaguely before him with unseeing eyes.

"Suppose," he murmured, "suppose I stand there under the pear trees at night and call her again and again, and each time the Answer comes nearer and nearer and I wait until at last one night, the supreme night of all, she—she—"

Suddenly the tension broke. With a sharp cry and a violent uncertain gesture of the hand Vanamee came to himself.

"Oh," he exclaimed, "what is it? Do I dare? What does it mean? There are times when it appals me and there are times when it thrills me with a sweetness and a happiness that I have not known since she died. The vagueness of it! How can I explain it to you, this that happens when I call to her across the night—that faint, far-off, unseen tremble in the darkness, that intangible, scarcely perceptible stir. Something neither heard nor seen, appealing to a sixth sense only. Listen, it is something like this: On Quien Sabe, all last week, we have been seeding the earth. The grain is there now under the earth buried in the dark, in the black stillness, under the clods. Can you imagine the first—the very first little quiver of life that the grain of wheat must feel after it is sown, when it answers to the call of the sun, down there in the dark of the earth, blind, deaf; the very first stir from the inert, long, long before any physical change has occurred,—long before the microscope could discover the slightest change,—when the shell first tightens with the first faint premonition of life? Well, it is something as illusive as that." He paused again, dreaming, lost in a reverie, then, just above a whisper, murmured:

"'That which thou sowest is not quickened except it die,'... and she, Angele... died."

"You could not have been mistaken?" said Presley. "You were sure that there was something? Imagination can do so much and the influence of the surroundings was strong. How impossible it would be that anything SHOULD happen. And you say you heard nothing, saw nothing."

"I believe," answered Vanamee, "in a sixth sense, or, rather, a whole system of other unnamed senses beyond the reach of our understanding. People who live much alone and close to nature experience the sensation of it. Perhaps it is something fundamental that we share with plants and animals. The same thing that sends the birds south long before the first colds, the same thing that makes the grain of wheat struggle up to meet the sun. And this sense never deceives. You may see wrong, hear wrong, but once touch this sixth sense and it acts with absolute fidelity, you are certain. No, I hear nothing in the Mission garden. I see nothing, nothing touches me, but I am CERTAIN for all that."

Presley hesitated for a moment, then he asked:

"Shall you go back to the garden again? Make the test again?"

"I don't know."

"Strange enough," commented Presley, wondering.

Vanamee sank back in his chair, his eyes growing vacant again:

"Strange enough," he murmured.

There was a long silence. Neither spoke nor moved. There, in that moribund, ancient town, wrapped in its siesta, flagellated with heat, deserted, ignored, baking in a noon-day silence, these two strange men, the one a poet by nature, the other by training, both out of tune with their world, dreamers, introspective, morbid, lost and unfamiliar at that end-of-the-century time, searching for a sign, groping and baffled amidst the perplexing obscurity of the Delusion, sat over empty wine glasses, silent with the pervading silence that surrounded them, hearing only the cooing of doves and the drone of bees, the quiet so profound, that at length they could plainly distinguish at intervals the puffing and coughing of a locomotive switching cars in the station yard of Bonneville.

It was, no doubt, this jarring sound that at length roused Presley from his lethargy. The two friends rose; Solotari very sleepily came forward; they paid for the luncheon, and stepping out into the heat and glare of the streets of the town, passed on through it and took the road that led northward across a corner of Dyke's hop fields. They were bound for the hills in the northeastern corner of Quien Sabe. It was the same walk which Presley had taken on the previous occasion when he had first met Vanamee herding the sheep. This encompassing detour around the whole country-side was a favorite pastime of his and he was anxious that Vanamee should share his pleasure in it.

But soon after leaving Guadalajara, they found themselves upon the land that Dyke had bought and upon which he was to raise his famous crop of hops. Dyke's house was close at hand, a very pleasant little cottage, painted white, with green blinds and deep porches, while near it and yet in process of construction, were two great storehouses and a drying and curing house, where the hops were to be stored and treated. All about were evidences that the former engineer had already been hard at work. The ground had been put in readiness to receive the crop and a bewildering, innumerable multitude of poles, connected with a maze of wire and twine, had been set out. Farther on at a turn of the road, they came upon Dyke himself, driving a farm wagon loaded with more poles. He was in his shirt sleeves, his massive, hairy arms bare to the elbow, glistening with sweat, red with heat. In his bell-like, rumbling voice, he was calling to his foreman and a boy at work in stringing the poles together. At sight of Presley and Vanamee he hailed them jovially, addressing them as "boys," and insisting that they should get into the wagon with him and drive to the house for a glass of beer. His mother had only the day before returned from Marysville, where she had been looking up a seminary for the little tad. She would be delighted to see the two boys; besides, Vanamee must see how the little tad had grown since he last set eyes on her; wouldn't know her for the same little girl; and the beer had been on ice since morning. Presley and Vanamee could not well refuse.

They climbed into the wagon and jolted over the uneven ground through the bare forest of hop-poles to the house. Inside they found Mrs. Dyke, an old lady with a very gentle face, who wore a cap and a very old-fashioned gown with hoop skirts, dusting the what-not in a corner of the parlor. The two men were presented and the beer was had from off the ice.

"Mother," said Dyke, as he wiped the froth from his great blond beard, "ain't Sid anywheres about? I want Mr. Vanamee to see how she has grown. Smartest little tad in Tulare County, boys. Can recite the whole of 'Snow Bound,' end to end, without skipping or looking at the book. Maybe you don't believe that. Mother, ain't I right—without skipping a line, hey?"

Mrs. Dyke nodded to say that it was so, but explained that Sidney was in Guadalajara. In putting on her new slippers for the first time the morning before, she had found a dime in the toe of one of them and had had the whole house by the ears ever since till she could spend it.

"Was it for licorice to make her licorice water?" inquired Dyke gravely.

"Yes," said Mrs. Dyke. "I made her tell me what she was going to get before she went, and it was licorice."

Dyke, though his mother protested that he was foolish and that Presley and Vanamee had no great interest in "young ones," insisted upon showing the visitors Sidney's copy-books. They were monuments of laborious, elaborate neatness, the trite moralities and ready-made aphorisms of the philanthropists and publicists, repeated from page to page with wearying insistence. "I, too, am an American Citizen. S. D.,"

"As the Twig is Bent the Tree is Inclined,"

"Truth Crushed to Earth Will Rise Again,"

"As for Me, Give Me Liberty or Give Me Death," and last of all, a strange intrusion amongst the mild, well-worn phrases, two legends. "My motto—Public Control of Public Franchises," and "The P. and S. W. is an Enemy of the State."

"I see," commented Presley, "you mean the little tad to understand 'the situation' early."

"I told him he was foolish to give that to Sid to copy," said Mrs. Dyke, with indulgent remonstrance. "What can she understand of public franchises?"

"Never mind," observed Dyke, "she'll remember it when she grows up and when the seminary people have rubbed her up a bit, and then she'll begin to ask questions and understand. And don't you make any mistake, mother," he went on, "about the little tad not knowing who her dad's enemies are. What do you think, boys? Listen, here. Precious little I've ever told her of the railroad or how I was turned off, but the other day I was working down by the fence next the railroad tracks and Sid was there. She'd brought her doll rags down and she was playing house behind a pile of hop poles. Well, along comes a through freight—mixed train from Missouri points and a string of empties from New Orleans,—and when it had passed, what do you suppose the tad did? SHE didn't know I was watching her. She goes to the fence and spits a little spit after the caboose and puts out her little head and, if you'll believe me, HISSES at the train; and mother says she does that same every time she sees a train go by, and never crosses the tracks that she don't spit her little spit on 'em. What do you THINK of THAT?"

"But I correct her every time," protested Mrs. Dyke seriously. "Where she picked up the trick of hissing I don't know. No, it's not funny. It seems dreadful to see a little girl who's as sweet and gentle as can be in every other way, so venomous. She says the other little girls at school and the boys, too, are all the same way. Oh, dear," she sighed, "why will the General Office be so unkind and unjust? Why, I couldn't be happy, with all the money in the world, if I thought that even one little child hated me—hated me so that it would spit and hiss at me. And it's not one child, it's all of them, so Sidney says; and think of all the grown people who hate the road, women and men, the whole county, the whole State, thousands and thousands of people. Don't the managers and the directors of the road ever think of that? Don't they ever think of all the hate that surrounds them, everywhere, everywhere, and the good people that just grit their teeth when the name of the road is mentioned? Why do they want to make the people hate them? No," she murmured, the tears starting to her eyes, "No, I tell you, Mr. Presley, the men who own the railroad are wicked, bad-hearted men who don't care how much the poor people suffer, so long as the road makes its eighteen million a year. They don't care whether the people hate them or love them, just so long as they are afraid of them. It's not right and God will punish them sooner or later."

A little after this the two young men took themselves away, Dyke obligingly carrying them in the wagon as far as the gate that opened into the Quien Sabe ranch. On the way, Presley referred to what Mrs. Dyke had said and led Dyke, himself, to speak of the P. and S. W.

"Well," Dyke said, "it's like this, Mr. Presley. I, personally, haven't got the right to kick. With you wheat-growing people I guess it's different, but hops, you see, don't count for much in the State. It's such a little business that the road don't want to bother themselves to tax it. It's the wheat growers that the road cinches. The rates on hops ARE FAIR. I've got to admit that; I was in to Bonneville a while ago to find out. It's two cents a pound, and Lord love you, that's reasonable enough to suit any man. No," he concluded, "I'm on the way to make money now. The road sacking me as they did was, maybe, a good thing for me, after all. It came just at the right time. I had a bit of money put by and here was the chance to go into hops with the certainty that hops would quadruple and quintuple in price inside the year. No, it was my chance, and though they didn't mean it by a long chalk, the railroad people did me a good turn when they gave me my time—and the tad'll enter the seminary next fall."

About a quarter of an hour after they had said goodbye to the one-time engineer, Presley and Vanamee, tramping briskly along the road that led northward through Quien Sabe, arrived at Annixter's ranch house. At once they were aware of a vast and unwonted bustle that revolved about the place. They stopped a few moments looking on, amused and interested in what was going forward.

The colossal barn was finished. Its freshly white-washed sides glared intolerably in the sun, but its interior was as yet innocent of paint and through the yawning vent of the sliding doors came a delicious odour of new, fresh wood and shavings. A crowd of men—Annixter's farm hands—were swarming all about it. Some were balanced on the topmost rounds of ladders, hanging festoons of Japanese lanterns from tree to tree, and all across the front of the barn itself. Mrs. Tree, her daughter Hilma and another woman were inside the barn cutting into long strips bolt after bolt of red, white and blue cambric and directing how these strips should be draped from the ceiling and on the walls; everywhere resounded the tapping of tack hammers. A farm wagon drove up loaded to overflowing with evergreens and with great bundles of palm leaves, and these were immediately seized upon and affixed as supplementary decorations to the tri-coloured cambric upon the inside walls of the barn. Two of the larger evergreen trees were placed on either side the barn door and their tops bent over to form an arch. In the middle of this arch it was proposed to hang a mammoth pasteboard escutcheon with gold letters, spelling the word WELCOME. Piles of chairs, rented from I.O.O.F. hall in Bonneville, heaped themselves in an apparently hopeless entanglement on the ground; while at the far extremity of the barn a couple of carpenters clattered about the impromptu staging which was to accommodate the band.

There was a strenuous gayety in the air; everybody was in the best of spirits. Notes of laughter continually interrupted the conversation on every hand. At every moment a group of men involved themselves in uproarious horse-play. They passed oblique jokes behind their hands to each other—grossly veiled double-meanings meant for the women—and bellowed with laughter thereat, stamping on the ground. The relations between the sexes grew more intimate, the women and girls pushing the young fellows away from their sides with vigorous thrusts of their elbows. It was passed from group to group that Adela Vacca, a division superintendent's wife, had lost her garter; the daughter of the foreman of the Home ranch was kissed behind the door of the dairy-house.

Annixter, in execrable temper, appeared from time to time, hatless, his stiff yellow hair in wild disorder. He hurried between the barn and the ranch house, carrying now a wickered demijohn, now a case of wine, now a basket of lemons and pineapples. Besides general supervision, he had elected to assume the responsibility of composing the punch—something stiff, by jingo, a punch that would raise you right out of your boots; a regular hairlifter.

The harness room of the barn he had set apart for: himself and intimates. He had brought a long table down from the house and upon it had set out boxes of cigars, bottles of whiskey and of beer and the great china bowls for the punch. It would be no fault of his, he declared, if half the number of his men friends were not uproarious before they left. His barn dance would be the talk of all Tulare County for years to come. For this one day he had resolved to put all thoughts of business out of his head. For the matter of that, things were going well enough. Osterman was back from Los Angeles with a favourable report as to his affair with Disbrow and Darrell. There had been another meeting of the committee. Harran Derrick had attended. Though he had taken no part in the discussion, Annixter was satisfied. The Governor had consented to allow Harran to "come in," if he so desired, and Harran had pledged himself to share one-sixth of the campaign expenses, providing these did not exceed a certain figure.

As Annixter came to the door of the barn to shout abuse at the distraught Chinese cook who was cutting up lemons in the kitchen, he caught sight of Presley and Vanamee and hailed them.

"Hello, Pres," he called. "Come over here and see how she looks;" he indicated the barn with a movement of his head. "Well, we're getting ready for you tonight," he went on as the two friends came up. "But how we are going to get straightened out by eight o'clock I don't know. Would you believe that pip Caraher is short of lemons—at this last minute and I told him I'd want three cases of 'em as much as a month ago, and here, just when I want a good lively saddle horse to get around on, somebody hikes the buckskin out the corral. STOLE her, by jingo. I'll have the law on that thief if it breaks me—and a sixty-dollar saddle 'n' head-stall gone with her; and only about half the number of Jap lanterns that I ordered have shown up and not candles enough for those. It's enough to make a dog sick. There's nothing done that you don't do yourself, unless you stand over these loafers with a club. I'm sick of the whole business—and I've lost my hat; wish to God I'd never dreamed of givin' this rotten fool dance. Clutter the whole place up with a lot of feemales. I sure did lose my presence of mind when I got THAT idea."

Then, ignoring the fact that it was he, himself, who had called the young men to him, he added:

"Well, this is my busy day. Sorry I can't stop and talk to you longer."

He shouted a last imprecation at the Chinaman and turned back into the barn. Presley and Vanamee went on, but Annixter, as he crossed the floor of the barn, all but collided with Hilma Tree, who came out from one of the stalls, a box of candles in her arms.

Gasping out an apology, Annixter reentered the harness room, closing the door behind him, and forgetting all the responsibility of the moment, lit a cigar and sat down in one of the hired chairs, his hands in his pockets, his feet on the table, frowning thoughtfully through the blue smoke.

Annixter was at last driven to confess to himself that he could not get the thought of Hilma Tree out of his mind. Finally she had "got a hold on him." The thing that of all others he most dreaded had happened. A feemale girl had got a hold on him, and now there was no longer for him any such thing as peace of mind. The idea of the young woman was with him continually. He went to bed with it; he got up with it. At every moment of the day he was pestered with it. It interfered with his work, got mixed up in his business. What a miserable confession for a man to make; a fine way to waste his time. Was it possible that only the other day he had stood in front of the music store in Bonneville and seriously considered making Hilma a present of a music-box? Even now, the very thought of it made him flush with shame, and this after she had told him plainly that she did not like him. He was running after her—he, Annixter! He ripped out a furious oath, striking the table with his boot heel. Again and again he had resolved to put the whole affair from out his mind. Once he had been able to do so, but of late it was becoming harder and harder with every successive day. He had only to close his eyes to see her as plain as if she stood before him; he saw her in a glory of sunlight that set a fine tinted lustre of pale carnation and gold on the silken sheen of her white skin, her hair sparkled with it, her thick, strong neck, sloping to her shoulders with beautiful, full curves, seemed to radiate the light; her eyes, brown, wide, innocent in expression, disclosing the full disc of the pupil upon the slightest provocation, flashed in this sunlight like diamonds.

Annixter was all bewildered. With the exception of the timid little creature in the glove-cleaning establishment in Sacramento, he had had no acquaintance with any woman. His world was harsh, crude, a world of men only—men who were to be combatted, opposed—his hand was against nearly every one of them. Women he distrusted with the instinctive distrust of the overgrown schoolboy. Now, at length, a young woman had come into his life. Promptly he was struck with discomfiture, annoyed almost beyond endurance, harassed, bedevilled, excited, made angry and exasperated. He was suspicious of the woman, yet desired her, totally ignorant of how to approach her, hating the sex, yet drawn to the individual, confusing the two emotions, sometimes even hating Hilma as a result of this confusion, but at all times disturbed, vexed, irritated beyond power of expression.

At length, Annixter cast his cigar from him and plunged again into the work of the day. The afternoon wore to evening, to the accompaniment of wearying and clamorous endeavour. In some unexplained fashion, the labour of putting the great barn in readiness for the dance was accomplished; the last bolt of cambric was hung in place from the rafters. The last evergreen tree was nailed to the joists of the walls; the last lantern hung, the last nail driven into the musicians' platform. The sun set. There was a great scurry to have supper and dress. Annixter, last of all the other workers, left the barn in the dusk of twilight. He was alone; he had a saw under one arm, a bag of tools was in his hand. He was in his shirt sleeves and carried his coat over his shoulder; a hammer was thrust into one of his hip pockets. He was in execrable temper. The day's work had fagged him out. He had not been able to find his hat.

"And the buckskin with sixty dollars' worth of saddle gone, too," he groaned. "Oh, ain't it sweet?"

At his house, Mrs. Tree had set out a cold supper for him, the inevitable dish of prunes serving as dessert. After supper Annixter bathed and dressed. He decided at the last moment to wear his usual town-going suit, a sack suit of black, made by a Bonneville tailor. But his hat was gone. There were other hats he might have worn, but because this particular one was lost he fretted about it all through his dressing and then decided to have one more look around the barn for it.

For over a quarter of an hour he pottered about the barn, going from stall to stall, rummaging the harness room and feed room, all to no purpose. At last he came out again upon the main floor, definitely giving up the search, looking about him to see if everything was in order.

The festoons of Japanese lanterns in and around the barn were not yet lighted, but some half-dozen lamps, with great, tin reflectors, that hung against the walls, were burning low. A dull half light pervaded the vast interior, hollow, echoing, leaving the corners and roof thick with impenetrable black shadows. The barn faced the west and through the open sliding doors was streaming a single bright bar from the after-glow, incongruous and out of all harmony with the dull flare of the kerosene lamps.

As Annixter glanced about him, he saw a figure step briskly out of the shadows of one corner of the building, pause for the fraction of one instant in the bar of light, then, at sight of him, dart back again. There was a sound of hurried footsteps.

Annixter, with recollections of the stolen buckskin in his mind, cried out sharply:

"Who's there?"

There was no answer. In a second his pistol was in his hand.

"Who's there? Quick, speak up or I'll shoot."

"No, no, no, don't shoot," cried an answering voice. "Oh, be careful. It's I—Hilma Tree."

Annixter slid the pistol into his pocket with a great qualm of apprehension. He came forward and met Hilma in the doorway.

"Good Lord," he murmured, "that sure did give me a start. If I HAD shot—"

Hilma stood abashed and confused before him. She was dressed in a white organdie frock of the most rigorous simplicity and wore neither flower nor ornament. The severity of her dress made her look even larger than usual, and even as it was her eyes were on a level with Annixter's. There was a certain fascination in the contradiction of stature and character of Hilma—a great girl, half-child as yet, but tall as a man for all that.

There was a moment's awkward silence, then Hilma explained:

"I—I came back to look for my hat. I thought I left it here this afternoon."

"And I was looking for my hat," cried Annixter. "Funny enough, hey?"

They laughed at this as heartily as children might have done. The constraint of the situation was a little relaxed and Annixter, with sudden directness, glanced sharply at the young woman and demanded:

"Well, Miss Hilma, hate me as much as ever?"

"Oh, no, sir," she answered, "I never said I hated you."

"Well,—dislike me, then; I know you said that."

"I—I disliked what you did—TRIED to do. It made me angry and it hurt me. I shouldn't have said what I did that time, but it was your fault."

"You mean you shouldn't have said you didn't like me?" asked Annixter. "Why?"

"Well, well,—I don't—I don't DISlike anybody," admitted Hilma.

"Then I can take it that you don't dislike ME? Is that it?"

"I don't dislike anybody," persisted Hilma.

"Well, I asked you more than that, didn't I?" queried Annixter uneasily. "I asked you to like me, remember, the other day. I'm asking you that again, now. I want you to like me."

Hilma lifted her eyes inquiringly to his. In her words was an unmistakable ring of absolute sincerity. Innocently she inquired:

"Why?"

Annixter was struck speechless. In the face of such candour, such perfect ingenuousness, he was at a loss for any words.

"Well—well," he stammered, "well—I don't know," he suddenly burst out. "That is," he went on, groping for his wits, "I can't quite say why." The idea of a colossal lie occurred to him, a thing actually royal.

"I like to have the people who are around me like me," he declared. "I—I like to be popular, understand? Yes, that's it," he continued, more reassured. "I don't like the idea of any one disliking me. That's the way I am. It's my nature."

"Oh, then," returned Hilma, "you needn't bother. No, I don't dislike you."

"Well, that's good," declared Annixter judicially. "That's good. But hold on," he interrupted, "I'm forgetting. It's not enough to not dislike me. I want you to like me. How about THAT?"

Hilma paused for a moment, glancing vaguely out of the doorway toward the lighted window of the dairy-house, her head tilted.

"I don't know that I ever thought about that," she said.

"Well, think about it now," insisted Annixter.

"But I never thought about liking anybody particularly," she observed. "It's because I like everybody, don't you see?"

"Well, you've got to like some people more than other people," hazarded Annixter, "and I want to be one of those 'some people,' savvy? Good Lord, I don't know how to say these fool things. I talk like a galoot when I get talking to feemale girls and I can't lay my tongue to anything that sounds right. It isn't my nature. And look here, I lied when I said I liked to have people like me—to be popular. Rot! I don't care a curse about people's opinions of me. But there's a few people that are more to me than most others—that chap Presley, for instance—and those people I DO want to have like me. What they think counts. Pshaw! I know I've got enemies; piles of them. I could name you half a dozen men right now that are naturally itching to take a shot at me. How about this ranch? Don't I know, can't I hear the men growling oaths under their breath after I've gone by? And in business ways, too," he went on, speaking half to himself, "in Bonneville and all over the county there's not a man of them wouldn't howl for joy if they got a chance to down Buck Annixter. Think I care? Why, I LIKE it. I run my ranch to suit myself and I play my game my own way. I'm a 'driver,' I know it, and a 'bully,' too. Oh, I know what they call me—'a brute beast, with a twist in my temper that would rile up a new-born lamb,' and I'm 'crusty' and 'pig-headed' and 'obstinate.' They say all that, but they've got to say, too, that I'm cleverer than any man-jack in the running. There's nobody can get ahead of me." His eyes snapped. "Let 'em grind their teeth. They can't 'down' me. When I shut my fist there's not one of them can open it. No, not with a CHISEL." He turned to Hilma again. "Well, when a man's hated as much as that, it stands to reason, don't it, Miss Hilma, that the few friends he has got he wants to keep? I'm not such an entire swine to the people that know me best—that jackass, Presley, for instance. I'd put my hand in the fire to do him a real service. Sometimes I get kind of lonesome; wonder if you would understand? It's my fault, but there's not a horse about the place that don't lay his ears back when I get on him; there's not a dog don't put his tail between his legs as soon as I come near him. The cayuse isn't foaled yet here on Quien Sabe that can throw me, nor the dog whelped that would dare show his teeth at me. I kick that Irish setter every time I see him—but wonder what I'd do, though, if he didn't slink so much, if he wagged his tail and was glad to see me? So it all comes to this: I'd like to have you—well, sort of feel that I was a good friend of yours and like me because of it."

The flame in the lamp on the wall in front of Hilma stretched upward tall and thin and began to smoke. She went over to where the lamp hung and, standing on tip-toe, lowered the wick. As she reached her hand up, Annixter noted how the sombre, lurid red of the lamp made a warm reflection on her smooth, round arm.

"Do you understand?" he queried.

"Yes, why, yes," she answered, turning around. "It's very good of you to want to be a friend of mine. I didn't think so, though, when you tried to kiss me. But maybe it's all right since you've explained things. You see I'm different from you. I like everybody to like me and I like to like everybody. It makes one so much happier. You wouldn't believe it, but you ought to try it, sir, just to see. It's so good to be good to people and to have people good to you. And everybody has always been so good to me. Mamma and papa, of course, and Billy, the stableman, and Montalegre, the Portugee foreman, and the Chinese cook, even, and Mr. Delaney—only he went away—and Mrs. Vacca and her little—"

"Delaney, hey?" demanded Annixter abruptly. "You and he were pretty good friends, were you?"

"Oh, yes," she answered. "He was just as GOOD to me. Every day in the summer time he used to ride over to the Seed ranch back of the Mission and bring me a great armful of flowers, the prettiest things, and I used to pretend to pay him for them with dollars made of cheese that I cut out of the cheese with a biscuit cutter. It was such fun. We were the best of friends."

"There's another lamp smoking," growled Annixter. "Turn it down, will you?—and see that somebody sweeps this floor here. It's all littered up with pine needles. I've got a lot to do. Good-bye."

"Good-bye, sir."

Annixter returned to the ranch house, his teeth clenched, enraged, his face flushed.

"Ah," he muttered, "Delaney, hey? Throwing it up to me that I fired him." His teeth gripped together more fiercely than ever. "The best of friends, hey? By God, I'll have that girl yet. I'll show that cow-puncher. Ain't I her employer, her boss? I'll show her—and Delaney, too. It would be easy enough—and then Delaney can have her—if he wants her—after me."

An evil light flashing from under his scowl, spread over his face. The male instincts of possession, unreasoned, treacherous, oblique, came twisting to the surface. All the lower nature of the man, ignorant of women, racked at one and the same time with enmity and desire, roused itself like a hideous and abominable beast. And at the same moment, Hilma returned to her house, humming to herself as she walked, her white dress glowing with a shimmer of faint saffron light in the last ray of the after-glow.

A little after half-past seven, the first carry-all, bearing the druggist of Bonneville and his women-folk, arrived in front of the new barn. Immediately afterward an express wagon loaded down with a swarming family of Spanish-Mexicans, gorgeous in red and yellow colours, followed. Billy, the stableman, and his assistant took charge of the teams, unchecking the horses and hitching them to a fence back of the barn. Then Caraher, the saloon-keeper, in "derby" hat, "Prince Albert" coat, pointed yellow shoes and inevitable red necktie, drove into the yard on his buckboard, the delayed box of lemons under the seat. It looked as if the whole array of invited guests was to arrive in one unbroken procession, but for a long half-hour nobody else appeared. Annixter and Caraher withdrew to the harness room and promptly involved themselves in a wrangle as to the make-up of the famous punch. From time to time their voices could be heard uplifted in clamorous argument.

"Two quarts and a half and a cupful of chartreuse."

"Rot, rot, I know better. Champagne straight and a dash of brandy."

The druggist's wife and sister retired to the feed room, where a bureau with a swinging mirror had been placed for the convenience of the women. The druggist stood awkwardly outside the door of the feed room, his coat collar turned up against the draughts that drifted through the barn, his face troubled, debating anxiously as to the propriety of putting on his gloves. The Spanish-Mexican family, a father, mother and five children and sister-in-law, sat rigid on the edges of the hired chairs, silent, constrained, their eyes lowered, their elbows in at their sides, glancing furtively from under their eyebrows at the decorations or watching with intense absorption young Vacca, son of one of the division superintendents, who wore a checked coat and white thread gloves and who paced up and down the length of the barn, frowning, very important, whittling a wax candle over the floor to make it slippery for dancing.

The musicians arrived, the City Band of Bonneville–Annixter having managed to offend the leader of the "Dirigo" Club orchestra, at the very last moment, to such a point that he had refused his services. These members of the City Band repaired at once to their platform in the corner. At every instant they laughed uproariously among themselves, joshing one of their number, a Frenchman, whom they called "Skeezicks." Their hilarity reverberated in a hollow, metallic roll among the rafters overhead. The druggist observed to young Vacca as he passed by that he thought them pretty fresh, just the same.

"I'm busy, I'm very busy," returned the young man, continuing on his way, still frowning and paring the stump of candle.

"Two quarts 'n' a half. Two quarts 'n' a half."

"Ah, yes, in a way, that's so; and then, again, in a way, it ISN'T. I know better."

All along one side of the barn were a row of stalls, fourteen of them, clean as yet, redolent of new cut wood, the sawdust still in the cracks of the flooring. Deliberately the druggist went from one to the other, pausing contemplatively before each. He returned down the line and again took up his position by the door of the feed room, nodding his head judicially, as if satisfied. He decided to put on his gloves.

By now it was quite dark. Outside, between the barn and the ranch houses one could see a group of men on step-ladders lighting the festoons of Japanese lanterns. In the darkness, only their faces appeared here and there, high above the ground, seen in a haze of red, strange, grotesque. Gradually as the multitude of lanterns were lit, the light spread. The grass underfoot looked like green excelsior. Another group of men invaded the barn itself, lighting the lamps and lanterns there. Soon the whole place was gleaming with points of light. Young Vacca, who had disappeared, returned with his pockets full of wax candles. He resumed his whittling, refusing to answer any questions, vociferating that he was busy.

Outside there was a sound of hoofs and voices. More guests had arrived. The druggist, seized with confusion, terrified lest he had put on his gloves too soon, thrust his hands into his pockets. It was Cutter, Magnus Derrick's division superintendent, who came, bringing his wife and her two girl cousins. They had come fifteen miles by the trail from the far distant division house on "Four" of Los Muertos and had ridden on horseback instead of driving. Mrs. Cutter could be heard declaring that she was nearly dead and felt more like going to bed than dancing. The two girl cousins, in dresses of dotted Swiss over blue sateen, were doing their utmost to pacify her. She could be heard protesting from moment to moment. One distinguished the phrases "straight to my bed," "back nearly broken in two," "never wanted to come in the first place." The druggist, observing Cutter take a pair of gloves from Mrs. Cutter's reticule, drew his hands from his pockets.

But abruptly there was an interruption. In the musicians' corner a scuffle broke out. A chair was overturned. There was a noise of imprecations mingled with shouts of derision. Skeezicks, the Frenchman, had turned upon the joshers.

"Ah, no," he was heard to exclaim, "at the end of the end it is too much. Kind of a bad canary—we will go to see about that. Aha, let him close up his face before I demolish it with a good stroke of the fist."

The men who were lighting the lanterns were obliged to intervene before he could be placated.

Hooven and his wife and daughters arrived. Minna was carrying little Hilda, already asleep, in her arms. Minna looked very pretty, striking even, with her black hair, pale face, very red lips and greenish-blue eyes. She was dressed in what had been Mrs. Hooven's wedding gown, a cheap affair of "farmer's satin." Mrs. Hooven had pendent earrings of imitation jet in her ears. Hooven was wearing an old frock coat of Magnus Derrick's, the sleeves too long, the shoulders absurdly too wide. He and Cutter at once entered into an excited conversation as to the ownership of a certain steer.

"Why, the brand—"

"Ach, Gott, der brendt," Hooven clasped his head, "ach, der brendt, dot maks me laugh some laughs. Dot's goot—der brendt—doand I see um—shoor der boole mit der bleck star bei der vore-head in der middle oaf. Any someones you esk tell you dot is mein boole. You esk any someones. Der brendt? To hell mit der brendt. You aindt got some memorie aboudt does ting I guess nodt."

"Please step aside, gentlemen," said young Vacca, who was still making the rounds of the floor.

Hooven whirled about. "Eh? What den," he exclaimed, still excited, willing to be angry at any one for the moment. "Doand you push soh, you. I tink berhapz you doand OWN dose barn, hey?"

"I'm busy, I'm very busy." The young man pushed by with grave preoccupation.

"Two quarts 'n' a half. Two quarts 'n' a half."

"I know better. That's all rot."

But the barn was filling up rapidly. At every moment there was a rattle of a newly arrived vehicle from outside. Guest after guest appeared in the doorway, singly or in couples, or in families, or in garrulous parties of five and six. Now it was Phelps and his mother from Los Muertos, now a foreman from Broderson's with his family, now a gayly apparelled clerk from a Bonneville store, solitary and bewildered, looking for a place to put his hat, now a couple of Spanish-Mexican girls from Guadalajara with coquettish effects of black and yellow about their dress, now a group of Osterman's tenants, Portuguese, swarthy, with plastered hair and curled mustaches, redolent of cheap perfumes. Sarria arrived, his smooth, shiny face glistening with perspiration. He wore a new cassock and carried his broad-brimmed hat under his arm. His appearance made quite a stir. He passed from group to group, urbane, affable, shaking hands right and left; he assumed a set smile of amiability which never left his face the whole evening.

But abruptly there was a veritable sensation. From out the little crowd that persistently huddled about the doorway came Osterman. He wore a dress-suit with a white waistcoat and patent leather pumps—what a wonder! A little qualm of excitement spread around the barn. One exchanged nudges of the elbow with one's neighbour, whispering earnestly behind the hand. What astonishing clothes! Catch on to the coat-tails! It was a masquerade costume, maybe; that goat Osterman was such a josher, one never could tell what he would do next.

The musicians began to tune up. From their corner came a medley of mellow sounds, the subdued chirps of the violins, the dull bourdon of the bass viol, the liquid gurgling of the flageolet and the deep-toned snarl of the big horn, with now and then a rasping stridulating of the snare drum. A sense of gayety began to spread throughout the assembly. At every moment the crowd increased. The aroma of new-sawn timber and sawdust began to be mingled with the feminine odour of sachet and flowers. There was a babel of talk in the air—male baritone and soprano chatter—varied by an occasional note of laughter and the swish of stiffly starched petticoats. On the row of chairs that went around three sides of the wall groups began to settle themselves. For a long time the guests huddled close to the doorway; the lower end of the floor was crowded! the upper end deserted; but by degrees the lines of white muslin and pink and blue sateen extended, dotted with the darker figures of men in black suits. The conversation grew louder as the timidity of the early moments wore off. Groups at a distance called back and forth; conversations were carried on at top voice. Once, even a whole party hurried across the floor from one side of the barn to the other.

Annixter emerged from the harness room, his face red with wrangling. He took a position to the right of the door, shaking hands with newcomers, inviting them over and over again to cut loose and whoop it along. Into the ears of his more intimate male acquaintances he dropped a word as to punch and cigars in the harness room later on, winking with vast intelligence. Ranchers from remoter parts of the country appeared: Garnett, from the Ruby rancho, Keast, from the ranch of the same name, Gethings, of the San Pablo, Chattern, of the Bonanza, and others and still others, a score of them—elderly men, for the most part, bearded, slow of speech, deliberate, dressed in broadcloth. Old Broderson, who entered with his wife on his arm, fell in with this type, and with them came a certain Dabney, of whom nothing but his name was known, a silent old man, who made no friends, whom nobody knew or spoke to, who was seen only upon such occasions as this, coming from no one knew where, going, no one cared to inquire whither.

Between eight and half-past, Magnus Derrick and his family were seen. Magnus's entry caused no little impression. Some said: "There's the Governor," and called their companions' attention to the thin, erect figure, commanding, imposing, dominating all in his immediate neighbourhood. Harran came with him, wearing a cut-away suit of black. He was undeniably handsome, young and fresh looking, his cheeks highly coloured, quite the finest looking of all the younger men; blond, strong, with that certain courtliness of manner that had always made him liked. He took his mother upon his arm and conducted her to a seat by the side of Mrs. Broderson.

Annie Derrick was very pretty that evening. She was dressed in a grey silk gown with a collar of pink velvet. Her light brown hair that yet retained so much of its brightness was transfixed by a high, shell comb, very Spanish. But the look of uneasiness in her large eyes—the eyes of a young girl—was deepening every day. The expression of innocence and inquiry which they so easily assumed, was disturbed by a faint suggestion of aversion, almost of terror. She settled herself in her place, in the corner of the hall, in the rear rank of chairs, a little frightened by the glare of lights, the hum of talk and the shifting crowd, glad to be out of the way, to attract no attention, willing to obliterate herself.

All at once Annixter, who had just shaken hands with Dyke, his mother and the little tad, moved abruptly in his place, drawing in his breath sharply. The crowd around the great, wide-open main door of the barn had somewhat thinned out and in the few groups that still remained there he had suddenly recognised Mr. and Mrs. Tree and Hilma, making their way towards some empty seats near the entrance of the feed room.

In the dusky light of the barn earlier in the evening, Annixter had not been able to see Hilma plainly. Now, however, as she passed before his eyes in the glittering radiance of the lamps and lanterns, he caught his breath in astonishment. Never had she appeared more beautiful in his eyes. It did not seem possible that this was the same girl whom he saw every day in and around the ranch house and dairy, the girl of simple calico frocks and plain shirt waists, who brought him his dinner, who made up his bed. Now he could not take his eyes from her. Hilma, for the first time, was wearing her hair done high upon her head. The thick, sweet-smelling masses, bitumen brown in the shadows, corruscated like golden filaments in the light. Her organdie frock was long, longer than any she had yet worn. It left a little of her neck and breast bare and all of her arm.

Annixter muttered an exclamation. Such arms! How did she manage to keep them hid on ordinary occasions. Big at the shoulder, tapering with delicious modulations to the elbow and wrist, overlaid with a delicate, gleaming lustre. As often as she turned her head the movement sent a slow undulation over her neck and shoulders, the pale amber-tinted shadows under her chin, coming and going over the creamy whiteness of the skin like the changing moire of silk. The pretty rose colour of her cheek had deepened to a pale carnation. Annixter, his hands clasped behind him, stood watching.

In a few moments Hilma was surrounded by a group of young men, clamouring for dances. They came from all corners of the barn, leaving the other girls precipitately, almost rudely. There could be little doubt as to who was to be the belle of the occasion. Hilma's little triumph was immediate, complete. Annixter could hear her voice from time to time, its usual velvety huskiness vibrating to a note of exuberant gayety.

All at once the orchestra swung off into a march—the Grand March. There was a great rush to secure "partners." Young Vacca, still going the rounds, was pushed to one side. The gayly apparelled clerk from the Bonneville store lost his head in the confusion. He could not find his "partner." He roamed wildly about the barn, bewildered, his eyes rolling. He resolved to prepare an elaborate programme card on the back of an old envelope. Rapidly the line was formed, Hilma and Harran Derrick in the lead, Annixter having obstinately refused to engage in either march, set or dance the whole evening. Soon the confused shuffling of feet settled to a measured cadence; the orchestra blared and wailed, the snare drum, rolling at exact intervals, the cornet marking the time. It was half-past eight o'clock.

Annixter drew a long breath:

"Good," he muttered, "the thing is under way at last."

Singularly enough, Osterman also refused to dance. The week before he had returned from Los Angeles, bursting with the importance of his mission. He had been successful. He had Disbrow "in his pocket." He was impatient to pose before the others of the committee as a skilful political agent, a manipulator. He forgot his attitude of the early part of the evening when he had drawn attention to himself with his wonderful clothes. Now his comic actor's face, with its brownish-red cheeks, protuberant ears and horizontal slit of a mouth, was overcast with gravity. His bald forehead was seamed with the wrinkles of responsibility. He drew Annixter into one of the empty stalls and began an elaborate explanation, glib, voluble, interminable, going over again in detail what he had reported to the committee in outline.

"I managed—I schemed—I kept dark—I lay low—"

But Annixter refused to listen.

"Oh, rot your schemes. There's a punch in the harness room that will make the hair grow on the top of your head in the place where the hair ought to grow. Come on, we'll round up some of the boys and walk into it."

They edged their way around the hall outside "The Grand March," toward the harness room, picking up on their way Caraher, Dyke, Hooven and old Broderson. Once in the harness room, Annixter shot the bolt.

"That affair outside," he observed, "will take care of itself, but here's a little orphan child that gets lonesome without company."

Annixter began ladling the punch, filling the glasses.

Osterman proposed a toast to Quien Sabe and the Biggest Barn. Their elbows crooked in silence. Old Broderson set down his glass, wiping his long beard and remarking:

"That—that certainly is very—very agreeable. I remember a punch I drank on Christmas day in '83, or no, it was '84—anyhow, that punch—it was in Ukiah—'TWAS '83—" He wandered on aimlessly, unable to stop his flow of speech, losing himself in details, involving his talk in a hopeless maze of trivialities to which nobody paid any attention.

"I don't drink myself," observed Dyke, "but just a taste of that with a lot of water wouldn't be bad for the little tad. She'd think it was lemonade." He was about to mix a glass for Sidney, but thought better of it at the last moment.

"It's the chartreuse that's lacking," commented Caraher, lowering at Annixter. The other flared up on the instant.

"Rot, rot. I know better. In some punches it goes; and then, again, in others it don't."

But it was left to Hooven to launch the successful phrase:

"Gesundheit," he exclaimed, holding out his second glass. After drinking, he replaced it on the table with a long breath. "Ach Gott!" he cried, "dat poonsch, say I tink dot poonsch mek some demn goot vertilizer, hey?"

Fertiliser! The others roared with laughter.

"Good eye, Bismarck," commented Annixter. The name had a great success. Thereafter throughout the evening the punch was invariably spoken of as the "Fertiliser." Osterman, having spilt the bottom of a glassful on the floor, pretended that he saw shoots of grain coming up on the spot. Suddenly he turned upon old Broderson. "I'm bald, ain't I? Want to know how I lost my hair? Promise you won't ask a single other question and I'll tell you. Promise your word of honour."

"Eh? What—wh—I—I don't understand. Your hair? Yes, I'll promise. How did you lose it?"

"It was bit off."

The other gazed at him stupefied; his jaw dropped. The company shouted, and old Broderson, believing he had somehow accomplished a witticism, chuckled in his beard, wagging his head. But suddenly he fell grave, struck with an idea. He demanded:

"Yes—I know—but—but what bit it off?"

"Ah," vociferated Osterman, "that's JUST what you promised not to ask."

The company doubled up with hilarity. Caraher leaned against the door, holding his sides, but Hooven, all abroad, unable to follow, gazed from face to face with a vacant grin, thinking it was still a question of his famous phrase.

"Vertilizer, hey? Dots some fine joke, hey? You bedt."

What with the noise of their talk and laughter, it was some time before Dyke, first of all, heard a persistent knocking on the bolted door. He called Annixter's attention to the sound. Cursing the intruder, Annixter unbolted and opened the door. But at once his manner changed.

"Hello. It's Presley. Come in, come in, Pres."

There was a shout of welcome from the others. A spirit of effusive cordiality had begun to dominate the gathering. Annixter caught sight of Vanamee back of Presley, and waiving for the moment the distinction of employer and employee, insisted that both the friends should come in.

"Any friend of Pres is my friend," he declared.

But when the two had entered and had exchanged greetings, Presley drew Annixter aside.

"Vanamee and I have just come from Bonneville," he explained. "We saw Delaney there. He's got the buckskin, and he's full of bad whiskey and dago-red. You should see him; he's wearing all his cow-punching outfit, hair trousers, sombrero, spurs and all the rest of it, and he has strapped himself to a big revolver. He says he wasn't invited to your barn dance but that he's coming over to shoot up the place. He says you promised to show him off Quien Sabe at the toe of your boot and that he's going to give you the chance to-night!"

"Ah," commented Annixter, nodding his head, "he is, is he?"

Presley was disappointed. Knowing Annixter's irascibility, he had expected to produce a more dramatic effect. He began to explain the danger of the business. Delaney had once knifed a greaser in the Panamint country. He was known as a "bad" man. But Annixter refused to be drawn.

"All right," he said, "that's all right. Don't tell anybody else. You might scare the girls off. Get in and drink."

Outside the dancing was by this time in full swing. The orchestra was playing a polka. Young Vacca, now at his fiftieth wax candle, had brought the floor to the slippery surface of glass. The druggist was dancing with one of the Spanish-Mexican girls with the solemnity of an automaton, turning about and about, always in the same direction, his eyes glassy, his teeth set. Hilma Tree was dancing for the second time with Harran Derrick. She danced with infinite grace. Her cheeks were bright red, her eyes half-closed, and through her parted lips she drew from time to time a long, tremulous breath of pure delight. The music, the weaving colours, the heat of the air, by now a little oppressive, the monotony of repeated sensation, even the pain of physical fatigue had exalted all her senses. She was in a dreamy lethargy of happiness. It was her "first ball." She could have danced without stopping until morning. Minna Hooven and Cutter were "promenading." Mrs. Hooven, with little Hilda already asleep on her knees, never took her eyes from her daughter's gown. As often as Minna passed near her she vented an energetic "pst! pst!" The metal tip of a white draw string was showing from underneath the waist of Minna's dress. Mrs. Hooven was on the point of tears.

The solitary gayly apparelled clerk from Bonneville was in a fever of agitation. He had lost his elaborate programme card. Bewildered, beside himself with trepidation, he hurried about the room, jostled by the dancing couples, tripping over the feet of those who were seated; he peered distressfully under the chairs and about the floor, asking anxious questions.

Magnus Derrick, the centre of a listening circle of ranchers—Garnett from the Ruby rancho, Keast from the ranch of the same name, Gethings and Chattern of the San Pablo and Bonanza—stood near the great open doorway of the barn, discussing the possibility of a shortage in the world's wheat crop for the next year.

Abruptly the orchestra ceased playing with a roll of the snare drum, a flourish of the cornet and a prolonged growl of the bass viol. The dance broke up, the couples hurrying to their seats, leaving the gayly apparelled clerk suddenly isolated in the middle of the floor, rolling his eyes. The druggist released the Spanish-Mexican girl with mechanical precision out amidst the crowd of dancers. He bowed, dropping his chin upon his cravat; throughout the dance neither had hazarded a word. The girl found her way alone to a chair, but the druggist, sick from continually revolving in the same direction, walked unsteadily toward the wall. All at once the barn reeled around him; he fell down. There was a great laugh, but he scrambled to his feet and disappeared abruptly out into the night through the doorway of the barn, deathly pale, his hand upon his stomach.

Dabney, the old man whom nobody knew, approached the group of ranchers around Magnus Derrick and stood, a little removed, listening gravely to what the governor was saying, his chin sunk in his collar, silent, offering no opinions.

But the leader of the orchestra, with a great gesture of his violin bow, cried out:

"All take partners for the lancers and promenade around the hall!"

However, there was a delay. A little crowd formed around the musicians' platform; voices were raised; there was a commotion. Skeezicks, who played the big horn, accused the cornet and the snare-drum of stealing his cold lunch. At intervals he could be heard expostulating:

"Ah, no! at the end of the end! Render me the sausages, you, or less I break your throat! Aha! I know you. You are going to play me there a bad farce. My sausages and the pork sandwich, else I go away from this place!"

He made an exaggerated show of replacing his big horn in its case, but the by-standers raised a great protest. The sandwiches and one sausage were produced; the other had disappeared. In the end Skeezichs allowed himself to be appeased. The dance was resumed.

Half an hour later the gathering in the harness room was considerably reinforced. It was the corner of the barn toward which the male guests naturally gravitated. Harran Derrick, who only cared to dance with Hilma Tree, was admitted. Garnett from the Ruby rancho and Gethings from the San Pablo, came in a little afterwards. A fourth bowl of punch was mixed, Annixter and Caraher clamouring into each other's face as to its ingredients. Cigars were lighted. Soon the air of the room became blue with an acrid haze of smoke. It was very warm. Ranged in their chairs around the side of the room, the guests emptied glass after glass.

Vanamee alone refused to drink. He sat a little to one side, disassociating himself from what was going forward, watching the others calmly, a little contemptuously, a cigarette in his fingers.

Hooven, after drinking his third glass, however, was afflicted with a great sadness; his breast heaved with immense sighs. He asserted that he was "obbressed;" Cutter had taken his steer. He retired to a corner and seated himself in a heap on his chair, his heels on the rungs, wiping the tears from his eyes, refusing to be comforted. Old Broderson startled Annixter, who sat next to him, out of all measure by suddenly winking at him with infinite craftiness.

"When I was a lad in Ukiah," he whispered hoarsely, "I was a devil of a fellow with the girls; but Lordy!" he nudged him slyly, "I wouldn't have it known!"

Of those who were drinking, Annixter alone retained all his wits. Though keeping pace with the others, glass for glass, the punch left him solid upon his feet, clear-headed. The tough, cross-grained fibre of him seemed proof against alcohol. Never in his life had he been drunk. He prided himself upon his power of resistance. It was his nature.

"Say!" exclaimed old Broderson, gravely addressing the company, pulling at his beard uneasily—"say! I—I—listen! I'm a devil of a fellow with the girls." He wagged his head doggedly, shutting his eyes in a knowing fashion. "Yes, sir, I am. There was a young lady in Ukiah—that was when I was a lad of seventeen. We used to meet in the cemetery in the afternoons. I was to go away to school at Sacramento, and the afternoon I left we met in the cemetery and we stayed so long I almost missed the train. Her name was Celestine."

There was a pause. The others waited for the rest of the story.

"And afterwards?" prompted Annixter.

"Afterwards? Nothing afterwards. I never saw her again. Her name was Celestine."

The company raised a chorus of derision, and Osterman cried ironically:

"Say! THAT'S a pretty good one! Tell us another."

The old man laughed with the rest, believing he had made another hit. He called Osterman to him, whispering in his ear:

"Sh! Look here! Some night you and I will go up to San Francisco—hey? We'll go skylarking. We'll be gay. Oh, I'm a—a—a rare old BUCK, I am! I ain't too old. You'll see."

Annixter gave over the making of the fifth bowl of punch to Osterman, who affirmed that he had a recipe for a "fertiliser" from Solotari that would take the plating off the ladle. He left him wrangling with Caraher, who still persisted in adding chartreuse, and stepped out into the dance to see how things were getting on.

It was the interval between two dances. In and around a stall at the farther end of the floor, where lemonade was being served, was a great throng of young men. Others hurried across the floor singly or by twos and threes, gingerly carrying overflowing glasses to their "partners," sitting in long rows of white and blue and pink against the opposite wall, their mothers and older sisters in a second dark-clothed rank behind them. A babel of talk was in the air, mingled with gusts of laughter. Everybody seemed having a good time. In the increasing heat the decorations of evergreen trees and festoons threw off a pungent aroma that suggested a Sunday-school Christmas festival. In the other stalls, lower down the barn, the young men had brought chairs, and in these deep recesses the most desperate love-making was in progress, the young man, his hair neatly parted, leaning with great solicitation over the girl, his "partner" for the moment, fanning her conscientiously, his arm carefully laid along the back of her chair.

By the doorway, Annixter met Sarria, who had stepped out to smoke a fat, black cigar. The set smile of amiability was still fixed on the priest's smooth, shiny face; the cigar ashes had left grey streaks on the front of his cassock. He avoided Annixter, fearing, no doubt, an allusion to his game cocks, and took up his position back of the second rank of chairs by the musicians' stand, beaming encouragingly upon every one who caught his eye.

Annixter was saluted right and left as he slowly went the round of the floor. At every moment he had to pause to shake hands and to listen to congratulations upon the size of his barn and the success of his dance. But he was distrait, his thoughts elsewhere; he did not attempt to hide his impatience when some of the young men tried to engage him in conversation, asking him to be introduced to their sisters, or their friends' sisters. He sent them about their business harshly, abominably rude, leaving a wake of angry disturbance behind him, sowing the seeds of future quarrels and renewed unpopularity. He was looking for Hilma Tree.

When at last he came unexpectedly upon her, standing near where Mrs. Tree was seated, some half-dozen young men hovering uneasily in her neighbourhood, all his audacity was suddenly stricken from him; his gruffness, his overbearing insolence vanished with an abruptness that left him cold. His old-time confusion and embarrassment returned to him. Instead of speaking to her as he intended, he affected not to see her, but passed by, his head in the air, pretending a sudden interest in a Japanese lantern that was about to catch fire.

But he had had a single distinct glimpse of her, definite, precise, and this glimpse was enough. Hilma had changed. The change was subtle, evanescent, hard to define, but not the less unmistakable. The excitement, the enchanting delight, the delicious disturbance of "the first ball," had produced its result. Perhaps there had only been this lacking. It was hard to say, but for that brief instant of time Annixter was looking at Hilma, the woman. She was no longer the young girl upon whom he might look down, to whom he might condescend, whose little, infantile graces were to be considered with amused toleration.

When Annixter returned to the harness room, he let himself into a clamour of masculine hilarity. Osterman had, indeed, made a marvellous "fertiliser," whiskey for the most part, diluted with champagne and lemon juice. The first round of this drink had been welcomed with a salvo of cheers. Hooven, recovering his spirits under its violent stimulation, spoke of "heving ut oudt mit Cudder, bei Gott," while Osterman, standing on a chair at the end of the room, shouted for a "few moments quiet, gentlemen," so that he might tell a certain story he knew. But, abruptly, Annixter discovered that the liquors—the champagne, whiskey, brandy, and the like—were running low. This would never do. He felt that he would stand disgraced if it could be said afterward that he had not provided sufficient drink at his entertainment. He slipped out, unobserved, and, finding two of his ranch hands near the doorway, sent them down to the ranch house to bring up all the cases of "stuff" they found there.

However, when this matter had been attended to, Annixter did not immediately return to the harness room. On the floor of the barn a square dance was under way, the leader of the City Band calling the figures. Young Vacca indefatigably continued the rounds of the barn, paring candle after candle, possessed with this single idea of duty, pushing the dancers out of his way, refusing to admit that the floor was yet sufficiently slippery. The druggist had returned indoors, and leaned dejected and melancholy against the wall near the doorway, unable to dance, his evening's enjoyment spoiled. The gayly apparelled clerk from Bonneville had just involved himself in a deplorable incident. In a search for his handkerchief, which he had lost while trying to find his programme card, he had inadvertently wandered into the feed room, set apart as the ladies' dressing room, at the moment when Mrs. Hooven, having removed the waist of Minna's dress, was relacing her corsets. There was a tremendous scene. The clerk was ejected forcibly, Mrs. Hooven filling all the neighbourhood with shrill expostulation. A young man, Minna's "partner," who stood near the feed room door, waiting for her to come out, had invited the clerk, with elaborate sarcasm, to step outside for a moment; and the clerk, breathless, stupefied, hustled from hand to hand, remained petrified, with staring eyes, turning about and about, looking wildly from face to face, speechless, witless, wondering what had happened.

But the square dance was over. The City Band was just beginning to play a waltz. Annixter assuring himself that everything was going all right, was picking his way across the floor, when he came upon Hilma Tree quite alone, and looking anxiously among the crowd of dancers.

"Having a good time, Miss Hilma?" he demanded, pausing for a moment.

"Oh, am I, JUST!" she exclaimed. "The best time—but I don't know what has become of my partner. See! I'm left all alone—the only time this whole evening," she added proudly. "Have you seen him—my partner, sir? I forget his name. I only met him this evening, and I've met SO many I can't begin to remember half of them. He was a young man from Bonneville—a clerk, I think, because I remember seeing him in a store there, and he wore the prettiest clothes!"

"I guess he got lost in the shuffle," observed Annixter. Suddenly an idea occurred to him. He took his resolution in both hands. He clenched his teeth.

"Say! look here, Miss Hilma. What's the matter with you and I stealing this one for ourselves? I don't mean to dance. I don't propose to make a jumping-jack of myself for some galoot to give me the laugh, but we'll walk around. Will you? What do you say?"

Hilma consented.

"I'm not so VERY sorry I missed my dance with that—that—little clerk," she said guiltily. "I suppose that's very bad of me, isn't it?"

Annixter fulminated a vigorous protest.

"I AM so warm!" murmured Hilma, fanning herself with her handkerchief; "and, oh! SUCH a good time as I have had! I was so afraid that I would be a wall-flower and sit up by mamma and papa the whole evening; and as it is, I have had every single dance, and even some dances I had to split. Oh-h!" she breathed, glancing lovingly around the barn, noting again the festoons of tri-coloured cambric, the Japanese lanterns, flaring lamps, and "decorations" of evergreen; "oh-h! it's all so lovely, just like a fairy story; and to think that it can't last but for one little evening, and that to-morrow morning one must wake up to the every-day things again!"

"Well," observed Annixter doggedly, unwilling that she should forget whom she ought to thank, "I did my best, and my best is as good as another man's, I guess."

Hilma overwhelmed him with a burst of gratitude which he gruffly pretended to deprecate. Oh, that was all right. It hadn't cost him much. He liked to see people having a good time himself, and the crowd did seem to be enjoying themselves. What did SHE think? Did things look lively enough? And how about herself—was she enjoying it?

Stupidly Annixter drove the question home again, at his wits' end as to how to make conversation. Hilma protested volubly she would never forget this night, adding:

"Dance! Oh, you don't know how I love it! I didn't know myself. I could dance all night and never stop once!"

Annixter was smitten with uneasiness. No doubt this "promenading" was not at all to her taste. Wondering what kind of a spectacle he was about to make of himself, he exclaimed:

"Want to dance now?"

"Oh, yes!" she returned.

They paused in their walk, and Hilma, facing him, gave herself into his arms. Annixter shut his teeth, the perspiration starting from his forehead. For five years he had abandoned dancing. Never in his best days had it been one of his accomplishments.

They hesitated a moment, waiting to catch the time from the musicians. Another couple bore down upon them at precisely the wrong moment, jostling them out of step. Annixter swore under his breath. His arm still about the young woman, he pulled her over to one corner.

"Now," he muttered, "we'll try again."

A second time, listening to the one-two-three, one-two-three cadence of the musicians, they endeavoured to get under way. Annixter waited the fraction of a second too long and stepped on Hilma's foot. On the third attempt, having worked out of the corner, a pair of dancers bumped into them once more, and as they were recovering themselves another couple caromed violently against Annixter so that he all but lost his footing. He was in a rage. Hilma, very embarrassed, was trying not to laugh, and thus they found themselves, out in the middle of the floor, continually jostled from their position, holding clumsily to each other, stammering excuses into one another's faces, when Delaney arrived.

He came with the suddenness of an explosion. There was a commotion by the doorway, a rolling burst of oaths, a furious stamping of hoofs, a wild scramble of the dancers to either side of the room, and there he was. He had ridden the buckskin at a gallop straight through the doorway and out into the middle of the floor of the barn.

Once well inside, Delaney hauled up on the cruel spade-bit, at the same time driving home the spurs, and the buckskin, without halting in her gait, rose into the air upon her hind feet, and coming down again with a thunder of iron hoofs upon the hollow floor, lashed out with both heels simultaneously, her back arched, her head between her knees. It was the running buck, and had not Delaney been the hardest buster in the county, would have flung him headlong like a sack of sand. But he eased off the bit, gripping the mare's flanks with his knees, and the buckskin, having long since known her master, came to hand quivering, the bloody spume dripping from the bit upon the slippery floor.

Delaney had arrayed himself with painful elaboration, determined to look the part, bent upon creating the impression, resolved that his appearance at least should justify his reputation of being "bad." Nothing was lacking—neither the campaign hat with upturned brim, nor the dotted blue handkerchief knotted behind the neck, nor the heavy gauntlets stitched with red, nor—this above all—the bear-skin "chaparejos," the hair trousers of the mountain cowboy, the pistol holster low on the thigh. But for the moment this holster was empty, and in his right hand, the hammer at full cock, the chamber loaded, the puncher flourished his teaser, an army Colt's, the lamplight dully reflected in the dark blue steel.

In a second of time the dance was a bedlam. The musicians stopped with a discord, and the middle of the crowded floor bared itself instantly. It was like sand blown from off a rock; the throng of guests, carried by an impulse that was not to be resisted, bore back against the sides of the barn, overturning chairs, tripping upon each other, falling down, scrambling to their feet again, stepping over one another, getting behind each other, diving under chairs, flattening themselves against the wall—a wild, clamouring pell-mell, blind, deaf, panic-stricken; a confused tangle of waving arms, torn muslin, crushed flowers, pale faces, tangled legs, that swept in all directions back from the centre of the floor, leaving Annixter and Hilma, alone, deserted, their arms about each other, face to face with Delaney, mad with alcohol, bursting with remembered insult, bent on evil, reckless of results.

After the first scramble for safety, the crowd fell quiet for the fraction of an instant, glued to the walls, afraid to stir, struck dumb and motionless with surprise and terror, and in the instant's silence that followed Annixter, his eyes on Delaney, muttered rapidly to Hilma:

"Get back, get away to one side. The fool MIGHT shoot."

There was a second's respite afforded while Delaney occupied himself in quieting the buckskin, and in that second of time, at this moment of crisis, the wonderful thing occurred. Hilma, turning from Delaney, her hands clasped on Annixter's arm, her eyes meeting his, exclaimed:

"You, too!"

And that was all; but to Annixter it was a revelation. Never more alive to his surroundings, never more observant, he suddenly understood. For the briefest lapse of time he and Hilma looked deep into each other's eyes, and from that moment on, Annixter knew that Hilma cared.

The whole matter was brief as the snapping of a finger. Two words and a glance and all was done. But as though nothing had occurred, Annixter pushed Hilma from him, repeating harshly:

"Get back, I tell you. Don't you see he's got a gun? Haven't I enough on my hands without you?"

He loosed her clasp and his eyes once more on Delaney, moved diagonally backwards toward the side of the barn, pushing Hilma from him. In the end he thrust her away so sharply that she gave back with a long stagger; somebody caught her arm and drew her in, leaving Annixter alone once more in the middle of the floor, his hands in his coat pockets, watchful, alert, facing his enemy.

But the cow-puncher was not ready to come to grapples yet. Fearless, his wits gambolling under the lash of the alcohol, he wished to make the most of the occasion, maintaining the suspense, playing for the gallery. By touches of the hand and knee he kept the buckskin in continual, nervous movement, her hoofs clattering, snorting, tossing her head, while he, himself, addressing himself to Annixter, poured out a torrent of invective.

"Well, strike me blind if it ain't old Buck Annixter! He was going to show me off Quien Sabe at the toe of his boot, was he? Well, here's your chance,—with the ladies to see you do it. Gives a dance, does he, high-falutin' hoe-down in his barn and forgets to invite his old broncho-bustin' friend. But his friend don't forget him; no, he don't. He remembers little things, does his broncho-bustin' friend. Likes to see a dance hisself on occasion, his friend does. Comes anyhow, trustin' his welcome will be hearty; just to see old Buck Annixter dance, just to show Buck Annixter's friends how Buck can dance—dance all by hisself, a little hen-on-a-hot-plate dance when his broncho-bustin' friend asks him so polite. A little dance for the ladies, Buck. This feature of the entertainment is alone worth the price of admission. Tune up, Buck. Attention now! I'll give you the key."

He "fanned" his revolver, spinning it about his index finger by the trigger-guard with incredible swiftness, the twirling weapon a mere blur of blue steel in his hand. Suddenly and without any apparent cessation of the movement, he fired, and a little splinter of wood flipped into the air at Annixter's feet.

"Time!" he shouted, while the buckskin reared to the report. "Hold on—wait a minute. This place is too light to suit. That big light yonder is in my eyes. Look out, I'm going to throw lead."

A second shot put out the lamp over the musicians' stand. The assembled guests shrieked, a frantic, shrinking quiver ran through the crowd like the huddling of frightened rabbits in their pen.

Annixter hardly moved. He stood some thirty paces from the buster, his hands still in his coat pockets, his eyes glistening, watchful. Excitable and turbulent in trifling matters, when actual bodily danger threatened he was of an abnormal quiet.

"I'm watching you," cried the other. "Don't make any mistake about that. Keep your hands in your COAT pockets, if you'd like to live a little longer, understand? And don't let me see you make a move toward your hip or your friends will be asked to identify you at the morgue to-morrow morning. When I'm bad, I'm called the Undertaker's Friend, so I am, and I'm that bad to-night that I'm scared of myself. They'll have to revise the census returns before I'm done with this place. Come on, now, I'm getting tired waiting. I come to see a dance."

"Hand over that horse, Delaney," said Annixter, without raising his voice, "and clear out."

The other affected to be overwhelmed with infinite astonishment, his eyes staring. He peered down from the saddle.

"Wh-a-a-t!" he exclaimed; "wh-a-a-t did you say? Why, I guess you must be looking for trouble; that's what I guess."

"There's where you're wrong, m'son," muttered Annixter, partly to Delaney, partly to himself. "If I was looking for trouble there wouldn't be any guess-work about it."

With the words he began firing. Delaney had hardly entered the barn before Annixter's plan had been formed. Long since his revolver was in the pocket of his coat, and he fired now through the coat itself, without withdrawing his hands.

Until that moment Annixter had not been sure of himself. There was no doubt that for the first few moments of the affair he would have welcomed with joy any reasonable excuse for getting out of the situation. But the sound of his own revolver gave him confidence. He whipped it from his pocket and fired again.

Abruptly the duel began, report following report, spurts of pale blue smoke jetting like the darts of short spears between the two men, expanding to a haze and drifting overhead in wavering strata. It was quite probable that no thought of killing each other suggested itself to either Annixter or Delaney. Both fired without aiming very deliberately. To empty their revolvers and avoid being hit was the desire common to both. They no longer vituperated each other. The revolvers spoke for them.

Long after, Annixter could recall this moment. For years he could with but little effort reconstruct the scene—the densely packed crowd flattened against the sides of the barn, the festoons of lanterns, the mingled smell of evergreens, new wood, sachets, and powder smoke; the vague clamour of distress and terror that rose from the throng of guests, the squealing of the buckskin, the uneven explosions of the revolvers, the reverberation of trampling hoofs, a brief glimpse of Harran Derrick's excited face at the door of the harness room, and in the open space in the centre of the floor, himself and Delaney, manoeuvring swiftly in a cloud of smoke.

Annixter's revolver contained but six cartridges. Already it seemed to him as if he had fired twenty times. Without doubt the next shot was his last. Then what? He peered through the blue haze that with every discharge thickened between him and the buster. For his own safety he must "place" at least one shot. Delaney's chest and shoulders rose suddenly above the smoke close upon him as the distraught buckskin reared again. Annixter, for the first time during the fight, took definite aim, but before he could draw the trigger there was a great shout and he was aware of the buckskin, the bridle trailing, the saddle empty, plunging headlong across the floor, crashing into the line of chairs. Delaney was scrambling off the floor. There was blood on the buster's wrist and he no longer carried his revolver. Suddenly he turned and ran. The crowd parted right and left before him as he made toward the doorway. He disappeared.

Twenty men promptly sprang to the buckskin's head, but she broke away, and wild with terror, bewildered, blind, insensate, charged into the corner of the barn by the musicians' stand. She brought up against the wall with cruel force and with impact of a sack of stones; her head was cut. She turned and charged again, bull-like, the blood streaming from her forehead. The crowd, shrieking, melted before her rush. An old man was thrown down and trampled. The buckskin trod upon the dragging bridle, somersaulted into a confusion of chairs in one corner, and came down with a terrific clatter in a wild disorder of kicking hoofs and splintered wood. But a crowd of men fell upon her, tugging at the bit, sitting on her head, shouting, gesticulating. For five minutes she struggled and fought; then, by degrees, she recovered herself, drawing great sobbing breaths at long intervals that all but burst the girths, rolling her eyes in bewildered, supplicating fashion, trembling in every muscle, and starting and shrinking now and then like a young girl in hysterics. At last she lay quiet. The men allowed her to struggle to her feet. The saddle was removed and she was led to one of the empty stalls, where she remained the rest of the evening, her head low, her pasterns quivering, turning her head apprehensively from time to time, showing the white of one eye and at long intervals heaving a single prolonged sigh.

And an hour later the dance was progressing as evenly as though nothing in the least extraordinary had occurred. The incident was closed—that abrupt swoop of terror and impending death dropping down there from out the darkness, cutting abruptly athwart the gayety of the moment, come and gone with the swiftness of a thunderclap. Many of the women had gone home, taking their men with them; but the great bulk of the crowd still remained, seeing no reason why the episode should interfere with the evening's enjoyment, resolved to hold the ground for mere bravado, if for nothing else. Delaney would not come back, of that everybody was persuaded, and in case he should, there was not found wanting fully half a hundred young men who would give him a dressing down, by jingo! They had been too surprised to act when Delaney had first appeared, and before they knew where they were at, the buster had cleared out. In another minute, just another second, they would have shown him—yes, sir, by jingo!—ah, you bet!

On all sides the reminiscences began to circulate. At least one man in every three had been involved in a gun fight at some time of his life. "Ah, you ought to have seen in Yuba County one time—" "Why, in Butte County in the early days—" "Pshaw! this to-night wasn't anything! Why, once in a saloon in Arizona when I was there—" and so on, over and over again. Osterman solemnly asserted that he had seen a greaser sawn in two in a Nevada sawmill. Old Broderson had witnessed a Vigilante lynching in '55 on California Street in San Francisco. Dyke recalled how once in his engineering days he had run over a drunk at a street crossing. Gethings of the San Pablo had taken a shot at a highwayman. Hooven had bayonetted a French Chasseur at Sedan. An old Spanish-Mexican, a centenarian from Guadalajara, remembered Fremont's stand on a mountain top in San Benito County. The druggist had fired at a burglar trying to break into his store one New Year's eve. Young Vacca had seen a dog shot in Guadalajara. Father Sarria had more than once administered the sacraments to Portuguese desperadoes dying of gunshot wounds. Even the women recalled terrible scenes. Mrs. Cutter recounted to an interested group how she had seen a claim jumped in Placer County in 1851, when three men were shot, falling in a fusillade of rifle shots, and expiring later upon the floor of her kitchen while she looked on. Mrs. Dyke had been in a stage hold-up, when the shotgun messenger was murdered. Stories by the hundreds went the round of the company. The air was surcharged with blood, dying groans, the reek of powder smoke, the crack of rifles. All the legends of '49, the violent, wild life of the early days, were recalled to view, defiling before them there in an endless procession under the glare of paper lanterns and kerosene lamps.

But the affair had aroused a combative spirit amongst the men of the assembly. Instantly a spirit of aggression, of truculence, swelled up underneath waistcoats and starched shirt bosoms. More than one offender was promptly asked to "step outside." It was like young bucks excited by an encounter of stags, lowering their horns upon the slightest provocation, showing off before the does and fawns. Old quarrels were remembered. One sought laboriously for slights and insults, veiled in ordinary conversation. The sense of personal honour became refined to a delicate, fine point. Upon the slightest pretext there was a haughty drawing up of the figure, a twisting of the lips into a smile of scorn. Caraher spoke of shooting S. Behrman on sight before the end of the week. Twice it became necessary to separate Hooven and Cutter, renewing their quarrel as to the ownership of the steer. All at once Minna Hooven's "partner" fell upon the gayly apparelled clerk from Bonneville, pummelling him with his fists, hustling him out of the hall, vociferating that Miss Hooven had been grossly insulted. It took three men to extricate the clerk from his clutches, dazed, gasping, his collar unfastened and sticking up into his face, his eyes staring wildly into the faces of the crowd.

But Annixter, bursting with pride, his chest thrown out, his chin in the air, reigned enthroned in a circle of adulation. He was the Hero. To shake him by the hand was an honour to be struggled for. One clapped him on the back with solemn nods of approval. "There's the BOY for you;" "There was nerve for you;" "What's the matter with Annixter?" "How about THAT for sand, and how was THAT for a SHOT?" "Why, Apache Kid couldn't have bettered that." "Cool enough." "Took a steady eye and a sure hand to make a shot like that." "There was a shot that would be told about in Tulare County fifty years to come."

Annixter had refrained from replying, all ears to this conversation, wondering just what had happened. He knew only that Delaney had run, leaving his revolver and a spatter of blood behind him. By degrees, however, he ascertained that his last shot but one had struck Delaney's pistol hand, shattering it and knocking the revolver from his grip. He was overwhelmed with astonishment. Why, after the shooting began he had not so much as seen Delaney with any degree of plainness. The whole affair was a whirl.

"Well, where did YOU learn to shoot THAT way?" some one in the crowd demanded. Annixter moved his shoulders with a gesture of vast unconcern.

"Oh," he observed carelessly, "it's not my SHOOTING that ever worried ME, m'son."

The crowd gaped with delight. There was a great wagging of heads.

"Well, I guess not."

"No, sir, not much."

"Ah, no, you bet not."

When the women pressed around him, shaking his hands, declaring that he had saved their daughters' lives, Annixter assumed a pose of superb deprecation, the modest self-obliteration of the chevalier. He delivered himself of a remembered phrase, very elegant, refined. It was Lancelot after the tournament, Bayard receiving felicitations after the battle.

"Oh, don't say anything about it," he murmured. "I only did what any man would have done in my place."

To restore completely the equanimity of the company, he announced supper. This he had calculated as a tremendous surprise. It was to have been served at mid-night, but the irruption of Delaney had dislocated the order of events, and the tables were brought in an hour ahead of time. They were arranged around three sides of the barn and were loaded down with cold roasts of beef, cold chickens and cold ducks, mountains of sandwiches, pitchers of milk and lemonade, entire cheeses, bowls of olives, plates of oranges and nuts. The advent of this supper was received with a volley of applause. The musicians played a quick step. The company threw themselves upon the food with a great scraping of chairs and a vast rustle of muslins, tarletans, and organdies; soon the clatter of dishes was a veritable uproar. The tables were taken by assault. One ate whatever was nearest at hand, some even beginning with oranges and nuts and ending with beef and chicken. At the end the paper caps were brought on, together with the ice cream. All up and down the tables the pulled "crackers" snapped continually like the discharge of innumerable tiny rifles.

The caps of tissue paper were put on—"Phrygian Bonnets," "Magicians' Caps," "Liberty Caps;" the young girls looked across the table at their vis-a-vis with bursts of laughter and vigorous clapping of the hands.

The harness room crowd had a table to themselves, at the head of which sat Annixter and at the foot Harran. The gun fight had sobered Presley thoroughly. He sat by the side of Vanamee, who ate but little, preferring rather to watch the scene with calm observation, a little contemptuous when the uproar around the table was too boisterous, savouring of intoxication. Osterman rolled bullets of bread and shot them with astonishing force up and down the table, but the others—Dyke, old Broderson, Caraher, Harran Derrick, Hooven, Cutter, Garnett of the Ruby rancho, Keast from the ranch of the same name, Gethings of the San Pablo, and Chattern of the Bonanza—occupied themselves with eating as much as they could before the supper gave out. At a corner of the table, speechless, unobserved, ignored, sat Dabney, of whom nothing was known but his name, the silent old man who made no friends. He ate and drank quietly, dipping his sandwich in his lemonade.

Osterman ate all the olives he could lay his hands on, a score of them, fifty of them, a hundred of them. He touched no crumb of anything else. Old Broderson stared at him, his jaw fallen. Osterman declared he had once eaten a thousand on a bet. The men called each others' attention to him. Delighted to create a sensation, Osterman persevered. The contents of an entire bowl disappeared in his huge, reptilian slit of a mouth. His cheeks of brownish red were extended, his bald forehead glistened. Colics seized upon him. His stomach revolted. It was all one with him. He was satisfied, contented. He was astonishing the people.

"Once I swallowed a tree toad." he told old Broderson, "by mistake. I was eating grapes, and the beggar lived in me three weeks. In rainy weather he would sing. You don't believe that," he vociferated. "Haven't I got the toad at home now in a bottle of alcohol."

And the old man, never doubting, his eyes starting, wagged his head in amazement.

"Oh, yes," cried Caraher, the length of the table, "that's a pretty good one. Tell us another."

"That reminds me of a story," hazarded old Broderson uncertainly; "once when I was a lad in Ukiah, fifty years."

"Oh, yes," cried half a dozen voices, "THAT'S a pretty good one. Tell us another."

"Eh—wh—what?" murmured Broderson, looking about him. "I—I don't know. It was Ukiah. You—you—you mix me all up."

As soon as supper was over, the floor was cleared again. The guests clamoured for a Virginia reel. The last quarter of the evening, the time of the most riotous fun, was beginning. The young men caught the girls who sat next to them. The orchestra dashed off into a rollicking movement. The two lines were formed. In a second of time the dance was under way again; the guests still wearing the Phrygian bonnets and liberty caps of pink and blue tissue paper.

But the group of men once more adjourned to the harness room. Fresh boxes of cigars were opened; the seventh bowl of fertiliser was mixed. Osterman poured the dregs of a glass of it upon his bald head, declaring that he could feel the hair beginning to grow.

But suddenly old Broderson rose to his feet.

"Aha," he cackled, "I'M going to have a dance, I am. Think I'm too old? I'll show you young fellows. I'm a regular old ROOSTER when I get started."

He marched out into the barn, the others following, holding their sides. He found an aged Mexican woman by the door and hustled her, all confused and giggling, into the Virginia reel, then at its height. Every one crowded around to see. Old Broderson stepped off with the alacrity of a colt, snapping his fingers, slapping his thigh, his mouth widening in an excited grin. The entire company of the guests shouted. The City Band redoubled their efforts; and the old man, losing his head, breathless, gasping, dislocated his stiff joints in his efforts. He became possessed, bowing, scraping, advancing, retreating, wagging his beard, cutting pigeons' wings, distraught with the music, the clamour, the applause, the effects of the fertiliser.

Annixter shouted:

"Nice eye, Santa Claus."

But Annixter's attention wandered. He searched for Hilma Tree, having still in mind the look in her eyes at that swift moment of danger. He had not seen her since then. At last he caught sight of her. She was not dancing, but, instead, was sitting with her "partner" at the end of the barn near her father and mother, her eyes wide, a serious expression on her face, her thoughts, no doubt, elsewhere. Annixter was about to go to her when he was interrupted by a cry.

Old Broderson, in the midst of a double shuffle, had clapped his hand to his side with a gasp, which he followed by a whoop of anguish. He had got a stitch or had started a twinge somewhere. With a gesture of resignation, he drew himself laboriously out of the dance, limping abominably, one leg dragging. He was heard asking for his wife. Old Mrs. Broderson took him in charge. She jawed him for making an exhibition of himself, scolding as though he were a ten-year-old.

"Well, I want to know!" she exclaimed, as he hobbled off, dejected and melancholy, leaning upon her arm, "thought he had to dance, indeed! What next? A gay old grandpa, this. He'd better be thinking of his coffin."

It was almost midnight. The dance drew towards its close in a storm of jubilation. The perspiring musicians toiled like galley slaves; the guests singing as they danced.

The group of men reassembled in the harness room. Even Magnus Derrick condescended to enter and drink a toast. Presley and Vanamee, still holding themselves aloof, looked on, Vanamee more and more disgusted. Dabney, standing to one side, overlooked and forgotten, continued to sip steadily at his glass, solemn, reserved. Garnett of the Ruby rancho, Keast from the ranch of the same name, Gethings of the San Pablo, and Chattern of the Bonanza, leaned back in their chairs, their waist-coats unbuttoned, their legs spread wide, laughing—they could not tell why. Other ranchers, men whom Annixter had never seen, appeared in the room, wheat growers from places as far distant as Goshen and Pixley; young men and old, proprietors of veritable principalities, hundreds of thousands of acres of wheat lands, a dozen of them, a score of them; men who were strangers to each other, but who made it a point to shake hands with Magnus Derrick, the "prominent man" of the valley. Old Broderson, whom every one had believed had gone home, returned, though much sobered, and took his place, refusing, however, to drink another spoonful.

Soon the entire number of Annixter's guests found themselves in two companies, the dancers on the floor of the barn, frolicking through the last figures of the Virginia reel and the boisterous gathering of men in the harness room, downing the last quarts of fertiliser. Both assemblies had been increased. Even the older people had joined in the dance, while nearly every one of the men who did not dance had found their way into the harness room. The two groups rivalled each other in their noise. Out on the floor of the barn was a very whirlwind of gayety, a tempest of laughter, hand-clapping and cries of amusement. In the harness room the confused shouting and singing, the stamping of heavy feet, set a quivering reverberation in the oil of the kerosene lamps, the flame of the candles in the Japanese lanterns flaring and swaying in the gusts of hilarity. At intervals, between the two, one heard the music, the wailing of the violins, the vigorous snarling of the cornet, and the harsh, incessant rasping of the snare drum.

And at times all these various sounds mingled in a single vague note, huge, clamorous, that rose up into the night from the colossal, reverberating compass of the barn and sent its echoes far off across the unbroken levels of the surrounding ranches, stretching out to infinity under the clouded sky, calm, mysterious, still.

Annixter, the punch bowl clasped in his arms, was pouring out the last spoonful of liquor into Caraher's glass when he was aware that some one was pulling at the sleeve of his coat. He set down the punch bowl.

"Well, where did YOU come from?" he demanded.

It was a messenger from Bonneville, the uniformed boy that the telephone company employed to carry messages. He had just arrived from town on his bicycle, out of breath and panting.

"Message for you, sir. Will you sign?"

He held the book to Annixter, who signed the receipt, wondering.

The boy departed, leaving a thick envelope of yellow paper in Annixter's hands, the address typewritten, the word "Urgent" written in blue pencil in one corner.

Annixter tore it open. The envelope contained other sealed envelopes, some eight or ten of them, addressed to Magnus Derrick, Osterman, Broderson, Garnett, Keast, Gethings, Chattern, Dabney, and to Annixter himself.

Still puzzled, Annixter distributed the envelopes, muttering to himself:

"What's up now?"

The incident had attracted attention. A comparative quiet followed, the guests following the letters with their eyes as they were passed around the table. They fancied that Annixter had arranged a surprise.

Magnus Derrick, who sat next to Annixter, was the first to receive his letter. With a word of excuse he opened it.

"Read it, read it, Governor," shouted a half-dozen voices. "No secrets, you know. Everything above board here to-night."

Magnus cast a glance at the contents of the letter, then rose to his feet and read:

Magnus Derrick,
Bonneville, Tulare Co., Cal.

Dear Sir:

By regrade of October 1st, the value of the railroad land you occupy, included in your ranch of Los Muertos, has been fixed at $27.00 per acre. The land is now for sale at that price to any one.

Yours, etc.,
CYRUS BLAKELEE RUGGLES,
Land Agent, P. and S. W. R. R.
S. BEHRMAN,
Local Agent, P. and S. W. R. R.

In the midst of the profound silence that followed, Osterman was heard to exclaim grimly:

"THAT'S a pretty good one. Tell us another."

But for a long moment this was the only remark.

The silence widened, broken only by the sound of torn paper as Annixter, Osterman, old Broderson, Garnett, Keast, Gethings, Chattern, and Dabney opened and read their letters. They were all to the same effect, almost word for word like the Governor's. Only the figures and the proper names varied. In some cases the price per acre was twenty-two dollars. In Annixter's case it was thirty.

"And—and the company promised to sell to me, to—to all of us," gasped old Broderson, "at TWO DOLLARS AND A HALF an acre."

It was not alone the ranchers immediately around Bonneville who would be plundered by this move on the part of the Railroad. The "alternate section" system applied throughout all the San Joaquin. By striking at the Bonneville ranchers a terrible precedent was established. Of the crowd of guests in the harness room alone, nearly every man was affected, every man menaced with ruin. All of a million acres was suddenly involved.

Then suddenly the tempest burst. A dozen men were on their feet in an instant, their teeth set, their fists clenched, their faces purple with rage. Oaths, curses, maledictions exploded like the firing of successive mines. Voices quivered with wrath, hands flung upward, the fingers hooked, prehensile, trembled with anger. The sense of wrongs, the injustices, the oppression, extortion, and pillage of twenty years suddenly culminated and found voice in a raucous howl of execration. For a second there was nothing articulate in that cry of savage exasperation, nothing even intelligent. It was the human animal hounded to its corner, exploited, harried to its last stand, at bay, ferocious, terrible, turning at last with bared teeth and upraised claws to meet the death grapple. It was the hideous squealing of the tormented brute, its back to the wall, defending its lair, its mate and its whelps, ready to bite, to rend, to trample, to batter out the life of The Enemy in a primeval, bestial welter of blood and fury.

The roar subsided to intermittent clamour, in the pauses of which the sounds of music and dancing made themselves audible once more.

"S. Behrman again," vociferated Harran Derrick.

"Chose his moment well," muttered Annixter. "Hits his hardest when we're all rounded up having a good time."

"Gentlemen, this is ruin."

"What's to be done now?"

"FIGHT! My God! do you think we are going to stand this? Do you think we CAN?"

The uproar swelled again. The clearer the assembly of ranchers understood the significance of this move on the part of the Railroad, the more terrible it appeared, the more flagrant, the more intolerable. Was it possible, was it within the bounds of imagination that this tyranny should be contemplated? But they knew—past years had driven home the lesson—the implacable, iron monster with whom they had to deal, and again and again the sense of outrage and oppression lashed them to their feet, their mouths wide with curses, their fists clenched tight, their throats hoarse with shouting.

"Fight! How fight? What ARE you going to do?"

"If there's a law in this land"

"If there is, it is in Shelgrim's pocket. Who owns the courts in California? Ain't it Shelgrim?"

"God damn him."

"Well, how long are you going to stand it? How long before you'll settle up accounts with six inches of plugged gas-pipe?"

"And our contracts, the solemn pledges of the corporation to sell to us first of all—"

"And now the land is for sale to anybody."

"Why, it is a question of my home. Am I to be turned out? Why, I have put eight thousand dollars into improving this land."

"And I six thousand, and now that I have, the Railroad grabs it."

"And the system of irrigating ditches that Derrick and I have been laying out. There's thousands of dollars in that!"

"I'll fight this out till I've spent every cent of my money."

"Where? In the courts that the company owns?"

"Think I am going to give in to this? Think I am to get off my land? By God, gentlemen, law or no law, railroad or no railroad, I—WILL—NOT."

"Nor I."

"Nor I."

"Nor I."

"This is the last. Legal means first; if those fail—the shotgun."

"They can kill me. They can shoot me down, but I'll die—die fighting for my home—before I'll give in to this."

At length Annixter made himself heard:

"All out of the room but the ranch owners," he shouted. "Hooven, Caraher, Dyke, you'll have to clear out. This is a family affair. Presley, you and your friend can remain."

Reluctantly the others filed through the door. There remained in the harness room—besides Vanamee and Presley—Magnus Derrick, Annixter, old Broderson Harran, Garnett from the Ruby rancho, Keast from the ranch of the same name, Gethings of the San Pablo, Chattern of the Bonanza, about a score of others, ranchers from various parts of the county, and, last of all, Dabney, ignored, silent, to whom nobody spoke and who, as yet, had not uttered a word. But the men who had been asked to leave the harness room spread the news throughout the barn. It was repeated from lip to lip. One by one the guests dropped out of the dance. Groups were formed. By swift degrees the gayety lapsed away. The Virginia reel broke up. The musicians ceased playing, and in the place of the noisy, effervescent revelry of the previous half hour, a subdued murmur filled all the barn, a mingling of whispers, lowered voices, the coming and going of light footsteps, the uneasy shifting of positions, while from behind the closed doors of the harness room came a prolonged, sullen hum of anger and strenuous debate. The dance came to an abrupt end. The guests, unwilling to go as yet, stunned, distressed, stood clumsily about, their eyes vague, their hands swinging at their sides, looking stupidly into each others' faces. A sense of impending calamity, oppressive, foreboding, gloomy, passed through the air overhead in the night, a long shiver of anguish and of terror, mysterious, despairing.

In the harness room, however, the excitement continued unchecked. One rancher after another delivered himself of a torrent of furious words. There was no order, merely the frenzied outcry of blind fury. One spirit alone was common to all—resistance at whatever cost and to whatever lengths.

Suddenly Osterman leaped to his feet, his bald head gleaming in the lamp-light, his red ears distended, a flood of words filling his great, horizontal slit of a mouth, his comic actor's face flaming. Like the hero of a melodrama, he took stage with a great sweeping gesture.

"ORGANISATION," he shouted, "that must be our watch-word. The curse of the ranchers is that they fritter away their strength. Now, we must stand together, now, NOW. Here's the crisis, here's the moment. Shall we meet it? I CALL FOR THE LEAGUE. Not next week, not to-morrow, not in the morning, but now, now, now, this very moment, before we go out of that door. Every one of us here to join it, to form the beginnings of a vast organisation, banded together to death, if needs be, for the protection of our rights and homes. Are you ready? Is it now or never? I call for the League."

Instantly there was a shout. With an actor's instinct, Osterman had spoken at the precise psychological moment. He carried the others off their feet, glib, dexterous, voluble. Just what was meant by the League the others did not know, but it was something, a vague engine, a machine with which to fight. Osterman had not done speaking before the room rang with outcries, the crowd of men shouting, for what they did not know.

"The League! The League!"

"Now, to-night, this moment; sign our names before we leave."

"He's right. Organisation! The League!"

"We have a committee at work already," Osterman vociferated. "I am a member, and also Mr. Broderson, Mr. Annixter, and Mr. Harran Derrick. What our aims are we will explain to you later. Let this committee be the nucleus of the League—temporarily, at least. Trust us. We are working for you and with you. Let this committee be merged into the larger committee of the League, and for President of the League"—he paused the fraction of a second—"for President there can be but one name mentioned, one man to whom we all must look as leader—Magnus Derrick."

The Governor's name was received with a storm of cheers. The harness room reechoed with shouts of:

"Derrick! Derrick!"

"Magnus for President!"

"Derrick, our natural leader."

"Derrick, Derrick, Derrick for President."

Magnus rose to his feet. He made no gesture. Erect as a cavalry officer, tall, thin, commanding, he dominated the crowd in an instant. There was a moment's hush. "Gentlemen," he said, "if organisation is a good word, moderation is a better one.

The matter is too grave for haste. I would suggest that we each and severally return to our respective homes for the night, sleep over what has happened, and convene again to-morrow, when we are calmer and can approach this affair in a more judicious mood. As for the honour with which you would inform me, I must affirm that that, too, is a matter for grave deliberation. This League is but a name as yet. To accept control of an organisation whose principles are not yet fixed is a heavy responsibility. I shrink from it—"

But he was allowed to proceed no farther. A storm of protest developed. There were shouts of:

"No, no. The League to-night and Derrick for President."

"We have been moderate too long."

"The League first, principles afterward."

"We can't wait," declared Osterman. "Many of us cannot attend a meeting to-morrow. Our business affairs would prevent it. Now we are all together. I propose a temporary chairman and secretary be named and a ballot be taken. But first the League. Let us draw up a set of resolutions to stand together, for the defence of our homes, to death, if needs be, and each man present affix his signature thereto."

He subsided amidst vigorous applause. The next quarter of an hour was a vague confusion, every one talking at once, conversations going on in low tones in various corners of the room. Ink, pens, and a sheaf of foolscap were brought from the ranch house. A set of resolutions was draughted, having the force of a pledge, organising the League of Defence. Annixter was the first to sign. Others followed, only a few holding back, refusing to join till they had thought the matter over. The roll grew; the paper circulated about the table; each signature was welcomed by a salvo of cheers. At length, it reached Harran Derrick, who signed amid tremendous uproar. He released the pen only to shake a score of hands.

"Now, Magnus Derrick."

"Gentlemen," began the Governor, once more rising, "I beg of you to allow me further consideration. Gentlemen—"

He was interrupted by renewed shouting.

"No, no, now or never. Sign, join the League."

"Don't leave us. We look to you to help."

But presently the excited throng that turned their faces towards the Governor were aware of a new face at his elbow. The door of the harness room had been left unbolted and Mrs. Derrick, unable to endure the heart-breaking suspense of waiting outside, had gathered up all her courage and had come into the room. Trembling, she clung to Magnus's arm, her pretty light-brown hair in disarray, her large young girl's eyes wide with terror and distrust. What was about to happen she did not understand, but these men were clamouring for Magnus to pledge himself to something, to some terrible course of action, some ruthless, unscrupulous battle to the death with the iron-hearted monster of steel and steam. Nerved with a coward's intrepidity, she, who so easily obliterated herself, had found her way into the midst of this frantic crowd, into this hot, close room, reeking of alcohol and tobacco smoke, into this atmosphere surcharged with hatred and curses. She seized her husband's arm imploring, distraught with terror.

"No, no," she murmured; "no, don't sign."

She was the feather caught in the whirlwind. En masse, the crowd surged toward the erect figure of the Governor, the pen in one hand, his wife's fingers in the other, the roll of signatures before him. The clamour was deafening; the excitement culminated brusquely. Half a hundred hands stretched toward him; thirty voices, at top pitch, implored, expostulated, urged, almost commanded. The reverberation of the shouting was as the plunge of a cataract.

It was the uprising of The People; the thunder of the outbreak of revolt; the mob demanding to be led, aroused at last, imperious, resistless, overwhelming. It was the blind fury of insurrection, the brute, many-tongued, red-eyed, bellowing for guidance, baring its teeth, unsheathing its claws, imposing its will with the abrupt, resistless pressure of the relaxed piston, inexorable, knowing no pity.

"No, no," implored Annie Derrick. "No, Magnus, don't sign."

"He must," declared Harran, shouting in her ear to make himself heard, "he must. Don't you understand?"

Again the crowd surged forward, roaring. Mrs. Derrick was swept back, pushed to one side. Her husband no longer belonged to her. She paid the penalty for being the wife of a great man. The world, like a colossal iron wedge, crushed itself between. She was thrust to the wall. The throng of men, stamping, surrounded Magnus; she could no longer see him, but, terror-struck, she listened. There was a moment's lull, then a vast thunder of savage jubilation. Magnus had signed.

Harran found his mother leaning against the wall, her hands shut over her ears; her eyes, dilated with fear, brimming with tears. He led her from the harness room to the outer room, where Mrs. Tree and Hilma took charge of her, and then, impatient, refusing to answer the hundreds of anxious questions that assailed him, hurried back to the harness room. Already the balloting was in progress, Osterman acting as temporary chairman on the very first ballot he was made secretary of the League pro tem., and Magnus unanimously chosen for its President. An executive committee was formed, which was to meet the next day at the Los Muertos ranch house.

It was half-past one o'clock. In the barn outside the greater number of the guests had departed. Long since the musicians had disappeared. There only remained the families of the ranch owners involved in the meeting in the harness room. These huddled in isolated groups in corners of the garish, echoing barn, the women in their wraps, the young men with their coat collars turned up against the draughts that once more made themselves felt.

For a long half hour the loud hum of eager conversation continued to issue from behind the door of the harness room. Then, at length, there was a prolonged scraping of chairs. The session was over. The men came out in groups, searching for their families.

At once the homeward movement began. Every one was worn out. Some of the ranchers' daughters had gone to sleep against their mothers' shoulders.

Billy, the stableman, and his assistant were awakened, and the teams were hitched up. The stable yard was full of a maze of swinging lanterns and buggy lamps. The horses fretted, champing the bits; the carry-alls creaked with the straining of leather and springs as they received their loads. At every instant one heard the rattle of wheels as vehicle after vehicle disappeared in the night.

A fine, drizzling rain was falling, and the lamps began to show dim in a vague haze of orange light.

Magnus Derrick was the last to go. At the doorway of the barn he found Annixter, the roll of names—which it had been decided he was to keep in his safe for the moment—under his arm. Silently the two shook hands. Magnus departed. The grind of the wheels of his carry-all grated sharply on the gravel of the driveway in front of the ranch house, then, with a hollow roll across a little plank bridge, gained the roadway. For a moment the beat of the horses' hoofs made itself heard on the roadway. It ceased. Suddenly there was a great silence.

Annixter, in the doorway of the great barn, stood looking about him for a moment, alone, thoughtful. The barn was empty. That astonishing evening had come to an end. The whirl of things and people, the crowd of dancers, Delaney, the gun fight, Hilma Tree, her eyes fixed on him in mute confession, the rabble in the harness room, the news of the regrade, the fierce outburst of wrath, the hasty organising of the League, all went spinning confusedly through his recollection. But he was exhausted. Time enough in the morning to think it all over. By now it was raining sharply. He put the roll of names into his inside pocket, threw a sack over his head and shoulders, and went down to the ranch house.

But in the harness room, lighted by the glittering lanterns and flaring lamps, in the midst of overturned chairs, spilled liquor, cigar stumps, and broken glasses, Vanamee and Presley still remained talking, talking. At length, they rose, and came out upon the floor of the barn and stood for a moment looking about them.

Billy, the stableman, was going the rounds of the walls, putting out light after light. By degrees, the vast interior was growing dim. Upon the roof overhead the rain drummed incessantly, the eaves dripping. The floor was littered with pine needles, bits of orange peel, ends and fragments of torn organdies and muslins and bits of tissue paper from the "Phrygian Bonnets" and "Liberty Caps." The buckskin mare in the stall, dozing on three legs, changed position with a long sigh. The sweat stiffening the hair upon her back and loins, as it dried, gave off a penetrating, ammoniacal odour that mingled with the stale perfume of sachet and wilted flowers.

Presley and Vanamee stood looking at the deserted barn. There was a long silence. Then Presley said:

"Well... what do you think of it all?"

"I think," answered Vanamee slowly, "I think that there was a dance in Brussels the night before Waterloo."

BOOK II

I

In his office at San Francisco, seated before a massive desk of polished redwood, very ornate, Lyman Derrick sat dictating letters to his typewriter, on a certain morning early in the spring of the year. The subdued monotone of his voice proceeded evenly from sentence to sentence, regular, precise, businesslike.

"I have the honour to acknowledge herewith your favour of the 14th instant, and in reply would state—"

"Please find enclosed draft upon New Orleans to be applied as per our understanding—"

"In answer to your favour No. 1107, referring to the case of the City and County of San Francisco against Excelsior Warehouse & Storage Co., I would say—"

His voice continued, expressionless, measured, distinct. While he spoke, he swung slowly back and forth in his leather swivel chair, his elbows resting on the arms, his pop eyes fixed vaguely upon the calendar on the opposite wall, winking at intervals when he paused, searching for a word.

"That's all for the present," he said at length.

Without reply, the typewriter rose and withdrew, thrusting her pencil into the coil of her hair, closing the door behind her, softly, discreetly.

When she had gone, Lyman rose, stretching himself putting up three fingers to hide his yawn. To further loosen his muscles, he took a couple of turns the length of he room, noting with satisfaction its fine appointments, the padded red carpet, the dull olive green tint of the walls, the few choice engravings—portraits of Marshall, Taney, Field, and a coloured lithograph—excellently done—of the Grand Canyon of the Colorado—the deep-seated leather chairs, the large and crowded bookcase (topped with a bust of James Lick, and a huge greenish globe), the waste basket of woven coloured grass, made by Navajo Indians, the massive silver inkstand on the desk, the elaborate filing cabinet, complete in every particular, and the shelves of tin boxes, padlocked, impressive, grave, bearing the names of clients, cases and estates.

He was between thirty-one and thirty-five years of age. Unlike Harran, he resembled his mother, but he was much darker than Annie Derrick and his eyes were much fuller, the eyeball protruding, giving him a pop-eyed, foreign expression, quite unusual and unexpected. His hair was black, and he wore a small, tight, pointed mustache, which he was in the habit of pushing delicately upward from the corners of his lips with the ball of his thumb, the little finger extended. As often as he made this gesture, he prefaced it with a little twisting gesture of the forearm in order to bring his cuff into view, and, in fact, this movement by itself was habitual.

He was dressed carefully, his trousers creased, a pink rose in his lapel. His shoes were of patent leather, his cutaway coat was of very rough black cheviot, his double-breasted waistcoat of tan covered cloth with buttons of smoked pearl. An Ascot scarf—a great puff of heavy black silk—was at his neck, the knot transfixed by a tiny golden pin set off with an opal and four small diamonds.

At one end of the room were two great windows of plate glass, and pausing at length before one of these, Lyman selected a cigarette from his curved box of oxydized silver, lit it and stood looking down and out, willing to be idle for a moment, amused and interested in the view.

His office was on the tenth floor of the EXCHANGE BUILDING, a beautiful, tower-like affair of white stone, that stood on the corner of Market Street near its intersection with Kearney, the most imposing office building of the city.

Below him the city swarmed tumultuous through its grooves, the cable-cars starting and stopping with a gay jangling of bells and a strident whirring of jostled glass windows. Drays and carts clattered over the cobbles, and an incessant shuffling of thousands of feet rose from the pavement. Around Lotta's fountain the baskets of the flower sellers, crammed with chrysanthemums, violets, pinks, roses, lilies, hyacinths, set a brisk note of colour in the grey of the street.

But to Lyman's notion the general impression of this centre of the city's life was not one of strenuous business activity. It was a continuous interest in small things, a people ever willing to be amused at trifles, refusing to consider serious matters—good-natured, allowing themselves to be imposed upon, taking life easily—generous, companionable, enthusiastic; living, as it were, from day to day, in a place where the luxuries of life were had without effort; in a city that offered to consideration the restlessness of a New York, without its earnestness; the serenity of a Naples, without its languor; the romance of a Seville, without its picturesqueness.

As Lyman turned from the window, about to resume his work, the office boy appeared at the door.

"The man from the lithograph company, sir," announced the boy.

"Well, what does he want?" demanded Lyman, adding, however, upon the instant: "Show him in."

A young man entered, carrying a great bundle, which he deposited on a chair, with a gasp of relief, exclaiming, all out of breath:

"From the Standard Lithograph Company."

"What is?"

"Don't know," replied the other. "Maps, I guess."

"I don't want any maps. Who sent them? I guess you're mistaken." Lyman tore the cover from the top of the package, drawing out one of a great many huge sheets of white paper, folded eight times. Suddenly, he uttered an exclamation:

"Ah, I see. They ARE maps. But these should not have come here. They are to go to the regular office for distribution." He wrote a new direction on the label of the package: "Take them to that address," he went on. "I'll keep this one here. The others go to that address. If you see Mr. Darrell, tell him that Mr. Derrick—you get the name—Mr. Derrick may not be able to get around this afternoon, but to go ahead with any business just the same."

The young man departed with the package and Lyman, spreading out the map upon the table, remained for some time studying it thoughtfully.

It was a commissioner's official railway map of the State of California, completed to March 30th of that year. Upon it the different railways of the State were accurately plotted in various colours, blue, green, yellow. However, the blue, the yellow, and the green were but brief traceries, very short, isolated, unimportant. At a little distance these could hardly be seen. The whole map was gridironed by a vast, complicated network of red lines marked P. and S. W. R. R. These centralised at San Francisco and thence ramified and spread north, east, and south, to every quarter of the State. From Coles, in the topmost corner of the map, to Yuma in the lowest, from Reno on one side to San Francisco on the other, ran the plexus of red, a veritable system of blood circulation, complicated, dividing, and reuniting, branching, splitting, extending, throwing out feelers, off-shoots, tap roots, feeders—diminutive little blood suckers that shot out from the main jugular and went twisting up into some remote county, laying hold upon some forgotten village or town, involving it in one of a myriad branching coils, one of a hundred tentacles, drawing it, as it were, toward that centre from which all this system sprang.

The map was white, and it seemed as if all the colour which should have gone to vivify the various counties, towns, and cities marked upon it had been absorbed by that huge, sprawling organism, with its ruddy arteries converging to a central point. It was as though the State had been sucked white and colourless, and against this pallid background the red arteries of the monster stood out, swollen with life-blood, reaching out to infinity, gorged to bursting; an excrescence, a gigantic parasite fattening upon the life-blood of an entire commonwealth.

However, in an upper corner of the map appeared the names of the three new commissioners: Jones McNish for the first district, Lyman Derrick for the second, and James Darrell for the third.

Nominated in the Democratic State convention in the fall of the preceding year, Lyman, backed by the coteries of San Francisco bosses in the pay of his father's political committee of ranchers, had been elected together with Darrell, the candidate of the Pueblo and Mojave road, and McNish, the avowed candidate of the Pacific and Southwestern. Darrell was rabidly against the P. and S. W., McNish rabidly for it. Lyman was supposed to be the conservative member of the board, the ranchers' candidate, it was true, and faithful to their interests, but a calm man, deliberative, swayed by no such violent emotions as his colleagues.

Osterman's dexterity had at last succeeded in entangling Magnus inextricably in the new politics. The famous League, organised in the heat of passion the night of Annixter's barn dance, had been consolidated all through the winter months. Its executive committee, of which Magnus was chairman, had been, through Osterman's manipulation, merged into the old committee composed of Broderson, Annixter, and himself. Promptly thereat he had resigned the chairmanship of this committee, thus leaving Magnus at its head. Precisely as Osterman had planned, Magnus was now one of them. The new committee accordingly had two objects in view: to resist the attempted grabbing of their lands by the Railroad, and to push forward their own secret scheme of electing a board of railroad commissioners who should regulate wheat rates so as to favour the ranchers of the San Joaquin. The land cases were promptly taken to the courts and the new grading—fixing the price of the lands at twenty and thirty dollars an acre instead of two—bitterly and stubbornly fought. But delays occurred, the process of the law was interminable, and in the intervals the committee addressed itself to the work of seating the "Ranchers' Commission," as the projected Board of Commissioners came to be called.

It was Harran who first suggested that his brother, Lyman, be put forward as the candidate for this district. At once the proposition had a great success. Lyman seemed made for the place. While allied by every tie of blood to the ranching interests, he had never been identified with them. He was city-bred. The Railroad would not be over-suspicious of him. He was a good lawyer, a good business man, keen, clear-headed, far-sighted, had already some practical knowledge of politics, having served a term as assistant district attorney, and even at the present moment occupying the position of sheriff's attorney. More than all, he was the son of Magnus Derrick; he could be relied upon, could be trusted implicitly to remain loyal to the ranchers' cause.

The campaign for Railroad Commissioner had been very interesting. At the very outset Magnus's committee found itself involved in corrupt politics. The primaries had to be captured at all costs and by any means, and when the convention assembled it was found necessary to buy outright the votes of certain delegates. The campaign fund raised by contributions from Magnus, Annixter, Broderson, and Osterman was drawn upon to the extent of five thousand dollars.

Only the committee knew of this corruption. The League, ignoring ways and means, supposed as a matter of course that the campaign was honorably conducted.

For a whole week after the consummation of this part of the deal, Magnus had kept to his house, refusing to be seen, alleging that he was ill, which was not far from the truth. The shame of the business, the loathing of what he had done, were to him things unspeakable. He could no longer look Harran in the face. He began a course of deception with his wife. More than once, he had resolved to break with the whole affair, resigning his position, allowing the others to proceed without him. But now it was too late. He was pledged. He had joined the League. He was its chief, and his defection might mean its disintegration at the very time when it needed all its strength to fight the land cases. More than a mere deal in bad politics was involved. There was the land grab. His withdrawal from an unholy cause would mean the weakening, perhaps the collapse, of another cause that he believed to be righteous as truth itself. He was hopelessly caught in the mesh. Wrong seemed indissolubly knitted into the texture of Right. He was blinded, dizzied, overwhelmed, caught in the current of events, and hurried along he knew not where. He resigned himself.

In the end, and after much ostentatious opposition on the part of the railroad heelers, Lyman was nominated and subsequently elected.

When this consummation was reached Magnus, Osterman, Broderson, and Annixter stared at each other. Their wildest hopes had not dared to fix themselves upon so easy a victory as this. It was not believable that the corporation would allow itself to be fooled so easily, would rush open-eyed into the trap. How had it happened?

Osterman, however, threw his hat into the air with wild whoops of delight. Old Broderson permitted himself a feeble cheer. Even Magnus beamed satisfaction. The other members of the League, present at the time, shook hands all around and spoke of opening a few bottles on the strength of the occasion. Annixter alone was recalcitrant.

"It's too easy," he declared. "No, I'm not satisfied. Where's Shelgrim in all this? Why don't he show his hand, damn his soul? The thing is yellow, I tell you. There's a big fish in these waters somewheres. I don't know his name, and I don't know his game, but he's moving round off and on, just out of sight. If you think you've netted him, I DON'T, that's all I've got to say."

But he was jeered down as a croaker. There was the Commission. He couldn't get around that, could he? There was Darrell and Lyman Derrick, both pledged to the ranches. Good Lord, he was never satisfied. He'd be obstinate till the very last gun was fired. Why, if he got drowned in a river he'd float upstream just to be contrary.

In the course of time, the new board was seated. For the first few months of its term, it was occupied in clearing up the business left over by the old board and in the completion of the railway map. But now, the decks were cleared. It was about to address itself to the consideration of a revision of the tariff for the carriage of grain between the San Joaquin Valley and tide-water.

Both Lyman and Darrell were pledged to an average ten per cent. cut of the grain rates throughout the entire State.

The typewriter returned with the letters for Lyman to sign, and he put away the map and took up his morning's routine of business, wondering, the while, what would become of his practice during the time he was involved in the business of the Ranchers' Railroad Commission.

But towards noon, at the moment when Lyman was drawing off a glass of mineral water from the siphon that stood at his elbow, there was an interruption. Some one rapped vigorously upon the door, which was immediately after opened, and Magnus and Harran came in, followed by Presley.

"Hello, hello!" cried Lyman, jumping up, extending his hands, "why, here's a surprise. I didn't expect you all till to-night. Come in, come in and sit down. Have a glass of sizz-water, Governor."

The others explained that they had come up from Bonneville the night before, as the Executive Committee of the League had received a despatch from the lawyers it had retained to fight the Railroad, that the judge of the court in San Francisco, where the test cases were being tried, might be expected to hand down his decision the next day.

Very soon after the announcement of the new grading of the ranchers' lands, the corporation had offered, through S. Behrman, to lease the disputed lands to the ranchers at a nominal figure. The offer had been angrily rejected, and the Railroad had put up the lands for sale at Ruggles's office in Bonneville. At the exorbitant price named, buyers promptly appeared—dummy buyers, beyond shadow of doubt, acting either for the Railroad or for S. Behrman—men hitherto unknown in the county, men without property, without money, adventurers, heelers. Prominent among them, and bidding for the railroad's holdings included on Annixter's ranch, was Delaney.

The farce of deeding the corporation's sections to these fictitious purchasers was solemnly gone through with at Ruggles's office, the Railroad guaranteeing them possession. The League refused to allow the supposed buyers to come upon the land, and the Railroad, faithful to its pledge in the matter of guaranteeing its dummies possession, at once began suits in ejectment in the district court in Visalia, the county seat.

It was the preliminary skirmish, the reconnaisance in force, the combatants feeling each other's strength, willing to proceed with caution, postponing the actual death-grip for a while till each had strengthened its position and organised its forces.

During the time the cases were on trial at Visalia, S. Behrman was much in evidence in and about the courts. The trial itself, after tedious preliminaries, was brief. The ranchers lost. The test cases were immediately carried up to the United States Circuit Court in San Francisco. At the moment the decision of this court was pending.

"Why, this is news," exclaimed Lyman, in response to the Governor's announcement; "I did not expect them to be so prompt. I was in court only last week and there seemed to be no end of business ahead. I suppose you are very anxious?"

Magnus nodded. He had seated himself in one of Lyman's deep chairs, his grey top-hat, with its wide brim, on the floor beside him. His coat of black broad-cloth that had been tightly packed in his valise, was yet wrinkled and creased; his trousers were strapped under his high boots. As he spoke, he stroked the bridge of his hawklike nose with his bent forefinger.

Leaning-back in his chair, he watched his two sons with secret delight. To his eye, both were perfect specimens of their class, intelligent, well-looking, resourceful. He was intensely proud of them. He was never happier, never more nearly jovial, never more erect, more military, more alert, and buoyant than when in the company of his two sons. He honestly believed that no finer examples of young manhood existed throughout the entire nation.

"I think we should win in this court," Harran observed, watching the bubbles break in his glass. "The investigation has been much more complete than in the Visalia trial. Our case this time is too good. It has made too much talk. The court would not dare render a decision for the Railroad. Why, there's the agreement in black and white—and the circulars the Railroad issued. How CAN one get around those?"

"Well, well, we shall know in a few hours now," remarked Magnus.

"Oh," exclaimed Lyman, surprised, "it is for this morning, then. Why aren't you at the court?"

"It seemed undignified, boy," answered the Governor. "We shall know soon enough."

"Good God!" exclaimed Harran abruptly, "when I think of what is involved. Why, Lyman, it's our home, the ranch house itself, nearly all Los Muertos, practically our whole fortune, and just now when there is promise of an enormous crop of wheat. And it is not only us. There are over half a million acres of the San Joaquin involved. In some cases of the smaller ranches, it is the confiscation of the whole of the rancher's land. If this thing goes through, it will absolutely beggar nearly a hundred men. Broderson wouldn't have a thousand acres to his name. Why, it's monstrous."

"But the corporations offered to lease these lands," remarked Lyman. "Are any of the ranchers taking up that offer—or are any of them buying outright?"

"Buying! At the new figure!" exclaimed Harran, "at twenty and thirty an acre! Why, there's not one in ten that CAN. They are land-poor. And as for leasing—leasing land they virtually own—no, there's precious few are doing that, thank God! That would be acknowledging the railroad's ownership right away—forfeiting their rights for good. None of the LEAGUERS are doing it, I know. That would be the rankest treachery."

He paused for a moment, drinking the rest of the mineral water, then interrupting Lyman, who was about to speak to Presley, drawing him into the conversation through politeness, said: "Matters are just romping right along to a crisis these days. It's a make or break for the wheat growers of the State now, no mistake. Here are the land cases and the new grain tariff drawing to a head at about the same time. If we win our land cases, there's your new freight rates to be applied, and then all is beer and skittles. Won't the San Joaquin go wild if we pull it off, and I believe we will."

"How we wheat growers are exploited and trapped and deceived at every turn," observed Magnus sadly. "The courts, the capitalists, the railroads, each of them in turn hoodwinks us into some new and wonderful scheme, only to betray us in the end. Well," he added, turning to Lyman, "one thing at least we can depend on. We will cut their grain rates for them, eh, Lyman?"

Lyman crossed his legs and settled himself in his office chair.

"I have wanted to have a talk with you about that, sir," he said. "Yes, we will cut the rates—an average 10 per cent. cut throughout the State, as we are pledged. But I am going to warn you, Governor, and you, Harran; don't expect too much at first. The man who, even after twenty years' training in the operation of railroads, can draw an equitable, smoothly working schedule of freight rates between shipping point and common point, is capable of governing the United States. What with main lines, and leased lines, and points of transfer, and the laws governing common carriers, and the rulings of the Inter-State Commerce Commission, the whole matter has become so confused that Vanderbilt himself couldn't straighten it out. And how can it be expected that railroad commissions who are chosen—well, let's be frank—as ours was, for instance, from out a number of men who don't know the difference between a switching charge and a differential rate, are going to regulate the whole business in six months' time? Cut rates; yes, any fool can do that; any fool can write one dollar instead of two, but if you cut too low by a fraction of one per cent. and if the railroad can get out an injunction, tie you up and show that your new rate prevents the road being operated at a profit, how are you any better off?"

"Your conscientiousness does you credit, Lyman," said the Governor. "I respect you for it, my son. I know you will be fair to the railroad. That is all we want. Fairness to the corporation is fairness to the farmer, and we won't expect you to readjust the whole matter out of hand. Take your time. We can afford to wait."

"And suppose the next commission is a railroad board, and reverses all our figures?"

The one-time mining king, the most redoubtable poker player of Calaveras County, permitted himself a momentary twinkle of his eyes.

"By then it will be too late. We will, all of us, have made our fortunes by then."

The remark left Presley astonished out of all measure He never could accustom himself to these strange lapses in the Governor's character. Magnus was by nature a public man, judicious, deliberate, standing firm for principle, yet upon rare occasion, by some such remark as this, he would betray the presence of a sub-nature of recklessness, inconsistent, all at variance with his creeds and tenets.

At the very bottom, when all was said and done, Magnus remained the Forty-niner.

Deep down in his heart the spirit of the Adventurer yet persisted. "We will all of us have made fortunes by then." That was it precisely. "After us the deluge." For all his public spirit, for all his championship of justice and truth, his respect for law, Magnus remained the gambler, willing to play for colossal stakes, to hazard a fortune on the chance of winning a million. It was the true California spirit that found expression through him, the spirit of the West, unwilling to occupy itself with details, refusing to wait, to be patient, to achieve by legitimate plodding; the miner's instinct of wealth acquired in a single night prevailed, in spite of all. It was in this frame of mind that Magnus and the multitude of other ranchers of whom he was a type, farmed their ranches. They had no love for their land. They were not attached to the soil. They worked their ranches as a quarter of a century before they had worked their mines. To husband the resources of their marvellous San Joaquin, they considered niggardly, petty, Hebraic. To get all there was out of the land, to squeeze it dry, to exhaust it, seemed their policy. When, at last, the land worn out, would refuse to yield, they would invest their money in something else; by then, they would all have made fortunes. They did not care. "After us the deluge."

Lyman, however, was obviously uneasy, willing to change the subject. He rose to his feet, pulling down his cuffs.

"By the way," he observed, "I want you three to lunch with me to-day at my club. It is close by. You can wait there for news of the court's decision as well as anywhere else, and I should like to show you the place. I have just joined."

At the club, when the four men were seated at a small table in the round window of the main room, Lyman's popularity with all classes was very apparent. Hardly a man entered that did not call out a salutation to him, some even coming over to shake his hand. He seemed to be every man's friend, and to all he seemed equally genial. His affability, even to those whom he disliked, was unfailing.

"See that fellow yonder," he said to Magnus, indicating a certain middle-aged man, flamboyantly dressed, who wore his hair long, who was afflicted with sore eyes, and the collar of whose velvet coat was sprinkled with dandruff, "that's Hartrath, the artist, a man absolutely devoid of even the commonest decency. How he got in here is a mystery to me."

Yet, when this Hartrath came across to say "How do you do" to Lyman, Lyman was as eager in his cordiality as his warmest friend could have expected.

"Why the devil are you so chummy with him, then?" observed Harran when Hartrath had gone away.

Lyman's explanation was vague. The truth of the matter was, that Magnus's oldest son was consumed by inordinate ambition. Political preferment was his dream, and to the realisation of this dream popularity was an essential. Every man who could vote, blackguard or gentleman, was to be conciliated, if possible. He made it his study to become known throughout the entire community—to put influential men under obligations to himself. He never forgot a name or a face. With everybody he was the hail-fellow-well-met. His ambition was not trivial. In his disregard for small things, he resembled his father. Municipal office had no attraction for him. His goal was higher. He had planned his life twenty years ahead. Already Sheriff's Attorney, Assistant District Attorney and Railroad Commissioner, he could, if he desired, attain the office of District Attorney itself. Just now, it was a question with him whether or not it would be politic to fill this office. Would it advance or sidetrack him in the career he had outlined for himself? Lyman wanted to be something better than District Attorney, better than Mayor, than State Senator, or even than member of the United States Congress. He wanted to be, in fact, what his father was only in name—to succeed where Magnus had failed. He wanted to be governor of the State. He had put his teeth together, and, deaf to all other considerations, blind to all other issues, he worked with the infinite slowness, the unshakable tenacity of the coral insect to this one end.

After luncheon was over, Lyman ordered cigars and liqueurs, and with the three others returned to the main room of the club. However, their former place in the round window was occupied. A middle-aged man, with iron grey hair and moustache, who wore a frock coat and a white waistcoat, and in some indefinable manner suggested a retired naval officer, was sitting at their table smoking a long, thin cigar. At sight of him, Presley became animated. He uttered a mild exclamation:

"Why, isn't that Mr. Cedarquist?"

"Cedarquist?" repeated Lyman Derrick. "I know him well. Yes, of course, it is," he continued. "Governor, you must know him. He is one of our representative men. You would enjoy talking to him. He was the head of the big Atlas Iron Works. They have shut down recently, you know. Not failed exactly, but just ceased to be a paying investment, and Cedarquist closed them out. He has other interests, though. He's a rich man—a capitalist."

Lyman brought the group up to the gentleman in question and introduced them. "Mr. Magnus Derrick, of course," observed Cedarquist, as he took the Governor's hand. "I've known you by repute for some time, sir. This is a great pleasure, I assure you." Then, turning to Presley, he added: "Hello, Pres, my boy. How is the great, the very great Poem getting on?"

"It's not getting on at all, sir," answered Presley, in some embarrassment, as they all sat down. "In fact, I've about given up the idea. There's so much interest in what you might call 'living issues' down at Los Muertos now, that I'm getting further and further from it every day."

"I should say as much," remarked the manufacturer, turning towards Magnus. "I'm watching your fight with Shelgrim, Mr. Derrick, with every degree of interest." He raised his drink of whiskey and soda. "Here's success to you."

As he replaced his glass, the artist Hartrath joined the group uninvited. As a pretext, he engaged Lyman in conversation. Lyman, he believed, was a man with a "pull" at the City Hall. In connection with a projected Million-Dollar Fair and Flower Festival, which at that moment was the talk of the city, certain statues were to be erected, and Hartrath bespoke Lyman's influence to further the pretensions of a sculptor friend of his, who wished to be Art Director of the affair. In the matter of this Fair and Flower Festival, Hartrath was not lacking in enthusiasm. He addressed the others with extravagant gestures, blinking his inflamed eyelids.

"A million dollars," he exclaimed. "Hey! think of that. Why, do you know that we have five hundred thousand practically pledged already? Talk about public spirit, gentlemen, this is the most public-spirited city on the continent. And the money is not thrown away. We will have Eastern visitors here by the thousands—capitalists—men with money to invest. The million we spend on our fair will be money in our pockets. Ah, you should see how the women of this city are taking hold of the matter. They are giving all kinds of little entertainments, teas, 'Olde Tyme Singing Skules,' amateur theatricals, gingerbread fetes, all for the benefit of the fund, and the business men, too—pouring out their money like water. It is splendid, splendid, to see a community so patriotic."

The manufacturer, Cedarquist, fixed the artist with a glance of melancholy interest.

"And how much," he remarked, "will they contribute—your gingerbread women and public-spirited capitalists, towards the blowing up of the ruins of the Atlas Iron Works?"

"Blowing up? I don't understand," murmured the artist, surprised. "When you get your Eastern capitalists out here with your Million-Dollar Fair," continued Cedarquist, "you don't propose, do you, to let them see a Million-Dollar Iron Foundry standing idle, because of the indifference of San Francisco business men? They might ask pertinent questions, your capitalists, and we should have to answer that our business men preferred to invest their money in corner lots and government bonds, rather than to back up a legitimate, industrial enterprise. We don't want fairs. We want active furnaces. We don't want public statues, and fountains, and park extensions and gingerbread fetes. We want business enterprise. Isn't it like us? Isn't it like us?" he exclaimed sadly. "What a melancholy comment! San Francisco! It is not a city—it is a Midway Plaisance. California likes to be fooled. Do you suppose Shelgrim could convert the whole San Joaquin Valley into his back yard otherwise? Indifference to public affairs—absolute indifference, it stamps us all. Our State is the very paradise of fakirs. You and your Million-Dollar Fair!" He turned to Hartrath with a quiet smile. "It is just such men as you, Mr. Hartrath, that are the ruin of us. You organise a sham of tinsel and pasteboard, put on fool's cap and bells, beat a gong at a street corner, and the crowd cheers you and drops nickels into your hat. Your ginger-bread fete; yes, I saw it in full blast the other night on the grounds of one of your women's places on Sutter Street. I was on my way home from the last board meeting of the Atlas Company. A gingerbread fete, my God! and the Atlas plant shutting down for want of financial backing. A million dollars spent to attract the Eastern investor, in order to show him an abandoned rolling mill, wherein the only activity is the sale of remnant material and scrap steel."

Lyman, however, interfered. The situation was becoming strained. He tried to conciliate the three men—the artist, the manufacturer, and the farmer, the warring elements. But Hartrath, unwilling to face the enmity that he felt accumulating against him, took himself away. A picture of his—"A Study of the Contra Costa Foot-hills"—was to be raffled in the club rooms for the benefit of the Fair. He, himself, was in charge of the matter. He disappeared.

Cedarquist looked after him with contemplative interest. Then, turning to Magnus, excused himself for the acridity of his words.

"He's no worse than many others, and the people of this State and city are, after all, only a little more addle-headed than other Americans." It was his favourite topic. Sure of the interest of his hearers, he unburdened himself.

"If I were to name the one crying evil of American life, Mr. Derrick," he continued, "it would be the indifference of the better people to public affairs. It is so in all our great centres. There are other great trusts, God knows, in the United States besides our own dear P. and S. W. Railroad. Every State has its own grievance. If it is not a railroad trust, it is a sugar trust, or an oil trust, or an industrial trust, that exploits the People, BECAUSE THE PEOPLE ALLOW IT. The indifference of the People is the opportunity of the despot. It is as true as that the whole is greater than the part, and the maxim is so old that it is trite—it is laughable. It is neglected and disused for the sake of some new ingenious and complicated theory, some wonderful scheme of reorganisation, but the fact remains, nevertheless, simple, fundamental, everlasting. The People have but to say 'No,' and not the strongest tyranny, political, religious, or financial, that was ever organised, could survive one week."

The others, absorbed, attentive, approved, nodding their heads in silence as the manufacturer finished.

"That's one reason, Mr. Derrick," the other resumed after a moment, "why I have been so glad to meet you. You and your League are trying to say 'No' to the trust. I hope you will succeed. If your example will rally the People to your cause, you will. Otherwise—" he shook his head.

"One stage of the fight is to be passed this very day," observed Magnus. "My sons and myself are expecting hourly news from the City Hall, a decision in our case is pending."

"We are both of us fighters, it seems, Mr. Derrick," said Cedarquist. "Each with his particular enemy. We are well met, indeed, the farmer and the manufacturer, both in the same grist between the two millstones of the lethargy of the Public and the aggression of the Trust, the two great evils of modern America. Pres, my boy, there is your epic poem ready to hand."

But Cedarquist was full of another idea. Rarely did so favourable an opportunity present itself for explaining his theories, his ambitions. Addressing himself to Magnus, he continued:

"Fortunately for myself, the Atlas Company was not my only investment. I have other interests. The building of ships—steel sailing ships—has been an ambition of mine,—for this purpose, Mr. Derrick, to carry American wheat. For years, I have studied this question of American wheat, and at last, I have arrived at a theory. Let me explain. At present, all our California wheat goes to Liverpool, and from that port is distributed over the world. But a change is coming. I am sure of it. You young men," he turned to Presley, Lyman, and Harran, "will live to see it. Our century is about done. The great word of this nineteenth century has been Production. The great word of the twentieth century will be—listen to me, you youngsters—Markets. As a market for our Production—or let me take a concrete example—as a market for our WHEAT, Europe is played out. Population in Europe is not increasing fast enough to keep up with the rapidity of our production. In some cases, as in France, the population is stationary. WE, however, have gone on producing wheat at a tremendous rate.

"The result is over-production. We supply more than Europe can eat, and down go the prices. The remedy is NOT in the curtailing of our wheat areas, but in this, we MUST HAVE NEW MARKETS, GREATER MARKETS. For years we have been sending our wheat from East to West, from California to Europe. But the time will come when we must send it from West to East. We must march with the course of empire, not against it. I mean, we must look to China. Rice in China is losing its nutritive quality. The Asiatics, though, must be fed; if not on rice, then on wheat. Why, Mr. Derrick, if only one-half the population of China ate a half ounce of flour per man per day all the wheat areas in California could not feed them. Ah, if I could only hammer that into the brains of every rancher of the San Joaquin, yes, and of every owner of every bonanza farm in Dakota and Minnesota. Send your wheat to China; handle it yourselves; do away with the middleman; break up the Chicago wheat pits and elevator rings and mixing houses. When in feeding China you have decreased the European shipments, the effect is instantaneous. Prices go up in Europe without having the least effect upon the prices in China. We hold the key, we have the wheat,—infinitely more than we ourselves can eat. Asia and Europe must look to America to be fed. What fatuous neglect of opportunity to continue to deluge Europe with our surplus food when the East trembles upon the verge of starvation!"

The two men, Cedarquist and Magnus, continued the conversation a little further. The manufacturer's idea was new to the Governor. He was greatly interested. He withdrew from the conversation. Thoughtful, he leaned back in his place, stroking the bridge of his beak-like nose with a crooked forefinger.

Cedarquist turned to Harran and began asking details as to the conditions of the wheat growers of the San Joaquin. Lyman still maintained an attitude of polite aloofness, yawning occasionally behind three fingers, and Presley was left to the company of his own thoughts.

There had been a day when the affairs and grievances of the farmers of his acquaintance—Magnus, Annixter, Osterman, and old Broderson—had filled him only with disgust. His mind full of a great, vague epic poem of the West, he had kept himself apart, disdainful of what he chose to consider their petty squabbles. But the scene in Annixter's harness room had thrilled and uplifted him. He was palpitating with excitement all through the succeeding months. He abandoned the idea of an epic poem. In six months he had not written a single verse. Day after day he trembled with excitement as the relations between the Trust and League became more and more strained. He saw the matter in its true light. It was typical. It was the world-old war between Freedom and Tyranny, and at times his hatred of the railroad shook him like a crisp and withered reed, while the languid indifference of the people of the State to the quarrel filled him with a blind exasperation.

But, as he had once explained to Vanamee, he must find expression. He felt that he would suffocate otherwise. He had begun to keep a journal. As the inclination spurred him, he wrote down his thoughts and ideas in this, sometimes every day, sometimes only three or four times a month. Also he flung aside his books of poems—Milton, Tennyson, Browning, even Homer—and addressed himself to Mill, Malthus, Young, Poushkin, Henry George, Schopenhauer. He attacked the subject of Social Inequality with unbounded enthusiasm. He devoured, rather than read, and emerged from the affair, his mind a confused jumble of conflicting notions, sick with over-effort, raging against injustice and oppression, and with not one sane suggestion as to remedy or redress.

The butt of his cigarette scorched his fingers and roused him from his brooding. In the act of lighting another, he glanced across the room and was surprised to see two very prettily dressed young women in the company of an older gentleman, in a long frock coat, standing before Hartrath's painting, examining it, their heads upon one side.

Presley uttered a murmur of surprise. He, himself, was a member of the club, and the presence of women within its doors, except on special occasions, was not tolerated. He turned to Lyman Derrick for an explanation, but this other had also seen the women and abruptly exclaimed:

"I declare, I had forgotten about it. Why, this is Ladies' Day, of course."

"Why, yes," interposed Cedarquist, glancing at the women over his shoulder. "Didn't you know? They let 'em in twice a year, you remember, and this is a double occasion. They are going to raffle Hartrath's picture,—for the benefit of the

Gingerbread Fair. Why, you are not up to date, Lyman. This is a sacred and religious rite,—an important public event."

"Of course, of course," murmured Lyman. He found means to survey Harran and Magnus. Certainly, neither his father nor his brother were dressed for the function that impended. He had been stupid. Magnus invariably attracted attention, and now with his trousers strapped under his boots, his wrinkled frock coat—Lyman twisted his cuffs into sight with an impatient, nervous movement of his wrists, glancing a second time at his brother's pink face, forward curling, yellow hair and clothes of a country cut. But there was no help for it. He wondered what were the club regulations in the matter of bringing in visitors on Ladies' Day. "Sure enough, Ladies' Day," he remarked, "I am very glad you struck it, Governor. We can sit right where we are. I guess this is as good a place as any to see the crowd. It's a good chance to see all the big guns of the city. Do you expect your people here, Mr. Cedarquist?"

"My wife may come, and my daughters," said the manufacturer.

"Ah," murmured Presley, "so much the better. I was going to give myself the pleasure of calling upon your daughters, Mr. Cedarquist, this afternoon."

"You can save your carfare, Pres," said Cedarquist, "you will see them here."

No doubt, the invitations for the occasion had appointed one o'clock as the time, for between that hour and two, the guests arrived in an almost unbroken stream. From their point of vantage in the round window of the main room, Magnus, his two sons, and Presley looked on very interested. Cedarquist had excused himself, affirming that he must look out for his women folk.

Of every ten of the arrivals, seven, at least, were ladies. They entered the room—this unfamiliar masculine haunt, where their husbands, brothers, and sons spent so much of their time—with a certain show of hesitancy and little, nervous, oblique glances, moving their heads from side to side like a file of hens venturing into a strange barn. They came in groups, ushered by a single member of the club, doing the honours with effusive bows and polite gestures, indicating the various objects of interest, pictures, busts, and the like, that decorated the room.

Fresh from his recollections of Bonneville, Guadalajara, and the dance in Annixter's barn, Presley was astonished at the beauty of these women and the elegance of their toilettes. The crowd thickened rapidly. A murmur of conversation arose, subdued, gracious, mingled with the soft rustle of silk, grenadines, velvet. The scent of delicate perfumes spread in the air, Violet de Parme, Peau d'Espagne. Colours of the most harmonious blends appeared and disappeared at intervals in the slowly moving press, touches of lavender-tinted velvets, pale violet crepes and cream-coloured appliqued laces.

There seemed to be no need of introductions. Everybody appeared to be acquainted. There was no awkwardness, no constraint. The assembly disengaged an impression of refined pleasure. On every hand, innumerable dialogues seemed to go forward easily and naturally, without break or interruption, witty, engaging, the couple never at a loss for repartee. A third party was gracefully included, then a fourth. Little groups were formed,—groups that divided themselves, or melted into other groups, or disintegrated again into isolated pairs, or lost themselves in the background of the mass,—all without friction, without embarrassment,—the whole affair going forward of itself, decorous, tactful, well-bred.

At a distance, and not too loud, a stringed orchestra sent up a pleasing hum. Waiters, with brass buttons on their full dress coats, went from group to group, silent, unobtrusive, serving salads and ices.

But the focus of the assembly was the little space before Hartrath's painting. It was called "A Study of the Contra Costa Foothills," and was set in a frame of natural redwood, the bark still adhering. It was conspicuously displayed on an easel at the right of the entrance to the main room of the club, and was very large. In the foreground, and to the left, under the shade of a live-oak, stood a couple of reddish cows, knee-deep in a patch of yellow poppies, while in the right-hand corner, to balance the composition, was placed a girl in a pink dress and white sunbonnet, in which the shadows were indicated by broad dashes of pale blue paint. The ladies and young girls examined the production with little murmurs of admiration, hazarding remembered phrases, searching for the exact balance between generous praise and critical discrimination, expressing their opinions in the mild technicalities of the Art Books and painting classes. They spoke of atmospheric effects, of middle distance, of "chiaro-oscuro," of fore-shortening, of the decomposition of light, of the subordination of individuality to fidelity of interpretation.

One tall girl, with hair almost white in its blondness, having observed that the handling of the masses reminded her strongly of Corot, her companion, who carried a gold lorgnette by a chain around her neck, answered:

"Ah! Millet, perhaps, but not Corot."

This verdict had an immediate success. It was passed from group to group. It seemed to imply a delicate distinction that carried conviction at once. It was decided formally that the reddish brown cows in the picture were reminiscent of Daubigny, and that the handling of the masses was altogether Millet, but that the general effect was not quite Corot.

Presley, curious to see the painting that was the subject of so much discussion, had left the group in the round window, and stood close by Hartrath, craning his head over the shoulders of the crowd, trying to catch a glimpse of the reddish cows, the milk-maid and the blue painted foothills. He was suddenly aware of Cedarquist's voice in his ear, and, turning about, found himself face to face with the manufacturer, his wife and his two daughters.

There was a meeting. Salutations were exchanged, Presley shaking hands all around, expressing his delight at seeing his old friends once more, for he had known the family from his boyhood, Mrs. Cedarquist being his aunt. Mrs. Cedarquist and her two daughters declared that the air of Los Muertos must certainly have done him a world of good. He was stouter, there could be no doubt of it. A little pale, perhaps. He was fatiguing himself with his writing, no doubt. Ah, he must take care. Health was everything, after all. Had he been writing any more verse? Every month they scanned the magazines, looking for his name.

Mrs. Cedarquist was a fashionable woman, the president or chairman of a score of clubs. She was forever running after fads, appearing continually in the society wherein she moved with new and astounding proteges—fakirs whom she unearthed no one knew where, discovering them long in advance of her companions. Now it was a Russian Countess, with dirty finger nails, who travelled throughout America and borrowed money; now an Aesthete who possessed a wonderful collection of topaz gems, who submitted decorative schemes for the interior arrangement of houses and who "received" in Mrs. Cedarquist's drawing-rooms dressed in a white velvet cassock; now a widow of some Mohammedan of Bengal or Rajputana, who had a blue spot in the middle of her forehead and who solicited contributions for her sisters in affliction; now a certain bearded poet, recently back from the Klondike; now a decayed musician who had been ejected from a young ladies' musical conservatory of Europe because of certain surprising pamphlets on free love, and who had come to San Francisco to introduce the community to the music of Brahms; now a Japanese youth who wore spectacles and a grey flannel shirt and who, at intervals, delivered himself of the most astonishing poems, vague, unrhymed, unmetrical lucubrations, incoherent, bizarre; now a Christian Scientist, a lean, grey woman, whose creed was neither Christian nor scientific; now a university professor, with the bristling beard of an anarchist chief-of-section, and a roaring, guttural voice, whose intenseness left him gasping and apoplectic; now a civilised Cherokee with a mission; now a female elocutionist, whose forte was Byron's Songs of Greece; now a high caste Chinaman; now a miniature painter; now a tenor, a pianiste, a mandolin player, a missionary, a drawing master, a virtuoso, a collector, an Armenian, a botanist with a new flower, a critic with a new theory, a doctor with a new treatment.

And all these people had a veritable mania for declamation and fancy dress. The Russian Countess gave talks on the prisons of Siberia, wearing the headdress and pinchbeck ornaments of a Slav bride; the Aesthete, in his white cassock, gave readings on obscure questions of art and ethics. The widow of India, in the costume of her caste, described the social life of her people at home. The bearded poet, perspiring in furs and boots of reindeer skin, declaimed verses of his own composition about the wild life of the Alaskan mining camps. The Japanese youth, in the silk robes of the Samurai two-sworded nobles, read from his own works—"The flat-bordered earth, nailed down at night, rusting under the darkness," "The brave, upright rains that came down like errands from iron-bodied yore-time." The

Christian Scientist, in funereal, impressive black, discussed the contra-will and pan-psychic hylozoism. The university professor put on a full dress suit and lisle thread gloves at three in the afternoon and before literary clubs and circles bellowed extracts from Goethe and Schiler in the German, shaking his fists, purple with vehemence. The Cherokee, arrayed in fringed buckskin and blue beads, rented from a costumer, intoned folk songs of his people in the vernacular. The elocutionist in cheese-cloth toga and tin bracelets, rendered "The Isles of Greece, where burning Sappho loved and sung." The Chinaman, in the robes of a mandarin, lectured on Confucius. The Armenian, in fez and baggy trousers, spoke of the Unspeakable Turk. The mandolin player, dressed like a bull fighter, held musical conversaziones, interpreting the peasant songs of Andalusia.

It was the Fake, the eternal, irrepressible Sham; glib, nimble, ubiquitous, tricked out in all the paraphernalia of imposture, an endless defile of charlatans that passed interminably before the gaze of the city, marshalled by "lady presidents," exploited by clubs of women, by literary societies, reading circles, and culture organisations. The attention the Fake received, the time devoted to it, the money which it absorbed, were incredible. It was all one that impostor after impostor was exposed; it was all one that the clubs, the circles, the societies were proved beyond doubt to have been swindled. The more the Philistine press of the city railed and guyed, the more the women rallied to the defence of their protege of the hour. That their favourite was persecuted, was to them a veritable rapture. Promptly they invested the apostle of culture with the glamour of a martyr.

The fakirs worked the community as shell-game tricksters work a county fair, departing with bursting pocket-books, passing on the word to the next in line, assured that the place was not worked out, knowing well that there was enough for all.

More frequently the public of the city, unable to think of more than one thing at one time, prostrated itself at the feet of a single apostle, but at other moments, such as the present, when a Flower Festival or a Million-Dollar Fair aroused enthusiasm in all quarters, the occasion was one of gala for the entire Fake. The decayed professors, virtuosi, litterateurs, and artists thronged to the place en masse. Their clamour filled all the air. On every hand one heard the scraping of violins, the tinkling of mandolins, the suave accents of "art talks," the incoherencies of poets, the declamation of elocutionists, the inarticulate wanderings of the Japanese, the confused mutterings of the Cherokee, the guttural bellowing of the German university professor, all in the name of the Million-Dollar Fair. Money to the extent of hundreds of thousands was set in motion.

Mrs. Cedarquist was busy from morning until night. One after another, she was introduced to newly arrived fakirs. To each poet, to each litterateur, to each professor she addressed the same question:

"How long have you known you had this power?"

She spent her days in one quiver of excitement and jubilation. She was "in the movement." The people of the city were awakening to a Realisation of the Beautiful, to a sense of the higher needs of life. This was Art, this was Literature, this was Culture and Refinement. The Renaissance had appeared in the West.

She was a short, rather stout, red-faced, very much over-dressed little woman of some fifty years. She was rich in her own name, even before her marriage, being a relative of Shelgrim himself and on familiar terms with the great financier and his family. Her husband, while deploring the policy of the railroad, saw no good reason for quarrelling with Shelgrim, and on more than one occasion had dined at his house. On this occasion, delighted that she had come upon a "minor poet," she insisted upon presenting him to Hartrath.

"You two should have so much in common," she explained.

Presley shook the flaccid hand of the artist, murmuring conventionalities, while Mrs. Cedarquist hastened to say:

"I am sure you know Mr. Presley's verse, Mr. Hartrath. You should, believe me. You two have much in common. I can see so much that is alike in your modes of interpreting nature. In Mr. Presley's sonnet, 'The Better Part,' there is the same note as in your picture, the same sincerity of tone, the same subtlety of touch, the same nuances,—ah."

"Oh, my dear Madame," murmured the artist, interrupting Presley's impatient retort; "I am a mere bungler. You don't mean quite that, I am sure. I am too sensitive. It is my cross. Beauty," he closed his sore eyes with a little expression of pain, "beauty unmans me."

But Mrs. Cedarquist was not listening. Her eyes were fixed on the artist's luxuriant hair, a thick and glossy mane, that all but covered his coat collar.

"Leonine!" she murmured— "leonine! Like Samson of old."

However, abruptly bestirring herself, she exclaimed a second later:

"But I must run away. I am selling tickets for you this afternoon, Mr. Hartrath. I am having such success. Twenty-five already. Mr. Presley, you will take two chances, I am sure, and, oh, by the way, I have such good news. You know I am one of the lady members of the subscription committee for our Fair, and you know we approached Mr. Shelgrim for a donation to help along. Oh, such a liberal patron, a real Lorenzo di' Medici. In the name of the Pacific and Southwestern he has subscribed, think of it, five thousand dollars; and yet they will talk of the meanness of the railroad."

"Possibly it is to his interest," murmured Presley. "The fairs and festivals bring people to the city over his railroad."

But the others turned on him, expostulating.

"Ah, you Philistine," declared Mrs. Cedarquist. "And this from YOU!, Presley; to attribute such base motives—"

"If the poets become materialised, Mr. Presley," declared Hartrath, "what can we say to the people?"

"And Shelgrim encourages your million-dollar fairs and fetes," said a voice at Presley's elbow, "because it is throwing dust in the people's eyes."

The group turned about and saw Cedarquist, who had come up unobserved in time to catch the drift of the talk. But he spoke without bitterness; there was even a good-humoured twinkle in his eyes.

"Yes," he continued, smiling, "our dear Shelgrim promotes your fairs, not only as Pres says, because it is money in his pocket, but because it amuses the people, distracts their attention from the doings of his railroad. When Beatrice was a baby and had little colics, I used to jingle my keys in front of her nose, and it took her attention from the pain in her tummy; so Shelgrim."

The others laughed good-humouredly, protesting, nevertheless, and Mrs. Cedarquist shook her finger in warning at the artist and exclaimed:

"The Philistines be upon thee, Samson!"

"By the way," observed Hartrath, willing to change the subject, "I hear you are on the Famine Relief Committee. Does your work progress?"

"Oh, most famously, I assure you," she said. "Such a movement as we have started. Those poor creatures. The photographs of them are simply dreadful. I had the committee to luncheon the other day and we passed them around. We are getting subscriptions from all over the State, and Mr. Cedarquist is to arrange for the ship."

The Relief Committee in question was one of a great number that had been formed in California—and all over the Union, for the matter of that—to provide relief for the victims of a great famine in Central India. The whole world had been struck with horror at the reports of suffering and mortality in the affected districts, and had hastened to send aid. Certain women of San Francisco, with Mrs. Cedarquist at their head, had organised a number of committees, but the manufacturer's wife turned the meetings of these committees into social affairs—luncheons, teas, where one discussed the ways and means of assisting the starving Asiatics over teacups and plates of salad.

Shortly afterward a mild commotion spread throughout the assemblage of the club's guests. The drawing of the numbers in the raffle was about to be made. Hartrath, in a flurry of agitation, excused himself. Cedarquist took Presley by the arm.

"Pres, let's get out of this," he said. "Come into the wine room and I will shake you for a glass of sherry."

They had some difficulty in extricating themselves. The main room where the drawing was to take place suddenly became densely thronged. All the guests pressed eagerly about the table near the picture, upon which one of the hall boys had just placed a ballot box containing the numbers. The ladies, holding their tickets in their hands, pushed forward. A staccato chatter of excited murmurs arose. "What became of Harran and Lyman and the Governor?" inquired Presley.

Lyman had disappeared, alleging a business engagement, but Magnus and his younger son had retired to the library of the club on the floor above. It was almost deserted. They were deep in earnest conversation.

"Harran," said the Governor, with decision, "there is a deal, there, in what Cedarquist says. Our wheat to China, hey, boy?"

"It is certainly worth thinking of, sir."

"It appeals to me, boy; it appeals to me. It's big and there's a fortune in it. Big chances mean big returns; and I know—your old father isn't a back number yet, Harran—I may not have so wide an outlook as our friend Cedarquist, but I am quick to see my chance. Boy, the whole East is opening, disintegrating before the Anglo-Saxon. It is time that bread stuffs, as well, should make markets for themselves in the Orient. Just at this moment, too, when Lyman will scale down freight rates so we can haul to tidewater at little cost."

Magnus paused again, his frown beetling, and in the silence the excited murmur from the main room of the club, the soprano chatter of a multitude of women, found its way to the deserted library.

"I believe it's worth looking into, Governor," asserted Harran.

Magnus rose, and, his hands behind him, paced the floor of the library a couple of times, his imagination all stimulated and vivid. The great gambler perceived his Chance, the kaleidoscopic shifting of circumstances that made a Situation. It had come silently, unexpectedly. He had not seen its approach. Abruptly he woke one morning to see the combination realised. But also he saw a vision. A sudden and abrupt revolution in the Wheat. A new world of markets discovered, the matter as important as the discovery of America. The torrent of wheat was to be diverted, flowing back upon itself in a sudden, colossal eddy, stranding the middleman, the ENTRE-PRENEUR, the elevator-and mixing-house men dry and despairing, their occupation gone. He saw the farmer suddenly emancipated, the world's food no longer at the mercy of the speculator, thousands upon thousands of men set free of the grip of Trust and ring and monopoly acting for themselves, selling their own wheat, organising into one gigantic trust, themselves, sending their agents to all the entry ports of China. Himself, Annixter, Broderson and Osterman would pool their issues. He would convince them of the magnificence of the new movement. They would be its pioneers. Harran would be sent to Hong Kong to represent the four. They would charter—probably buy—a ship, perhaps one of Cedarquist's, American built, the nation's flag at the peak, and the sailing of that ship, gorged with the crops from Broderson's and Osterman's ranches, from Quien Sabe and Los Muertos, would be like the sailing of the caravels from Palos. It would mark a new era; it would make an epoch.

With this vision still expanding before the eye of his mind, Magnus, with Harran at his elbow, prepared to depart.

They descended to the lower floor and involved themselves for a moment in the throng of fashionables that blocked the hallway and the entrance to the main room, where the numbers of the raffle were being drawn. Near the head of the stairs they encountered Presley and Cedarquist, who had just come out of the wine room.

Magnus, still on fire with the new idea, pressed a few questions upon the manufacturer before bidding him good-bye. He wished to talk further upon the great subject, interested as to details, but Cedarquist was vague in his replies. He was no farmer, he hardly knew wheat when he saw it, only he knew the trend of the world's affairs; he felt them to be setting inevitably eastward.

However, his very vagueness was a further inspiration to the Governor. He swept details aside. He saw only the grand coup, the huge results, the East conquered, the march of empire rolling westward, finally arriving at its starting point, the vague, mysterious Orient.

He saw his wheat, like the crest of an advancing billow, crossing the Pacific, bursting upon Asia, flooding the Orient in a golden torrent. It was the new era. He had lived to see the death of the old and the birth of the new; first the mine, now the ranch; first gold, now wheat. Once again he became the pioneer, hardy, brilliant, taking colossal chances, blazing the way, grasping a fortune—a million in a single day. All the bigness of his nature leaped up again within him. At the magnitude of the inspiration he felt young again, indomitable, the leader at last, king of his fellows, wresting from fortune at this eleventh hour, before his old age, the place of high command which so long had been denied him. At last he could achieve.

Abruptly Magnus was aware that some one had spoken his name. He looked about and saw behind him, at a little distance, two gentlemen, strangers to him. They had withdrawn from the crowd into a little recess. Evidently having no women to look after, they had lost interest in the afternoon's affair. Magnus realised that they had not seen him. One of them was reading aloud to his companion from an evening edition of that day's newspaper. It was in the course of this reading that Magnus caught the sound of his name. He paused, listening, and Presley, Harran and Cedarquist followed his example. Soon they all understood. They were listening to the report of the judge's decision, for which Magnus was waiting—the decision in the case of the League vs. the Railroad. For the moment, the polite clamour of the raffle hushed itself—the winning number was being drawn. The guests held their breath, and in the ensuing silence Magnus and the others heard these words distinctly:

".... It follows that the title to the lands in question is in the plaintiff—the Pacific and Southwestern Railroad, and the defendants have no title, and their possession is wrongful. There must be findings and judgment for the plaintiff, and it is so ordered."

In spite of himself, Magnus paled. Harran shut his teeth with an oath. Their exaltation of the previous moment collapsed like a pyramid of cards. The vision of the new movement of the wheat, the conquest of the East, the invasion of the Orient, seemed only the flimsiest mockery. With a brusque wrench, they were snatched back to reality. Between them and the vision, between the fecund San Joaquin, reeking with fruitfulness, and the millions of Asia crowding toward the verge of starvation, lay the iron-hearted monster of steel and steam, implacable, insatiable, huge—its entrails gorged with the life blood that it sucked from an entire commonwealth, its ever hungry maw glutted with the harvests that should have fed the famished bellies of the whole world of the Orient.

But abruptly, while the four men stood there, gazing into each other's faces, a vigorous hand-clapping broke out. The raffle of Hartrath's picture was over, and as Presley turned about he saw Mrs. Cedarquist and her two daughters signalling eagerly to the manufacturer, unable to reach him because of the intervening crowd. Then Mrs. Cedarquist raised her voice and cried:

"I've won. I've won."

Unnoticed, and with but a brief word to Cedarquist, Magnus and Harran went down the marble steps leading to the street door, silent, Harran's arm tight around his father's shoulder.

At once the orchestra struck into a lively air. A renewed murmur of conversation broke out, and Cedarquist, as he said good-bye to Presley, looked first at the retreating figures of the ranchers, then at the gayly dressed throng of beautiful women and debonair young men, and indicating the whole scene with a single gesture, said, smiling sadly as he spoke:

"Not a city, Presley, not a city, but a Midway Plaisance."

II

Underneath the Long Trestle where Broderson Creek cut the line of the railroad and the Upper Road, the ground was low and covered with a second growth of grey green willows. Along the borders of the creek were occasional marshy spots, and now and then Hilma Tree came here to gather water-cresses, which she made into salads.

The place was picturesque, secluded, an oasis of green shade in all the limitless, flat monotony of the surrounding wheat lands. The creek had eroded deep into the little gully, and no matter how hot it was on the baking, shimmering levels of the ranches above, down here one always found one's self enveloped in an odorous, moist coolness. From time to time, the incessant murmur of the creek, pouring over and around the larger stones, was interrupted by the thunder of trains roaring out upon the trestle overhead, passing on with the furious gallop of their hundreds of iron wheels, leaving in the air a taint of hot oil, acrid smoke, and reek of escaping steam.

On a certain afternoon, in the spring of the year, Hilma was returning to Quien

Sabe from Hooven's by the trail that led from Los Muertos to Annixter's ranch houses, under the trestle. She had spent the afternoon with Minna Hooven, who, for the time being, was kept indoors because of a wrenched ankle. As Hilma descended into the gravel flats and thickets of willows underneath the trestle, she decided that she would gather some cresses for her supper that night. She found a spot around the base of one of the supports of the trestle where the cresses grew thickest, and plucked a couple of handfuls, washing them in the creek and pinning them up in her handkerchief. It made a little, round, cold bundle, and Hilma, warm from her walk, found a delicious enjoyment in pressing the damp ball of it to her cheeks and neck.

For all the change that Annixter had noted in her upon the occasion of the barn dance, Hilma remained in many things a young child. She was never at loss for enjoyment, and could always amuse herself when left alone. Just now, she chose to drink from the creek, lying prone on the ground, her face half-buried in the water, and this, not because she was thirsty, but because it was a new way to drink. She imagined herself a belated traveller, a poor girl, an outcast, quenching her thirst at the wayside brook, her little packet of cresses doing duty for a bundle of clothes. Night was coming on. Perhaps it would storm. She had nowhere to go. She would apply at a hut for shelter.

Abruptly, the temptation to dabble her feet in the creek presented itself to her. Always she had liked to play in the water. What a delight now to take off her shoes and stockings and wade out into the shallows near the bank! She had worn low shoes that afternoon, and the dust of the trail had filtered in above the edges. At times, she felt the grit and grey sand on the soles of her feet, and the sensation had set her teeth on edge. What a delicious alternative the cold, clean water suggested, and how easy it would be to do as she pleased just then, if only she were a little girl. In the end, it was stupid to be grown up.

Sitting upon the bank, one finger tucked into the heel of her shoe, Hilma hesitated. Suppose a train should come! She fancied she could see the engineer leaning from the cab with a great grin on his face, or the brakeman shouting gibes at her from the platform. Abruptly she blushed scarlet. The blood throbbed in her temples. Her heart beat. Since the famous evening of the barn dance, Annixter had spoken to her but twice. Hilma no longer looked after the ranch house these days. The thought of setting foot within Annixter's dining-room and bed-room terrified her, and in the end her mother had taken over that part of her work. Of the two meetings with the master of Quien Sabe, one had been a mere exchange of good mornings as the two happened to meet over by the artesian well; the other, more complicated, had occurred in the dairy-house again, Annixter, pretending to look over the new cheese press, asking about details of her work. When this had happened on that previous occasion, ending with Annixter's attempt to kiss her, Hilma had been talkative enough, chattering on from one subject to another, never at a loss for a theme. But this last time was a veritable ordeal. No sooner had Annixter appeared than her heart leaped and quivered like that of the hound-harried doe. Her speech failed her. Throughout the whole brief interview she had been miserably tongue-tied, stammering monosyllables, confused, horribly awkward, and when Annixter had gone away, she had fled to her little room, and bolting the door, had flung herself face downward on the bed and wept as though her heart were breaking, she did not know why.

That Annixter had been overwhelmed with business all through the winter was an inexpressible relief to Hilma. His affairs took him away from the ranch continually. He was absent sometimes for weeks, making trips to San Francisco, or to Sacramento, or to Bonneville. Perhaps he was forgetting her, overlooking her; and while, at first, she told herself that she asked nothing better, the idea of it began to occupy her mind. She began to wonder if it was really so.

She knew his trouble. Everybody did. The news of the sudden forward movement of the Railroad's forces, inaugurating the campaign, had flared white-hot and blazing all over the country side. To Hilma's notion, Annixter's attitude was heroic beyond all expression. His courage in facing the Railroad, as he had faced Delaney in the barn, seemed to her the pitch of sublimity. She refused to see any auxiliaries aiding him in his fight. To her imagination, the great League, which all the ranchers were joining, was a mere form. Single-handed, Annixter fronted the monster. But for him the corporation would gobble Quien Sabe, as a whale would a minnow. He was a hero who stood between them all and destruction. He was a protector of her family. He was her champion. She began to mention him in her prayers every night, adding a further petition to the effect that he would become a good man, and that he should not swear so much, and that he should never meet Delaney again.

However, as Hilma still debated the idea of bathing her feet in the creek, a train did actually thunder past overhead—the regular evening Overland,—the through express, that never stopped between Bakersfield and Fresno. It stormed by with a deafening clamour, and a swirl of smoke, in a long succession of way-coaches, and chocolate coloured Pullmans, grimy with the dust of the great deserts of the Southwest. The quivering of the trestle's supports set a tremble in the ground underfoot. The thunder of wheels drowned all sound of the flowing of the creek, and also the noise of the buckskin mare's hoofs descending from the trail upon the gravel about the creek, so that Hilma, turning about after the passage of the train, saw Annixter close at hand, with the abruptness of a vision.

He was looking at her, smiling as he rarely did, the firm line of his out-thrust lower lip relaxed good-humouredly. He had taken off his campaign hat to her, and though his stiff, yellow hair was twisted into a bristling mop, the little persistent tuft on the crown, usually defiantly erect as an Apache's scalp-lock, was nowhere in sight.

"Hello, it's you, is it, Miss Hilma?" he exclaimed, getting down from the buckskin, and allowing her to drink.

Hilma nodded, scrambling to her feet, dusting her skirt with nervous pats of both hands.

Annixter sat down on a great rock close by and, the loop of the bridle over his arm, lit a cigar, and began to talk. He complained of the heat of the day, the bad condition of the Lower Road, over which he had come on his way from a committee meeting of the League at Los Muertos; of the slowness of the work on the irrigating ditch, and, as a matter of course, of the general hard times.

"Miss Hilma," he said abruptly, "never you marry a ranchman. He's never out of trouble."

Hilma gasped, her eyes widening till the full round of the pupil was disclosed. Instantly, a certain, inexplicable guiltiness overpowered her with incredible confusion. Her hands trembled as she pressed the bundle of cresses into a hard ball between her palms.

Annixter continued to talk. He was disturbed and excited himself at this unexpected meeting. Never through all the past winter months of strenuous activity, the fever of political campaigns, the harrowing delays and ultimate defeat in one law court after another, had he forgotten the look in Hilma's face as he stood with one arm around her on the floor of his barn, in peril of his life from the buster's revolver. That dumb confession of Hilma's wide-open eyes had been enough for him. Yet, somehow, he never had had a chance to act upon it. During the short period when he could be on his ranch Hilma had always managed to avoid him. Once, even, she had spent a month, about Christmas time, with her mother's father, who kept a hotel in San Francisco.

Now, to-day, however, he had her all to himself. He would put an end to the situation that troubled him, and vexed him, day after day, month after month. Beyond question, the moment had come for something definite, he could not say precisely what. Readjusting his cigar between his teeth, he resumed his speech. It suited his humour to take the girl into his confidence, following an instinct which warned him that this would bring about a certain closeness of their relations, a certain intimacy.

"What do you think of this row, anyways, Miss Hilma,—this railroad fuss in general? Think Shelgrim and his rushers are going to jump Quien Sabe—are going to run us off the ranch?"

"Oh, no, sir," protested Hilma, still breathless. "Oh, no, indeed not."

"Well, what then?"

Hilma made a little uncertain movement of ignorance.

"I don't know what."

"Well, the League agreed to-day that if the test cases were lost in the Supreme Court—you know we've appealed to the Supreme Court, at Washington—we'd fight."

"Fight?"

"Yes, fight."

"Fight like—like you and Mr. Delaney that time with—oh, dear—with guns?"

"I don't know," grumbled Annixter vaguely. "What do YOU think?"

Hilma's low-pitched, almost husky voice trembled a little as she replied, "Fighting—with guns—that's so terrible. Oh, those revolvers in the barn! I can hear them yet. Every shot seemed like the explosion of tons of powder."

"Shall we clear out, then? Shall we let Delaney have possession, and S. Behrman, and all that lot? Shall we give in to them?"

"Never, never," she exclaimed, her great eyes flashing.

"YOU wouldn't like to be turned out of your home, would you, Miss Hilma, because Quien Sabe is your home isn't it? You've lived here ever since you were as big as a minute. You wouldn't like to have S. Behrman and the rest of 'em turn you out?"

"N-no," she murmured. "No, I shouldn't like that. There's mamma and—"

"Well, do you think for one second I'm going to let 'em?" cried Annixter, his teeth tightening on his cigar. "You stay right where you are. I'll take care of you, right enough. Look here," he demanded abruptly, "you've no use for that roaring lush, Delaney, have you?"

"I think he is a wicked man," she declared. "I know the Railroad has pretended to sell him part of the ranch, and he lets Mr. S. Behrman and Mr. Ruggles just use him."

"Right. I thought you wouldn't be keen on him."

There was a long pause. The buckskin began blowing among the pebbles, nosing for grass, and Annixter shifted his cigar to the other corner of his mouth.

"Pretty place," he muttered, looking around him. Then he added: "Miss Hilma, see here, I want to have a kind of talk with you, if you don't mind. I don't know just how to say these sort of things, and if I get all balled up as I go along, you just set it down to the fact that I've never had any experience in dealing with feemale girls; understand? You see, ever since the barn dance—yes, and long before then—I've been thinking a lot about you. Straight, I have, and I guess you know it. You're about the only girl that I ever knew well, and I guess," he declared deliberately, "you're about the only one I want to know. It's my nature. You didn't say anything that time when we stood there together and Delaney was playing the fool, but, somehow, I got the idea that you didn't want Delaney to do for me one little bit; that if he'd got me then you would have been sorrier than if he'd got any one else. Well, I felt just that way about you. I would rather have had him shoot any other girl in the room than you; yes, or in the whole State. Why, if anything should happen to you, Miss Hilma—well, I wouldn't care to go on with anything. S. Behrman could jump Quien Sabe, and welcome. And Delaney could shoot me full of holes whenever he got good and ready. I'd quit. I'd lay right down. I wouldn't care a whoop about anything any more. You are the only girl for me in the whole world. I didn't think so at first. I didn't want to. But seeing you around every day, and seeing how pretty you were, and how clever, and hearing your voice and all, why, it just got all inside of me somehow, and now I can't think of anything else. I hate to go to San Francisco, or Sacramento, or Visalia, or even Bonneville, for only a day, just because you aren't there, in any of those places, and I just rush what I've got to do so as I can get back here. While you were away that Christmas time, why, I was as lonesome as—oh, you don't know anything about it. I just scratched off the days on the calendar every night, one by one, till you got back. And it just comes to this, I want you with me all the time. I want you should have a home that's my home, too. I want to take care of you, and have you all for myself, you understand. What do you say?"

Hilma, standing up before him, retied a knot in her handkerchief bundle with elaborate precaution, blinking at it through her tears.

"What do you say, Miss Hilma?" Annixter repeated. "How about that? What do you say?"

Just above a whisper, Hilma murmured:

"I—I don't know."

"Don't know what? Don't you think we could hit it off together?"

"I don't know."

"I know we could, Hilma. I don't mean to scare you. What are you crying for?"

"I don't know."

Annixter got up, cast away his cigar, and dropping the buckskin's bridle, came and stood beside her, putting a hand on her shoulder. Hilma did not move, and he felt her trembling. She still plucked at the knot of the handkerchief. "I can't do without you, little girl," Annixter continued, "and I want you. I want you bad. I don't get much fun out of life ever. It, sure, isn't my nature, I guess. I'm a hard man. Everybody is trying to down me, and now I'm up against the Railroad. I'm fighting 'em all, Hilma, night and day, lock, stock, and barrel, and I'm fighting now for my home, my land, everything I have in the world. If I win out, I want somebody to be glad with me. If I don't—I want somebody to be sorry for me, sorry with me,—and that somebody is you. I am dog-tired of going it alone. I want some one to back me up. I want to feel you alongside of me, to give me a touch of the shoulder now and then. I'm tired of fighting for THINGS—land, property, money. I want to fight for some PERSON—somebody beside myself. Understand? want to feel that it isn't all selfishness—that there are other interests than mine in the game—that there's some one dependent on me, and that's thinking of me as I'm thinking of them—some one I can come home to at night and put my arm around—like this, and have her put her two arms around me—like—" He paused a second, and once again, as it had been in that moment of imminent peril, when he stood with his arm around her, their eyes met,—"put her two arms around me," prompted Annixter, half smiling, "like—like what, Hilma?"

"I don't know."

"Like what, Hilma?" he insisted.

"Like—like this?" she questioned. With a movement of infinite tenderness and affection she slid her arms around his neck, still crying a little.

The sensation of her warm body in his embrace, the feeling of her smooth, round arm, through the thinness of her sleeve, pressing against his cheek, thrilled Annixter with a delight such as he had never known. He bent his head and kissed her upon the nape of her neck, where the delicate amber tint melted into the thick, sweet smelling mass of her dark brown hair. She shivered a little, holding him closer, ashamed as yet to look up. Without speech, they stood there for a long minute, holding each other close. Then Hilma pulled away from him, mopping her tear-stained cheeks with the little moist ball of her handkerchief.

"What do you say? Is it a go?" demanded Annixter jovially.

"I thought I hated you all the time," she said, and the velvety huskiness of her voice never sounded so sweet to him.

"And I thought it was that crockery smashing goat of a lout of a cow-puncher."

"Delaney? The idea! Oh, dear! I think it must always have been you."

"Since when, Hilma?" he asked, putting his arm around her. "Ah, but it is good to have you, my girl," he exclaimed, delighted beyond words that she permitted this freedom. "Since when? Tell us all about it."

"Oh, since always. It was ever so long before I came to think of you—to, well, to think about—I mean to remember—oh, you know what I mean. But when I did, oh, THEN!"

"Then what?"

"I don't know—I haven't thought—that way long enough to know."

"But you said you thought it must have been me always."

"I know; but that was different—oh, I'm all mixed up. I'm so nervous and trembly now. Oh," she cried suddenly, her face overcast with a look of earnestness and great seriousness, both her hands catching at his wrist, "Oh, you WILL be good to me, now, won't you? I'm only a little, little child in so many ways, and I've given myself to you, all in a minute, and I can't go back of it now, and it's for always. I don't know how it happened or why. Sometimes I think I didn't wish it, but now it's done, and I am glad and happy. But NOW if you weren't good to me—oh, think of how it would be with me. You are strong, and big, and rich, and I am only a servant of yours, a little nobody, but I've given all I had to you—myself—and you must be so good to me now. Always remember that. Be good to me and be gentle and kind to me in LITTLE things,—in everything, or you will break my heart."

Annixter took her in his arms. He was speechless. No words that he had at his command seemed adequate. All he could say was:

"That's all right, little girl. Don't you be frightened. I'll take care of you. That's all right, that's all right."

For a long time they sat there under the shade of the great trestle, their arms about each other, speaking only at intervals. An hour passed. The buckskin, finding no feed to her taste, took the trail stablewards, the bridle dragging. Annixter let her go. Rather than to take his arm from around Hilma's waist he would have lost his whole stable. At last, however, he bestirred himself and began to talk. He thought it time to formulate some plan of action.

"Well, now, Hilma, what are we going to do?"

"Do?" she repeated. "Why, must we do anything? Oh, isn't this enough?"

"There's better ahead," he went on. "I want to fix you up somewhere where you can have a bit of a home all to yourself. Let's see; Bonneville wouldn't do. There's always a lot of yaps about there that know us, and they would begin to cackle first off. How about San Francisco. We might go up next week and have a look around. I would find rooms you could take somewheres, and we would fix 'em up as lovely as how-do-you-do."

"Oh, but why go away from Quien Sabe?" she protested. "And, then, so soon, too. Why must we have a wedding trip, now that you are so busy? Wouldn't it be better—oh, I tell you, we could go to Monterey after we were married, for a little week, where mamma's people live, and then come back here to the ranch house and settle right down where we are and let me keep house for you. I wouldn't even want a single servant."

Annixter heard and his face grew troubled.

"Hum," he said, "I see."

He gathered up a handful of pebbles and began snapping them carefully into the creek. He fell thoughtful. Here was a phase of the affair he had not planned in the least. He had supposed all the time that Hilma took his meaning. His old suspicion that she was trying to get a hold on him stirred again for a moment. There was no good of such talk as that. Always these feemale girls seemed crazy to get married, bent on complicating the situation.

"Isn't that best?" said Hilma, glancing at him.

"I don't know," he muttered gloomily.

"Well, then, let's not. Let's come right back to Quien Sabe without going to Monterey. Anything that you want I want."

"I hadn't thought of it in just that way," he observed.

"In what way, then?"

"Can't we—can't we wait about this marrying business?"

"That's just it," she said gayly. "I said it was too soon. There would be so much to do between whiles. Why not say at the end of the summer?"

"Say what?"

"Our marriage, I mean."

"Why get married, then? What's the good of all that fuss about it? I don't go anything upon a minister puddling round in my affairs. What's the difference, anyhow? We understand each other. Isn't that enough? Pshaw, Hilma, I'M no marrying man."

She looked at him a moment, bewildered, then slowly she took his meaning. She rose to her feet, her eyes wide, her face paling with terror. He did not look at her, but he could hear the catch in her throat.

"Oh!" she exclaimed, with a long, deep breath, and again "Oh!" the back of her hand against her lips.

It was a quick gasp of a veritable physical anguish. Her eyes brimmed over. Annixter rose, looking at her.

"Well?" he said, awkwardly, "Well?"

Hilma leaped back from him with an instinctive recoil of her whole being, throwing out her hands in a gesture of defence, fearing she knew not what. There was as yet no sense of insult in her mind, no outraged modesty. She was only terrified. It was as though searching for wild flowers she had come suddenly upon a snake.

She stood for an instant, spellbound, her eyes wide, her bosom swelling; then, all at once, turned and fled, darting across the plank that served for a foot bridge over the creek, gaining the opposite bank and disappearing with a brisk rustle of underbrush, such as might have been made by the flight of a frightened fawn.

Abruptly Annixter found himself alone. For a moment he did not move, then he picked up his campaign hat, carefully creased its limp crown and put it on his head and stood for a moment, looking vaguely at the ground on both sides of him. He went away without uttering a word, without change of countenance, his hands in his pockets, his feet taking great strides along the trail in the direction of the ranch house.

He had no sight of Hilma again that evening, and the next morning he was up early and did not breakfast at the ranch house. Business of the League called him to Bonneville to confer with Magnus and the firm of lawyers retained by the League to fight the land-grabbing cases. An appeal was to be taken to the Supreme Court at Washington, and it was to be settled that day which of the cases involved should be considered as test cases.

Instead of driving or riding into Bonneville, as he usually did, Annixter took an early morning train, the Bakersfield-Fresno local at Guadalajara, and went to Bonneville by rail, arriving there at twenty minutes after seven and breakfasting by appointment with Magnus Derrick and Osterman at the Yosemite House, on Main Street.

The conference of the committee with the lawyers took place in a front room of the Yosemite, one of the latter bringing with him his clerk, who made a stenographic report of the proceedings and took carbon copies of all letters written. The conference was long and complicated, the business transacted of the utmost moment, and it was not until two o'clock that Annixter found himself at liberty.

However, as he and Magnus descended into the lobby of the hotel, they were aware of an excited and interested group collected about the swing doors that opened from the lobby of the Yosemite into the bar of the same name. Dyke was there—even at a distance they could hear the reverberation of his deep-toned voice, uplifted in wrath and furious expostulation. Magnus and Annixter joined the group wondering, and all at once fell full upon the first scene of a drama.

That same morning Dyke's mother had awakened him according to his instructions at daybreak. A consignment of his hop poles from the north had arrived at the freight office of the P. and S. W. in Bonneville, and he was to drive in on his farm wagon and bring them out. He would have a busy day.

"Hello, hello," he said, as his mother pulled his ear to arouse him; "morning, mamma."

"It's time," she said, "after five already. Your breakfast is on the stove."

He took her hand and kissed it with great affection. He loved his mother devotedly, quite as much as he did the little tad. In their little cottage, in the forest of green hops that surrounded them on every hand, the three led a joyous and secluded life, contented, industrious, happy, asking nothing better. Dyke, himself, was a big-hearted, jovial man who spread an atmosphere of good-humour wherever he went. In the evenings he played with Sidney like a big boy, an older brother, lying on the bed, or the sofa, taking her in his arms. Between them they had invented a great game. The ex-engineer, his boots removed, his huge legs in the air, hoisted the little tad on the soles of his stockinged feet like a circus acrobat, dandling her there, pretending he was about to let her fall. Sidney, choking with delight, held on nervously, with little screams and chirps of excitement, while he shifted her gingerly from one foot to another, and thence, the final act, the great gallery play, to the palm of one great hand. At this point Mrs. Dyke was called in, both father and daughter, children both, crying out that she was to come in and look, look. She arrived out of breath from the kitchen, the potato masher in her hand. "Such children," she murmured, shaking her head at them, amused for all that, tucking the potato masher under her arm and clapping her hands. In the end, it was part of the game that Sidney should tumble down upon Dyke, whereat he invariably vented a great bellow as if in pain, declaring that his ribs were broken. Gasping, his eyes shut, he pretended to be in the extreme of dissolution—perhaps he was dying. Sidney, always a little uncertain, amused but distressed, shook him nervously, tugging at his beard, pushing open his eyelid with one finger, imploring him not to frighten her, to wake up and be good.

On this occasion, while yet he was half-dressed, Dyke tiptoed into his mother's room to look at Sidney fast asleep in her little iron cot, her arm under her head, her lips parted. With infinite precaution he kissed her twice, and then finding one little stocking, hung with its mate very neatly over the back of a chair, dropped into it a dime, rolled up in a wad of paper. He winked all to himself and went out again, closing the door with exaggerated carefulness.

He breakfasted alone, Mrs. Dyke pouring his coffee and handing him his plate of ham and eggs, and half an hour later took himself off in his springless, skeleton wagon, humming a tune behind his beard and cracking the whip over the backs of his staid and solid farm horses.

The morning was fine, the sun just coming up. He left Guadalajara, sleeping and lifeless, on his left, and going across lots, over an angle of Quien Sabe, came out upon the Upper Road, a mile below the Long Trestle. He was in great spirits, looking about him over the brown fields, ruddy with the dawn. Almost directly in front of him, but far off, the gilded dome of the court-house at Bonneville was glinting radiant in the first rays of the sun, while a few miles distant, toward the north, the venerable campanile of the Mission San Juan stood silhouetted in purplish black against the flaming east. As he proceeded, the great farm horses jogging forward, placid, deliberate, the country side waked to another day. Crossing the irrigating ditch further on, he met a gang of Portuguese, with picks and shovels over their shoulders, just going to work. Hooven, already abroad, shouted him a "Goot mornun" from behind the fence of Los Muertos. Far off, toward the southwest, in the bare expanse of the open fields, where a clump of eucalyptus and cypress trees set a dark green note, a thin stream of smoke rose straight into the air from the kitchen of Derrick's ranch houses.

But a mile or so beyond the Long Trestle he was surprised to see Magnus Derrick's protege, the one-time shepherd, Vanamee, coming across Quien Sabe, by a trail from one of Annixter's division houses. Without knowing exactly why, Dyke received the impression that the young man had not been in bed all of that night.

As the two approached each other, Dyke eyed the young fellow. He was distrustful of Vanamee, having the country-bred suspicion of any person he could not understand. Vanamee was, beyond doubt, no part of the life of ranch and country town. He was an alien, a vagabond, a strange fellow who came and went in mysterious fashion, making no friends, keeping to himself. Why did he never wear a hat, why indulge in a fine, black, pointed beard, when either a round beard or a mustache was the invariable custom? Why did he not cut his hair? Above all, why did he prowl about so much at night? As the two passed each other, Dyke, for all his good-nature, was a little blunt in his greeting and looked back at the ex-shepherd over his shoulder.

Dyke was right in his suspicion. Vanamee's bed had not been disturbed for three nights. On the Monday of that week he had passed the entire night in the garden of the Mission, overlooking the Seed ranch, in the little valley. Tuesday evening had found him miles away from that spot, in a deep arroyo in the Sierra foothills to the eastward, while Wednesday he had slept in an abandoned 'dobe on Osterman's stock range, twenty miles from his resting place of the night before.

The fact of the matter was that the old restlessness had once more seized upon Vanamee. Something began tugging at him; the spur of some unseen rider touched his flank. The instinct of the wanderer woke and moved. For some time now he had been a part of the Los Muertos staff. On Quien Sabe, as on the other ranches, the slack season was at hand. While waiting for the wheat to come up no one was doing much of anything. Vanamee had come over to Los Muertos and spent most of his days on horseback, riding the range, rounding up and watching the cattle in the fourth division of the ranch. But if the vagabond instinct now roused itself in the strange fellow's nature, a counter influence had also set in. More and more Vanamee frequented the Mission garden after nightfall, sometimes remaining there till the dawn began to whiten, lying prone on the ground, his chin on his folded arms, his eyes searching the darkness over the little valley of the Seed ranch, watching, watching. As the days went by, he became more reticent than ever. Presley often came to find him on the stock range, a lonely figure in the great wilderness of bare, green hillsides, but Vanamee no longer took him into his confidence. Father Sarria alone heard his strange stories.

Dyke drove on toward Bonneville, thinking over the whole matter. He knew, as every one did in that part of the country, the legend of Vanamee and Angele, the romance of the Mission garden, the mystery of the Other, Vanamee's flight to the deserts of the southwest, his periodic returns, his strange, reticent, solitary character, but, like many another of the country people, he accounted for Vanamee by a short and easy method. No doubt, the fellow's wits were turned. That was the long and short of it.

The ex-engineer reached the Post Office in Bonneville towards eleven o'clock, but he did not at once present his notice of the arrival of his consignment at Ruggles's office. It entertained him to indulge in an hour's lounging about the streets. It was seldom he got into town, and when he did he permitted himself the luxury of enjoying his evident popularity. He met friends everywhere, in the Post Office, in the drug store, in the barber shop and around the court-house. With each one he held a moment's conversation; almost invariably this ended in the same way:

"Come on 'n have a drink."

"Well, I don't care if I do."

And the friends proceeded to the Yosemite bar, pledging each other with punctilious ceremony. Dyke, however, was a strictly temperate man. His life on the engine had trained him well. Alcohol he never touched, drinking instead ginger ale, sarsaparilla-and-iron—soft drinks.

At the drug store, which also kept a stock of miscellaneous stationery, his eye was caught by a "transparent slate," a child's toy, where upon a little pane of frosted glass one could trace with considerable elaboration outline figures of cows, ploughs, bunches of fruit and even rural water mills that were printed on slips of paper underneath.

"Now, there's an idea, Jim," he observed to the boy behind the soda-water fountain; "I know a little tad that would just about jump out of her skin for that. Think I'll have to take it with me."

"How's Sidney getting along?" the other asked, while wrapping up the package.

Dyke's enthusiasm had made of his little girl a celebrity throughout Bonneville.

The ex-engineer promptly became voluble, assertive, doggedly emphatic.

"Smartest little tad in all Tulare County, and more fun! A regular whole show in herself."

"And the hops?" inquired the other.

"Bully," declared Dyke, with the good-natured man's readiness to talk of his private affairs to any one who would listen. "Bully. I'm dead sure of a bonanza crop by now. The rain came JUST right. I actually don't know as I can store the crop in those barns I built, it's going to be so big. That foreman of mine was a daisy. Jim, I'm going to make money in that deal. After I've paid off the mortgage—you know I had to mortgage, yes, crop and homestead both, but I can pay it off and all the interest to boot, lovely,—well, and as I was saying, after all expenses are paid off I'll clear big money, m' son. Yes, sir. I KNEW there was boodle in hops. You know the crop is contracted for already. Sure, the foreman managed that. He's a daisy. Chap in San Francisco will take it all and at the advanced price. I wanted to hang on, to see if it wouldn't go to six cents, but the foreman said, 'No, that's good enough.' So I signed. Ain't it bully, hey?"

"Then what'll you do?"

"Well, I don't know. I'll have a lay-off for a month or so and take the little tad and mother up and show 'em the city—'Frisco—until it's time for the schools to open, and then we'll put Sid in the seminary at Marysville. Catch on?"

"I suppose you'll stay right by hops now?"

"Right you are, m'son. I know a good thing when I see it. There's plenty others going into hops next season. I set 'em the example. Wouldn't be surprised if it came to be a regular industry hereabouts. I'm planning ahead for next year already. I can let the foreman go, now that I've learned the game myself, and I think I'll buy a piece of land off Quien Sabe and get a bigger crop, and build a couple more barns, and, by George, in about five years time I'll have things humming. I'm going to make MONEY, Jim."

He emerged once more into the street and went up the block leisurely, planting his feet squarely. He fancied that he could feel he was considered of more importance nowadays. He was no longer a subordinate, an employee. He was his own man, a proprietor, an owner of land, furthering a successful enterprise. No one had helped him; he had followed no one's lead. He had struck out unaided for himself, and his success was due solely to his own intelligence, industry, and foresight. He squared his great shoulders till the blue gingham of his jumper all but cracked. Of late, his great blond beard had grown and the work in the sun had made his face very red. Under the visor of his cap—relic of his engineering days—his blue eyes twinkled with vast good-nature. He felt that he made a fine figure as he went by a group of young girls in lawns and muslins and garden hats on their way to the Post Office. He wondered if they looked after him, wondered if they had heard that he was in a fair way to become a rich man.

But the chronometer in the window of the jewelry store warned him that time was passing. He turned about, and, crossing the street, took his way to Ruggles's office, which was the freight as well as the land office of the P. and S. W. Railroad.

As he stood for a moment at the counter in front of the wire partition, waiting for the clerk to make out the order for the freight agent at the depot, Dyke was surprised to see a familiar figure in conference with Ruggles himself, by a desk inside the railing.

The figure was that of a middle-aged man, fat, with a great stomach, which he stroked from time to time. As he turned about, addressing a remark to the clerk, Dyke recognised S. Behrman. The banker, railroad agent, and political manipulator seemed to the ex-engineer's eyes to be more gross than ever. His smooth-shaven jowl stood out big and tremulous on either side of his face; the roll of fat on the nape of his neck, sprinkled with sparse, stiff hairs, bulged out with greater prominence. His great stomach, covered with a light brown linen vest, stamped with innumerable interlocked horseshoes, protruded far in advance, enormous, aggressive. He wore his inevitable round-topped hat of stiff brown straw, varnished so bright that it reflected the light of the office windows like a helmet, and even from where he stood Dyke could hear his loud breathing and the clink of the hollow links of his watch chain upon the vest buttons of imitation pearl, as his stomach rose and fell.

Dyke looked at him with attention. There was the enemy, the representative of the Trust with which Derrick's League was locking horns. The great struggle had begun to invest the combatants with interest. Daily, almost hourly, Dyke was in touch with the ranchers, the wheat-growers. He heard their denunciations, their growls of exasperation and defiance. Here was the other side—this placid, fat man, with a stiff straw hat and linen vest, who never lost his temper, who smiled affably upon his enemies, giving them good advice, commiserating with them in one defeat after another, never ruffled, never excited, sure of his power, conscious that back of him was the Machine, the colossal force, the inexhaustible coffers of a mighty organisation, vomiting millions to the League's thousands.

The League was clamorous, ubiquitous, its objects known to every urchin on the streets, but the Trust was silent, its ways inscrutable, the public saw only results. It worked on in the dark, calm, disciplined, irresistible. Abruptly Dyke received the impression of the multitudinous ramifications of the colossus. Under his feet the ground seemed mined; down there below him in the dark the huge tentacles went silently twisting and advancing, spreading out in every direction, sapping the strength of all opposition, quiet, gradual, biding the time to reach up and out and grip with a sudden unleashing of gigantic strength.

"I'll be wanting some cars of you people before the summer is out," observed Dyke to the clerk as he folded up and put away the order that the other had handed him. He remembered perfectly well that he had arranged the matter of transporting his crop some months before, but his role of proprietor amused him and he liked to busy himself again and again with the details of his undertaking.

"I suppose," he added, "you'll be able to give 'em to me. There'll be a big wheat crop to move this year and I don't want to be caught in any car famine."

"Oh, you'll get your cars," murmured the other.

"I'll be the means of bringing business your way," Dyke went on; "I've done so well with my hops that there are a lot of others going into the business next season. Suppose," he continued, struck with an idea, "suppose we went into some sort of pool, a sort of shippers' organisation, could you give us special rates, cheaper rates—say a cent and a half?"

The other looked up.

"A cent and a half! Say FOUR cents and a half and maybe I'll talk business with you."

"Four cents and a half," returned Dyke, "I don't see it. Why, the regular rate is only two cents."

"No, it isn't," answered the clerk, looking him gravely in the eye, "it's five cents."

"Well, there's where you are wrong, m'son," Dyke retorted, genially. "You look it up. You'll find the freight on hops from Bonneville to 'Frisco is two cents a pound for car load lots. You told me that yourself last fall."

"That was last fall," observed the clerk. There was a silence. Dyke shot a glance of suspicion at the other. Then, reassured, he remarked:

"You look it up. You'll see I'm right."

S. Behrman came forward and shook hands politely with the ex-engineer.

"Anything I can do for you, Mr. Dyke?"

Dyke explained. When he had done speaking, the clerk turned to S. Behrman and observed, respectfully:

"Our regular rate on hops is five cents."

"Yes," answered S. Behrman, pausing to reflect; "yes, Mr. Dyke, that's right—five cents."

The clerk brought forward a folder of yellow paper and handed it to Dyke. It was inscribed at the top "Tariff Schedule No. 8," and underneath these words, in brackets, was a smaller inscription, "SUPERSEDES NO. 7 OF AUG. 1"

"See for yourself," said S. Behrman. He indicated an item under the head of "Miscellany."

"The following rates for carriage of hops in car load lots," read Dyke, "take effect June 1, and will remain in force until superseded by a later tariff. Those quoted beyond Stockton are subject to changes in traffic arrangements with carriers by water from that point."

In the list that was printed below, Dyke saw that the rate for hops between Bonneville or Guadalajara and San Francisco was five cents.

For a moment Dyke was confused. Then swiftly the matter became clear in his mind. The Railroad had raised the freight on hops from two cents to five.

All his calculations as to a profit on his little investment he had based on a freight rate of two cents a pound. He was under contract to deliver his crop. He could not draw back. The new rate ate up every cent of his gains. He stood there ruined.

"Why, what do you mean?" he burst out. "You promised me a rate of two cents and I went ahead with my business with that understanding. What do you mean?"

S. Behrman and the clerk watched him from the other side of the counter.

"The rate is five cents," declared the clerk doggedly.

"Well, that ruins me," shouted Dyke. "Do you understand? I won't make fifty cents. MAKE! Why, I will OWE,—I'll be—be—That ruins me, do you understand?"

The other, raised a shoulder.

"We don't force you to ship. You can do as you like. The rate is five cents."

"Well—but—damn you, I'm under contract to deliver. What am I going to do? Why, you told me—you promised me a two-cent rate."

"I don't remember it," said the clerk. "I don't know anything about that. But I know this; I know that hops have gone up. I know the German crop was a failure and that the crop in New York wasn't worth the hauling. Hops have gone up to nearly a dollar. You don't suppose we don't know that, do you, Mr. Dyke?"

"What's the price of hops got to do with you?"

"It's got THIS to do with us," returned the other with a sudden aggressiveness, "that the freight rate has gone up to meet the price. We're not doing business for our health. My orders are to raise your rate to five cents, and I think you are getting off easy."

Dyke stared in blank astonishment. For the moment, the audacity of the affair was what most appealed to him. He forgot its personal application.

"Good Lord," he murmured, "good Lord! What will you people do next? Look here. What's your basis of applying freight rates, anyhow?" he suddenly vociferated with furious sarcasm. "What's your rule? What are you guided by?"

But at the words, S. Behrman, who had kept silent during the heat of the discussion, leaned abruptly forward. For the only time in his knowledge, Dyke saw his face inflamed with anger and with the enmity and contempt of all this farming element with whom he was contending.

"Yes, what's your rule? What's your basis?" demanded Dyke, turning swiftly to him.

S. Behrman emphasised each word of his reply with a tap of one forefinger on the counter before him:

"All—the—traffic—will—bear."

The ex-engineer stepped back a pace, his fingers on the ledge of the counter, to steady himself. He felt himself grow pale, his heart became a mere leaden weight in his chest, inert, refusing to beat.

In a second the whole affair, in all its bearings, went speeding before the eye of his imagination like the rapid unrolling of a panorama. Every cent of his earnings was sunk in this hop business of his. More than that, he had borrowed money to carry it on, certain of success—borrowed of S. Behrman, offering his crop and his little home as security. Once he failed to meet his obligations, S. Behrman would foreclose. Not only would the Railroad devour every morsel of his profits, but also it would take from him his home; at a blow he would be left penniless and without a home. What would then become of his mother—and what would become of the little tad? She, whom he had been planning to educate like a veritable lady. For all that year he had talked of his ambition for his little daughter to every one he met. All Bonneville knew of it. What a mark for gibes he had made of himself. The workingman turned farmer! What a target for jeers—he who had fancied he could elude the Railroad! He remembered he had once said the great Trust had overlooked his little enterprise, disdaining to plunder such small fry. He should have known better than that. How had he ever imagined the Road would permit him to make any money?

Anger was not in him yet; no rousing of the blind, white-hot wrath that leaps to the attack with prehensile fingers, moved him. The blow merely crushed, staggered, confused.

He stepped aside to give place to a coatless man in a pink shirt, who entered, carrying in his hands an automatic door-closing apparatus.

"Where does this go?" inquired the man.

Dyke sat down for a moment on a seat that had been removed from a worn-out railway car to do duty in Ruggles's office. On the back of a yellow envelope he made some vague figures with a stump of blue pencil, multiplying, subtracting, perplexing himself with many errors.

S. Behrman, the clerk, and the man with the door-closing apparatus involved themselves in a long argument, gazing intently at the top panel of the door. The man who had come to fix the apparatus was unwilling to guarantee it, unless a sign was put on the outside of the door, warning incomers that the door was self-closing. This sign would cost fifteen cents extra.

"But you didn't say anything about this when the thing was ordered," declared S. Behrman. "No, I won't pay it, my friend. It's an overcharge."

"You needn't think," observed the clerk, "that just because you are dealing with the Railroad you are going to work us."

Genslinger came in, accompanied by Delaney. S. Behrman and the clerk, abruptly dismissing the man with the door-closing machine, put themselves behind the counter and engaged in conversation with these two. Genslinger introduced Delaney. The buster had a string of horses he was shipping southward. No doubt he had come to make arrangements with the Railroad in the matter of stock cars. The conference of the four men was amicable in the extreme.

Dyke, studying the figures on the back of the envelope, came forward again. Absorbed only in his own distress, he ignored the editor and the cow-puncher.

"Say," he hazarded, "how about this? I make out–

"We've told you what our rates are, Mr. Dyke," exclaimed the clerk angrily. "That's all the arrangement we will make. Take it or leave it." He turned again to Genslinger, giving the ex-engineer his back.

Dyke moved away and stood for a moment in the centre of the room, staring at the figures on the envelope.

"I don't see," he muttered, "just what I'm going to do. No, I don't see what I'm going to do at all."

Ruggles came in, bringing with him two other men in whom Dyke recognised dummy buyers of the Los Muertos and Osterman ranchos. They brushed by him, jostling his elbow, and as he went out of the door he heard them exchange jovial greetings with Delaney, Genslinger, and S. Behrman.

Dyke went down the stairs to the street and proceeded onward aimlessly in the direction of the Yosemite House, fingering the yellow envelope and looking vacantly at the sidewalk.

There was a stoop to his massive shoulders. His great arms dangled loosely at his sides, the palms of his hands open.

As he went along, a certain feeling of shame touched him. Surely his predicament must be apparent to every passer-by. No doubt, every one recognised the unsuccessful man in the very way he slouched along. The young girls in lawns, muslins, and garden hats, returning from the Post Office, their hands full of letters, must surely see in him the type of the failure, the bankrupt.

Then brusquely his tardy rage flamed up. By God, NO, it was not his fault; he had made no mistake. His energy, industry, and foresight had been sound. He had been merely the object of a colossal trick, a sordid injustice, a victim of the insatiate greed of the monster, caught and choked by one of those millions of tentacles suddenly reaching up from below, from out the dark beneath his feet, coiling around his throat, throttling him, strangling him, sucking his blood. For a moment he thought of the courts, but instantly laughed at the idea. What court was immune from the power of the monster? Ah, the rage of helplessness, the fury of impotence! No help, no hope,—ruined in a brief instant—he a veritable giant, built of great sinews, powerful, in the full tide of his manhood, having all his health, all his wits. How could he now face his home? How could he tell his mother of this catastrophe? And Sidney—the little tad; how could he explain to her this wretchedness—how soften her disappointment? How keep the tears from out her eyes—how keep alive her confidence in him—her faith in his resources?

Bitter, fierce, ominous, his wrath loomed up in his heart. His fists gripped tight together, his teeth clenched. Oh, for a moment to have his hand upon the throat of S. Behrman, wringing the breath from him, wrenching out the red life of him—staining the street with the blood sucked from the veins of the People!

To the first friend that he met, Dyke told the tale of the tragedy, and to the next, and to the next. The affair went from mouth to mouth, spreading with electrical swiftness, overpassing and running ahead of Dyke himself, so that by the time he reached the lobby of the Yosemite House, he found his story awaiting him. A group formed about him. In his immediate vicinity business for the instant was suspended. The group swelled. One after another of his friends added themselves to it. Magnus Derrick joined it, and Annixter. Again and again, Dyke recounted the matter, beginning with the time when he was discharged from the same corporation's service for refusing to accept an unfair wage. His voice quivered with exasperation; his heavy frame shook with rage; his eyes were injected, bloodshot; his face flamed vermilion, while his deep bass rumbled throughout the running comments of his auditors like the thunderous reverberation of diapason.

From all points of view, the story was discussed by those who listened to him, now in the heat of excitement, now calmly, judicially. One verdict, however, prevailed. It was voiced by Annixter: "You're stuck. You can roar till you're black in the face, but you can't buck against the Railroad. There's nothing to be done."

"You can shoot the ruffian, you can shoot S. Behrman," clamoured one of the group. "Yes, sir; by the Lord, you can shoot him."

"Poor fool," commented Annixter, turning away.

Nothing to be done. No, there was nothing to be done—not one thing. Dyke, at last alone and driving his team out of the town, turned the business confusedly over in his mind from end to end. Advice, suggestion, even offers of financial aid had been showered upon him from all directions. Friends were not wanting who heatedly presented to his consideration all manner of ingenious plans, wonderful devices.

They were worthless. The tentacle held fast. He was stuck.

By degrees, as his wagon carried him farther out into the country, and open empty fields, his anger lapsed, and the numbness of bewilderment returned. He could not look one hour ahead into the future; could formulate no plans even for the next day. He did not know what to do. He was stuck.

With the limpness and inertia of a sack of sand, the reins slipping loosely in his dangling fingers, his eyes fixed, staring between the horses' heads, he allowed himself to be carried aimlessly along. He resigned himself. What did he care? What was the use of going on? He was stuck.

The team he was driving had once belonged to the Los Muertos stables and unguided as the horses were, they took the county road towards Derrick's ranch house. Dyke, all abroad, was unaware of the fact till, drawn by the smell of water, the horses halted by the trough in front of Caraher's saloon.

The ex-engineer dismounted, looking about him, realising where he was. So much the worse; it did not matter. Now that he had come so far it was as short to go home by this route as to return on his tracks. Slowly he unchecked the horses and stood at their heads, watching them drink.

"I don't see," he muttered, "just what I am going to do."

Caraher appeared at the door of his place, his red face, red beard, and flaming cravat standing sharply out from the shadow of the doorway. He called a welcome to Dyke.

"Hello, Captain."

Dyke looked up, nodding his head listlessly.

"Hello, Caraher," he answered.

"Well," continued the saloonkeeper, coming forward a step, "what's the news in town?"

Dyke told him. Caraher's red face suddenly took on a darker colour. The red glint in his eyes shot from under his eyebrows. Furious, he vented a rolling explosion of oaths.

"And now it's your turn," he vociferated. "They ain't after only the big wheat-growers, the rich men. By God, they'll even pick the poor man's pocket. Oh, they'll get their bellies full some day. It can't last forever. They'll wake up the wrong kind of man some morning, the man that's got guts in him, that will hit back when he's kicked and that will talk to 'em with a torch in one hand and a stick of dynamite in the other." He raised his clenched fists in the air. "So help me, God," he cried, "when I think it all over I go crazy, I see red. Oh, if the people only knew their strength. Oh, if I could wake 'em up. There's not only Shelgrim, but there's others. All the magnates, all the butchers, all the blood-suckers, by the thousands. Their day will come, by God, it will."

By now, the ex-engineer and the bar-keeper had retired to the saloon back of the grocery to talk over the details of this new outrage. Dyke, still a little dazed, sat down by one of the tables, preoccupied, saying but little, and Caraher as a matter of course set the whiskey bottle at his elbow.

It happened that at this same moment, Presley, returning to Los Muertos from Bonneville, his pockets full of mail, stopped in at the grocery to buy some black lead for his bicycle. In the saloon, on the other side of the narrow partition, he overheard the conversation between Dyke and Caraher. The door was open. He caught every word distinctly.

"Tell us all about it, Dyke," urged Caraher.

For the fiftieth time Dyke told the story. Already it had crystallised into a certain form. He used the same phrases with each repetition, the same sentences, the same words. In his mind it became set. Thus he would tell it to any one who would listen from now on, week after week, year after year, all the rest of his life—"And I based my calculations on a two-cent rate. So soon as they saw I was to make money they doubled the tariff—all the traffic would bear—and I mortgaged to S. Behrman—ruined me with a turn of the hand—stuck, cinched, and not one thing to be done."

As he talked, he drank glass after glass of whiskey, and the honest rage, the open, above-board fury of his mind coagulated, thickened, and sunk to a dull, evil hatred, a wicked, oblique malevolence. Caraher, sure now of winning a disciple, replenished his glass.

"Do you blame us now," he cried, "us others, the Reds? Ah, yes, it's all very well for your middle class to preach moderation. I could do it, too. You could do it, too, if your belly was fed, if your property was safe, if your wife had not been murdered if your children were not starving. Easy enough then to preach law-abiding methods, legal redress, and all such rot. But how about US?" he vociferated. "Ah, yes, I'm a loud-mouthed rum-seller, ain't I? I'm a wild-eyed striker, ain't I? I'm a blood-thirsty anarchist, ain't I? Wait till you've seen your wife brought home to you with the face you used to kiss smashed in by a horse's hoof—killed by the Trust, as it happened to me. Then talk about moderation! And you, Dyke, black-listed engineer, discharged employee, ruined agriculturist, wait till you see your little tad and your mother turned out of doors when S. Behrman forecloses. Wait till you see 'em getting thin and white, and till you hear your little girl ask you why you all don't eat a little more and that she wants her dinner and you can't give it to her. Wait till you see—at the same time that your family is dying for lack of bread—a hundred thousand acres of wheat—millions of bushels of food—grabbed and gobbled by the Railroad Trust, and then talk of moderation. That talk is just what the Trust wants to hear. It ain't frightened of that. There's one thing only it does listen to, one thing it is frightened of—the people with dynamite in their hands,—six inches of plugged gaspipe. THAT talks."

Dyke did not reply. He filled another pony of whiskey and drank it in two gulps.

His frown had lowered to a scowl, his face was a dark red, his head had sunk, bull-like, between his massive shoulders; without winking he gazed long and with troubled eyes at his knotted, muscular hands, lying open on the table before him, idle, their occupation gone.

Presley forgot his black lead. He listened to Caraher. Through the open door he caught a glimpse of Dyke's back, broad, muscled, bowed down, the great shoulders stooping.

The whole drama of the doubled freight rate leaped salient and distinct in the eye of his mind. And this was but one instance, an isolated case. Because he was near at hand he happened to see it. How many others were there, the length and breadth of the State? Constantly this sort of thing must occur—little industries choked out in their very beginnings, the air full of the death rattles of little enterprises, expiring unobserved in far-off counties, up in canyons and arroyos of the foothills, forgotten by every one but the monster who was daunted by the magnitude of no business, however great, who overlooked no opportunity of plunder, however petty, who with one tentacle grabbed a hundred thousand acres of wheat, and with another pilfered a pocketful of growing hops.

He went away without a word, his head bent, his hands clutched tightly on the cork grips of the handle bars of his bicycle. His lips were white. In his heart a blind demon of revolt raged tumultuous, shrieking blasphemies.

At Los Muertos, Presley overtook Annixter. As he guided his wheel up the driveway to Derrick's ranch house, he saw the master of Quien Sabe and Harran in conversation on the steps of the porch. Magnus stood in the doorway, talking to his wife.

Occupied with the press of business and involved in the final conference with the League's lawyers on the eve of the latter's departure for Washington, Annixter had missed the train that was to take him back to Guadalajara and Quien Sabe. Accordingly, he had accepted the Governor's invitation to return with him on his buck-board to Los Muertos, and before leaving Bonneville had telephoned to his ranch to have young Vacca bring the buckskin, by way of the Lower Road, to meet him at Los Muertos. He found her waiting there for him, but before going on, delayed a few moments to tell Harran of Dyke's affair.

"I wonder what he will do now?" observed Harran when his first outburst of indignation had subsided.

"Nothing," declared Annixter. "He's stuck."

"That eats up every cent of Dyke's earnings," Harran went on. "He has been ten years saving them. Oh, I told him to make sure of the Railroad when he first spoke to me about growing hops."

"I've just seen him," said Presley, as he joined the others. "He was at Caraher's. I only saw his back. He was drinking at a table and his back was towards me. But the man looked broken—absolutely crushed. It is terrible, terrible."

"He was at Caraher's, was he?" demanded Annixter.

"Yes."

"Drinking, hey?"

"I think so. Yes, I saw a bottle."

"Drinking at Caraher's," exclaimed Annixter, rancorously; "I can see HIS finish."

There was a silence. It seemed as if nothing more was to be said. They paused, looking thoughtfully on the ground.

In silence, grim, bitter, infinitely sad, the three men as if at that moment actually standing in the bar-room of Caraher's roadside saloon, contemplated the slow sinking, the inevitable collapse and submerging of one of their companions, the wreck of a career, the ruin of an individual; an honest man, strong, fearless, upright, struck down by a colossal power, perverted by an evil influence, go reeling to his ruin.

"I see his finish," repeated Annixter. "Exit Dyke, and score another tally for S. Behrman, Shelgrim and Co."

He moved away impatiently, loosening the tie-rope with which the buckskin was fastened. He swung himself up.

"God for us all," he declared as he rode away, "and the devil take the hindmost. Good-bye, I'm going home. I still have one a little longer."

He galloped away along the Lower Road, in the direction of Quien Sabe, emerging from the grove of cypress and eucalyptus about the ranch house, and coming out upon the bare brown plain of the wheat land, stretching away from him in apparent barrenness on either hand.

It was late in the day, already his shadow was long upon the padded dust of the road in front of him. On ahead, a long ways off, and a little to the north, the venerable campanile of the Mission San Juan was glinting radiant in the last rays of the sun, while behind him, towards the north and west, the gilded dome of the courthouse at Bonneville stood silhouetted in purplish black against the flaming west. Annixter spurred the buck-skin forward. He feared he might be late to his supper. He wondered if it would be brought to him by Hilma.

Hilma! The name struck across in his brain with a pleasant, glowing tremour. All through that day of activity, of strenuous business, the minute and cautious planning of the final campaign in the great war of the League and the Trust, the idea of her and the recollection of her had been the undercurrent of his thoughts. At last he was alone. He could put all other things behind him and occupy himself solely with her.

In that glory of the day's end, in that chaos of sunshine, he saw her again. Unimaginative, crude, direct, his fancy, nevertheless, placed her before him, steeped in sunshine, saturated with glorious light, brilliant, radiant, alluring. He saw the sweet simplicity of her carriage, the statuesque evenness of the contours of her figure, the single, deep swell of her bosom, the solid masses of her hair. He remembered the small contradictory suggestions of feminine daintiness he had so often remarked about her, her slim, narrow feet, the little steel buckles of her low shoes, the knot of black ribbon she had begun to wear of late on the back of her head, and he heard her voice, low-pitched, velvety, a sweet, murmuring huskiness that seemed to come more from her chest than from her throat.

The buckskin's hoofs clattered upon the gravelly flats of Broderson's Creek underneath the Long Trestle. Annixter's mind went back to the scene of the previous evening, when he had come upon her at this place. He set his teeth with anger and disappointment. Why had she not been able to understand? What was the matter with these women, always set upon this marrying notion? Was it not enough that he wanted her more than any other girl he knew and that she wanted him? She had said as much. Did she think she was going to be mistress of Quien Sabe? Ah, that was it. She was after his property, was for marrying him because of his money. His unconquerable suspicion of the woman, his innate distrust of the feminine element would not be done away with. What fathomless duplicity was hers, that she could appear so innocent. It was almost unbelievable; in fact, was it believable?

For the first time doubt assailed him. Suppose Hilma was indeed all that she appeared to be. Suppose it was not with her a question of his property, after all; it was a poor time to think of marrying him for his property when all Quien Sabe hung in the issue of the next few months. Suppose she had been sincere. But he caught himself up. Was he to be fooled by a feemale girl at this late date? He, Buck Annixter, crafty, hard-headed, a man of affairs? Not much. Whatever transpired he would remain the master.

He reached Quien Sabe in this frame of mind. But at this hour, Annixter, for all his resolutions, could no longer control his thoughts. As he stripped the saddle from the buckskin and led her to the watering trough by the stable corral, his heart was beating thick at the very notion of being near Hilma again. It was growing dark, but covertly he glanced here and there out of the corners of his eyes to see if she was anywhere about. Annixter—how, he could not tell—had become possessed of the idea that Hilma would not inform her parents of what had passed between them the previous evening under the Long Trestle. He had no idea that matters were at an end between himself and the young woman. He must apologise, he saw that clearly enough, must eat crow, as he told himself. Well, he would eat crow. He was not afraid of her any longer, now that she had made her confession to him. He would see her as soon as possible and get this business straightened out, and begin again from a new starting point. What he wanted with Hilma, Annixter did not define clearly in his mind. At one time he had known perfectly well what he wanted. Now, the goal of his desires had become vague. He could not say exactly what it was. He preferred that things should go forward without much idea of consequences; if consequences came, they would do so naturally enough, and of themselves; all that he positively knew was that Hilma occupied his thoughts morning, noon, and night; that he was happy when he was with her, and miserable when away from her.

The Chinese cook served his supper in silence. Annixter ate and drank and lighted a cigar, and after his meal sat on the porch of his house, smoking and enjoying the twilight. The evening was beautiful, warm, the sky one powder of stars. From the direction of the stables he heard one of the Portuguese hands picking a guitar.

But he wanted to see Hilma. The idea of going to bed without at least a glimpse of her became distasteful to him. Annixter got up and descending from the porch began to walk aimlessly about between the ranch buildings, with eye and ear alert. Possibly he might meet her somewheres.

The Trees' little house, toward which inevitably Annixter directed his steps, was dark. Had they all gone to bed so soon? He made a wide circuit about it, listening, but heard no sound. The door of the dairy-house stood ajar. He pushed it open, and stepped into the odorous darkness of its interior. The pans and deep cans of polished metal glowed faintly from the corners and from the walls. The smell of new cheese was pungent in his nostrils. Everything was quiet. There was nobody there. He went out again, closing the door, and stood for a moment in the space between the dairy-house and the new barn, uncertain as to what he should do next.

As he waited there, his foreman came out of the men's bunk house, on the other side of the kitchens, and crossed over toward the barn. "Hello, Billy," muttered Annixter as he passed.

"Oh, good evening, Mr. Annixter," said the other, pausing in front of him. "I didn't know you were back. By the way," he added, speaking as though the matter was already known to Annixter, "I see old man Tree and his family have left us. Are they going to be gone long? Have they left for good?"

"What's that?" Annixter exclaimed. "When did they go? Did all of them go, all three?"

"Why, I thought you knew. Sure, they all left on the afternoon train for San Francisco. Cleared out in a hurry—took all their trunks. Yes, all three went—the young lady, too. They gave me notice early this morning. They ain't ought to have done that. I don't know who I'm to get to run the dairy on such short notice. Do you know any one, Mr. Annixter?"

"Well, why in hell did you let them go?" vociferated Annixter. "Why didn't you keep them here till I got back? Why didn't you find out if they were going for good? I can't be everywhere. What do I feed you for if it ain't to look after things I can't attend to?"

He turned on his heel and strode away straight before him, not caring where he was going. He tramped out from the group of ranch buildings; holding on over the open reach of his ranch, his teeth set, his heels digging furiously into the ground. The minutes passed. He walked on swiftly, muttering to himself from time to time.

"Gone, by the Lord. Gone, by the Lord. By the Lord Harry, she's cleared out."

As yet his head was empty of all thought. He could not steady his wits to consider this new turn of affairs. He did not even try.

"Gone, by the Lord," he exclaimed. "By the Lord, she's cleared out."

He found the irrigating ditch, and the beaten path made by the ditch tenders that bordered it, and followed it some five minutes; then struck off at right angles over the rugged surface of the ranch land, to where a great white stone jutted from the ground. There he sat down, and leaning forward, rested his elbows on his knees, and looked out vaguely into the night, his thoughts swiftly readjusting themselves.

He was alone. The silence of the night, the infinite repose of the flat, bare earth—two immensities—widened around and above him like illimitable seas. A grey half-light, mysterious, grave, flooded downward from the stars.

Annixter was in torment. Now, there could be no longer any doubt—now it was Hilma or nothing. Once out of his reach, once lost to him, and the recollection of her assailed him with unconquerable vehemence. Much as she had occupied his mind, he had never realised till now how vast had been the place she had filled in his life. He had told her as much, but even then he did not believe it.

Suddenly, a bitter rage against himself overwhelmed him as he thought of the hurt he had given her the previous evening. He should have managed differently. How, he did not know, but the sense of the outrage he had put upon her abruptly recoiled against him with cruel force. Now, he was sorry for it, infinitely sorry, passionately sorry. He had hurt her. He had brought the tears to her eyes. He had so flagrantly insulted her that she could no longer bear to breathe the same air with him. She had told her parents all. She had left Quien Sabe—had left him for good, at the very moment when he believed he had won her. Brute, beast that he was, he had driven her away.

An hour went by; then two, then four, then six. Annixter still sat in his place, groping and battling in a confusion of spirit, the like of which he had never felt before. He did not know what was the matter with him. He could not find his way out of the dark and out of the turmoil that wheeled around him. He had had no experience with women. There was no precedent to guide him. How was he to get out of this? What was the clew that would set everything straight again?

That he would give Hilma up, never once entered his head. Have her he would. She had given herself to him. Everything should have been easy after that, and instead, here he was alone in the night, wrestling with himself, in deeper trouble than ever, and Hilma farther than ever away from him.

It was true, he might have Hilma, even now, if he was willing to marry her. But marriage, to his mind, had been always a vague, most remote possibility, almost as vague and as remote as his death,—a thing that happened to some men, but that would surely never occur to him, or, if it did, it would be after long years had passed, when he was older, more settled, more mature—an event that belonged to the period of his middle life, distant as yet.

He had never faced the question of his marriage. He had kept it at an immense distance from him. It had never been a part of his order of things. He was not a marrying man.

But Hilma was an ever-present reality, as near to him as his right hand. Marriage was a formless, far distant abstraction. Hilma a tangible, imminent fact. Before he could think of the two as one; before he could consider the idea of marriage, side by side with the idea of Hilma, measureless distances had to be traversed, things as disassociated in his mind as fire and water, had to be fused together; and between the two he was torn as if upon a rack.

Slowly, by imperceptible degrees, the imagination, unused, unwilling machine, began to work. The brain's activity lapsed proportionately. He began to think less, and feel more. In that rugged composition, confused, dark, harsh, a furrow had been driven deep, a little seed planted, a little seed at first weak, forgotten, lost in the lower dark places of his character.

But as the intellect moved slower, its functions growing numb, the idea of self dwindled. Annixter no longer considered himself; no longer considered the notion of marriage from the point of view of his own comfort, his own wishes, his own advantage. He realised that in his newfound desire to make her happy, he was sincere. There was something in that idea, after all. To make some one happy—how about that now? It was worth thinking of.

Far away, low down in the east, a dim belt, a grey light began to whiten over the horizon. The tower of the Mission stood black against it. The dawn was coming. The baffling obscurity of the night was passing. Hidden things were coming into view.

Annixter, his eyes half-closed, his chin upon his fist, allowed his imagination full play. How would it be if he should take Hilma into his life, this beautiful young girl, pure as he now knew her to be; innocent, noble with the inborn nobility of dawning womanhood? An overwhelming sense of his own unworthiness suddenly bore down upon him with crushing force, as he thought of this. He had gone about the whole affair wrongly. He had been mistaken from the very first. She was infinitely above him. He did not want—he should not desire to be the master. It was she, his servant, poor, simple, lowly even, who should condescend to him.

Abruptly there was presented to his mind's eye a picture of the years to come, if he now should follow his best, his highest, his most unselfish impulse. He saw Hilma, his own, for better or for worse, for richer or for poorer, all barriers down between them, he giving himself to her as freely, as nobly, as she had given herself to him. By a supreme effort, not of the will, but of the emotion, he fought his way across that vast gulf that for a time had gaped between Hilma and the idea of his marriage. Instantly, like the swift blending of beautiful colours, like the harmony of beautiful chords of music, the two ideas melted into one, and in that moment into his harsh, unlovely world a new idea was born. Annixter stood suddenly upright, a mighty tenderness, a gentleness of spirit, such as he had never conceived of, in his heart strained, swelled, and in a moment seemed to burst. Out of the dark furrows of his soul, up from the deep rugged recesses of his being, something rose, expanding. He opened his arms wide. An immense happiness overpowered him. Actual tears came to his eyes. Without knowing why, he was not ashamed of it. This poor, crude fellow, harsh, hard, narrow, with his unlovely nature, his fierce truculency, his selfishness, his obstinacy, abruptly knew that all the sweetness of life, all the great vivifying eternal force of humanity had burst into life within him.

The little seed, long since planted, gathering strength quietly, had at last germinated.

Then as the realisation of this hardened into certainty, in the growing light of the new day that had just dawned for him, Annixter uttered a cry. Now at length, he knew the meaning of it all.

"Why—I—I, I LOVE her," he cried. Never until then had it occurred to him. Never until then, in all his thoughts of Hilma, had that great word passed his lips.

It was a Memnonian cry, the greeting of the hard, harsh image of man, rough-hewn, flinty, granitic, uttering a note of joy, acclaiming the new risen sun.

By now it was almost day. The east glowed opalescent. All about him Annixter saw the land inundated with light. But there was a change. Overnight something had occurred. In his perturbation the change seemed to him, at first, elusive, almost fanciful, unreal. But now as the light spread, he looked again at the gigantic scroll of ranch lands unrolled before him from edge to edge of the horizon. The change was not fanciful. The change was real. The earth was no longer bare. The land was no longer barren,—no longer empty, no longer dull brown. All at once Annixter shouted aloud.

There it was, the Wheat, the Wheat! The little seed long planted, germinating in the deep, dark furrows of the soil, straining, swelling, suddenly in one night had burst upward to the light. The wheat had come up. It was there before him, around him, everywhere, illimitable, immeasurable. The winter brownness of the ground was overlaid with a little shimmer of green. The promise of the sowing was being fulfilled. The earth, the loyal mother, who never failed, who never disappointed, was keeping her faith again. Once more the strength of nations was renewed. Once more the force of the world was revivified. Once more the Titan, benignant, calm, stirred and woke, and the morning abruptly blazed into glory upon the spectacle of a man whose heart leaped exuberant with the love of a woman, and an exulting earth gleaming transcendent with the radiant magnificence of an inviolable pledge.

III

Presley's room in the ranch house of Los Muertos was in the second story of the building. It was a corner room; one of its windows facing the south, the other the east. Its appointments were of the simplest. In one angle was the small white painted iron bed, covered with a white counterpane. The walls were hung with a white paper figured with knots of pale green leaves, very gay and bright. There was a straw matting on the floor. White muslin half-curtains hung in the windows, upon the sills of which certain plants bearing pink waxen flowers of which Presley did not know the name, grew in oblong green boxes. The walls were unadorned, save by two pictures, one a reproduction of the "Reading from Homer," the other a charcoal drawing of the Mission of San Juan de Guadalajara, which Presley had made himself. By the east window stood the plainest of deal tables, innocent of any cloth or covering, such as might have been used in a kitchen. It was Presley's work table, and was invariably littered with papers, half-finished manuscripts, drafts of poems, notebooks, pens, half-smoked cigarettes, and the like. Near at hand, upon a shelf, were his books. There were but two chairs in the room—the straight backed wooden chair, that stood in front of the table, angular, upright, and in which it was impossible to take one's ease, and the long comfortable wicker steamer chair, stretching its length in front of the south window. Presley was immensely fond of this room. It amused and interested him to maintain its air of rigorous simplicity and freshness. He abhorred cluttered bric-a-brac and meaningless objets d'art. Once in so often he submitted his room to a vigorous inspection; setting it to rights, removing everything but the essentials, the few ornaments which, in a way, were part of his life.

His writing had by this time undergone a complete change. The notes for his great Song of the West, the epic poem he once had hoped to write he had flung aside, together with all the abortive attempts at its beginning. Also he had torn up a great quantity of "fugitive" verses, preserving only a certain half-finished poem, that he called "The Toilers." This poem was a comment upon the social fabric, and had been inspired by the sight of a painting he had seen in Cedarquist's art gallery. He had written all but the last verse.

On the day that he had overheard the conversation between Dyke and Caraher, in the latter's saloon, which had acquainted him with the monstrous injustice of the increased tariff, Presley had returned to Los Muertos, white and trembling, roused to a pitch of exaltation, the like of which he had never known in all his life. His wrath was little short of even Caraher's. He too "saw red"; a mighty spirit of revolt heaved tumultuous within him. It did not seem possible that this outrage could go on much longer. The oppression was incredible; the plain story of it set down in truthful statement of fact would not be believed by the outside world.

He went up to his little room and paced the floor with clenched fists and burning face, till at last, the repression of his contending thoughts all but suffocated him, and he flung himself before his table and began to write. For a time, his pen seemed to travel of itself; words came to him without searching, shaping themselves into phrases,—the phrases building themselves up to great, forcible sentences, full of eloquence, of fire, of passion. As his prose grew more exalted, it passed easily into the domain of poetry. Soon the cadence of his paragraphs settled to an ordered beat and rhythm, and in the end Presley had thrust aside his journal and was once more writing verse.

He picked up his incomplete poem of "The Toilers," read it hastily a couple of times to catch its swing, then the Idea of the last verse—the Idea for which he so long had sought in vain—abruptly springing to his brain, wrote it off without so much as replenishing his pen with ink. He added still another verse, bringing the poem to a definite close, resuming its entire conception, and ending with a single majestic thought, simple, noble, dignified, absolutely convincing.

Presley laid down his pen and leaned back in his chair, with the certainty that for one moment he had touched untrod heights. His hands were cold, his head on fire, his heart leaping tumultuous in his breast.

Now at last, he had achieved. He saw why he had never grasped the inspiration for his vast, vague, IMPERSONAL Song of the West. At the time when he sought for it, his convictions had not been aroused; he had not then cared for the People. His sympathies had not been touched. Small wonder that he had missed it. Now he was of the People; he had been stirred to his lowest depths. His earnestness was almost a frenzy. He BELIEVED, and so to him all things were possible at once.

Then the artist in him reasserted itself. He became more interested in his poem, as such, than in the cause that had inspired it. He went over it again, retouching it carefully, changing a word here and there, and improving its rhythm. For the moment, he forgot the People, forgot his rage, his agitation of the previous hour, he remembered only that he had written a great poem.

Then doubt intruded. After all, was it so great? Did not its sublimity overpass a little the bounds of the ridiculous? Had he seen true? Had he failed again? He re-read the poem carefully; and it seemed all at once to lose force.

By now, Presley could not tell whether what he had written was true poetry or doggerel. He distrusted profoundly his own judgment. He must have the opinion of some one else, some one competent to judge. He could not wait; to-morrow would not do. He must know to a certainty before he could rest that night.

He made a careful copy of what he had written, and putting on his hat and laced boots, went down stairs and out upon the lawn, crossing over to the stables. He found Phelps there, washing down the buckboard.

"Do you know where Vanamee is to-day?" he asked the latter. Phelps put his chin in the air.

"Ask me something easy," he responded. "He might be at Guadalajara, or he might be up at Osterman's, or he might be a hundred miles away from either place. I know where he ought to be, Mr. Presley, but that ain't saying where the crazy gesabe is. He OUGHT to be range-riding over east of Four, at the head waters of Mission Creek."

"I'll try for him there, at all events," answered Presley. "If you see Harran when he comes in, tell him I may not be back in time for supper."

Presley found the pony in the corral, cinched the saddle upon him, and went off over the Lower Road, going eastward at a brisk canter.

At Hooven's he called a "How do you do" to Minna, whom he saw lying in a slat hammock under the mammoth live oak, her foot in bandages; and then galloped on over the bridge across the irrigating ditch, wondering vaguely what would become of such a pretty girl as Minna, and if in the end she would marry the Portuguese foreman in charge of the ditching-gang. He told himself that he hoped she would, and that speedily. There was no lack of comment as to Minna Hooven about the ranches. Certainly she was a good girl, but she was seen at all hours here and there about Bonneville and Guadalajara, skylarking with the Portuguese farm hands of Quien Sabe and Los Muertos. She was very pretty; the men made fools of themselves over her. Presley hoped they would not end by making a fool of her.

Just beyond the irrigating ditch, Presley left the Lower Road, and following a trail that branched off southeasterly from this point, held on across the Fourth Division of the ranch, keeping the Mission Creek on his left. A few miles farther on, he went through a gate in a barbed wire fence, and at once engaged himself in a system of little arroyos and low rolling hills, that steadily lifted and increased in size as he proceeded. This higher ground was the advance guard of the Sierra foothills, and served as the stock range for Los Muertos. The hills were huge rolling hummocks of bare ground, covered only by wild oats. At long intervals, were isolated live oaks. In the canyons and arroyos, the chaparral and manzanita grew in dark olive-green thickets. The ground was honey-combed with gopher-holes, and the gophers themselves were everywhere. Occasionally a jack rabbit bounded across the open, from one growth of chaparral to another, taking long leaps, his ears erect. High overhead, a hawk or two swung at anchor, and once, with a startling rush of wings, a covey of quail flushed from the brush at the side of the trail.

On the hillsides, in thinly scattered groups were the cattle, grazing deliberately, working slowly toward the water-holes for their evening drink, the horses keeping to themselves, the colts nuzzling at their mothers' bellies, whisking their tails, stamping their unshod feet. But once in a remoter field, solitary, magnificent, enormous, the short hair curling tight upon his forehead, his small red eyes twinkling, his vast neck heavy with muscles, Presley came upon the monarch, the king, the great Durham bull, maintaining his lonely state, unapproachable, austere.

Presley found the one-time shepherd by a water-hole, in a far distant corner of the range. He had made his simple camp for the night. His blue-grey army blanket lay spread under a live oak, his horse grazed near at hand. He himself sat on his heels before a little fire of dead manzanita roots, cooking his coffee and bacon. Never had Presley conceived so keen an impression of loneliness as his crouching figure presented. The bald, bare landscape widened about him to infinity. Vanamee was a spot in it all, a tiny dot, a single atom of human organisation, floating endlessly on the ocean of an illimitable nature.

The two friends ate together, and Vanamee, having snared a brace of quails, dressed and then roasted them on a sharpened stick. After eating, they drank great refreshing draughts from the water-hole. Then, at length, Presley having lit his cigarette, and Vanamee his pipe, the former said:

"Vanamee, I have been writing again."

Vanamee turned his lean ascetic face toward him, his black eyes fixed attentively.

"I know," he said, "your journal."

"No, this is a poem. You remember, I told you about it once. 'The Toilers,' I called it."

"Oh, verse! Well, I am glad you have gone back to it. It is your natural vehicle."

"You remember the poem?" asked Presley. "It was unfinished."

"Yes, I remember it. There was better promise in it than anything you ever wrote. Now, I suppose, you have finished it."

Without reply, Presley brought it from out the breast pocket of his shooting coat. The moment seemed propitious. The stillness of the vast, bare hills was profound. The sun was setting in a cloudless brazier of red light; a golden dust pervaded all the landscape. Presley read his poem aloud. When he had finished, his friend looked at him.

"What have you been doing lately?" he demanded. Presley, wondering, told of his various comings and goings.

"I don't mean that," returned the other. "Something has happened to you, something has aroused you. I am right, am I not? Yes, I thought so. In this poem of yours, you have not been trying to make a sounding piece of literature. You wrote it under tremendous stress. Its very imperfections show that. It is better than a mere rhyme. It is an Utterance—a Message. It is Truth. You have come back to the primal heart of things, and you have seen clearly. Yes, it is a great poem."

"Thank you," exclaimed Presley fervidly. "I had begun to mistrust myself."

"Now," observed Vanamee, "I presume you will rush it into print. To have formulated a great thought, simply to have accomplished, is not enough."

"I think I am sincere," objected Presley. "If it is good it will do good to others. You said yourself it was a Message. If it has any value, I do not think it would be right to keep it back from even a very small and most indifferent public."

"Don't publish it in the magazines at all events," Vanamee answered. "Your inspiration has come FROM the People. Then let it go straight TO the People—not the literary readers of the monthly periodicals, the rich, who would only be indirectly interested. If you must publish it, let it be in the daily press. Don't interrupt. I know what you will say. It will be that the daily press is common, is vulgar, is undignified; and I tell you that such a poem as this of yours, called as it is, 'The Toilers,' must be read BY the Toilers. It MUST BE common; it must be vulgarised. You must not stand upon your dignity with the People, if you are to reach them."

"That is true, I suppose," Presley admitted, "but I can't get rid of the idea that it would be throwing my poem away. The great magazine gives me such—a—background; gives me such weight."

"Gives YOU such weight, gives you such background. Is it YOURSELF you think of? You helper of the helpless. Is that your sincerity? You must sink yourself; must forget yourself and your own desire of fame, of admitted success. It is your POEM, your MESSAGE, that must prevail,—not YOU, who wrote it. You preach a doctrine of abnegation, of self-obliteration, and you sign your name to your words as high on the tablets as you can reach, so that all the world may see, not the poem, but the poet. Presley, there are many like you. The social reformer writes a book on the iniquity of the possession of land, and out of the proceeds, buys a corner lot. The economist who laments the hardships of the poor, allows himself to grow rich upon the sale of his book."

But Presley would hear no further.

"No," he cried, "I know I am sincere, and to prove it to you, I will publish my poem, as you say, in the daily press, and I will accept no money for it."

They talked on for about an hour, while the evening wore away. Presley very soon noticed that Vanamee was again preoccupied. More than ever of late, his silence, his brooding had increased. By and by he rose abruptly, turning his head to the north, in the direction of the Mission church of San Juan. "I think," he said to Presley, "that I must be going."

"Going? Where to at this time of night?"

"Off there." Vanamee made an uncertain gesture toward the north. "Good-bye," and without another word he disappeared in the grey of the twilight. Presley was left alone wondering. He found his horse, and, tightening the girths, mounted and rode home under the sheen of the stars, thoughtful, his head bowed. Before he went to bed that night he sent "The Toilers" to the Sunday Editor of a daily newspaper in San Francisco.

Upon leaving Presley, Vanamee, his thumbs hooked into his empty cartridge belt, strode swiftly down from the hills of the Los Muertos stock-range and on through the silent town of Guadalajara. His lean, swarthy face, with its hollow cheeks, fine, black, pointed beard, and sad eyes, was set to the northward. As was his custom, he was bareheaded, and the rapidity of his stride made a breeze in his long, black hair. He knew where he was going. He knew what he must live through that night.

Again, the deathless grief that never slept leaped out of the shadows, and fastened upon his shoulders. It was scourging him back to that scene of a vanished happiness, a dead romance, a perished idyl,—the Mission garden in the shade of the venerable pear trees.

But, besides this, other influences tugged at his heart. There was a mystery in the garden. In that spot the night was not always empty, the darkness not always silent. Something far off stirred and listened to his cry, at times drawing nearer to him. At first this presence had been a matter for terror; but of late, as he felt it gradually drawing nearer, the terror had at long intervals given place to a feeling of an almost ineffable sweetness. But distrusting his own senses, unwilling to submit himself to such torturing, uncertain happiness, averse to the terrible confusion of spirit that followed upon a night spent in the garden, Vanamee had tried to keep away from the place. However, when the sorrow of his life reassailed him, and the thoughts and recollections of Angele brought the ache into his heart, and the tears to his eyes, the temptation to return to the garden invariably gripped him close. There were times when he could not resist. Of themselves, his footsteps turned in that direction. It was almost as if he himself had been called.

Guadalajara was silent, dark. Not even in Solotari's was there a light. The town was asleep. Only the inevitable guitar hummed from an unseen 'dobe. Vanamee pushed on. The smell of the fields and open country, and a distant scent of flowers that he knew well, came to his nostrils, as he emerged from the town by way of the road that led on towards the Mission through Quien Sabe. On either side of him lay the brown earth, silently nurturing the implanted seed. Two days before it had rained copiously, and the soil, still moist, disengaged a pungent aroma of fecundity.

Vanamee, following the road, passed through the collection of buildings of Annixter's home ranch. Everything slept. At intervals, the aer-motor on the artesian well creaked audibly, as it turned in a languid breeze from the northeast. A cat, hunting field-mice, crept from the shadow of the gigantic barn and paused uncertainly in the open, the tip of her tail twitching. From within the barn itself came the sound of the friction of a heavy body and a stir of hoofs, as one of the dozing cows lay down with a long breath.

Vanamee left the ranch house behind him and proceeded on his way. Beyond him, to the right of the road, he could make out the higher ground in the Mission enclosure, and the watching tower of the Mission itself. The minutes passed. He went steadily forward. Then abruptly he paused, his head in the air, eye and ear alert. To that strange sixth sense of his, responsive as the leaves of the sensitive plant, had suddenly come the impression of a human being near at hand. He had neither seen nor heard, but for all that he stopped an instant in his tracks; then, the sensation confirmed, went on again with slow steps, advancing warily.

At last, his swiftly roving eyes lighted upon an object, just darker than the grey-brown of the night-ridden land. It was at some distance from the roadside. Vanamee approached it cautiously, leaving the road, treading carefully upon the moist clods of earth underfoot. Twenty paces distant, he halted.

Annixter was there, seated upon a round, white rock, his back towards him. He was leaning forward, his elbows on his knees, his chin in his hands. He did not move. Silent, motionless, he gazed out upon the flat, sombre land.

It was the night wherein the master of Quien Sabe wrought out his salvation, struggling with Self from dusk to dawn. At the moment when Vanamee came upon him, the turmoil within him had only begun. The heart of the man had not yet wakened. The night was young, the dawn far distant, and all around him the fields of upturned clods lay bare and brown, empty of all life, unbroken by a single green shoot.

For a moment, the life-circles of these two men, of so widely differing characters, touched each other, there in the silence of the night under the stars. Then silently Vanamee withdrew, going on his way, wondering at the trouble that, like himself, drove this hardheaded man of affairs, untroubled by dreams, out into the night to brood over an empty land.

Then speedily he forgot all else. The material world drew off from him. Reality dwindled to a point and vanished like the vanishing of a star at moonrise. Earthly things dissolved and disappeared, as a strange, unnamed essence flowed in upon him. A new atmosphere for him pervaded his surroundings. He entered the world of the Vision, of the Legend, of the Miracle, where all things were possible. He stood at the gate of the Mission garden.

Above him rose the ancient tower of the Mission church. Through the arches at its summit, where swung the Spanish queen's bells, he saw the slow-burning stars. The silent bats, with flickering wings, threw their dancing shadows on the pallid surface of the venerable facade.

Not the faintest chirring of a cricket broke the silence. The bees were asleep. In the grasses, in the trees, deep in the calix of punka flower and magnolia bloom, the gnats, the caterpillars, the beetles, all the microscopic, multitudinous life of the daytime drowsed and dozed. Not even the minute scuffling of a lizard over the warm, worn pavement of the colonnade disturbed the infinite repose, the profound stillness. Only within the garden, the intermittent trickling of the fountain made itself heard, flowing steadily, marking off the lapse of seconds, the progress of hours, the cycle of years, the inevitable march of centuries. At one time, the doorway before which Vanamee now stood had been hermetically closed. But he, himself, had long since changed that. He stood before it for a moment, steeping himself in the mystery and romance of the place, then raising he latch, pushed open the gate, entered, and closed it softly behind him. He was in the cloister garden.

The stars were out, strewn thick and close in the deep blue of the sky, the milky way glowing like a silver veil. Ursa Major wheeled gigantic in the north. The great nebula in Orion was a whorl of shimmering star dust. Venus flamed a lambent disk of pale saffron, low over the horizon. From edge to edge of the world marched the constellations, like the progress of emperors, and from the innumerable glory of their courses a mysterious sheen of diaphanous light disengaged itself, expanding over all the earth, serene, infinite, majestic.

The little garden revealed itself but dimly beneath the brooding light, only half emerging from the shadow. The polished surfaces of the leaves of the pear trees winked faintly back the reflected light as the trees just stirred in the uncertain breeze. A blurred shield of silver marked the ripples of the fountain. Under the flood of dull blue lustre, the gravelled walks lay vague amid the grasses, like webs of white satin on the bed of a lake. Against the eastern wall the headstones of the graves, an indistinct procession of grey cowls ranged themselves.

Vanamee crossed the garden, pausing to kiss the turf upon Angele's grave. Then he approached the line of pear trees, and laid himself down in their shadow, his chin propped upon his hands, his eyes wandering over the expanse of the little valley that stretched away from the foot of the hill upon which the Mission was built.

Once again he summoned the Vision. Once again he conjured up the Illusion. Once again, tortured with doubt, racked with a deathless grief, he craved an Answer of the night. Once again, mystic that he was, he sent his mind out from him across the enchanted sea of the Supernatural. Hope, of what he did not know, roused up within him. Surely, on such a night as this, the hallucination must define itself. Surely, the Manifestation must be vouchsafed.

His eyes closed, his will girding itself to a supreme effort, his senses exalted to a state of pleasing numbness, he called upon Angele to come to him, his voiceless cry penetrating far out into that sea of faint, ephemeral light that floated tideless over the little valley beneath him. Then motionless, prone upon the ground, he waited.

Months had passed since that first night when, at length, an Answer had come to Vanamee. At first, startled out of all composure, troubled and stirred to his lowest depths, because of the very thing for which he sought, he resolved never again to put his strange powers to the test. But for all that, he had come a second night to the garden, and a third, and a fourth. At last, his visits were habitual. Night after night he was there, surrendering himself to the influences of the place, gradually convinced that something did actually answer when he called. His faith increased as the winter grew into spring. As the spring advanced and the nights became shorter, it crystallised into certainty. Would he have her again, his love, long dead? Would she come to him once more out of the grave, out of the night? He could not tell; he could only hope. All that he knew was that his cry found an answer, that his outstretched hands, groping in the darkness, met the touch of other fingers. Patiently he waited. The nights became warmer as the spring drew on. The stars shone clearer.

The nights seemed brighter. For nearly a month after the occasion of his first answer nothing new occurred. Some nights it failed him entirely; upon others it was faint, illusive.

Then, at last, the most subtle, the barest of perceptible changes began. His groping mind far-off there, wandering like a lost bird over the valley, touched upon some thing again, touched and held it and this time drew it a single step closer to him. His heart beating, the blood surging in his temples, he watched with the eyes of his imagination, this gradual approach. What was coming to him? Who was coming to him? Shrouded in the obscurity of the night, whose was the face now turned towards his? Whose the footsteps that with such infinite slowness drew nearer to where he waited? He did not dare to say.

His mind went back many years to that time before the tragedy of Angele's death, before the mystery of the Other. He waited then as he waited now. But then he had not waited in vain. Then, as now, he had seemed to feel her approach, seemed to feel her drawing nearer and nearer to their rendezvous. Now, what would happen? He did not know. He waited. He waited, hoping all things. He waited, believing all things. He waited, enduring all things. He trusted in the Vision.

Meanwhile, as spring advanced, the flowers in the Seed ranch began to come to life. Over the five hundred acres whereon the flowers were planted, the widening growth of vines and bushes spread like the waves of a green sea. Then, timidly, colours of the faintest tints began to appear. Under the moonlight, Vanamee saw them expanding, delicate pink, faint blue, tenderest variations of lavender and yellow, white shimmering with reflections of gold, all subdued and pallid in the moonlight.

By degrees, the night became impregnated with the perfume of the flowers. Illusive at first, evanescent as filaments of gossamer; then as the buds opened, emphasising itself, breathing deeper, stronger. An exquisite mingling of many odours passed continually over the Mission, from the garden of the Seed ranch, meeting and blending with the aroma of its magnolia buds and punka blossoms.

As the colours of the flowers of the Seed ranch deepened, and as their odours penetrated deeper and more distinctly, as the starlight of each succeeding night grew brighter and the air became warmer, the illusion defined itself. By imperceptible degrees, as Vanamee waited under the shadows of the pear trees, the Answer grew nearer and nearer. He saw nothing but the distant glimmer of the flowers. He heard nothing but the drip of the fountain. Nothing moved about him but the invisible, slow-passing breaths of perfume; yet he felt the approach of the Vision.

It came first to about the middle of the Seed ranch itself, some half a mile away, where the violets grew; shrinking, timid flowers, hiding close to the ground. Then it passed forward beyond the violets, and drew nearer and stood amid the mignonette, hardier blooms that dared look heavenward from out the leaves. A few nights later it left the mignonette behind, and advanced into the beds of white iris that pushed more boldly forth from the earth, their waxen petals claiming the attention. It advanced then a long step into the proud, challenging beauty of the carnations and roses; and at last, after many nights, Vanamee felt that it paused, as if trembling at its hardihood, full in the superb glory of the royal lilies themselves, that grew on the extreme border of the Seed ranch nearest to him. After this, there was a certain long wait. Then, upon a dark midnight, it advanced again. Vanamee could scarcely repress a cry. Now, the illusion emerged from the flowers. It stood, not distant, but unseen, almost at the base of the hill upon whose crest he waited, in a depression of the ground where the shadows lay thickest. It was nearly within earshot.

The nights passed. The spring grew warmer. In the daytime intermittent rains freshened all the earth. The flowers of the Seed ranch grew rapidly. Bud after bud burst forth, while those already opened expanded to full maturity. The colour of the Seed ranch deepened.

One night, after hours of waiting, Vanamee felt upon his cheek the touch of a prolonged puff of warm wind, breathing across the little valley from out the east. It reached the Mission garden and stirred the branches of the pear trees. It seemed veritably to be compounded of the very essence of the flowers. Never had the aroma been so sweet, so pervasive. It passed and faded, leaving in its wake an absolute silence. Then, at length, the silence of the night, that silence to which Vanamee had so long appealed, was broken by a tiny sound. Alert, half-risen from the ground, he listened; for now, at length, he heard something. The sound repeated itself. It came from near at hand, from the thick shadow at the foot of the hill. What it was, he could not tell, but it did not belong to a single one of the infinite similar noises of the place with which he was so familiar. It was neither the rustle of a leaf, the snap of a parted twig, the drone of an insect, the dropping of a magnolia blossom. It was a vibration merely, faint, elusive, impossible of definition; a minute notch in the fine, keen edge of stillness.

Again the nights passed. The summer stars became brighter. The warmth increased. The flowers of the Seed ranch grew still more. The five hundred acres of the ranch were carpeted with them.

At length, upon a certain midnight, a new light began to spread in the sky. The thin scimitar of the moon rose, veiled and dim behind the earth-mists. The light increased. Distant objects, until now hidden, came into view, and as the radiance brightened, Vanamee, looking down upon the little valley, saw a spectacle of incomparable beauty. All the buds of the Seed ranch had opened. The faint tints of the flowers had deepened, had asserted themselves. They challenged the eye. Pink became a royal red. Blue rose into purple. Yellow flamed into orange. Orange glowed golden and brilliant. The earth disappeared under great bands and fields of resplendent colour. Then, at length, the moon abruptly soared zenithward from out the veiling mist, passing from one filmy haze to another. For a moment there was a gleam of a golden light, and Vanamee, his eyes searching the shade at the foot of the hill, felt his heart suddenly leap, and then hang poised, refusing to beat. In that instant of passing light, something had caught his eye. Something that moved, down there, half in and half out of the shadow, at the hill's foot. It had come and gone in an instant. The haze once more screened the moonlight. The shade again engulfed the vision. What was it he had seen? He did not know. So brief had been that movement, the drowsy brain had not been quick enough to interpret the cipher message of the eye. Now it was gone. But something had been there. He had seen it. Was it the lifting of a strand of hair, the wave of a white hand, the flutter of a garment's edge? He could not tell, but it did not belong to any of those sights which he had seen so often in that place. It was neither the glancing of a moth's wing, the nodding of a wind-touched blossom, nor the noiseless flitting of a bat. It was a gleam merely, faint, elusive, impossible of definition, an intangible agitation, in the vast, dim blur of the darkness.

And that was all. Until now no single real thing had occurred, nothing that Vanamee could reduce to terms of actuality, nothing he could put into words. The manifestation, when not recognisable to that strange sixth sense of his, appealed only to the most refined, the most delicate perception of eye and ear. It was all ephemeral, filmy, dreamy, the mystic forming of the Vision—the invisible developing a concrete nucleus, the starlight coagulating, the radiance of the flowers thickening to something actual; perfume, the most delicious fragrance, becoming a tangible presence.

But into that garden the serpent intruded. Though cradled in the slow rhythm of the dream, lulled by this beauty of a summer's night, heavy with the scent of flowers, the silence broken only by a rippling fountain, the darkness illuminated by a world of radiant blossoms, Vanamee could not forget the tragedy of the Other; that terror of many years ago,—that prowler of the night, that strange, fearful figure with the unseen face, swooping in there from out the darkness, gone in an instant, yet leaving behind the trail and trace of death and of pollution.

Never had Vanamee seen this more clearly than when leaving Presley on the stock range of Los Muertos, he had come across to the Mission garden by way of the Quien Sabe ranch.

It was the same night in which Annixter out-watched the stars, coming, at last, to himself.

As the hours passed, the two men, far apart, ignoring each other, waited for the Manifestation,—Annixter on the ranch, Vanamee in the garden.

Prone upon his face, under the pear trees, his forehead buried in the hollow of his arm, Vanamee lay motionless. For the last time, raising his head, he sent his voiceless cry out into the night across the multi-coloured levels of the little valley, calling upon the miracle, summoning the darkness to give Angele back to him, resigning himself to the hallucination. He bowed his head upon his arm again and waited. The minutes passed. The fountain dripped steadily. Over the hills a haze of saffron light foretold the rising of the full moon. Nothing stirred. The silence was profound.

Then, abruptly, Vanamee's right hand shut tight upon his wrist. There—there it was. It began again, his invocation was answered. Far off there, the ripple formed again upon the still, black pool of the night. No sound, no sight; vibration merely, appreciable by some sublimated faculty of the mind as yet unnamed. Rigid, his nerves taut, motionless, prone on the ground, he waited.

It advanced with infinite slowness. Now it passed through the beds of violets, now through the mignonette. A moment later, and he knew it stood among the white iris. Then it left those behind. It was in the splendour of the red roses and carnations. It passed like a moving star into the superb abundance, the imperial opulence of the royal lilies. It was advancing slowly, but there was no pause. He held his breath, not daring to raise his head. It passed beyond the limits of the Seed ranch, and entered the shade at the foot of the hill below him. Would it come farther than this? Here it had always stopped hitherto, stopped for a moment, and then, in spite of his efforts, had slipped from his grasp and faded back into the night. But now he wondered if he had been willing to put forth his utmost strength, after all. Had there not always been an element of dread in the thought of beholding the mystery face to face? Had he not even allowed the Vision to dissolve, the Answer to recede into the obscurity whence it came?

But never a night had been so beautiful as this. It was the full period of the spring. The air was a veritable caress. The infinite repose of the little garden, sleeping under the night, was delicious beyond expression. It was a tiny corner of the world, shut off, discreet, distilling romance, a garden of dreams, of enchantments.

Below, in the little valley, the resplendent colourations of the million flowers, roses, lilies, hyacinths, carnations, violets, glowed like incandescence in the golden light of the rising moon. The air was thick with the perfume, heavy with it, clogged with it. The sweetness filled the very mouth. The throat choked with it. Overhead wheeled the illimitable procession of the constellations. Underfoot, the earth was asleep. The very flowers were dreaming. A cathedral hush overlay all the land, and a sense of benediction brooded low,—a divine kindliness manifesting itself in beauty, in peace, in absolute repose.

It was a time for visions. It was the hour when dreams come true, and lying deep in the grasses beneath the pear trees, Vanamee, dizzied with mysticism, reaching up and out toward the supernatural, felt, as it were, his mind begin to rise upward from out his body. He passed into a state of being the like of which he had not known before. He felt that his imagination was reshaping itself, preparing to receive an impression never experienced until now. His body felt light to him, then it dwindled, vanished. He saw with new eyes, heard with new ears, felt with a new heart.

"Come to me," he murmured.

Then slowly he felt the advance of the Vision. It was approaching. Every instant it drew gradually nearer. At last, he was to see. It had left the shadow at the base of the hill; it was on the hill itself. Slowly, steadily, it ascended the slope; just below him there, he heard a faint stirring. The grasses rustled under the touch of a foot. The leaves of the bushes murmured, as a hand brushed against them; a slender twig creaked. The sounds of approach were more distinct. They came nearer. They reached the top of the hill. They were within whispering distance.

Vanamee, trembling, kept his head buried in his arm. The sounds, at length, paused definitely. The Vision could come no nearer. He raised his head and looked. The moon had risen. Its great shield of gold stood over the eastern horizon. Within six feet of Vanamee, clear and distinct, against the disk of the moon, stood the figure of a young girl. She was dressed in a gown of scarlet silk, with flowing sleeves, such as Japanese wear, embroidered with flowers and figures of birds worked in gold threads. On either side of her face, making three-cornered her round, white forehead, hung the soft masses of her hair of gold. Her hands hung limply at her sides. But from between her parted lips—lips of almost an Egyptian fulness—her breath came slow and regular, and her eyes, heavy lidded, slanting upwards toward the temples, perplexing, oriental, were closed. She was asleep.

From out this life of flowers, this world of colour, this atmosphere oppressive with perfume, this darkness clogged and cloyed, and thickened with sweet odours, she came to him. She came to him from out of the flowers, the smell of the roses in her hair of gold, the aroma and the imperial red of the carnations in her lips, the whiteness of the lilies, the perfume of the lilies, and the lilies' slender, balancing grace in her neck. Her hands disengaged the scent of the heliotrope. The folds of her scarlet gown gave off the enervating smell of poppies. Her feet were redolent of hyacinth. She stood before him, a Vision realised—a dream come true. She emerged from out the invisible. He beheld her, a figure of gold and pale vermilion, redolent of perfume, poised motionless in the faint saffron sheen of the new-risen moon. She, a creation of sleep, was herself asleep. She, a dream, was herself dreaming.

Called forth from out the darkness, from the grip of the earth, the embrace of the grave, from out the memory of corruption, she rose into light and life, divinely pure. Across that white forehead was no smudge, no trace of an earthly pollution—no mark of a terrestrial dishonour. He saw in her the same beauty of untainted innocence he had known in his youth. Years had made no difference with her. She was still young. It was the old purity that returned, the deathless beauty, the ever-renascent life, the eternal consecrated and immortal youth. For a few seconds, she stood there before him, and he, upon the ground at her feet, looked up at her, spellbound. Then, slowly she withdrew. Still asleep, her eyelids closed, she turned from him, descending the slope. She was gone.

Vanamee started up, coming, as it were, to himself, looking wildly about him. Sarria was there.

"I saw her," said the priest. "It was Angele, the little girl, your Angele's daughter. She is like her mother."

But Vanamee scarcely heard. He walked as if in a trance, pushing by Sarria, going forth from the garden. Angele or Angele's daughter, it was all one with him. It was She. Death was overcome. The grave vanquished. Life, ever-renewed, alone existed. Time was naught; change was naught; all things were immortal but evil; all things eternal but grief.

Suddenly, the dawn came; the east burned roseate toward the zenith. Vanamee walked on, he knew not where. The dawn grew brighter. At length, he paused upon the crest of a hill overlooking the ranchos, and cast his eye below him to the southward. Then, suddenly flinging up his arms, he uttered a great cry.

There it was. The Wheat! The Wheat! In the night it had come up. It was there, everywhere, from margin to margin of the horizon. The earth, long empty, teemed with green life. Once more the pendulum of the seasons swung in its mighty arc, from death back to life. Life out of death, eternity rising from out dissolution. There was the lesson. Angele was not the symbol, but the PROOF of immortality. The seed dying, rotting and corrupting in the earth; rising again in life unconquerable, and in immaculate purity,–Angele dying as she gave birth to her little daughter, life springing from her death,–the pure, unconquerable, coming forth from the defiled. Why had he not had the knowledge of God? Thou fool, that which thou sowest is not quickened except it die. So the seed had died. So died Angele. And that which thou sowest, thou sowest not that body that shall be, but bare grain. It may chance of wheat, or of some other grain. The wheat called forth from out the darkness, from out the grip of the earth, of the grave, from out corruption, rose triumphant into light and life. So Angele, so life, so also the resurrection of the dead. It is sown in corruption. It is raised in incorruption. It is sown in dishonour. It is raised in glory. It is sown in weakness. It is raised in power. Death was swallowed up in Victory.

The sun rose. The night was over. The glory of the terrestrial was one, and the glory of the celestial was another. Then, as the glory of sun banished the lesser glory of moon and stars, Vanamee, from his mountain top, beholding the eternal green life of the growing Wheat, bursting its bonds, and in his heart exulting in his triumph over the grave, flung out his arms with a mighty shout:

"Oh, Death, where is thy sting? Oh, Grave, where is thy victory?"

IV

Presley's Socialistic poem, "The Toilers," had an enormous success. The editor of the Sunday supplement of the San Francisco paper to which it was sent, printed it in Gothic type, with a scare-head title so decorative as to be almost illegible, and furthermore caused the poem to be illustrated by one of the paper's staff artists in a most impressive fashion. The whole affair occupied an entire page. Thus advertised, the poem attracted attention. It was promptly copied in New York, Boston, and Chicago papers. It was discussed, attacked, defended, eulogised, ridiculed. It was praised with the most fulsome adulation; assailed with the most violent condemnation. Editorials were written upon it. Special articles, in literary pamphlets, dissected its rhetoric and prosody. The phrases were quoted,–were used as texts for revolutionary sermons, reactionary speeches. It was parodied; it was distorted so as to read as an advertisement for patented cereals and infants' foods. Finally, the editor of an enterprising monthly magazine reprinted the poem, supplementing it by a photograph and biography of Presley himself.

Presley was stunned, bewildered. He began to wonder at himself. Was he actually the "greatest American poet since Bryant"? He had had no thought of fame while composing "The Toilers." He had only been moved to his heart's foundations,–thoroughly in earnest, seeing clearly,–and had addressed himself to the poem's composition in a happy moment when words came easily to him, and the elaboration of fine sentences was not difficult. Was it thus fame was achieved? For a while he was tempted to cross the continent and go to New York and there come unto his own, enjoying the triumph that awaited him. But soon he denied himself this cheap reward. Now he was too much in earnest. He wanted to help his People, the community in which he lived–the little world of the San Joaquin, at grapples with the Railroad. The struggle had found its poet. He told himself that his place was here. Only the words of the manager of a lecture bureau troubled him for a moment. To range the entire nation, telling all his countrymen of the drama that was working itself out on this fringe of the continent, this ignored and distant Pacific Coast, rousing their interest and stirring them up to action–appealed to him. It might do great good. To devote himself to "the Cause," accepting no penny of remuneration; to give his life to loosing the grip of the iron-hearted monster of steel and steam would be beyond question heroic. Other States than California had their grievances. All over the country the family of cyclops was growing. He would declare himself the champion of the People in their opposition to the Trust. He would be an apostle, a prophet, a martyr of Freedom.

But Presley was essentially a dreamer, not a man of affairs. He hesitated to act at this precise psychological moment, striking while the iron was yet hot, and while he hesitated, other affairs near at hand began to absorb his attention.

One night, about an hour after he had gone to bed, he was awakened by the sound of voices on the porch of the ranch house, and, descending, found Mrs. Dyke there with Sidney. The ex-engineer's mother was talking to Magnus and Harran, and crying as she talked. It seemed that Dyke was missing. He had gone into town early that afternoon with the wagon and team, and was to have been home for supper. By now it was ten o'clock and there was no news of him. Mrs. Dyke told how she first had gone to Quien Sabe, intending to telephone from there to Bonneville, but Annixter was in San Francisco, and in his absence the house was locked up, and the over-seer, who had a duplicate key, was himself in Bonneville. She had telegraphed three times from Guadalajara to Bonneville for news of her son, but without result. Then, at last, tortured with anxiety, she had gone to Hooven's, taking Sidney with her, and had prevailed upon "Bismarck" to hitch up and drive her across Los Muertos to the Governor's, to beg him to telephone into Bonneville, to know what had become of Dyke.

While Harran rang up Central in town, Mrs. Dyke told Presley and Magnus of the lamentable change in Dyke.

"They have broken my son's spirit, Mr. Derrick," she said. "If you were only there to see. Hour after hour, he sits on the porch with his hands lying open in his lap, looking at them without a word. He won't look me in the face any more, and he don't sleep. Night after night, he has walked the floor until morning. And he will go on that way for days together, very silent, without a word, and sitting still in his chair, and then, all of a sudden, he will break out—oh, Mr. Derrick, it is terrible—into an awful rage, cursing, swearing, grinding his teeth, his hands clenched over his head, stamping so that the house shakes, and saying that if S. Behrman don't give him back his money, he will kill him with his two hands. But that isn't the worst, Mr. Derrick. He goes to Mr. Caraher's saloon now, and stays there for hours, and listens to Mr. Caraher. There is something on my son's mind; I know there is—something that he and Mr. Caraher have talked over together, and I can't find out what it is. Mr. Caraher is a bad man, and my son has fallen under his influence." The tears filled her eyes. Bravely, she turned to hide them, turning away to take Sidney in her arms, putting her head upon the little girl's shoulder.

"I—I haven't broken down before, Mr. Derrick," she said, "but after we have been so happy in our little house, just us three—and the future seemed so bright—oh, God will punish the gentlemen who own the railroad for being so hard and cruel."

Harran came out on the porch, from the telephone, and she interrupted herself, fixing her eyes eagerly upon him.

"I think it is all right, Mrs. Dyke," he said, reassuringly. "We know where he is, I believe. You and the little tad stay here, and Hooven and I will go after him."

About two hours later, Harran brought Dyke back to Los Muertos in Hooven's wagon. He had found him at Caraher's saloon, very drunk.

There was nothing maudlin about Dyke's drunkenness. In him the alcohol merely roused the spirit of evil, vengeful, reckless.

As the wagon passed out from under the eucalyptus trees about the ranch house, taking Mrs. Dyke, Sidney, and the one-time engineer back to the hop ranch, Presley leaning from his window heard the latter remark:

"Caraher is right. There is only one thing they listen to, and that's dynamite."

The following day Presley drove Magnus over to Guadalajara to take the train for San Francisco. But after he had said good-bye to the Governor, he was moved to go on to the hop ranch to see the condition of affairs in that quarter. He returned to Los Muertos overwhelmed with sadness and trembling with anger. The hop ranch that he had last seen in the full tide of prosperity was almost a ruin. Work had evidently been abandoned long since. Weeds were already choking the vines. Everywhere the poles sagged and drooped. Many had even fallen, dragging the vines with them, spreading them over the ground in an inextricable tangle of dead leaves, decaying tendrils, and snarled string. The fence was broken; the unfinished storehouse, which never was to see completion, was a lamentable spectacle of gaping doors and windows—a melancholy skeleton. Last of all, Presley had caught a glimpse of Dyke himself, seated in his rocking chair on the porch, his beard and hair unkempt, motionless, looking with vague eyes upon his hands that lay palm upwards and idle in his lap.

Magnus on his way to San Francisco was joined at Bonneville by Osterman. Upon seating himself in front of the master of Los Muertos in the smoking-car of the train, this latter, pushing back his hat and smoothing his bald head, observed:

"Governor, you look all frazeled out. Anything wrong these days?"

The other answered in the negative, but, for all that, Osterman was right. The Governor had aged suddenly. His former erectness was gone, the broad shoulders stooped a little, the strong lines of his thin-lipped mouth were relaxed, and his hand, as it clasped over the yellowed ivory knob of his cane, had an unwonted tremulousness not hitherto noticeable. But the change in Magnus was more than physical. At last, in the full tide of power, President of the League, known and talked of in every county of the State, leader in a great struggle, consulted, deferred to as the "Prominent Man," at length attaining that position, so long and vainly sought for, he yet found no pleasure in his triumph, and little but bitterness in life. His success had come by devious methods, had been reached by obscure means.

He was a briber. He could never forget that. To further his ends, disinterested, public-spirited, even philanthropic as those were, he had connived with knavery, he, the politician of the old school, of such rigorous integrity, who had abandoned a "career" rather than compromise with honesty. At this eleventh hour, involved and entrapped in the fine-spun web of a new order of things, bewildered by Osterman's dexterity, by his volubility and glibness, goaded and harassed beyond the point of reason by the aggression of the Trust he fought, he had at last failed. He had fallen he had given a bribe. He had thought that, after all, this would make but little difference with him. The affair was known only to Osterman, Broderson, and Annixter; they would not judge him, being themselves involved. He could still preserve a bold front; could still hold his head high. As time went on the affair would lose its point.

But this was not so. Some subtle element of his character had forsaken him. He felt it. He knew it. Some certain stiffness that had given him all his rigidity, that had lent force to his authority, weight to his dominance, temper to his fine, inflexible hardness, was diminishing day by day. In the decisions which he, as President of the League, was called upon to make so often, he now hesitated. He could no longer be arrogant, masterful, acting upon his own judgment, independent of opinion. He began to consult his lieutenants, asking their advice, distrusting his own opinions. He made mistakes, blunders, and when those were brought to his notice, took refuge in bluster. He knew it to be bluster—knew that sooner or later his subordinates would recognise it as such. How long could he maintain his position? So only he could keep his grip upon the lever of control till the battle was over, all would be well. If not, he would fall, and, once fallen, he knew that now, briber that he was, he would never rise again.

He was on his way at this moment to the city to consult with Lyman as to a certain issue of the contest between the Railroad and the ranchers, which, of late, had been brought to his notice.

When appeal had been taken to the Supreme Court by the League's Executive Committee, certain test cases had been chosen, which should represent all the lands in question. Neither Magnus nor Annixter had so appealed, believing, of course, that their cases were covered by the test cases on trial at Washington. Magnus had here blundered again, and the League's agents in San Francisco had written to warn him that the Railroad might be able to take advantage of a technicality, and by pretending that neither Quien Sabe nor Los Muertos were included in the appeal, attempt to put its dummy buyers in possession of the two ranches before the Supreme Court handed down its decision. The ninety days allowed for taking this appeal were nearly at an end and after then the Railroad could act. Osterman and Magnus at once decided to go up to the city, there joining Annixter (who had been absent from Quien Sabe for the last ten days), and talk the matter over with Lyman. Lyman, because of his position as Commissioner, might be cognisant of the Railroad's plans, and, at the same time, could give sound legal advice as to what was to be done should the new rumour prove true.

"Say," remarked Osterman, as the train pulled out of the Bonneville station, and the two men settled themselves for the long journey, "say Governor, what's all up with Buck Annixter these days? He's got a bean about something, sure."

"I had not noticed," answered Magnus. "Mr. Annixter has been away some time lately. I cannot imagine what should keep him so long in San Francisco."

"That's it," said Osterman, winking. "Have three guesses. Guess right and you get a cigar. I guess g-i-r-l spells Hilma Tree. And a little while ago she quit Quien Sabe and hiked out to 'Frisco. So did Buck. Do I draw the cigar? It's up to you."

"I have noticed her," observed Magnus. "A fine figure of a woman. She would make some man a good wife."

"Hoh! Wife! Buck Annixter marry! Not much. He's gone a-girling at last, old Buck! It's as funny as twins. Have to josh him about it when I see him, sure."

But when Osterman and Magnus at last fell in with Annixter in the vestibule of the Lick House, on Montgomery Street, nothing could be got out of him. He was in an execrable humour. When Magnus had broached the subject of business, he had declared that all business could go to pot, and when Osterman, his tongue in his cheek, had permitted himself a most distant allusion to a feemale girl, Annixter had cursed him for a "busy-face" so vociferously and tersely, that even Osterman was cowed.

"Well," insinuated Osterman, "what are you dallying 'round 'Frisco so much for?"

"Cat fur, to make kitten-breeches," retorted Annixter with oracular vagueness.

Two weeks before this time, Annixter had come up to the city and had gone at once to a certain hotel on Bush Street, behind the First National Bank, that he knew was kept by a family connection of the Trees. In his conjecture that Hilma and her parents would stop here, he was right. Their names were on the register. Ignoring custom, Annixter marched straight up to their rooms, and before he was well aware of it, was "eating crow" before old man Tree.

Hilma and her mother were out at the time. Later on, Mrs. Tree returned alone, leaving Hilma to spend the day with one of her cousins who lived far out on Stanyan Street in a little house facing the park.

Between Annixter and Hilma's parents, a reconciliation had been effected, Annixter convincing them both of his sincerity in wishing to make Hilma his wife. Hilma, however, refused to see him. As soon as she knew he had followed her to San Francisco she had been unwilling to return to the hotel and had arranged with her cousin to spend an indefinite time at her house.

She was wretchedly unhappy during all this time; would not set foot out of doors, and cried herself to sleep night after night. She detested the city. Already she was miserably homesick for the ranch. She remembered the days she had spent in the little dairy-house, happy in her work, making butter and cheese; skimming the great pans of milk, scouring the copper vessels and vats, plunging her arms, elbow deep, into the white curds; coming and going in that atmosphere of freshness, cleanliness, and sunlight, gay, singing, supremely happy just because the sun shone. She remembered her long walks toward the Mission late in the afternoons, her excursions for cresses underneath the Long Trestle, the crowing of the cocks, the distant whistle of the passing trains, the faint sounding of the Angelus. She recalled with infinite longing the solitary expanse of the ranches, the level reaches between the horizons, full of light and silence; the heat at noon, the cloudless iridescence of the sunrise and sunset. She had been so happy in that life! Now, all those days were passed. This crude, raw city, with its crowding houses all of wood and tin, its blotting fogs, its uproarious trade winds, disturbed and saddened her. There was no outlook for the future.

At length, one day, about a week after Annixter's arrival in the city, she was prevailed upon to go for a walk in the park. She went alone, putting on for the first time the little hat of black straw with its puff of white silk her mother had bought for her, a pink shirtwaist, her belt of imitation alligator skin, her new skirt of brown cloth, and her low shoes, set off with their little steel buckles.

She found a tiny summer house, built in Japanese fashion, around a diminutive pond, and sat there for a while, her hands folded in her lap, amused with watching the goldfish, wishing—she knew not what.

Without any warning, Annixter sat down beside her. She was too frightened to move. She looked at him with wide eyes that began to fill with tears.

"Oh," she said, at last, "oh—I didn't know."

"Well," exclaimed Annixter, "here you are at last. I've been watching that blamed house till I was afraid the policeman would move me on. By the Lord," he suddenly cried, "you're pale. You—you, Hilma, do you feel well?"

"Yes—I am well," she faltered.

"No, you're not," he declared. "I know better. You are coming back to Quien Sabe with me. This place don't agree with you. Hilma, what's all the matter? Why haven't you let me see you all this time? Do you know—how things are with me? Your mother told you, didn't she? Do you know how sorry I am? Do you know that I see now that I made the mistake of my life there, that time, under the Long Trestle? I found it out the night after you went away. I sat all night on a stone out on the ranch somewhere and I don't know exactly what happened, but I've been a different man since then. I see things all different now. Why, I've only begun to live since then. I know what love means now, and instead of being ashamed of it, I'm proud of it. If I never was to see you again I would be glad I'd lived through that night, just the same. I just woke up that night. I'd been absolutely and completely selfish up to the moment I realised I really loved you, and now, whether you'll let me marry you or not, I mean to live—I don't know, in a different way. I've GOT to live different. I—well—oh, I can't make you understand, but just loving you has changed my life all around. It's made it easier to do the straight, clean thing. I want to do it, it's fun doing it. Remember, once I said I was proud of being a hard man, a driver, of being glad that people hated me and were afraid of me? Well, since I've loved you I'm ashamed of it all. I don't want to be hard any more, and nobody is going to hate me if I can help it. I'm happy and I want other people so. I love you," he suddenly exclaimed; "I love you, and if you will forgive me, and if you will come down to such a beast as I am, I want to be to you the best a man can be to a woman, Hilma. Do you understand, little girl? I want to be your husband."

Hilma looked at the goldfishes through her tears.

"Have you got anything to say to me, Hilma?" he asked, after a while.

"I don't know what you want me to say," she murmured.

"Yes, you do," he insisted. "I've followed you 'way up here to hear it. I've waited around in these beastly, draughty picnic grounds for over a week to hear it. You know what I want to hear, Hilma."

"Well—I forgive you," she hazarded.

"That will do for a starter," he answered. "But that's not IT."

"Then, I don't know what."

"Shall I say it for you?"

She hesitated a long minute, then:

"You mightn't say it right," she replied.

"Trust me for that. Shall I say it for you, Hilma?"

"I don't know what you'll say."

"I'll say what you are thinking of. Shall I say it?"

There was a very long pause. A goldfish rose to the surface of the little pond, with a sharp, rippling sound. The fog drifted overhead. There was nobody about.

"No," said Hilma, at length. "I—I—I can say it for myself. I—" All at once she turned to him and put her arms around his neck. "Oh, DO you love me?" she cried. "Is it really true? Do you mean every word of it? And you are sorry and you WILL be good to me if I will be your wife? You will be my dear, dear husband?"

The tears sprang to Annixter's eyes. He took her in his arms and held her there for a moment. Never in his life had he felt so unworthy, so undeserving of this clean, pure girl who forgave him and trusted his spoken word and believed him to be the good man he could only wish to be. She was so far above him, so exalted, so noble that he should have bowed his forehead to her feet, and instead, she took him in her arms, believing him to be good, to be her equal. He could think of no words to say. The tears overflowed his eyes and ran down upon his cheeks. She drew away from him and held him a second at arm's length, looking at him, and he saw that she, too, had been crying.

"I think," he said, "we are a couple of softies."

"No, no," she insisted. "I want to cry and want you to cry, too. Oh, dear, I haven't a handkerchief."

"Here, take mine."

They wiped each other's eyes like two children and for a long time sat in the deserted little Japanese pleasure house, their arms about each other, talking, talking, talking.

On the following Saturday they were married in an uptown Presbyterian church, and spent the week of their honeymoon at a small, family hotel on Sutter Street. As a matter of course, they saw the sights of the city together. They made the inevitable bridal trip to the Cliff House and spent an afternoon in the grewsome and made-to-order beauties of Sutro's Gardens; they went through Chinatown, the Palace Hotel, the park museum—where Hilma resolutely refused to believe in the Egyptian mummy—and they drove out in a hired hack to the Presidio and the Golden Gate.

On the sixth day of their excursions, Hilma abruptly declared they had had enough of "playing out," and must be serious and get to work.

This work was nothing less than the buying of the furniture and appointments for the rejuvenated ranch house at Quien Sabe, where they were to live. Annixter had telegraphed to his overseer to have the building repainted, replastered, and reshingled and to empty the rooms of everything but the telephone and safe. He also sent instructions to have the dimensions of each room noted down and the result forwarded to him. It was the arrival of these memoranda that had roused Hilma to action.

Then ensued a most delicious week. Armed with formidable lists, written by Annixter on hotel envelopes, they two descended upon the department stores of the city, the carpet stores, the furniture stores. Right and left they bought and bargained, sending each consignment as soon as purchased to Quien Sabe. Nearly an entire car load of carpets, curtains, kitchen furniture, pictures, fixtures, lamps, straw matting, chairs, and the like were sent down to the ranch, Annixter making a point that their new home should be entirely equipped by San Francisco dealers.

The furnishings of the bedroom and sitting-room were left to the very last. For the former, Hilma bought a "set" of pure white enamel, three chairs, a washstand and bureau, a marvellous bargain of thirty dollars, discovered by wonderful accident at a "Friday Sale." The bed was a piece by itself, bought elsewhere, but none the less a wonder. It was of brass, very brave and gay, and actually boasted a canopy! They bought it complete, just as it stood in the window of the department store and Hilma was in an ecstasy over its crisp, clean, muslin curtains, spread, and shams. Never was there such a bed, the luxury of a princess, such a bed as she had dreamed about her whole life.

Next the appointments of the sitting-room occupied her—since Annixter, himself, bewildered by this astonishing display, unable to offer a single suggestion himself, merely approved of all she bought. In the sitting-room was to be a beautiful blue and white paper, cool straw matting, set off with white wool rugs, a stand of flowers in the window, a globe of goldfish, rocking chairs, a sewing machine, and a great, round centre table of yellow oak whereon should stand a lamp covered with a deep shade of crinkly red tissue paper. On the walls were to hang several pictures—lovely affairs, photographs from life, all properly tinted—of choir boys in robes, with beautiful eyes; pensive young girls in pink gowns, with flowing yellow hair, drooping over golden harps; a coloured reproduction of "Rouget de Lisle, Singing the Marseillaise," and two "pieces" of wood carving, representing a quail and a wild duck, hung by one leg in the midst of game bags and powder horns,—quite masterpieces, both.

At last everything had been bought, all arrangements made, Hilma's trunks packed with her new dresses, and the tickets to Bonneville bought.

"We'll go by the Overland, by Jingo," declared Annixter across the table to his wife, at their last meal in the hotel where they had been stopping; "no way trains or locals for us, hey?"

"But we reach Bonneville at SUCH an hour," protested Hilma. "Five in the morning!"

"Never mind," he declared, "we'll go home in PULLMAN'S, Hilma. I'm not going to have any of those slobs in Bonneville say I didn't know how to do the thing in style, and we'll have Vacca meet us with the team. No, sir, it is Pullman's or nothing. When it comes to buying furniture, I don't shine, perhaps, but I know what's due my wife."

He was obdurate, and late one afternoon the couple boarded the Transcontinental (the crack Overland Flyer of the Pacific and Southwestern) at the Oakland mole. Only Hilma's parents were there to say good-bye. Annixter knew that Magnus and Osterman were in the city, but he had laid his plans to elude them. Magnus, he could trust to be dignified, but that goat Osterman, one could never tell what he would do next. He did not propose to start his journey home in a shower of rice. Annixter marched down the line of cars, his hands encumbered with wicker telescope baskets, satchels, and valises, his tickets in his mouth, his hat on wrong side foremost, Hilma and her parents hurrying on behind him, trying to keep up. Annixter was in a turmoil of nerves lest something should go wrong; catching a train was always for him a little crisis. He rushed ahead so furiously that when he had found his Pullman he had lost his party. He set down his valises to mark the place and charged back along the platform, waving his arms.

"Come on," he cried, when, at length, he espied the others. "We've no more time."

He shouldered and urged them forward to where he had set his valises, only to find one of them gone. Instantly he raised an outcry. Aha, a fine way to treat passengers! There was P. and S. W. management for you. He would, by the Lord, he would—but the porter appeared in the vestibule of the car to placate him. He had already taken his valises inside.

Annixter would not permit Hilma's parents to board the car, declaring that the train might pull out any moment. So he and his wife, following the porter down the narrow passage by the stateroom, took their places and, raising the window, leaned out to say good-bye to Mr. and Mrs. Tree. These latter would not return to Quien Sabe. Old man Tree had found a business chance awaiting him in the matter of supplying his relative's hotel with dairy products. But Bonneville was not too far from San Francisco; the separation was by no means final.

The porters began taking up the steps that stood by the vestibule of each sleeping-car.

"Well, have a good time, daughter," observed her father; "and come up to see us whenever you can."

From beyond the enclosure of the depot's reverberating roof came the measured clang of a bell.

"I guess we're off," cried Annixter. "Good-bye, Mrs. Tree."

"Remember your promise, Hilma," her mother hastened to exclaim, "to write every Sunday afternoon."

There came a prolonged creaking and groan of straining wood and iron work, all along the length of the train. They all began to cry their good-byes at once. The train stirred, moved forward, and gathering slow headway, rolled slowly out into the sunlight. Hilma leaned out of the window and as long as she could keep her mother in sight waved her handkerchief. Then at length she sat back in her seat and looked at her husband.

"Well," she said.

"Well," echoed Annixter, "happy?" for the tears rose in her eyes.

She nodded energetically, smiling at him bravely.

"You look a little pale," he declared, frowning uneasily; "feel well?"

"Pretty well."

Promptly he was seized with uneasiness. "But not ALL well, hey? Is that it?"

It was true that Hilma had felt a faint tremour of seasickness on the ferry-boat coming from the city to the Oakland mole. No doubt a little nausea yet remained with her. But Annixter refused to accept this explanation. He was distressed beyond expression.

"Now you're going to be sick," he cried anxiously.

"No, no," she protested, "not a bit."

"But you said you didn't feel very well. Where is it you feel sick?"

"I don't know. I'm not sick. Oh, dear me, why will you bother?"

"Headache?"

"Not the least."

"You feel tired, then. That's it. No wonder, the way rushed you 'round to-day."

"Dear, I'm NOT tired, and I'm NOT sick, and I'm all RIGHT."

"No, no; I can tell. I think we'd best have the berth made up and you lie down."

"That would be perfectly ridiculous."

"Well, where is it you feel sick? Show me; put your hand on the place. Want to eat something?"

With elaborate minuteness, he cross-questioned her, refusing to let the subject drop, protesting that she had dark circles under her eyes; that she had grown thinner.

"Wonder if there's a doctor on board," he murmured, looking uncertainly about the car. "Let me see your tongue. I know—a little whiskey is what you want, that and some pru—"

"No, no, NO," she exclaimed. "I'm as well as I ever was in all my life. Look at me. Now, tell me, do I look likee a sick lady?"

He scrutinised her face distressfully.

"Now, don't I look the picture of health?" she challenged.

"In a way you do," he began, "and then again—"

Hilma beat a tattoo with her heels upon the floor, shutting her fists, the thumbs tucked inside. She closed her eyes, shaking her head energetically.

"I won't listen, I won't listen, I won't listen," she cried.

"But, just the same—"

"Gibble—gibble—gibble," she mocked. "I won't Listen, I won't listen." She put a hand over his mouth. "Look, here's the dining-car waiter, and the first call for supper, and your wife is hungry."

They went forward and had supper in the diner, while the long train, now out upon the main line, settled itself to its pace, the prolonged, even gallop that it would hold for the better part of the week, spinning out the miles as a cotton spinner spins thread.

It was already dark when Antioch was left behind. Abruptly the sunset appeared to wheel in the sky and readjusted itself to the right of the track behind Mount Diablo, here visible almost to its base. The train had turned southward. Neroly was passed, then Brentwood, then Byron. In the gathering dusk, mountains began to build themselves up on either hand, far off, blocking the horizon. The train shot forward, roaring. Between the mountains the land lay level, cut up into farms, ranches. These continually grew larger; growing wheat began to appear, billowing in the wind of the train's passage. The mountains grew higher, the land richer, and by the time the moon rose, the train was well into the northernmost limits of the valley of the San Joaquin.

Annixter had engaged an entire section, and after he and his wife went to bed had the porter close the upper berth. Hilma sat up in bed to say her prayers, both hands over her face, and then kissing Annixter good-night, went to sleep with the directness of a little child, holding his hand in both her own.

Annixter, who never could sleep on the train, dozed and tossed and fretted for hours, consulting his watch and time-table whenever there was a stop; twice he rose to get a drink of ice water, and between whiles was forever sitting up in the narrow berth, stretching himself and yawning, murmuring with uncertain relevance:

"Oh, Lord! Oh-h-h LORD!"

There were some dozen other passengers in the car—a lady with three children, a group of school-teachers, a couple of drummers, a stout gentleman with whiskers, and a well-dressed young man in a plaid travelling cap, whom Annixter had observed before supper time reading Daudet's "Tartarin" in the French.

But by nine o'clock, all these people were in their berths. Occasionally, above the rhythmic rumble of the wheels, Annixter could hear one of the lady's children fidgeting and complaining. The stout gentleman snored monotonously in two notes, one a rasping bass, the other a prolonged treble. At intervals, a brakeman or the passenger conductor pushed down the aisle, between the curtains, his red and white lamp over his arm. Looking out into the car Annixter saw in an end section where the berths had not been made up, the porter, in his white duck coat, dozing, his mouth wide open, his head on his shoulder.

The hours passed. Midnight came and went. Annixter, checking off the stations, noted their passage of Modesto, Merced, and Madeira. Then, after another broken nap, he lost count. He wondered where they were. Had they reached Fresno yet? Raising the window curtain, he made a shade with both hands on either side of his face and looked out. The night was thick, dark, clouded over. A fine rain was falling, leaving horizontal streaks on the glass of the outside window. Only the faintest grey blur indicated the sky. Everything else was impenetrable blackness.

"I think sure we must have passed Fresno," he muttered. He looked at his watch. It was about half-past three. "If we have passed Fresno," he said to himself, "I'd better wake the little girl pretty soon. She'll need about an hour to dress. Better find out for sure."

He drew on his trousers and shoes, got into his coat, and stepped out into the aisle. In the seat that had been occupied by the porter, the Pullman conductor, his cash box and car-schedules before him, was checking up his berths, a blue pencil behind his ear.

"What's the next stop, Captain?" inquired Annixter, coming up. "Have we reached Fresno yet?"

"Just passed it," the other responded, looking at Annixter over his spectacles.

"What's the next stop?"

"Goshen. We will be there in about forty-five minutes."

"Fair black night, isn't it?"

"Black as a pocket. Let's see, you're the party in upper and lower 9."

Annixter caught at the back of the nearest seat, just in time to prevent a fall, and the conductor's cash box was shunted off the surface of the plush seat and came clanking to the floor. The Pintsch lights overhead vibrated with blinding rapidity in the long, sliding jar that ran through the train from end to end, and the momentum of its speed suddenly decreasing, all but pitched the conductor from his seat. A hideous ear-splitting rasp made itself heard from the clamped-down Westinghouse gear underneath, and Annixter knew that the wheels had ceased to revolve and that the train was sliding forward upon the motionless flanges.

"Hello, hello," he exclaimed, "what's all up now?"

"Emergency brakes," declared the conductor, catching up his cash box and thrusting his papers and tickets into it. "Nothing much; probably a cow on the track."

He disappeared, carrying his lantern with him.

But the other passengers, all but the stout gentleman, were awake; heads were thrust from out the curtains, and Annixter, hurrying back to Hilma, was assailed by all manner of questions.

"What was that?"

"Anything wrong?"

"What's up, anyways?"

Hilma was just waking as Annixter pushed the curtain aside.

"Oh, I was so frightened. What's the matter, dear?" she exclaimed.

"I don't know," he answered. "Only the emergency brakes. Just a cow on the track, I guess. Don't get scared. It isn't anything."

But with a final shriek of the Westinghouse appliance, the train came to a definite halt.

At once the silence was absolute. The ears, still numb with the long-continued roar of wheels and clashing iron, at first refused to register correctly the smaller noises of the surroundings. Voices came from the other end of the car, strange and unfamiliar, as though heard at a great distance across the water. The stillness of the night outside was so profound that the rain, dripping from the car roof upon the road-bed underneath, was as distinct as the ticking of a clock.

"Well, we've sure stopped," observed one of the drummers.

"What is it?" asked Hilma again. "Are you sure there's nothing wrong?"

"Sure," said Annixter. Outside, underneath their window, they heard the sound of hurried footsteps crushing into the clinkers by the side of the ties. They passed on, and Annixter heard some one in the distance shout:

"Yes, on the other side."

Then the door at the end of their car opened and a brakeman with a red beard ran down the aisle and out upon the platform in front. The forward door closed. Everything was quiet again. In the stillness the fat gentleman's snores made themselves heard once more.

The minutes passed; nothing stirred. There was no sound but the dripping rain. The line of cars lay immobilised and inert under the night. One of the drummers, having stepped outside on the platform for a look around, returned, saying:

"There sure isn't any station anywheres about and no siding. Bet you they have had an accident of some kind."

"Ask the porter."

"I did. He don't know."

"Maybe they stopped to take on wood or water, or something."

"Well, they wouldn't use the emergency brakes for that, would they? Why, this train stopped almost in her own length. Pretty near slung me out the berth. Those were the emergency brakes. I heard some one say so."

From far out towards the front of the train, near the locomotive, came the sharp, incisive report of a revolver; then two more almost simultaneously; then, after a long interval, a fourth.

"Say, that's SHOOTING. By God, boys, they're shooting. Say, this is a hold-up."

Instantly a white-hot excitement flared from end to end of the car. Incredibly sinister, heard thus in the night, and in the rain, mysterious, fearful, those four pistol shots started confusion from out the sense of security like a frightened rabbit hunted from her burrow. Wide-eyed, the passengers of the car looked into each other's faces. It had come to them at last, this, they had so often read about. Now they were to see the real thing, now they were to face actuality, face this danger of the night, leaping in from out the blackness of the roadside, masked, armed, ready to kill. They were facing it now. They were held up.

Hilma said nothing, only catching Annixter's hand, looking squarely into his eyes.

"Steady, little girl," he said. "They can't hurt you. I won't leave you. By the Lord," he suddenly exclaimed, his excitement getting the better of him for a moment. "By the Lord, it's a hold-up."

The school-teachers were in the aisle of the car, in night gown, wrapper, and dressing sack, huddled together like sheep, holding on to each other, looking to the men, silently appealing for protection. Two of them were weeping, white to the lips.

"Oh, oh, oh, it's terrible. Oh, if they only won't hurt me."

But the lady with the children looked out from her berth, smiled reassuringly, and said:

"I'm not a bit frightened. They won't do anything to us if we keep quiet. I've my watch and jewelry all ready for them in my little black bag, see?"

She exhibited it to the passengers. Her children were all awake. They were quiet, looking about them with eager faces, interested and amused at this surprise. In his berth, the fat gentleman with whiskers snored profoundly.

"Say, I'm going out there," suddenly declared one of the drummers, flourishing a pocket revolver.

His friend caught his arm.

"Don't make a fool of yourself, Max," he said.

"They won't come near us," observed the well-dressed young man; "they are after the Wells-Fargo box and the registered mail. You won't do any good out there."

But the other loudly protested. No; he was going out. He didn't propose to be buncoed without a fight. He wasn't any coward.

"Well, you don't go, that's all," said his friend, angrily. "There's women and children in this car. You ain't going to draw the fire here."

"Well, that's to be thought of," said the other, allowing himself to be pacified, but still holding his pistol.

"Don't let him open that window," cried Annixter sharply from his place by Hilma's side, for the drummer had made as if to open the sash in one of the sections that had not been made up.

"Sure, that's right," said the others. "Don't open any windows. Keep your head in. You'll get us all shot if you aren't careful."

However, the drummer had got the window up and had leaned out before the others could interfere and draw him away.

"Say, by jove," he shouted, as he turned back to the car, "our engine's gone. We're standing on a curve and you can see the end of the train. She's gone, I tell you. Well, look for yourself."

In spite of their precautions, one after another, his friends looked out. Sure enough, the train was without a locomotive.

"They've done it so we can't get away," vociferated the drummer with the pistol. "Now, by jiminy-Christmas, they'll come through the cars and stand us up. They'll be in here in a minute. LORD! WHAT WAS THAT?"

From far away up the track, apparently some half-mile ahead of the train, came the sound of a heavy explosion. The windows of the car vibrated with it.

"Shooting again."

"That isn't shooting," exclaimed Annixter. "They've pulled the express and mail car on ahead with the engine and now they are dynamiting her open."

"That must be it. Yes, sure, that's just what they are doing."

The forward door of the car opened and closed and the school-teachers shrieked and cowered. The drummer with the revolver faced about, his eyes bulging. However, it was only the train conductor, hatless, his lantern in his hand. He was soaked with rain. He appeared in the aisle.

"Is there a doctor in this car?" he asked.

Promptly the passengers surrounded him, voluble with questions. But he was in a bad temper.

"I don't know anything more than you," he shouted angrily. "It was a hold-up. I guess you know that, don't you? Well, what more do you want to know? I ain't got time to fool around. They cut off our express car and have cracked it open, and they shot one of our train crew, that's all, and I want a doctor."

"Did they shoot him—kill him, do you mean?"

"Is he hurt bad?"

"Did the men get away?"

"Oh, shut up, will you all?" exclaimed the conductor.

"What do I know? Is there a DOCTOR in this car, that's what I want to know?"

The well-dressed young man stepped forward.

"I'm a doctor," he said. "Well, come along then," returned the conductor, in a surly voice, "and the passengers in this car," he added, turning back at the door and nodding his head menacingly, "will go back to bed and STAY there. It's all over and there's nothing to see."

He went out, followed by the young doctor.

Then ensued an interminable period of silence. The entire train seemed deserted. Helpless, bereft of its engine, a huge, decapitated monster it lay, half-way around a curve, rained upon, abandoned.

There was more fear in this last condition of affairs, more terror in the idea of this prolonged line of sleepers, with their nickelled fittings, their plate glass, their upholstery, vestibules, and the like, loaded down with people, lost and forgotten in the night and the rain, than there had been when the actual danger threatened.

What was to become of them now? Who was there to help them? Their engine was gone; they were helpless. What next was to happen?

Nobody came near the car. Even the porter had disappeared. The wait seemed endless, and the persistent snoring of the whiskered gentleman rasped the nerves like the scrape of a file.

"Well, how long are we going to stick here now?" began one of the drummers. "Wonder if they hurt the engine with their dynamite?"

"Oh, I know they will come through the car and rob us," wailed the school-teachers.

The lady with the little children went back to bed, and Annixter, assured that the trouble was over, did likewise. But nobody slept. From berth to berth came the sound of suppressed voices talking it all over, formulating conjectures. Certain points seemed to be settled upon, no one knew how, as indisputable. The highwaymen had been four in number and had stopped the train by pulling the bell cord. A brakeman had attempted to interfere and had been shot. The robbers had been on the train all the way from San Francisco. The drummer named Max remembered to have seen four "suspicious-looking characters" in the smoking-car at Lathrop, and had intended to speak to the conductor about them. This drummer had been in a hold-up before, and told the story of it over and over again.

At last, after what seemed to have been an hour's delay, and when the dawn had already begun to show in the east, the locomotive backed on to the train again with a reverberating jar that ran from car to car. At the jolting, the school-teachers screamed in chorus, and the whiskered gentleman stopped snoring and thrust his head from his curtains, blinking at the Pintsch lights. It appeared that he was an Englishman.

"I say," he asked of the drummer named Max, "I say, my friend, what place is this?"

The others roared with derision.

"We were HELD UP, sir, that's what we were. We were held up and you slept through it all. You missed the show of your life."

The gentleman fixed the group with a prolonged gaze. He said never a word, but little by little he was convinced that the drummers told the truth. All at once he grew wrathful, his face purpling. He withdrew his head angrily, buttoning his curtains together in a fury. The cause of his rage was inexplicable, but they could hear him resettling himself upon his pillows with exasperated movements of his head and shoulders. In a few moments the deep bass and shrill treble of his snoring once more sounded through the car.

At last the train got under way again, with useless warning blasts of the engine's whistle. In a few moments it was tearing away through the dawn at a wonderful speed, rocking around curves, roaring across culverts, making up time.

And all the rest of that strange night the passengers, sitting up in their unmade beds, in the swaying car, lighted by a strange mingling of pallid dawn and trembling Pintsch lights, rushing at break-neck speed through the misty rain, were oppressed by a vision of figures of terror, far behind them in the night they had left, masked, armed, galloping toward the mountains pistol in hand, the booty bound to the saddle bow, galloping, galloping on, sending a thrill of fear through all the country side.

The young doctor returned. He sat down in the smoking-room, lighting a cigarette, and Annixter and the drummers pressed around him to know the story of the whole affair.

"The man is dead," he declared, "the brakeman. He was shot through the lungs twice. They think the fellow got away with about five thousand in gold coin."

"The fellow? Wasn't there four of them?"

"No; only one. And say, let me tell you, he had his nerve with him. It seems he was on the roof of the express car all the time, and going as fast as we were, he jumped from the roof of the car down on to the coal on the engine's tender, and crawled over that and held up the men in the cab with his gun, took their guns from 'em and made 'em stop the train. Even ordered 'em to use the emergency gear, seems he knew all about it. Then he went back and uncoupled the express car himself.

"While he was doing this, a brakeman—you remember that brakeman that came through here once or twice—had a red mustache."

"THAT chap?"

"Sure. Well, as soon as the train stopped, this brakeman guessed something was wrong and ran up, saw the fellow cutting off the express car and took a couple of shots at him, and the fireman says the fellow didn't even take his hand off the coupling-pin; just turned around as cool as how-do-you-do and NAILED the brakeman right there. They weren't five feet apart when they began shooting. The brakeman had come on him unexpected, had no idea he was so close."

"And the express messenger, all this time?"

"Well, he did his best. Jumped out with his repeating shot-gun, but the fellow had him covered before he could turn round. Held him up and took his gun away from him. Say, you know I call that nerve, just the same. One man standing up a whole train-load, like that. Then, as soon as he'd cut the express car off, he made the engineer run her up the track about half a mile to a road crossing, WHERE HE HAD A HORSE TIED. What do you think of that? Didn't he have it all figured out close? And when he got there, he dynamited the safe and got the Wells-Fargo box. He took five thousand in gold coin; the messenger says it was railroad money that the company were sending down to Bakersfield to pay off with. It was in a bag. He never touched the registered mail, nor a whole wad of greenbacks that were in the safe, but just took the coin, got on his horse, and lit out. The engineer says he went to the east'ard."

"He got away, did he?"

"Yes, but they think they'll get him. He wore a kind of mask, but the brakeman recognised him positively. We got his ante-mortem statement. The brakeman said the fellow had a grudge against the road. He was a discharged employee, and lives near Bonneville."

"Dyke, by the Lord!" exclaimed Annixter.

"That's the name," said the young doctor.

When the train arrived at Bonneville, forty minutes behind time, it landed Annixter and Hilma in the midst of the very thing they most wished to avoid—an enormous crowd. The news that the Overland had been held up thirty miles south of Fresno, a brakeman killed and the safe looted, and that Dyke alone was responsible for the night's work, had been wired on ahead from Fowler, the train conductor throwing the despatch to the station agent from the flying train.

Before the train had come to a standstill under the arched roof of the Bonneville depot, it was all but taken by assault. Annixter, with Hilma on his arm, had almost to fight his way out of the car. The depot was black with people. S. Behrman was there, Delaney, Cyrus Ruggles, the town marshal, the mayor. Genslinger, his hat on the back of his head, ranged the train from cab to rear-lights, note-book in hand, interviewing, questioning, collecting facts for his extra. As Annixter descended finally to the platform, the editor, alert as a black-and-tan terrier, his thin, osseous hands quivering with eagerness, his brown, dry face working with excitement, caught his elbow.

"Can I have your version of the affair, Mr. Annixter?"

Annixter turned on him abruptly.

"Yes!" he exclaimed fiercely. "You and your gang drove Dyke from his job because he wouldn't work for starvation wages. Then you raised freight rates on him and robbed him of all he had. You ruined him and drove him to fill himself up with Caraher's whiskey. He's only taken back what you plundered him of, and now you're going to hound him over the State, hunt him down like a wild animal, and bring him to the gallows at San Quentin. That's my version of the affair, Mister Genslinger, but it's worth your subsidy from the P. and S. W. to print it."

There was a murmur of approval from the crowd that stood around, and Genslinger, with an angry shrug of one shoulder, took himself away.

At length, Annixter brought Hilma through the crowd to where young Vacca was waiting with the team. However, they could not at once start for the ranch, Annixter wishing to ask some questions at the freight office about a final consignment of chairs. It was nearly eleven o'clock before they could start home. But to gain the Upper Road to Quien Sabe, it was necessary to traverse all of Main Street, running through the heart of Bonneville.

The entire town seemed to be upon the sidewalks. By now the rain was over and the sun shining. The story of the hold-up—the work of a man whom every one knew and liked—was in every mouth. How had Dyke come to do it? Who would have believed it of him? Think of his poor mother and the little tad. Well, after all, he was not so much to blame; the railroad people had brought it on themselves. But he had shot a man to death. Ah, that was a serious business. Good-natured, big, broad-shouldered, jovial Dyke, the man they knew, with whom they had shaken hands only yesterday, yes, and drank with him. He had shot a man, killed him, had stood there in the dark and in the rain while they were asleep in their beds, and had killed a man. Now where was he? Instinctively eyes were turned eastward, over the tops of the houses, or down vistas of side streets to where the foot-hills of the mountains rose dim and vast over the edge of the valley. He was in amongst them; somewhere, in all that pile of blue crests and purple canyons he was hidden away. Now for weeks of searching, false alarms, clews, trailings, watchings, all the thrill and heart-bursting excitement of a man-hunt. Would he get away? Hardly a man on the sidewalks of the town that day who did not hope for it.

As Annixter's team trotted through the central portion of the town, young Vacca pointed to a denser and larger crowd around the rear entrance of the City Hall. Fully twenty saddle horses were tied to the iron rail underneath the scant, half-grown trees near by, and as Annixter and Hilma drove by, the crowd parted and a dozen men with revolvers on their hips pushed their way to the curbstone, and, mounting their horses, rode away at a gallop.

"It's the posse," said young Vacca.

Outside the town limits the ground was level. There was nothing to obstruct the view, and to the north, in the direction of Osterman's ranch, Vacca made out another party of horsemen, galloping eastward, and beyond these still another.

"There're the other posses," he announced. "That further one is Archie Moore's. He's the sheriff. He came down from Visalia on a special engine this morning."

When the team turned into the driveway to the ranch house, Hilma uttered a little cry, clasping her hands joyfully. The house was one glitter of new white paint, the driveway had been freshly gravelled, the flower-beds replenished. Mrs. Vacca and her daughter, who had been busy putting on the finishing touches, came to the door to welcome them.

"What's this case here?" asked Annixter, when, after helping his wife from the carry-all, his eye fell upon a wooden box of some three by five feet that stood on the porch and bore the red Wells-Fargo label.

"It came here last night, addressed to you, sir," exclaimed Mrs. Vacca. "We were sure it wasn't any of your furniture, so we didn't open it."

"Oh, maybe it's a wedding present," exclaimed Hilma, her eyes sparkling.

"Well, maybe it is," returned her husband. "Here, m' son, help me in with this."

Annixter and young Vacca bore the case into the sitting-room of the house, and Annixter, hammer in hand, attacked it vigorously. Vacca discreetly withdrew on signal from his mother, closing the door after him. Annixter and his wife were left alone.

"Oh, hurry, hurry," cried Hilma, dancing around him.

"I want to see what it is. Who do you suppose could have sent it to us? And so heavy, too. What do you think it can be?"

Annixter put the claw of the hammer underneath the edge of the board top and wrenched with all his might. The boards had been clamped together by a transverse bar and the whole top of the box came away in one piece. A layer of excelsior was disclosed, and on it a letter addressed by typewriter to Annixter. It bore the trade-mark of a business firm of Los Angeles. Annixter glanced at this and promptly caught it up before Hilma could see, with an exclamation of intelligence.

"Oh, I know what this is," he observed, carelessly trying to restrain her busy hands. "It isn't anything. Just some machinery. Let it go." But already she had pulled away the excelsior. Underneath, in temporary racks, were two dozen Winchester repeating rifles.

"Why—what—what—" murmured Hilma blankly.

"Well, I told you not to mind," said Annixter. "It isn't anything. Let's look through the rooms."

"But you said you knew what it was," she protested, bewildered. "You wanted to make believe it was machinery. Are you keeping anything from me? Tell me what it all means. Oh, why are you getting—these?"

She caught his arm, looking with intense eagerness into his face. She half understood already. Annixter saw that.

"Well," he said, lamely, "YOU know—it may not come to anything at all, but you know—well, this League of ours—suppose the Railroad tries to jump Quien Sabe or Los Muertos or any of the other ranches—we made up our minds—the Leaguers have—that we wouldn't let it. That's all."

"And I thought," cried Hilma, drawing back fearfully from the case of rifles, "and I thought it was a wedding present."

And that was their home-coming, the end of their bridal trip. Through the terror of the night, echoing with pistol shots, through that scene of robbery and murder, into this atmosphere of alarms, a man-hunt organising, armed horsemen silhouetted against the horizons, cases of rifles where wedding presents should have been, Annixter brought his young wife to be mistress of a home he might at any moment be called upon to defend with his life.

The days passed. Soon a week had gone by. Magnus Derrick and Osterman returned from the city without any definite idea as to the Corporation's plans. Lyman had been reticent. He knew nothing as to the progress of the land cases in Washington. There was no news. The Executive Committee of the League held a perfunctory meeting at Los Muertos at which nothing but routine business was transacted. A scheme put forward by Osterman for a conference with the railroad managers fell through because of the refusal of the company to treat with the ranchers upon any other basis than that of the new grading. It was impossible to learn whether or not the company considered Los Muertos, Quien Sabe, and the ranches around Bonneville covered by the test cases then on appeal.

Meanwhile there was no decrease in the excitement that Dyke's hold-up had set loose over all the county. Day after day it was the one topic of conversation, at street corners, at cross-roads, over dinner tables, in office, bank, and store. S. Behrman placarded the town with a notice of $500.00 reward for the ex-engineer's capture, dead or alive, and the express company supplemented this by another offer of an equal amount. The country was thick with parties of horsemen, armed with rifles and revolvers, recruited from Visalia, Goshen, and the few railroad sympathisers around Bonneville and Guadlajara. One after another of these returned, empty-handed, covered with dust and mud, their horses exhausted, to be met and passed by fresh posses starting out to continue the pursuit. The sheriff of Santa Clara County sent down his bloodhounds from San Jose—small, harmless-looking dogs, with a terrific bay—to help in the chase. Reporters from the San Francisco papers appeared, interviewing every one, sometimes even accompanying the searching bands. Horse hoofs clattered over the roads at night; bells were rung, the "Mercury" issued extra after extra; the bloodhounds bayed, gun butts clashed on the asphalt pavements of Bonneville; accidental discharges of revolvers brought the whole town into the street; farm hands called to each other across the fences of ranch-divisions—in a word, the country-side was in an uproar.

And all to no effect. The hoof-marks of Dyke's horse had been traced in the mud of the road to within a quarter of a mile of the foot-hills and there irretrievably lost. Three days after the hold-up, a sheep-herder was found who had seen the highwayman on a ridge in the higher mountains, to the northeast of Taurusa. And that was absolutely all. Rumours were thick, promising clews were discovered, new trails taken up, but nothing transpired to bring the pursuers and pursued any closer together. Then, after ten days of strain, public interest began to flag. It was believed that Dyke had succeeded in getting away. If this was true, he had gone to the southward, after gaining the mountains, and it would be his intention to work out of the range somewhere near the southern part of the San Joaquin, near Bakersfield. Thus, the sheriffs, marshals, and deputies decided. They had hunted too many criminals in these mountains before not to know the usual courses taken. In time, Dyke MUST come out of the mountains to get water and provisions. But this time passed, and from not one of the watched points came any word of his appearance. At last the posses began to disband. Little by little the pursuit was given up.

Only S. Behrman persisted. He had made up his mind to bring Dyke in. He succeeded in arousing the same degree of determination in Delaney—by now, a trusted aide of the Railroad—and of his own cousin, a real estate broker, named Christian, who knew the mountains and had once been marshal of Visalia in the old stock-raising days. These two went into the Sierras, accompanied by two hired deputies, and carrying with them a month's provisions and two of the bloodhounds loaned by the Santa Clara sheriff.

On a certain Sunday, a few days after the departure of Christian and Delaney, Annixter, who had been reading "David Copperfield" in his hammock on the porch of the ranch house, put down the book and went to find Hilma, who was helping Louisa Vacca set the table for dinner. He found her in the dining-room, her hands full of the gold-bordered china plates, only used on special occasions and which Louisa was forbidden to touch.

His wife was more than ordinarily pretty that day. She wore a dress of flowered organdie over pink sateen with pink ribbons about her waist and neck, and on her slim feet the low shoes she always affected, with their smart, bright buckles. Her thick, brown, sweet-smelling hair was heaped high upon her head and set off with a bow of black velvet, and underneath the shadow of its coils, her wide-open eyes, rimmed with the thin, black line of her lashes, shone continually, reflecting the sunlight. Marriage had only accentuated the beautiful maturity of Hilma's figure—now no longer precocious—defining the single, deep swell from her throat to her waist, the strong, fine amplitude of her hips, the sweet feminine undulation of her neck and shoulders. Her cheeks were pink with health, and her large round arms carried the piled-up dishes with never a tremour. Annixter, observant enough where his wife was concerned noted how the reflection of the white china set a glow of pale light underneath her chin.

"Hilma," he said, "I've been wondering lately about things. We're so blamed happy ourselves it won't do for us to forget about other people who are down, will it? Might change our luck. And I'm just likely to forget that way, too. It's my nature."

His wife looked up at him joyfully. Here was the new Annixter, certainly.

"In all this hullabaloo about Dyke," he went on "there's some one nobody ain't thought about at all. That's MRS. Dyke—and the little tad. I wouldn't be surprised if they were in a hole over there. What do you say we drive over to the hop ranch after dinner and see if she wants anything?"

Hilma put down the plates and came around the table and kissed him without a word.

As soon as their dinner was over, Annixter had the carry-all hitched up, and, dispensing with young Vacca, drove over to the hop ranch with Hilma.

Hilma could not keep back the tears as they passed through the lamentable desolation of the withered, brown vines, symbols of perished hopes and abandoned effort, and Annixter swore between his teeth.

Though the wheels of the carry-all grated loudly on the roadway in front of the house, nobody came to the door nor looked from the windows. The place seemed tenantless, infinitely lonely, infinitely sad. Annixter tied the team, and with Hilma approached the wide-open door, scuffling and tramping on the porch to attract attention. Nobody stirred. A Sunday stillness pervaded the place. Outside, the withered hop-leaves rustled like dry paper in the breeze. The quiet was ominous. They peered into the front room from the doorway, Hilma holding her husband's hand. Mrs. Dyke was there. She sat at the table in the middle of the room, her head, with its white hair, down upon her arm. A clutter of unwashed dishes were strewed over the red and white tablecloth. The unkempt room, once a marvel of neatness, had not been cleaned for days. Newspapers, Genslinger's extras and copies of San Francisco and Los Angeles dailies were scattered all over the room. On the table itself were crumpled yellow telegrams, a dozen of them, a score of them, blowing about in the draught from the door. And in the midst of all this disarray, surrounded by the published accounts of her son's crime, the telegraphed answers to her pitiful appeals for tidings fluttering about her head, the highwayman's mother, worn out, abandoned and forgotten, slept through the stillness of the Sunday afternoon.

Neither Hilma nor Annixter ever forgot their interview with Mrs. Dyke that day. Suddenly waking, she had caught sight of Annixter, and at once exclaimed eagerly:

"Is there any news?"

For a long time afterwards nothing could be got from her. She was numb to all other issues than the one question of Dyke's capture. She did not answer their questions nor reply to their offers of assistance. Hilma and Annixter conferred together without lowering their voices, at her very elbow, while she looked vacantly at the floor, drawing one hand over the other in a persistent, maniacal gesture. From time to time she would start suddenly from her chair, her eyes wide, and as if all at once realising Annixter's presence, would cry out:

"Is there any news?"

"Where is Sidney, Mrs. Dyke?" asked Hilma for the fourth time. "Is she well? Is she taken care of?"

"Here's the last telegram," said Mrs. Dyke, in a loud, monotonous voice. "See, it says there is no news. He didn't do it," she moaned, rocking herself back and forth, drawing one hand over the other, "he didn't do it, he didn't do it, he didn't do it. I don't know where he is."

When at last she came to herself, it was with a flood of tears. Hilma put her arms around the poor, old woman, as she bowed herself again upon the table, sobbing and weeping.

"Oh, my son, my son," she cried, "my own boy, my only son! If I could have died for you to have prevented this. I remember him when he was little. Such a splendid little fellow, so brave, so loving, with never an unkind thought, never a mean action. So it was all his life. We were never apart. It was always 'dear little son,' and 'dear mammy' between us—never once was he unkind, and he loved me and was the gentlest son to me. And he was a GOOD man. He is now, he is now. They don't understand him. They are not even sure that he did this. He never meant it. They don't know my son. Why, he wouldn't have hurt a kitten. Everybody loved him. He was driven to it. They hounded him down, they wouldn't let him alone. He was not right in his mind. They hounded him to it," she cried fiercely, "they hounded him to it. They drove him and goaded him till he couldn't stand it any longer, and now they mean to kill him for turning on them. They are hunting him with dogs; night after night I have stood on the porch and heard the dogs baying far off. They are tracking my boy with dogs like a wild animal. May God never forgive them." She rose to her feet, terrible, her white hair unbound. "May God punish them as they deserve, may they never prosper—on my knees I shall pray for it every night—may their money be a curse to them, may their sons, their first-born, only sons, be taken from them in their youth."

But Hilma interrupted, begging her to be silent, to be quiet. The tears came again then and the choking sobs. Hilma took her in her arms.

"Oh, my little boy, my little boy," she cried. "My only son, all that I had, to have come to this! He was not right in his mind or he would have known it would break my heart. Oh, my son, my son, if I could have died for you."

Sidney came in, clinging to her dress, weeping, imploring her not to cry, protesting that they never could catch her papa, that he would come back soon. Hilma took them both, the little child and the broken-down old woman, in the great embrace of her strong arms, and they all three sobbed together.

Annixter stood on the porch outside, his back turned, looking straight before him into the wilderness of dead vines, his teeth shut hard, his lower lip thrust out.

"I hope S. Behrman is satisfied with all this," he muttered. "I hope he is satisfied now, damn his soul!"

All at once an idea occurred to him. He turned about and reentered the room.

"Mrs Dyke," he began, "I want you and Sidney to come over and live at Quien Sabe. I know—you can't make me believe that the reporters and officers and officious busy-faces that pretend to offer help just so as they can satisfy their curiosity aren't nagging you to death. I want you to let me take care of you and the little tad till all this trouble of yours is over with. There's plenty of place for you. You can have the house my wife's people used to live in. You've got to look these things in the face. What are you going to do to get along? You must be very short of money. S. Behrman will foreclose on you and take the whole place in a little while, now. I want you to let me help you, let Hilma and me be good friends to you. It would be a privilege."

Mrs. Dyke tried bravely to assume her pride, insisting that she could manage, but her spirit was broken. The whole affair ended unexpectedly, with Annixter and Hilma bringing Dyke's mother and little girl back to Quien Sabe in the carry-all.

Mrs. Dyke would not take with her a stick of furniture nor a single ornament. It would only serve to remind her of a vanished happiness. She packed a few clothes of her own and Sidney's in a little trunk, Hilma helping her, and Annixter stowed the trunk under the carry-all's back seat. Mrs. Dyke turned the key in the door of the house and Annixter helped her to her seat beside his wife. They drove through the sear, brown hop vines. At the angle of the road Mrs. Dyke turned around and looked back at the ruin of the hop ranch, the roof of the house just showing above the trees. She never saw it again.

As soon as Annixter and Hilma were alone, after their return to Quien Sabe—Mrs. Dyke and Sidney having been installed in the Trees' old house—Hilma threw her arms around her husband's neck.

"Fine," she exclaimed, "oh, it was fine of you, dear to think of them and to be so good to them. My husband is such a GOOD man. So unselfish. You wouldn't have thought of being kind to Mrs. Dyke and Sidney a little while ago. You wouldn't have thought of them at all. But you did now, and it's just because you love me true, isn't it? Isn't it? And because it's made you a better man. I'm so proud and glad to think it's so. It is so, isn't it? Just because you love me true."

"You bet it is, Hilma," he told her.

As Hilma and Annixter were sitting down to the supper which they found waiting for them, Louisa Vacca came to the door of the dining-room to say that Harran Derrick had telephoned over from Los Muertos for Annixter, and had left word for him to ring up Los Muertos as soon as he came in.

"He said it was important," added Louisa Vacca.

"Maybe they have news from Washington," suggested Hilma.

Annixter would not wait to have supper, but telephoned to Los Muertos at once. Magnus answered the call. There was a special meeting of the Executive Committee of the League summoned for the next day, he told Annixter. It was for the purpose of considering the new grain tariff prepared by the Railroad Commissioners. Lyman had written that the schedule of this tariff had just been issued, that he had not been able to construct it precisely according to the wheat-growers' wishes, and that he, himself, would come down to Los Muertos and explain its apparent discrepancies. Magnus said Lyman would be present at the session.

Annixter, curious for details, forbore, nevertheless, to question. The connection from Los Muertos to Quien Sabe was made through Bonneville, and in those troublesome times no one could be trusted. It could not be known who would overhear conversations carried on over the lines. He assured Magnus that he would be on hand. The time for the Committee meeting had been set for seven o'clock in the evening, in order to accommodate Lyman, who wrote that he would be down on the evening train, but would be compelled, by pressure of business, to return to the city early the next morning.

At the time appointed, the men composing the Committee gathered about the table in the dining-room of the Los Muertos ranch house. It was almost a reproduction of the scene of the famous evening when Osterman had proposed the plan of the Ranchers' Railroad Commission. Magnus Derrick sat at the head of the table, in his buttoned frock coat. Whiskey bottles and siphons of soda-water were within easy reach. Presley, who by now was considered the confidential friend of every member of the Committee, lounged as before on the sofa, smoking cigarettes, the cat Nathalie on his knee. Besides Magnus and Annixter, Osterman was present, and old Broderson and Harran; Garnet from the Ruby Rancho and Gethings of the San Pablo, who were also members of the Executive Committee, were on hand, preoccupied, bearded men, smoking black cigars, and, last of all, Dabney, the silent old man, of whom little was known but his name, and who had been made a member of the Committee, nobody could tell why.

"My son Lyman should be here, gentlemen, within at least ten minutes. I have sent my team to meet him at Bonneville," explained Magnus, as he called the meeting to order. "The Secretary will call the roll."

Osterman called the roll, and, to fill in the time, read over the minutes of the previous meeting. The treasurer was making his report as to the funds at the disposal of the League when Lyman arrived.

Magnus and Harran went forward to meet him, and the Committee rather awkwardly rose and remained standing while the three exchanged greetings, the members, some of whom had never seen their commissioner, eyeing him out of the corners of their eyes.

Lyman was dressed with his usual correctness. His cravat was of the latest fashion, his clothes of careful design and unimpeachable fit. His shoes, of patent leather, reflected the lamplight, and he carried a drab overcoat over his arm. Before being introduced to the Committee, he excused himself a moment and ran to see his mother, who waited for him in the adjoining sitting-room. But in a few moments he returned, asking pardon for the delay.

He was all affability; his protruding eyes, that gave such an unusual, foreign appearance to his very dark face, radiated geniality. He was evidently anxious to please, to produce a good impression upon the grave, clumsy farmers before whom he stood. But at the same time, Presley, watching him from his place on the sofa, could imagine that he was rather nervous. He was too nimble in his cordiality, and the little gestures he made in bringing his cuffs into view and in touching the ends of his tight, black mustache with the ball of his thumb were repeated with unnecessary frequency.

"Mr. Broderson, my son, Lyman, my eldest son. Mr. Annixter, my son, Lyman."

The Governor introduced him to the ranchers, proud of Lyman's good looks, his correct dress, his ease of manner. Lyman shook hands all around, keeping up a flow of small talk, finding a new phrase for each member, complimenting Osterman, whom he already knew, upon his talent for organisation, recalling a mutual acquaintance to the mind of old Broderson. At length, however, he sat down at the end of the table, opposite his brother. There was a silence.

Magnus rose to recapitulate the reasons for the extra session of the Committee, stating again that the Board of Railway Commissioners which they—the ranchers—had succeeded in seating had at length issued the new schedule of reduced rates, and that Mr. Derrick had been obliging enough to offer to come down to Los Muertos in person to acquaint the wheat-growers of the San Joaquin with the new rates for the carriage of their grain.

But Lyman very politely protested, addressing his father punctiliously as "Mr. Chairman," and the other ranchers as "Gentlemen of the Executive Committee of the League." He had no wish, he said, to disarrange the regular proceedings of the Committee. Would it not be preferable to defer the reading of his report till "new business" was called for? In the meanwhile, let the Committee proceed with its usual work. He understood the necessarily delicate nature of this work, and would be pleased to withdraw till the proper time arrived for him to speak.

"Good deal of backing and filling about the reading of a column of figures," muttered Annixter to the man at his elbow.

Lyman "awaited the Committee's decision." He sat down, touching the ends of his mustache.

"Oh, play ball," growled Annixter.

Gethings rose to say that as the meeting had been called solely for the purpose of hearing and considering the new grain tariff, he was of the opinion that routine business could be dispensed with and the schedule read at once. It was so ordered.

Lyman rose and made a long speech. Voluble as Osterman himself, he, nevertheless, had at his command a vast number of ready-made phrases, the staples of a political speaker, the stock in trade of the commercial lawyer, which rolled off his tongue with the most persuasive fluency. By degrees, in the course of his speech, he began to insinuate the idea that the wheat-growers had never expected to settle their difficulties with the Railroad by the work of a single commission; that they had counted upon a long, continued campaign of many years, railway commission succeeding railway commission, before the desired low rates should be secured; that the present Board of Commissioners was only the beginning and that too great results were not expected from them. All this he contrived to mention casually, in the talk, as if it were a foregone conclusion, a matter understood by all.

As the speech continued, the eyes of the ranchers around the table were fixed with growing attention upon this well-dressed, city-bred young man, who spoke so fluently and who told them of their own intentions. A feeling of perplexity began to spread, and the first taint of distrust invaded their minds.

"But the good work has been most auspiciously inaugurated," continued Lyman. "Reforms so sweeping as the one contemplated cannot be accomplished in a single night. Great things grow slowly, benefits to be permanent must accrue gradually. Yet, in spite of all this, your commissioners have done much. Already the phalanx of the enemy is pierced, already his armour is dinted. Pledged as were your commissioners to an average ten per cent. reduction in rates for the carriage of grain by the Pacific and Southwestern Railroad, we have rigidly adhered to the demands of our constituency, we have obeyed the People. The main problem has not yet been completely solved; that is for later, when we shall have gathered sufficient strength to attack the enemy in his very stronghold; BUT AN AVERAGE TEN PER CENT. CUT HAS BEEN MADE ALL OVER THE STATE. We have made a great advance, have taken a great step forward, and if the work is carried ahead, upon the lines laid down by the present commissioners and their constituents, there is every reason to believe that within a very few years equitable and stable rates for the shipment of grain from the San Joaquin Valley to Stockton, Port Costa, and tidewater will be permanently imposed."

"Well, hold on," exclaimed Annixter, out of order and ignoring the Governor's reproof, "hasn't your commission reduced grain rates in the San Joaquin?"

"We have reduced grain rates by ten per cent. all over the State," rejoined Lyman. "Here are copies of the new schedule."

He drew them from his valise and passed them around the table.

"You see," he observed, "the rate between Mayfield and Oakland, for instance, has been reduced by twenty-five cents a ton."

"Yes—but—but—" said old Broderson, "it is rather unusual, isn't it, for wheat in that district to be sent to Oakland?"

"Why, look here," exclaimed Annixter, looking up from the schedule, "where is there any reduction in rates in the San Joaquin—from Bonneville and Guadalajara, for instance? I don't see as you've made any reduction at all. Is this right? Did you give me the right schedule?"

"Of course, ALL the points in the State could not be covered at once," returned Lyman. "We never expected, you know, that we could cut rates in the San Joaquin the very first move; that is for later. But you will see we made very material reductions on shipments from the upper Sacramento Valley; also the rate from Ione to Marysville has been reduced eighty cents a ton."

"Why, rot," cried Annixter, "no one ever ships wheat that way."

"The Salinas rate," continued Lyman, "has been lowered seventy-five cents; the St. Helena rate fifty cents, and please notice the very drastic cut from Red Bluff, north, along the Oregon route, to the Oregon State Line."

"Where not a carload of wheat is shipped in a year," commented Gethings of the San Pablo.

"Oh, you will find yourself mistaken there, Mr. Gethings," returned Lyman courteously. "And for the matter of that, a low rate would stimulate wheat-production in that district."

The order of the meeting was broken up, neglected; Magnus did not even pretend to preside. In the growing excitement over the inexplicable schedule, routine was not thought of. Every one spoke at will.

"Why, Lyman," demanded Magnus, looking across the table to his son, "is this schedule correct? You have not cut rates in the San Joaquin at all. We—these gentlemen here and myself, we are no better off than we were before we secured your election as commissioner."

"We were pledged to make an average ten per cent. cut, sir—"

"It IS an average ten per cent. cut," cried Osterman. "Oh, yes, that's plain. It's an average ten per cent. cut all right, but you've made it by cutting grain rates between points where practically no grain is shipped. We, the wheat-growers in the San Joaquin, where all the wheat is grown, are right where we were before. The Railroad won't lose a nickel. By Jingo, boys," he glanced around the table, "I'd like to know what this means."

"The Railroad, if you come to that," returned Lyman, "has already lodged a protest against the new rate."

Annixter uttered a derisive shout.

"A protest! That's good, that is. When the P. and S. W. objects to rates it don't 'protest,' m' son. The first you hear from Mr. Shelgrim is an injunction from the courts preventing the order for new rates from taking effect. By the Lord," he cried angrily, leaping to his feet, "I would like to know what all this means, too. Why didn't you reduce our grain rates? What did we elect you for?"

"Yes, what did we elect you for?" demanded Osterman and Gethings, also getting to their feet.

"Order, order, gentlemen," cried Magnus, remembering the duties of his office and rapping his knuckles on the table. "This meeting has been allowed to degenerate too far already."

"You elected us," declared Lyman doggedly, "to make an average ten per cent. cut on grain rates. We have done it. Only because you don't benefit at once, you object. It makes a difference whose ox is gored, it seems."

"Lyman!"

It was Magnus who spoke. He had drawn himself to his full six feet. His eyes were flashing direct into his son's. His voice rang with severity.

"Lyman, what does this mean?"

The other spread out his hands.

"As you see, sir. We have done our best. I warned you not to expect too much. I told you that this question of transportation was difficult. You would not wish to put rates so low that the action would amount to confiscation of property."

"Why did you not lower rates in the valley of the San Joaquin?"

"That was not a PROMINENT issue in the affair," responded Lyman, carefully emphasising his words. "I understand, of course, it was to be approached IN TIME. The main point was AN AVERAGE TEN PER CENT. REDUCTION. Rates WILL be lowered in the San Joaquin. The ranchers around Bonneville will be able to ship to Port Costa at equitable rates, but so radical a measure as that cannot be put through in a turn of the hand. We must study—"

"You KNEW the San Joaquin rate was an issue," shouted Annixter, shaking his finger across the table. "What do we men who backed you care about rates up in Del Norte and Siskiyou Counties? Not a whoop in hell. It was the San Joaquin rate we were fighting for, and we elected you to reduce that. You didn't do it and you don't intend to, and, by the Lord Harry, I want to know why."

"You'll know, sir—" began Lyman.

"Well, I'll tell you why," vociferated Osterman. "I'll tell you why. It's because we have been sold out. It's because the P. and S. W. have had their spoon in this boiling. It's because our commissioners have betrayed us. It's because we're a set of damn fool farmers and have been cinched again."

Lyman paled under his dark skin at the direct attack. He evidently had not expected this so soon. For the fraction of one instant he lost his poise. He strove to speak, but caught his breath, stammering.

"What have you to say, then?" cried Harran, who, until now, had not spoken.

"I have this to say," answered Lyman, making head as best he might, "that this is no proper spirit in which to discuss business. The Commission has fulfilled its obligations. It has adjusted rates to the best of its ability. We have been at work for two months on the preparation of this schedule—"

"That's a lie," shouted Annixter, his face scarlet; "that's a lie. That schedule was drawn in the offices of the Pacific and Southwestern and you know it. It's a scheme of rates made for the Railroad and by the Railroad and you were bought over to put your name to it."

There was a concerted outburst at the words. All the men in the room were on their feet, gesticulating and vociferating.

"Gentlemen, gentlemen," cried Magnus, "are we schoolboys, are we ruffians of the street?"

"We're a set of fool farmers and we've been betrayed," cried Osterman.

"Well, what have you to say? What have you to say?" persisted Harran, leaning across the table toward his brother. "For God's sake, Lyman, you've got SOME explanation."

"You've misunderstood," protested Lyman, white and trembling. "You've misunderstood. You've expected too much. Next year,—next year,—soon now, the Commission will take up the—the Commission will consider the San Joaquin rate. We've done our best, that is all."

"Have you, sir?" demanded Magnus.

The Governor's head was in a whirl; a sensation, almost of faintness, had seized upon him. Was it possible? Was it possible?

"Have you done your best?" For a second he compelled Lyman's eye. The glances of father and son met, and, in spite of his best efforts, Lyman's eyes wavered. He began to protest once more, explaining the matter over again from the beginning. But Magnus did not listen. In that brief lapse of time he was convinced that the terrible thing had happened, that the unbelievable had come to pass. It was in the air. Between father and son, in some subtle fashion, the truth that was a lie stood suddenly revealed. But even then Magnus would not receive it. Lyman do this! His son, his eldest son, descend to this! Once more and for the last time he turned to him and in his voice there was that ring that compelled silence.

"Lyman," he said, "I adjure you—I—I demand of you as you are my son and an honourable man, explain yourself. What is there behind all this? It is no longer as Chairman of the Committee I speak to you, you a member of the Railroad Commission. It is your father who speaks, and I address you as my son. Do you understand the gravity of this crisis; do you realise the responsibility of your position; do you not see the importance of this moment? Explain yourself."

"There is nothing to explain."

"You have not reduced rates in the San Joaquin? You have not reduced rates between Bonneville and tidewater?"

"I repeat, sir, what I said before. An average ten per cent. cut—"

"Lyman, answer me, yes or no. Have you reduced the Bonneville rate?"

"It could not be done so soon. Give us time. We—"

"Yes or no! By God, sir, do you dare equivocate with me? Yes or no; have you reduced the Bonneville rate?"

"No."

"And answer ME," shouted Harran, leaning far across the table, "answer ME. Were you paid by the Railroad to leave the San Joaquin rate untouched?"

Lyman, whiter than ever, turned furious upon his brother.

"Don't you dare put that question to me again."

"No, I won't," cried Harran, "because I'll TELL you to your villain's face that you WERE paid to do it."

On the instant the clamour burst forth afresh. Still on their feet, the ranchers had, little by little, worked around the table, Magnus alone keeping his place. The others were in a group before Lyman, crowding him, as it were, to the wall, shouting into his face with menacing gestures. The truth that was a lie, the certainty of a trust betrayed, a pledge ruthlessly broken, was plain to every one of them.

"By the Lord! men have been shot for less than this," cried Osterman. "You've sold us out, you, and if you ever bring that dago face of yours on a level with mine again, I'll slap it."

"Keep your hands off," exclaimed Lyman quickly, the aggressiveness of the cornered rat flaming up within him. "No violence. Don't you go too far."

"How much were you paid? How much were you paid?" vociferated Harran.

"Yes, yes, what was your price?" cried the others. They were beside themselves with anger; their words came harsh from between their set teeth; their gestures were made with their fists clenched.

"You know the Commission acted in good faith," retorted Lyman. "You know that all was fair and above board."

"Liar," shouted Annixter; "liar, bribe-eater. You were bought and paid for," and with the words his arm seemed almost of itself to leap out from his shoulder. Lyman received the blow squarely in the face and the force of it sent him staggering backwards toward the wall. He tripped over his valise and fell half way, his back supported against the closed door of the room. Magnus sprang forward. His son had been struck, and the instincts of a father rose up in instant protest; rose for a moment, then forever died away in his heart. He checked the words that flashed to his mind. He lowered his upraised arm. No, he had but one son. The poor, staggering creature with the fine clothes, white face, and blood-streaked lips was no longer his. A blow could not dishonour him more than he had dishonoured himself.

But Gethings, the older man, intervened, pulling Annixter back, crying:

"Stop, this won't do. Not before his father."

"I am no father to this man, gentlemen," exclaimed Magnus. "From now on, I have but one son. You, sir," he turned to Lyman, "you, sir, leave my house."

Lyman, his handkerchief to his lips, his smart cravat in disarray, caught up his hat and coat. He was shaking with fury, his protruding eyes were blood-shot. He swung open the door.

"Ruffians," he shouted from the threshold, "ruffians, bullies. Do your own dirty business yourselves after this. I'm done with you. How is it, all of a sudden you talk about honour? How is it that all at once you're so clean and straight? You weren't so particular at Sacramento just before the nominations. How was the Board elected? I'm a bribe-eater, am I? Is it any worse than GIVING a bribe? Ask Magnus Derrick what he thinks about that. Ask him how much he paid the Democratic bosses at Sacramento to swing the convention."

He went out, slamming the door.

Presley followed. The whole affair made him sick at heart, filled him with infinite disgust, infinite weariness. He wished to get away from it all. He left the dining-room and the excited, clamouring men behind him and stepped out on the porch of the ranch house, closing the door behind him. Lyman was nowhere in sight. Presley was alone. It was late, and after the lamp-heated air of the dining-room, the coolness of the night was delicious, and its vast silence, after the noise and fury of the committee meeting, descended from the stars like a benediction. Presley stepped to the edge of the porch, looking off to southward.

And there before him, mile after mile, illimitable, covering the earth from horizon to horizon, lay the Wheat. The growth, now many days old, was already high from the ground. There it lay, a vast, silent ocean, shimmering a pallid green under the moon and under the stars; a mighty force, the strength of nations, the life of the world. There in the night, under the dome of the sky, it was growing steadily. To Presley's mind, the scene in the room he had just left dwindled to paltry insignificance before this sight. Ah, yes, the Wheat—it was over this that the Railroad, the ranchers, the traitor false to his trust, all the members of an obscure conspiracy, were wrangling. As if human agency could affect this colossal power! What were these heated, tiny squabbles, this feverish, small bustle of mankind, this minute swarming of the human insect, to the great, majestic, silent ocean of the Wheat itself! Indifferent, gigantic, resistless, it moved in its appointed grooves. Men, Liliputians, gnats in the sunshine, buzzed impudently in their tiny battles, were born, lived through their little day, died, and were forgotten; while the Wheat, wrapped in Nirvanic calm, grew steadily under the night, alone with the stars and with God.

V

Jack-rabbits were a pest that year and Presley occasionally found amusement in hunting them with Harran's half-dozen greyhounds, following the chase on horseback. One day, between two and three months after Lyman s visit to Los Muertos, as he was returning toward the ranch house from a distant and lonely quarter of Los Muertos, he came unexpectedly upon a strange sight.

Some twenty men, Annixter's and Osterman's tenants, and small ranchers from east of Guadalajara—all members of the League—were going through the manual of arms under Harran Derrick's supervision. They were all equipped with new Winchester rifles. Harran carried one of these himself and with it he illustrated the various commands he gave. As soon as one of the men under his supervision became more than usually proficient, he was told off to instruct a file of the more backward. After the manual of arms, Harran gave the command to take distance as skirmishers, and when the line had opened out so that some half-dozen feet intervened between each man, an advance was made across the field, the men stooping low and snapping the hammers of their rifles at an imaginary enemy.

The League had its agents in San Francisco, who watched the movements of the Railroad as closely as was possible, and some time before this, Annixter had received word that the Marshal and his deputies were coming down to Bonneville to put the dummy buyers of his ranch in possession. The report proved to be but the first of many false alarms, but it had stimulated the League to unusual activity, and some three or four hundred men were furnished with arms and from time to time were drilled in secret.

Among themselves, the ranchers said that if the Railroad managers did not believe they were terribly in earnest in the stand they had taken, they were making a fatal mistake.

Harran reasserted this statement to Presley on the way home to the ranch house that same day. Harran had caught up with him by the time he reached the Lower Road, and the two jogged homeward through the miles of standing wheat.

"They may jump the ranch, Pres," he said, "if they try hard enough, but they will never do it while I am alive. By the way," he added, "you know we served notices yesterday upon S. Behrman and Cy. Ruggles to quit the country. Of course, they won't do it, but they won't be able to say they didn't have warning."

About an hour later, the two reached the ranch house, but as Harran rode up the driveway, he uttered an exclamation.

"Hello," he said, "something is up. That's Genslinger's buckboard."

In fact, the editor's team was tied underneath the shade of a giant eucalyptus tree near by. Harran, uneasy under this unexpected visit of the enemy's friend, dismounted without stabling his horse, and went at once to the dining-room, where visitors were invariably received. But the dining-room was empty, and his mother told him that Magnus and the editor were in the "office." Magnus had said they were not to be disturbed.

Earlier in the afternoon, the editor had driven up to the porch and had asked Mrs. Derrick, whom he found reading a book of poems on the porch, if he could see Magnus. At the time, the Governor had gone with Phelps to inspect the condition of the young wheat on Hooven's holding, but within half an hour he returned, and

Genslinger had asked him for a "few moments' talk in private."

The two went into the "office," Magnus locking the door behind him. "Very complete you are here, Governor," observed the editor in his alert, jerky manner, his black, bead-like eyes twinkling around the room from behind his glasses. "Telephone, safe, ticker, account-books—well, that's progress, isn't it? Only way to manage a big ranch these days. But the day of the big ranch is over. As the land appreciates in value, the temptation to sell off small holdings will be too strong. And then the small holding can be cultivated to better advantage. I shall have an editorial on that some day."

"The cost of maintaining a number of small holdings," said Magnus, indifferently, "is, of course, greater than if they were all under one management."

"That may be, that may be," rejoined the other.

There was a long pause. Genslinger leaned back in his chair and rubbed a knee. Magnus, standing erect in front of the safe, waited for him to speak.

"This is an unfortunate business, Governor," began the editor, "this misunderstanding between the ranchers and the Railroad. I wish it could be adjusted. HERE are two industries that MUST be in harmony with one another, or we all go to pot."

"I should prefer not to be interviewed on the subject, Mr. Genslinger," said Magnus.

"Oh, no, oh, no. Lord love you, Governor, I don't want to interview you. We all know how you stand."

Again there was a long silence. Magnus wondered what this little man, usually so garrulous, could want of him. At length, Genslinger began again. He did not look at Magnus, except at long intervals.

"About the present Railroad Commission," he remarked. "That was an interesting campaign you conducted in Sacramento and San Francisco."

Magnus held his peace, his hands shut tight. Did Genslinger know of Lyman's disgrace? Was it for this he had come? Would the story of it be the leading article in to-morrow's Mercury?

"An interesting campaign," repeated Genslinger, slowly; "a very interesting campaign. I watched it with every degree of interest. I saw its every phase, Mr. Derrick."

"The campaign was not without its interest," admitted Magnus.

"Yes," said Genslinger, still more deliberately, "and some phases of it were—more interesting than others, as, for instance, let us say the way in which you—personally—secured the votes of certain chairmen of delegations—NEED I particularise further? Yes, those men—the way you got their votes. Now, THAT I should say, Mr. Derrick, was the most interesting move in the whole game—to you. Hm, curious," he murmured, musingly. "Let's see. You deposited two one-thousand dollar bills and four five-hundred dollar bills in a box—three hundred and eight was the number—in a box in the Safety Deposit Vaults in San Francisco, and then—let's see, you gave a key to this box to each of the gentlemen in question, and after the election the box was empty. Now, I call that interesting—curious, because it's a new, safe, and highly ingenious method of bribery. How did you happen to think of it, Governor?"

"Do you know what you are doing, sir?" Magnus burst forth. "Do you know what you are insinuating, here, in my own house?"

"Why, Governor," returned the editor, blandly, "I'm not INSINUATING anything. I'm talking about what I KNOW."

"It's a lie."

Genslinger rubbed his chin reflectively.

"Well," he answered, "you can have a chance to prove it before the Grand Jury, if you want to."

"My character is known all over the State," blustered Magnus. "My politics are pure politics. My—"

"No one needs a better reputation for pure politics than the man who sets out to be a briber," interrupted Genslinger, "and I might as well tell you, Governor, that you can't shout me down. I can put my hand on the two chairmen you bought before it's dark to-day. I've had their depositions in my safe for the last six weeks. We could make the arrests to-morrow, if we wanted. Governor, you sure did a risky thing when you went into that Sacramento fight, an awful risky thing. Some men can afford to have bribery charges preferred against them, and it don't hurt one little bit, but YOU—Lord, it would BUST you, Governor, bust you dead. I know all about the whole shananigan business from A to Z, and if you don't believe it—here," he drew a long strip of paper from his pocket, "here's a galley proof of the story."

Magnus took it in his hands. There, under his eyes, scare-headed, double-leaded, the more important clauses printed in bold type, was the detailed account of the "deal" Magnus had made with the two delegates. It was pitiless, remorseless, bald. Every statement was substantiated, every statistic verified with Genslinger's meticulous love for exactness. Besides all that, it had the ring of truth. It was exposure, ruin, absolute annihilation.

"That's about correct, isn't it?" commented Genslinger, as Derrick finished reading. Magnus did not reply. "I think it is correct enough," the editor continued. "But I thought it would only be fair to you to let you see it before it was published."

The one thought uppermost in Derrick's mind, his one impulse of the moment was, at whatever cost, to preserve his dignity, not to allow this man to exult in the sight of one quiver of weakness, one trace of defeat, one suggestion of humiliation. By an effort that put all his iron rigidity to the test, he forced himself to look straight into Genslinger's eyes.

"I congratulate you," he observed, handing back the proof, "upon your journalistic enterprise. Your paper will sell to-morrow."

"Oh, I don't know as I want to publish this story," remarked the editor, indifferently, putting away the galley. "I'm just like that. The fun for me is running a good story to earth, but once I've got it, I lose interest. And, then, I wouldn't like to see you—holding the position you do, President of the League and a leading man of the county—I wouldn't like to see a story like this smash you over. It's worth more to you to keep it out of print than for me to put it in. I've got nothing much to gain but a few extra editions, but you—Lord, you would lose everything. Your committee was in the deal right enough. But your League, all the San Joaquin Valley, everybody in the State believes the commissioners were fairly elected."

"Your story," suddenly exclaimed Magnus, struck with an idea, "will be thoroughly discredited just so soon as the new grain tariff is published. I have means of knowing that the San Joaquin rate—the issue upon which the board was elected—is not to be touched. Is it likely the ranchers would secure the election of a board that plays them false?"

"Oh, we know all about that," answered Genslinger, smiling. "You thought you were electing Lyman easily. You thought you had got the Railroad to walk right into your trap. You didn't understand how you could pull off your deal so easily. Why, Governor, LYMAN WAS PLEDGED TO THE RAILROAD TWO YEARS AGO. He was THE ONE PARTICULAR man the corporation wanted for commissioner. And your people elected him—saved the Railroad all the trouble of campaigning for him. And you can't make any counter charge of bribery there. No, sir, the corporation don't use such amateurish methods as that. Confidentially and between us two, all that the Railroad has done for Lyman, in order to attach him to their interests, is to promise to back him politically in the next campaign for Governor. It's too bad," he continued, dropping his voice, and changing his position. "It really is too bad to see good men trying to bunt a stone wall over with their bare heads. You couldn't have won at any stage of the game. I wish I could have talked to you and your friends before you went into that Sacramento fight. I could have told you then how little chance you had. When will you people realise that you can't buck against the Railroad? Why, Magnus, it's like me going out in a paper boat and shooting peas at a battleship."

"Is that all you wished to see me about, Mr. Genslinger?" remarked Magnus, bestirring himself. "I am rather occupied to-day."

"Well," returned the other, "you know what the publication of this article would mean for you." He paused again, took off his glasses, breathed on them, polished the lenses with his handkerchief and readjusted them on his nose. "I've been thinking, Governor," he began again, with renewed alertness, and quite irrelevantly, "of enlarging the scope of the 'Mercury.' You see, I'm midway between the two big centres of the State, San Francisco and Los Angeles, and I want to extend the 'Mercury's' sphere of influence as far up and down the valley as I can. I want to illustrate the paper. You see, if I had a photo-engraving plant of my own, I could do a good deal of outside jobbing as well, and the investment would pay ten per cent. But it takes money to make money. I wouldn't want to put in any dinky, one-horse affair. I want a good plant. I've been figuring out the business. Besides the plant, there would be the expense of a high grade paper. Can't print half-tones on anything but coated paper, and that COSTS. Well, what with this and with that and running expenses till the thing began to pay, it would cost me about ten thousand dollars, and I was wondering if, perhaps, you couldn't see your way clear to accommodating me."

"Ten thousand?"

"Yes. Say five thousand down, and the balance within sixty days."

Magnus, for the moment blind to what Genslinger had in mind, turned on him in astonishment.

"Why, man, what security could you give me for such an amount?"

"Well, to tell the truth," answered the editor, "I hadn't thought much about securities. In fact, I believed you would see how greatly it was to your advantage to talk business with me. You see, I'm not going to print this article about you, Governor, and I'm not going to let it get out so as any one else can print it, and it seems to me that one good turn deserves another. You understand?"

Magnus understood. An overwhelming desire suddenly took possession of him to grip this blackmailer by the throat, to strangle him where he stood; or, if not, at least to turn upon him with that old-time terrible anger, before which whole conventions had once cowered. But in the same moment the Governor realised this was not to be. Only its righteousness had made his wrath terrible; only the justice of his anger had made him feared. Now the foundation was gone from under his feet; he had knocked it away himself. Three times feeble was he whose quarrel was unjust. Before this country editor, this paid speaker of the Railroad, he stood, convicted. The man had him at his mercy. The detected briber could not resent an insult. Genslinger rose, smoothing his hat.

"Well," he said, "of course, you want time to think it over, and you can't raise money like that on short notice. I'll wait till Friday noon of this week. We begin to set Saturday's paper at about four, Friday afternoon, and the forms are locked about two in the morning. I hope," he added, turning back at the door of the room, "that you won't find anything disagreeable in your Saturday morning 'Mercury,' Mr. Derrick."

He went out, closing the door behind him, and in a moment, Magnus heard the wheels of his buckboard grating on the driveway.

The following morning brought a letter to Magnus from Gethings, of the San Pueblo ranch, which was situated very close to Visalia. The letter was to the effect that all around Visalia, upon the ranches affected by the regrade of the Railroad, men were arming and drilling, and that the strength of the League in that quarter was undoubted. "But to refer," continued the letter, "to a most painful recollection. You will, no doubt, remember that, at the close of our last committee meeting, specific charges were made as to fraud in the nomination and election of one of our commissioners, emanating, most unfortunately, from the commissioner himself. These charges, my dear Mr. Derrick, were directed at yourself. How the secrets of the committee have been noised about, I cannot understand. You may be, of course, assured of my own unquestioning confidence and loyalty. However, I regret exceedingly to state not only that the rumour of the charges referred to above is spreading in this district, but that also they are made use of by the enemies of the League. It is to be deplored that some of the Leaguers themselves—you know, we number in our ranks many small farmers, ignorant Portuguese and foreigners—have listened to these stories and have permitted a feeling of uneasiness to develop among them. Even though it were admitted that fraudulent means had been employed in the elections, which, of course, I personally do not admit, I do not think it would make very much difference in the confidence which the vast majority of the Leaguers repose in their chiefs. Yet we have so insisted upon the probity of our position as opposed to Railroad chicanery, that I believe it advisable to quell this distant suspicion at once; to publish a denial of these rumoured charges would only be to give them too much importance. However, can you not write me a letter, stating exactly how the campaign was conducted, and the commission nominated and elected? I could show this to some of the more disaffected, and it would serve to allay all suspicion on the instant. I think it would be well to write as though the initiative came, not from me, but from yourself, ignoring this present letter. I offer this only as a suggestion, and will confidently endorse any decision you may arrive at."

The letter closed with renewed protestations of confidence.

Magnus was alone when he read this. He put it carefully away in the filing cabinet in his office, and wiped the sweat from his forehead and face. He stood for one moment, his hands rigid at his sides, his fists clinched.

"This is piling up," he muttered, looking blankly at the opposite wall. "My God, this is piling up. What am I to do?"

Ah, the bitterness of unavailing regret, the anguish of compromise with conscience, the remorse of a bad deed done in a moment of excitement. Ah, the humiliation of detection, the degradation of being caught, caught like a schoolboy pilfering his fellows' desks, and, worse than all, worse than all, the consciousness of lost self-respect, the knowledge of a prestige vanishing, a dignity impaired, knowledge that the grip which held a multitude in check was trembling, that control was wavering, that command was being weakened. Then the little tricks to deceive the crowd, the little subterfuges, the little pretences that kept up appearances, the lies, the bluster, the pose, the strut, the gasconade, where once was iron authority; the turning of the head so as not to see that which could not be prevented; the suspicion of suspicion, the haunting fear of the Man on the Street, the uneasiness of the direct glance, the questioning as to motives—why had this been said, what was meant by that word, that gesture, that glance?

Wednesday passed, and Thursday. Magnus kept to himself, seeing no visitors, avoiding even his family. How to break through the mesh of the net, how to regain the old position, how to prevent discovery? If there were only some way, some vast, superhuman effort by which he could rise in his old strength once more, crushing Lyman with one hand, Genslinger with the other, and for one more moment, the last, to stand supreme again, indomitable, the leader; then go to his death, triumphant at the end, his memory untarnished, his fame undimmed. But the plague-spot was in himself, knitted forever into the fabric of his being. Though Genslinger should be silenced, though Lyman should be crushed, though even the League should overcome the Railroad, though he should be the acknowledged leader of a resplendent victory, yet the plague-spot would remain. There was no success for him now. However conspicuous the outward achievement, he, he himself, Magnus Derrick, had failed, miserably and irredeemably.

Petty, material complications intruded, sordid considerations. Even if Genslinger was to be paid, where was the money to come from? His legal battles with the Railroad, extending now over a period of many years, had cost him dear; his plan of sowing all of Los Muertos to wheat, discharging the tenants, had proved expensive, the campaign resulting in Lyman's election had drawn heavily upon his account. All along he had been relying upon a "bonanza crop" to reimburse him. It was not believable that the Railroad would "jump" Los Muertos, but if this should happen, he would be left without resources. Ten thousand dollars! Could he raise the amount? Possibly. But to pay it out to a blackmailer! To be held up thus in road-agent fashion, without a single means of redress! Would it not cripple him financially? Genslinger could do his worst. He, Magnus, would brave it out. Was not his character above suspicion?

Was it? This letter of Gethings's. Already the murmur of uneasiness made itself heard. Was this not the thin edge of the wedge? How the publication of Genslinger's story would drive it home! How the spark of suspicion would flare into the blaze of open accusation! There would be investigations. Investigation! There was terror in the word. He could not stand investigation. Magnus groaned aloud, covering his head with his clasped hands. Briber, corrupter of government, ballot-box stuffer, descending to the level of back-room politicians, of bar-room heelers, he, Magnus Derrick, statesman of the old school, Roman in his iron integrity, abandoning a career rather than enter the "new politics," had, in one moment of weakness, hazarding all, even honour, on a single stake, taking great chances to achieve great results, swept away the work of a lifetime.

Gambler that he was, he had at last chanced his highest stake, his personal honour, in the greatest game of his life, and had lost.

It was Presley's morbidly keen observation that first noticed the evidence of a new trouble in the Governor's face and manner. Presley was sure that Lyman's defection had not so upset him. The morning after the committee meeting, Magnus had called Harran and Annie Derrick into the office, and, after telling his wife of Lyman's betrayal, had forbidden either of them to mention his name again. His attitude towards his prodigal son was that of stern, unrelenting resentment. But now, Presley could not fail to detect traces of a more deep-seated travail. Something was in the wind, the times were troublous. What next was about to happen? What fresh calamity impended?

One morning, toward the very end of the week, Presley woke early in his small, white-painted iron bed. He hastened to get up and dress. There was much to be done that day. Until late the night before, he had been at work on a collection of some of his verses, gathered from the magazines in which they had first appeared. Presley had received a liberal offer for the publication of these verses in book form. "The Toilers" was to be included in this book, and, indeed, was to give it its name—" The Toilers and Other Poems." Thus it was that, until the previous midnight, he had been preparing the collection for publication, revising, annotating, arranging. The book was to be sent off that morning.

But also Presley had received a typewritten note from Annixter, inviting him to Quien Sabe that same day. Annixter explained that it was Hilma's birthday, and that he had planned a picnic on the high ground of his ranch, at the headwaters of Broderson Creek. They were to go in the carry-all, Hilma, Presley, Mrs. Dyke, Sidney, and himself, and were to make a day of it. They would leave Quien Sabe at ten in the morning. Presley had at once resolved to go. He was immensely fond of Annixter—more so than ever since his marriage with Hilma and the astonishing transformation of his character. Hilma, as well, was delightful as Mrs. Annixter; and Mrs. Dyke and the little tad had always been his friends. He would have a good time.

But nobody was to go into Bonneville that morning with the mail, and if he wished to send his manuscript, he would have to take it in himself. He had resolved to do this, getting an early start, and going on horseback to Quien Sabe, by way of Bonneville.

It was barely six o'clock when Presley sat down to his coffee and eggs in the dining-room of Los Muertos. The day promised to be hot, and for the first time, Presley had put on a new khaki riding suit, very English-looking, though in place of the regulation top-boots, he wore his laced knee-boots, with a great spur on the left heel. Harran joined him at breakfast, in his working clothes of blue canvas. He was bound for the irrigating ditch to see how the work was getting on there.

"How is the wheat looking?" asked Presley.

"Bully," answered the other, stirring his coffee. "The Governor has had his usual luck. Practically, every acre of the ranch was sown to wheat, and everywhere the stand is good. I was over on Two, day before yesterday, and if nothing happens, I believe it will go thirty sacks to the acre there. Cutter reports that there are spots on Four where we will get forty-two or three. Hooven, too, brought up some wonderful fine ears for me to look at. The grains were just beginning to show. Some of the ears carried twenty grains. That means nearly forty bushels of wheat to every acre. I call it a bonanza year."

"Have you got any mail?" said Presley, rising. "I'm going into town."

Harran shook his head, and took himself away, and Presley went down to the stable-corral to get his pony.

As he rode out of the stable-yard and passed by the ranch house, on the driveway, he was surprised to see Magnus on the lowest step of the porch.

"Good morning, Governor," called Presley. "Aren't you up pretty early?"

"Good morning, Pres, my boy." The Governor came forward and, putting his hand on the pony's withers, walked along by his side.

"Going to town, Pres?" he asked.

"Yes, sir. Can I do anything for you, Governor?"

Magnus drew a sealed envelope from his pocket.

"I wish you would drop in at the office of the Mercury for me," he said, "and see Mr. Genslinger personally, and give him this envelope. It is a package of papers, but they involve a considerable sum of money, and you must be careful of them. A few years ago, when our enmity was not so strong, Mr. Genslinger and I had some business dealings with each other. I thought it as well just now, considering that we are so openly opposed, to terminate the whole affair, and break off relations. We came to a settlement a few days ago. These are the final papers. They must be given to him in person, Presley. You understand."

Presley cantered on, turning into the county road and holding northward by the mammoth watering tank and Broderson's popular windbreak. As he passed Caraher's, he saw the saloon-keeper in the doorway of his place, and waved him a salutation which the other returned.

By degrees, Presley had come to consider Caraher in a more favourable light. He found, to his immense astonishment, that Caraher knew something of Mill and Bakounin, not, however, from their books, but from extracts and quotations from their writings, reprinted in the anarchistic journals to which he subscribed. More than once, the two had held long conversations, and from Caraher's own lips, Presley heard the terrible story of the death of his wife, who had been accidentally killed by Pinkertons during a "demonstration" of strikers. It invested the saloon-keeper, in Presley's imagination, with all the dignity of the tragedy. He could not blame Caraher for being a "red." He even wondered how it was the saloon-keeper had not put his theories into practice, and adjusted his ancient wrong with his "six inches of plugged gas-pipe." Presley began to conceive of the man as a "character."

"You wait, Mr. Presley," the saloon-keeper had once said, when Presley had protested against his radical ideas. "You don't know the Railroad yet. Watch it and its doings long enough, and you'll come over to my way of thinking, too."

It was about half-past seven when Presley reached Bonneville. The business part of the town was as yet hardly astir; he despatched his manuscript, and then hurried to the office of the "Mercury." Genslinger, as he feared, had not yet put in appearance, but the janitor of the building gave Presley the address of the editor's residence, and it was there he found him in the act of sitting down to breakfast. Presley was hardly courteous to the little man, and abruptly refused his offer of a drink. He delivered Magnus's envelope to him and departed.

It had occurred to him that it would not do to present himself at Quien Sabe on Hilma's birthday, empty-handed, and, on leaving Genslinger's house, he turned his pony's head toward the business part of the town again pulling up in front of the jeweller's, just as the clerk was taking down the shutters.

At the jeweller's, he purchased a little brooch for Hilma and at the cigar stand in the lobby of the Yosemite House, a box of superfine cigars, which, when it was too late, he realised that the master of Quien Sabe would never smoke, holding, as he did, with defiant inconsistency, to miserable weeds, black, bitter, and flagrantly doctored, which he bought, three for a nickel, at Guadalajara.

Presley arrived at Quien Sabe nearly half an hour behind the appointed time; but, as he had expected, the party were in no way ready to start. The carry-all, its horses covered with white fly-nets, stood under a tree near the house, young Vacca dozing on the seat. Hilma and Sidney, the latter exuberant with a gayety that all but brought the tears to Presley's eyes, were making sandwiches on the back porch. Mrs. Dyke was nowhere to be seen, and Annixter was shaving himself in his bedroom.

This latter put a half-lathered face out of the window as Presley cantered through the gate, and waved his razor with a beckoning motion.

"Come on in, Pres," he cried. "Nobody's ready yet. You're hours ahead of time."

Presley came into the bedroom, his huge spur clinking on the straw matting. Annixter was without coat, vest or collar, his blue silk suspenders hung in loops over either hip, his hair was disordered, the crown lock stiffer than ever.

"Glad to see you, old boy," he announced, as Presley came in. "No, don't shake hands, I'm all lather. Here, find a chair, will you? I won't be long."

"I thought you said ten o'clock," observed Presley, sitting down on the edge of the bed.

"Well, I did, but–"

"But, then again, in a way, you didn't, hey?" his friend interrupted.

Annixter grunted good-humouredly, and turned to strop his razor. Presley looked with suspicious disfavour at his suspenders.

"Why is it," he observed, "that as soon as a man is about to get married, he buys himself pale blue suspenders, silk ones? Think of it. You, Buck Annixter, with sky-blue, silk suspenders. It ought to be a strap and a nail."

"Old fool," observed Annixter, whose repartee was the heaving of brick bats. "Say," he continued, holding the razor from his face, and jerking his head over his shoulder, while he looked at Presley's reflection in his mirror; "say, look around. Isn't this a nifty little room? We refitted the whole house, you know. Notice she's all painted?"

"I have been looking around," answered Presley, sweeping the room with a series of glances. He forebore criticism. Annixter was so boyishly proud of the effect that it would have been unkind to have undeceived him. Presley looked at the marvellous, department-store bed of brass, with its brave, gay canopy; the mill-made wash-stand, with its pitcher and bowl of blinding red and green china, the straw-framed lithographs of symbolic female figures against the multi-coloured, new wall-paper; the inadequate spindle chairs of white and gold; the sphere of tissue paper hanging from the gas fixture, and the plumes of pampas grass tacked to the wall at artistic angles, and overhanging two astonishing oil paintings, in dazzling golden frames.

"Say, how about those paintings, Pres?" inquired Annixter a little uneasily. "I don't know whether they're good or not. They were painted by a three-fingered Chinaman in Monterey, and I got the lot for thirty dollars, frames thrown in. Why, I think the frames alone are worth thirty dollars."

"Well, so do I," declared Presley. He hastened to change the subject.

"Buck," he said, "I hear you've brought Mrs. Dyke and Sidney to live with you. You know, I think that's rather white of you."

"Oh, rot, Pres," muttered Annixter, turning abruptly to his shaving.

"And you can't fool me, either, old man," Presley continued. "You're giving this picnic as much for Mrs. Dyke and the little tad as you are for your wife, just to cheer them up a bit."

"Oh, pshaw, you make me sick."

"Well, that's the right thing to do, Buck, and I'm as glad for your sake as I am for theirs. There was a time when you would have let them all go to grass, and never so much as thought of them. I don't want to seem to be officious, but you've changed for the better, old man, and I guess I know why. She—" Presley caught his friend's eye, and added gravely, "She's a good woman, Buck."

Annixter turned around abruptly, his face flushing under its lather.

"Pres," he exclaimed, "she's made a man of me. I was a machine before, and if another man, or woman, or child got in my way, I rode 'em down, and I never

DREAMED of anybody else but myself. But as soon as I woke up to the fact that I really loved her, why, it was glory hallelujah all in a minute, and, in a way, I kind of loved everybody then, and wanted to be everybody's friend. And I began to see that a fellow can't live FOR himself any more than he can live BY himself. He's got to think of others. If he's got brains, he's got to think for the poor ducks that haven't 'em, and not give 'em a boot in the backsides because they happen to be stupid; and if he's got money, he's got to help those that are busted, and if he's got a house, he's got to think of those that ain't got anywhere to go. I've got a whole lot of ideas since I began to love Hilma, and just as soon as I can, I'm going to get in and HELP people, and I'm going to keep to that idea the rest of my natural life. That ain't much of a religion, but it's the best I've got, and Henry Ward Beecher couldn't do any more than that. And it's all come about because of Hilma, and because we cared for each other."

Presley jumped up, and caught Annixter about the shoulders with one arm, gripping his hand hard. This absurd figure, with dangling silk suspenders, lathered chin, and tearful eyes, seemed to be suddenly invested with true nobility. Beside this blundering struggle to do right, to help his fellows, Presley's own vague schemes, glittering systems of reconstruction, collapsed to ruin, and he himself, with all his refinement, with all his poetry, culture, and education, stood, a bungler at the world's workbench.

"You're all RIGHT, old man," he exclaimed, unable to think of anything adequate. "You're all right. That's the way to talk, and here, by the way, I brought you a box of cigars."

Annixter stared as Presley laid the box on the edge of the washstand.

"Old fool," he remarked, "what in hell did you do that for?"

"Oh, just for fun."

"I suppose they're rotten stinkodoras, or you wouldn't give 'em away."

"This cringing gratitude—" Presley began.

"Shut up," shouted Annixter, and the incident was closed.

Annixter resumed his shaving, and Presley lit a cigarette.

"Any news from Washington?" he queried.

"Nothing that's any good," grunted Annixter. "Hello," he added, raising his head, "there's somebody in a hurry for sure."

The noise of a horse galloping so fast that the hoof-beats sounded in one uninterrupted rattle, abruptly made itself heard. The noise was coming from the direction of the road that led from the Mission to Quien Sabe. With incredible swiftness, the hoof-beats drew nearer. There was that in their sound which brought Presley to his feet. Annixter threw open the window.

"Runaway," exclaimed Presley.

Annixter, with thoughts of the Railroad, and the "Jumping" of the ranch, flung his hand to his hip pocket.

"What is it, Vacca?" he cried.

Young Vacca, turning in his seat in the carryall, was looking up the road. All at once, he jumped from his place, and dashed towards the window. "Dyke," he shouted. "Dyke, it's Dyke."

While the words were yet in his mouth, the sound of the hoof-beats rose to a roar, and a great, bell-toned voice shouted:

"Annixter, Annixter, Annixter!"

It was Dyke's voice, and the next instant he shot into view in the open square in front of the house.

"Oh, my God!" cried Presley.

The ex-engineer threw the horse on its haunches, springing from the saddle; and, as he did so, the beast collapsed, shuddering, to the ground. Annixter sprang from the window, and ran forward, Presley following.

There was Dyke, hatless, his pistol in his hand, a gaunt terrible figure the beard immeasurably long, the cheeks fallen in, the eyes sunken. His clothes ripped and torn by weeks of flight and hiding in the chaparral, were ragged beyond words, the boots were shreds of leather, bloody to the ankle with furious spurring.

"Annixter," he shouted, and again, rolling his sunken eyes, "Annixter, Annixter!"

"Here, here," cried Annixter.

The other turned, levelling his pistol.

"Give me a horse, give me a horse, quick, do you hear? Give me a horse, or I'll shoot."

"Steady, steady. That won't do. You know me, Dyke. We're friends here."

The other lowered his weapon.

"I know, I know," he panted. "I'd forgotten. I'm unstrung, Mr. Annixter, and I'm running for my life. They're not ten minutes behind me."

"Come on, come on," shouted Annixter, dashing stablewards, his suspenders flying.

"Here's a horse."

"Mine?" exclaimed Presley. "He wouldn't carry you a mile."

Annixter was already far ahead, trumpeting orders.

"The buckskin," he yelled. "Get her out, Billy. Where's the stable-man? Get out that buckskin. Get out that saddle."

Then followed minutes of furious haste, Presley, Annixter, Billy the stable-man, and Dyke himself, darting hither and thither about the yellow mare, buckling, strapping, cinching, their lips pale, their fingers trembling with excitement.

"Want anything to eat?" Annixter's head was under the saddle flap as he tore at the cinch. "Want anything to eat? Want any money? Want a gun?"

"Water," returned Dyke. "They've watched every spring. I'm killed with thirst."

"There's the hydrant. Quick now."

"I got as far as the Kern River, but they turned me back," he said between breaths as he drank.

"Don't stop to talk."

"My mother, and the little tad—"

"I'm taking care of them. They're stopping with me."

Here?

"You won't see 'em; by the Lord, you won't. You'll get away. Where's that back cinch strap, BILLY? God damn it, are you going to let him be shot before he can get away? Now, Dyke, up you go. She'll kill herself running before they can catch you."

"God bless you, Annixter. Where's the little tad? Is she well, Annixter, and the mother? Tell them—"

"Yes, yes, yes. All clear, Pres? Let her have her own gait, Dyke. You're on the best horse in the county now. Let go her head, Billy. Now, Dyke,—shake hands? You bet I will. That's all right. Yes, God bless you. Let her go. You're OFF."

Answering the goad of the spur, and already quivering with the excitement of the men who surrounded her, the buckskin cleared the stable-corral in two leaps; then, gathering her legs under her, her head low, her neck stretched out, swung into the road from out the driveway disappearing in a blur of dust.

With the agility of a monkey, young Vacca swung himself into the framework of the artesian well, clambering aloft to its very top. He swept the country with a glance.

"Well?" demanded Annixter from the ground. The others cocked their heads to listen.

"I see him; I see him!" shouted Vacca. "He's going like the devil. He's headed for Guadalajara."

"Look back, up the road, toward the Mission. Anything there?"

The answer came down in a shout of apprehension.

"There's a party of men. Three or four—on horse-back. There's dogs with 'em. They're coming this way. Oh, I can hear the dogs. And, say, oh, say, there's another party coming down the Lower Road, going towards Guadalajara, too. They got guns. I can see the shine of the barrels. And, oh, Lord, say, there's three more men on horses coming down on the jump from the hills on the Los Muertos stock range. They're making towards Guadalajara. And I can hear the courthouse bell in Bonneville ringing. Say, the whole county is up."

As young Vacca slid down to the ground, two small black-and-tan hounds, with flapping ears and lolling tongues, loped into view on the road in front of the house. They were grey with dust, their noses were to the ground. At the gate where Dyke had turned into the ranch house grounds, they halted in confusion a moment. One started to follow the highwayman's trail towards the stable corral, but the other, quartering over the road with lightning swiftness, suddenly picked up the new scent leading on towards Guadalajara. He tossed his head in the air, and Presley abruptly shut his hands over his ears.

Ah, that terrible cry! deep-toned, reverberating like the bourdon of a great bell. It was the trackers exulting on the trail of the pursued, the prolonged, raucous howl, eager, ominous, vibrating with the alarm of the tocsin, sullen with the heavy muffling note of death. But close upon the bay of the hounds, came the gallop of horses. Five men, their eyes upon the hounds, their rifles across their pommels, their horses reeking and black with sweat, swept by in a storm of dust, glinting hoofs, and streaming manes.

"That was Delaney's gang," exclaimed Annixter. "I saw him."

"The other was that chap Christian," said Vacca, "S. Behrman's cousin. He had two deputies with him; and the chap in the white slouch hat was the sheriff from Visalia."

"By the Lord, they aren't far behind," declared Annixter.

As the men turned towards the house again they saw Hilma and Mrs. Dyke in the doorway of the little house where the latter lived. They were looking out, bewildered, ignorant of what had happened. But on the porch of the Ranch house itself, alone, forgotten in the excitement, Sidney—the little tad—stood, with pale face and serious, wide-open eyes. She had seen everything, and had understood. She said nothing. Her head inclined towards the roadway, she listened to the faint and distant baying of the dogs.

Dyke thundered across the railway tracks by the depot at Guadalajara not five minutes ahead of his pursuers. Luck seemed to have deserted him. The station, usually so quiet, was now occupied by the crew of a freight train that lay on the down track; while on the up line, near at hand and headed in the same direction, was a detached locomotive, whose engineer and fireman recognized him, he was sure, as the buckskin leaped across the rails.

He had had no time to formulate a plan since that morning, when, tortured with thirst, he had ventured near the spring at the headwaters of Broderson Creek, on Quien Sabe, and had all but fallen into the hands of the posse that had been watching for that very move. It was useless now to regret that he had tried to foil pursuit by turning back on his tracks to regain the mountains east of Bonneville. Now Delaney was almost on him. To distance that posse, was the only thing to be thought of now. It was no longer a question of hiding till pursuit should flag; they had driven him out from the shelter of the mountains, down into this populous countryside, where an enemy might be met with at every turn of the road. Now it was life or death. He would either escape or be killed. He knew very well that he would never allow himself to be taken alive. But he had no mind to be killed—to turn and fight—till escape was blocked. His one thought was to leave pursuit behind.

Weeks of flight had sharpened Dyke's every sense. As he turned into the Upper

Road beyond Guadalajara, he saw the three men galloping down from Derrick's stock range, making for the road ahead of him. They would cut him off there. He swung the buckskin about. He must take the Lower Road across Los Muertos from Guadalajara, and he must reach it before Delaney's dogs and posse. Back he galloped, the buckskin measuring her length with every leap. Once more the station came in sight. Rising in his stirrups, he looked across the fields in the direction of the Lower Road. There was a cloud of dust there. From a wagon? No, horses on the run, and their riders were armed! He could catch the flash of gun barrels. They were all closing in on him, converging on Guadalajara by every available road. The Upper Road west of Guadalajara led straight to Bonneville. That way was impossible. Was he in a trap? Had the time for fighting come at last?

But as Dyke neared the depot at Guadalajara, his eye fell upon the detached locomotive that lay quietly steaming on the up line, and with a thrill of exultation, he remembered that he was an engineer born and bred. Delaney's dogs were already to be heard, and the roll of hoofs on the Lower Road was dinning in his ears, as he leaped from the buckskin before the depot. The train crew scattered like frightened sheep before him, but Dyke ignored them. His pistol was in his hand as, once more on foot, he sprang toward the lone engine.

"Out of the cab," he shouted. "Both of you. Quick, or I'll kill you both."

The two men tumbled from the iron apron of the tender as Dyke swung himself up, dropping his pistol on the floor of the cab and reaching with the old instinct for the familiar levers. The great compound hissed and trembled as the steam was released, and the huge drivers stirred, turning slowly on the tracks. But there was a shout. Delaney's posse, dogs and men, swung into view at the turn of the road, their figures leaning over as they took the curve at full speed. Dyke threw everything wide open and caught up his revolver. From behind came the challenge of a Winchester. The party on the Lower Road were even closer than Delaney. They had seen his manoeuvre, and the first shot of the fight shivered the cab windows above the engineer's head.

But spinning futilely at first, the drivers of the engine at last caught the rails. The engine moved, advanced, travelled past the depot and the freight train, and gathering speed, rolled out on the track beyond. Smoke, black and boiling, shot skyward from the stack; not a joint that did not shudder with the mighty strain of the steam; but the great iron brute—one of Baldwin's newest and best—came to call, obedient and docile as soon as ever the great pulsing heart of it felt a master hand upon its levers. It gathered its speed, bracing its steel muscles, its thews of iron, and roared out upon the open track, filling the air with the rasp of its tempest-breath, blotting the sunshine with the belch of its hot, thick smoke. Already it was lessening in the distance, when Delaney, Christian, and the sheriff of Visalia dashed up to the station.

The posse had seen everything.

"Stuck. Curse the luck!" vociferated the cow-Puncher.

But the sheriff was already out of the saddle and into the telegraph office.

"There's a derailing switch between here and Pixley, isn't there?" he cried.

"Yes."

"Wire ahead to open it. We'll derail him there. Come on;" he turned to Delaney and the others. They sprang into the cab of the locomotive that was attached to the freight train.

"Name of the State of California," shouted the sheriff to the bewildered engineer. "Cut off from your train."

The sheriff was a man to be obeyed without hesitating. Time was not allowed the crew of the freight train for debating as to the right or the wrong of requisitioning the engine, and before anyone thought of the safety or danger of the affair, the freight engine was already flying out upon the down line, hot in pursuit of Dyke, now far ahead upon the up track.

"I remember perfectly well there's a derailing switch between here and Pixley," shouted the sheriff above the roar of the locomotive. "They use it in case they have to derail runaway engines. It runs right off into the country. We'll pile him up there. Ready with your guns, boys."

"If we should meet another train coming up on this track—" protested the frightened engineer.

"Then we'd jump or be smashed. Hi! look! There he is." As the freight engine rounded a curve, Dyke's engine came into view, shooting on some quarter of a mile ahead of them, wreathed in whirling smoke.

"The switch ain't much further on," clamoured the engineer. "You can see Pixley now."

Dyke, his hand on the grip of the valve that controlled the steam, his head out of the cab window, thundered on. He was back in his old place again; once more he was the engineer; once more he felt the engine quiver under him; the familiar noises were in his ears; the familiar buffeting of the wind surged, roaring at his face; the familiar odours of hot steam and smoke reeked in his nostrils, and on either side of him, parallel panoramas, the two halves of the landscape sliced, as it were, in two by the clashing wheels of his engine, streamed by in green and brown blurs.

He found himself settling to the old position on the cab seat, leaning on his elbow from the window, one hand on the controller. All at once, the instinct of the pursuit that of late had become so strong within him, prompted him to shoot a glance behind. He saw the other engine on the down line, plunging after him, rocking from side to side with the fury of its gallop. Not yet had he shaken the trackers from his heels; not yet was he out of the reach of danger. He set his teeth and, throwing open the fire-door, stoked vigorously for a few moments. The indicator of the steam gauge rose; his speed increased; a glance at the telegraph poles told him he was doing his fifty miles an hour. The freight engine behind him was never built for that pace. Barring the terrible risk of accident, his chances were good.

But suddenly—the engineer dominating the highway-man—he shut off his steam and threw back his brake to the extreme notch. Directly ahead of him rose a semaphore, placed at a point where evidently a derailing switch branched from the line. The semaphore's arm was dropped over the track, setting the danger signal that showed the switch was open.

In an instant, Dyke saw the trick. They had meant to smash him here; had been clever enough, quick-witted enough to open the switch, but had forgotten the automatic semaphore that worked simultaneously with the movement of the rails. To go forward was certain destruction. Dyke reversed. There was nothing for it but to go back. With a wrench and a spasm of all its metal fibres, the great compound braced itself, sliding with rigid wheels along the rails. Then, as Dyke applied the reverse, it drew back from the greater danger, returning towards the less. Inevitably now the two engines, one on the up, the other on the down line, must meet and pass each other.

Dyke released the levers, reaching for his revolver. The engineer once more became the highwayman, in peril of his life. Now, beyond all doubt, the time for fighting was at hand.

The party in the heavy freight engine, that lumbered after in pursuit, their eyes fixed on the smudge of smoke on ahead that marked the path of the fugitive, suddenly raised a shout.

"He's stopped. He's broke down. Watch, now, and see if he jumps off."

"Broke NOTHING. HE'S COMING BACK. Ready, now, he's got to pass us."

The engineer applied the brakes, but the heavy freight locomotive, far less mobile than Dyke's flyer, was slow to obey. The smudge on the rails ahead grew swiftly larger.

"He's coming. He's coming—look out, there's a shot. He's shooting already."

A bright, white sliver of wood leaped into the air from the sooty window sill of the cab.

"Fire on him! Fire on him!"

While the engines were yet two hundred yards apart, the duel began, shot answering shot, the sharp staccato reports punctuating the thunder of wheels and the clamour of steam.

Then the ground trembled and rocked; a roar as of heavy ordnance developed with the abruptness of an explosion. The two engines passed each other, the men firing the while, emptying their revolvers, shattering wood, shivering glass, the bullets clanging against the metal work as they struck and struck and struck. The men leaned from the cabs towards each other, frantic with excitement, shouting curses, the engines rocking, the steam roaring; confusion whirling in the scene like the whirl of a witch's dance, the white clouds of steam, the black eddies from the smokestack, the blue wreaths from the hot mouths of revolvers, swirling together in a blinding maze of vapour, spinning around them, dazing them, dizzying them, while the head rang with hideous clamour and the body twitched and trembled with the leap and jar of the tumult of machinery.

Roaring, clamouring, reeking with the smell of powder and hot oil, spitting death, resistless, huge, furious, an abrupt vision of chaos, faces, rage-distorted, peering through smoke, hands gripping outward from sudden darkness, prehensile, malevolent; terrible as thunder, swift as lightning, the two engines met and passed.

"He's hit," cried Delaney. "I know I hit him. He can't go far now. After him again. He won't dare go through Bonneville."

It was true. Dyke had stood between cab and tender throughout all the duel, exposed, reckless, thinking only of attack and not of defence, and a bullet from one of the pistols had grazed his hip. How serious was the wound he did not know, but he had no thought of giving up. He tore back through the depot at Guadalajara in a storm of bullets, and, clinging to the broken window ledge of his cab, was carried towards Bonneville, on over the Long Trestle and Broderson Creek and through the open country between the two ranches of Los Muertos and Quien Sabe.

But to go on to Bonneville meant certain death. Before, as well as behind him, the roads were now blocked. Once more he thought of the mountains. He resolved to abandon the engine and make another final attempt to get into the shelter of the hills in the northernmost corner of Quien Sabe. He set his teeth. He would not give in. There was one more fight left in him yet. Now to try the final hope.

He slowed the engine down, and, reloading his revolver, jumped from the platform to the road. He looked about him, listening. All around him widened an ocean of wheat. There was no one in sight.

The released engine, alone, unattended, drew slowly away from him, jolting ponderously over the rail joints. As he watched it go, a certain indefinite sense of abandonment, even in that moment, came over Dyke. His last friend, that also had been his first, was leaving him. He remembered that day, long ago, when he had opened the throttle of his first machine. To-day, it was leaving him alone, his last friend turning against him. Slowly it was going back towards Bonneville, to the shops of the Railroad, the camp of the enemy, that enemy that had ruined him and wrecked him. For the last time in his life, he had been the engineer. Now, once more, he became the highwayman, the outlaw against whom all hands were raised, the fugitive skulking in the mountains, listening for the cry of dogs.

But he would not give in. They had not broken him yet. Never, while he could fight, would he allow S. Behrman the triumph of his capture.

He found his wound was not bad. He plunged into the wheat on Quien Sabe, making northward for a division house that rose with its surrounding trees out of the wheat like an island. He reached it, the blood squelching in his shoes. But the sight of two men, Portuguese farm-hands, staring at him from an angle of the barn, abruptly roused him to action. He sprang forward with peremptory commands, demanding a horse.

At Guadalajara, Delaney and the sheriff descended from the freight engine.

"Horses now," declared the sheriff. "He won't go into Bonneville, that's certain. He'll leave the engine between here and there, and strike off into the country. We'll follow after him now in the saddle. Soon as he leaves his engine, HE'S on foot. We've as good as got him now."

Their horses, including even the buckskin mare that Dyke had ridden, were still at the station. The party swung themselves up, Delaney exclaiming, "Here's MY mount," as he bestrode the buckskin.

At Guadalajara, the two bloodhounds were picked up again. Urging the jaded horses to a gallop, the party set off along the Upper Road, keeping a sharp lookout to right and left for traces of Dyke's abandonment of the engine.

Three miles beyond the Long Trestle, they found S. Behrman holding his saddle horse by the bridle, and looking attentively at a trail that had been broken through the standing wheat on Quien Sabe. The party drew rein.

"The engine passed me on the tracks further up, and empty," said S. Behrman. "Boys, I think he left her here."

But before anyone could answer, the bloodhounds gave tongue again, as they picked up the scent.

"That's him," cried S. Behrman. "Get on, boys."

They dashed forward, following the hounds. S. Behrman laboriously climbed to his saddle, panting, perspiring, mopping the roll of fat over his coat collar, and turned in after them, trotting along far in the rear, his great stomach and tremulous jowl shaking with the horse's gait.

"What a day," he murmured. "What a day."

Dyke's trail was fresh, and was followed as easily as if made on new-fallen snow. In a short time, the posse swept into the open space around the division house. The two Portuguese were still there, wide-eyed, terribly excited.

Yes, yes, Dyke had been there not half an hour since, had held them up, taken a horse and galloped to the northeast, towards the foothills at the headwaters of Broderson Creek.

On again, at full gallop, through the young wheat, trampling it under the flying hoofs; the hounds hot on the scent, baying continually; the men, on fresh mounts, secured at the division house, bending forward in their saddles, spurring relentlessly. S. Behrman jolted along far in the rear.

And even then, harried through an open country, where there was no place to hide, it was a matter of amazement how long a chase the highwayman led them. Fences were passed; fences whose barbed wire had been slashed apart by the fugitive's knife. The ground rose under foot; the hills were at hand; still the pursuit held on. The sun, long past the meridian, began to turn earthward. Would night come on before they were up with him?

"Look! Look! There he is! Quick, there he goes!"

High on the bare slope of the nearest hill, all the posse, looking in the direction of Delaney's gesture, saw the figure of a horseman emerge from an arroyo, filled with chaparral, and struggle at a labouring gallop straight up the slope. Suddenly, every member of the party shouted aloud. The horse had fallen, pitching the rider from the saddle. The man rose to his feet, caught at the bridle, missed it and the horse dashed on alone. The man, pausing for a second looked around, saw the chase drawing nearer, then, turning back, disappeared in the chaparral. Delaney raised a great whoop.

"We've got you now." Into the slopes and valleys of the hills dashed the band of horsemen, the trail now so fresh that it could be easily discerned by all. On and on it led them, a furious, wild scramble straight up the slopes. The minutes went by. The dry bed of a rivulet was passed; then another fence; then a tangle of manzanita; a meadow of wild oats, full of agitated cattle; then an arroyo, thick with chaparral and scrub oaks, and then, without warning, the pistol shots ripped out and ran from rider to rider with the rapidity of a gatling discharge, and one of the deputies bent forward in the saddle, both hands to his face, the blood jetting from between his fingers.

Dyke was there, at bay at last, his back against a bank of rock, the roots of a fallen tree serving him as a rampart, his revolver smoking in his hand.

"You're under arrest, Dyke," cried the sheriff. "It's not the least use to fight. The whole country is up."

Dyke fired again, the shot splintering the foreleg of the horse the sheriff rode.

The posse, four men all told—the wounded deputy having crawled out of the fight after Dyke's first shot—fell back after the preliminary fusillade, dismounted, and took shelter behind rocks and trees. On that rugged ground, fighting from the saddle was impracticable. Dyke, in the meanwhile, held his fire, for he knew that, once his pistol was empty, he would never be allowed time to reload.

"Dyke," called the sheriff again, "for the last time, I summon you to surrender."

Dyke did not reply. The sheriff, Delaney, and the man named Christian conferred together in a low voice. Then Delaney and Christian left the others, making a wide detour up the sides of the arroyo, to gain a position to the left and somewhat to the rear of Dyke.

But it was at this moment that S. Behrman arrived. It could not be said whether it was courage or carelessness that brought the Railroad's agent within reach of

Dyke's revolver. Possibly he was really a brave man; possibly occupied with keeping an uncertain seat upon the back of his labouring, scrambling horse, he had not noticed that he was so close upon that scene of battle. He certainly did not observe the posse lying upon the ground behind sheltering rocks and trees, and before anyone could call a warning, he had ridden out into the open, within thirty paces of Dyke's intrenchment.

Dyke saw. There was the arch-enemy; the man of all men whom he most hated; the man who had ruined him, who had exasperated him and driven him to crime, and who had instigated tireless pursuit through all those past terrible weeks. Suddenly, inviting death, he leaped up and forward; he had forgotten all else, all other considerations, at the sight of this man. He would die, gladly, so only that S. Behrman died before him.

"I've got YOU, anyway," he shouted, as he ran forward.

The muzzle of the weapon was not ten feet from S. Behrman's huge stomach as Dyke drew the trigger. Had the cartridge exploded, death, certain and swift, would have followed, but at this, of all moments, the revolver missed fire.

S. Behrman, with an unexpected agility, leaped from the saddle, and, keeping his horse between him and Dyke, ran, dodging and ducking, from tree to tree. His first shot a failure, Dyke fired again and again at his enemy, emptying his revolver, reckless of consequences. His every shot went wild, and before he could draw his knife, the whole posse was upon him.

Without concerted plans, obeying no signal but the promptings of the impulse that snatched, unerring, at opportunity—the men, Delaney and Christian from one side, the sheriff and the deputy from the other, rushed in. They did not fire. It was Dyke alive they wanted. One of them had a riata snatched from a saddle-pommel, and with this they tried to bind him.

The fight was four to one—four men with law on their side, to one wounded freebooter, half-starved, exhausted by days and nights of pursuit, worn down with loss of sleep, thirst, privation, and the grinding, nerve-racking consciousness of an ever-present peril.

They swarmed upon him from all sides, gripping at his legs, at his arms, his throat, his head, striking, clutching, kicking, falling to the ground, rolling over and over, now under, now above, now staggering forward, now toppling back. Still Dyke fought. Through that scrambling, struggling group, through that maze of twisting bodies, twining arms, straining legs, S. Behrman saw him from moment to moment, his face flaming, his eyes bloodshot, his hair matted with sweat. Now he was down, pinned under, two men across his legs, and now half-way up again, struggling to one knee. Then upright again, with half his enemies hanging on his back. His colossal strength seemed doubled; when his arms were held, he fought bull-like with his head. A score of times, it seemed as if they were about to secure him finally and irrevocably, and then he would free an arm, a leg, a shoulder, and the group that, for the fraction of an instant, had settled, locked and rigid, on its prey, would break up again as he flung a man from him, reeling and bloody, and he himself twisting, squirming, dodging, his great fists working like pistons, backed away, dragging and carrying the others with him.

More than once, he loosened almost every grip, and for an instant stood nearly free, panting, rolling his eyes, his clothes torn from his body, bleeding, dripping with sweat, a terrible figure, nearly free. The sheriff, under his breath, uttered an exclamation:

"By God, he'll get away yet."

S. Behrman watched the fight complacently.

"That all may show obstinacy," he commented, "but it don't show common sense."

Yet, however Dyke might throw off the clutches and fettering embraces that encircled him, however he might disintegrate and scatter the band of foes that heaped themselves upon him, however he might gain one instant of comparative liberty, some one of his assailants always hung, doggedly, blindly to an arm, a leg, or a foot, and the others, drawing a second's breath, closed in again, implacable, unconquerable, ferocious, like hounds upon a wolf.

At length, two of the men managed to bring Dyke's wrists close enough together to allow the sheriff to snap the handcuffs on. Even then, Dyke, clasping his hands, and using the handcuffs themselves as a weapon, knocked down Delaney by the crushing impact of the steel bracelets upon the cow-puncher's forehead. But he could no longer protect himself from attacks from behind, and the riata was finally passed around his body, pinioning his arms to his sides. After this it was useless to resist.

The wounded deputy sat with his back to a rock, holding his broken jaw in both hands. The sheriff's horse, with its splintered foreleg, would have to be shot. Delaney's head was cut from temple to cheekbone. The right wrist of the sheriff was all but dislocated. The other deputy was so exhausted he had to be helped to his horse. But Dyke was taken.

He himself had suddenly lapsed into semi-unconsciousness, unable to walk. They sat him on the buckskin, S. Behrman supporting him, the sheriff, on foot, leading the horse by the bridle. The little procession formed, and descended from the hills, turning in the direction of Bonneville. A special train, one car and an engine, would be made up there, and the highwayman would sleep in the Visalia jail that night.

Delaney and S. Behrman found themselves in the rear of the cavalcade as it moved off. The cow-puncher turned to his chief:

"Well, captain," he said, still panting, as he bound up his forehead; "well—we GOT him."

VI

Osterman cut his wheat that summer before any of the other ranchers, and as soon as his harvest was over organized a jack-rabbit drive. Like Annixter's barn-dance, it was to be an event in which all the country-side should take part. The drive was to begin on the most western division of the Osterman ranch, whence it would proceed towards the southeast, crossing into the northern part of Quien Sabe—on which Annixter had sown no wheat—and ending in the hills at the headwaters of Broderson Creek, where a barbecue was to be held.

Early on the morning of the day of the drive, as Harran and Presley were saddling their horses before the stables on Los Muertos, the foreman, Phelps, remarked:

"I was into town last night, and I hear that Christian has been after Ruggles early and late to have him put him in possession here on Los Muertos, and Delaney is doing the same for Quien Sabe."

It was this man Christian, the real estate broker, and cousin of S. Behrman, one of the main actors in the drama of Dyke's capture, who had come forward as a purchaser of Los Muertos when the Railroad had regraded its holdings on the ranches around Bonneville.

"He claims, of course," Phelps went on, "that when he bought Los Muertos of the Railroad he was guaranteed possession, and he wants the place in time for the harvest."

"That's almost as thin," muttered Harran as he thrust the bit into his horse's mouth, "as Delaney buying Annixter's Home ranch. That slice of Quien Sabe, according to the Railroad's grading, is worth about ten thousand dollars; yes, even fifteen, and I don't believe Delaney is worth the price of a good horse. Why, those people don't even try to preserve appearances. Where would Christian find the money to buy Los Muertos? There's no one man in all Bonneville rich enough to do it. Damned rascals! as if we didn't see that Christian and Delaney are S. Behrman's right and left hands. Well, he'll get 'em cut off," he cried with sudden fierceness, "if he comes too near the machine."

"How is it, Harran," asked Presley as the two young men rode out of the stable yard, "how is it the Railroad gang can do anything before the Supreme Court hands down a decision?"

"Well, you know how they talk," growled Harran. "They have claimed that the cases taken up to the Supreme Court were not test cases as WE claim they ARE, and that because neither Annixter nor the Governor appealed, they've lost their cases by default. It's the rottenest kind of sharp practice, but it won't do any good. The League is too strong. They won't dare move on us yet awhile. Why, Pres, the moment they'd try to jump any of these ranches around here, they would have six hundred rifles cracking at them as quick as how-do-you-do. Why, it would take a regiment of U. S. soldiers to put any one of us off our land. No, sir; they know the League means business this time."

As Presley and Harran trotted on along the county road they continually passed or overtook other horsemen, or buggies, carry-alls, buck-boards or even farm wagons, going in the same direction. These were full of the farming people from all the country round about Bonneville, on their way to the rabbit drive—the same people seen at the barn-dance—in their Sunday finest, the girls in muslin frocks and garden hats, the men with linen dusters over their black clothes; the older women in prints and dotted calicoes. Many of these latter had already taken off their bonnets—the day was very hot—and pinning them in newspapers, stowed them under the seats. They tucked their handkerchiefs into the collars of their dresses, or knotted them about their fat necks, to keep out the dust. From the axle trees of the vehicles swung carefully covered buckets of galvanised iron, in which the lunch was packed. The younger children, the boys with great frilled collars, the girls with ill-fitting shoes cramping their feet, leaned from the sides of buggy and carry-all, eating bananas and "macaroons," staring about with ox-like stolidity. Tied to the axles, the dogs followed the horses' hoofs with lolling tongues coated with dust.

The California summer lay blanket-wise and smothering over all the land. The hills, bone-dry, were browned and parched. The grasses and wild-oats, sear and yellow, snapped like glass filaments under foot. The roads, the bordering fences, even the lower leaves and branches of the trees, were thick and grey with dust. All colour had been burned from the landscape, except in the irrigated patches, that in the waste of brown and dull yellow glowed like oases.

The wheat, now close to its maturity, had turned from pale yellow to golden yellow, and from that to brown. Like a gigantic carpet, it spread itself over all the land. There was nothing else to be seen but the limitless sea of wheat as far as the eye could reach, dry, rustling, crisp and harsh in the rare breaths of hot wind out of the southeast. As Harran and Presley went along the county road, the number of vehicles and riders increased. They overtook and passed Hooven and his family in the former's farm wagon, a saddled horse tied to the back board. The little Dutchman, wearing the old frock coat of Magnus Derrick, and a new broad-brimmed straw hat, sat on the front seat with Mrs. Hooven. The little girl Hilda, and the older daughter Minna, were behind them on a board laid across the sides of the wagon. Presley and Harran stopped to shake hands. "Say," cried Hooven, exhibiting an old, but extremely well kept, rifle, "say, bei Gott, me, I tek some schatz at dose rebbit, you bedt. Ven he hef shtop to run und sit oop soh, bei der hind laigs on, I oop mit der guhn und—bing! I cetch um."

"The marshals won't allow you to shoot, Bismarck," observed Presley, looking at Minna.

Hooven doubled up with merriment.

"Ho! dot's hell of some fine joak. Me, I'M ONE OAF DOSE MAIRSCHELL

MINE-SELLUF," he roared with delight, beating his knee. To his notion, the joke was irresistible. All day long, he could be heard repeating it. "Und Mist'r Praicelie, he say, 'Dose mairschell woand led you schoot, Bismarck,' und ME, ach Gott, ME, aindt I mine-selluf one oaf dose mairschell?"

As the two friends rode on, Presley had in his mind the image of Minna Hooven, very pretty in a clean gown of pink gingham, a cheap straw sailor hat from a Bonneville store on her blue black hair. He remembered her very pale face, very red lips and eyes of greenish blue,—a pretty girl certainly, always trailing a group of men behind her. Her love affairs were the talk of all Los Muertos.

"I hope that Hooven girl won't go to the bad," Presley said to Harran.

"Oh, she's all right," the other answered. "There's nothing vicious about Minna, and I guess she'll marry that foreman on the ditch gang, right enough."

"Well, as a matter of course, she's a good girl," Presley hastened to reply, "only she's too pretty for a poor girl, and too sure of her prettiness besides. That's the kind," he continued, "who would find it pretty easy to go wrong if they lived in a city."

Around Caraher's was a veritable throng. Saddle horses and buggies by the score were clustered underneath the shed or hitched to the railings in front of the watering trough. Three of Broderson's Portuguese tenants and a couple of workmen from the railroad shops in Bonneville were on the porch, already very drunk.

Continually, young men, singly or in groups, came from the door-way, wiping their lips with sidelong gestures of the hand. The whole place exhaled the febrile bustle of the saloon on a holiday morning.

The procession of teams streamed on through Bonneville, reenforced at every street corner. Along the Upper Road from Quien Sabe and Guadalajara came fresh auxiliaries, Spanish-Mexicans from the town itself,—swarthy young men on capering horses, dark-eyed girls and matrons, in red and black and yellow, more Portuguese in brand-new overalls, smoking long thin cigars. Even Father Sarria appeared.

"Look," said Presley, "there goes Annixter and Hilma. He's got his buckskin back." The master of Quien Sabe, in top laced boots and campaign hat, a cigar in his teeth, followed along beside the carry-all. Hilma and Mrs. Derrick were on the back seat, young Vacca driving. Harran and Presley bowed, taking off their hats.

"Hello, hello, Pres," cried Annixter, over the heads of the intervening crowd, standing up in his stirrups and waving a hand, "Great day! What a mob, hey? Say when this thing is over and everybody starts to walk into the barbecue, come and have lunch with us. I'll look for you, you and Harran. Hello, Harran, where's the Governor?"

"He didn't come to-day," Harran shouted back, as the crowd carried him further away from Annixter. "Left him and old Broderson at Los Muertos."

The throng emerged into the open country again, spreading out upon the

Osterman ranch. From all directions could be seen horses and buggies driving across the stubble, converging upon the rendezvous. Osterman's Ranch house was left to the eastward; the army of the guests hurrying forward—for it began to be late—to where around a flag pole, flying a red flag, a vast crowd of buggies and horses was already forming. The marshals began to appear. Hooven, descending from the farm wagon, pinned his white badge to his hat brim and mounted his horse. Osterman, in marvellous riding clothes of English pattern, galloped up and down upon his best thoroughbred, cracking jokes with everybody, chaffing, joshing, his great mouth distended in a perpetual grin of amiability.

"Stop here, stop here," he vociferated, dashing along in front of Presley and Harran, waving his crop. The procession came to a halt, the horses' heads pointing eastward. The line began to be formed. The marshals perspiring, shouting, fretting, galloping about, urging this one forward, ordering this one back, ranged the thousands of conveyances and cavaliers in a long line, shaped like a wide open crescent. Its wings, under the command of lieutenants, were slightly advanced. Far out before its centre Osterman took his place, delighted beyond expression at his conspicuousness, posing for the gallery, making his horse dance.

"Wail, aindt dey gowun to gommence den bretty soohn," exclaimed Mrs. Hooven, who had taken her husband's place on the forward seat of the wagon.

"I never was so warm," murmured Minna, fanning herself with her hat. All seemed in readiness. For miles over the flat expanse of stubble, curved the interminable lines of horses and vehicles. At a guess, nearly five thousand people were present. The drive was one of the largest ever held. But no start was made; immobilized, the vast crescent stuck motionless under the blazing sun. Here and there could be heard voices uplifted in jocular remonstrance.

"Oh, I say, get a move on, somebody."

"ALL aboard."

"Say, I'll take root here pretty soon."

Some took malicious pleasure in starting false alarms.

"Ah, HERE we go."

"Off, at last."

"We're off."

Invariably these jokes fooled some one in the line. An old man, or some old woman, nervous, hard of hearing, always gathered up the reins and started off, only to be hustled and ordered back into the line by the nearest marshal. This manoeuvre never failed to produce its effect of hilarity upon those near at hand. Everybody laughed at the blunderer, the joker jeering audibly.

"Hey, come back here."

"Oh, he's easy."

"Don't be in a hurry, Grandpa."

"Say, you want to drive all the rabbits yourself."

Later on, a certain group of these fellows started a huge "josh."

"Say, that's what we're waiting for, the 'do-funny.'"

"The do-funny?"

"Sure, you can't drive rabbits without the 'do-funny.'"

"What's the do-funny?"

"Oh, say, she don't know what the do-funny is. We can't start without it, sure. Pete went back to get it."

"Oh, you're joking me, there's no such thing."

"Well, aren't we WAITING for it?"

"Oh, look, look," cried some women in a covered rig. "See, they are starting already 'way over there."

In fact, it did appear as if the far extremity of the line was in motion. Dust rose in the air above it.

"They ARE starting. Why don't we start?"

"No, they've stopped. False alarm."

"They've not, either. Why don't we move?"

But as one or two began to move off, the nearest marshal shouted wrathfully:

"Get back there, get back there."

"Well, they've started over there."

"Get back, I tell you."

"Where's the 'do-funny?'"

"Say, we're going to miss it all. They've all started over there."

A lieutenant came galloping along in front of the line, shouting:

"Here, what's the matter here? Why don't you start?"

There was a great shout. Everybody simultaneously uttered a prolonged "Oh-h."

"We're off."

"Here we go for sure this time."

"Remember to keep the alignment," roared the lieutenant. "Don't go too fast."

And the marshals, rushing here and there on their sweating horses to points where the line bulged forward, shouted, waving their arms: "Not too fast, not too fast....Keep back here....Here, keep closer together here. Do you want to let all the rabbits run back between you?"

A great confused sound rose into the air,—the creaking of axles, the jolt of iron tires over the dry clods, the click of brittle stubble under the horses' hoofs, the barking of dogs, the shouts of conversation and laughter.

The entire line, horses, buggies, wagons, gigs, dogs, men and boys on foot, and armed with clubs, moved slowly across the fields, sending up a cloud of white dust, that hung above the scene like smoke. A brisk gaiety was in the air. Everyone was in the best of humor, calling from team to team, laughing, skylarking, joshing. Garnett, of the Ruby Rancho, and Gethings, of the San Pablo, both on horseback, found themselves side by side. Ignoring the drive and the spirit of the occasion, they kept up a prolonged and serious conversation on an expected rise in the price of wheat. Dabney, also on horseback, followed them, listening attentively to every word, but hazarding no remark.

Mrs. Derrick and Hilma sat in the back seat of the carry-all, behind young Vacca. Mrs. Derrick, a little disturbed by such a great concourse of people, frightened at the idea of the killing of so many rabbits, drew back in her place, her young-girl eyes troubled and filled with a vague distress. Hilma, very much excited, leaned from the carry-all, anxious to see everything, watching for rabbits, asking innumerable questions of Annixter, who rode at her side.

The change that had been progressing in Hilma, ever since the night of the famous barn-dance, now seemed to be approaching its climax; first the girl, then the woman, last of all the Mother. Conscious dignity, a new element in her character, developed. The shrinking, the timidity of the girl just awakening to the consciousness of sex, passed away from her. The confusion, the troublous complexity of the woman, a mystery even to herself, disappeared. Motherhood dawned, the old simplicity of her maiden days came back to her. It was no longer a simplicity of ignorance, but of supreme knowledge, the simplicity of the perfect, the simplicity of greatness. She looked the world fearlessly in the eyes. At last, the confusion of her ideas, like frightened birds, re-settling, adjusted itself, and she emerged from the trouble calm, serene, entering into her divine right, like a queen into the rule of a realm of perpetual peace.

And with this, with the knowledge that the crown hung poised above her head, there came upon Hilma a gentleness infinitely beautiful, infinitely pathetic; a sweetness that touched all who came near her with the softness of a caress. She moved surrounded by an invisible atmosphere of Love. Love was in her wide-opened brown eyes, Love—the dim reflection of that descending crown poised over her head—radiated in a faint lustre from her dark, thick hair. Around her beautiful neck, sloping to her shoulders with full, graceful curves, Love lay encircled like a necklace—Love that was beyond words, sweet, breathed from her parted lips. From her white, large arms downward to her pink finger-tips—Love, an invisible electric fluid, disengaged itself, subtle, alluring. In the velvety huskiness of her voice, Love vibrated like a note of unknown music.

Annixter, her uncouth, rugged husband, living in this influence of a wife, who was also a mother, at all hours touched to the quick by this sense of nobility, of gentleness and of love, the instincts of a father already clutching and tugging at his heart, was trembling on the verge of a mighty transformation. The hardness and inhumanity of the man was fast breaking up. One night, returning late to the Ranch house, after a compulsory visit to the city, he had come upon Hilma asleep. He had never forgotten that night. A realization of his boundless happiness in this love he gave and received, the thought that Hilma TRUSTED him, a knowledge of his own unworthiness, a vast and humble thankfulness that his God had chosen him of all men for this great joy, had brought him to his knees for the first time in all his troubled, restless life of combat and aggression. He prayed, he knew not what,—vague words, wordless thoughts, resolving fiercely to do right, to make some return for God's gift thus placed within his hands.

Where once Annixter had thought only of himself, he now thought only of Hilma. The time when this thought of another should broaden and widen into thought of OTHERS, was yet to come; but already it had expanded to include the unborn child—already, as in the case of Mrs. Dyke, it had broadened to enfold another child and another mother bound to him by no ties other than those of humanity and pity. In time, starting from this point it would reach out more and more till it should take in all men and all women, and the intolerant selfish man, while retaining all of his native strength, should become tolerant and generous, kind and forgiving.

For the moment, however, the two natures struggled within him. A fight was to be fought, one more, the last, the fiercest, the attack of the enemy who menaced his very home and hearth, was to be resisted. Then, peace attained, arrested development would once more proceed.

Hilma looked from the carry-all, scanning the open plain in front of the advancing line of the drive.

"Where are the rabbits?" she asked of Annixter. "I don't see any at all."

"They are way ahead of us yet," he said. "Here, take the glasses."

He passed her his field glasses, and she adjusted them.

"Oh, yes," she cried, "I see. I can see five or six, but oh, so far off."

"The beggars run 'way ahead, at first."

"I should say so. See them run,—little specks. Every now and then they sit up, their ears straight up, in the air."

"Here, look, Hilma, there goes one close by."

From out of the ground apparently, some twenty yards distant, a great jack sprang into view, bounding away with tremendous leaps, his black-tipped ears erect. He disappeared, his grey body losing itself against the grey of the ground.

"Oh, a big fellow."

"Hi, yonder's another."

"Yes, yes, oh, look at him run." From off the surface of the ground, at first apparently empty of all life, and seemingly unable to afford hiding place for so much as a field-mouse, jack-rabbits started up at every moment as the line went forward. At first, they appeared singly and at long intervals; then in twos and threes, as the drive continued to advance. They leaped across the plain, and stopped in the distance, sitting up with straight ears, then ran on again, were joined by others; sank down flush to the soil—their ears flattened; started up again, ran to the side, turned back once more, darted away with incredible swiftness, and were lost to view only to be replaced by a score of others.

Gradually, the number of jacks to be seen over the expanse of stubble in front of the line of teams increased. Their antics were infinite. No two acted precisely alike. Some lay stubbornly close in a little depression between two clods, till the horses' hoofs were all but upon them, then sprang out from their hiding-place at the last second. Others ran forward but a few yards at a time, refusing to take flight, scenting a greater danger before them than behind. Still others, forced up at the last moment, doubled with lightning alacrity in their tracks, turning back to scuttle between the teams, taking desperate chances. As often as this occurred, it was the signal for a great uproar.

"Don't let him get through; don t let him get through."

"Look out for him, there he goes."

Horns were blown, bells rung, tin pans clamorously beaten. Either the jack escaped, or confused by the noise, darted back again, fleeing away as if his life depended on the issue of the instant. Once even, a bewildered rabbit jumped fair into Mrs. Derrick's lap as she sat in the carry-all, and was out again like a flash.

"Poor frightened thing," she exclaimed; and for a long time afterward, she retained upon her knees the sensation of the four little paws quivering with excitement, and the feel of the trembling furry body, with its wildly beating heart, pressed against her own.

By noon the number of rabbits discernible by Annixter's field glasses on ahead was far into the thousands. What seemed to be ground resolved itself, when seen through the glasses, into a maze of small, moving bodies, leaping, ducking, doubling, running back and forth—a wilderness of agitated ears, white tails and twinkling legs. The outside wings of the curved line of vehicles began to draw in a little; Osterman's ranch was left behind, the drive continued on over Quien Sabe.

As the day advanced, the rabbits, singularly enough, became less wild. When flushed, they no longer ran so far nor so fast, limping off instead a few feet at a time, and crouching down, their ears close upon their backs. Thus it was, that by degrees the teams began to close up on the main herd. At every instant the numbers increased. It was no longer thousands, it was tens of thousands. The earth was alive with rabbits.

Denser and denser grew the throng. In all directions nothing was to be seen but the loose mass of the moving jacks. The horns of the crescent of teams began to contract. Far off the corral came into sight. The disintegrated mass of rabbits commenced, as it were, to solidify, to coagulate. At first, each jack was some three feet distant from his nearest neighbor, but this space diminished to two feet, then to one, then to but a few inches. The rabbits began leaping over one another.

Then the strange scene defined itself. It was no longer a herd covering the earth. It was a sea, whipped into confusion, tossing incessantly, leaping, falling, agitated by unseen forces. At times the unexpected tameness of the rabbits all at once vanished. Throughout certain portions of the herd eddies of terror abruptly burst forth. A panic spread; then there would ensue a blind, wild rushing together of thousands of crowded bodies, and a furious scrambling over backs, till the scuffing thud of innumerable feet over the earth rose to a reverberating murmur as of distant thunder, here and there pierced by the strange, wild cry of the rabbit in distress.

The line of vehicles was halted. To go forward now meant to trample the rabbits under foot. The drive came to a standstill while the herd entered the corral. This took time, for the rabbits were by now too crowded to run. However, like an opened sluice-gate, the extending flanks of the entrance of the corral slowly engulfed the herd. The mass, packed tight as ever, by degrees diminished, precisely as a pool of water when a dam is opened. The last stragglers went in with a rush, and the gate was dropped.

"Come, just have a lock in here," called Annixter.

Hilma, descending from the carry-all and joined by Presley and Harran, approached and looked over the high board fence.

"Oh, did you ever see anything like that?" she exclaimed.

The corral, a really large enclosure, had proved all too small for the number of rabbits collected by the drive. Inside it was a living, moving, leaping, breathing, twisting mass. The rabbits were packed two, three, and four feet deep. They were in constant movement; those beneath struggling to the top, those on top sinking and disappearing below their fellows. All wildness, all fear of man, seemed to have entirely disappeared. Men and boys reaching over the sides of the corral, picked up a jack in each hand, holding them by the ears, while two reporters from San Francisco papers took photographs of the scene. The noise made by the tens of thousands of moving bodies was as the noise of wind in a forest, while from the hot and sweating mass there rose a strange odor, penetrating, ammoniacal, savouring of wild life.

On signal, the killing began. Dogs that had been brought there for that purpose when let into the corral refused, as had been half expected, to do the work. They snuffed curiously at the pile, then backed off, disturbed, perplexed. But the men and boys—Portuguese for the most part—were more eager. Annixter drew Hilma away, and, indeed, most of the people set about the barbecue at once.

In the corral, however, the killing went forward. Armed with a club in each hand, the young fellows from Guadalajara and Bonneville, and the farm boys from the ranches, leaped over the rails of the corral. They walked unsteadily upon the myriad of crowding bodies underfoot, or, as space was cleared, sank almost waist deep into the mass that leaped and squirmed about them. Blindly, furiously, they struck and struck. The Anglo-Saxon spectators round about drew back in disgust, but the hot, degenerated blood of Portuguese, Mexican, and mixed Spaniard boiled up in excitement at this wholesale slaughter.

But only a few of the participants of the drive cared to look on. All the guests betook themselves some quarter of a mile farther on into the hills.

The picnic and barbecue were to be held around the spring where Broderson Creek took its rise. Already two entire beeves were roasting there; teams were hitched, saddles removed, and men, women, and children, a great throng, spread out under the shade of the live oaks. A vast confused clamour rose in the air, a babel of talk, a clatter of tin plates, of knives and forks. Bottles were uncorked, napkins and oil-cloths spread over the ground. The men lit pipes and cigars, the women seized the occasion to nurse their babies.

Osterman, ubiquitous as ever, resplendent in his boots and English riding breeches, moved about between the groups, keeping up an endless flow of talk, cracking jokes, winking, nudging, gesturing, putting his tongue in his cheek, never at a loss for a reply, playing the goat.

"That josher, Osterman, always at his monkey-shines, but a good fellow for all that; brainy too. Nothing stuck up about him either, like Magnus Derrick."

"Everything all right, Buck?" inquired Osterman, coming up to where Annixter, Hilma and Mrs. Derrick were sitting down to their lunch.

"Yes, yes, everything right. But we've no cork-screw."

"No screw-cork—no scare-crow? Here you are," and he drew from his pocket a silver-plated jack-knife with a cork-screw attachment. Harran and Presley came up, bearing between them a great smoking, roasted portion of beef just off the fire. Hilma hastened to put forward a huge china platter.

Osterman had a joke to crack with the two boys, a joke that was rather broad, but as he turned about, the words almost on his lips, his glance fell upon Hilma herself, whom he had not seen for more than two months.

She had handed Presley the platter, and was now sitting with her back against the tree, between two boles of the roots. The position was a little elevated and the supporting roots on either side of her were like the arms of a great chair—a chair of state. She sat thus, as on a throne, raised above the rest, the radiance of the unseen crown of motherhood glowing from her forehead, the beauty of the perfect woman surrounding her like a glory.

And the josh died away on Osterman's lips, and unconsciously and swiftly he bared his head. Something was passing there in the air about him that he did not understand, something, however, that imposed reverence and profound respect. For the first time in his life, embarrassment seized upon him, upon this joker, this wearer of clothes, this teller of funny stories, with his large, red ears, bald head and comic actor's face. He stammered confusedly and took himself away, for the moment abstracted, serious, lost in thought.

By now everyone was eating. It was the feeding of the People, elemental, gross, a great appeasing of appetite, an enormous quenching of thirst. Quarters of beef, roasts, ribs, shoulders, haunches were consumed, loaves of bread by the thousands disappeared, whole barrels of wine went down the dry and dusty throats of the multitude. Conversation lagged while the People ate, while hunger was appeased. Everybody had their fill. One ate for the sake of eating, resolved that there should be nothing left, considering it a matter of pride to exhibit a clean plate.

After dinner, preparations were made for games. On a flat plateau at the top of one of the hills the contestants were to strive. There was to be a footrace of young girls under seventeen, a fat men's race, the younger fellows were to put the shot, to compete in the running broad jump, and the standing high jump, in the hop, skip, and step and in wrestling.

Presley was delighted with it all. It was Homeric, this feasting, this vast consuming of meat and bread and wine, followed now by games of strength. An epic simplicity and directness, an honest Anglo-Saxon mirth and innocence, commended it. Crude it was; coarse it was, but no taint of viciousness was here. These people were good people, kindly, benignant even, always readier to give than to receive, always more willing to help than to be helped. They were good stock. Of such was the backbone of the nation—sturdy Americans everyone of them. Where else in the world round were such strong, honest men, such strong, beautiful women?

Annixter, Harran, and Presley climbed to the level plateau where the games were to be held, to lay out the courses, and mark the distances. It was the very place where once Presley had loved to lounge entire afternoons, reading his books of poems, smoking and dozing. From this high point one dominated the entire valley to the south and west. The view was superb. The three men paused for a moment on the crest of the hill to consider it.

Young Vacca came running and panting up the hill after them, calling for Annixter.

"Well, well, what is it?"

"Mr. Osterman's looking for you, sir, you and Mr. Harran. Vanamee, that cow-boy over at Derrick's, has just come from the Governor with a message. I guess it's important."

"Hello, what's up now?" muttered Annixter, as they turned back.

They found Osterman saddling his horse in furious haste. Near-by him was Vanamee holding by the bridle an animal that was one lather of sweat. A few of the picnickers were turning their heads curiously in that direction. Evidently something of moment was in the wind.

"What's all up?" demanded Annixter, as he and Harran, followed by Presley, drew near.

"There's hell to pay," exclaimed Osterman under his breath. "Read that. Vanamee just brought it."

He handed Annixter a sheet of note paper, and turned again to the cinching of his saddle.

"We've got to be quick," he cried. "They've stolen a march on us."

Annixter read the note, Harran and Presley looking over his shoulder.

"Ah, it's them, is it," exclaimed Annixter.

Harran set his teeth. "Now for it," he exclaimed. "They've been to your place already, Mr. Annixter," said Vanamee. "I passed by it on my way up. They have put Delaney in possession, and have set all your furniture out in the road."

Annixter turned about, his lips white. Already Presley and Harran had run to their horses.

"Vacca," cried Annixter, "where's Vacca? Put the saddle on the buckskin, QUICK. Osterman, get as many of the League as are here together at THIS spot, understand. I'll be back in a minute. I must tell Hilma this."

Hooven ran up as Annixter disappeared. His little eyes were blazing, he was dragging his horse with him.

"Say, dose fellers come, hey? Me, I'm alretty, see I hev der guhn."

"They've jumped the ranch, little girl," said Annixter, putting one arm around Hilma. "They're in our house now. I'm off. Go to Derrick's and wait for me there."

She put her arms around his neck.

"You're going?" she demanded.

"I must. Don't be frightened. It will be all right. Go to Derrick's and—good-bye."

She said never a word. She looked once long into his eyes, then kissed him on the mouth.

Meanwhile, the news had spread. The multitude rose to its feet. Women and men, with pale faces, looked at each other speechless, or broke forth into inarticulate exclamations. A strange, unfamiliar murmur took the place of the tumultuous gaiety of the previous moments. A sense of dread, of confusion, of impending terror weighed heavily in the air. What was now to happen?

When Annixter got back to Osterman, he found a number of the Leaguers already assembled. They were all mounted. Hooven was there and Harran, and besides these, Garnett of the Ruby ranch and Gethings of the San Pablo, Phelps the foreman of Los Muertos, and, last of all, Dabney, silent as ever, speaking to no one. Presley came riding up.

"Best keep out of this, Pres," cried Annixter.

"Are we ready?" exclaimed Gethings.

"Ready, ready, we're all here."

"ALL. Is this all of us?" cried Annixter. "Where are the six hundred men who were going to rise when this happened?"

They had wavered, these other Leaguers. Now, when the actual crisis impended, they were smitten with confusion. Ah, no, they were not going to stand up and be shot at just to save Derrick's land. They were not armed. What did Annixter and Osterman take them for? No, sir; the Railroad had stolen a march on them. After all his big talk Derrick had allowed them to be taken by surprise. The only thing to do was to call a meeting of the Executive Committee. That was the only thing. As for going down there with no weapons in their hands, NO, sir. That was asking a little TOO much. "Come on, then, boys," shouted Osterman, turning his back on the others. "The Governor says to meet him at Hooven's. We'll make for the Long Trestle and strike the trail to Hooven's there."

They set off. It was a terrible ride. Twice during the scrambling descent from the hills, Presley's pony fell beneath him. Annixter, on his buckskin, and Osterman, on his thoroughbred, good horsemen both, led the others, setting a terrific pace. The hills were left behind. Broderson Creek was crossed and on the levels of Quien Sabe, straight through the standing wheat, the nine horses, flogged and spurred, stretched out to their utmost. Their passage through the wheat sounded like the rip and tear of a gigantic web of cloth. The landscape on either hand resolved itself into a long blur. Tears came to the eyes, flying pebbles, clods of earth, grains of wheat flung up in the flight, stung the face like shot. Osterman's thoroughbred took the second crossing of Broderson's Creek in a single leap. Down under the Long Trestle tore the cavalcade in a shower of mud and gravel; up again on the further bank, the horses blowing like steam engines; on into the trail to Hooven's, single file now, Presley's pony lagging, Hooven's horse bleeding at the eyes, the buckskin, game as a fighting cock, catching her second wind, far in the lead now, distancing even the English thoroughbred that Osterman rode.

At last Hooven's unpainted house, beneath the enormous live oak tree, came in sight. Across the Lower Road, breaking through fences and into the yard around the house, thundered the Leaguers. Magnus was waiting for them.

The riders dismounted, hardly less exhausted than their horses.

"Why, where's all the men?" Annixter demanded of Magnus.

"Broderson is here and Cutter," replied the Governor, "no one else. I thought YOU would bring more men with you."

"There are only nine of us."

"And the six hundred Leaguers who were going to rise when this happened!" exclaimed Garnett, bitterly.

"Rot the League," cried Annixter. "It's gone to pot—went to pieces at the first touch."

"We have been taken by surprise, gentlemen, after all," said Magnus. "Totally off our guard. But there are eleven of us. It is enough."

"Well, what's the game? Has the marshal come? How many men are with him?"

"The United States marshal from San Francisco," explained Magnus, "came down early this morning and stopped at Guadalajara. We learned it all through our friends in Bonneville about an hour ago. They telephoned me and Mr. Broderson. S. Behrman met him and provided about a dozen deputies. Delaney, Ruggles, and Christian joined them at Guadalajara. They left Guadalajara, going towards Mr. Annixter's ranch house on Quien Sabe. They are serving the writs in ejectment and putting the dummy buyers in possession. They are armed. S. Behrman is with them."

"Where are they now?"

"Cutter is watching them from the Long Trestle. They returned to Guadalajara. They are there now."

"Well," observed Gethings, "From Guadalajara they can only go to two places. Either they will take the Upper Road and go on to Osterman's next, or they will take the Lower Road to Mr. Derrick's."

"That is as I supposed," said Magnus. "That is why I wanted you to come here. From Hooven's, here, we can watch both roads simultaneously."

"Is anybody on the lookout on the Upper Road?"

"Cutter. He is on the Long Trestle."

"Say," observed Hooven, the instincts of the old-time soldier stirring him, "say, dose feller pretty demn schmart, I tink. We got to put some picket way oudt bei der Lower Roadt alzoh, und he tek dose glassus Mist'r Ennixt'r got bei um. Say, look at dose irregation ditsch. Dot ditsch he run righd across BOTH dose road, hey? Dat's some fine entrenchment, you bedt. We fighd um from dose ditsch."

In fact, the dry irrigating ditch was a natural trench, admirably suited to the purpose, crossing both roads as Hooven pointed out and barring approach from Guadalajara to all the ranches save Annixter's—which had already been seized.

Gethings departed to join Cutter on the Long Trestle, while Phelps and Harran, taking Annixter's field glasses with them, and mounting their horses, went out towards Guadalajara on the Lower Road to watch for the marshal's approach from that direction.

After the outposts had left them, the party in Hooven's cottage looked to their weapons. Long since, every member of the League had been in the habit of carrying his revolver with him. They were all armed and, in addition, Hooven had his rifle. Presley alone carried no weapon.

The main room of Hooven's house, in which the Leaguers were now assembled, was barren, poverty-stricken, but tolerably clean. An old clock ticked vociferously on a shelf. In one corner was a bed, with a patched, faded quilt. In the centre of the room, straddling over the bare floor, stood a pine table. Around this the men gathered, two or three occupying chairs, Annixter sitting sideways on the table, the rest standing.

"I believe, gentlemen," said Magnus, "that we can go through this day without bloodshed. I believe not one shot need be fired. The Railroad will not force the issue, will not bring about actual fighting. When the marshal realises that we are thoroughly in earnest, thoroughly determined, I am convinced that he will withdraw."

There were murmurs of assent.

"Look here," said Annixter, "if this thing can by any means be settled peaceably, I say let's do it, so long as we don't give in."

The others stared. Was this Annixter who spoke—the Hotspur of the League, the quarrelsome, irascible fellow who loved and sought a quarrel? Was it Annixter, who now had been the first and only one of them all to suffer, whose ranch had been seized, whose household possessions had been flung out into the road?

"When you come right down to it," he continued, "killing a man, no matter what he's done to you, is a serious business. I propose we make one more attempt to stave this thing off. Let's see if we can't get to talk with the marshal himself; at any rate, warn him of the danger of going any further. Boys, let's not fire the first shot. What do you say?"

The others agreed unanimously and promptly; and old Broderson, tugging uneasily at his long beard, added:

"No—no—no violence, no UNNECESSARY violence, that is. I should hate to have innocent blood on my hands—that is, if it IS innocent. I don't know, that S. Behrman—ah, he is a—a—surely he had innocent blood on HIS head. That Dyke affair, terrible, terrible; but then Dyke WAS in the wrong—driven to it, though; the Railroad did drive him to it. I want to be fair and just to everybody."

"There's a team coming up the road from Los Muertos," announced Presley from the door.

"Fair and just to everybody," murmured old Broderson, wagging his head, frowning perplexedly. "I don't want to—to—to harm anybody unless they harm me."

"Is the team going towards Guadalajara?" enquired Garnett, getting up and coming to the door.

"Yes, it's a Portuguese, one of the garden truck men."

"We must turn him back," declared Osterman. "He can't go through here. We don't want him to take any news on to the marshal and S. Behrman."

"I'll turn him back," said Presley.

He rode out towards the market cart, and the others, watching from the road in front of Hooven's, saw him halt it. An excited interview followed. They could hear the Portuguese expostulating volubly, but in the end he turned back.

"Martial law on Los Muertos, isn't it?" observed Osterman. "Steady all," he exclaimed as he turned about, "here comes Harran."

Harran rode up at a gallop. The others surrounded him.

"I saw them," he cried. "They are coming this way. S. Behrman and Ruggles are in a two-horse buggy. All the others are on horseback. There are eleven of them. Christian and Delaney are with them. Those two have rifles. I left Hooven watching them."

"Better call in Gethings and Cutter right away," said Annixter. "We'll need all our men."

"I'll call them in," Presley volunteered at once. "Can I have the buckskin? My pony is about done up."

He departed at a brisk gallop, but on the way met Gethings and Cutter returning. They, too, from their elevated position, had observed the marshal's party leaving Guadalajara by the Lower Road. Presley told them of the decision of the Leaguers not to fire until fired upon.

"All right," said Gethings. "But if it comes to a gun-fight, that means it's all up with at least one of us. Delaney never misses his man."

When they reached Hooven's again, they found that the Leaguers had already taken their position in the ditch. The plank bridge across it had been torn up. Magnus, two long revolvers lying on the embankment in front of him, was in the middle, Harran at his side. On either side, some five feet intervening between each man, stood the other Leaguers, their revolvers ready. Dabney, the silent old man, had taken off his coat.

"Take your places between Mr. Osterman and Mr. Broderson," said Magnus, as the three men rode up. "Presley," he added, "I forbid you to take any part in this affair."

"Yes, keep him out of it," cried Annixter from his position at the extreme end of the line. "Go back to Hooven's house, Pres, and look after the horses," he added. "This is no business of yours. And keep the road behind us clear. Don't let ANY ONE come near, not ANY ONE, understand?"

Presley withdrew, leading the buckskin and the horses that Gethings and Cutter had ridden. He fastened them under the great live oak and then came out and stood in the road in front of the house to watch what was going on.

In the ditch, shoulder deep, the Leaguers, ready, watchful, waited in silence, their eyes fixed on the white shimmer of the road leading to Guadalajara.

"Where's Hooven?" enquired Cutter.

"I don't know," Osterman replied. "He was out watching the Lower Road with Harran Derrick. Oh, Harran," he called, "isn't Hooven coming in?"

"I don't know what he is waiting for," answered Harran. "He was to have come in just after me. He thought maybe the marshal's party might make a feint in this direction, then go around by the Upper Road, after all. He wanted to watch them a little longer. But he ought to be here now."

"Think he'll take a shot at them on his own account?"

"Oh, no, he wouldn't do that."

"Maybe they took him prisoner."

"Well, that's to be thought of, too."

Suddenly there was a cry. Around the bend of the road in front of them came a cloud of dust. From it emerged a horse's head.

"Hello, hello, there's something."

"Remember, we are not to fire first."

"Perhaps that's Hooven; I can't see. Is it? There only seems to be one horse."

"Too much dust for one horse."

Annixter, who had taken his field glasses from Harran, adjusted them to his eyes.

"That's not them," he announced presently, "nor Hooven either. That's a cart." Then after another moment, he added, "The butcher's cart from Guadalajara."

The tension was relaxed. The men drew long breaths, settling back in their places.

"Do we let him go on, Governor?"

"The bridge is down. He can't go by and we must not let him go back. We shall have to detain him and question him. I wonder the marshal let him pass."

The cart approached at a lively trot.

"Anybody else in that cart, Mr. Annixter?" asked Magnus. "Look carefully. It may be a ruse. It is strange the marshal should have let him pass."

The Leaguers roused themselves again. Osterman laid his hand on his revolver.

"No," called Annixter, in another instant, "no, there's only one man in it."

The cart came up, and Cutter and Phelps, clambering from the ditch, stopped it as it arrived in front of the party.

"Hey—what—what?" exclaimed the young butcher, pulling up. "Is that bridge broke?"

But at the idea of being held, the boy protested at top voice, badly frightened, bewildered, not knowing what was to happen next.

"No, no, I got my meat to deliver. Say, you let me go. Say, I ain't got nothing to do with you."

He tugged at the reins, trying to turn the cart about. Cutter, with his jack-knife, parted the reins just back of the bit.

"You'll stay where you are, m' son, for a while. We're not going to hurt you. But you are not going back to town till we say so. Did you pass anybody on the road out of town?"

In reply to the Leaguers' questions, the young butcher at last told them he had passed a two-horse buggy and a lot of men on horseback just beyond the railroad tracks. They were headed for Los Muertos.

"That's them, all right," muttered Annixter. "They're coming by this road, sure."

The butcher's horse and cart were led to one side of the road, and the horse tied to the fence with one of the severed lines. The butcher, himself, was passed over to Presley, who locked him in Hooven's barn.

"Well, what the devil," demanded Osterman, "has become of Bismarck?"

In fact, the butcher had seen nothing of Hooven. The minutes were passing, and still he failed to appear.

"What's he up to, anyways?"

"Bet you what you like, they caught him. Just like that crazy Dutchman to get excited and go too near. You can always depend on Hooven to lose his head."

Five minutes passed, then ten. The road towards Guadalajara lay empty, baking and white under the sun.

"Well, the marshal and S. Behrman don't seem to be in any hurry, either."

"Shall I go forward and reconnoitre, Governor?" asked Harran.

But Dabney, who stood next to Annixter, touched him on the shoulder and, without speaking, pointed down the road. Annixter looked, then suddenly cried out:

"Here comes Hooven."

The German galloped into sight, around the turn of the road, his rifle laid across his saddle. He came on rapidly, pulled up, and dismounted at the ditch.

"Dey're commen," he cried, trembling with excitement. "I watch um long dime bei der side oaf der roadt in der busches. Dey shtop bei der gate oder side der relroadt trecks and talk long dime mit one n'udder. Den dey gome on. Dey're gowun sure do zum monkey-doodle pizeness. Me, I see Gritschun put der kertridges in his guhn. I tink dey gowun to gome MY blace first. Dey gowun to try put me off, tek my home, bei Gott."

"All right, get down in here and keep quiet, Hooven. Don't fire unless—"

"Here they are."

A half-dozen voices uttered the cry at once.

There could be no mistake this time. A buggy, drawn by two horses, came into view around the curve of the road. Three riders accompanied it, and behind these, seen at intervals in a cloud of dust were two—three—five—six others.

This, then, was S. Behrman with the United States marshal and his posse. The event that had been so long in preparation, the event which it had been said would never come to pass, the last trial of strength, the last fight between the Trust and the People, the direct, brutal grapple of armed men, the law defied, the Government ignored, behold, here it was close at hand.

Osterman cocked his revolver, and in the profound silence that had fallen upon the scene, the click was plainly audible from end to end of the line.

"Remember our agreement, gentlemen," cried Magnus, in a warning voice. "Mr. Osterman, I must ask you to let down the hammer of your weapon."

No one answered. In absolute quiet, standing motionless in their places, the Leaguers watched the approach of the marshal.

Five minutes passed. The riders came on steadily. They drew nearer. The grind of the buggy wheels in the grit and dust of the road, and the prolonged clatter of the horses' feet began to make itself heard. The Leaguers could distinguish the faces of their enemies.

In the buggy were S. Behrman and Cyrus Ruggles, the latter driving. A tall man in a frock coat and slouched hat—the marshal, beyond question—rode at the left of the buggy; Delaney, carrying a Winchester, at the right. Christian, the real estate broker, S. Behrman's cousin, also with a rifle, could be made out just behind the marshal. Back of these, riding well up, was a group of horsemen, indistinguishable in the dust raised by the buggy's wheels.

Steadily the distance between the Leaguers and the posse diminished.

"Don't let them get too close, Governor," whispered Harran.

When S. Behrman's buggy was about one hundred yards distant from the irrigating ditch, Magnus sprang out upon the road, leaving his revolvers behind him. He beckoned Garnett and Gethings to follow, and the three ranchers, who, with the exception of Broderson, were the oldest men present, advanced, without arms, to meet the marshal.

Magnus cried aloud:

"Halt where you are."

From their places in the ditch, Annixter, Osterman, Dabney, Harran, Hooven, Broderson, Cutter, and Phelps, their hands laid upon their revolvers, watched silently, alert, keen, ready for anything.

At the Governor's words, they saw Ruggles pull sharply on the reins. The buggy came to a standstill, the riders doing likewise. Magnus approached the marshal, still followed by Garnett and Gethings, and began to speak. His voice was audible to the men in the ditch, but his words could not be made out. They heard the marshal reply quietly enough and the two shook hands. Delaney came around from the side of the buggy, his horse standing before the team across the road. He leaned from the saddle, listening to what was being said, but made no remark. From time to time, S. Behrman and Ruggles, from their seats in the buggy, interposed a sentence or two into the conversation, but at first, so far as the Leaguers could discern, neither Magnus nor the marshal paid them any attention. They saw, however, that the latter repeatedly shook his head and once they heard him exclaim in a loud voice:

"I only know my duty, Mr. Derrick."

Then Gethings turned about, and seeing Delaney close at hand, addressed an unheard remark to him. The cow-puncher replied curtly and the words seemed to anger Gethings. He made a gesture, pointing back to the ditch, showing the intrenched Leaguers to the posse. Delaney appeared to communicate the news that the Leaguers were on hand and prepared to resist, to the other members of the party. They all looked toward the ditch and plainly saw the ranchers there, standing to their arms.

But meanwhile Ruggles had addressed himself more directly to Magnus, and between the two an angry discussion was going forward. Once even Harran heard his father exclaim:

"The statement is a lie and no one knows it better than yourself."

"Here," growled Annixter to Dabney, who stood next him in the ditch, "those fellows are getting too close. Look at them edging up. Don't Magnus see that?"

The other members of the marshal's force had come forward from their places behind the buggy and were spread out across the road. Some of them were gathered about Magnus, Garnett, and Gethings; and some were talking together, looking and pointing towards the ditch. Whether acting upon signal or not, the Leaguers in the ditch could not tell, but it was certain that one or two of the posse had moved considerably forward. Besides this, Delaney had now placed his horse between Magnus and the ditch, and two others riding up from the rear had followed his example. The posse surrounded the three ranchers, and by now, everybody was talking at once.

"Look here," Harran called to Annixter, "this won't do. I don't like the looks of this thing. They all seem to be edging up, and before we know it they may take the Governor and the other men prisoners."

"They ought to come back," declared Annixter.

"Somebody ought to tell them that those fellows are creeping up."

By now, the angry argument between the Governor and Ruggles had become more heated than ever. Their voices were raised; now and then they made furious gestures.

"They ought to come back," cried Osterman. "We couldn't shoot now if anything should happen, for fear of hitting them."

"Well, it sounds as though something were going to happen pretty soon."

They could hear Gethings and Delaney wrangling furiously; another deputy joined in.

"I'm going to call the Governor back," exclaimed Annixter, suddenly clambering out of the ditch. "No, no," cried Osterman, "keep in the ditch. They can't drive us out if we keep here."

Hooven and Harran, who had instinctively followed Annixter, hesitated at Osterman's words and the three halted irresolutely on the road before the ditch, their weapons in their hands.

"Governor," shouted Harran, "come on back. You can't do anything."

Still the wrangle continued, and one of the deputies, advancing a little from out the group, cried out:

"Keep back there! Keep back there, you!"

"Go to hell, will you?" shouted Harran on the instant. "You're on my land."

"Oh, come back here, Harran," called Osterman. "That ain't going to do any good."

"There—listen," suddenly exclaimed Harran. "The Governor is calling us. Come on; I'm going."

Osterman got out of the ditch and came forward, catching Harran by the arm and pulling him back.

"He didn't call. Don't get excited. You'll ruin everything. Get back into the ditch again."

But Cutter, Phelps, and the old man Dabney, misunderstanding what was happening, and seeing Osterman leave the ditch, had followed his example. All the Leaguers were now out of the ditch, and a little way down the road, Hooven, Osterman, Annixter, and Harran in front, Dabney, Phelps, and Cutter coming up from behind.

"Keep back, you," cried the deputy again.

In the group around S. Behrman's buggy, Gethings and Delaney were yet quarrelling, and the angry debate between Magnus, Garnett, and the marshal still continued.

Till this moment, the real estate broker, Christian, had taken no part in the argument, but had kept himself in the rear of the buggy. Now, however, he pushed forward. There was but little room for him to pass, and, as he rode by the buggy, his horse scraped his flank against the hub of the wheel. The animal recoiled sharply, and, striking against Garnett, threw him to the ground. Delaney's horse stood between the buggy and the Leaguers gathered on the road in front of the ditch; the incident, indistinctly seen by them, was misinterpreted.

Garnett had not yet risen when Hooven raised a great shout:

"HOCH, DER KAISER! HOCH, DER VATERLAND!"

With the words, he dropped to one knee, and sighting his rifle carefully, fired into the group of men around the buggy.

Instantly the revolvers and rifles seemed to go off of themselves. Both sides, deputies and Leaguers, opened fire simultaneously. At first, it was nothing but a confused roar of explosions; then the roar lapsed to an irregular, quick succession of reports, shot leaping after shot; then a moment's silence, and, last of all, regular as clock-ticks, three shots at exact intervals. Then stillness.

Delaney, shot through the stomach, slid down from his horse, and, on his hands and knees, crawled from the road into the standing wheat. Christian fell backward from the saddle toward the buggy, and hung suspended in that position, his head and shoulders on the wheel, one stiff leg still across his saddle. Hooven, in attempting to rise from his kneeling position, received a rifle ball squarely in the throat, and rolled forward upon his face. Old Broderson, crying out, "Oh, they've shot me, boys," staggered sideways, his head bent, his hands rigid at his sides, and fell into the ditch. Osterman, blood running from his mouth and nose, turned about and walked back. Presley helped him across the irrigating ditch and Osterman laid himself down, his head on his folded arms. Harran Derrick dropped where he stood, turning over on his face, and lay motionless, groaning terribly, a pool of blood forming under his stomach. The old man Dabney, silent as ever, received his death, speechless. He fell to his knees, got up again, fell once more, and died without a word. Annixter, instantly killed, fell his length to the ground, and lay without movement, just as he had fallen, one arm across his face.

VII

On their way to Derrick's ranch house, Hilma and Mrs. Derrick heard the sounds of distant firing.

"Stop!" cried Hilma, laying her hand upon young Vacca's arm. "Stop the horses. Listen, what was that?"

The carry-all came to a halt and from far away across the rustling wheat came the faint rattle of rifles and revolvers.

"Say," cried Vacca, rolling his eyes, "oh, say, they're fighting over there."

Mrs. Derrick put her hands over her face.

"Fighting," she cried, "oh, oh, it's terrible. Magnus is there—and Harran."

"Where do you think it is?" demanded Hilma. "That's over toward Hooven's."

"I'm going. Turn back. Drive to Hooven's, quick."

"Better not, Mrs. Annixter," protested the young man. "Mr. Annixter said we were to go to Derrick's. Better keep away from Hooven's if there's trouble there. We wouldn't get there till it's all over, anyhow."

"Yes, yes, let's go home," cried Mrs. Derrick, "I'm afraid. Oh, Hilma, I'm afraid."

"Come with me to Hooven's then."

"There, where they are fighting? Oh, I couldn't. I—I can't. It would be all over before we got there as Vacca says."

"Sure," repeated young Vacca.

"Drive to Hooven's," commanded Hilma. "If you won't, I'll walk there." She threw off the lap-robes, preparing to descend. "And you," she exclaimed, turning to Mrs. Derrick, "how CAN you—when Harran and your husband may be—may—are in danger."

Grumbling, Vacca turned the carry-all about and drove across the open fields till he reached the road to Guadalajara, just below the Mission.

"Hurry!" cried Hilma.

The horses started forward under the touch of the whip. The ranch houses of Quien Sabe came in sight.

"Do you want to stop at the house?" inquired Vacca over his shoulder.

"No, no; oh, go faster—make the horses run."

They dashed through the houses of the Home ranch.

"Oh, oh," cried Hilma suddenly, "look, look there. Look what they have done."

Vacca pulled the horses up, for the road in front of Annixter's house was blocked.

A vast, confused heap of household effects was there—chairs, sofas, pictures, fixtures, lamps. Hilma's little home had been gutted; everything had been taken from it and ruthlessly flung out upon the road, everything that she and her husband had bought during that wonderful week after their marriage. Here was the white enamelled "set" of the bedroom furniture, the three chairs, wash-stand and bureau,—the bureau drawers falling out, spilling their contents into the dust; there were the white wool rugs of the sitting-room, the flower stand, with its pots all broken, its flowers wilting; the cracked goldfish globe, the fishes already dead; the rocking chair, the sewing machine, the great round table of yellow oak, the lamp with its deep shade of crinkly red tissue paper, the pretty tinted photographs that had hung on the wall—the choir boys with beautiful eyes, the pensive young girls in pink gowns—the pieces of wood carving that represented quails and ducks, and, last of all, its curtains of crisp, clean muslin, cruelly torn and crushed—the bed, the wonderful canopied bed so brave and gay, of which Hilma had been so proud, thrust out there into the common road, torn from its place, from the discreet intimacy of her bridal chamber, violated, profaned, flung out into the dust and garish sunshine for all men to stare at, a mockery and a shame.

To Hilma it was as though something of herself, of her person, had been thus exposed and degraded; all that she held sacred pilloried, gibbeted, and exhibited to the world's derision. Tears of anguish sprang to her eyes, a red flame of outraged modesty overspread her face.

"Oh," she cried, a sob catching her throat, "oh, how could they do it?" But other fears intruded; other greater terrors impended.

"Go on," she cried to Vacca, "go on quickly."

But Vacca would go no further. He had seen what had escaped Hilma's attention, two men, deputies, no doubt, on the porch of the ranch house. They held possession there, and the evidence of the presence of the enemy in this raid upon Quien Sabe had daunted him.

"No, SIR," he declared, getting out of the carry-all, "I ain't going to take you anywhere where you're liable to get hurt. Besides, the road's blocked by all this stuff. You can't get the team by."

Hilma sprang from the carry-all.

"Come," she said to Mrs. Derrick.

The older woman, trembling, hesitating, faint with dread, obeyed, and Hilma, picking her way through and around the wreck of her home, set off by the trail towards the Long Trestle and Hooven's.

When she arrived, she found the road in front of the German's house, and, indeed, all the surrounding yard, crowded with people. An overturned buggy lay on the side of the road in the distance, its horses in a tangle of harness, held by two or three men. She saw Caraher's buckboard under the live oak and near it a second buggy which she recognised as belonging to a doctor in Guadalajara.

"Oh, what has happened; oh, what has happened?" moaned Mrs. Derrick.

"Come," repeated Hilma. The young girl took her by the hand and together they pushed their way through the crowd of men and women and entered the yard.

The throng gave way before the two women, parting to right and left without a word.

"Presley," cried Mrs. Derrick, as she caught sight of him in the doorway of the house, "oh, Presley, what has happened? Is Harran safe? Is Magnus safe? Where are they?"

"Don't go in, Mrs. Derrick," said Presley, coming forward, "don't go in."

"Where is my husband?" demanded Hilma.

Presley turned away and steadied himself against the jamb of the door.

Hilma, leaving Mrs. Derrick, entered the house. The front room was full of men. She was dimly conscious of Cyrus Ruggles and S. Behrman, both deadly pale, talking earnestly and in whispers to Cutter and Phelps. There was a strange, acrid odour of an unfamiliar drug in the air. On the table before her was a satchel, surgical instruments, rolls of bandages, and a blue, oblong paper box full of cotton. But above the hushed noises of voices and footsteps, one terrible sound made itself heard—the prolonged, rasping sound of breathing, half choked, laboured, agonised.

"Where is my husband?" she cried. She pushed the men aside. She saw Magnus, bareheaded, three or four men lying on the floor, one half naked, his body swathed in white bandages; the doctor in shirt sleeves, on one knee beside a figure of a man stretched out beside him.

Garnett turned a white face to her.

"Where is my husband?"

The other did not reply, but stepped aside and Hilma saw the dead body of her husband lying upon the bed. She did not cry out. She said no word. She went to the bed, and sitting upon it, took Annixter's head in her lap, holding it gently between her hands. Thereafter she did not move, but sat holding her dead husband's head in her lap, looking vaguely about from face to face of those in the room, while, without a sob, without a cry, the great tears filled her wide-opened eyes and rolled slowly down upon her cheeks.

On hearing that his wife was outside, Magnus came quickly forward. She threw herself into his arms.

"Tell me, tell me," she cried, "is Harran—is—"

"We don't know yet," he answered. "Oh, Annie—"

Then suddenly the Governor checked himself. He, the indomitable, could not break down now.

"The doctor is with him," he said; "we are doing all we can. Try and be brave, Annie. There is always hope. This is a terrible day's work. God forgive us all."

She pressed forward, but he held her back.

"No, don't see him now. Go into the next room. Garnett, take care of her."

But she would not be denied. She pushed by Magnus, and, breaking through the group that surrounded her son, sank on her knees beside him, moaning, in compassion and terror.

Harran lay straight and rigid upon the floor, his head propped by a pillow, his coat that had been taken off spread over his chest. One leg of his trousers was soaked through and through with blood. His eyes were half-closed, and with the regularity of a machine, the eyeballs twitched and twitched. His face was so white that it made his yellow hair look brown, while from his opened mouth, there issued that loud and terrible sound of guttering, rasping, laboured breathing that gagged and choked and gurgled with every inhalation.

"Oh, Harrie, Harrie," called Mrs. Derrick, catching at one of his hands.

The doctor shook his head.

"He is unconscious, Mrs. Derrick."

"Where was he—where is—the—the—"

"Through the lungs."

"Will he get well? Tell me the truth."

"I don't know. Mrs. Derrick."

She had all but fainted, and the old rancher, Garnett, half-carrying, half-leading her, took her to the one adjoining room—Minna Hooven's bedchamber. Dazed, numb with fear, she sat down on the edge of the bed, rocking herself back and forth, murmuring:

"Harrie, Harrie, oh, my son, my little boy."

In the outside room, Presley came and went, doing what he could to be of service, sick with horror, trembling from head to foot.

The surviving members of both Leaguers and deputies—the warring factions of the Railroad and the People—mingled together now with no thought of hostility. Presley helped the doctor to cover Christian's body. S. Behrman and Ruggles held bowls of water while Osterman was attended to. The horror of that dreadful business had driven all other considerations from the mind. The sworn foes of the last hour had no thought of anything but to care for those whom, in their fury, they had shot down. The marshal, abandoning for that day the attempt to serve the writs, departed for San Francisco.

The bodies had been brought in from the road where they fell. Annixter's corpse had been laid upon the bed; those of Dabney and Hooven, whose wounds had all been in the face and head, were covered with a tablecloth. Upon the floor, places were made for the others. Cutter and Ruggles rode into Guadalajara to bring out the doctor there, and to telephone to Bonneville for others.

Osterman had not at any time since the shooting, lost consciousness. He lay upon the floor of Hooven's house, bare to the waist, bandages of adhesive tape reeved about his abdomen and shoulder. His eyes were half-closed. Presley, who looked after him, pending the arrival of a hack from Bonneville that was to take him home, knew that he was in agony.

But this poser, this silly fellow, this cracker of jokes, whom no one had ever taken very seriously, at the last redeemed himself. When at length, the doctor had arrived, he had, for the first time, opened his eyes.

"I can wait," he said. "Take Harran first." And when at length, his turn had come, and while the sweat rolled from his forehead as the doctor began probing for the bullet, he had reached out his free arm and taken Presley's hand in his, gripping it harder and harder, as the probe entered the wound. His breath came short through his nostrils; his face, the face of a comic actor, with its high cheek bones, bald forehead, and salient ears, grew paler and paler, his great slit of a mouth shut tight, but he uttered no groan.

When the worst anguish was over and he could find breath to speak, his first words had been:

"Were any of the others badly hurt?"

As Presley stood by the door of the house after bringing in a pail of water for the doctor, he was aware of a party of men who had struck off from the road on the other side of the irrigating ditch and were advancing cautiously into the field of wheat. He wondered what it meant and Cutter, coming up at that moment, Presley asked him if he knew.

"It's Delaney," said Cutter. "It seems that when he was shot he crawled off into the wheat. They are looking for him there."

Presley had forgotten all about the buster and had only a vague recollection of seeing him slide from his horse at the beginning of the fight. Anxious to know what had become of him, he hurried up and joined the party of searchers.

"We better look out," said one of the young men, "how we go fooling around in here. If he's alive yet he's just as liable as not to think we're after him and take a shot at us."

"I guess there ain't much fight left in him," another answered. "Look at the wheat here."

"Lord! He's bled like a stuck pig."

"Here's his hat," abruptly exclaimed the leader of the party. "He can't be far off. Let's call him."

They called repeatedly without getting any answer, then proceeded cautiously. All at once the men in advance stopped so suddenly that those following carromed against them. There was an outburst of exclamation.

"Here he is!"

"Good Lord! Sure, that's him."

"Poor fellow, poor fellow."

The cow-puncher lay on his back, deep in the wheat, his knees drawn up, his eyes wide open, his lips brown. Rigidly gripped in one hand was his empty revolver.

The men, farm hands from the neighbouring ranches, young fellows from Guadalajara, drew back in instinctive repulsion. One at length ventured near, peering down into the face.

"Is he dead?" inquired those in the rear.

"I don't know."

"Well, put your hand on his heart."

"No! I—I don't want to."

"What you afraid of?"

"Well, I just don't want to touch him, that's all. It's bad luck. YOU feel his heart."

"You can't always tell by that."

"How can you tell, then? Pshaw, you fellows make me sick. Here, let me get there. I'll do it."

There was a long pause, as the other bent down and laid his hand on the cow-puncher's breast.

"Well?"

"I can't tell. Sometimes I think I feel it beat and sometimes I don't. I never saw a dead man before."

"Well, you can't tell by the heart."

"What's the good of talking so blame much. Dead or not, let's carry him back to the house."

Two or three ran back to the road for planks from the broken bridge. When they returned with these a litter was improvised, and throwing their coats over the body, the party carried it back to the road. The doctor was summoned and declared the cow-puncher to have been dead over half an hour.

"What did I tell you?" exclaimed one of the group.

"Well, I never said he wasn't dead," protested the other. "I only said you couldn't always tell by whether his heart beat or not."

But all at once there was a commotion. The wagon containing Mrs. Hooven, Minna, and little Hilda drove up.

"Eh, den, my men," cried Mrs. Hooven, wildly interrogating the faces of the crowd. "Whadt has happun? Sey, den, dose vellers, hev dey hurdt my men, eh, whadt?"

She sprang from the wagon, followed by Minna with Hilda in her arms. The crowd bore back as they advanced, staring at them in silence.

"Eh, whadt has happun, whadt has happun?" wailed Mrs. Hooven, as she hurried on, her two hands out before her, the fingers spread wide. "Eh, Hooven, eh, my men, are you alle righdt?"

She burst into the house. Hooven's body had been removed to an adjoining room, the bedroom of the house, and to this room Mrs. Hooven—Minna still at her heels—proceeded, guided by an instinct born of the occasion. Those in the outside room, saying no word, made way for them. They entered, closing the door behind them, and through all the rest of that terrible day, no sound nor sight of them was had by those who crowded into and about that house of death. Of all the main actors of the tragedy of the fight in the ditch, they remained the least noted, obtruded themselves the least upon the world's observation. They were, for the moment, forgotten.

But by now Hooven's house was the centre of an enormous crowd. A vast concourse of people from Bonneville, from Guadalajara, from the ranches, swelled by the thousands who had that morning participated in the rabbit drive, surged about the place; men and women, young boys, young girls, farm hands, villagers, townspeople, ranchers, railroad employees, Mexicans, Spaniards, Portuguese. Presley, returning from the search for Delaney's body, had to fight his way to the house again.

And from all this multitude there rose an indefinable murmur. As yet, there was no menace in it, no anger. It was confusion merely, bewilderment, the first long-drawn "oh!" that greets the news of some great tragedy. The people had taken no thought as yet. Curiosity was their dominant impulse. Every one wanted to see what had been done; failing that, to hear of it, and failing that, to be near the scene of the affair. The crowd of people packed the road in front of the house for nearly a quarter of a mile in either direction. They balanced themselves upon the lower strands of the barbed wire fence in their effort to see over each others' shoulders; they stood on the seats of their carts, buggies, and farm wagons, a few even upon the saddles of their riding horses. They crowded, pushed, struggled, surged forward and back without knowing why, converging incessantly upon Hooven's house.

When, at length, Presley got to the gate, he found a carry-all drawn up before it. Between the gate and the door of the house a lane had been formed, and as he paused there a moment, a group of Leaguers, among whom were Garnett and Gethings, came slowly from the door carrying old Broderson in their arms. The doctor, bareheaded and in his shirt sleeves, squinting in the sunlight, attended them, repeating at every step:

"Slow, slow, take it easy, gentlemen."

Old Broderson was unconscious. His face was not pale, no bandages could be seen. With infinite precautions, the men bore him to the carry-all and deposited him on the back seat; the rain flaps were let down on one side to shut off the gaze of the multitude.

But at this point a moment of confusion ensued. Presley, because of half a dozen people who stood in his way, could not see what was going on. There were exclamations, hurried movements. The doctor uttered a sharp command and a man ran back to the house returning on the instant with the doctor's satchel. By this time, Presley was close to the wheels of the carry-all and could see the doctor inside the vehicle bending over old Broderson.

"Here it is, here it is," exclaimed the man who had been sent to the house.

"I won't need it," answered the doctor, "he's dying now."

At the words a great hush widened throughout the throng near at hand. Some men took off their hats.

"Stand back," protested the doctor quietly, "stand back, good people, please."

The crowd bore back a little. In the silence, a woman began to sob. The seconds passed, then a minute. The horses of the carry-all shifted their feet and whisked their tails, driving off the flies. At length, the doctor got down from the carry-all, letting down the rain-flaps on that side as well.

"Will somebody go home with the body?" he asked. Gethings stepped forward and took his place by the driver. The carry-all drove away.

Presley reentered the house. During his absence it had been cleared of all but one or two of the Leaguers, who had taken part in the fight. Hilma still sat on the bed with Annixter's head in her lap. S. Behrman, Ruggles, and all the railroad party had gone. Osterman had been taken away in a hack and the tablecloth over Dabney's body replaced with a sheet. But still unabated, agonised, raucous, came the sounds of Harran's breathing. Everything possible had already been done. For the moment it was out of the question to attempt to move him. His mother and father were at his side, Magnus, with a face of stone, his look fixed on those persistently twitching eyes, Annie Derrick crouching at her son's side, one of his hands in hers, fanning his face continually with the crumpled sheet of an old newspaper.

Presley on tip-toes joined the group, looking on attentively. One of the surgeons who had been called from Bonneville stood close by, watching Harran's face, his arms folded.

"How is he?" Presley whispered.

"He won't live," the other responded.

By degrees the choke and gurgle of the breathing became more irregular and the lids closed over the twitching eyes. All at once the breath ceased. Magnus shot an inquiring glance at the surgeon.

"He is dead, Mr. Derrick," the surgeon replied.

Annie Derrick, with a cry that rang through all the house, stretched herself over the body of her son, her head upon his breast, and the Governor's great shoulders bowed never to rise again.

"God help me and forgive me," he groaned.

Presley rushed from the house, beside himself with grief, with horror, with pity, and with mad, insensate rage. On the porch outside Caraher met him.

"Is he—is he—" began the saloon-keeper.

"Yes, he's dead," cried Presley. "They're all dead, murdered, shot down, dead, dead, all of them. Whose turn is next?"

"That's the way they killed my wife, Presley."

"Caraher," cried Presley, "give me your hand. I've been wrong all the time. The League is wrong. All the world is wrong. You are the only one of us all who is right. I'm with you from now on. BY GOD, I TOO, I'M A RED!"

In course of time, a farm wagon from Bonneville arrived at Hooven's. The bodies of Annixter and Harran were placed in it, and it drove down the Lower Road towards the Los Muertos ranch houses.

The bodies of Delaney and Christian had already been carried to Guadalajara and thence taken by train to Bonneville.

Hilma followed the farm wagon in the Derricks' carry-all, with Magnus and his wife. During all that ride none of them spoke a word. It had been arranged that, since Quien Sabe was in the hands of the Railroad, Hilma should come to Los Muertos. To that place also Annixter's body was carried.

Later on in the day, when it was almost evening, the undertaker's black wagon passed the Derricks' Home ranch on its way from Hooven's and turned into the county road towards Bonneville. The initial excitement of the affair of the irrigating ditch had died down; the crowd long since had dispersed. By the time the wagon passed Caraher's saloon, the sun had set. Night was coming on.

And the black wagon went on through the darkness, unattended, ignored, solitary, carrying the dead body of Dabney, the silent old man of whom nothing was known but his name, who made no friends, whom nobody knew or spoke to, who had come from no one knew whence and who went no one knew whither.

Towards midnight of that same day, Mrs. Dyke was awakened by the sounds of groaning in the room next to hers. Magnus Derrick was not so occupied by Harran's death that he could not think of others who were in distress, and when he had heard that Mrs. Dyke and Sidney, like Hilma, had been turned out of Quien Sabe, he had thrown open Los Muertos to them.

"Though," he warned them, "it is precarious hospitality at the best."

Until late, Mrs. Dyke had sat up with Hilma, comforting her as best she could, rocking her to and fro in her arms, crying with her, trying to quiet her, for once having given way to her grief, Hilma wept with a terrible anguish and a violence that racked her from head to foot, and at last, worn out, a little child again, had sobbed herself to sleep in the older woman's arms, and as a little child, Mrs. Dyke had put her to bed and had retired herself.

Aroused a few hours later by the sounds of a distress that was physical, as well as mental, Mrs. Dyke hurried into Hilma's room, carrying the lamp with her. Mrs. Dyke needed no enlightenment. She woke Presley and besought him to telephone to Bonneville at once, summoning a doctor. That night Hilma in great pain suffered a miscarriage.

Presley did not close his eyes once during the night; he did not even remove his clothes. Long after the doctor had departed and that house of tragedy had quieted down, he still remained in his place by the open window of his little room, looking off across the leagues of growing wheat, watching the slow kindling of the dawn. Horror weighed intolerably upon him. Monstrous things, huge, terrible, whose names he knew only too well, whirled at a gallop through his imagination, or rose spectral and grisly before the eyes of his mind. Harran dead, Annixter dead, Broderson dead, Osterman, perhaps, even at that moment dying. Why, these men had made up his world. Annixter had been his best friend, Harran, his almost daily companion; Broderson and Osterman were familiar to him as brothers. They were all his associates, his good friends, the group was his environment, belonging to his daily life. And he, standing there in the dust of the road by the irrigating ditch, had seen them shot. He found himself suddenly at his table, the candle burning at his elbow, his journal before him, writing swiftly, the desire for expression, the craving for outlet to the thoughts that clamoured tumultuous at his brain, never more insistent, more imperious. Thus he wrote:

"Dabney dead, Hooven dead, Harran dead, Annixter dead, Broderson dead, Osterman dying, S. Behrman alive, successful; the Railroad in possession of Quien Sabe. I saw them shot. Not twelve hours since I stood there at the irrigating ditch. Ah, that terrible moment of horror and confusion! powder smoke—flashing pistol barrels—blood stains—rearing horses—men staggering to their death—Christian in a horrible posture, one rigid leg high in the air across his saddle—Broderson falling sideways into the ditch—Osterman laying himself down, his head on his arms, as if tired, tired out. These things, I have seen them. The picture of this day's work is from henceforth part of my mind, part of ME. They have done it, S. Behrman and the owners of the railroad have done it, while all the world looked on, while the people of these United States looked on. Oh, come now and try your theories upon us, us of the ranchos, us, who have suffered, us, who KNOW. Oh, talk to US now of the 'rights of Capital,' talk to US of the Trust, talk to US of the 'equilibrium between the classes.' Try your ingenious ideas upon us. WE KNOW. I cannot tell whether or not your theories are excellent. I do not know if your ideas are plausible. I do not know how practical is your scheme of society. I do not know if the Railroad has a right to our lands, but I DO know that Harran is dead, that Annixter is dead, that Broderson is dead, that Hooven is dead, that Osterman is dying, and that S. Behrman is alive, successful, triumphant; that he has ridden into possession of a principality over the dead bodies of five men shot down by his hired associates.

"I can see the outcome. The Railroad will prevail. The Trust will overpower us. Here in this corner of a great nation, here, on the edge of the continent, here, in this valley of the West, far from the great centres, isolated, remote, lost, the great iron hand crushes life from us, crushes liberty and the pursuit of happiness from us, and our little struggles, our moment's convulsion of death agony causes not one jar in the vast, clashing machinery of the nation's life; a fleck of grit in the wheels, perhaps, a grain of sand in the cogs—the momentary creak of the axle is the mother's wail of bereavement, the wife's cry of anguish—and the great wheel turns, spinning smooth again, even again, and the tiny impediment of a second, scarce noticed, is forgotten. Make the people believe that the faint tremour in their great engine is a menace to its function? What a folly to think of it. Tell them of the danger and they will laugh at you. Tell them, five years from now, the story of the fight between the League of the San Joaquin and the Railroad and it will not be believed. What! a pitched battle between Farmer and Railroad, a battle that cost the lives of seven men? Impossible, it could not have happened. Your story is fiction—is exaggerated.

"Yet it is Lexington—God help us, God enlighten us, God rouse us from our lethargy—it is Lexington; farmers with guns in their hands fighting for Liberty. Is our State of California the only one that has its ancient and hereditary foe? Are there no other Trusts between the oceans than this of the Pacific and Southwestern Railroad? Ask yourselves, you of the Middle West, ask yourselves, you of the North, ask yourselves, you of the East, ask yourselves, you of the South—ask yourselves, every citizen of every State from Maine to Mexico, from the Dakotas to the Carolinas, have you not the monster in your boundaries? If it is not a Trust of transportation, it is only another head of the same Hydra. Is not our death struggle typical? Is it not one of many, is it not symbolical of the great and terrible conflict that is going on everywhere in these United States? Ah, you people, blind, bound, tricked, betrayed, can you not see it? Can you not see how the monsters have plundered your treasures and holding them in the grip of their iron claws, dole them out to you only at the price of your blood, at the price of the lives of your wives and your little children? You give your babies to Moloch for the loaf of bread you have kneaded yourselves. You offer your starved wives to Juggernaut for the iron nail you have yourselves compounded."

He spent the night over his journal, writing down such thoughts as these or walking the floor from wall to wall, or, seized at times with unreasoning horror and blind rage, flinging himself face downward upon his bed, vowing with inarticulate cries that neither S. Behrman nor Shelgrim should ever live to consummate their triumph.

Morning came and with it the daily papers and news. Presley did not even glance at the "Mercury." Bonneville published two other daily journals that professed to voice the will and reflect the temper of the people and these he read eagerly.

Osterman was yet alive and there were chances of his recovery. The League—some three hundred of its members had gathered at Bonneville over night and were patrolling the streets and, still resolved to keep the peace, were even guarding the railroad shops and buildings. Furthermore, the Leaguers had issued manifestoes, urging all citizens to preserve law and order, yet summoning an indignation meeting to be convened that afternoon at the City Opera House.

It appeared from the newspapers that those who obstructed the marshal in the discharge of his duty could be proceeded against by the District Attorney on information or by bringing the matter before the Grand Jury. But the Grand Jury was not at that time in session, and it was known that there were no funds in the marshal's office to pay expenses for the summoning of jurors or the serving of processes. S. Behrman and Ruggles in interviews stated that the Railroad withdrew entirely from the fight; the matter now, according to them, was between the Leaguers and the United States Government; they washed their hands of the whole business. The ranchers could settle with Washington. But it seemed that Congress had recently forbade the use of troops for civil purposes; the whole matter of the League-Railroad contest was evidently for the moment to be left in status quo.

But to Presley's mind the most important piece of news that morning was the report of the action of the Railroad upon hearing of the battle.

Instantly Bonneville had been isolated. Not a single local train was running, not one of the through trains made any halt at the station. The mails were not moved. Further than this, by some arrangement difficult to understand, the telegraph operators at Bonneville and Guadalajara, acting under orders, refused to receive any telegrams except those emanating from railway officials. The story of the fight, the story creating the first impression, was to be told to San Francisco and the outside world by S. Behrman, Ruggles, and the local P. and S. W. agents.

An hour before breakfast, the undertakers arrived and took charge of the bodies of Harran and Annixter. Presley saw neither Hilma, Magnus, nor Mrs. Derrick. The doctor came to look after Hilma. He breakfasted with Mrs. Dyke and Presley, and from him Presley learned that Hilma would recover both from the shock of her husband's death and from her miscarriage of the previous night.

"She ought to have her mother with her," said the physician. "She does nothing but call for her or beg to be allowed to go to her. I have tried to get a wire through to Mrs. Tree, but the company will not take it, and even if I could get word to her, how could she get down here? There are no trains."

But Presley found that it was impossible for him to stay at Los Muertos that day. Gloom and the shadow of tragedy brooded heavy over the place. A great silence pervaded everything, a silence broken only by the subdued coming and going of the undertaker and his assistants. When Presley, having resolved to go into Bonneville, came out through the doorway of the house, he found the undertaker tying a long strip of crape to the bell-handle.

Presley saddled his pony and rode into town. By this time, after long hours of continued reflection upon one subject, a sombre brooding malevolence, a deep-seated desire of revenge, had grown big within his mind. The first numbness had passed off; familiarity with what had been done had blunted the edge of horror, and now the impulse of retaliation prevailed. At first, the sullen anger of defeat, the sense of outrage, had only smouldered, but the more he brooded, the fiercer flamed his rage. Sudden paroxysms of wrath gripped him by the throat; abrupt outbursts of fury injected his eyes with blood. He ground his teeth, his mouth filled with curses, his hands clenched till they grew white and bloodless. Was the Railroad to triumph then in the end? After all those months of preparation, after all those grandiloquent resolutions, after all the arrogant presumption of the League! The League! what a farce; what had it amounted to when the crisis came? Was the Trust to crush them all so easily? Was S. Behrman to swallow Los Muertos? S. Behrman! Presley saw him plainly, huge, rotund, white; saw his jowl tremulous and obese, the roll of fat over his collar sprinkled with sparse hairs, the great stomach with its brown linen vest and heavy watch chain of hollow links, clinking against the buttons of imitation pearl. And this man was to crush Magnus Derrick—had already stamped the life from such men as Harran and Annixter. This man, in the name of the Trust, was to grab Los Muertos as he had grabbed Quien Sabe, and after Los Muertos, Broderson's ranch, then Osterman's, then others, and still others, the whole valley, the whole State.

Presley beat his forehead with his clenched fist as he rode on.

"No," he cried, "no, kill him, kill him, kill him with my hands."

The idea of it put him beside himself. Oh, to sink his fingers deep into the white, fat throat of the man, to clutch like iron into the great puffed jowl of him, to wrench out the life, to batter it out, strangle it out, to pay him back for the long years of extortion and oppression, to square accounts for bribed jurors, bought judges, corrupted legislatures, to have justice for the trick of the Ranchers' Railroad Commission, the charlatanism of the "ten per cent. cut," the ruin of Dyke, the seizure of Quien Sabe, the murder of Harran, the assassination of Annixter!

It was in such mood that he reached Caraher's. The saloon-keeper had just opened his place and was standing in his doorway, smoking his pipe. Presley dismounted and went in and the two had a long talk.

When, three hours later, Presley came out of the saloon and rode on towards Bonneville, his face was very pale, his lips shut tight, resolute, determined. His manner was that of a man whose mind is made up. The hour for the mass meeting at the Opera House had been set for one o'clock, but long before noon the street in front of the building and, in fact, all the streets in its vicinity, were packed from side to side with a shifting, struggling, surging, and excited multitude. There were few women in the throng, but hardly a single male inhabitant of either Bonneville or Guadalajara was absent. Men had even come from Visalia and Pixley. It was no longer the crowd of curiosity seekers that had thronged around Hooven's place by the irrigating ditch; the People were no longer confused, bewildered. A full realisation of just what had been done the day before was clear now in the minds of all. Business was suspended; nearly all the stores were closed. Since early morning the members of the League had put in an appearance and rode from point to point, their rifles across their saddle pommels. Then, by ten o'clock, the streets had begun to fill up, the groups on the corners grew and merged into one another; pedestrians, unable to find room on the sidewalks, took to the streets. Hourly the crowd increased till shoulders touched and elbows, till free circulation became impeded, then congested, then impossible. The crowd, a solid mass, was wedged tight from store front to store front. And from all this throng, this single unit, this living, breathing organism—the People—there rose a droning, terrible note. It was not yet the wild, fierce clamour of riot and insurrection, shrill, high pitched; but it was a beginning, the growl of the awakened brute, feeling the iron in its flank, heaving up its head with bared teeth, the throat vibrating to the long, indrawn snarl of wrath.

Thus the forenoon passed, while the people, their bulk growing hourly vaster, kept to the streets, moving slowly backward and forward, oscillating in the grooves of the thoroughfares, the steady, low-pitched growl rising continually into the hot, still air.

Then, at length, about twelve o'clock, the movement of the throng assumed definite direction. It set towards the Opera House. Presley, who had left his pony at the City livery stable, found himself caught in the current and carried slowly forward in its direction. His arms were pinioned to his sides by the press, the crush against his body was all but rib-cracking, he could hardly draw his breath. All around him rose and fell wave after wave of faces, hundreds upon hundreds, thousands upon thousands, red, lowering, sullen. All were set in one direction and slowly, slowly they advanced, crowding closer, till they almost touched one another. For reasons that were inexplicable, great, tumultuous heavings, like ground-swells of an incoming tide, surged over and through the multitude. At times, Presley, lifted from his feet, was swept back, back, back, with the crowd, till the entrance of the Opera House was half a block away; then, the returning billow beat back again and swung him along, gasping, staggering, clutching, till he was landed once more in the vortex of frantic action in front of the foyer. Here the waves were shorter, quicker, the crushing pressure on all sides of his body left him without strength to utter the cry that rose to his lips; then, suddenly the whole mass of struggling, stamping, fighting, writhing men about him seemed, as it were, to rise, to lift, multitudinous, swelling, gigantic. A mighty rush dashed Presley forward in its leap. There was a moment's whirl of confused sights, congested faces, opened mouths, bloodshot eyes, clutching hands; a moment's outburst of furious sound, shouts, cheers, oaths; a moment's jam wherein Presley veritably believed his ribs must snap like pipestems and he was carried, dazed, breathless, helpless, an atom on the crest of a storm-driven wave, up the steps of the Opera House, on into the vestibule, through the doors, and at last into the auditorium of the house itself.

There was a mad rush for places; men disdaining the aisle, stepped from one orchestra chair to another, striding over the backs of seats, leaving the print of dusty feet upon the red plush cushions. In a twinkling the house was filled from stage to topmost gallery. The aisles were packed solid, even on the edge of the stage itself men were sitting, a black fringe on either side of the footlights.

The curtain was up, disclosing a half-set scene,—the flats, leaning at perilous angles,—that represented some sort of terrace, the pavement, alternate squares of black and white marble, while red, white, and yellow flowers were represented as growing from urns and vases. A long, double row of chairs stretched across the scene from wing to wing, flanking a table covered with a red cloth, on which was set a pitcher of water and a speaker's gavel.

Promptly these chairs were filled up with members of the League, the audience cheering as certain well-known figures made their appearance—Garnett of the Ruby ranch, Gethings of the San Pablo, Keast of the ranch of the same name, Chattern of the Bonanza, elderly men, bearded, slow of speech, deliberate.

Garnett opened the meeting; his speech was plain, straightforward, matter-of-fact. He simply told what had happened. He announced that certain resolutions were to be drawn up. He introduced the next speaker.

This one pleaded for moderation. He was conservative. All along he had opposed the idea of armed resistance except as the very last resort. He "deplored" the terrible affair of yesterday. He begged the people to wait in patience, to attempt no more violence. He informed them that armed guards of the League were, at that moment, patrolling Los Muertos, Broderson's, and Osterman's. It was well known that the United States marshal confessed himself powerless to serve the writs. There would be no more bloodshed.

"We have had," he continued, "bloodshed enough, and I want to say right here that I am not so sure but what yesterday's terrible affair might have been avoided. A gentleman whom we all esteem, who from the first has been our recognised leader, is, at this moment, mourning the loss of a young son, killed before his eyes. God knows that I sympathise, as do we all, in the affliction of our President. I am sorry for him. My heart goes out to him in this hour of distress, but, at the same time, the position of the League must be defined. We owe it to ourselves, we owe it to the people of this county. The League armed for the very purpose of preserving the peace, not of breaking it. We believed that with six hundred armed and drilled men at our disposal, ready to muster at a moment's call, we could so overawe any attempt to expel us from our lands that such an attempt would not be made until the cases pending before the Supreme Court had been decided. If when the enemy appeared in our midst yesterday they had been met by six hundred rifles, it is not conceivable that the issue would have been forced. No fight would have ensued, and to-day we would not have to mourn the deaths of four of our fellow-citizens. A mistake has been made and we of the League must not be held responsible."

The speaker sat down amidst loud applause from the Leaguers and less pronounced demonstrations on the part of the audience.

A second Leaguer took his place, a tall, clumsy man, half-rancher, half-politician.

"I want to second what my colleague has just said," he began. "This matter of resisting the marshal when he tried to put the Railroad dummies in possession on the ranches around here, was all talked over in the committee meetings of the League long ago. It never was our intention to fire a single shot. No such absolute authority as was assumed yesterday was delegated to anybody. Our esteemed President is all right, but we all know that he is a man who loves authority and who likes to go his own gait without accounting to anybody. We—the rest of us Leaguers—never were informed as to what was going on. We supposed, of course, that watch was being kept on the Railroad so as we wouldn't be taken by surprise as we were yesterday. And it seems no watch was kept at all, or if there was, it was mighty ineffective. Our idea was to forestall any movement on the part of the Railroad and then when we knew the marshal was coming down, to call a meeting of our Executive Committee and decide as to what should be done. We ought to have had time to call out the whole League. Instead of that, what happens? While we're all off chasing rabbits, the Railroad is allowed to steal a march on us and when it is too late, a handful of Leaguers is got together and a fight is precipitated and our men killed. I'M sorry for our President, too. No one is more so, but I want to put myself on record as believing he did a hasty and inconsiderate thing. If he had managed right, he could have had six hundred men to oppose the Railroad and there would not have been any gun fight or any killing. He DIDN'T manage right and there WAS a killing and I don't see as how the League ought to be held responsible. The idea of the League, the whole reason why it was organised, was to protect ALL the ranches of this valley from the Railroad, and it looks to me as if the lives of our fellow-citizens had been sacrificed, not in defending ALL of our ranches, but just in defence of one of them—Los Muertos—the one that Mr. Derrick owns."

The speaker had no more than regained his seat when a man was seen pushing his way from the back of the stage towards Garnett. He handed the rancher a note, at the same time whispering in his ear. Garnett read the note, then came forward to the edge of the stage, holding up his hand. When the audience had fallen silent he said:

"I have just received sad news. Our friend and fellow-citizen, Mr. Osterman, died this morning between eleven and twelve o'clock."

Instantly there was a roar. Every man in the building rose to his feet, shouting, gesticulating. The roar increased, the Opera House trembled to it, the gas jets in the lighted chandeliers vibrated to it. It was a raucous howl of execration, a bellow of rage, inarticulate, deafening.

A tornado of confusion swept whirling from wall to wall and the madness of the moment seized irresistibly upon Presley. He forgot himself; he no longer was master of his emotions or his impulses. All at once he found himself upon the stage, facing the audience, flaming with excitement, his imagination on fire, his arms uplifted in fierce, wild gestures, words leaping to his mind in a torrent that could not be withheld.

"One more dead," he cried, "one more. Harran dead, Annixter dead, Broderson dead, Dabney dead, Osterman dead, Hooven dead; shot down, killed, killed in the defence of their homes, killed in the defence of their rights, killed for the sake of liberty. How long must it go on? How long must we suffer? Where is the end; what is the end? How long must the iron-hearted monster feed on our life's blood? How long must this terror of steam and steel ride upon our necks? Will you never be satisfied, will you never relent, you, our masters, you, our lords, you, our kings, you, our task-masters, you, our Pharoahs. Will you never listen to that command 'LET MY PEOPLE GO'? Oh, that cry ringing down the ages. Hear it, hear it. It is the voice of the Lord God speaking in his prophets. Hear it, hear it—'Let My people go!' Rameses heard it in his pylons at Thebes, Caesar heard it on the Palatine, the Bourbon Louis heard it at Versailles, Charles Stuart heard it at Whitehall, the white Czar heard it in the Kremlin,—'LET MY PEOPLE GO.' It is the cry of the nations, the great voice of the centuries; everywhere it is raised. The voice of God is the voice of the People. The people cry out 'Let us, the People, God's people, go.' You, our masters, you, our kings, you, our tyrants, don't you hear us? Don't you hear God speaking in us? Will you never let us go? How long at length will you abuse our patience? How long will you drive us? How long will you harass us? Will nothing daunt you? Does nothing check you? Do you not know that to ignore our cry too long is to wake the Red Terror? Rameses refused to listen to it and perished miserably. Caesar refused to listen and was stabbed in the Senate House. The Bourbon Louis refused to listen and died on the guillotine; Charles Stuart refused to listen and died on the block; the white Czar refused to listen and was blown up in his own capital. Will you let it come to that? Will you drive us to it? We who boast of our land of freedom, we who live in the country of liberty? Go on as you have begun and it WILL come to that. Turn a deaf ear to that cry of 'Let My people go' too long and another cry will be raised, that you cannot choose but hear, a cry that you cannot shut out. It will be the cry of the man on the street, the 'a la Bastille' that wakes the Red Terror and unleashes Revolution. Harassed, plundered, exasperated, desperate, the people will turn at last as they have turned so many, many times before. You, our lords, you, our task-masters, you, our kings; you have caught your Samson, you have made his strength your own. You have shorn his head; you have put out his eyes; you have set him to turn your millstones, to grind the grist for your mills; you have made him a shame and a mock. Take care, oh, as you love your lives, take care, lest some day calling upon the Lord his God he reach not out his arms for the pillars of your temples."

The audience, at first bewildered, confused by this unexpected invective, suddenly took fire at his last words. There was a roar of applause; then, more significant than mere vociferation, Presley's listeners, as he began to speak again, grew suddenly silent. His next sentences were uttered in the midst of a profound stillness.

"They own us, these task-masters of ours; they own our homes, they own our legislatures. We cannot escape from them. There is no redress. We are told we can defeat them by the ballot-box. They own the ballot-box. We are told that we must look to the courts for redress; they own the courts. We know them for what they are,—ruffians in politics, ruffians in finance, ruffians in law, ruffians in trade, bribers, swindlers, and tricksters. No outrage too great to daunt them, no petty larceny too small to shame them; despoiling a government treasury of a million dollars, yet picking the pockets of a farm hand of the price of a loaf of bread.

"They swindle a nation of a hundred million and call it Financiering; they levy a blackmail and call it Commerce; they corrupt a legislature and call it Politics; they bribe a judge and call it Law; they hire blacklegs to carry out their plans and call it Organisation; they prostitute the honour of a State and call it Competition.

"And this is America. We fought Lexington to free ourselves; we fought Gettysburg to free others. Yet the yoke remains; we have only shifted it to the other shoulder. We talk of liberty—oh, the farce of it, oh, the folly of it! We tell ourselves and teach our children that we have achieved liberty, that we no longer need fight for it. Why, the fight is just beginning and so long as our conception of liberty remains as it is to-day, it will continue.

"For we conceive of Liberty in the statues we raise to her as a beautiful woman, crowned, victorious, in bright armour and white robes, a light in her uplifted hand—a serene, calm, conquering goddess. Oh, the farce of it, oh, the folly of it! Liberty is NOT a crowned goddess, beautiful, in spotless garments, victorious, supreme. Liberty is the Man In the Street, a terrible figure, rushing through powder smoke, fouled with the mud and ordure of the gutter, bloody, rampant, brutal, yelling curses, in one hand a smoking rifle, in the other, a blazing torch.

"Freedom is NOT given free to any who ask; Liberty is not born of the gods. She is a child of the People, born in the very height and heat of battle, born from death, stained with blood, grimed with powder. And she grows to be not a goddess, but a Fury, a fearful figure, slaying friend and foe alike, raging, insatiable, merciless, the Red Terror."

Presley ceased speaking. Weak, shaking, scarcely knowing what he was about, he descended from the stage. A prolonged explosion of applause followed, the Opera House roaring to the roof, men cheering, stamping, waving their hats. But it was not intelligent applause. Instinctively as he made his way out, Presley knew that, after all, he had not once held the hearts of his audience. He had talked as he would have written; for all his scorn of literature, he had been literary. The men who listened to him, ranchers, country people, store-keepers, attentive though they were, were not once sympathetic. Vaguely they had felt that here was something which other men—more educated—would possibly consider eloquent. They applauded vociferously but perfunctorily, in order to appear to understand.

Presley, for all his love of the people, saw clearly for one moment that he was an outsider to their minds. He had not helped them nor their cause in the least; he never would.

Disappointed, bewildered, ashamed, he made his way slowly from the Opera House and stood on the steps outside, thoughtful, his head bent.

He had failed, thus he told himself. In that moment of crisis, that at the time he believed had been an inspiration, he had failed. The people would not consider him, would not believe that he could do them service. Then suddenly he seemed to remember. The resolute set of his lips returned once more. Pushing his way through the crowded streets, he went on towards the stable where he had left his pony.

Meanwhile, in the Opera House, a great commotion had occurred. Magnus Derrick had appeared.

Only a sense of enormous responsibility, of gravest duty could have prevailed upon Magnus to have left his house and the dead body of his son that day. But he was the President of the League, and never since its organisation had a meeting of such importance as this one been held. He had been in command at the irrigating ditch the day before. It was he who had gathered the handful of Leaguers together. It was he who must bear the responsibility of the fight.

When he had entered the Opera House, making his way down the central aisle towards the stage, a loud disturbance had broken out, partly applause, partly a meaningless uproar. Many had pressed forward to shake his hand, but others were not found wanting who, formerly his staunch supporters, now scenting opposition in the air, held back, hesitating, afraid to compromise themselves by adhering to the fortunes of a man whose actions might be discredited by the very organisation of which he was the head.

Declining to take the chair of presiding officer which Garnett offered him, the Governor withdrew to an angle of the stage, where he was joined by Keast.

This one, still unalterably devoted to Magnus, acquainted him briefly with the tenor of the speeches that had been made.

"I am ashamed of them, Governor," he protested indignantly, "to lose their nerve now! To fail you now! it makes my blood boil. If you had succeeded yesterday, if all had gone well, do you think we would have heard of any talk of 'assumption of authority,' or 'acting without advice and consent'? As if there was any time to call a meeting of the Executive Committee. If you hadn't acted as you did, the whole county would have been grabbed by the Railroad. Get up, Governor, and bring 'em all up standing. Just tear 'em all to pieces, show 'em that you are the head, the boss. That's what they need. That killing yesterday has shaken the nerve clean out of them."

For the instant the Governor was taken all aback. What, his lieutenants were failing him? What, he was to be questioned, interpolated upon yesterday's "irrepressible conflict"? Had disaffection appeared in the ranks of the League—at this, of all moments? He put from him his terrible grief. The cause was in danger. At the instant he was the President of the League only, the chief, the master. A royal anger surged within him, a wide, towering scorn of opposition. He would crush this disaffection in its incipiency, would vindicate himself and strengthen the cause at one and the same time. He stepped forward and stood in the speaker's place, turning partly toward the audience, partly toward the assembled Leaguers.

"Gentlemen of the League," he began, "citizens of Bonneville"

But at once the silence in which the Governor had begun to speak was broken by a shout. It was as though his words had furnished a signal. In a certain quarter of the gallery, directly opposite, a man arose, and in a voice partly of derision, partly of defiance, cried out:

"How about the bribery of those two delegates at Sacramento? Tell us about that. That's what we want to hear about."

A great confusion broke out. The first cry was repeated not only by the original speaker, but by a whole group of which he was but a part. Others in the audience, however, seeing in the disturbance only the clamour of a few Railroad supporters, attempted to howl them down, hissing vigorously and exclaiming:

"Put 'em out, put 'em out."

"Order, order," called Garnett, pounding with his gavel. The whole Opera House was in an uproar.

But the interruption of the Governor's speech was evidently not unpremeditated. It began to look like a deliberate and planned attack. Persistently, doggedly, the group in the gallery vociferated: "Tell us how you bribed the delegates at Sacramento. Before you throw mud at the Railroad, let's see if you are clean yourself."

"Put 'em out, put 'em out."

"Briber, briber—Magnus Derrick, unconvicted briber! Put him out."

Keast, beside himself with anger, pushed down the aisle underneath where the recalcitrant group had its place and, shaking his fist, called up at them:

"You were paid to break up this meeting. If you have anything to say; you will be afforded the opportunity, but if you do not let the gentleman proceed, the police will be called upon to put you out."

But at this, the man who had raised the first shout leaned over the balcony rail, and, his face flaming with wrath, shouted:

"YAH! talk to me of your police. Look out we don't call on them first to arrest your President for bribery. You and your howl about law and justice and corruption! Here"—he turned to the audience—" read about him, read the story of how the

Sacramento convention was bought by Magnus Derrick, President of the San Joaquin League. Here's the facts printed and proved."

With the words, he stooped down and from under his seat dragged forth a great package of extra editions of the "Bonneville Mercury," not an hour off the presses. Other equally large bundles of the paper appeared in the hands of the surrounding group. The strings were cut and in handfuls and armfuls the papers were flung out over the heads of the audience underneath. The air was full of the flutter of the newly printed sheets. They swarmed over the rim of the gallery like clouds of monstrous, winged insects, settled upon the heads and into the hands of the audience, were passed swiftly from man to man, and within five minutes of the first outbreak every one in the Opera House had read Genslinger's detailed and substantiated account of Magnus Derrick's "deal" with the political bosses of the Sacramento convention.

Genslinger, after pocketing the Governor's hush money, had "sold him out."

Keast, one quiver of indignation, made his way back upon the stage. The Leaguers were in wild confusion. Half the assembly of them were on their feet, bewildered, shouting vaguely. From proscenium wall to foyer, the Opera House was a tumult of noise. The gleam of the thousands of the "Mercury" extras was like the flash of white caps on a troubled sea.

Keast faced the audience.

"Liars," he shouted, striving with all the power of his voice to dominate the clamour, "liars and slanderers. Your paper is the paid organ of the corporation. You have not one shadow of proof to back you up. Do you choose this, of all times, to heap your calumny upon the head of an honourable gentleman, already prostrated by your murder of his son? Proofs—we demand your proofs!"

"We've got the very assemblymen themselves," came back the answering shout. "Let Derrick speak. Where is he hiding? If this is a lie, let him deny it. Let HIM DISPROVE the charge."

"Derrick, Derrick," thundered the Opera House.

Keast wheeled about. Where was Magnus? He was not in sight upon the stage. He had disappeared. Crowding through the throng of Leaguers, Keast got from off the stage into the wings. Here the crowd was no less dense. Nearly every one had a copy of the "Mercury." It was being read aloud to groups here and there, and once Keast overheard the words, "Say, I wonder if this is true, after all?"

"Well, and even if it was," cried Keast, turning upon the speaker, "we should be the last ones to kick. In any case, it was done for our benefit. It elected the Ranchers' Commission."

"A lot of benefit we got out of the Ranchers' Commission," retorted the other.

"And then," protested a third speaker, "that ain't the way to do—if he DID do it—bribing legislatures. Why, we were bucking against corrupt politics. We couldn't afford to be corrupt."

Keast turned away with a gesture of impatience. He pushed his way farther on. At last, opening a small door in a hallway back of the stage, he came upon Magnus.

The room was tiny. It was a dressing-room. Only two nights before it had been used by the leading actress of a comic opera troupe which had played for three nights at Bonneville. A tattered sofa and limping toilet table occupied a third of the space. The air was heavy with the smell of stale grease paint, ointments, and sachet. Faded photographs of young women in tights and gauzes ornamented the mirror and the walls. Underneath the sofa was an old pair of corsets. The spangled skirt of a pink dress, turned inside out, hung against the wall.

And in the midst of such environment, surrounded by an excited group of men who gesticulated and shouted in his very face, pale, alert, agitated, his thin lips pressed tightly together, stood Magnus Derrick.

"Here," cried Keast, as he entered, closing the door behind him, "where's the Governor? Here, Magnus, I've been looking for you. The crowd has gone wild out there. You've got to talk 'em down. Come out there and give those blacklegs the lie. They are saying you are hiding."

But before Magnus could reply, Garnett turned to Keast.

"Well, that's what we want him to do, and he won't do it."

"Yes, yes," cried the half-dozen men who crowded around Magnus, "yes, that's what we want him to do."

Keast turned to Magnus.

"Why, what's all this, Governor?" he exclaimed. "You've got to answer that. Hey? why don't you give 'em the lie?"

"I—I," Magnus loosened the collar about his throat "it is a lie. I will not stoop—I would not—would be—it would be beneath my—my—it would be beneath me."

Keast stared in amazement. Was this the Great Man the Leader, indomitable, of Roman integrity, of Roman valour, before whose voice whole conventions had quailed? Was it possible he was AFRAID to face those hired villifiers?

"Well, how about this?" demanded Garnett suddenly. "It is a lie, isn't it? That Commission was elected honestly, wasn't it?"

"How dare you, sir!" Magnus burst out. "How dare you question me—call me to account! Please understand, sir, that I tolerate—"

"Oh, quit it!" cried a voice from the group. "You can't scare us, Derrick. That sort of talk was well enough once, but it don't go any more. We want a yes or no answer."

It was gone—that old-time power of mastery, that faculty of command. The ground crumbled beneath his feet. Long since it had been, by his own hand, undermined. Authority was gone. Why keep up this miserable sham any longer? Could they not read the lie in his face, in his voice? What a folly to maintain the wretched pretence! He had failed. He was ruined. Harran was gone. His ranch would soon go; his money was gone. Lyman was worse than dead. His own honour had been prostituted. Gone, gone, everything he held dear, gone, lost, and swept away in that fierce struggle. And suddenly and all in a moment the last remaining shells of the fabric of his being, the sham that had stood already wonderfully long, cracked and collapsed.

"Was the Commission honestly elected?" insisted Garnett. "Were the delegates—did you bribe the delegates?"

"We were obliged to shut our eyes to means," faltered Magnus. "There was no other way to—" Then suddenly and with the last dregs of his resolution, he concluded with: "Yes, I gave them two thousand dollars each."

"Oh, hell! Oh, my God!" exclaimed Keast, sitting swiftly down upon the ragged sofa.

There was a long silence. A sense of poignant embarrassment descended upon those present. No one knew what to say or where to look. Garnett, with a laboured attempt at nonchalance, murmured:

"I see. Well, that's what I was trying to get at. Yes, I see."

"Well," said Gethings at length, bestirring himself, "I guess I'LL go home."

There was a movement. The group broke up, the men making for the door. One by one they went out. The last to go was Keast. He came up to Magnus and shook the Governor's limp hand.

"Good-bye, Governor," he said. "I'll see you again pretty soon. Don't let this discourage you. They'll come around all right after a while. So long."

He went out, shutting the door.

And seated in the one chair of the room, Magnus Derrick remained a long time, looking at his face in the cracked mirror that for so many years had reflected the painted faces of soubrettes, in this atmosphere of stale perfume and mouldy rice powder.

It had come—his fall, his ruin. After so many years of integrity and honest battle, his life had ended here—in an actress's dressing-room, deserted by his friends, his son murdered, his dishonesty known, an old man, broken, discarded, discredited, and abandoned. Before nightfall of that day, Bonneville was further excited by an astonishing bit of news. S. Behrman lived in a detached house at some distance from the town, surrounded by a grove of live oak and eucalyptus trees. At a little after half-past six, as he was sitting down to his supper, a bomb was thrown through the window of his dining-room, exploding near the doorway leading into the hall. The room was wrecked and nearly every window of the house shattered. By a miracle, S. Behrman, himself, remained untouched.

VIII

On a certain afternoon in the early part of July, about a month after the fight at the irrigating ditch and the mass meeting at Bonneville, Cedarquist, at the moment opening his mail in his office in San Francisco, was genuinely surprised to receive a visit from Presley.

"Well, upon my word, Pres," exclaimed the manufacturer, as the young man came in through the door that the office boy held open for him, "upon my word, have you been sick? Sit down, my boy. Have a glass of sherry. I always keep a bottle here."

Presley accepted the wine and sank into the depths of a great leather chair near by.

"Sick?" he answered. "Yes, I have been sick. I'm sick now. I'm gone to pieces, sir."

His manner was the extreme of listlessness—the listlessness of great fatigue. "Well, well," observed the other. "I'm right sorry to hear that. What's the trouble, Pres?"

"Oh, nerves mostly, I suppose, and my head, and insomnia, and weakness, a general collapse all along the line, the doctor tells me. 'Over-cerebration,' he says; 'over-excitement.' I fancy I rather narrowly missed brain fever."

"Well, I can easily suppose it," answered Cedarquist gravely, "after all you have been through."

Presley closed his eyes—they were sunken in circles of dark brown flesh—and pressed a thin hand to the back of his head.

"It is a nightmare," he murmured. "A frightful nightmare, and it's not over yet. You have heard of it all only through the newspaper reports. But down there, at Bonneville, at Los Muertos—oh, you can have no idea of it, of the misery caused by the defeat of the ranchers and by this decision of the Supreme Court that dispossesses them all. We had gone on hoping to the last that we would win there. We had thought that in the Supreme Court of the United States, at least, we could find justice. And the news of its decision was the worst, last blow of all. For Magnus it was the last—positively the very last."

"Poor, poor Derrick," murmured Cedarquist. "Tell me about him, Pres. How does he take it? What is he going to do?"

"It beggars him, sir. He sunk a great deal more than any of us believed in his ranch, when he resolved to turn off most of the tenants and farm the ranch himself. Then the fight he made against the Railroad in the Courts and the political campaign he went into, to get Lyman on the Railroad Commission, took more of it. The money that Genslinger blackmailed him of, it seems, was about all he had left. He had been gambling—you know the Governor—on another bonanza crop this year to recoup him. Well, the bonanza came right enough—just in time for S. Behrman and the Railroad to grab it. Magnus is ruined."

"What a tragedy! what a tragedy!" murmured the other. "Lyman turning rascal, Harran killed, and now this; and all within so short a time—all at the SAME time, you might almost say."

"If it had only killed him," continued Presley; "but that is the worst of it."

"How the worst?"

"I'm afraid, honestly, I'm afraid it is going to turn his wits, sir. It's broken him; oh, you should see him, you should see him. A shambling, stooping, trembling old man, in his dotage already. He sits all day in the dining-room, turning over papers, sorting them, tying them up, opening them again, forgetting them—all fumbling and mumbling and confused. And at table sometimes he forgets to eat. And, listen, you know, from the house we can hear the trains whistling for the Long Trestle. As often as that happens the Governor seems to be—oh, I don't know, frightened. He will sink his head between his shoulders, as though he were dodging something, and he won't fetch a long breath again till the train is out of hearing. He seems to have conceived an abject, unreasoned terror of the Railroad."

"But he will have to leave Los Muertos now, of course?"

"Yes, they will all have to leave. They have a fortnight more. The few tenants that were still on Los Muertos are leaving. That is one thing that brings me to the city. The family of one of the men who was killed—Hooven was his name—have come to the city to find work. I think they are liable to be in great distress, unless they have been wonderfully lucky, and I am trying to find them in order to look after them."

"You need looking after yourself, Pres."

"Oh, once away from Bonneville and the sight of the ruin there, I'm better. But I intend to go away. And that makes me think, I came to ask you if you could help me. If you would let me take passage on one of your wheat ships. The Doctor says an ocean voyage would set me up."

"Why, certainly, Pres," declared Cedarquist. "But I'm sorry you'll have to go. We expected to have you down in the country with us this winter."

Presley shook his head. "No," he answered. "I must go. Even if I had all my health, I could not bring myself to stay in California just now. If you can introduce me to one of your captains—"

"With pleasure. When do you want to go? You may have to wait a few weeks. Our first ship won't clear till the end of the month."

"That would do very well. Thank you, sir."

But Cedarquist was still interested in the land troubles of the Bonneville farmers, and took the first occasion to ask:

"So, the Railroad are in possession on most of the ranches?"

"On all of them," returned Presley. "The League went all to pieces, so soon as Magnus was forced to resign. The old story—they got quarrelling among themselves. Somebody started a compromise party, and upon that issue a new president was elected. Then there were defections. The Railroad offered to lease the lands in question to the ranchers—the ranchers who owned them," he exclaimed bitterly, "and because the terms were nominal—almost nothing—plenty of the men took the chance of saving themselves. And, of course, once signing the lease, they acknowledged the Railroad's title. But the road would not lease to Magnus. S. Behrman takes over Los Muertos in a few weeks now."

"No doubt, the road made over their title in the property to him," observed Cedarquist, "as a reward of his services."

"No doubt," murmured Presley wearily. He rose to go.

"By the way," said Cedarquist, "what have you on hand for, let us say, Friday evening? Won't you dine with us then? The girls are going to the country Monday of next week, and you probably won't see them again for some time if you take that ocean voyage of yours."

"I'm afraid I shall be very poor company, sir," hazarded Presley. "There's no 'go,' no life in me at all these days. I am like a clock with a broken spring."

"Not broken, Pres, my boy;" urged the other, "only run down. Try and see if we can't wind you up a bit. Say that we can expect you. We dine at seven."

"Thank you, sir. Till Friday at seven, then."

Regaining the street, Presley sent his valise to his club (where he had engaged a room) by a messenger boy, and boarded a Castro Street car. Before leaving Bonneville, he had ascertained, by strenuous enquiry, Mrs. Hooven's address in the city, and thitherward he now directed his steps.

When Presley had told Cedarquist that he was ill, that he was jaded, worn out, he had only told half the truth. Exhausted he was, nerveless, weak, but this apathy was still invaded from time to time with fierce incursions of a spirit of unrest and revolt, reactions, momentary returns of the blind, undirected energy that at one time had prompted him to a vast desire to acquit himself of some terrible deed of readjustment, just what, he could not say, some terrifying martyrdom, some awe-inspiring immolation, consummate, incisive, conclusive. He fancied himself to be fired with the purblind, mistaken heroism of the anarchist, hurling his victim to destruction with full knowledge that the catastrophe shall sweep him also into the vortex it creates.

But his constitutional irresoluteness obstructed his path continually; brain-sick, weak of will, emotional, timid even, he temporised, procrastinated, brooded; came to decisions in the dark hours of the night, only to abandon them in the morning.

Once only he had ACTED. And at this moment, as he was carried through the windy, squalid streets, he trembled at the remembrance of it. The horror of "what might have been" incompatible with the vengeance whose minister he fancied he was, oppressed him. The scene perpetually reconstructed itself in his imagination. He saw himself under the shade of the encompassing trees and shrubbery, creeping on his belly toward the house, in the suburbs of Bonneville, watching his chances, seizing opportunities, spying upon the lighted windows where the raised curtains afforded a view of the interior. Then had come the appearance in the glare of the gas of the figure of the man for whom he waited. He saw himself rise and run forward. He remembered the feel and weight in his hand of Caraher's bomb—the six inches of plugged gas pipe. His upraised arm shot forward. There was a shiver of smashed window-panes, then—a void—a red whirl of confusion, the air rent, the ground rocking, himself flung headlong, flung off the spinning circumference of things out into a place of terror and vacancy and darkness. And then after a long time the return of reason, the consciousness that his feet were set upon the road to Los Muertos, and that he was fleeing terror-stricken, gasping, all but insane with hysteria. Then the never-to-be-forgotten night that ensued, when he descended into the pit, horrified at what he supposed he had done, at one moment ridden with remorse, at another raging against his own feebleness, his lack of courage, his wretched, vacillating spirit. But morning had come, and with it the knowledge that he had failed, and the baser assurance that he was not even remotely suspected. His own escape had been no less miraculous than that of his enemy, and he had fallen on his knees in inarticulate prayer, weeping, pouring out his thanks to God for the deliverance from the gulf to the very brink of which his feet had been drawn.

After this, however, there had come to Presley a deep-rooted suspicion that he was—of all human beings, the most wretched—a failure. Everything to which he had set his mind failed—his great epic, his efforts to help the people who surrounded him, even his attempted destruction of the enemy, all these had come to nothing. Girding his shattered strength together, he resolved upon one last attempt to live up to the best that was in him, and to that end had set himself to lift out of the despair into which they had been thrust, the bereaved family of the German, Hooven.

After all was over, and Hooven, together with the seven others who had fallen at the irrigating ditch, was buried in the Bonneville cemetery, Mrs. Hooven, asking no one's aid or advice, and taking with her Minna and little Hilda, had gone to San Francisco—had gone to find work, abandoning Los Muertos and her home forever. Presley only learned of the departure of the family after fifteen days had elapsed.

At once, however, the suspicion forced itself upon him that Mrs. Hooven—and Minna, too for the matter of that—country-bred, ignorant of city ways, might easily come to grief in the hard, huge struggle of city life. This suspicion had swiftly hardened to a conviction, acting at last upon which Presley had followed them to San Francisco, bent upon finding and assisting them.

The house to which Presley was led by the address in his memorandum book was a cheap but fairly decent hotel near the power house of the Castro Street cable. He inquired for Mrs. Hooven.

The landlady recollected the Hoovens perfectly.

"German woman, with a little girl-baby, and an older daughter, sure. The older daughter was main pretty. Sure I remember them, but they ain't here no more. They left a week ago. I had to ask them for their room. As it was, they owed a week's room-rent. Mister, I can't afford—"

"Well, do you know where they went? Did you hear what address they had their trunk expressed to?"

"Ah, yes, their trunk," vociferated the woman, clapping her hands to her hips, her face purpling. "Their trunk, ah, sure. I got their trunk, and what are you going to do about it? I'm holding it till I get my money. What have you got to say about it? Let's hear it."

Presley turned away with a gesture of discouragement, his heart sinking. On the street corner he stood for a long time, frowning in trouble and perplexity. His suspicions had been only too well founded. So long ago as a week, the Hoovens had exhausted all their little store of money. For seven days now they had been without resources, unless, indeed, work had been found; "and what," he asked himself, "what work in God's name could they find to do here in the city?"

Seven days! He quailed at the thought of it. Seven days without money, knowing not a soul in all that swarming city. Ignorant of city life as both Minna and her mother were, would they even realise that there were institutions built and generously endowed for just such as they? He knew them to have their share of pride, the dogged sullen pride of the peasant; even if they knew of charitable organisations, would they, could they bring themselves to apply there? A poignant anxiety thrust itself sharply into Presley's heart. Where were they now? Where had they slept last night? Where breakfasted this morning? Had there even been any breakfast this morning? Had there even been any bed last night? Lost, and forgotten in the plexus of the city's life, what had befallen them? Towards what fate was the ebb tide of the streets drifting them?

Was this to be still another theme wrought out by iron hands upon the old, the world-old, world-wide keynote? How far were the consequences of that dreadful day's work at the irrigating ditch to reach? To what length was the tentacle of the monster to extend?

Presley returned toward the central, the business quarter of the city, alternately formulating and dismissing from his mind plan after plan for the finding and aiding of Mrs. Hooven and her daughters. He reached Montgomery Street, and turned toward his club, his imagination once more reviewing all the causes and circumstances of the great battle of which for the last eighteen months he had been witness.

All at once he paused, his eye caught by a sign affixed to the wall just inside the street entrance of a huge office building, and smitten with an idea, stood for an instant motionless, upon the sidewalk, his eyes wide, his fists shut tight.

The building contained the General Office of the Pacific and Southwestern Railroad. Large though it was, it nevertheless, was not pretentious, and during his visits to the city, Presley must have passed it, unheeding, many times.

But for all that it was the stronghold of the enemy—the centre of all that vast ramifying system of arteries that drained the life-blood of the State; the nucleus of the web in which so many lives, so many fortunes, so many destinies had been enmeshed. From this place—so he told himself—had emanated that policy of extortion, oppression and injustice that little by little had shouldered the ranchers from their rights, till, their backs to the wall, exasperated and despairing they had turned and fought and died. From here had come the orders to S. Behrman, to Cyrus Ruggles and to Genslinger, the orders that had brought Dyke to a prison, that had killed Annixter, that had ruined Magnus, that had corrupted Lyman. Here was the keep of the castle, and here, behind one of those many windows, in one of those many offices, his hand upon the levers of his mighty engine, sat the master, Shelgrim himself.

Instantly, upon the realisation of this fact an ungovernable desire seized upon Presley, an inordinate curiosity. Why not see, face to face, the man whose power was so vast, whose will was so resistless, whose potency for evil so limitless, the man who for so long and so hopelessly they had all been fighting. By reputation he knew him to be approachable; why should he not then approach him? Presley took his resolution in both hands. If he failed to act upon this impulse, he knew he would never act at all. His heart beating, his breath coming short, he entered the building, and in a few moments found himself seated in an ante-room, his eyes fixed with hypnotic intensity upon the frosted pane of an adjoining door, whereon in gold letters was inscribed the word, "PRESIDENT."

In the end, Presley had been surprised to find that Shelgrim was still in. It was already very late, after six o'clock, and the other offices in the building were in the act of closing. Many of them were already deserted. At every instant, through the open door of the ante-room, he caught a glimpse of clerks, office boys, book-keepers, and other employees hurrying towards the stairs and elevators, quitting business for the day. Shelgrim, it seemed, still remained at his desk, knowing no fatigue, requiring no leisure.

"What time does Mr. Shelgrim usually go home?" inquired Presley of the young man who sat ruling forms at the table in the ante-room.

"Anywhere between half-past six and seven," the other answered, adding, "Very often he comes back in the evening."

And the man was seventy years old. Presley could not repress a murmur of astonishment. Not only mentally, then, was the President of the P. and S. W. a giant. Seventy years of age and still at his post, holding there with the energy, with a concentration of purpose that would have wrecked the health and impaired the mind of many men in the prime of their manhood.

But the next instant Presley set his teeth.

"It is an ogre's vitality," he said to himself. "Just so is the man-eating tiger strong. The man should have energy who has sucked the life-blood from an entire People."

A little electric bell on the wall near at hand trilled a warning. The young man who was ruling forms laid down his pen, and opening the door of the President's office, thrust in his head, then after a word exchanged with the unseen occupant of the room, he swung the door wide, saying to Presley:

"Mr. Shelgrim will see you, sir."

Presley entered a large, well lighted, but singularly barren office. A well-worn carpet was on the floor, two steel engravings hung against the wall, an extra chair or two stood near a large, plain, littered table. That was absolutely all, unless he excepted the corner wash-stand, on which was set a pitcher of ice water, covered with a clean, stiff napkin. A man, evidently some sort of manager's assistant, stood at the end of the table, leaning on the back of one of the chairs. Shelgrim himself sat at the table.

He was large, almost to massiveness. An iron-grey beard and a mustache that completely hid the mouth covered the lower part of his face. His eyes were a pale blue, and a little watery; here and there upon his face were moth spots. But the enormous breadth of the shoulders was what, at first, most vividly forced itself upon Presley's notice. Never had he seen a broader man; the neck, however, seemed in a manner to have settled into the shoulders, and furthermore they were humped and rounded, as if to bear great responsibilities, and great abuse.

At the moment he was wearing a silk skull-cap, pushed to one side and a little awry, a frock coat of broadcloth, with long sleeves, and a waistcoat from the lower buttons of which the cloth was worn and, upon the edges, rubbed away, showing the metal underneath. At the top this waistcoat was unbuttoned and in the shirt front disclosed were two pearl studs.

Presley, uninvited, unnoticed apparently, sat down. The assistant manager was in the act of making a report. His voice was not lowered, and Presley heard every word that was spoken.

The report proved interesting. It concerned a book-keeper in the office of the auditor of disbursements. It seems he was at most times thoroughly reliable, hard-working, industrious, ambitious. But at long intervals the vice of drunkenness seized upon the man and for three days rode him like a hag. Not only during the period of this intemperance, but for the few days immediately following, the man was useless, his work untrustworthy. He was a family man and earnestly strove to rid himself of his habit; he was, when sober, valuable. In consideration of these facts, he had been pardoned again and again.

"You remember, Mr. Shelgrim," observed the manager, "that you have more than once interfered in his behalf, when we were disposed to let him go. I don't think we can do anything with him, sir. He promises to reform continually, but it is the same old story. This last time we saw nothing of him for four days. Honestly, Mr. Shelgrim, I think we ought to let Tentell out. We can't afford to keep him. He is really losing us too much money. Here's the order ready now, if you care to let it go."

There was a pause. Presley all attention, listened breathlessly. The assistant manager laid before his President the typewritten order in question. The silence lengthened; in the hall outside, the wrought-iron door of the elevator cage slid to with a clash. Shelgrim did not look at the order. He turned his swivel chair about and faced the windows behind him, looking out with unseeing eyes. At last he spoke:

"Tentell has a family, wife and three children. How much do we pay him?"

"One hundred and thirty."

"Let's double that, or say two hundred and fifty. Let's see how that will do."

"Why—of course—if you say so, but really, Mr. Shelgrim"

"Well, we'll try that, anyhow."

Presley had not time to readjust his perspective to this new point of view of the President of the P. and S. W. before the assistant manager had withdrawn. Shelgrim wrote a few memoranda on his calendar pad, and signed a couple of letters before turning his attention to Presley. At last, he looked up and fixed the young man with a direct, grave glance. He did not smile. It was some time before he spoke. At last, he said:

"Well, sir."

Presley advanced and took a chair nearer at hand. Shelgrim turned and from his desk picked up and consulted Presley's card. Presley observed that he read without the use of glasses.

"You," he said, again facing about, "you are the young man who wrote the poem called 'The Toilers.'"

"Yes, sir."

"It seems to have made a great deal of talk. I've read it, and I've seen the picture in Cedarquist's house, the picture you took the idea from."

Presley, his senses never more alive, observed that, curiously enough, Shelgrim did not move his body. His arms moved, and his head, but the great bulk of the man remained immobile in its place, and as the interview proceeded and this peculiarity emphasised itself, Presley began to conceive the odd idea that Shelgrim had, as it were, placed his body in the chair to rest, while his head and brain and hands went on working independently. A saucer of shelled filberts stood near his elbow, and from time to time he picked up one of these in a great thumb and forefinger and put it between his teeth.

"I've seen the picture called 'The Toilers,'" continued Shelgrim, "and of the two, I like the picture better than the poem."

"The picture is by a master," Presley hastened to interpose.

"And for that reason," said Shelgrim, "it leaves nothing more to be said. You might just as well have kept quiet. There's only one best way to say anything. And what has made the picture of 'The Toilers' great is that the artist said in it the BEST that could be said on the subject."

"I had never looked at it in just that light," observed Presley. He was confused, all at sea, embarrassed. What he had expected to find in Shelgrim, he could not have exactly said. But he had been prepared to come upon an ogre, a brute, a terrible man of blood and iron, and instead had discovered a sentimentalist and an art critic. No standards of measurement in his mental equipment would apply to the actual man, and it began to dawn upon him that possibly it was not because these standards were different in kind, but that they were lamentably deficient in size. He began to see that here was the man not only great, but large; many-sided, of vast sympathies, who understood with equal intelligence, the human nature in an habitual drunkard, the ethics of a masterpiece of painting, and the financiering and operation of ten thousand miles of railroad.

"I had never looked at it in just that light," repeated Presley. "There is a great deal in what you say."

"If I am to listen," continued Shelgrim, "to that kind of talk, I prefer to listen to it first hand. I would rather listen to what the great French painter has to say, than to what YOU have to say about what he has already said."

His speech, loud and emphatic at first, when the idea of what he had to say was fresh in his mind, lapsed and lowered itself at the end of his sentences as though he had already abandoned and lost interest in that thought, so that the concluding words were indistinct, beneath the grey beard and mustache. Also at times there was the faintest suggestion of a lisp.

"I wrote that poem," hazarded Presley, "at a time when I was terribly upset. I live," he concluded, "or did live on the Los Muertos ranch in Tulare County–Magnus Derrick's ranch."

"The Railroad's ranch LEASED to Mr. Derrick," observed Shelgrim.

Presley spread out his hands with a helpless, resigned gesture.

"And," continued the President of the P. and S. W. with grave intensity, looking at Presley keenly, "I suppose you believe I am a grand old rascal."

"I believe," answered Presley, "I am persuaded–" He hesitated, searching for his words.

"Believe this, young man," exclaimed Shelgrim, laying a thick powerful forefinger on the table to emphasise his words, "try to believe this–to begin with–THAT RAILROADS BUILD THEMSELVES. Where there is a demand sooner or later there will be a supply. Mr. Derrick, does he grow his wheat? The Wheat grows itself. What does he count for? Does he supply the force? What do I count for? Do I build the Railroad? You are dealing with forces, young man, when you speak of Wheat and the Railroads, not with men. There is the Wheat, the supply. It must be carried to feed the People. There is the demand. The Wheat is one force, the Railroad, another, and there is the law that governs them–supply and demand. Men have only little to do in the whole business. Complications may arise, conditions that bear hard on the individual–crush him maybe–BUT THE WHEAT WILL BE CARRIED TO FEED THE PEOPLE as inevitably as it will grow. If you want to fasten the blame of the affair at Los Muertos on any one person, you will make a mistake. Blame conditions, not men."

"But—but," faltered Presley, "you are the head, you control the road."

"You are a very young man. Control the road! Can I stop it? I can go into bankruptcy if you like. But otherwise if I run my road, as a business proposition, I can do nothing. I can not control it. It is a force born out of certain conditions, and I—no man—can stop it or control it. Can your Mr. Derrick stop the Wheat growing? He can burn his crop, or he can give it away, or sell it for a cent a bushel—just as I could go into bankruptcy—but otherwise his Wheat must grow. Can any one stop the Wheat? Well, then no more can I stop the Road."

Presley regained the street stupefied, his brain in a whirl. This new idea, this new conception dumfounded him. Somehow, he could not deny it. It rang with the clear reverberation of truth. Was no one, then, to blame for the horror at the irrigating ditch? Forces, conditions, laws of supply and demand—were these then the enemies, after all? Not enemies; there was no malevolence in Nature. Colossal indifference only, a vast trend toward appointed goals. Nature was, then, a gigantic engine, a vast cyclopean power, huge, terrible, a leviathan with a heart of steel, knowing no compunction, no forgiveness, no tolerance; crushing out the human atom standing in its way, with nirvanic calm, the agony of destruction sending never a jar, never the faintest tremour through all that prodigious mechanism of wheels and cogs. He went to his club and ate his supper alone, in gloomy agitation. He was sombre, brooding, lost in a dark maze of gloomy reflections. However, just as he was rising from the table an incident occurred that for the moment roused him and sharply diverted his mind.

His table had been placed near a window and as he was sipping his after-dinner coffee, he happened to glance across the street. His eye was at once caught by the sight of a familiar figure. Was it Minna Hooven? The figure turned the street corner and was lost to sight; but it had been strangely like. On the moment, Presley had risen from the table and, clapping on his hat, had hurried into the streets, where the lamps were already beginning to shine.

But search though he would, Presley could not again come upon the young woman, in whom he fancied he had seen the daughter of the unfortunate German. At last, he gave up the hunt, and returning to his club—at this hour almost deserted—smoked a few cigarettes, vainly attempted to read from a volume of essays in the library, and at last, nervous, distraught, exhausted, retired to his bed.

But none the less, Presley had not been mistaken. The girl whom he had tried to follow had been indeed Minna Hooven.

When Minna, a week before this time, had returned to the lodging house on Castro Street, after a day's unsuccessful effort to find employment, and was told that her mother and Hilda had gone, she was struck speechless with surprise and dismay.

She had never before been in any town larger than Bonneville, and now knew not which way to turn nor how to account for the disappearance of her mother and little Hilda. That the landlady was on the point of turning them out, she understood, but it had been agreed that the family should be allowed to stay yet one more day, in the hope that Minna would find work. Of this she reminded the land-lady. But this latter at once launched upon her such a torrent of vituperation, that the girl was frightened to speechless submission.

"Oh, oh," she faltered, "I know. I am sorry. I know we owe you money, but where did my mother go? I only want to find her."

"Oh, I ain't going to be bothered," shrilled the other. "How do I know?"

The truth of the matter was that Mrs. Hooven, afraid to stay in the vicinity of the house, after her eviction, and threatened with arrest by the landlady if she persisted in hanging around, had left with the woman a note scrawled on an old blotter, to be given to Minna when she returned. This the landlady had lost. To cover her confusion, she affected a vast indignation, and a turbulent, irascible demeanour.

"I ain't going to be bothered with such cattle as you," she vociferated in Minna's face. "I don't know where your folks is. Me, I only have dealings with honest people. I ain't got a word to say so long as the rent is paid. But when I'm soldiered out of a week's lodging, then I'm done. You get right along now. I don't know you. I ain't going to have my place get a bad name by having any South of Market Street chippies hanging around. You get along, or I'll call an officer."

Minna sought the street, her head in a whirl. It was about five o'clock. In her pocket was thirty-five cents, all she had in the world. What now?

All at once, the Terror of the City, that blind, unreasoned fear that only the outcast knows, swooped upon her, and clutched her vulture-wise, by the throat.

Her first few days' experience in the matter of finding employment, had taught her just what she might expect from this new world upon which she had been thrown. What was to become of her? What was she to do, where was she to go? Unanswerable, grim questions, and now she no longer had herself to fear for. Her mother and the baby, little Hilda, both of them equally unable to look after themselves, what was to become of them, where were they gone? Lost, lost, all of them, herself as well. But she rallied herself, as she walked along. The idea of her starving, of her mother and Hilda starving, was out of all reason. Of course, it would not come to that, of course not. It was not thus that starvation came. Something would happen, of course, it would–in time. But meanwhile, meanwhile, how to get through this approaching night, and the next few days. That was the thing to think of just now.

The suddenness of it all was what most unnerved her. During all the nineteen years of her life, she had never known what it meant to shift for herself. Her father had always sufficed for the family; he had taken care of her, then, all of a sudden, her father had been killed, her mother snatched from her. Then all of a sudden there was no help anywhere. Then all of a sudden a terrible voice demanded of her, "Now just what can you do to keep yourself alive?" Life faced her; she looked the huge stone image squarely in the lustreless eyes.

It was nearly twilight. Minna, for the sake of avoiding observation—for it seemed to her that now a thousand prying glances followed her—assumed a matter-of-fact demeanour, and began to walk briskly toward the business quarter of the town.

She was dressed neatly enough, in a blue cloth skirt with a blue plush belt, fairly decent shoes, once her mother's, a pink shirt waist, and jacket and a straw sailor. She was, in an unusual fashion, pretty. Even her troubles had not dimmed the bright light of her pale, greenish-blue eyes, nor faded the astonishing redness of her lips, nor hollowed her strangely white face. Her blue-black hair was trim. She carried her well-shaped, well-rounded figure erectly. Even in her distress, she observed that men looked keenly at her, and sometimes after her as she went along. But this she noted with a dim sub-conscious faculty. The real Minna, harassed, terrified, lashed with a thousand anxieties, kept murmuring under her breath:

"What shall I do, what shall I do, oh, what shall I do, now?"

After an interminable walk, she gained Kearney Street, and held it till the well-lighted, well-kept neighbourhood of the shopping district gave place to the vice-crowded saloons and concert halls of the Barbary Coast. She turned aside in avoidance of this, only to plunge into the purlieus of Chinatown, whence only she emerged, panic-stricken and out of breath, after a half hour of never-to-be-forgotten terrors, and at a time when it had grown quite dark.

On the corner of California and Dupont streets, she stood a long moment, pondering.

"I MUST do something," she said to herself. "I must do SOMETHING." She was tired out by now, and the idea occurred to her to enter the Catholic church in whose shadow she stood, and sit down and rest. This she did. The evening service was just being concluded. But long after the priests and altar boys had departed from the chancel, Minna still sat in the dim, echoing interior, confronting her desperate situation as best she might.

Two or three hours later, the sexton woke her. The church was being closed; she must leave. Once more, chilled with the sharp night air, numb with long sitting in the same attitude, still oppressed with drowsiness, confused, frightened, Minna found herself on the pavement. She began to be hungry, and, at length, yielding to the demand that every moment grew more imperious, bought and eagerly devoured a five-cent bag of fruit. Then, once more she took up the round of walking.

At length, in an obscure street that branched from Kearney Street, near the corner of the Plaza, she came upon an illuminated sign, bearing the inscription, "Beds for the Night, 15 and 25 cents."

Fifteen cents! Could she afford it? It would leave her with only that much more, that much between herself and a state of privation of which she dared not think; and, besides, the forbidding look of the building frightened her. It was dark, gloomy, dirty, a place suggestive of obscure crimes and hidden terrors. For twenty minutes or half an hour, she hesitated, walking twice and three times around the block. At last, she made up her mind. Exhaustion such as she had never known, weighed like lead upon her shoulders and dragged at her heels. She must sleep. She could not walk the streets all night. She entered the door-way under the sign, and found her way up a filthy flight of stairs. At the top, a man in a blue checked "jumper" was filling a lamp behind a high desk. To him Minna applied.

"I should like," she faltered, "to have a room—a bed for the night. One of those for fifteen cents will be good enough, I think."

"Well, this place is only for men," said the man, looking up from the lamp.

"Oh," said Minna, "oh—I—I didn't know."

She looked at him stupidly, and he, with equal stupidity, returned the gaze. Thus, for a long moment, they held each other's eyes.

"I—I didn't know," repeated Minna.

"Yes, it's for men," repeated the other. She slowly descended the stairs, and once more came out upon the streets.

And upon those streets that, as the hours advanced, grew more and more deserted, more and more silent, more and more oppressive with the sense of the bitter hardness of life towards those who have no means of living, Minna Hooven spent the first night of her struggle to keep her head above the ebb-tide of the city's sea, into which she had been plunged.

Morning came, and with it renewed hunger. At this time, she had found her way uptown again, and towards ten o'clock was sitting upon a bench in a little park full of nurse-maids and children. A group of the maids drew their baby-buggies to Minna's bench, and sat down, continuing a conversation they had already begun. Minna listened. A friend of one of the maids had suddenly thrown up her position, leaving her "madame" in what would appear to have been deserved embarrassment.

"Oh," said Minna, breaking in, and lying with sudden unwonted fluency, "I am a nurse-girl. I am out of a place. Do you think I could get that one?"

The group turned and fixed her—so evidently a country girl—with a supercilious indifference.

"Well, you might try," said one of them. "Got good references?"

"References?" repeated Minna blankly. She did not know what this meant.

"Oh, Mrs. Field ain't the kind to stick about references," spoke up the other, "she's that soft. Why, anybody could work her."

"I'll go there," said Minna. "Have you the address?" It was told to her.

"Lorin," she murmured. "Is that out of town?"

"Well, it's across the Bay."

"Across the Bay."

"Um. You're from the country, ain't you?"

"Yes. How—how do I get there? Is it far?"

"Well, you take the ferry at the foot of Market Street, and then the train on the other side. No, it ain't very far. Just ask any one down there. They'll tell you."

It was a chance; but Minna, after walking down to the ferry slips, found that the round trip would cost her twenty cents. If the journey proved fruitless, only a dime would stand between her and the end of everything. But it was a chance; the only one that had, as yet, presented itself. She made the trip.

And upon the street-railway cars, upon the ferryboats, on the locomotives and way-coaches of the local trains, she was reminded of her father's death, and of the giant power that had reduced her to her present straits, by the letters, P. and S. W. R. R. To her mind, they occurred everywhere. She seemed to see them in every direction. She fancied herself surrounded upon every hand by the long arms of the monster.

Minute after minute, her hunger gnawed at her. She could not keep her mind from it. As she sat on the boat, she found herself curiously scanning the faces of the passengers, wondering how long since such a one had breakfasted, how long before this other should sit down to lunch.

When Minna descended from the train, at Lorin on the other side of the Bay, she found that the place was one of those suburban towns, not yet become fashionable, such as may be seen beyond the outskirts of any large American city. All along the line of the railroad thereabouts, houses, small villas—contractors' ventures—were scattered, the advantages of suburban lots and sites for homes being proclaimed in seven-foot letters upon mammoth bill-boards close to the right of way. Without much trouble, Minna found the house to which she had been directed, a pretty little cottage, set back from the street and shaded by palms, live oaks, and the inevitable eucalyptus. Her heart warmed at the sight of it. Oh, to find a little niche for herself here, a home, a refuge from those horrible city streets, from the rat of famine, with its relentless tooth. How she would work, how strenuously she would endeavour to please, how patient of rebuke she would be, how faithful, how conscientious. Nor were her pretensions altogether false; upon her, while at home, had devolved almost continually the care of the baby Hilda, her little sister. She knew the wants and needs of children.

Her heart beating, her breath failing, she rang the bell set squarely in the middle of the front door.

The lady of the house herself, an elderly lady, with pleasant, kindly face, opened the door. Minna stated her errand.

"But I have already engaged a girl," she said.

"Oh," murmured Minna, striving with all her might to maintain appearances. "Oh–I thought perhaps–" She turned away.

"I'm sorry," said the lady. Then she added, "Would you care to look after so many as three little children, and help around in light housework between whiles?"

"Yes, ma'am."

"Because my sister–she lives in North Berkeley, above here–she's looking far a girl. Have you had lots of experience? Got good references?"

"Yes, ma'am."

"Well, I'll give you the address. She lives up in North Berkeley."

She turned back into the house a moment, and returned, handing Minna a card.

"That's where she lives–careful not to BLOT it, child, the ink's wet yet–you had better see her."

"Is it far? Could I walk there?"

"My, no; you better take the electric cars, about six blocks above here."

When Minna arrived in North Berkeley, she had no money left. By a cruel mistake, she had taken a car going in the wrong direction, and though her error was rectified easily enough, it had cost her her last five-cent piece. She was now to try her last hope. Promptly it crumbled away. Like the former, this place had been already filled, and Minna left the door of the house with the certainty that her chance had come to naught, and that now she entered into the last struggle with life–the death struggle–shorn of her last pitiful defence, her last safeguard, her last penny.

As she once more resumed her interminable walk, she realised she was weak, faint; and she knew that it was the weakness of complete exhaustion, and the faintness of approaching starvation. Was this the end coming on? Terror of death aroused her.

"I MUST, I MUST do something, oh, anything. I must have something to eat."

At this late hour, the idea of pawning her little jacket occurred to her, but now she was far away from the city and its pawnshops, and there was no getting back.

She walked on. An hour passed. She lost her sense of direction, became confused, knew not where she was going, turned corners and went up by-streets without knowing why, anything to keep moving, for she fancied that so soon as she stood still, the rat in the pit of her stomach gnawed more eagerly.

At last, she entered what seemed to be, if not a park, at least some sort of public enclosure. There were many trees; the place was beautiful; well-kept roads and walks led sinuously and invitingly underneath the shade. Through the trees upon the other side of a wide expanse of turf, brown and sear under the summer sun, she caught a glimpse of tall buildings and a flagstaff. The whole place had a vaguely public, educational appearance, and Minna guessed, from certain notices affixed to the trees, warning the public against the picking of flowers, that she had found her way into the grounds of the State University. She went on a little further. The path she was following led her, at length, into a grove of gigantic live oaks, whose lower branches all but swept the ground. Here the grass was green, the few flowers in bloom, the shade very thick. A more lovely spot she had seldom seen. Near at hand was a bench, built around the trunk of the largest live oak, and here, at length, weak from hunger, exhausted to the limits of her endurance, despairing, abandoned, Minna Hooven sat down to enquire of herself what next she could do.

But once seated, the demands of the animal—so she could believe—became more clamorous, more insistent. To eat, to rest, to be safely housed against another night, above all else, these were the things she craved; and the craving within her grew so mighty that she crisped her poor, starved hands into little fists, in an agony of desire, while the tears ran from her eyes, and the sobs rose thick from her breast and struggled and strangled in her aching throat.

But in a few moments Minna was aware that a woman, apparently of some thirty years of age, had twice passed along the walk in front of the bench where she sat, and now, as she took more notice of her, she remembered that she had seen her on the ferry-boat coming over from the city.

The woman was gowned in silk, tightly corseted, and wore a hat of rather ostentatious smartness. Minna became convinced that the person was watching her, but before she had a chance to act upon this conviction she was surprised out of all countenance by the stranger coming up to where she sat and speaking to her.

"Here is a coincidence," exclaimed the new-comer, as she sat down; "surely you are the young girl who sat opposite me on the boat. Strange I should come across you again. I've had you in mind ever since."

On this nearer view Minna observed that the woman's face bore rather more than a trace of enamel and that the atmosphere about was impregnated with sachet. She was not otherwise conspicuous, but there was a certain hardness about her mouth and a certain droop of fatigue in her eyelids which, combined with an indefinite self-confidence of manner, held Minna's attention.

"Do you know," continued the woman, "I believe you are in trouble. I thought so when I saw you on the boat, and I think so now. Are you? Are you in trouble? You're from the country, ain't you?"

Minna, glad to find a sympathiser, even in this chance acquaintance, admitted that she was in distress; that she had become separated from her mother, and that she was indeed from the country.

"I've been trying to find a situation," she hazarded in conclusion, "but I don't seem to succeed. I've never been in a city before, except Bonneville."

"Well, it IS a coincidence," said the other. "I know I wasn't drawn to you for nothing. I am looking for just such a young girl as you. You see, I live alone a good deal and I've been wanting to find a nice, bright, sociable girl who will be a sort of COMPANION to me. Understand? And there's something about you that I like. I took to you the moment I saw you on the boat. Now shall we talk this over?"

Towards the end of the week, one afternoon, as Presley was returning from his club, he came suddenly face to face with Minna upon a street corner.

"Ah," he cried, coming toward her joyfully. "Upon my word, I had almost given you up. I've been looking everywhere for you. I was afraid you might not be getting along, and I wanted to see if there was anything I could do. How are your mother and Hilda? Where are you stopping? Have you got a good place?"

"I don't know where mamma is," answered Minna. "We got separated, and I never have been able to find her again."

Meanwhile, Presley had been taking in with a quick eye the details of Minna's silk dress, with its garniture of lace, its edging of velvet, its silver belt-buckle. Her hair was arranged in a new way and on her head was a wide hat with a flare to one side, set off with a gilt buckle and a puff of bright blue plush. He glanced at her sharply.

"Well, but—but how are you getting on?" he demanded.

Minna laughed scornfully.

"I?" she cried. "Oh, I'VE gone to hell. It was either that or starvation."

Presley regained his room at the club, white and trembling. Worse than the worst he had feared had happened. He had not been soon enough to help. He had failed again. A superstitious fear assailed him that he was, in a manner, marked; that he was foredoomed to fail. Minna had come—had been driven to this; and he, acting too late upon his tardy resolve, had not been able to prevent it. Were the horrors, then, never to end? Was the grisly spectre of consequence to forever dance in his vision? Were the results, the far-reaching results of that battle at the irrigating ditch to cross his path forever? When would the affair be terminated, the incident closed? Where was that spot to which the tentacle of the monster could not reach?

By now, he was sick with the dread of it all. He wanted to get away, to be free from that endless misery, so that he might not see what he could no longer help. Cowardly he now knew himself to be. He thought of himself only with loathing.

Bitterly self-contemptuous that he could bring himself to a participation in such trivialities, he began to dress to keep his engagement to dine with the Cedarquists.

He arrived at the house nearly half an hour late, but before he could take off his overcoat, Mrs. Cedarquist appeared in the doorway of the drawing-room at the end of the hall. She was dressed as if to go out.

"My DEAR Presley," she exclaimed, her stout, over-dressed body bustling toward him with a great rustle of silk. "I never was so glad. You poor, dear poet, you are thin as a ghost. You need a better dinner than I can give you, and that is just what you are to have."

"Have I blundered?" Presley hastened to exclaim. "Did not Mr. Cedarquist mention Friday evening?"

"No, no, no," she cried; "it was he who blundered. YOU blundering in a social amenity! Preposterous! No; Mr. Cedarquist forgot that we were dining out ourselves to-night, and when he told me he had asked you here for the same evening, I fell upon the man, my dear, I did actually, tooth and nail. But I wouldn't hear of his wiring you. I just dropped a note to our hostess, asking if I could not bring you, and when I told her who you WERE, she received the idea with, oh, empressement. So, there it is, all settled. Cedarquist and the girls are gone on ahead, and you are to take the old lady like a dear, dear poet. I believe I hear the carriage. Allons! En voiture!"

Once settled in the cool gloom of the coupe, odorous of leather and upholstery, Mrs. Cedarquist exclaimed:

"And I've never told you who you were to dine with; oh, a personage, really. Fancy, you will be in the camp of your dearest foes. You are to dine with the Gerard people, one of the Vice-Presidents of your bete noir, the P. and S. W. Railroad."

Presley started, his fists clenching so abruptly as to all but split his white gloves. He was not conscious of what he said in reply, and Mrs. Cedarquist was so taken up with her own endless stream of talk that she did not observe his confusion.

"Their daughter Honora is going to Europe next week; her mother is to take her, and Mrs. Gerard is to have just a few people to dinner—very informal, you know—ourselves, you and, oh, I don't know, two or three others. Have you ever seen Honora? The prettiest little thing, and will she be rich? Millions, I would not dare say how many. Tiens. Nous voici."

The coupe drew up to the curb, and Presley followed Mrs. Cedarquist up the steps to the massive doors of the great house. In a confused daze, he allowed one of the footmen to relieve him of his hat and coat; in a daze he rejoined Mrs. Cedarquist in a room with a glass roof, hung with pictures, the art gallery, no doubt, and in a daze heard their names announced at the entrance of another room, the doors of which were hung with thick, blue curtains.

He entered, collecting his wits for the introductions and presentations that he foresaw impended.

The room was very large, and of excessive loftiness. Flat, rectagonal pillars of a rose-tinted, variegated marble, rose from the floor almost flush with the walls, finishing off at the top with gilded capitals of a Corinthian design, which supported the ceiling. The ceiling itself, instead of joining the walls at right angles, curved to meet them, a device that produced a sort of dome-like effect. This ceiling was a maze of golden involutions in very high relief, that adjusted themselves to form a massive framing for a great picture, nymphs and goddesses, white doves, golden chariots and the like, all wreathed about with clouds and garlands of roses. Between the pillars around the sides of the room were hangings of silk, the design—of a Louis Quinze type—of beautiful simplicity and faultless taste. The fireplace was a marvel. It reached from floor to ceiling; the lower parts, black marble, carved into crouching Atlases, with great muscles that upbore the superstructure. The design of this latter, of a kind of purple marble, shot through with white veinings, was in the same style as the design of the silk hangings. In its midst was a bronze escutcheon, bearing an undecipherable monogram and a Latin motto. Andirons of brass, nearly six feet high, flanked the hearthstone.

The windows of the room were heavily draped in sombre brocade and ecru lace, in which the initials of the family were very beautifully worked. But directly opposite the fireplace, an extra window, lighted from the adjoining conservatory, threw a wonderful, rich light into the apartment. It was a Gothic window of stained glass, very large, the centre figures being armed warriors, Parsifal and Lohengrin; the one with a banner, the other with a swan. The effect was exquisite, the window a veritable masterpiece, glowing, flaming, and burning with a hundred tints and colours—opalescent, purple, wine-red, clouded pinks, royal blues, saffrons, violets so dark as to be almost black.

Under foot, the carpet had all the softness of texture of grass; skins (one of them of an enormous polar bear) and rugs of silk velvet were spread upon the floor. A Renaissance cabinet of ebony, many feet taller than Presley's head, and inlaid with ivory and silver, occupied one corner of the room, while in its centre stood a vast table of Flemish oak, black, heavy as iron, massive. A faint odour of sandalwood pervaded the air. From the conservatory near-by, came the splashing of a fountain. A row of electric bulbs let into the frieze of the walls between the golden capitals, and burning dimly behind hemispheres of clouded glass, threw a subdued light over the whole scene.

Mrs. Gerard came forward.

"This is Mr. Presley, of course, our new poet of whom we are all so proud. I was so afraid you would be unable to come. You have given me a real pleasure in allowing me to welcome you here."

The footman appeared at her elbow.

"Dinner is served, madame," he announced.

When Mrs. Hooven had left the boarding-house on Castro Street, she had taken up a position on a neighbouring corner, to wait for Minna's reappearance. Little Hilda, at this time hardly more than six years of age, was with her, holding to her hand.

Mrs. Hooven was by no means an old woman, but hard work had aged her. She no longer had any claim to good looks. She no longer took much interest in her personal appearance. At the time of her eviction from the Castro Street boarding-house, she wore a faded black bonnet, garnished with faded artificial flowers of dirty pink. A plaid shawl was about her shoulders. But this day of misfortune had set Mrs. Hooven adrift in even worse condition than her daughter. Her purse, containing a miserable handful of dimes and nickels, was in her trunk, and her trunk was in the hands of the landlady. Minna had been allowed such reprieve as her thirty-five cents would purchase. The destitution of Mrs. Hooven and her little girl had begun from the very moment of her eviction.

While she waited for Minna, watching every street car and every approaching pedestrian, a policeman appeared, asked what she did, and, receiving no satisfactory reply, promptly moved her on.

Minna had had little assurance in facing the life struggle of the city. Mrs. Hooven had absolutely none. In her, grief, distress, the pinch of poverty, and, above all, the nameless fear of the turbulent, fierce life of the streets, had produced a numbness, an embruted, sodden, silent, speechless condition of dazed mind, and clogged, unintelligent speech. She was dumb, bewildered, stupid, animated but by a single impulse. She clung to life, and to the life of her little daughter Hilda, with the blind tenacity of purpose of a drowning cat.

Thus, when ordered to move on by the officer, she had silently obeyed, not even attempting to explain her situation. She walked away to the next street-crossing. Then, in a few moments returned, taking up her place on the corner near the boarding-house, spying upon the approaching cable cars, peeping anxiously down the length of the sidewalks.

Once more, the officer ordered her away, and once more, unprotesting, she complied. But when for the third time the policeman found her on the forbidden spot, he had lost his temper. This time when Mrs. Hooven departed, he had followed her, and when, bewildered, persistent, she had attempted to turn back, he caught her by the shoulder.

"Do you want to get arrested, hey?" he demanded. "Do you want me to lock you up? Say, do you, speak up?"

The ominous words at length reached Mrs. Hooven's comprehension. Arrested! She was to be arrested. The countrywoman's fear of the Jail nipped and bit eagerly at her unwilling heels. She hurried off, thinking to return to her post after the policeman should have gone away. But when, at length, turning back, she tried to find the boarding-house, she suddenly discovered that she was on an unfamiliar street. Unwittingly, no doubt, she had turned a corner. She could not retrace her steps. She and Hilda were lost.

"Mammy, I'm tired," Hilda complained.

Her mother picked her up.

"Mammy, where're we gowun, mammy?"

Where, indeed? Stupefied, Mrs. Hooven looked about her at the endless blocks of buildings, the endless procession of vehicles in the streets, the endless march of pedestrians on the sidewalks. Where was Minna; where was she and her baby to sleep that night? How was Hilda to be fed?

She could not stand still. There was no place to sit down; but one thing was left, walk.

Ah, that via dolorosa of the destitute, that chemin de la croix of the homeless. Ah, the mile after mile of granite pavement that MUST be, MUST be traversed. Walk they must. Move, they must; onward, forward, whither they cannot tell; why, they do not know. Walk, walk, walk with bleeding feet and smarting joints; walk with aching back and trembling knees; walk, though the senses grow giddy with fatigue, though the eyes droop with sleep, though every nerve, demanding rest, sets in motion its tiny alarm of pain. Death is at the end of that devious, winding maze of paths, crossed and re-crossed and crossed again. There is but one goal to the via dolorosa; there is no escape from the central chamber of that labyrinth. Fate guides the feet of them that are set therein. Double on their steps though they may, weave in and out of the myriad corners of the city's streets, return, go forward, back, from side to side, here, there, anywhere, dodge, twist, wind, the central chamber where Death sits is reached inexorably at the end.

Sometimes leading and sometimes carrying Hilda, Mrs. Hooven set off upon her objectless journey. Block after block she walked, street after street. She was afraid to stop, because of the policemen. As often as she so much as slackened her pace, she was sure to see one of these terrible figures in the distance, watching her, so it seemed to her, waiting for her to halt for the fraction of a second, in order that he might have an excuse to arrest her.

Hilda fretted incessantly.

"Mammy, where're we gowun? Mammy, I'm tired." Then, at last, for the first time, that plaint that stabbed the mother's heart:

"Mammy, I'm hungry."

"Be qui-ut, den," said Mrs. Hooven. "Bretty soon we'll hev der subber."

Passers-by on the sidewalk, men and women in the great six o'clock homeward march, jostled them as they went along. With dumb, dull curiousness, she looked into one after another of the limitless stream of faces, and she fancied she saw in them every emotion but pity. The faces were gay, were anxious, were sorrowful, were mirthful, were lined with thought, or were merely flat and expressionless, but not one was turned toward her in compassion. The expressions of the faces might be various, but an underlying callousness was discoverable beneath every mask. The people seemed removed from her immeasurably; they were infinitely above her. What was she to them, she and her baby, the crippled outcasts of the human herd, the unfit, not able to survive, thrust out on the heath to perish?

To beg from these people did not yet occur to her. There was no pride, however, in the matter. She would have as readily asked alms of so many sphinxes.

She went on. Without willing it, her feet carried her in a wide circle. Soon she began to recognise the houses; she had been in that street before. Somehow, this was distasteful to her; so, striking off at right angles, she walked straight before her for over a dozen blocks. By now, it was growing darker. The sun had set. The hands of a clock on the power-house of a cable line pointed to seven. No doubt, Minna had come long before this time, had found her mother gone, and had—just what had she done, just what COULD she do? Where was her daughter now? Walking the streets herself, no doubt. What was to become of Minna, pretty girl that she was, lost, houseless and friendless in the maze of these streets? Mrs. Hooven, roused from her lethargy, could not repress an exclamation of anguish. Here was misfortune indeed; here was calamity. She bestirred herself, and remembered the address of the boarding-house. She might inquire her way back thither. No doubt, by now the policeman would be gone home for the night. She looked about. She was in the district of modest residences, and a young man was coming toward her, carrying a new garden hose looped around his shoulder.

"Say, Meest'r; say, blease—"

The young man gave her a quick look and passed on, hitching the coil of hose over his shoulder. But a few paces distant, he slackened in his walk and fumbled in his vest pocket with his fingers. Then he came back to Mrs. Hooven and put a quarter into her hand.

Mrs. Hooven stared at the coin stupefied. The young man disappeared. He thought, then, that she was begging. It had come to that; she, independent all her life, whose husband had held five hundred acres of wheat land, had been taken for a beggar. A flush of shame shot to her face. She was about to throw the money after its giver. But at the moment, Hilda again exclaimed:

"Mammy, I'm hungry."

With a movement of infinite lassitude and resigned acceptance of the situation, Mrs. Hooven put the coin in her pocket. She had no right to be proud any longer. Hilda must have food.

That evening, she and her child had supper at a cheap restaurant in a poor quarter of the town, and passed the night on the benches of a little uptown park.

Unused to the ways of the town, ignorant as to the customs and possibilities of eating-houses, she spent the whole of her quarter upon supper for herself and Hilda, and had nothing left wherewith to buy a lodging.

The night was dreadful; Hilda sobbed herself to sleep on her mother's shoulder, waking thereafter from hour to hour, to protest, though wrapped in her mother's shawl, that she was cold, and to enquire why they did not go to bed. Drunken men snored and sprawled near at hand. Towards morning, a loafer, reeking of alcohol, sat down beside her, and indulged in an incoherent soliloquy, punctuated with oaths and obscenities. It was not till far along towards daylight that she fell asleep.

She awoke to find it broad day. Hilda—mercifully—slept. Her mother's limbs were stiff and lame with cold and damp; her head throbbed. She moved to another bench which stood in the rays of the sun, and for a long two hours sat there in the thin warmth, till the moisture of the night that clung to her clothes was evaporated.

A policeman came into view. She woke Hilda, and carrying her in her arms, took herself away.

"Mammy," began Hilda as soon as she was well awake; "Mammy, I'm hungry. I want mein breakfest."

"Sure, sure, soon now, leedle tochter."

She herself was hungry, but she had but little thought of that. How was Hilda to be fed? She remembered her experience of the previous day, when the young man with the hose had given her money. Was it so easy, then, to beg? Could charity be had for the asking? So it seemed; but all that was left of her sturdy independence revolted at the thought. SHE beg! SHE hold out the hand to strangers!

"Mammy, I'm hungry."

There was no other way. It must come to that in the end. Why temporise, why put off the inevitable? She sought out a frequented street where men and women were on their way to work. One after another, she let them go by, searching their faces, deterred at the very last moment by some trifling variation of expression, a firm set mouth, a serious, level eyebrow, an advancing chin. Then, twice, when she had made a choice, and brought her resolution to the point of speech, she quailed, shrinking, her ears tingling, her whole being protesting against the degradation. Every one must be looking at her. Her shame was no doubt the object of an hundred eyes.

"Mammy, I'm hungry," protested Hilda again.

She made up her mind. What, though, was she to say? In what words did beggars ask for assistance?

She tried to remember how tramps who had appeared at her back door on Los Muertos had addressed her; how and with what formula certain mendicants of Bonneville had appealed to her. Then, having settled upon a phrase, she approached a whiskered gentleman with a large stomach, walking briskly in the direction of the town.

"Say, den, blease hellup a boor womun."

The gentleman passed on.

"Perhaps he doand hear me," she murmured.

Two well-dressed women advanced, chattering gayly.

"Say, say, den, blease hellup a boor womun."

One of the women paused, murmuring to her companion, and from her purse extracted a yellow ticket which she gave to Mrs. Hooven with voluble explanations. But Mrs. Hooven was confused, she did not understand. What could the ticket mean? The women went on their way.

The next person to whom she applied was a young girl of about eighteen, very prettily dressed.

"Say, say, den, blease hellup a boor womun."

In evident embarrassment, the young girl paused and searched in her little pocketbook. "I think I have—I think—I have just ten cents here somewhere," she murmured again and again.

In the end, she found a dime, and dropped it into Mrs. Hooven's palm.

That was the beginning. The first step once taken, the others became easy. All day long, Mrs. Hooven and Hilda followed the streets, begging, begging. Here it was a nickel, there a dime, here a nickel again. But she was not expert in the art, nor did she know where to buy food the cheapest; and the entire day's work resulted only in barely enough for two meals of bread, milk, and a wretchedly cooked stew. Tuesday night found the pair once more shelterless.

Once more, Mrs. Hooven and her baby passed the night on the park benches. But early on Wednesday morning, Mrs. Hooven found herself assailed by sharp pains and cramps in her stomach. What was the cause she could not say; but as the day went on, the pains increased, alternating with hot flushes over all her body, and a certain weakness and faintness. As the day went on, the pain and the weakness increased. When she tried to walk, she found she could do so only with the greatest difficulty. Here was fresh misfortune. To beg, she must walk. Dragging herself forward a half-block at a time, she regained the street once more. She succeeded in begging a couple of nickels, bought a bag of apples from a vender, and, returning to the park, sank exhausted upon a bench.

Here she remained all day until evening, Hilda alternately whimpering for her bread and milk, or playing languidly in the gravel walk at her feet. In the evening, she started out again. This time, it was bitter hard. Nobody seemed inclined to give. Twice she was "moved on" by policemen. Two hours' begging elicited but a single dime. With this, she bought Hilda's bread and milk, and refusing herself to eat, returned to the bench—the only home she knew—and spent the night shivering with cold, burning with fever.

From Wednesday morning till Friday evening, with the exception of the few apples she had bought, and a quarter of a loaf of hard bread that she found in a greasy newspaper—scraps of a workman's dinner—Mrs. Hooven had nothing to eat. In her weakened condition, begging became hourly more difficult, and such little money as was given her, she resolutely spent on Hilda's bread and milk in the morning and evening.

By Friday afternoon, she was very weak, indeed. Her eyes troubled her. She could no longer see distinctly, and at times there appeared to her curious figures, huge crystal goblets of the most graceful shapes, floating and swaying in the air in front of her, almost within arm's reach. Vases of elegant forms, made of shimmering glass, bowed and courtesied toward her. Glass bulbs took graceful and varying shapes before her vision, now rounding into globes, now evolving into hour-glasses, now twisting into pretzel-shaped convolutions.

"Mammy, I'm hungry," insisted Hilda, passing her hands over her face. Mrs. Hooven started and woke. It was Friday evening. Already the street lamps were being lit.

"Gome, den, leedle girl," she said, rising and taking Hilda's hand. "Gome, den, we go vind subber, hey?"

She issued from the park and took a cross street, directly away from the locality where she had begged the previous days. She had had no success there of late. She would try some other quarter of the town. After a weary walk, she came out upon Van Ness Avenue, near its junction with Market Street. She turned into the avenue, and went on toward the Bay, painfully traversing block after block, begging of all whom she met (for she no longer made any distinction among the passers-by).

"Say, say, den, blease hellup a boor womun."

"Mammy, mammy, I'm hungry."

It was Friday night, between seven and eight. The great deserted avenue was already dark. A sea fog was scudding overhead, and by degrees descending lower. The warmth was of the meagerest, and the street lamps, birds of fire in cages of glass, fluttered and danced in the prolonged gusts of the trade wind that threshed and weltered in the city streets from off the ocean.

Presley entered the dining-room of the Gerard mansion with little Miss Gerard on his arm. The other guests had preceded them—Cedarquist with Mrs. Gerard; a pale-faced, languid young man (introduced to Presley as Julian Lambert) with Presley's cousin Beatrice, one of the twin daughters of Mr. and Mrs. Cedarquist; his brother Stephen, whose hair was straight as an Indian's, but of a pallid straw color, with Beatrice's sister; Gerard himself, taciturn, bearded, rotund, loud of breath, escorted Mrs. Cedarquist. Besides these, there were one or two other couples, whose names Presley did not remember.

The dining-room was superb in its appointments. On three sides of the room, to the height of some ten feet, ran a continuous picture, an oil painting, divided into long sections by narrow panels of black oak. The painting represented the personages in the Romaunt de la Rose, and was conceived in an atmosphere of the most delicate, most ephemeral allegory. One saw young chevaliers, blue-eyed, of elemental beauty and purity; women with crowns, gold girdles, and cloudy wimples; young girls, entrancing in their loveliness, wearing snow-white kerchiefs, their golden hair unbound and flowing, dressed in white samite, bearing armfuls of flowers; the whole procession defiling against a background of forest glades, venerable oaks, half-hidden fountains, and fields of asphodel and roses.

Otherwise, the room was simple. Against the side of the wall unoccupied by the picture stood a sideboard of gigantic size, that once had adorned the banquet hall of an Italian palace of the late Renaissance. It was black with age, and against its sombre surfaces glittered an array of heavy silver dishes and heavier cut-glass bowls and goblets.

The company sat down to the first course of raw Blue Point oysters, served upon little pyramids of shaved ice, and the two butlers at once began filling the glasses of the guests with cool Haut Sauterne.

Mrs. Gerard, who was very proud of her dinners, and never able to resist the temptation of commenting upon them to her guests, leaned across to Presley and Mrs. Cedarquist, murmuring, "Mr. Presley, do you find that Sauterne too cold? I always believe it is so bourgeois to keep such a delicate wine as Sauterne on the ice, and to ice Bordeaux or Burgundy—oh, it is nothing short of a crime."

"This is from your own vineyard, is it not?" asked Julian Lambert. "I think I recognise the bouquet."

He strove to maintain an attitude of fin gourmet, unable to refrain from comment upon the courses as they succeeded one another.

Little Honora Gerard turned to Presley:

"You know," she explained, "Papa has his own vineyards in southern France. He is so particular about his wines; turns up his nose at California wines. And I am to go there next summer. Ferrieres is the name of the place where our vineyards are, the dearest village!" She was a beautiful little girl of a dainty porcelain type, her colouring low in tone. She wore no jewels, but her little, undeveloped neck and shoulders, of an exquisite immaturity, rose from the tulle bodice of her first decollete gown.

"Yes," she continued; "I'm to go to Europe for the first time. Won't it be gay? And I am to have my own bonne, and Mamma and I are to travel—so many places, Baden, Homburg, Spa, the Tyrol. Won't it be gay?"

Presley assented in meaningless words. He sipped his wine mechanically, looking about that marvellous room, with its subdued saffron lights, its glitter of glass and silver, its beautiful women in their elaborate toilets, its deft, correct servants; its array of tableware—cut glass, chased silver, and Dresden crockery. It was Wealth, in all its outward and visible forms, the signs of an opulence so great that it need never be husbanded. It was the home of a railway "Magnate," a Railroad King. For this, then, the farmers paid. It was for this that S. Behrman turned the screw, tightened the vise. It was for this that Dyke had been driven to outlawry and a jail. It was for this that Lyman Derrick had been bought, the Governor ruined and broken, Annixter shot down, Hooven killed.

The soup, puree a la Derby, was served, and at the same time, as hors d'oeuvres, ortolan patties, together with a tiny sandwich made of browned toast and thin slices of ham, sprinkled over with Parmesan cheese. The wine, so Mrs. Gerard caused it to be understood, was Xeres, of the 1815 vintage.

Mrs. Hooven crossed the avenue. It was growing late. Without knowing it, she had come to a part of the city that experienced beggars shunned. There was nobody about. Block after block of residences stretched away on either hand, lighted, full of people. But the sidewalks were deserted.

"Mammy," whimpered Hilda. "I'm tired, carry me."

Using all her strength, Mrs. Hooven picked her up and moved on aimlessly.

Then again that terrible cry, the cry of the hungry child appealing to the helpless mother:

"Mammy, I'm hungry."

"Ach, Gott, leedle girl," exclaimed Mrs. Hooven, holding her close to her shoulder, the tears starting from her eyes. "Ach, leedle tochter. Doand, doand, doand. You praik my hairt. I cen't vind any subber. We got noddings to eat, noddings, noddings."

"When do we have those bread'n milk again, Mammy?"

"To-morrow—soon—py-and-py, Hilda. I doand know what pecome oaf us now, what pecome oaf my leedle babby."

She went on, holding Hilda against her shoulder with one arm as best she might, one hand steadying herself against the fence railings along the sidewalk. At last, a solitary pedestrian came into view, a young man in a top hat and overcoat, walking rapidly. Mrs. Hooven held out a quivering hand as he passed her.

"Say, say, den, Meest'r, blease hellup a boor womun."

The other hurried on.

The fish course was grenadins of bass and small salmon, the latter stuffed, and cooked in white wine and mushroom liquor.

"I have read your poem, of course, Mr. Presley," observed Mrs. Gerard. "'The Toilers,' I mean. What a sermon you read us, you dreadful young man. I felt that I ought at once to 'sell all that I have and give to the poor.' Positively, it did stir me up. You may congratulate yourself upon making at least one convert. Just because of that poem Mrs. Cedarquist and I have started a movement to send a whole shipload of wheat to the starving people in India. Now, you horrid reactionnaire, are you satisfied?"

"I am very glad," murmured Presley.

"But I am afraid," observed Mrs. Cedarquist, "that we may be too late. They are dying so fast, those poor people. By the time our ship reaches India the famine may be all over."

"One need never be afraid of being 'too late' in the matter of helping the destitute," answered Presley. "Unfortunately, they are always a fixed quantity. 'The poor ye have always with you.'"

"How very clever that is," said Mrs. Gerard.

Mrs. Cedarquist tapped the table with her fan in mild applause.

"Brilliant, brilliant," she murmured, "epigrammatical."

"Honora," said Mrs. Gerard, turning to her daughter, at that moment in conversation with the languid Lambert, "Honora, entends-tu, ma cherie, l'esprit de notre jeune Lamartine."

Mrs. Hooven went on, stumbling from street to street, holding Hilda to her breast.

Famine gnawed incessantly at her stomach; walk though she might, turn upon her tracks up and down the streets, back to the avenue again, incessantly and relentlessly the torture dug into her vitals. She was hungry, hungry, and if the want of food harassed and rended her, full-grown woman that she was, what must it be in the poor, starved stomach of her little girl? Oh, for some helping hand now, oh, for one little mouthful, one little nibble! Food, food, all her wrecked body clamoured for nourishment; anything to numb those gnawing teeth—an abandoned loaf, hard, mouldered; a half-eaten fruit, yes, even the refuse of the gutter, even the garbage of the ash heap. On she went, peering into dark corners, into the areaways, anywhere, everywhere, watching the silent prowling of cats, the intent rovings of stray dogs. But she was growing weaker; the pains and cramps in her stomach returned. Hilda's weight bore her to the pavement. More than once a great giddiness, a certain wheeling faintness all but overcame her. Hilda, however, was asleep. To wake her would only mean to revive her to the consciousness of hunger; yet how to carry her further? Mrs. Hooven began to fear that she would fall with her child in her arms. The terror of a collapse upon those cold pavements glistening with fog-damp roused her; she must make an effort to get through the night. She rallied all her strength, and pausing a moment to shift the weight of her baby to the other arm, once more set off through the night. A little while later she found on the edge of the sidewalk the peeling of a banana. It had been trodden upon and it was muddy, but joyfully she caught it up.

"Hilda," she cried, "wake oop, leedle girl. See, loog den, dere's somedings to eat. Look den, hey? Dat's goot, ain't it? Zum bunaner."

But it could not be eaten. Decayed, dirty, all but rotting, the stomach turned from the refuse, nauseated.

"No, no," cried Hilda, "that's not good. I can't eat it. Oh, Mammy, please gif me those bread'n milk."

By now the guests of Mrs. Gerard had come to the entrees—Londonderry pheasants, escallops of duck, and rissolettes a la pompadour. The wine was Chateau Latour.

All around the table conversations were going forward gayly. The good wines had broken up the slight restraint of the early part of the evening and a spirit of good humour and good fellowship prevailed. Young Lambert and Mr. Gerard were deep in reminiscences of certain mutual duck-shooting expeditions. Mrs. Gerard and Mrs. Cedarquist discussed a novel—a strange mingling of psychology, degeneracy, and analysis of erotic conditions—which had just been translated from the Italian. Stephen Lambert and Beatrice disputed over the merits of a Scotch collie just given to the young lady. The scene was gay, the electric bulbs sparkled, the wine flashing back the light. The entire table was a vague glow of white napery, delicate china, and glass as brilliant as crystal. Behind the guests the serving-men came and went, filling the glasses continually, changing the covers, serving the entrees, managing the dinner without interruption, confusion, or the slightest unnecessary noise.

But Presley could find no enjoyment in the occasion. From that picture of feasting, that scene of luxury, that atmosphere of decorous, well-bred refinement, his thoughts went back to Los Muertos and Quien Sabe and the irrigating ditch at Hooven's. He saw them fall, one by one, Harran, Annixter, Osterman, Broderson, Hooven. The clink of the wine glasses was drowned in the explosion of revolvers. The Railroad might indeed be a force only, which no man could control and for which no man was responsible, but his friends had been killed, but years of extortion and oppression had wrung money from all the San Joaquin, money that had made possible this very scene in which he found himself. Because Magnus had been beggared, Gerard had become Railroad King; because the farmers of the valley were poor, these men were rich.

The fancy grew big in his mind, distorted, caricatured, terrible. Because the farmers had been killed at the irrigation ditch, these others, Gerard and his family, fed full. They fattened on the blood of the People, on the blood of the men who had been killed at the ditch. It was a half-ludicrous, half-horrible "dog eat dog," an unspeakable cannibalism. Harran, Annixter, and Hooven were being devoured there under his eyes. These dainty women, his cousin Beatrice and little Miss Gerard, frail, delicate; all these fine ladies with their small fingers and slender necks, suddenly were transfigured in his tortured mind into harpies tearing human flesh. His head swam with the horror of it, the terror of it. Yes, the People WOULD turn some day, and turning, rend those who now preyed upon them. It would be "dog eat dog" again, with positions reversed, and he saw for one instant of time that splendid house sacked to its foundations, the tables overturned, the pictures torn, the hangings blazing, and Liberty, the red-handed Man in the Street, grimed with powder smoke, foul with the gutter, rush yelling, torch in hand, through every door.

At ten o'clock Mrs. Hooven fell.

Luckily she was leading Hilda by the hand at the time and the little girl was not hurt. In vain had Mrs. Hooven, hour after hour, walked the streets. After a while she no longer made any attempt to beg; nobody was stirring, nor did she even try to hunt for food with the stray dogs and cats. She had made up her mind to return to the park in order to sit upon the benches there, but she had mistaken the direction, and following up Sacramento Street, had come out at length, not upon the park, but upon a great vacant lot at the very top of the Clay Street hill. The ground was unfenced and rose above her to form the cap of the hill, all overgrown with bushes and a few stunted live oaks. It was in trying to cross this piece of ground that she fell. She got upon her feet again.

"Ach, Mammy, did you hurt yourself?" asked Hilda.

"No, no."

"Is that house where we get those bread'n milk?"

Hilda pointed to a single rambling building just visible in the night, that stood isolated upon the summit of the hill in a grove of trees.

"No, no, dere aindt no braid end miluk, leedle tochter."

Hilda once more began to sob.

"Ach, Mammy, please, PLEASE, I want it. I'm hungry."

The jangled nerves snapped at last under the tension, and Mrs. Hooven, suddenly shaking Hilda roughly, cried out: "Stop, stop. Doand say ut egen, you. My Gott, you kill me yet."

But quick upon this came the reaction. The mother caught her little girl to her, sinking down upon her knees, putting her arms around her, holding her close.

"No, no, gry all so mudge es you want. Say dot you are hongry. Say ut egen, say ut all de dime, ofer end ofer egen. Say ut, poor, starfing, leedle babby. Oh, mein poor, leedle tochter. My Gott, oh, I go crazy bretty soon, I guess. I cen't hellup you. I cen't ged you noddings to eat, noddings, noddings. Hilda, we gowun to die togedder. Put der arms roundt me, soh, tighd, leedle babby. We gowun to die, we gowun to vind Popper. We aindt gowun to be hongry eny more."

"Vair we go now?" demanded Hilda.

"No places. Mommer's soh tiredt. We stop heir, leedle while, end rest."

Underneath a large bush that afforded a little shelter from the wind, Mrs. Hooven lay down, taking Hilda in her arms and wrapping her shawl about her. The infinite, vast night expanded gigantic all around them. At this elevation they were far above the city. It was still. Close overhead whirled the chariots of the fog, galloping landward, smothering lights, blurring outlines. Soon all sight of the town was shut out; even the solitary house on the hilltop vanished. There was nothing left but grey, wheeling fog, and the mother and child, alone, shivering in a little strip of damp ground, an island drifting aimlessly in empty space.

Hilda's fingers touched a leaf from the bush and instinctively closed upon it and carried it to her mouth.

"Mammy," she said, "I'm eating those leaf. Is those good?"

Her mother did not reply.

"You going to sleep, Mammy?" inquired Hilda, touching her face.

Mrs. Hooven roused herself a little.

"Hey? Vat you say? Asleep? Yais, I guess I wass asleep."

Her voice trailed unintelligibly to silence again. She was not, however, asleep. Her eyes were open. A grateful numbness had begun to creep over her, a pleasing semi-insensibility. She no longer felt the pain and cramps of her stomach, even the hunger was ceasing to bite.

"These stuffed artichokes are delicious, Mrs. Gerard," murmured young Lambert, wiping his lips with a corner of his napkin. "Pardon me for mentioning it, but your dinner must be my excuse."

"And this asparagus—since Mr. Lambert has set the bad example," observed Mrs. Cedarquist, "so delicate, such an exquisite flavour. How do you manage?"

"We get all our asparagus from the southern part of the State, from one particular ranch," explained Mrs. Gerard. "We order it by wire and get it only twenty hours after cutting. My husband sees to it that it is put on a special train. It stops at this ranch just to take on our asparagus. Extravagant, isn't it, but I simply cannot eat asparagus that has been cut more than a day."

"Nor I," exclaimed Julian Lambert, who posed as an epicure. "I can tell to an hour just how long asparagus has been picked."

"Fancy eating ordinary market asparagus," said Mrs. Gerard, "that has been fingered by Heaven knows how many hands."

"Mammy, mammy, wake up," cried Hilda, trying to push open Mrs. Hooven's eyelids, at last closed. "Mammy, don't. You're just trying to frighten me."

Feebly Hilda shook her by the shoulder. At last Mrs. Hooven's lips stirred. Putting her head down, Hilda distinguished the whispered words:

"I'm sick. Go to schleep....Sick....Noddings to eat."

The dessert was a wonderful preparation of alternate layers of biscuit glaces, ice cream, and candied chestnuts.

"Delicious, is it not?" observed Julian Lambert, partly to himself, partly to Miss Cedarquist. "This Moscovite fouette—upon my word, I have never tasted its equal."

"And you should know, shouldn't you?" returned the young lady.

"Mammy, mammy, wake up," cried Hilda. "Don't sleep so. I'm frightenedt."

Repeatedly she shook her; repeatedly she tried to raise the inert eyelids with the point of her finger. But her mother no longer stirred. The gaunt, lean body, with its bony face and sunken eye-sockets, lay back, prone upon the ground, the feet upturned and showing the ragged, worn soles of the shoes, the forehead and grey hair beaded with fog, the poor, faded bonnet awry, the poor, faded dress soiled and torn. Hilda drew close to her mother, kissing her face, twining her arms around her neck. For a long time, she lay that way, alternately sobbing and sleeping. Then, after a long time, there was a stir. She woke from a doze to find a police officer and two or three other men bending over her. Some one carried a lantern. Terrified, smitten dumb, she was unable to answer the questions put to her. Then a woman, evidently a mistress of the house on the top of the hill, arrived and took Hilda in her arms and cried over her.

"I'll take the little girl," she said to the police officer.

"But the mother, can you save her? Is she too far gone?"

"I've sent for a doctor," replied the other.

Just before the ladies left the table, young Lambert raised his glass of Madeira. Turning towards the wife of the Railroad King, he said:

"My best compliments for a delightful dinner."

The doctor who had been bending over Mrs. Hooven, rose.

"It's no use," he said; "she has been dead some time—exhaustion from starvation."

IX

On Division Number Three of the Los Muertos ranch the wheat had already been cut, and S. Behrman on a certain morning in the first week of August drove across the open expanse of stubble toward the southwest, his eyes searching the horizon for the feather of smoke that would mark the location of the steam harvester. However, he saw nothing. The stubble extended onward apparently to the very margin of the world.

At length, S. Behrman halted his buggy and brought out his field glasses from beneath the seat. He stood up in his place and, adjusting the lenses, swept the prospect to the south and west. It was the same as though the sea of land were, in reality, the ocean, and he, lost in an open boat, were scanning the waste through his glasses, looking for the smoke of a steamer, hull down, below the horizon. "Wonder," he muttered, "if they're working on Four this morning?"

At length, he murmured an "Ah" of satisfaction. Far to the south into the white sheen of sky, immediately over the horizon, he made out a faint smudge—the harvester beyond doubt.

Thither S. Behrman turned his horse's head. It was all of an hour's drive over the uneven ground and through the crackling stubble, but at length he reached the harvester. He found, however, that it had been halted. The sack sewers, together with the header-man, were stretched on the ground in the shade of the machine, while the engineer and separator-man were pottering about a portion of the works.

"What's the matter, Billy?" demanded S. Behrman reining up.

The engineer turned about.

"The grain is heavy in here. We thought we'd better increase the speed of the cup-carrier, and pulled up to put in a smaller sprocket."

S. Behrman nodded to say that was all right, and added a question.

"How is she going?"

"Anywheres from twenty-five to thirty sacks to the acre right along here; nothing the matter with THAT I guess."

"Nothing in the world, Bill."

One of the sack sewers interposed:

"For the last half hour we've been throwing off three bags to the minute."

"That's good, that's good."

It was more than good; it was "bonanza," and all that division of the great ranch was thick with just such wonderful wheat. Never had Los Muertos been more generous, never a season more successful. S. Behrman drew a long breath of satisfaction. He knew just how great was his share in the lands which had just been absorbed by the corporation he served, just how many thousands of bushels of this marvellous crop were his property. Through all these years of confusion, bickerings, open hostility and, at last, actual warfare he had waited, nursing his patience, calm with the firm assurance of ultimate success. The end, at length, had come; he had entered into his reward and saw himself at last installed in the place he had so long, so silently coveted; saw himself chief of a principality, the Master of the Wheat.

The sprocket adjusted, the engineer called up the gang and the men took their places. The fireman stoked vigorously, the two sack sewers resumed their posts on the sacking platform, putting on the goggles that kept the chaff from their eyes. The separator-man and header-man gripped their levers.

The harvester, shooting a column of thick smoke straight upward, vibrating to the top of the stack, hissed, clanked, and lurched forward. Instantly, motion sprang to life in all its component parts; the header knives, cutting a thirty-six foot swath, gnashed like teeth; beltings slid and moved like smooth flowing streams; the separator whirred, the agitator jarred and crashed; cylinders, augers, fans, seeders and elevators, drapers and chaff-carriers clattered, rumbled, buzzed, and clanged. The steam hissed and rasped; the ground reverberated a hollow note, and the thousands upon thousands of wheat stalks sliced and slashed in the clashing shears of the header, rattled like dry rushes in a hurricane, as they fell inward, and were caught up by an endless belt, to disappear into the bowels of the vast brute that devoured them.

It was that and no less. It was the feeding of some prodigious monster, insatiable, with iron teeth, gnashing and threshing into the fields of standing wheat; devouring always, never glutted, never satiated, swallowing an entire harvest, snarling and slobbering in a welter of warm vapour, acrid smoke, and blinding, pungent clouds of chaff. It moved belly-deep in the standing grain, a hippopotamus, half-mired in river ooze, gorging rushes, snorting, sweating; a dinosaur wallowing through thick, hot grasses, floundering there, crouching, grovelling there as its vast jaws crushed and tore, and its enormous gullet swallowed, incessant, ravenous, and inordinate.

S. Behrman, very much amused, changed places with one of the sack sewers, allowing him to hold his horse while he mounted the sacking platform and took his place. The trepidation and jostling of the machine shook him till his teeth chattered in his head. His ears were shocked and assaulted by a myriad-tongued clamour, clashing steel, straining belts, jarring woodwork, while the impalpable chaff powder from the separators settled like dust in his hair, his ears, eyes, and mouth.

Directly in front of where he sat on the platform was the chute from the cleaner, and from this into the mouth of a half-full sack spouted an unending gush of grain, winnowed, cleaned, threshed, ready for the mill.

The pour from the chute of the cleaner had for S. Behrman an immense satisfaction. Without an instant's pause, a thick rivulet of wheat rolled and dashed tumultuous into the sack. In half a minute—sometimes in twenty seconds—the sack was full, was passed over to the second sewer, the mouth reeved up, and the sack dumped out upon the ground, to be picked up by the wagons and hauled to the railroad.

S. Behrman, hypnotised, sat watching that river of grain. All that shrieking, bellowing machinery, all that gigantic organism, all the months of labour, the ploughing, the planting, the prayers for rain, the years of preparation, the heartaches, the anxiety, the foresight, all the whole business of the ranch, the work of horses, of steam, of men and boys, looked to this spot—the grain chute from the harvester into the sacks. Its volume was the index of failure or success, of riches or poverty. And at this point, the labour of the rancher ended. Here, at the lip of the chute, he parted company with his grain, and from here the wheat streamed forth to feed the world. The yawning mouths of the sacks might well stand for the unnumbered mouths of the People, all agape for food; and here, into these sacks, at first so lean, so flaccid, attenuated like starved stomachs, rushed the living stream of food, insistent, interminable, filling the empty, fattening the shrivelled, making it sleek and heavy and solid.

Half an hour later, the harvester stopped again. The men on the sacking platform had used up all the sacks. But S. Behrman's foreman, a new man on Los Muertos, put in an appearance with the report that the wagon bringing a fresh supply was approaching.

"How is the grain elevator at Port Costa getting on, sir?"

"Finished," replied S. Behrman.

The new master of Los Muertos had decided upon accumulating his grain in bulk in a great elevator at the tide-water port, where the grain ships for Liverpool and the East took on their cargoes. To this end, he had bought and greatly enlarged a building at Port Costa, that was already in use for that purpose, and to this elevator all the crop of Los Muertos was to be carried. The P. and S. W. made S. Behrman a special rate.

"By the way," said S. Behrman to his superintendent, "we're in luck. Fallon's buyer was in Bonneville yesterday. He's buying for Fallon and for Holt, too. I happened to run into him, and I've sold a ship load."

"A ship load!"

"Of Los Muertos wheat. He's acting for some Indian Famine Relief Committee—lot of women people up in the city—and wanted a whole cargo. I made a deal with him. There's about fifty thousand tons of disengaged shipping in San Francisco Bay right now, and ships are fighting for charters. I wired McKissick and got a long distance telephone from him this morning. He got me a barque, the 'Swanhilda.' She'll dock day after to-morrow, and begin loading."

"Hadn't I better take a run up," observed the superintendent, "and keep an eye on things?"

"No," answered S. Behrman, "I want you to stop down here, and see that those carpenters hustle the work in the ranch house. Derrick will be out by then. You see this deal is peculiar. I'm not selling to any middle-man—not to Fallon's buyer. He only put me on to the thing. I'm acting direct with these women people, and I've got to have some hand in shipping this stuff myself. But I made my selling figure cover the price of a charter. It's a queer, mixed-up deal, and I don't fancy it much, but there's boodle in it. I'll go to Port Costa myself."

A little later on in the day, when S. Behrman had satisfied himself that his harvesting was going forward favourably, he reentered his buggy and driving to the County Road turned southward towards the Los Muertos ranch house. He had not gone far, however, before he became aware of a familiar figure on horse-back, jogging slowly along ahead of him. He recognised Presley; he shook the reins over his horse's back and very soon ranging up by the side of the young man passed the time of day with him.

"Well, what brings you down here again, Mr. Presley?" he observed. "I thought we had seen the last of you."

"I came down to say good-bye to my friends," answered Presley shortly.

"Going away?"

"Yes—to India."

"Well, upon my word. For your health, hey?"

"Yes."

"You LOOK knocked up," asserted the other. "By the way," he added, "I suppose you've heard the news?"

Presley shrank a little. Of late the reports of disasters had followed so swiftly upon one another that he had begun to tremble and to quail at every unexpected bit of information.

"What news do you mean?" he asked.

"About Dyke. He has been convicted. The judge sentenced him for life."

For life! Riding on by the side of this man through the ranches by the County Road, Presley repeated these words to himself till the full effect of them burst at last upon him.

Jailed for life! No outlook. No hope for the future. Day after day, year after year, to tread the rounds of the same gloomy monotony. He saw the grey stone walls, the iron doors; the flagging of the "yard" bare of grass or trees—the cell, narrow, bald, cheerless; the prison garb, the prison fare, and round all the grim granite of insuperable barriers, shutting out the world, shutting in the man with outcasts, with the pariah dogs of society, thieves, murderers, men below the beasts, lost to all decency, drugged with opium, utter reprobates. To this, Dyke had been brought, Dyke, than whom no man had been more honest, more courageous, more jovial.

This was the end of him, a prison; this was his final estate, a criminal.

Presley found an excuse for riding on, leaving S. Behrman behind him. He did not stop at Caraher's saloon, for the heat of his rage had long since begun to cool, and dispassionately, he saw things in their true light. For all the tragedy of his wife's death, Caraher was none the less an evil influence among the ranchers, an influence that worked only to the inciting of crime. Unwilling to venture himself, to risk his own life, the anarchist saloon-keeper had goaded Dyke and Presley both to murder; a bad man, a plague spot in the world of the ranchers, poisoning the farmers' bodies with alcohol and their minds with discontent.

At last, Presley arrived at the ranch house of Los Muertos. The place was silent; the grass on the lawn was half dead and over a foot high; the beginnings of weeds showed here and there in the driveway. He tied his horse to a ring in the trunk of one of the larger eucalyptus trees and entered the house.

Mrs. Derrick met him in the dining-room. The old look of uneasiness, almost of terror, had gone from her wide-open brown eyes. There was in them instead, the expression of one to whom a contingency, long dreaded, has arrived and passed. The stolidity of a settled grief, of an irreparable calamity, of a despair from which there was no escape was in her look, her manner, her voice. She was listless, apathetic, calm with the calmness of a woman who knows she can suffer no further.

"We are going away," she told Presley, as the two sat down at opposite ends of the dining table. "Just Magnus and myself—all there is left of us. There is very little money left; Magnus can hardly take care of himself, to say nothing of me. I must look after him now. We are going to Marysville."

"Why there?"

"You see," she explained, "it happens that my old place is vacant in the Seminary there. I am going back to teach—literature." She smiled wearily. "It is beginning all over again, isn't it? Only there is nothing to look forward to now. Magnus is an old man already, and I must take care of him."

"He will go with you, then," Presley said, "that will be some comfort to you at least."

"I don't know," she said slowly, "you have not seen Magnus lately."

"Is he—how do you mean? Isn't he any better?"

"Would you like to see him? He is in the office. You can go right in."

Presley rose. He hesitated a moment, then:

"Mrs. Annixter," he asked, "Hilma—is she still with you? I should like to see her before I go."

"Go in and see Magnus," said Mrs. Derrick. "I will tell her you are here."

Presley stepped across the stone-paved hallway with the glass roof, and after knocking three times at the office door pushed it open and entered.

Magnus sat in the chair before the desk and did not look up as Presley entered. He had the appearance of a man nearer eighty than sixty. All the old-time erectness was broken and bent. It was as though the muscles that once had held the back rigid, the chin high, had softened and stretched. A certain fatness, the obesity of inertia, hung heavy around the hips and abdomen, the eye was watery and vague, the cheeks and chin unshaven and unkempt, the grey hair had lost its forward curl towards the temples and hung thin and ragged around the ears. The hawk-like nose seemed hooked to meet the chin; the lips were slack, the mouth half-opened.

Where once the Governor had been a model of neatness in his dress, the frock coat buttoned, the linen clean, he now sat in his shirt sleeves, the waistcoat open and showing the soiled shirt. His hands were stained with ink, and these, the only members of his body that yet appeared to retain their activity, were busy with a great pile of papers,—oblong, legal documents, that littered the table before him. Without a moment's cessation, these hands of the Governor's came and went among the papers, deft, nimble, dexterous.

Magnus was sorting papers. From the heap upon his left hand he selected a document, opened it, glanced over it, then tied it carefully, and laid it away upon a second pile on his right hand. When all the papers were in one pile, he reversed the process, taking from his right hand to place upon his left, then back from left to right again, then once more from right to left. He spoke no word, he sat absolutely still, even his eyes did not move, only his hands, swift, nervous, agitated, seemed alive.

"Why, how are you, Governor?" said Presley, coming forward. Magnus turned slowly about and looked at him and at the hand in which he shook his own.

"Ah," he said at length, "Presley...yes."

Then his glance fell, and he looked aimlessly about upon the floor. "I've come to say good-bye, Governor," continued Presley, "I'm going away."

"Going away...yes, why it's Presley. Good-day, Presley."

"Good-day, Governor. I'm going away. I've come to say good-bye."

"Good-bye?" Magnus bent his brows, "what are you saying good-bye for?"

"I'm going away, sir."

The Governor did not answer. Staring at the ledge of the desk, he seemed lost in thought. There was a long silence. Then, at length, Presley said:

"How are you getting on, Governor?"

Magnus looked up slowly.

"Why it's Presley," he said. "How do you do, Presley."

"Are you getting on all right, sir?"

"Yes," said Magnus after a while, "yes, all right. I am going away. I've come to say good-bye. No—" He interrupted himself with a deprecatory smile, "YOU said THAT, didn't you?"

"Well, you are going away, too, your wife tells me."

"Yes, I'm going away. I can't stay on..." he hesitated a long time, groping for the right word, "I can't stay on—on—what's the name of this place?"

"Los Muertos," put in Presley.

"No, it isn't. Yes, it is, too, that's right, Los Muertos. I don't know where my memory has gone to of late."

"Well, I hope you will be better soon, Governor."

As Presley spoke the words, S. Behrman entered the room, and the Governor sprang up with unexpected agility and stood against the wall, drawing one long breath after another, watching the railroad agent with intent eyes.

S. Behrman saluted both men affably and sat down near the desk, drawing the links of his heavy watch chain through his fat fingers.

"There wasn't anybody outside when I knocked, but I heard your voice in here, Governor, so I came right in. I wanted to ask you, Governor, if my carpenters can begin work in here day after to-morrow. I want to take down that partition there, and throw this room and the next into one. I guess that will be O. K., won't it? You'll be out of here by then, won't you?"

There was no vagueness about Magnus's speech or manner now. There was that same alertness in his demeanour that one sees in a tamed lion in the presence of its trainer.

"Yes, yes," he said quickly, "you can send your men here. I will be gone by to-morrow."

"I don't want to seem to hurry you, Governor."

"No, you will not hurry me. I am ready to go now."

"Anything I can do for you, Governor?"

"Nothing."

"Yes, there is, Governor," insisted S. Behrman. "I think now that all is over we ought to be good friends. I think I can do something for you. We still want an assistant in the local freight manager's office. Now, what do you say to having a try at it? There's a salary of fifty a month goes with it. I guess you must be in need of money now, and there's always the wife to support; what do you say? Will you try the place?"

Presley could only stare at the man in speechless wonder. What was he driving at? What reason was there back of this new move, and why should it be made thus openly and in his hearing? An explanation occurred to him. Was this merely a pleasantry on the part of S. Behrman, a way of enjoying to the full his triumph; was he testing the completeness of his victory, trying to see just how far he could go, how far beneath his feet he could push his old-time enemy?

"What do you say?" he repeated. "Will you try the place?"

"You—you INSIST?" inquired the Governor.

"Oh, I'm not insisting on anything," cried S. Behrman. "I'm offering you a place, that's all. Will you take it?"

"Yes, yes, I'll take it."

"You'll come over to our side?"

"Yes, I'll come over."

"You'll have to turn 'railroad,' understand?"

"I'll turn railroad."

"Guess there may be times when you'll have to take orders from me."

"I'll take orders from you."

"You'll have to be loyal to railroad, you know. No funny business."

"I'll be loyal to the railroad."

"You would like the place then?"

"Yes."

S. Behrman turned from Magnus, who at once resumed his seat and began again to sort his papers.

"Well, Presley," said the railroad agent: "I guess I won't see you again."

"I hope not," answered the other.

"Tut, tut, Presley, you know you can't make me angry."

He put on his hat of varnished straw and wiped his fat forehead with his handkerchief. Of late, he had grown fatter than ever, and the linen vest, stamped with a multitude of interlocked horseshoes, strained tight its imitation pearl buttons across the great protuberant stomach.

Presley looked at the man a moment before replying.

But a few weeks ago he could not thus have faced the great enemy of the farmers without a gust of blind rage blowing tempestuous through all his bones. Now, however, he found to his surprise that his fury had lapsed to a profound contempt, in which there was bitterness, but no truculence. He was tired, tired to death of the whole business.

"Yes," he answered deliberately, "I am going away. You have ruined this place for me. I couldn't live here where I should have to see you, or the results of what you have done, whenever I stirred out of doors."

"Nonsense, Presley," answered the other, refusing to become angry. "That's foolishness, that kind of talk; though, of course, I understand how you feel. I guess it was you, wasn't it, who threw that bomb into my house?"

"It was."

"Well, that don't show any common sense, Presley," returned S. Behrman with perfect aplomb. "What could you have gained by killing me?"

"Not so much probably as you have gained by killing Harran and Annixter. But that's all passed now. You're safe from me." The strangeness of this talk, the oddity of the situation burst upon him and he laughed aloud. "It don't seem as though you could be brought to book, S. Behrman, by anybody, or by any means, does it? They can't get at you through the courts,—the law can't get you, Dyke's pistol missed fire for just your benefit, and you even escaped Caraher's six inches of plugged gas pipe. Just what are we going to do with you?"

"Best give it up, Pres, my boy," returned the other. "I guess there ain't anything can touch me. Well, Magnus," he said, turning once more to the Governor. "Well, I'll think over what you say, and let you know if I can get the place for you in a day or two. You see," he added, "you're getting pretty old, Magnus Derrick."

Presley flung himself from the room, unable any longer to witness the depths into which Magnus had fallen. What other scenes of degradation were enacted in that room, how much further S. Behrman carried the humiliation, he did not know. He suddenly felt that the air of the office was choking him.

He hurried up to what once had been his own room. On his way he could not but note that much of the house was in disarray, a great packing-up was in progress; trunks, half-full, stood in the hallways, crates and cases in a litter of straw encumbered the rooms. The servants came and went with armfuls of books, ornaments, articles of clothing.

Presley took from his room only a few manuscripts and note-books, and a small valise full of his personal effects; at the doorway he paused and, holding the knob of the door in his hand, looked back into the room a very long time.

He descended to the lower floor and entered the dining-room. Mrs. Derrick had disappeared. Presley stood for a long moment in front of the fireplace, looking about the room, remembering the scenes that he had witnessed there—the conference when Osterman had first suggested the fight for Railroad Commissioner and then later the attack on Lyman Derrick and the sudden revelation of that inconceivable treachery. But as he stood considering these things a door to his right opened and Hilma entered the room.

Presley came forward, holding out his hand, all unable to believe his eyes. It was a woman, grave, dignified, composed, who advanced to meet him. Hilma was dressed in black, the cut and fashion of the gown severe, almost monastic. All the little feminine and contradictory daintinesses were nowhere to be seen. Her statuesque calm evenness of contour yet remained, but it was the calmness of great sorrow, of infinite resignation. Beautiful she still remained, but she was older. The seriousness of one who has gained the knowledge of the world—knowledge of its evil—seemed to envelope her. The calm gravity of a great suffering past, but not forgotten, sat upon her. Not yet twenty-one, she exhibited the demeanour of a woman of forty.

The one-time amplitude of her figure, the fulness of hip and shoulder, the great deep swell from waist to throat were gone. She had grown thinner and, in consequence, seemed unusually, almost unnaturally tall. Her neck was slender, the outline of her full lips and round chin was a little sharp; her arms, those wonderful, beautiful arms of hers, were a little shrunken. But her eyes were as wide open as always, rimmed as ever by the thin, intensely black line of the lashes and her brown, fragrant hair was still thick, still, at times, glittered and coruscated in the sun. When she spoke, it was with the old-time velvety huskiness of voice that Annixter had learned to love so well.

"Oh, it is you," she said, giving him her hand. "You were good to want to see me before you left. I hear that you are going away."

She sat down upon the sofa.

"Yes," Presley answered, drawing a chair near to her, "yes, I felt I could not stay—down here any longer. I am going to take a long ocean voyage. My ship sails in a few days. But you, Mrs. Annixter, what are you going to do? Is there any way I can serve you?"

"No," she answered, "nothing. Papa is doing well. We are living here now."

"You are well?"

She made a little helpless gesture with both her hands, smiling very sadly.

"As you see," she answered.

As he talked, Presley was looking at her intently. Her dignity was a new element in her character and the certain slender effect of her figure, emphasised now by the long folds of the black gown she wore, carried it almost superbly. She conveyed something of the impression of a queen in exile. But she had lost none of her womanliness; rather, the contrary. Adversity had softened her, as well as deepened her. Presley saw that very clearly. Hilma had arrived now at her perfect maturity; she had known great love and she had known great grief, and the woman that had awakened in her with her affection for Annixter had been strengthened and infinitely ennobled by his death. What if things had been different? Thus, as he conversed with her, Presley found himself wondering. Her sweetness, her beautiful gentleness, and tenderness were almost like palpable presences. It was almost as if a caress had been laid softly upon his cheek, as if a gentle hand closed upon his. Here, he knew, was sympathy; here, he knew, was an infinite capacity for love.

Then suddenly all the tired heart of him went out towards her. A longing to give the best that was in him to the memory of her, to be strong and noble because of her, to reshape his purposeless, half-wasted life with her nobility and purity and gentleness for his inspiration leaped all at once within him, leaped and stood firm, hardening to a resolve stronger than any he had ever known.

For an instant he told himself that the suddenness of this new emotion must be evidence of its insincerity. He was perfectly well aware that his impulses were abrupt and of short duration. But he knew that this was not sudden. Without realising it, he had been from the first drawn to Hilma, and all through these last terrible days, since the time he had seen her at Los Muertos, just after the battle at the ditch, she had obtruded continually upon his thoughts. The sight of her to-day, more beautiful than ever, quiet, strong, reserved, had only brought matters to a culmination.

"Are you," he asked her, "are you so unhappy, Hilma, that you can look forward to no more brightness in your life?"

"Unless I could forget—forget my husband," she answered, "how can I be happy? I would rather be unhappy in remembering him than happy in forgetting him. He was my whole world, literally and truly. Nothing seemed to count before I knew him, and nothing can count for me now, after I have lost him."

"You think now," he answered, "that in being happy again you would be disloyal to him. But you will find after a while—years from now—that it need not be so. The part of you that belonged to your husband can always keep him sacred, that part of you belongs to him and he to it. But you are young; you have all your life to live yet. Your sorrow need not be a burden to you. If you consider it as you should—as you WILL some day, believe me—it will only be a great help to you. It will make you more noble, a truer woman, more generous."

"I think I see," she answered, "and I never thought about it in that light before."

"I want to help you," he answered, "as you have helped me. I want to be your friend, and above all things I do not want to see your life wasted. I am going away and it is quite possible I shall never see you again, but you will always be a help to me."

"I do not understand," she answered, "but I know you mean to be very, very kind to me. Yes, I hope when you come back—if you ever do—you will still be that. I do not know why you should want to be so kind, unless—yes, of course—you were my husband's dearest friend."

They talked a little longer, and at length Presley rose.

"I cannot bring myself to see Mrs. Derrick again," he said. "It would only serve to make her very unhappy. Will you explain that to her? I think she will understand."

"Yes," answered Hilma. "Yes, I will."

There was a pause. There seemed to be nothing more for either of them to say. Presley held out his hand.

"Good-bye," she said, as she gave him hers.

He carried it to his lips.

"Good-bye," he answered. "Good-bye and may God bless you."

He turned away abruptly and left the room. But as he was quietly making his way out of the house, hoping to get to his horse unobserved, he came suddenly upon Mrs. Dyke and Sidney on the porch of the house. He had forgotten that since the affair at the ditch, Los Muertos had been a home to the engineer's mother and daughter.

"And you, Mrs. Dyke," he asked as he took her hand, "in this break-up of everything, where do you go?"

"To the city," she answered, "to San Francisco. I have a sister there who will look after the little tad."

"But you, how about yourself, Mrs. Dyke?"

She answered him in a quiet voice, monotonous, expressionless:

"I am going to die very soon, Mr. Presley. There is no reason why I should live any longer. My son is in prison for life, everything is over for me, and I am tired, worn out."

"You mustn't talk like that, Mrs. Dyke," protested Presley, "nonsense; you will live long enough to see the little tad married." He tried to be cheerful. But he knew his words lacked the ring of conviction. Death already overshadowed the face of the engineer's mother. He felt that she spoke the truth, and as he stood there speaking to her for the last time, his arm about little Sidney's shoulder, he knew that he was seeing the beginnings of the wreck of another family and that, like Hilda Hooven, another baby girl was to be started in life, through no fault of hers, fearfully handicapped, weighed down at the threshold of existence with a load of disgrace. Hilda Hooven and Sidney Dyke, what was to be their histories? the one, sister of an outcast; the other, daughter of a convict. And he thought of that other young girl, the little Honora Gerard, the heiress of millions, petted, loved, receiving adulation from all who came near to her, whose only care was to choose from among the multitude of pleasures that the world hastened to present to her consideration.

"Good-bye," he said, holding out his hand.

"Good-bye."

"Good-bye, Sidney."

He kissed the little girl, clasped Mrs. Dyke's hand a moment with his; then, slinging his satchel about his shoulders by the long strap with which it was provided, left the house, and mounting his horse rode away from Los Muertos never to return.

Presley came out upon the County Road. At a little distance to his left he could see the group of buildings where once Broderson had lived. These were being remodelled, at length, to suit the larger demands of the New Agriculture. A strange man came out by the road gate; no doubt, the new proprietor. Presley turned away, hurrying northwards along the County Road by the mammoth watering-tank and the long wind-break of poplars.

He came to Caraher's place. There was no change here. The saloon had weathered the storm, indispensable to the new as well as to the old regime. The same dusty buggies and buckboards were tied under the shed, and as Presley hurried by he could distinguish Caraher's voice, loud as ever, still proclaiming his creed of annihilation.

Bonneville Presley avoided. He had no associations with the town. He turned aside from the road, and crossing the northwest corner of Los Muertos and the line of the railroad, turned back along the Upper Road till he came to the Long Trestle and Annixter's,—Silence, desolation, abandonment.

A vast stillness, profound, unbroken, brooded low over all the place. No living thing stirred. The rusted wind-mill on the skeleton-like tower of the artesian well was motionless; the great barn empty; the windows of the ranch house, cook house, and dairy boarded up. Nailed upon a tree near the broken gateway was a board, white painted, with stencilled letters, bearing the inscription:

"Warning. ALL PERSONS FOUND TRESPASSING ON THESE PREMISES WILL BE PROSECUTED TO THE FULLEST EXTENT OF THE LAW. By order P. and S. W. R. R."

As he had planned, Presley reached the hills by the head waters of Broderson's Creek late in the afternoon. Toilfully he climbed them, reached the highest crest, and turning about, looked long and for the last time at all the reach of the valley unrolled beneath him. The land of the ranches opened out forever and forever under the stimulus of that measureless range of vision. The whole gigantic sweep of the San Joaquin expanded Titanic before the eye of the mind, flagellated with heat, quivering and shimmering under the sun's red eye. It was the season after the harvest, and the great earth, the mother, after its period of reproduction, its pains of labour, delivered of the fruit of its loins, slept the sleep of exhaustion in the infinite repose of the colossus, benignant, eternal, strong, the nourisher of nations, the feeder of an entire world.

And as Presley looked there came to him strong and true the sense and the significance of all the enigma of growth. He seemed for one instant to touch the explanation of existence. Men were nothings, mere animalculae, mere ephemerides that fluttered and fell and were forgotten between dawn and dusk. Vanamee had said there was no death. But for one second Presley could go one step further. Men were naught, death was naught, life was naught; FORCE only existed—FORCE that brought men into the world, FORCE that crowded them out of it to make way for the succeeding generation, FORCE that made the wheat grow, FORCE that garnered it from the soil to give place to the succeeding crop.

It was the mystery of creation, the stupendous miracle of recreation; the vast rhythm of the seasons, measured, alternative, the sun and the stars keeping time as the eternal symphony of reproduction swung in its tremendous cadences like the colossal pendulum of an almighty machine—primordial energy flung out from the hand of the Lord God himself, immortal, calm, infinitely strong.

But as he stood thus looking down upon the great valley he was aware of the figure of a man, far in the distance, moving steadily towards the Mission of San Juan. The man was hardly more than a dot, but there was something unmistakably familiar in his gait; and besides this, Presley could fancy that he was hatless. He touched his pony with his spur. The man was Vanamee beyond all doubt, and a little later Presley, descending the maze of cow-paths and cattle-trails that led down towards the Broderson Creek, overtook his friend.

Instantly Presley was aware of an immense change. Vanamee's face was still that of an ascetic, still glowed with the rarefied intelligence of a young seer, a half-inspired shepherd-prophet of Hebraic legends; but the shadow of that great sadness which for so long had brooded over him was gone; the grief that once he had fancied deathless was, indeed, dead, or rather swallowed up in a victorious joy that radiated like sunlight at dawn from the deep-set eyes, and the hollow, swarthy cheeks. They talked together till nearly sundown, but to Presley's questions as to the reasons for Vanamee's happiness, the other would say nothing. Once only he allowed himself to touch upon the subject.

"Death and grief are little things," he said. "They are transient. Life must be before death, and joy before grief. Else there are no such things as death or grief. These are only negatives. Life is positive. Death is only the absence of life, just as night is only the absence of day, and if this is so, there is no such thing as death. There is only life, and the suppression of life, that we, foolishly, say is death. 'Suppression,' I say, not extinction. I do not say that life returns. Life never departs. Life simply IS. For certain seasons, it is hidden in the dark, but is that death, extinction, annihilation? I take it, thank God, that it is not. Does the grain of wheat, hidden for certain seasons in the dark, die? The grain we think is dead RESUMES AGAIN; but how? Not as one grain, but as twenty. So all life. Death is only real for all the detritus of the world, for all the sorrow, for all the injustice, for all the grief. Presley, the good never dies; evil dies, cruelty, oppression, selfishness, greed—these die; but nobility, but love, but sacrifice, but generosity, but truth, thank God for it, small as they are, difficult as it is to discover them—these live forever, these are eternal. You are all broken, all cast down by what you have seen in this valley, this hopeless struggle, this apparently hopeless despair. Well, the end is not yet. What is it that remains after all is over, after the dead are buried and the hearts are broken? Look at it all from the vast height of humanity—'the greatest good to the greatest numbers.' What remains? Men perish, men are corrupted, hearts are rent asunder, but what remains untouched, unassailable, undefiled? Try to find that, not only in this, but in every crisis of the world's life, and you will find, if your view be large enough, that it is not evil, but good, that in the end remains."

There was a long pause. Presley, his mind full of new thoughts, held his peace, and Vanamee added at length:

"I believed Angele dead. I wept over her grave; mourned for her as dead in corruption. She has come back to me, more beautiful than ever. Do not ask me any further. To put this story, this idyl, into words, would, for me, be a profanation. This must suffice you. Angele has returned to me, and I am happy. Adios."

He rose suddenly. The friends clasped each other's hands.

"We shall probably never meet again," said Vanamee; "but if these are the last words I ever speak to you, listen to them, and remember them, because I know I speak the truth. Evil is short-lived. Never judge of the whole round of life by the mere segment you can see. The whole is, in the end, perfect."

Abruptly he took himself away. He was gone. Presley, alone, thoughtful, his hands clasped behind him, passed on through the ranches—here teeming with ripened wheat—his face set from them forever.

Not so Vanamee. For hours he roamed the countryside, now through the deserted cluster of buildings that had once been Annixter's home; now through the rustling and, as yet, uncut wheat of Quien Sabe! now treading the slopes of the hills far to the north, and again following the winding courses of the streams. Thus he spent the night.

At length, the day broke, resplendent, cloudless. The night was passed. There was all the sparkle and effervescence of joy in the crystal sunlight as the dawn expanded roseate, and at length flamed dazzling to the zenith when the sun moved over the edge of the world and looked down upon all the earth like the eye of God the Father.

At the moment, Vanamee stood breast-deep in the wheat in a solitary corner of the Quien Sabe rancho. He turned eastward, facing the celestial glory of the day and sent his voiceless call far from him across the golden grain out towards the little valley of flowers.

Swiftly the answer came. It advanced to meet him. The flowers of the Seed ranch were gone, dried and parched by the summer's sun, shedding their seed by handfuls to be sown again and blossom yet another time. The Seed ranch was no longer royal with colour. The roses, the lilies, the carnations, the hyacinths, the poppies, the violets, the mignonette, all these had vanished, the little valley was without colour; where once it had exhaled the most delicious perfume, it was now odourless. Under the blinding light of the day it stretched to its hillsides, bare, brown, unlovely. The romance of the place had vanished, but with it had vanished the Vision.

It was no longer a figment of his imagination, a creature of dreams that advanced to meet Vanamee. It was Reality—it was Angele in the flesh, vital, sane, material, who at last issued forth from the entrance of the little valley. Romance had vanished, but better than romance was here. Not a manifestation, not a dream, but her very self. The night was gone, but the sun had risen; the flowers had disappeared, but strong, vigorous, noble, the wheat had come.

In the wheat he waited for her. He saw her coming. She was simply dressed. No fanciful wreath of tube-roses was about her head now, no strange garment of red and gold enveloped her now. It was no longer an ephemeral illusion of the night, evanescent, mystic, but a simple country girl coming to meet her lover. The vision of the night had been beautiful, but what was it compared to this? Reality was better than Romance. The simple honesty of a loving, trusting heart was better than a legend of flowers, an hallucination of the moonlight. She came nearer. Bathed in sunlight, he saw her face to face, saw her hair hanging in two straight plaits on either side of her face, saw the enchanting fulness of her lips, the strange, balancing movement of her head upon her slender neck. But now she was no longer asleep. The wonderful eyes, violet blue, heavy-lidded, with their perplexing, oriental slant towards the temples, were wide open and fixed upon his.

From out the world of romance, out of the moonlight and the star sheen, out of the faint radiance of the lilies and the still air heavy with perfume, she had at last come to him. The moonlight, the flowers, and the dream were all vanished away. Angele was realised in the Wheat. She stood forth in the sunlight, a fact, and no longer a fancy.

He ran forward to meet her and she held out her arms to him. He caught her to him, and she, turning her face to his, kissed him on the mouth.

"I love you, I love you," she murmured.

Upon descending from his train at Port Costa, S. Behrman asked to be directed at once to where the bark "Swanhilda" was taking on grain. Though he had bought and greatly enlarged his new elevator at this port, he had never seen it. The work had been carried on through agents, S. Behrman having far too many and more pressing occupations to demand his presence and attention. Now, however, he was to see the concrete evidence of his success for the first time.

He picked his way across the railroad tracks to the line of warehouses that bordered the docks, numbered with enormous Roman numerals and full of grain in bags. The sight of these bags of grain put him in mind of the fact that among all the other shippers he was practically alone in his way of handling his wheat. They handled the grain in bags; he, however, preferred it in the bulk. Bags were sometimes four cents apiece, and he had decided to build his elevator and bulk his grain therein, rather than to incur this expense. Only a small part of his wheat—that on Number Three division—had been sacked. All the rest, practically two-thirds of the entire harvest of Los Muertos, now found itself warehoused in his enormous elevator at Port Costa.

To a certain degree it had been the desire of observing the working of his system of handling the wheat in bulk that had drawn S. Behrman to Port Costa. But the more powerful motive had been curiosity, not to say downright sentiment. So long had he planned for this day of triumph, so eagerly had he looked forward to it, that now, when it had come, he wished to enjoy it to its fullest extent, wished to miss no feature of the disposal of the crop. He had watched it harvested, he had watched it hauled to the railway, and now would watch it as it poured into the hold of the ship, would even watch the ship as she cleared and got under way.

He passed through the warehouses and came out upon the dock that ran parallel with the shore of the bay. A great quantity of shipping was in view, barques for the most part, Cape Horners, great, deep sea tramps, whose iron-shod forefeet had parted every ocean the world round from Rangoon to Rio Janeiro, and from Melbourne to Christiania. Some were still in the stream, loaded with wheat to the

Plimsoll mark, ready to depart with the next tide. But many others laid their great flanks alongside the docks and at that moment were being filled by derrick and crane with thousands upon thousands of bags of wheat. The scene was brisk; the cranes creaked and swung incessantly with a rattle of chains; stevedores and wharfingers toiled and perspired; boatswains and dock-masters shouted orders, drays rumbled, the water lapped at the piles; a group of sailors, painting the flanks of one of the great ships, raised an occasional chanty; the trade wind sang aeolian in the cordages, filling the air with the nimble taint of salt. All around were the noises of ships and the feel and flavor of the sea.

S. Behrman soon discovered his elevator. It was the largest structure discernible, and upon its red roof, in enormous white letters, was his own name. Thither, between piles of grain bags, halted drays, crates and boxes of merchandise, with an occasional pyramid of salmon cases, S. Behrman took his way. Cabled to the dock, close under his elevator, lay a great ship with lofty masts and great spars. Her stern was toward him as he approached, and upon it, in raised golden letters, he could read the words "Swanhilda–Liverpool."

He went aboard by a very steep gangway and found the mate on the quarter deck. S. Behrman introduced himself.

"Well," he added, "how are you getting on?"

"Very fairly, sir," returned the mate, who was an Englishman. "We'll have her all snugged down tight by this time, day after to-morrow. It's a great saving of time shunting the stuff in her like that, and three men can do the work of seven."

"I'll have a look 'round, I believe," returned S. Behrman.

"Right–oh," answered the mate with a nod.

S. Behrman went forward to the hatch that opened down into the vast hold of the ship. A great iron chute connected this hatch with the elevator, and through it was rushing a veritable cataract of wheat.

It came from some gigantic bin within the elevator itself, rushing down the confines of the chute to plunge into the roomy, gloomy interior of the hold with an incessant, metallic roar, persistent, steady, inevitable. No men were in sight. The place was deserted. No human agency seemed to be back of the movement of the wheat. Rather, the grain seemed impelled with a force of its own, a resistless, huge force, eager, vivid, impatient for the sea.

S. Behrman stood watching, his ears deafened with the roar of the hard grains against the metallic lining of the chute. He put his hand once into the rushing tide, and the contact rasped the flesh of his fingers and like an undertow drew his hand after it in its impetuous dash.

Cautiously he peered down into the hold. A musty odour rose to his nostrils, the vigorous, pungent aroma of the raw cereal. It was dark. He could see nothing; but all about and over the opening of the hatch the air was full of a fine, impalpable dust that blinded the eyes and choked the throat and nostrils.

As his eyes became used to the shadows of the cavern below him, he began to distinguish the grey mass of the wheat, a great expanse, almost liquid in its texture, which, as the cataract from above plunged into it, moved and shifted in long, slow eddies. As he stood there, this cataract on a sudden increased in volume. He turned about, casting his eyes upward toward the elevator to discover the cause. His foot caught in a coil of rope, and he fell headforemost into the hold.

The fall was a long one and he struck the surface of the wheat with the sodden impact of a bundle of damp clothes. For the moment he was stunned. All the breath was driven from his body. He could neither move nor cry out. But, by degrees, his wits steadied themselves and his breath returned to him. He looked about and above him. The daylight in the hold was dimmed and clouded by the thick, chaff-dust thrown off by the pour of grain, and even this dimness dwindled to twilight at a short distance from the opening of the hatch, while the remotest quarters were lost in impenetrable blackness. He got upon his feet only to find that he sunk ankle deep in the loose packed mass underfoot.

"Hell," he muttered, "here's a fix."

Directly underneath the chute, the wheat, as it poured in, raised itself in a conical mound, but from the sides of this mound it shunted away incessantly in thick layers, flowing in all directions with the nimbleness of water. Even as S. Behrman spoke, a wave of grain poured around his legs and rose rapidly to the level of his knees. He stepped quickly back. To stay near the chute would soon bury him to the waist.

No doubt, there was some other exit from the hold, some companion ladder that led up to the deck. He scuffled and waded across the wheat, groping in the dark with outstretched hands. With every inhalation he choked, filling his mouth and nostrils more with dust than with air. At times he could not breathe at all, but gagged and gasped, his lips distended. But search as he would he could find no outlet to the hold, no stairway, no companion ladder. Again and again, staggering along in the black darkness, he bruised his knuckles and forehead against the iron sides of the ship. He gave up the attempt to find any interior means of escape and returned laboriously to the space under the open hatchway. Already he could see that the level of the wheat was raised.

"God," he said, "this isn't going to do at all." He uttered a great shout. "Hello, on deck there, somebody. For God's sake."

The steady, metallic roar of the pouring wheat drowned out his voice. He could scarcely hear it himself above the rush of the cataract. Besides this, he found it impossible to stay under the hatch. The flying grains of wheat, spattering as they fell, stung his face like wind-driven particles of ice. It was a veritable torture; his hands smarted with it. Once he was all but blinded. Furthermore, the succeeding waves of wheat, rolling from the mound under the chute, beat him back, swirling and dashing against his legs and knees, mounting swiftly higher, carrying him off his feet.

Once more he retreated, drawing back from beneath the hatch. He stood still for a moment and shouted again. It was in vain. His voice returned upon him, unable to penetrate the thunder of the chute, and horrified, he discovered that so soon as he stood motionless upon the wheat, he sank into it. Before he knew it, he was knee-deep again, and a long swirl of grain sweeping outward from the ever-breaking, ever-reforming pyramid below the chute, poured around his thighs, immobolising him.

A frenzy of terror suddenly leaped to life within him. The horror of death, the Fear of The Trap, shook him like a dry reed. Shouting, he tore himself free of the wheat and once more scrambled and struggled towards the hatchway. He stumbled as he reached it and fell directly beneath the pour. Like a storm of small shot, mercilessly, pitilessly, the unnumbered multitude of hurtling grains flagellated and beat and tore his flesh. Blood streamed from his forehead and, thickening with the powder-like chaff-dust, blinded his eyes. He struggled to his feet once more. An avalanche from the cone of wheat buried him to his thighs. He was forced back and back and back, beating the air, falling, rising, howling for aid. He could no longer see; his eyes, crammed with dust, smarted as if transfixed with needles whenever he opened them. His mouth was full of the dust, his lips were dry with it; thirst tortured him, while his outcries choked and gagged in his rasped throat.

And all the while without stop, incessantly, inexorably, the wheat, as if moving with a force all its own, shot downward in a prolonged roar, persistent, steady, inevitable.

He retreated to a far corner of the hold and sat down with his back against the iron hull of the ship and tried to collect his thoughts, to calm himself. Surely there must be some way of escape; surely he was not to die like this, die in this dreadful substance that was neither solid nor fluid. What was he to do? How make himself heard?

But even as he thought about this, the cone under the chute broke again and sent a great layer of grain rippling and tumbling toward him. It reached him where he sat and buried his hand and one foot.

He sprang up trembling and made for another corner.

"By God," he cried, "by God, I must think of something pretty quick!"

Once more the level of the wheat rose and the grains began piling deeper about him. Once more he retreated. Once more he crawled staggering to the foot of the cataract, screaming till his ears sang and his eyeballs strained in their sockets, and once more the relentless tide drove him back.

Then began that terrible dance of death; the man dodging, doubling, squirming, hunted from one corner to another, the wheat slowly, inexorably flowing, rising, spreading to every angle, to every nook and cranny. It reached his middle. Furious and with bleeding hands and broken nails, he dug his way out to fall backward, all but exhausted, gasping for breath in the dust-thickened air. Roused again by the slow advance of the tide, he leaped up and stumbled away, blinded with the agony in his eyes, only to crash against the metal hull of the vessel. He turned about, the blood streaming from his face, and paused to collect his senses, and with a rush, another wave swirled about his ankles and knees. Exhaustion grew upon him. To stand still meant to sink; to lie or sit meant to be buried the quicker; and all this in the dark, all this in an air that could scarcely be breathed, all this while he fought an enemy that could not be gripped, toiling in a sea that could not be stayed.

Guided by the sound of the falling wheat, S. Behrman crawled on hands and knees toward the hatchway. Once more he raised his voice in a shout for help. His bleeding throat and raw, parched lips refused to utter but a wheezing moan. Once more he tried to look toward the one patch of faint light above him. His eye-lids, clogged with chaff, could no longer open. The Wheat poured about his waist as he raised himself upon his knees.

Reason fled. Deafened with the roar of the grain, blinded and made dumb with its chaff, he threw himself forward with clutching fingers, rolling upon his back, and lay there, moving feebly, the head rolling from side to side. The Wheat, leaping continuously from the chute, poured around him. It filled the pockets of the coat, it crept up the sleeves and trouser legs, it covered the great, protuberant stomach, it ran at last in rivulets into the distended, gasping mouth. It covered the face. Upon the surface of the Wheat, under the chute, nothing moved but the Wheat itself. There was no sign of life. Then, for an instant, the surface stirred. A hand, fat, with short fingers and swollen veins, reached up, clutching, then fell limp and prone. In another instant it was covered. In the hold of the "Swanhilda" there was no movement but the widening ripples that spread flowing from the ever-breaking, ever-reforming cone; no sound, but the rushing of the Wheat that continued to plunge incessantly from the iron chute in a prolonged roar, persistent, steady, inevitable.

CONCLUSION

The "Swanhilda" cast off from the docks at Port Costa two days after Presley had left Bonneville and the ranches and made her way up to San Francisco, anchoring in the stream off the City front. A few hours after her arrival, Presley, waiting at his club, received a despatch from Cedarquist to the effect that she would clear early the next morning and that he must be aboard of her before midnight.

He sent his trunks aboard and at once hurried to Cedarquist's office to say good-bye. He found the manufacturer in excellent spirits.

"What do you think of Lyman Derrick now, Presley?" he said, when Presley had sat down. "He's in the new politics with a vengeance, isn't he? And our own dear Railroad openly acknowledges him as their candidate. You've heard of his canvass."

"Yes, yes," answered Presley. "Well, he knows his business best."

But Cedarquist was full of another idea: his new venture—the organizing of a line of clipper wheat ships for Pacific and Oriental trade—was prospering.

"The 'Swanhilda' is the mother of the fleet, Pres. I had to buy HER, but the keel of her sister ship will be laid by the time she discharges at Calcutta. We'll carry our wheat into Asia yet. The Anglo-Saxon started from there at the beginning of everything and it's manifest destiny that he must circle the globe and fetch up where he began his march. You are up with procession, Pres, going to India this way in a wheat ship that flies American colours. By the way, do you know where the money is to come from to build the sister ship of the 'Swanhilda'? From the sale of the plant and scrap iron of the Atlas Works. Yes, I've given it up definitely, that business. The people here would not back me up. But I'm working off on this new line now. It may break me, but we'll try it on. You know the 'Million Dollar Fair' was formally opened yesterday. There is," he added with a wink, "a Midway Pleasance in connection with the thing. Mrs. Cedarquist and our friend Hartrath 'got up a subscription' to construct a figure of California—heroic size—out of dried apricots. I assure you," he remarked With prodigious gravity, "it is a real work of art and quite a 'feature' of the Fair. Well, good luck to you, Pres. Write to me from Honolulu, and bon voyage. My respects to the hungry Hindoo. Tell him 'we're coming, Father Abraham, a hundred thousand more.' Tell the men of the East to look out for the men of the West. The irrepressible Yank is knocking at the doors of their temples and he will want to sell 'em carpet-sweepers for their harems and electric light plants for their temple shrines. Good-bye to you."

"Good-bye, sir."

"Get fat yourself while you're about it, Presley," he observed, as the two stood up and shook hands.

"There shouldn't be any lack of food on a wheat ship. Bread enough, surely."

"Little monotonous, though. 'Man cannot live by bread alone.' Well, you're really off. Good-bye."

"Good-bye, sir."

And as Presley issued from the building and stepped out into the street, he was abruptly aware of a great wagon shrouded in white cloth, inside of which a bass drum was being furiously beaten. On the cloth, in great letters, were the words:

"Vote for Lyman Derrick, Regular Republican Nominee for Governor of California."

The "Swanhilda" lifted and rolled slowly, majestically on the ground swell of the Pacific, the water hissing and boiling under her forefoot, her cordage vibrating and droning in the steady rush of the trade winds. It was drawing towards evening and her lights had just been set. The master passed Presley, who was leaning over the rail smoking a cigarette, and paused long enough to remark:

"The land yonder, if you can make it out, is Point Gordo, and if you were to draw a line from our position now through that point and carry it on about a hundred miles further, it would just about cross Tulare County not very far from where you used to live."

"I see," answered Presley, "I see. Thanks. I am glad to know that."

The master passed on, and Presley, going up to the quarter deck, looked long and earnestly at the faint line of mountains that showed vague and bluish above the waste of tumbling water.

Those were the mountains of the Coast range and beyond them was what once had been his home. Bonneville was there, and Guadalajara and Los Muertos and Quien Sabe, the Mission of San Juan, the Seed ranch, Annixter's desolated home and Dyke's ruined hop-fields.

Well, it was all over now, that terrible drama through which he had lived. Already it was far distant from him; but once again it rose in his memory, portentous, sombre, ineffaceable. He passed it all in review from the day of his first meeting with Vanamee to the day of his parting with Hilma. He saw it all—the great sweep of country opening to view from the summit of the hills at the head waters of Broderson's Creek; the barn dance at Annixter's, the harness room with its jam of furious men; the quiet garden of the Mission; Dyke's house, his flight upon the engine, his brave fight in the chaparral; Lyman Derrick at bay in the dining-room of the ranch house; the rabbit drive; the fight at the irrigating ditch, the shouting mob in the Bonneville Opera House. The drama was over. The fight of Ranch and Railroad had been wrought out to its dreadful close. It was true, as Shelgrim had said, that forces rather than men had locked horns in that struggle, but for all that the men of the Ranch and not the men of the Railroad had suffered. Into the prosperous valley, into the quiet community of farmers, that galloping monster, that terror of steel and steam had burst, shooting athwart the horizons, flinging the echo of its thunder over all the ranches of the valley, leaving blood and destruction in its path.

Yes, the Railroad had prevailed. The ranches had been seized in the tentacles of the octopus; the iniquitous burden of extortionate freight rates had been imposed like a yoke of iron. The monster had killed Harran, had killed Osterman, had killed Broderson, had killed Hooven. It had beggared Magnus and had driven him to a state of semi-insanity after he had wrecked his honour in the vain attempt to do evil that good might come. It had enticed Lyman into its toils to pluck from him his manhood and his honesty, corrupting him and poisoning him beyond redemption; it had hounded Dyke from his legitimate employment and had made of him a highwayman and criminal. It had cast forth Mrs. Hooven to starve to death upon the City streets. It had driven Minna to prostitution. It had slain Annixter at the very moment when painfully and manfully he had at last achieved his own salvation and stood forth resolved to do right, to act unselfishly and to live for others. It had widowed Hilma in the very dawn of her happiness. It had killed the very babe within the mother's womb, strangling life ere yet it had been born, stamping out the spark ordained by God to burn through all eternity.

What then was left? Was there no hope, no outlook for the future, no rift in the black curtain, no glimmer through the night? Was good to be thus overthrown? Was evil thus to be strong and to prevail? Was nothing left?

Then suddenly Vanamee's words came back to his mind. What was the larger view, what contributed the greatest good to the greatest numbers? What was the full round of the circle whose segment only he beheld? In the end, the ultimate, final end of all, what was left? Yes, good issued from this crisis, untouched, unassailable, undefiled.

Men—motes in the sunshine—perished, were shot down in the very noon of life, hearts were broken, little children started in life lamentably handicapped; young girls were brought to a life of shame; old women died in the heart of life for lack of food. In that little, isolated group of human insects, misery, death, and anguish spun like a wheel of fire.

BUT THE WHEAT REMAINED. Untouched, unassailable, undefiled, that mighty world-force, that nourisher of nations, wrapped in Nirvanic calm, indifferent to the human swarm, gigantic, resistless, moved onward in its appointed grooves. Through the welter of blood at the irrigation ditch, through the sham charity and shallow philanthropy of famine relief committees, the great harvest of Los Muertos rolled like a flood from the Sierras to the Himalayas to feed thousands of starving scarecrows on the barren plains of India.

Falseness dies; injustice and oppression in the end of everything fade and vanish away. Greed, cruelty, selfishness, and inhumanity are short-lived; the individual suffers, but the race goes on. Annixter dies, but in a far distant corner of the world a thousand lives are saved. The larger view always and through all shams, all wickednesses, discovers the Truth that will, in the end, prevail, and all things, surely, inevitably, resistlessly work together for good.

The Pit: a Story of Chicago

I

At eight o'clock in the inner vestibule of the Auditorium Theatre by the window of the box office, Laura Dearborn, her younger sister Page, and their aunt—Aunt Wess'—were still waiting for the rest of the theatre-party to appear. A great, slow-moving press of men and women in evening dress filled the vestibule from one wall to another. A confused murmur of talk and the shuffling of many feet arose on all sides, while from time to time, when the outside and inside doors of the entrance chanced to be open simultaneously, a sudden draught of air gushed in, damp, glacial, and edged with the penetrating keenness of a Chicago evening at the end of February.

The Italian Grand Opera Company gave one of the most popular pieces of its repertoire on that particular night, and the Cresslers had invited the two sisters and their aunt to share their box with them. It had been arranged that the party should assemble in the Auditorium vestibule at a quarter of eight; but by now the quarter was gone and the Cresslers still failed to arrive.

"I don't see," murmured Laura anxiously for the last time, "what can be keeping them. Are you sure Page that Mrs. Cressler meant here—inside?"

She was a tall young girl of about twenty-two or three, holding herself erect and with fine dignity. Even beneath the opera cloak it was easy to infer that her neck and shoulders were beautiful. Her almost extreme slenderness was, however, her characteristic; the curves of her figure, the contour of her shoulders, the swell of hip and breast were all low; from head to foot one could discover no pronounced salience. Yet there was no trace, no suggestion of angularity. She was slender as a willow shoot is slender—and equally graceful, equally erect.

Next to this charming tenuity, perhaps her paleness was her most noticeable trait. But it was not a paleness of lack of colour. Laura Dearborn's pallour was in itself a colour. It was a tint rather than a shade, like ivory; a warm white, blending into an exquisite, delicate brownness towards the throat. Set in the middle of this paleness of brow and cheek, her deep brown eyes glowed lambent and intense. They were not large, but in some indefinable way they were important. It was very natural to speak of her eyes, and in speaking to her, her friends always found that they must look squarely into their pupils. And all this beauty of pallid face and brown eyes was crowned by, and sharply contrasted with, the intense blackness of her hair, abundant, thick, extremely heavy, continually coruscating with sombre, murky reflections, tragic, in a sense vaguely portentous,—the coiffure of a heroine of romance, doomed to dark crises.

On this occasion at the side of the topmost coil, a white aigrette scintillated and trembled with her every movement. She was unquestionably beautiful. Her mouth was a little large, the lips firm set, and one would not have expected that she would smile easily; in fact, the general expression of her face was rather serious.

"Perhaps," continued Laura, "they would look for us outside." But Page shook her head. She was five years younger than Laura, just turned seventeen. Her hair, dressed high for the first time this night, was brown. But Page's beauty was no less marked than her sister's. The seriousness of her expression, however, was more noticeable. At times it amounted to undeniable gravity. She was straight, and her figure, all immature as yet, exhibited hardly any softer outlines than that of a boy.

"No, no," she said, in answer to Laura's question. "They would come in here; they wouldn't wait outside—not on such a cold night as this. Don't you think so, Aunt Wess'?"

But Mrs. Wessels, a lean, middle-aged little lady, with a flat, pointed nose, had no suggestions to offer. She disengaged herself from any responsibility in the situation and, while waiting, found a vague amusement in counting the number of people who filtered in single file through the wicket where the tickets were presented. A great, stout gentleman in evening dress, perspiring, his cravatte limp, stood here, tearing the checks from the tickets, and without ceasing, maintaining a continuous outcry that dominated the murmur of the throng:

"Have your tickets ready, please! Have your tickets ready."

"Such a crowd," murmured Page. "Did you ever see—and every one you ever knew or heard of. And such toilettes!"

With every instant the number of people increased; progress became impossible, except an inch at a time. The women were, almost without exception, in light-coloured gowns, white, pale blue, Nile green, and pink, while over these costumes were thrown opera cloaks and capes of astonishing complexity and elaborateness. Nearly all were bare-headed, and nearly all wore aigrettes; a score of these, a hundred of them, nodded and vibrated with an incessant agitation over the heads of the crowd and flashed like mica flakes as the wearers moved. Everywhere the eye was arrested by the luxury of stuffs, the brilliance and delicacy of fabrics, laces as white and soft as froth, crisp, shining silks, suave satins, heavy gleaming velvets, and brocades and plushes, nearly all of them white—violently so—dazzling and splendid under the blaze of the electrics. The gentlemen, in long, black overcoats, and satin mufflers, and opera hats; their hands under the elbows of their women-folk, urged or guided them forward, distressed, preoccupied, adjuring their parties to keep together; in their white-gloved fingers they held their tickets ready. For all the icy blasts that burst occasionally through the storm doors, the vestibule was uncomfortably warm, and into this steam-heated atmosphere a multitude of heavy odours exhaled—the scent of crushed flowers, of perfume, of sachet, and even—occasionally—the strong smell of damp seal-skin.

Outside it was bitterly cold. All day a freezing wind had blown from off the Lake, and since five in the afternoon a fine powder of snow had been falling. The coachmen on the boxes of the carriages that succeeded one another in an interminable line before the entrance of the theatre, were swathed to the eyes in furs. The spume and froth froze on the bits of the horses, and the carriage wheels crunching through the dry, frozen snow gave off a shrill staccato whine. Yet for all this, a crowd had collected about the awning on the sidewalk, and even upon the opposite side of the street, peeping and peering from behind the broad shoulders of policemen—a crowd of miserables, shivering in rags and tattered comforters, who found, nevertheless, an unexplainable satisfaction in watching this prolonged defile of millionaires.

So great was the concourse of teams, that two blocks distant from the theatre they were obliged to fall into line, advancing only at intervals, and from door to door of the carriages thus immobilised ran a score of young men, their arms encumbered with pamphlets, shouting: "Score books, score books and librettos; score books with photographs of all the artists."

However, in the vestibule the press was thinning out. It was understood that the overture had begun. Other people who were waiting like Laura and her sister had been joined by their friends and had gone inside. Laura, for whom this opera night had been an event, a thing desired and anticipated with all the eagerness of a girl who had lived for twenty-two years in a second-class town of central Massachusetts, was in great distress. She had never seen Grand Opera, she would not have missed a note, and now she was in a fair way to lose the whole overture.

"Oh, dear," she cried. "Isn't it too bad. I can't imagine why they don't come."

Page, more metropolitan, her keenness of appreciation a little lost by two years of city life and fashionable schooling, tried to reassure her.

"You won't lose much," she said. "The air of the overture is repeated in the first act—I've heard it once before."

"If we even see the first act," mourned Laura. She scanned the faces of the late comers anxiously. Nobody seemed to mind being late. Even some of the other people who were waiting, chatted calmly among themselves. Directly behind them two men, their faces close together, elaborated an interminable conversation, of which from time to time they could overhear a phrase or two.

"—and I guess he'll do well if he settles for thirty cents on the dollar. I tell you, dear boy, it was a smash!"

"Never should have tried to swing a corner. The short interest was too small and the visible supply was too great."

Page nudged her sister and whispered: "That's the Helmick failure they're talking about, those men. Landry Court told me all about it. Mr. Helmick had a corner in corn, and he failed to-day, or will fail soon, or something."

But Laura, preoccupied with looking for the Cresslers, hardly listened. Aunt Wess', whose count was confused by all these figures murmured just behind her, began over again, her lips silently forming the words, "sixty-one, sixty-two, and two is sixty-four." Behind them the voice continued:

"They say Porteous will peg the market at twenty-six."

"Well he ought to. Corn is worth that."

"Never saw such a call for margins in my life. Some of the houses called eight cents."

Page turned to Mrs. Wessels: "By the way, Aunt Wess'; look at that man there by the box office window, the one with his back towards us, the one with his hands in his overcoat pockets. Isn't that Mr. Jadwin? The gentleman we are going to meet to-night. See who I mean?"

"Who? Mr. Jadwin? I don't know. I don't know, child. I never saw him, you know."

"Well I think it is he," continued Page. "He was to be with our party to-night. I heard Mrs. Cressler say she would ask him. That's Mr. Jadwin, I'm sure. He's waiting for them, too."

"Oh, then ask him about it, Page," exclaimed Laura. "We're missing everything."

But Page shook her head:

"I only met him once, ages ago; he wouldn't know me. It was at the Cresslers, and we just said 'How do you do.' And then maybe it isn't Mr. Jadwin."

"Oh, I wouldn't bother, girls," said Mrs. Wessels. "It's all right. They'll be here in a minute. I don't believe the curtain has gone up yet."

But the man of whom they spoke turned around at the moment and cast a glance about the vestibule. They saw a gentleman of an indeterminate age—judged by his face he might as well have been forty as thirty-five. A heavy mustache touched with grey covered his lips. The eyes were twinkling and good-tempered. Between his teeth he held an unlighted cigar.

"It is Mr. Jadwin," murmured Page, looking quickly away. "But he don't recognise me."

Laura also averted her eyes.

"Well, why not go right up to him and introduce ourself, or recall yourself to him?" she hazarded.

"Oh, Laura, I couldn't," gasped Page. "I wouldn't for worlds."

"Couldn't she, Aunt Wess'?" appealed Laura. "Wouldn't it be all right?"

But Mrs. Wessels, ignoring forms and customs, was helpless. Again she withdrew from any responsibility in the matter.

"I don't know anything about it," she answered. "But Page oughtn't to be bold."

"Oh, bother; it isn't that," protested Page. "But it's just because—I don't know, I don't want to—Laura, I should just die," she exclaimed with abrupt irrelevance, "and besides, how would that help any?" she added.

"Well, we're just going to miss it all," declared Laura decisively. There were actual tears in her eyes. "And I had looked forward to it so."

"Well," hazarded Aunt Wess', "you girls can do just as you please. Only I wouldn't be bold."

"Well, would it be bold if Page, or if—if I were to speak to him? We're going to meet him anyways in just a few minutes."

"Better wait, hadn't you, Laura," said Aunt Wess', "and see. Maybe he'll come up and speak to us."

"Oh, as if!" contradicted Laura. "He don't know us,—just as Page says. And if he did, he wouldn't. He wouldn't think it polite."

"Then I guess, girlie, it wouldn't be polite for you."

"I think it would," she answered. "I think it would be a woman's place. If he's a gentleman, he would feel that he just couldn't speak first. I'm going to do it," she announced suddenly.

"Just as you think best, Laura," said her aunt.

But nevertheless Laura did not move, and another five minutes went by.

Page took advantage of the interval to tell Laura about Jadwin. He was very rich, but a bachelor, and had made his money in Chicago real estate. Some of his holdings in the business quarter of the city were enormous; Landry Court had told her about him. Jadwin, unlike Mr. Cressler, was not opposed to speculation. Though not a member of the Board of Trade, he nevertheless at very long intervals took part in a "deal" in wheat, or corn, or provisions. He believed that all corners were doomed to failure, however, and had predicted Helmick's collapse six months ago. He had influence, was well known to all Chicago people, what he said carried weight, financiers consulted him, promoters sought his friendship, his name on the board of directors of a company was an all-sufficing endorsement; in a word, a "strong" man.

"I can't understand," exclaimed Laura distrait, referring to the delay on the part of the Cresslers. "This was the night, and this was the place, and it is long past the time. We could telephone to the house, you know," she said, struck with an idea, "and see if they've started, or what has happened."

"I don't know—I don't know," murmured Mrs. Wessels vaguely. No one seemed ready to act upon Laura's suggestion, and again the minutes passed.

"I'm going," declared Laura again, looking at the other two, as if to demand what they had to say against the idea.

"I just couldn't," declared Page flatly.

"Well," continued Laura, "I'll wait just three minutes more, and then if the Cresslers are not here I will speak to him. It seems to me to be perfectly natural, and not at all bold."

She waited three minutes, and the Cresslers still failing to appear, temporised yet further, for the twentieth time repeating:

"I don't see—I can't understand."

Then, abruptly drawing her cape about her, she crossed the vestibule and came up to Jadwin.

As she approached she saw him catch her eye. Then, as he appeared to understand that this young woman was about to speak to him, she noticed an expression of suspicion, almost of distrust, come into his face. No doubt he knew nothing of this other party who were to join the Cresslers in the vestibule. Why should this girl speak to him? Something had gone wrong, and the instinct of the man, no longer very young, to keep out of strange young women's troubles betrayed itself in the uneasy glance that he shot at her from under his heavy eyebrows. But the look faded as quickly as it had come. Laura guessed that he had decided that in such a place as this he need have no suspicions. He took the cigar from his mouth, and she, immensely relieved, realised that she had to do with a man who was a gentleman. Full of trepidation as she had been in crossing the vestibule, she was quite mistress of herself when the instant came for her to speak, and it was in a steady voice and without embarrassment that she said:

"I beg your pardon, but I believe this is Mr. Jadwin."

He took off his hat, evidently a little nonplussed that she should know his name, and by now she was ready even to browbeat him a little should it be necessary.

"Yes, yes," he answered, now much more confused than she, "my name is Jadwin."

"I believe," continued Laura steadily, "we were all to be in the same party to-night with the Cresslers. But they don't seem to come, and we—my sister and my aunt and I—don't know what to do."

She saw that he was embarrassed, convinced, and the knowledge that she controlled the little situation, that she could command him, restored her all her equanimity.

"My name is Miss Dearborn," she continued. "I believe you know my sister Page."

By some trick of manner she managed to convey to him the impression that if he did not know her sister Page, that if for one instant he should deem her to be bold, he would offer a mortal affront. She had not yet forgiven him that stare of suspicion when first their eyes had met; he should pay her for that yet.

"Miss Page,—your sister,—Miss Page Dearborn? Certainly I know her," he answered. "And you have been waiting, too? What a pity!" And he permitted himself the awkwardness of adding: "I did not know that you were to be of our party."

"No," returned Laura upon the instant, "I did not know you were to be one of us to-night—until Page told me." She accented the pronouns a little, but it was enough for him to know that he had been rebuked. How, he could not just say; and for what it was impossible for him at the moment to determine; and she could see that he began to experience a certain distress, was beating a retreat, was ceding place to her. Who was she, then, this tall and pretty young woman, with the serious, unsmiling face, who was so perfectly at ease, and who hustled him about and made him feel as though he were to blame for the Cresslers' non-appearance; as though it was his fault that she must wait in the draughty vestibule. She had a great air with her; how had he offended her? If he had introduced himself to her, had forced himself upon her, she could not be more lofty, more reserved.

"I thought perhaps you might telephone," she observed.

"They haven't a telephone, unfortunately," he answered.

"Oh!"

This was quite the last slight, the Cresslers had not a telephone! He was to blame for that, too, it seemed. At his wits' end, he entertained for an instant the notion of dashing out into the street in a search for a messenger boy, who would take a note to Cressler and set him right again; and his agitation was not allayed when Laura, in frigid tones, declared:

"It seems to me that something might be done."

"I don't know," he replied helplessly. "I guess there's nothing to be done but just wait. They are sure to be along."

In the background, Page and Mrs. Wessels had watched the interview, and had guessed that Laura was none too gracious. Always anxious that her sister should make a good impression, the little girl was now in great distress.

"Laura is putting on her 'grand manner,'" she lamented. "I just know how she's talking. The man will hate the very sound of her name all the rest of his life." Then all at once she uttered a joyful exclamation: "At last, at last," she cried, "and about time, too!"

The Cresslers and the rest of the party—two young men—had appeared, and Page and her aunt came up just in time to hear Mrs. Cressler—a fine old lady, in a wonderful ermine-trimmed cape, whose hair was powdered—exclaim at the top of her voice, as if the mere declaration of fact was final, absolutely the last word upon the subject, "The bridge was turned!"

The Cresslers lived on the North Side. The incident seemed to be closed with the abruptness of a slammed door.

Page and Aunt Wess' were introduced to Jadwin, who was particular to announce that he remembered the young girl perfectly. The two young men were already acquainted with the Dearborn sisters and Mrs. Wessels. Page and Laura knew one of them well enough to address him familiarly by his Christian name.

This was Landry Court, a young fellow just turned twenty-three, who was "connected with" the staff of the great brokerage firm of Gretry, Converse and Co. He was astonishingly good-looking, small-made, wiry, alert, nervous, debonair, with blond hair and dark eyes that snapped like a terrier's. He made friends almost at first sight, and was one of those fortunate few who were favoured equally of men and women. The healthiness of his eye and skin persuaded to a belief in the healthiness of his mind; and, in fact, Landry was as clean without as within. He was frank, open-hearted, full of fine sentiments and exaltations and enthusiasms. Until he was eighteen he had cherished an ambition to become the President of the United States.

"Yes, yes," he said to Laura, "the bridge was turned. It was an imposition. We had to wait while they let three tows through. I think two at a time is as much as is legal. And we had to wait for three. Yes, sir; three, think of that! I shall look into that to-morrow. Yes, sir; don't you be afraid of that. I'll look into it." He nodded his head with profound seriousness.

"Well," announced Mr. Cressler, marshalling the party, "shall we go in? I'm afraid, Laura, we've missed the overture."

Smiling, she shrugged her shoulders, while they moved to the wicket, as if to say that it could not be helped now.

Cressler, tall, lean, bearded, and stoop-shouldered, belonging to the same physical type that includes Lincoln—the type of the Middle West—was almost a second father to the parentless Dearborn girls. In Massachusetts, thirty years before this time, he had been a farmer, and the miller Dearborn used to grind his grain regularly. The two had been boys together, and had always remained fast friends, almost brothers. Then, in the years just before the War, had come the great movement westward, and Cressler had been one of those to leave an "abandoned" New England farm behind him, and with his family emigrate toward the Mississippi. He had come to Sangamon County in Illinois. For a time he tried wheat-raising, until the War, which skied the prices of all food-stuffs, had made him—for those days—a rich man. Giving up farming, he came to live in Chicago, bought a seat on the Board of Trade, and in a few years was a millionaire. At the time of the Turco-Russian War he and two Milwaukee men had succeeded in cornering all the visible supply of spring wheat. At the end of the thirtieth day of the corner the clique figured out its profits at close upon a million; a week later it looked like a million and a half. Then the three lost their heads; they held the corner just a fraction of a month too long, and when the time came that the three were forced to take profits, they found that they were unable to close out their immense holdings without breaking the price. In two days wheat that they had held at a dollar and ten cents collapsed to sixty. The two Milwaukee men were ruined, and two-thirds of Cressler's immense fortune vanished like a whiff of smoke.

But he had learned his lesson. Never since then had he speculated. Though keeping his seat on the Board, he had confined himself to commission trading, uninfluenced by fluctuations in the market. And he was never wearied of protesting against the evil and the danger of trading in margins. Speculation he abhorred as the small-pox, believing it to be impossible to corner grain by any means or under any circumstances. He was accustomed to say: "It can't be done; first, for the reason that there is a great harvest of wheat somewhere in the world for every month in the year; and, second, because the smart man who runs the corner has every other smart man in the world against him. And, besides, it's wrong; the world's food should not be at the mercy of the Chicago wheat pit."

As the party filed in through the wicket, the other young man who had come with Landry Court managed to place himself next to Laura. Meeting her eyes, he murmured:

"Ah, you did not wear them after all. My poor little flowers."

But she showed him a single American Beauty, pinned to the shoulder of her gown beneath her cape.

"Yes, Mr. Corthell," she answered, "one. I tried to select the prettiest, and I think I succeeded—don't you? It was hard to choose."

"Since you have worn it, it is the prettiest," he answered.

He was a slightly built man of about twenty-eight or thirty; dark, wearing a small, pointed beard, and a mustache that he brushed away from his lips like a Frenchman. By profession he was an artist, devoting himself more especially to the designing of stained windows. In this, his talent was indisputable. But he was by no means dependent upon his profession for a living, his parents—long since dead—having left him to the enjoyment of a very considerable fortune. He had a beautiful studio in the Fine Arts Building, where he held receptions once every two months, or whenever he had a fine piece of glass to expose. He had travelled, read, studied, occasionally written, and in matters pertaining to the colouring and fusing of glass was cited as an authority. He was one of the directors of the new Art Gallery that had taken the place of the old Exposition Building on the Lake Front.

Laura had known him for some little time. On the occasion of her two previous visits to Page he had found means to see her two or three times each week. Once, even, he had asked her to marry him, but she, deep in her studies at the time, consumed with vague ambitions to be a great actress of Shakespearian roles, had told him she could care for nothing but her art. He had smiled and said that he could wait, and, strangely enough, their relations had resumed again upon the former footing. Even after she had gone away they had corresponded regularly, and he had made and sent her a tiny window—a veritable jewel—illustrative of a scene from "Twelfth Night."

In the foyer, as the gentlemen were checking their coats, Laura overheard Jadwin say to Mr. Cressler:

"Well, how about Helmick?"

The other made an impatient movement of his shoulders.

"Ask me, what was the fool thinking of—a corner! Pshaw!"

There were one or two other men about, making their overcoats and opera hats into neat bundles preparatory to checking them; and instantly there was a flash of a half-dozen eyes in the direction of the two men. Evidently the collapse of the Helmick deal was in the air. All the city seemed interested.

But from behind the heavy curtains that draped the entrance to the theatre proper, came a muffled burst of music, followed by a long salvo of applause. Laura's cheeks flamed with impatience, she hurried after Mrs. Cressler; Corthell drew the curtains for her to pass, and she entered.

Inside it was dark, and a prolonged puff of hot air, thick with the mingled odours of flowers, perfume, upholstery, and gas, enveloped her upon the instant. It was the unmistakable, unforgettable, entrancing aroma of the theatre, that she had known only too seldom, but that in a second set her heart galloping.

Every available space seemed to be occupied. Men, even women, were standing up, compacted into a suffocating pressure, and for the moment everybody was applauding vigorously. On all sides Laura heard:

"Bravo!"

"Good, good!"

"Very well done!"

"Encore! Encore!"

Between the peoples' heads and below the low dip of the overhanging balcony—a brilliant glare in the surrounding darkness—she caught a glimpse of the stage. It was set for a garden; at the back and in the distance a chateau; on the left a bower, and on the right a pavilion. Before the footlights, a famous contralto, dressed as a boy, was bowing to the audience, her arms full of flowers.

"Too bad," whispered Corthell to Laura, as they followed the others down the side-aisle to the box. "Too bad, this is the second act already; you've missed the whole first act—and this song. She'll sing it over again, though, just for you, if I have to lead the applause myself. I particularly wanted you to hear that."

Once in the box, the party found itself a little crowded, and Jadwin and Cressler were obliged to stand, in order to see the stage. Although they all spoke in whispers, their arrival was the signal for certain murmurs of "Sh! Sh!" Mrs. Cressler made Laura occupy the front seat. Jadwin took her cloak from her, and she settled herself in her chair and looked about her. She could see but little of the house or audience. All the lights were lowered; only through the gloom the swaying of a multitude of fans, pale coloured, like night-moths balancing in the twilight, defined itself.

But soon she turned towards the stage. The applause died away, and the contralto once more sang the aria. The melody was simple, the tempo easily followed; it was not a very high order of music. But to Laura it was nothing short of a revelation.

She sat spell-bound, her hands clasped tight, her every faculty of attention at its highest pitch. It was wonderful, such music as that; wonderful, such a voice; wonderful, such orchestration; wonderful, such exaltation inspired by mere beauty of sound. Never, never was this night to be forgotten, this her first night of Grand Opera. All this excitement, this world of perfume, of flowers, of exquisite costumes, of beautiful women, of fine, brave men. She looked back with immense pity to the narrow little life of her native town she had just left forever, the restricted horizon, the petty round of petty duties, the rare and barren pleasures—the library, the festival, the few concerts, the trivial plays. How easy it was to be good and noble when music such as this had become a part of one's life; how desirable was wealth when it could make possible such exquisite happiness as hers of the moment. Nobility, purity, courage, sacrifice seemed much more worth while now than a few moments ago. All things not positively unworthy became heroic, all things and all men. Landry Court was a young chevalier, pure as Galahad. Corthell was a beautiful artist-priest of the early Renaissance. Even Jadwin was a merchant prince, a great financial captain. And she herself—ah, she did not know; she dreamed of another Laura, a better, gentler, more beautiful Laura, whom everybody, everybody loved dearly and tenderly, and who loved everybody, and who should die beautifully, gently, in some garden far away—die because of a great love—beautifully, gently in the midst of flowers, die of a broken heart, and all the world should be sorry for her, and would weep over her when they found her dead and beautiful in her garden, amid the flowers and the birds, in some far-off place, where it was always early morning and where there was soft music. And she was so sorry for herself, and so hurt with the sheer strength of her longing to be good and true, and noble and womanly, that as she sat in the front of the Cresslers' box on that marvellous evening, the tears ran down her cheeks again and again, and dropped upon her tight-shut, white-gloved fingers.

But the contralto had disappeared, and in her place the tenor held the stage—a stout, short young man in red plush doublet and grey silk tights. His chin advanced, an arm extended, one hand pressed to his breast, he apostrophised the pavilion, that now and then swayed a little in the draught from the wings.

The aria was received with furor; thrice he was obliged to repeat it. Even Corthell, who was critical to extremes, approved, nodding his head. Laura and Page clapped their hands till the very last. But Landry Court, to create an impression, assumed a certain disaffection.

"He's not in voice to-night. Too bad. You should have heard him Friday in 'Aida.'"

The opera continued. The great soprano, the prima donna, appeared and delivered herself of a song for which she was famous with astonishing eclat. Then in a little while the stage grew dark, the orchestration lapsed to a murmur, and the tenor and the soprano reentered. He clasped her in his arms and sang a half-dozen bars, then holding her hand, one arm still about her waist, withdrew from her gradually, till she occupied the front-centre of the stage. He assumed an attitude of adoration and wonderment, his eyes uplifted as if entranced, and she, very softly, to the accompaniment of the sustained, dreamy chords of the orchestra, began her solo.

Laura shut her eyes. Never had she felt so soothed, so cradled and lulled and languid. Ah, to love like that! To love and be loved. There was no such love as that to-day. She wished that she could loose her clasp upon the sordid, material modern life that, perforce, she must hold to, she knew not why, and drift, drift off into the past, far away, through rose-coloured mists and diaphanous veils, or resign herself, reclining in a silver skiff drawn by swans, to the gentle current of some smooth-flowing river that ran on forever and forever.

But a discordant element developed. Close by—the lights were so low she could not tell where—a conversation, kept up in low whispers, began by degrees to intrude itself upon her attention. Try as she would, she could not shut it out, and now, as the music died away fainter and fainter, till voice and orchestra blended together in a single, barely audible murmur, vibrating with emotion, with romance, and with sentiment, she heard, in a hoarse, masculine whisper, the words:

"The shortage is a million bushels at the very least. Two hundred carloads were to arrive from Milwaukee last night."

She made a little gesture of despair, turning her head for an instant, searching the gloom about her. But she could see no one not interested in the stage. Why could not men leave their business outside, why must the jar of commerce spoil all the harmony of this moment.

However, all sounds were drowned suddenly in a long burst of applause. The tenor and soprano bowed and smiled across the footlights. The soprano vanished, only to reappear on the balcony of the pavilion, and while she declared that the stars and the night-bird together sang "He loves thee," the voices close at hand continued:

"—one hundred and six carloads—"

"—paralysed the bulls—"

"—fifty thousand dollars—"

Then all at once the lights went up. The act was over.

Laura seemed only to come to herself some five minutes later. She and Corthell were out in the foyer behind the boxes. Everybody was promenading. The air was filled with the staccato chatter of a multitude of women. But she herself seemed far away—she and Sheldon Corthell. His face, dark, romantic, with the silky beard and eloquent eyes, appeared to be all she cared to see, while his low voice, that spoke close to her ear, was in a way a mere continuation of the melody of the duet just finished.

Instinctively she knew what he was about to say, for what he was trying to prepare her. She felt, too, that he had not expected to talk thus to her to-night. She knew that he loved her, that inevitably, sooner or later, they must return to a subject that for long had been excluded from their conversations, but it was to have been when they were alone, remote, secluded, not in the midst of a crowd, brilliant electrics dazzling their eyes, the humming of the talk of hundreds assaulting their ears. But it seemed as if these important things came of themselves, independent of time and place, like birth and death. There was nothing to do but to accept the situation, and it was without surprise that at last, from out the murmur of Corthell's talk, she was suddenly conscious of the words:

"So that it is hardly necessary, is it, to tell you once more that I love you?"

She drew a long breath.

"I know. I know you love me."

They had sat down on a divan, at one end of the promenade; and Corthell, skilful enough in the little arts of the drawing-room, made it appear as though they talked of commonplaces; as for Laura, exalted, all but hypnotised with this marvellous evening, she hardly cared; she would not even stoop to maintain appearances.

"Yes, yes," she said; "I know you love me."

"And is that all you can say?" he urged. "Does it mean nothing to you that you are everything to me?"

She was coming a little to herself again. Love was, after all, sweeter in the actual—even in this crowded foyer, in this atmosphere of silk and jewels, in this show-place of a great city's society—than in a mystic garden of some romantic dreamland. She felt herself a woman again, modern, vital, and no longer a maiden of a legend of chivalry.

"Nothing to me?" she answered. "I don't know. I should rather have you love me than—not."

"Let me love you then for always," he went on. "You know what I mean. We have understood each other from the very first. Plainly, and very simply, I love you with all my heart. You know now that I speak the truth, you know that you can trust me. I shall not ask you to share your life with mine. I ask you for the great happiness"—he raised his head sharply, suddenly proud—"the great honour of the opportunity of giving you all that I have of good. God give me humility, but that is much since I have known you. If I were a better man because of myself, I would not presume to speak of it, but if I am in anything less selfish, if I am more loyal, if I am stronger, or braver, it is only something of you that has become a part of me, and made me to be born again. So when I offer myself to you, I am only bringing back to you the gift you gave me for a little while. I have tried to keep it for you, to keep it bright and sacred and un-spotted. It is yours again now if you will have it."

There was a long pause; a group of men in opera hats and white gloves came up the stairway close at hand. The tide of promenaders set towards the entrances of the theatre. A little electric bell shrilled a note of warning.

Laura looked up at length, and as their glances met, he saw that there were tears in her eyes. This declaration of his love for her was the last touch to the greatest exhilaration of happiness she had ever known. Ah yes, she was loved, just as that young girl of the opera had been loved. For this one evening, at least, the beauty of life was unmarred, and no cruel word of hers should spoil it. The world was beautiful. All people were good and noble and true. To-morrow, with the material round of duties and petty responsibilities and cold, calm reason, was far, far away.

Suddenly she turned to him, surrendering to the impulse, forgetful of consequences.

"Oh, I am glad, glad," she cried, "glad that you love me!"

But before Corthell could say anything more Landry Court and Page came up.

"We've been looking for you," said the young girl quietly. Page was displeased. She took herself and her sister—in fact, the whole scheme of existence—with extraordinary seriousness. She had no sense of humour. She was not tolerant; her ideas of propriety and the amenities were as immutable as the fixed stars. A fine way for Laura to act, getting off into corners with Sheldon Corthell. It would take less than that to make talk. If she had no sense of her obligations to Mrs. Cressler, at least she ought to think of the looks of things.

"They're beginning again," she said solemnly. "I should think you'd feel as though you had missed about enough of this opera."

They returned to the box. The rest of the party were reassembling.

"Well, Laura," said Mrs. Cressler, when they had sat down, "do you like it?"

"I don't want to leave it—ever," she answered. "I could stay here always."

"I like the young man best," observed Aunt Wess'. "The one who seems to be the friend of the tall fellow with a cloak. But why does he seem so sorry? Why don't he marry the young lady? Let's see, I don't remember his name."

"Beastly voice," declared Landry Court. "He almost broke there once. Too bad. He's not what he used to be. It seems he's terribly dissipated—drinks. Yes, sir, like a fish. He had delirium tremens once behind the scenes in Philadelphia, and stabbed a scene shifter with his stage dagger. A bad lot, to say the least."

"Now, Landry," protested Mrs. Cressler, "you're making it up as you go along." And in the laugh that followed Landry himself joined.

"After all," said Corthell, "this music seems to be just the right medium between the naive melody of the Italian school and the elaborate complexity of Wagner. I can't help but be carried away with it at times—in spite of my better judgment."

Jadwin, who had been smoking a cigar in the vestibule during the entr'acte, rubbed his chin reflectively.

"Well," he said, "it's all very fine. I've no doubt of that, but I give you my word I would rather hear my old governor take his guitar and sing 'Father, oh father, come home with me now,' than all the fiddle-faddle, tweedle-deedle opera business in the whole world."

But the orchestra was returning, the musicians crawling out one by one from a little door beneath the stage hardly bigger than the entrance of a rabbit hutch. They settled themselves in front of their racks, adjusting their coat-tails, fingering their sheet music. Soon they began to tune up, and a vague bourdon of many sounds—the subdued snarl of the cornets, the dull mutter of the bass viols, the liquid gurgling of the flageolets and wood-wind instruments, now and then pierced by the strident chirps and cries of the violins, rose into the air dominating the incessant clamour of conversation that came from all parts of the theatre.

Then suddenly the house lights sank and the footlights rose. From all over the theatre came energetic whispers of "Sh! Sh!" Three strokes, as of a great mallet, sepulchral, grave, came from behind the wings; the leader of the orchestra raised his baton, then brought it slowly down, and while from all the instruments at once issued a prolonged minor chord, emphasised by a muffled roll of the kettle-drum, the curtain rose upon a mediaeval public square. The soprano was seated languidly upon a bench. Her grande scene occurred in this act. Her hair was un-bound; she wore a loose robe of cream white, with flowing sleeves, which left the arms bare to the shoulder. At the waist it was caught in by a girdle of silk rope.

"This is the great act," whispered Mrs. Cressler, leaning over Laura's shoulder. "She is superb later on. Superb."

"I wish those men would stop talking," murmured Laura, searching the darkness distressfully, for between the strains of the music she had heard the words:

"—Clearing House balance of three thousand dollars."

Meanwhile the prima donna, rising to her feet, delivered herself of a lengthy recitative, her chin upon her breast, her eyes looking out from under her brows, an arm stretched out over the footlights. The baritone entered, striding to the left of the footlights, apostrophising the prima donna in a rage. She clasped her hands imploringly, supplicating him to leave her, exclaiming from time to time:

"Va via, va via—Vel chieco per pieta."

Then all at once, while the orchestra blared, they fell into each other's arms.

"Why do they do that?" murmured Aunt Wess' perplexed. "I thought the gentleman with the beard didn't like her at all."

"Why, that's the duke, don't you see, Aunt Wess'?" said Laura trying to explain. "And he forgives her. I don't know exactly. Look at your libretto."

"—a conspiracy of the Bears ... seventy cents ... and naturally he busted."

The mezzo-soprano, the confidante of the prima donna, entered, and a trio developed that had but a mediocre success. At the end the baritone abruptly drew his sword, and the prima donna fell to her knees, chanting:

"Io tremo, ahime!"

"And now he's mad again," whispered Aunt Wess', consulting her libretto, all at sea once more. "I can't understand. She says—the opera book says she says, 'I tremble.' I don't see why."

"Look now," said Page, "here comes the tenor. Now they're going to have it out."

The tenor, hatless, debouched suddenly upon the scene, and furious, addressed himself to the baritone, leaning forward, his hands upon his chest. Though the others sang in Italian, the tenor, a Parisian, used the French book continually, and now villified the baritone, crying out:

"O traitre infame
O lache et coupable"

"I don't see why he don't marry the young lady and be done with it," commented Aunt Wess'.

The act drew to its close. The prima donna went through her "great scene," wherein her voice climbed to C in alt, holding the note so long that Aunt Wess' became uneasy. As she finished, the house rocked with applause, and the soprano, who had gone out supported by her confidante, was recalled three times. A duel followed between the baritone and tenor, and the latter, mortally wounded, fell into the arms of his friends uttering broken, vehement notes. The chorus—made up of the city watch and town's people—crowded in upon the back of the stage. The soprano and her confidante returned. The basso, a black-bearded, bull necked man, sombre, mysterious, parted the chorus to right and left, and advanced to the footlights. The contralto, dressed as a boy, appeared. The soprano took stage, and abruptly the closing scene of the act developed.

The violins raged and wailed in unison, all the bows moving together like parts of a well-regulated machine. The kettle-drums, marking the cadences, rolled at exact intervals. The director beat time furiously, as though dragging up the notes and chords with the end of his baton, while the horns and cornets blared, the bass viols growled, and the flageolets and piccolos lost themselves in an amazing complication of liquid gurgles and modulated roulades.

On the stage every one was singing. The soprano in the centre, vocalised in her highest register, bringing out the notes with vigorous twists of her entire body, and tossing them off into the air with sharp flirts of her head. On the right, the basso, scowling, could be heard in the intervals of the music repeating

"Il perfido, l'ingrato"

while to the left of the soprano, the baritone intoned indistinguishable, sonorous phrases, striking his breast and pointing to the fallen tenor with his sword. At the extreme left of the stage the contralto, in tights and plush doublet, turned to the audience, extending her hands, or flinging back her arms. She raised her eyebrows with each high note, and sunk her chin into her ruff when her voice descended. At certain intervals her notes blended with those of the soprano's while she sang:

"Addio, felicita del ciel!"

The tenor, raised upon one hand, his shoulders supported by his friends, sustained the theme which the soprano led with the words:

"Je me meurs
Ah malheur
Ah je souffre
Mon ame s'envole."

The chorus formed a semi-circle just behind him. The women on one side, the men on the other. They left much to be desired; apparently scraped hastily together from heaven knew what sources, after the manner of a management suddenly become economical. The women were fat, elderly, and painfully homely; the men lean, osseous, and distressed, in misfitting hose. But they had been conscientiously drilled. They made all their gestures together, moved in masses simultaneously, and, without ceasing, chanted over and over again:

"O terror, O blasfema."

The finale commenced. Everybody on the stage took a step forward, beginning all over again upon a higher key. The soprano's voice thrilled to the very chandelier. The orchestra redoubled its efforts, the director beating time with hands, head, and body.

"Il perfido, l'ingrato"

thundered the basso.

"Ineffabil mistero,"

answered the baritone, striking his breast and pointing with his sword; while all at once the soprano's voice, thrilling out again, ran up an astonishing crescendo that evoked veritable gasps from all parts of the audience, then jumped once more to her famous C in alt, and held it long enough for the chorus to repeat

"O terror, O blasfema"

four times.

Then the director's baton descended with the violence of a blow. There was a prolonged crash of harmony, a final enormous chord, to which every voice and every instrument contributed. The singers struck tableau attitudes, the tenor fell back with a last wail:

"Je me meurs,"

and the soprano fainted into the arms of her confidante. The curtain fell.

The house roared with applause. The scene was recalled again and again. The tenor, scrambling to his feet, joined hands with the baritone, soprano, and other artists, and all bowed repeatedly. Then the curtain fell for the last time, the lights of the great chandelier clicked and blazed up, and from every quarter of the house came the cries of the programme sellers:

"Opera books. Books of the opera. Words and music of the opera."

During this, the last entr'acte, Laura remained in the box with Mrs. Cressler, Corthell, and Jadwin. The others went out to look down upon the foyer from a certain balcony.

In the box the conversation turned upon stage management, and Corthell told how, in "L'Africaine," at the Opera, in Paris, the entire superstructure of the stage—wings, drops, and backs—turned when Vasco da Gama put the ship about. Jadwin having criticised the effect because none of the actors turned with it, was voted a Philistine by Mrs. Cressler and Corthell. But as he was about to answer, Mrs. Cressler turned to the artist, passing him her opera glasses, and asking:

"Who are those people down there in the third row of the parquet—see, on the middle aisle—the woman is in red. Aren't those the Gretrys?"

This left Jadwin and Laura out of the conversation, and the capitalist was quick to seize the chance of talking to her. Soon she was surprised to notice that he was trying hard to be agreeable, and before they had exchanged a dozen sentences, he had turned an awkward compliment. She guessed by his manner that paying attention to young girls was for him a thing altogether unusual. Intuitively she divined that she, on this, the very first night of their acquaintance, had suddenly interested him.

She had had neither opportunity nor inclination to observe him closely during their interview in the vestibule, but now, as she sat and listened to him talk, she could not help being a little attracted. He was a heavy-built man, would have made two of Corthell, and his hands were large and broad, the hands of a man of affairs, who knew how to grip, and, above all, how to hang on. Those broad, strong hands, and keen, calm eyes would enfold and envelop a Purpose with tremendous strength, and they would persist and persist and persist, unswerving, unwavering, untiring, till the Purpose was driven home. And the two long, lean, fibrous arms of him; what a reach they could attain, and how wide and huge and even formidable would be their embrace of affairs. One of those great manoeuvres of a fellow money-captain had that very day been concluded, the Helmick failure, and between the chords and bars of a famous opera men talked in excited whispers, and one great leader lay at that very moment, broken and spent, fighting with his last breath for bare existence. Jadwin had seen it all. Uninvolved in the crash, he had none the less been close to it, watching it, in touch with it, foreseeing each successive collapse by which it reeled fatally to the final catastrophe. The voices of the two men that had so annoyed her in the early part of the evening were suddenly raised again:

"—It was terrific, there on the floor of the Board this morning. By the Lord! they fought each other when the Bears began throwing the grain at 'em—in carload lots."

And abruptly, midway between two phases of that music-drama, of passion and romance, there came to Laura the swift and vivid impression of that other drama that simultaneously—even at that very moment—was working itself out close at hand, equally picturesque, equally romantic, equally passionate; but more than that, real, actual, modern, a thing in the very heart of the very life in which she moved. And here he sat, this Jadwin, quiet, in evening dress, listening good-naturedly to this beautiful music, for which he did not care, to this rant and fustian, watching quietly all this posing and attitudinising. How small and petty it must all seem to him!

Laura found time to be astonished. What! She had first met this man haughtily, in all the panoply of her "grand manner," and had promised herself that she would humble him, and pay him for that first mistrustful stare at her. And now, behold, she was studying him, and finding the study interesting. Out of harmony though she knew him to be with those fine emotions of hers of the early part of the evening, she nevertheless found much in him to admire. It was always just like that. She told herself that she was forever doing the unexpected thing, the inconsistent thing. Women were queer creatures, mysterious even to themselves.

"I am so pleased that you are enjoying it all," said Corthell's voice at her shoulder. "I knew you would. There is nothing like music such as this to appeal to the emotions, the heart—and with your temperament."

Straightway he made her feel her sex. Now she was just a woman again, with all a woman's limitations, and her relations with Corthell could never be—so she realised—any other than sex-relations. With Jadwin somehow it had been different. She had felt his manhood more than her womanhood, her sex side. And between them it was more a give-and-take affair, more equality, more companionship. Corthell spoke only of her heart and to her heart. But Jadwin made her feel—or rather she made herself feel when he talked to her—that she had a head as well as a heart.

And the last act of the opera did not wholly absorb her attention. The artists came and went, the orchestra wailed and boomed, the audience applauded, and in the end the tenor, fired by a sudden sense of duty and of stern obligation, tore himself from the arms of the soprano, and calling out upon remorseless fate and upon heaven, and declaiming about the vanity of glory, and his heart that broke yet disdained tears, allowed himself to be dragged off the scene by his friend the basso. For the fifth time during the piece the soprano fainted into the arms of her long-suffering confidante. The audience, suddenly remembering hats and wraps, bestirred itself, and many parties were already upon their feet and filing out at the time the curtain fell.

The Cresslers and their friends were among the last to regain the vestibule. But as they came out from the foyer, where the first draughts of outside air began to make themselves felt, there were exclamations:

"It's raining."

"Why, it's raining right down."

It was true. Abruptly the weather had moderated, and the fine, dry snow that had been falling since early evening had changed to a lugubrious drizzle. A wave of consternation invaded the vestibule for those who had not come in carriages, or whose carriages had not arrived. Tempers were lost; women, cloaked to the ears, their heads protected only by fichus or mantillas, quarrelled with husbands or cousins or brothers over the question of umbrellas. The vestibules were crowded to suffocation, and the aigrettes nodded and swayed again in alternate gusts, now of moist, chill atmosphere from without, and now of stale, hot air that exhaled in long puffs from the inside doors of the theatre itself. Here and there in the press, footmen, their top hats in rubber cases, their hands full of umbrellas, searched anxiously for their masters.

Outside upon the sidewalks and by the curbs, an apparently inextricable confusion prevailed; policemen with drawn clubs laboured and objurgated: anxious, preoccupied young men, their opera hats and gloves beaded with rain, hurried to and fro, searching for their carriages. At the edge of the awning, the caller, a gigantic fellow in gold-faced uniform, shouted the numbers in a roaring, sing-song that dominated every other sound. Coachmen, their wet rubber coats reflecting the lamplight, called back and forth, furious quarrels broke out between hansom drivers and the police officers, steaming horses with jingling bits, their backs covered with dark green cloths, plunged and pranced, carriage doors banged, and the roll of wheels upon the pavement was as the reverberation of artillery caissons.

"Get your carriage, sir?" cried a ragged, half-grown arab at Cressler's elbow.

"Hurry up, then," said Cressler. Then, raising his voice, for the clamour was increasing with every second: "What's your number, Laura? You girls first. Ninety-three? Get that, boy? Ninety-three. Quick now."

The carriage appeared. Hastily they said good-by; hastily Laura expressed to Mrs. Cressler her appreciation and enjoyment. Corthell saw them to the carriage, and getting in after them shut the door behind him. They departed.

Laura sank back in the cool gloom of the carriage's interior redolent of damp leather and upholstery.

"What an evening! What an evening!" she murmured.

On the way home both she and Page appealed to the artist, who knew the opera well, to hum or whistle for them the arias that had pleased them most. Each time they were enthusiastic. Yes, yes, that was the air. Wasn't it pretty, wasn't it beautiful?

But Aunt Wess' was still unsatisfied.

"I don't see yet," she complained, "why the young man, the one with the pointed beard, didn't marry that lady and be done with it. Just as soon as they'd seem to have it all settled, he'd begin to take on again, and strike his breast and go away. I declare, I think it was all kind of foolish."

"Why, the duke—don't you see. The one who sang bass—" Page laboured to explain.

"Oh, I didn't like him at all," said Aunt Wess'. "He stamped around so." But the audience itself had interested her, and the decollete gowns had been particularly impressing.

"I never saw such dressing in all my life," she declared. "And that woman in the box next ours. Well! did you notice that!" She raised her eyebrows and set her lips together. "Well, I don't want to say anything."

The carriage rolled on through the darkened downtown streets, towards the North Side, where the Dearborns lived. They could hear the horses plashing through the layer of slush—mud, half-melted snow and rain—that encumbered the pavement. In the gloom the girls' wraps glowed pallid and diaphanous. The rain left long, slanting parallels on the carriage windows. They passed on down Wabash Avenue, and crossed over to State Street and Clarke Street, dark, deserted.

Laura, after a while, lost in thought, spoke but little. It had been a great evening—because of other things than mere music. Corthell had again asked her to marry him, and she, carried away by the excitement of the moment, had answered him encouragingly. On the heels of this she had had that little talk with the capitalist Jadwin, and somehow since then she had been steadied, calmed. The cold air and the rain in her face had cooled her flaming cheeks and hot temples. She asked herself now if she did really, honestly love the artist. No, she did not; really and honestly she did not; and now as the carriage rolled on through the deserted streets of the business districts, she knew very well that she did not want to marry him. She had done him an injustice; but in the matter of righting herself with him, correcting his false impression, she was willing to procrastinate. She wanted him to love her, to pay her all those innumerable little attentions which he managed with such faultless delicacy. To say: "No, Mr. Corthell, I do not love you, I will never be your wife," would—this time—be final. He would go away, and she had no intention of allowing him to do that.

But abruptly her reflections were interrupted. While she thought it all over she had been looking out of the carriage window through a little space where she had rubbed the steam from the pane. Now, all at once, the strange appearance of the neighbourhood as the carriage turned north from out Jackson Street into La Salle, forced itself upon her attention. She uttered an exclamation.

The office buildings on both sides of the street were lighted from basement to roof. Through the windows she could get glimpses of clerks and book-keepers in shirt-sleeves bending over desks. Every office was open, and every one of them full of a feverish activity. The sidewalks were almost as crowded as though at noontime. Messenger boys ran to and fro, and groups of men stood on the corners in earnest conversation. The whole neighbourhood was alive, and this, though it was close upon one o'clock in the morning!

"Why, what is it all?" she murmured.

Corthell could not explain, but all at once Page cried:

"Oh, oh, I know. See this is Jackson and La Salle streets. Landry was telling me. The 'commission district,' he called it. And these are the brokers' offices working overtime—that Helmick deal, you know."

Laura looked, suddenly stupefied. Here it was, then, that other drama, that other tragedy, working on there furiously, fiercely through the night, while she and all those others had sat there in that atmosphere of flowers and perfume, listening to music. Suddenly it loomed portentous in the eye of her mind, terrible, tremendous. Ah, this drama of the "Provision Pits," where the rush of millions of bushels of grain, and the clatter of millions of dollars, and the tramping and the wild shouting of thousands of men filled all the air with the noise of battle! Yes, here was drama in deadly earnest—drama and tragedy and death, and the jar of mortal fighting. And the echoes of it invaded the very sanctuary of art, and cut athwart the music of Italy and the cadence of polite conversation, and the shock of it endured when all the world should have slept, and galvanised into vivid life all these sombre piles of office buildings. It was dreadful, this labour through the night. It had all the significance of field hospitals after the battle—hospitals and the tents of commanding generals. The wounds of the day were being bound up, the dead were being counted, while, shut in their headquarters, the captains and the commanders drew the plans for the grapple of armies that was to recommence with daylight.

"Yes, yes, that's just what it is," continued Page. "See, there's the Rookery, and there's the Constable Building, where Mr. Helmick has his offices. Landry showed me it all one day. And, look back." She raised the flap that covered the little window at the back of the carriage. "See, down there, at the end of the street. There's the Board of Trade Building, where the grain speculating is done,—where the wheat pits and corn pits are."

Laura turned and looked back. On either side of the vista in converging lines stretched the blazing office buildings. But over the end of the street the lead-coloured sky was rifted a little. A long, faint bar of light stretched across the prospect, and silhouetted against this rose a sombre mass, unbroken by any lights, rearing a black and formidable facade against the blur of light behind it.

And this was her last impression of the evening. The lighted office buildings, the murk of rain, the haze of light in the heavens, and raised against it the pile of the Board of Trade Building, black, grave, monolithic, crouching on its foundations, like a monstrous sphinx with blind eyes, silent, grave,—crouching there without a sound, without sign of life under the night and the drifting veil of rain.

II

Laura Dearborn's native town was Barrington, in Worcester County, Massachusetts. Both she and Page had been born there, and there had lived until the death of their father, at a time when Page was ready for the High School. The mother, a North Carolina girl, had died long before.

Laura's education had been unusual. After leaving the High School her father had for four years allowed her a private tutor (an impecunious graduate from the Harvard Theological School). She was ambitious, a devoted student, and her instructor's task was rather to guide than to enforce her application. She soon acquired a reading knowledge of French, and knew her Racine in the original almost as well as her Shakespeare. Literature became for her an actual passion. She delved into Tennyson and the Victorian poets, and soon was on terms of intimacy with the poets and essayists of New England. The novelists of the day she ignored almost completely, and voluntarily. Only occasionally, and then as a concession, she permitted herself a reading of Mr. Howells.

Moderately prosperous while he himself was conducting his little mill, Dearborn had not been able to put by any money to speak of, and when Laura and the local lawyer had come to close up the business, to dispose of the mill, and to settle the claims against what the lawyer grandiloquently termed "the estate," there was just enough money left to pay for Page's tickets to Chicago and a course of tuition for her at a seminary.

The Cresslers on the event of Dearborn's death had advised both sisters to come West, and had pledged themselves to look after Page during the period of her schooling. Laura had sent the little girl on at once, but delayed taking the step herself.

Fortunately, the two sisters were not obliged to live upon their inheritance. Dearborn himself had a sister—a twin of Aunt Wess'—who had married a wealthy woollen merchant of Boston, and this one, long since, had provided for the two girls. A large sum had been set aside, which was to be made over to them when the father died. For years now this sum had been accumulating interest. So that when Laura and Page faced the world, alone, upon the steps of the Barrington cemetery, they had the assurance that, at least, they were independent.

For two years, in the solidly built colonial dwelling, with its low ceilings and ample fireplaces, where once the minute-men had swung their kettles, Laura, alone, thought it all over. Mother and father were dead; even the Boston aunt was dead. Of all her relations, Aunt Wess' alone remained. Page was at her finishing school at Geneva Lake, within two hours of Chicago. The Cresslers were the dearest friends of the orphan girls. Aunt Wess', herself a widow, living also in Chicago, added her entreaties to Mrs. Cressler's. All things seemed to point her westward, all things seemed to indicate that one phase of her life was ended.

Then, too, she had her ambitions. These hardly took definite shape in her mind; but vaguely she chose to see herself, at some far-distant day, an actress, a tragedienne, playing the roles of Shakespeare's heroines. This idea of hers was more a desire than an ambition, but it could not be realised in Barrington, Massachusetts. For a year she temporised, procrastinated, loth to leave the old home, loth to leave the grave in the cemetery back of the Methodist-Episcopal chapel. Twice during this time she visited Page, and each time the great grey city threw the spell of its fascination about her. Each time she returned to Barrington the town dwindled in her estimation. It was picturesque, but lamentably narrow. The life was barren, the "New England spirit" prevailed in all its severity; and this spirit seemed to her a veritable cult, a sort of religion, wherein the Old Maid was the priestess, the Spinster the officiating devotee, the thing worshipped the Great Unbeautiful, and the ritual unremitting, unrelenting Housework. She detested it.

That she was an Episcopalian, and preferred to read her prayers rather than to listen to those written and memorised by the Presbyterian minister, seemed to be regarded as a relic of heathenish rites—a thing almost cannibalistic. When she elected to engage a woman and a "hired man" to manage her house, she felt the disapprobation of the entire village, as if she had sunk into some decadent and enervating Lower-Empire degeneracy.

The crisis came when Laura travelled alone to Boston to hear Modjeska in "Marie Stuart" and "Macbeth," and upon returning full of enthusiasm, allowed it to be understood that she had a half-formed desire of emulating such an example. A group of lady-deaconesses, headed by the Presbyterian minister, called upon her, with some intention of reasoning and labouring with her.

They got no farther than the statement of the cause of this visit. The spirit and temper of the South, that she had from her mother, flamed up in Laura at last, and the members of the "committee," before they were well aware, came to themselves in the street outside the front gate, dazed and bewildered, staring at each other, all confounded and stunned by the violence of an outbreak of long-repressed emotion and long-restrained anger, that like an actual physical force had swept them out of the house.

At the same moment Laura, thrown across her bed, wept with a vehemence that shook her from head to foot. But she had not the least compunction for what she had said, and before the month was out had said good-by to Barrington forever, and was on her way to Chicago, henceforth to be her home.

A house was bought on the North Side, and it was arranged that Aunt Wess' should live with her two nieces. Pending the installation Laura and Page lived at a little family hotel in the same neighbourhood. The Cresslers' invitation to join the theatre party at the Auditorium had fallen inopportunely enough, squarely in the midst of the ordeal of moving in. Indeed the two girls had already passed one night in the new home, and they must dress for the affair by lamplight in their unfurnished quarters and under inconceivable difficulties. Only the lure of Italian opera, heard from a box, could have tempted them to have accepted the invitation at such a time and under such circumstances.

The morning after the opera, Laura woke in her bed—almost the only article of furniture that was in place in the whole house—with the depressing consciousness of a hard day's work at hand. Outside it was still raining, the room was cold, heated only by an inadequate oil stove, and through the slats of the inside shutters, which, pending the hanging of the curtains they had been obliged to close, was filtering a gloomy light of a wet Chicago morning.

It was all very mournful, and she regretted now that she had not abided by her original decision to remain at the hotel until the new house was ready for occupancy. But it had happened that their month at the hotel was just up, and rather than engage the rooms for another four weeks she had thought it easier as well as cheaper to come to the house. It was all a new experience for her, and she had imagined that everything could be moved in, put in place, and the household running smoothly in a week's time.

She sat up in bed, hugging her shoulders against the chill of the room and looking at her theatre gown, that—in default of a clean closet—she had hung from the gas fixture the night before. From the direction of the kitchen came the sounds of the newly engaged "girl" making the fire for breakfast, while through the register a thin wisp of blue smoke curled upward to prove that the "hired man" was tinkering with the unused furnace. The room itself was in lamentable confusion. Crates and packing boxes encumbered the uncarpeted floor; chairs wrapped in excelsior and jute were piled one upon another; a roll of carpet leaned in one corner and a pile of mattresses occupied another.

As Laura considered the prospect she realised her blunder.

"Why, and oh, why," she murmured, "didn't we stay at the hotel till all this was straightened out?"

But in an adjoining room she heard Aunt Wess' stirring. She turned to Page, who upon the pillows beside her still slept, her stocking around her neck as a guarantee against draughts.

"Page, Page! Wake up, girlie. It's late, and there's worlds to do."

Page woke blinking.

"Oh, it's freezing cold, Laura. Let's light the oil stove and stay in bed till the room gets warm. Oh, dear, aren't you sleepy, and, oh, wasn't last night lovely? Which one of us will get up to light the stove? We'll count for it. Lie down, sissie, dear," she begged, "you're letting all the cold air in."

Laura complied, and the two sisters, their noses all but touching, the bedclothes up to their ears, put their arms about each other to keep the warmer.

Amused at the foolishness, they "counted" to decide as to who should get up to light the oil stove, Page beginning:

"Eeny—meeny—myny—mo—"

But before the "count" was decided Aunt Wess' came in, already dressed, and in a breath the two girls implored her to light the stove. While she did so, Aunt Wess' remarked, with the alacrity of a woman who observes the difficulties of a proceeding in which she has no faith:

"I don't believe that hired girl knows her business. She says now she can't light a fire in that stove. My word, Laura, I do believe you'll have enough of all this before you're done. You know I advised you from the very first to take a flat."

"Nonsense, Aunt Wess'," answered Laura, good-naturedly. "We'll work it out all right. I know what's the matter with that range. I'll be right down and see to it so soon as I'm dressed."

It was nearly ten o'clock before breakfast, such as it was, was over. They ate it on the kitchen table, with the kitchen knives and forks, and over the meal, Page having remarked: "Well, what will we do first?" discussed the plan of campaign.

"Landry Court does not have to work to-day—he told me why, but I've forgotten—and he said he was coming up to help," observed Laura, and at once Aunt Wess' smiled. Landry Court was openly and strenuously in love with Laura, and no one of the new household ignored the fact. Aunt Wess' chose to consider the affair as ridiculous, and whenever the subject was mentioned spoke of Landry as "that boy."

Page, however, bridled with seriousness as often as the matter came up. Yes, that was all very well, but Landry was a decent, hard-working young fellow, with all his way to make and no time to waste, and if Laura didn't mean that it should come to anything it wasn't very fair to him to keep him dangling along like that.

"I guess," Laura was accustomed to reply, looking significantly at Aunt Wess', "that our little girlie has a little bit of an eye on a certain hard-working young fellow herself." And the answer invariably roused Page.

"Now, Laura," she would cry, her eyes snapping, her breath coming fast. "Now, Laura, that isn't right at all, and you know I don't like it, and you just say it because you know it makes me cross. I won't have you insinuate that I would run after any man or care in the least whether he's in love or not. I just guess I've got some self-respect; and as for Landry Court, we're no more nor less than just good friends, and I appreciate his business talents and the way he rustles 'round, and he merely respects me as a friend, and it don't go any farther than that. 'An eye on him,' I do declare! As if I hadn't yet to see the man I'd so much as look at a second time."

And Laura, remembering her "Shakespeare," was ever ready with the words:

"The lady doth protest too much, methinks."

Just after breakfast, in fact, Landry did appear.

"Now," he began, with a long breath, addressing Laura, who was unwrapping the pieces of cut glass and bureau ornaments as Page passed them to her from the depths of a crate. "Now, I've done a lot already. That's what made me late. I've ordered your newspaper sent here, and I've telephoned the hotel to forward any mail that comes for you to this address, and I sent word to the gas company to have your gas turned on—"

"Oh, that's good," said Laura.

"Yes, I thought of that; the man will be up right away to fix it, and I've ordered a cake of ice left here every day, and told the telephone company that you wanted a telephone put in. Oh, yes, and the bottled-milk man—I stopped in at a dairy on the way up. Now, what do we do first?"

He took off his coat, rolled up his shirt sleeves, and plunged into the confusion of crates and boxes that congested the rooms and hallways on the first floor of the house. The two sisters could hear him attacking his task with tremendous blows of the kitchen hammer. From time to time he called up the stairway:

"Hey, what do you want done with this jardiniere thing? ... Where does this hanging lamp go, Laura?"

Laura, having unpacked all the cut-glass ornaments, came down-stairs, and she and Landry set about hanging the parlour curtains.

Landry fixed the tops of the window mouldings with a piercing eye, his arms folded.

"I see, I see," he answered to Laura's explanations. "I see. Now where's a screw-driver, and a step-ladder? Yes, and I'll have to have some brass nails, and your hired man must let me have that hammer again."

He sent the cook after the screw-driver, called the hired man from the furnace, shouted upstairs to Page to ask for the whereabouts of the brass nails, and delegated Laura to steady the step-ladder.

"Now, Landry," directed Laura, "those rods want to be about three inches from the top."

"Well," he said, climbing up, "I'll mark the place with the screw and you tell me if it is right."

She stepped back, her head to one side.

"No; higher, Landry. There, that's about it—or a little lower—so. That's just right. Come down now and help me put the hooks in."

They pulled a number of sofa cushions together and sat down on the floor side by side, Landry snapping the hooks in place where Laura had gathered the pleats. Inevitably his hands touched hers, and their heads drew close together. Page and Mrs. Wessels were unpacking linen in the upstairs hall. The cook and hired man raised a great noise of clanking stove lids and grates as they wrestled with the range in the kitchen.

"Well," said Landry, "you are going to have a pretty home." He was meditating a phrase of which he purposed delivering himself when opportunity afforded. It had to do with Laura's eyes, and her ability of understanding him. She understood him; she was to know that he thought so, that it was of immense importance to him. It was thus he conceived of the manner of love making. The evening before that palavering artist seemed to have managed to monopolise her about all of the time. Now it was his turn, and this day of household affairs, of little domestic commotions, appeared to him to be infinitely more desirous than the pomp and formality of evening dress and opera boxes. This morning the relations between himself and Laura seemed charming, intimate, unconventional, and full of opportunities. Never had she appeared prettier to him. She wore a little pink flannel dressing-sack with full sleeves, and her hair, carelessly twisted into great piles, was in a beautiful disarray, curling about her cheeks and ears. "I didn't see anything of you at all last night," he grumbled.

"Well, you didn't try."

"Oh, it was the Other Fellow's turn," he went on. "Say," he added, "how often are you going to let me come to see you when you get settled here? Twice a week—three times?"

"As if you wanted to see me as often as that. Why, Landry, I'm growing up to be an old maid. You can't want to lose your time calling on old maids."

He was voluble in protestations. He was tired of young girls. They were all very well to dance with, but when a man got too old for that sort of thing, he wanted some one with sense to talk to. Yes, he did. Some one with sense. Why, he would rather talk five minutes with her—

"Honestly, Landry?" she asked, as though he were telling a thing incredible.

He swore to her it was true. His eyes snapped. He struck his palm with his fist.

"An old maid like me?" repeated Laura.

"Old maid nothing!" he vociferated. "Ah," he cried, "you seem to understand me. When I look at you, straight into your eyes—"

From the doorway the cook announced that the man with the last load of furnace coal had come, and handed Laura the voucher to sign. Then needs must that Laura go with the cook to see if the range was finally and properly adjusted, and while she was gone the man from the gas company called to turn on the meter, and Landry was obliged to look after him. It was half an hour before he and Laura could once more settle themselves on the cushions in the parlour.

"Such a lot of things to do," she said; "and you are such a help, Landry. It was so dear of you to want to come."

"I would do anything in the world for you, Laura," he exclaimed, encouraged by her words; "anything. You know I would. It isn't so much that I want you to care for me—and I guess I want that bad enough—but it's because I love to be with you, and be helping you, and all that sort of thing. Now, all this," he waved a hand at the confusion of furniture, "all this to-day—I just feel," he declared with tremendous earnestness, "I just feel as though I were entering into your life. And just sitting here beside you and putting in these curtain hooks, I want you to know that it's inspiring to me. Yes, it is, inspiring; it's elevating. You don't know how it makes a man feel to have the companionship of a good and lovely woman."

"Landry, as though I were all that. Here, put another hook in here."

She held the fold towards him. But he took her hand as their fingers touched and raised it to his lips and kissed it. She did not withdraw it, nor rebuke him, crying out instead, as though occupied with quite another matter:

"Landry, careful, my dear boy; you'll make me prick my fingers. Ah—there, you did."

He was all commiseration and self-reproach at once, and turned her hand palm upwards, looking for the scratch.

"Um!" she breathed. "It hurts."

"Where now," he cried, "where was it? Ah, I was a beast; I'm so ashamed." She indicated a spot on her wrist instead of her fingers, and very naturally Landry kissed it again.

"How foolish!" she remonstrated. "The idea! As if I wasn't old enough to be—"

"You're not so old but what you're going to marry me some day," he declared.

"How perfectly silly, Landry!" she retorted. "Aren't you done with my hand yet?"

"No, indeed," he cried, his clasp tightening over her fingers. "It's mine. You can't have it till I say—or till you say that—some day—you'll give it to me for good—for better or for worse."

"As if you really meant that," she said, willing to prolong the little situation. It was very sweet to have this clean, fine-fibred young boy so earnestly in love with her, very sweet that the lifting of her finger, the mere tremble of her eyelid should so perturb him.

"Mean it! Mean it!" he vociferated. "You don't know how much I do mean it. Why, Laura, why—why, I can't think of anything else."

"You!" she mocked. "As if I believed that. How many other girls have you said it to this year?"

Landry compressed his lips.

"Miss Dearborn, you insult me."

"Oh, my!" exclaimed Laura, at last withdrawing her hand.

"And now you're mocking me. It isn't kind. No, it isn't; it isn't kind."

"I never answered your question yet," she observed.

"What question?"

"About your coming to see me when we were settled. I thought you wanted to know."

"How about lunch?" said Page, from the doorway. "Do you know it's after twelve?"

"The girl has got something for us," said Laura. "I told her about it. Oh, just a pick-up lunch—coffee, chops. I thought we wouldn't bother to-day. We'll have to eat in the kitchen."

"Well, let's be about it," declared Landry, "and finish with these curtains afterward. Inwardly I'm a ravening wolf."

It was past one o'clock by the time that luncheon, "picked up" though it was, was over. By then everybody was very tired. Aunt Wess' exclaimed that she could not stand another minute, and retired to her room. Page, indefatigable, declaring they never would get settled if they let things dawdle along, set to work unpacking her trunk and putting her clothes away. Her fox terrier, whom the family, for obscure reasons, called the Pig, arrived in the middle of the afternoon in a crate, and shivering with the chill of the house, was tied up behind the kitchen range, where, for all the heat, he still trembled and shuddered at long intervals, his head down, his eyes rolled up, bewildered and discountenanced by so much confusion and so many new faces.

Outside the weather continued lamentable. The rain beat down steadily upon the heaps of snow on the grass-plats by the curbstones, melting it, dirtying it, and reducing it to viscid slush. The sky was lead grey; the trees, bare and black as though built of iron and wire, dripped incessantly. The sparrows, huddling under the house-eaves or in interstices of the mouldings, chirped feebly from time to time, sitting disconsolate, their feathers puffed out till their bodies assumed globular shapes. Delivery wagons trundled up and down the street at intervals, the horses and drivers housed in oil-skins.

The neighborhood was quiet. There was no sound of voices in the streets. But occasionally, from far away in the direction of the river or the Lake Front, came the faint sounds of steamer and tug whistles. The sidewalks in either direction were deserted. Only a solitary policeman, his star pinned to the outside of his dripping rubber coat, his helmet shedding rivulets, stood on the corner absorbed in the contemplation of the brown torrent of the gutter plunging into a sewer vent.

Landry and Laura were in the library at the rear of the house, a small room, two sides of which were occupied with book-cases. They were busy putting the books in place. Laura stood half-way up the step-ladder taking volume after volume from Landry as he passed them to her.

"Do you wipe them carefully, Landry?" she asked.

He held a strip of cloth torn from an old sheet in his hand, and rubbed the dust from each book before he handed it to her.

"Yes, yes; very carefully," he assured her. "Say," he added, "where are all your modern novels? You've got Scott and Dickens and Thackeray, of course, and Eliot—yes, and here's Hawthorne and Poe. But I haven't struck anything later than Oliver Wendell Holmes."

Laura put up her chin. "Modern novels—no indeed. When I've yet to read 'Jane Eyre,' and have only read 'Ivanhoe' and 'The Newcomes' once."

She made a point of the fact that her taste was the extreme of conservatism, refusing to acknowledge hardly any fiction that was not almost classic. Even Stevenson aroused her suspicions.

"Well, here's 'The Wrecker,'" observed Landry, handing it up to her. "I read it last summer-vacation at Waukesha. Just about took the top of my head off."

"I tried to read it," she answered. "Such an outlandish story, no love story in it, and so coarse, so brutal, and then so improbable. I couldn't get interested."

But abruptly Landry uttered an exclamation:

"Well, what do you call this? 'Wanda,' by Ouida. How is this for modern?"

She blushed to her hair, snatching the book from him.

"Page brought it home. It's hers."

But her confusion betrayed her, and Landry shouted derisively.

"Well, I did read it then," she suddenly declared defiantly. "No, I'm not ashamed. Yes, I read it from cover to cover. It made me cry like I haven't cried over a book since I was a little tot. You can say what you like, but it's beautiful—a beautiful love story—and it does tell about noble, unselfish people. I suppose it has its faults, but it makes you feel better for reading it, and that's what all your 'Wreckers' in the world would never do."

"Well," answered Landry, "I don't know much about that sort of thing. Corthell does. He can talk you blind about literature. I've heard him run on by the hour. He says the novel of the future is going to be the novel without a love story."

But Laura nodded her head incredulously.

"It will be long after I am dead—that's one consolation," she said.

"Corthell is full of crazy ideas anyhow," Landry went on, still continuing to pass the books up to her. "He's a good sort, and I like him well enough, but he's the kind of man that gets up a reputation for being clever and artistic by running down the very one particular thing that every one likes, and cracking up some book or picture or play that no one has ever heard of. Just let anything get popular once and Sheldon Corthell can't speak of it without shuddering. But he'll go over here to some Archer Avenue pawn shop, dig up an old brass stewpan, or coffee-pot that some greasy old Russian Jew has chucked away, and he'll stick it up in his studio and regularly kow-tow to it, and talk about the 'decadence of American industrial arts.' I've heard him. I say it's pure affectation, that's what it is, pure affectation."

But the book-case meanwhile had been filling up, and now Laura remarked:

"No more, Landry. That's all that will go here."

She prepared to descend from the ladder. In filling the higher shelves she had mounted almost to the topmost step.

"Careful now," said Landry, as he came forward. "Give me your hand."

She gave it to him, and then, as she descended, Landry had the assurance to put his arm around her waist as if to steady her. He was surprised at his own audacity, for he had premeditated nothing, and his arm was about her before he was well aware. He yet found time to experience a qualm of apprehension. Just how would Laura take it? Had he gone too far?

But Laura did not even seem to notice, all her attention apparently fixed upon coming safely down to the floor. She descended and shook out her skirts.

"There," she said, "that's over with. Look, I'm all dusty."

There was a knock at the half-open door. It was the cook.

"What are you going to have for supper, Miss Dearborn?" she inquired. "There's nothing in the house."

"Oh, dear," said Laura with sudden blankness, "I never thought of supper. Isn't there anything?"

"Nothing but some eggs and coffee." The cook assumed an air of aloofness, as if the entire affair were totally foreign to any interest or concern of hers. Laura dismissed her, saying that she would see to it.

"We'll have to go out and get some things," she said. "We'll all go. I'm tired of staying in the house."

"No, I've a better scheme," announced Landry. "I'll invite you all out to dine with me. I know a place where you can get the best steak in America. It has stopped raining. See," he showed her the window.

"But, Landry, we are all so dirty and miserable."

"We'll go right now and get there early. There will be nobody there, and we can have a room to ourselves. Oh, it's all right," he declared. "You just trust me."

"We'll see what Page and Aunt Wess' say. Of course Aunt Wess' would have to come."

"Of course," he said. "I wouldn't think of asking you unless she could come."

A little later the two sisters, Mrs. Wessels, and Landry came out of the house, but before taking their car they crossed to the opposite side of the street, Laura having said that she wanted to note the effect of her parlour curtains from the outside.

"I think they are looped up just far enough," she declared. But Landry was observing the house itself.

"It is the best-looking place on the block," he answered.

In fact, the house was not without a certain attractiveness. It occupied a corner lot at the intersection of Huron and North State streets. Directly opposite was St. James' Church, and at one time the house had served as the rectory. For the matter of that, it had been built for just that purpose. Its style of architecture was distantly ecclesiastic, with a suggestion of Gothic to some of the doors and windows. The material used was solid, massive, the walls thick, the foundation heavy. It did not occupy the entire lot, the original builder seeming to have preferred garden space to mere amplitude of construction, and in addition to the inevitable "back yard," a lawn bordered it on three sides. It gave the place a certain air of distinction and exclusiveness. Vines grew thick upon the southern walls; in the summer time fuchsias, geraniums, and pansies would flourish in the flower beds by the front stoop. The grass plat by the curb boasted a couple of trees. The whole place was distinctive, individual, and very homelike, and came as a grateful relief to the endless lines of houses built of yellow Michigan limestone that pervaded the rest of the neighbourhood in every direction.

"I love the place," exclaimed Laura. "I think it's as pretty a house as I have seen in Chicago."

"Well, it isn't so spick and span," commented Page. "It gives you the idea that we're not new-rich and showy and all."

But Aunt Wess' was not yet satisfied.

"You may see, Laura," she remarked, "how you are going to heat all that house with that one furnace, but I declare I don't."

Their car, or rather their train of cars, coupled together in threes, in Chicago style, came, and Landry escorted them down town. All the way Laura could not refrain from looking out of the windows, absorbed in the contemplation of the life and aspects of the streets.

"You will give yourself away," said Page. "Everybody will know you're from the country."

"I am," she retorted. "But there's a difference between just mere 'country' and Massachusetts, and I'm not ashamed of it."

Chicago, the great grey city, interested her at every instant and under every condition. As yet she was not sure that she liked it; she could not forgive its dirty streets, the unspeakable squalor of some of its poorer neighbourhoods that sometimes developed, like cancerous growths, in the very heart of fine residence districts. The black murk that closed every vista of the business streets oppressed her, and the soot that stained linen and gloves each time she stirred abroad was a never-ending distress.

But the life was tremendous. All around, on every side, in every direction the vast machinery of Commonwealth clashed and thundered from dawn to dark and from dark till dawn. Even now, as the car carried her farther into the business quarter, she could hear it, see it, and feel in her every fibre the trepidation of its motion. The blackened waters of the river, seen an instant between stanchions as the car trundled across the State Street bridge, disappeared under fleets of tugs, of lake steamers, of lumber barges from Sheboygan and Mackinac, of grain boats from Duluth, of coal scows that filled the air with impalpable dust, of cumbersome schooners laden with produce, of grimy rowboats dodging the prows and paddles of the larger craft, while on all sides, blocking the horizon, red in color and designated by Brobdignag letters, towered the hump-shouldered grain elevators.

Just before crossing the bridge on the north side of the river she had caught a glimpse of a great railway terminus. Down below there, rectilinear, scientifically paralleled and squared, the Yard disclosed itself. A system of grey rails beyond words complicated opened out and spread immeasurably. Switches, semaphores, and signal towers stood here and there. A dozen trains, freight and passenger, puffed and steamed, waiting the word to depart. Detached engines hurried in and out of sheds and roundhouses, seeking their trains, or bunted the ponderous freight cars into switches; trundling up and down, clanking, shrieking, their bells filling the air with the clangour of tocsins. Men in visored caps shouted hoarsely, waving their arms or red flags; drays, their big dappled horses, feeding in their nose bags, stood backed up to the open doors of freight cars and received their loads. A train departed roaring. Before midnight it would be leagues away boring through the Great Northwest, carrying Trade—the life blood of nations—into communities of which Laura had never heard. Another train, reeking with fatigue, the air brakes screaming, arrived and halted, debouching a flood of passengers, business men, bringing Trade—a galvanising elixir—from the very ends and corners of the continent.

Or, again, it was South Water Street—a jam of delivery wagons and market carts backed to the curbs, leaving only a tortuous path between the endless files of horses, suggestive of an actual barrack of cavalry. Provisions, market produce, "garden truck" and fruits, in an infinite welter of crates and baskets, boxes, and sacks, crowded the sidewalks. The gutter was choked with an overflow of refuse cabbage leaves, soft oranges, decaying beet tops. The air was thick with the heavy smell of vegetation. Food was trodden under foot, food crammed the stores and warehouses to bursting. Food mingled with the mud of the highway. The very dray horses were gorged with an unending nourishment of snatched mouthfuls picked from backboard, from barrel top, and from the edge of the sidewalk. The entire locality reeked with the fatness of a hundred thousand furrows. A land of plenty, the inordinate abundance of the earth itself emptied itself upon the asphalt and cobbles of the quarter. It was the Mouth of the City, and drawn from all directions, over a territory of immense area, this glut of crude subsistence was sucked in, as if into a rapacious gullet, to feed the sinews and to nourish the fibres of an immeasurable colossus.

Suddenly the meaning and significance of it all dawned upon Laura. The Great Grey City, brooking no rival, imposed its dominion upon a reach of country larger than many a kingdom of the Old World. For, thousands of miles beyond its confines was its influence felt. Out, far out, far away in the snow and shadow of Northern Wisconsin forests, axes and saws bit the bark of century-old trees, stimulated by this city's energy. Just as far to the southward pick and drill leaped to the assault of veins of anthracite, moved by her central power. Her force turned the wheels of harvester and seeder a thousand miles distant in Iowa and Kansas. Her force spun the screws and propellers of innumerable squadrons of lake steamers crowding the Sault Sainte Marie. For her and because of her all the Central States, all the Great Northwest roared with traffic and industry; sawmills screamed; factories, their smoke blackening the sky, clashed and flamed; wheels turned, pistons leaped in their cylinders; cog gripped cog; beltings clasped the drums of mammoth wheels; and converters of forges belched into the clouded air their tempest breath of molten steel.

It was Empire, the resistless subjugation of all this central world of the lakes and the prairies. Here, mid-most in the land, beat the Heart of the Nation, whence inevitably must come its immeasurable power, its infinite, infinite, inexhaustible vitality. Here, of all her cities, throbbed the true life—the true power and spirit of America; gigantic, crude with the crudity of youth, disdaining rivalry; sane and healthy and vigorous; brutal in its ambition, arrogant in the new-found knowledge of its giant strength, prodigal of its wealth, infinite in its desires. In its capacity boundless, in its courage indomitable; subduing the wilderness in a single generation, defying calamity, and through the flame and the debris of a commonwealth in ashes, rising suddenly renewed, formidable, and Titanic.

Laura, her eyes dizzied, her ears stunned, watched tirelessly.

"There is something terrible about it," she murmured, half to herself, "something insensate. In a way, it doesn't seem human. It's like a great tidal wave. It's all very well for the individual just so long as he can keep afloat, but once fallen, how horribly quick it would crush him, annihilate him, how horribly quick, and with such horrible indifference! I suppose it's civilisation in the making, the thing that isn't meant to be seen, as though it were too elemental, too—primordial; like the first verses of Genesis."

The impression remained long with her, and not even the gaiety of their little supper could altogether disperse it. She was a little frightened—frightened of the vast, cruel machinery of the city's life, and of the men who could dare it, who conquered it. For a moment they seemed, in a sense, more terrible than the city itself—men for whom all this crash of conflict and commerce had no terrors. Those who could subdue it to their purposes, must they not be themselves more terrible, more pitiless, more brutal? She shrank a little. What could women ever know of the life of men, after all? Even Landry, extravagant as he was, so young, so exuberant, so seemingly innocent—she knew that he was spoken of as a good business man. He, too, then had his other side. For him the Battle of the Street was an exhilaration. Beneath that boyish exterior was the tough coarseness, the male hardness, the callousness that met the brunt and withstood the shock of onset.

Ah, these men of the city, what could women ever know of them, of their lives, of that other existence through which—freed from the influence of wife or mother, or daughter or sister—they passed every day from nine o'clock till evening? It was a life in which women had no part, and in which, should they enter it, they would no longer recognise son or husband, or father or brother. The gentle-mannered fellow, clean-minded, clean-handed, of the breakfast or supper table was one man. The other, who and what was he? Down there in the murk and grime of the business district raged the Battle of the Street, and therein he was a being transformed, case hardened, supremely selfish, asking no quarter; no, nor giving any. Fouled with the clutchings and grapplings of the attack, besmirched with the elbowing of low associates and obscure allies, he set his feet toward conquest, and mingled with the marchings of an army that surged forever forward and back; now in merciless assault, beating the fallen enemy under foot, now in repulse, equally merciless, trampling down the auxiliaries of the day before, in a panic dash for safety; always cruel, always selfish, always pitiless.

To contrast these men with such as Corthell was inevitable. She remembered him, to whom the business district was an unexplored country, who kept himself far from the fighting, his hands unstained, his feet unsullied. He passed his life gently, in the calm, still atmosphere of art, in the cult of the beautiful, unperturbed, tranquil; painting, reading, or, piece by piece, developing his beautiful stained glass. Him women could know, with him they could sympathise. And he could enter fully into their lives and help and stimulate them. Of the two existences which did she prefer, that of the business man, or that of the artist?

Then suddenly Laura surprised herself. After all, she was a daughter of the frontier, and the blood of those who had wrestled with a new world flowed in her body. Yes, Corthell's was a beautiful life; the charm of dim painted windows, the attraction of darkened studios with their harmonies of color, their orientalisms, and their arabesques was strong. No doubt it all had its place. It fascinated her at times, in spite of herself. To relax the mind, to indulge the senses, to live in an environment of pervading beauty was delightful. But the men to whom the woman in her turned were not those of the studio. Terrible as the Battle of the Street was, it was yet battle. Only the strong and the brave might dare it, and the figure that held her imagination and her sympathy was not the artist, soft of hand and of speech, elaborating graces of sound and color and form, refined, sensitive, and temperamental; but the fighter, unknown and un-knowable to women as he was; hard, rigorous, panoplied in the harness of the warrior, who strove among the trumpets, and who, in the brunt of conflict, conspicuous, formidable, set the battle in a rage around him, and exulted like a champion in the shoutings of the captains.

They were not long at table, and by the time they were ready to depart it was about half-past five. But when they emerged into the street, it was discovered that once more the weather had abruptly changed. It was snowing thickly. Again a bitter wind from off the Lake tore through the streets. The slush and melted snow was freezing, and the north side of every lamp post and telegraph pole was sheeted with ice.

To add to their discomfort, the North State Street cars were blocked. When they gained the corner of Washington Street they could see where the congestion began, a few squares distant.

"There's nothing for it," declared Landry, "but to go over and get the Clarke Street cars—and at that you may have to stand up all the way home, at this time of day."

They paused, irresolute, a moment on the corner. It was the centre of the retail quarter. Close at hand a vast dry goods house, built in the old "iron-front" style, towered from the pavement, and through its hundreds of windows presented to view a world of stuffs and fabrics, upholsteries and textiles, kaleidoscopic, gleaming in the fierce brilliance of a multitude of lights. From each street doorway was pouring an army of "shoppers," women for the most part; and these—since the store catered to a rich clientele—fashionably dressed. Many of them stood for a moment on the threshold of the storm-doorways, turning up the collars of their sealskins, settling their hands in their muffs, and searching the street for their coupes and carriages.

Among the number of those thus engaged, one, suddenly catching sight of Laura, waved a muff in her direction, then came quickly forward. It was Mrs. Cressler.

"Laura, my dearest girl! Of all the people. I am so glad to see you!" She kissed Laura on the cheek, shook hands all around, and asked about the sisters' new home. Did they want anything, or was there anything she could do to help? Then interrupting herself, and laying a glove on Laura's arm:

"I've got more to tell you."

She compressed her lips and stood off from Laura, fixing her with a significant glance.

"Me? To tell me?"

"Where are you going now?"

"Home; but our cars are stopped. We must go over to—"

"Fiddlesticks! You and Page and Mrs. Wessels—all of you are coming home and dine with me."

"But we've had dinner already," they all cried, speaking at once.

Page explained the situation, but Mrs. Cressler would not be denied.

"The carriage is right here," she said. "I don't have to call for Charlie. He's got a man from Cincinnati in tow, and they are going to dine at the Calumet Club."

It ended by the two sisters and Mrs. Wessels getting into Mrs. Cressler's carriage. Landry excused himself. He lived on the South Side, on Michigan Avenue, and declaring that he knew they had had enough of him for one day, took himself off.

But whatever Mrs. Cressler had to tell Laura, she evidently was determined to save for her ears only. Arrived at the Dearborns' home, she sent her footman in to tell the "girl" that the family would not be home that night. The Cresslers lived hard by on the same street, and within ten minutes' walk of the Dearborns. The two sisters and their aunt would be back immediately after breakfast.

When they had got home with Mrs. Cressler, this latter suggested hot tea and sandwiches in the library, for the ride had been cold. But the others, worn out, declared for bed as soon as Mrs. Cressler herself had dined.

"Oh, bless you, Carrie," said Aunt Wess'; "I couldn't think of tea. My back is just about broken, and I'm going straight to my bed."

Mrs. Cressler showed them to their rooms. Page and Mrs. Wessels elected to sleep together, and once the door had closed upon them the little girl unburdened herself.

"I suppose Laura thinks it's all right, running off like this for the whole blessed night, and no one to look after the house but those two servants that nobody knows anything about. As though there weren't heaven knows what all to tend to there in the morning. I just don't see," she exclaimed decisively, "how we're going to get settled at all. That Landry Court! My goodness, he's more hindrance than help. Did you ever see! He just dashes in as though he were doing it all, and messes everything up, and loses things, and gets things into the wrong place, and forgets this and that, and then he and Laura sit down and spoon. I never saw anything like it. First it's Corthell and then Landry, and next it will be somebody else. Laura regularly mortifies me; a great, grown-up girl like that, flirting, and letting every man she meets think that he's just the one particular one of the whole earth. It's not good form. And Landry—as if he didn't know we've got more to do now than just to dawdle and dawdle. I could slap him. I like to see a man take life seriously and try to amount to something, and not waste the best years of his life trailing after women who are old enough to be his grandmother, and don't mean that it will ever come to anything."

In her room, in the front of the house, Laura was partly undressed when Mrs. Cressler knocked at her door. The latter had put on a wrapper of flowered silk, and her hair was bound in "invisible nets."

"I brought you a dressing-gown," she said. She hung it over the foot of the bed, and sat down on the bed itself, watching Laura, who stood before the glass of the bureau, her head bent upon her breast, her hands busy with the back of her hair. From time to time the hairpins clicked as she laid them down in the silver trays close at hand. Then putting her chin in the air, she shook her head, and the great braids, unlooped, fell to her waist.

"What pretty hair you have, child," murmured Mrs. Cressler. She was settling herself for a long talk with her protege. She had much to tell, but now that they had the whole night before them, could afford to take her time.

Between the two women the conversation began slowly, with detached phrases and observations that did not call necessarily for answers—mere beginnings that they did not care to follow up.

"They tell me," said Mrs. Cressler, "that that Gretry girl smokes ten cigarettes every night before she goes to bed. You know the Gretrys—they were at the opera the other night."

Laura permitted herself an indefinite murmur of interest. Her head to one side, she drew the brush in slow, deliberate movements downward underneath the long, thick strands of her hair. Mrs. Cressler watched her attentively.

"Why don't you wear your hair that new way, Laura," she remarked, "farther down on your neck? I see every one doing it now."

The house was very still. Outside the double windows they could hear the faint murmuring click of the frozen snow. A radiator in the hallway clanked and strangled for a moment, then fell quiet again.

"What a pretty room this is," said Laura. "I think I'll have to do our guest room something like this—a sort of white and gold effect. My hair? Oh, I don't know. Wearing it low that way makes it catch so on the hooks of your collar, and, besides, I was afraid it would make my head look so flat."

There was a silence. Laura braided a long strand, with quick, regular motions of both hands, and letting it fall over her shoulder, shook it into place with a twist of her head. She stepped out of her skirt, and Mrs. Cressler handed her her dressing-gown, and brought out a pair of quilted slippers of red satin from the wardrobe.

In the grate, the fire that had been lighted just before they had come upstairs was crackling sharply. Laura drew up an armchair and sat down in front of it, her chin in her hand. Mrs. Cressler stretched herself upon the bed, an arm behind her head.

"Well, Laura," she began at length, "I have some real news for you. My dear, I believe you've made a conquest."

"I!" murmured Laura, looking around. She feigned a surprise, though she guessed at once that Mrs. Cressler had Corthell in mind.

"That Mr. Jadwin—the one you met at the opera."

Genuinely taken aback, Laura sat upright and stared wide-eyed.

"Mr. Jadwin!" she exclaimed. "Why, we didn't have five minutes' talk. Why, I hardly know the man. I only met him last night."

But Mrs. Cressler shook her head, closing her eyes and putting her lips together.

"That don't make any difference, Laura. Trust me to tell when a man is taken with a girl. My dear, you can have him as easy as that." She snapped her fingers.

"Oh, I'm sure you're mistaken, Mrs. Cressler."

"Not in the least. I've known Curtis Jadwin now for fifteen years—nobody better. He's as old a family friend as Charlie and I have. I know him like a book. And I tell you the man is in love with you."

"Well, I hope he didn't tell you as much," cried Laura, promising herself to be royally angry if such was the case. But Mrs. Cressler hastened to reassure her.

"Oh my, no. But all the way home last night—he came home with us, you know—he kept referring to you, and just so soon as the conversation got on some other subject he would lose interest. He wanted to know all about you—oh, you know how a man will talk," she exclaimed. "And he said you had more sense and more intelligence than any girl he had ever known."

"Oh, well," answered Laura deprecatingly, as if to say that that did not count for much with her.

"And that you were simply beautiful. He said that he never remembered to have seen a more beautiful woman."

Laura turned her head away, a hand shielding her cheek. She did not answer immediately, then at length:

"Has he—this Mr. Jadwin—has he ever been married before?"

"No, no. He's a bachelor, and rich! He could buy and sell us. And don't think, Laura dear, that I'm jumping at conclusions. I hope I'm woman of the world enough to know that a man who's taken with a pretty face and smart talk isn't going to rush right into matrimony because of that. It wasn't so much what Curtis Jadwin said—though, dear me suz, he talked enough about you—as what he didn't say. I could tell. He was thinking hard. He was hit, Laura. I know he was. And Charlie said he spoke about you again this morning at breakfast. Charlie makes me tired sometimes," she added irrelevantly.

"Charlie?" repeated Laura.

"Well, of course I spoke to him about Jadwin, and how taken he seemed with you, and the man roared at me."

"He didn't believe it, then."

"Yes he did—when I could get him to talk seriously about it, and when I made him remember how Mr. Jadwin had spoken in the carriage coming home."

Laura curled her leg under her and sat nursing her foot and looking into the fire. For a long time neither spoke. A little clock of brass and black marble began to chime, very prettily, the half hour of nine. Mrs. Cressler observed:

"That Sheldon Corthell seems to be a very agreeable kind of a young man, doesn't he?"

"Yes," replied Laura thoughtfully, "he is agreeable."

"And a talented fellow, too," continued Mrs. Cressler. "But somehow it never impressed me that there was very much to him."

"Oh," murmured Laura indifferently, "I don't know."

"I suppose," Mrs. Cressler went on, in a tone of resignation, "I suppose he thinks the world and all of you?"

Laura raised a shoulder without answering.

"Charlie can't abide him," said Mrs. Cressler. "Funny, isn't it what prejudices men have? Charlie always speaks of him as though he were a higher order of glazier. Curtis Jadwin seems to like him.... What do you think of him, Laura—of Mr. Jadwin?"

"I don't know," she answered, looking vaguely into the fire. "I thought he was a strong man—mentally I mean, and that he would be kindly and—and—generous. Somehow," she said, musingly, "I didn't think he would be the sort of man that women would take to, at first—but then I don't know. I saw very little of him, as I say. He didn't impress me as being a woman's man."

"All the better," said the other. "Who would want to marry a woman's man? I wouldn't. Sheldon Corthell is that. I tell you one thing, Laura, and when you are as old as I am, you'll know it's true: the kind of a man that men like—not women—is the kind of a man that makes the best husband."

Laura nodded her head.

"Yes," she answered, listlessly, "I suppose that's true."

"You said Jadwin struck you as being a kindly man, a generous man. He's just that, and that charitable! You know he has a Sunday-school over on the West Side, a Sunday-school for mission children, and I do believe he's more interested in that than in his business. He wants to make it the biggest Sunday-school in Chicago. It's an ambition of his. I don't want you to think that he's good in a goody-goody way, because he's not. Laura," she exclaimed, "he's a fine man. I didn't intend to brag him up to you, because I wanted you to like him. But no one knows—as I say—no one knows Curtis Jadwin better than Charlie and I, and we just love him. The kindliest, biggest-hearted fellow—oh, well, you'll know him for yourself, and then you'll see. He passes the plate in our church."

"Dr. Wendell's church?" asked Laura.

"Yes you know—the Second Presbyterian."

"I'm Episcopalian myself," observed Laura, still thoughtfully gazing into the fire.

"I know, I know. But Jadwin isn't the blue-nosed sort. And now see here, Laura, I want to tell you. J.—that's what Charlie and I call Jadwin—J. was talking to us the other day about supporting a ward in the Children's Hospital for the children of his Sunday-school that get hurt or sick. You see he has nearly eight hundred boys and girls in his school, and there's not a week passes that he don't hear of some one of them who has been hurt or taken sick. And he wants to start a ward at the Children's Hospital, that can take care of them. He says he wants to get other people interested, too, and so he wants to start a contribution. He says he'll double any amount that's raised in the next six months—that is, if there's two thousand raised, he'll make it four thousand; understand? And so Charlie and I and the Gretrys are going to get up an amateur play—a charity affair—and raise as much money as we can. J. thinks it's a good idea, and—here's the point—we were talking about it coming home in the carriage, and J. said he wondered if that Miss Dearborn wouldn't take part. And we are all wild to have you. You know you do that sort of thing so well. Now don't say yes or no to-night. You sleep over it. J. is crazy to have you in it."

"I'd love to do it," answered Laura. "But I would have to see—it takes so long to get settled, and there's so much to do about a big house like ours, I might not have time. But I will let you know."

Mrs. Cressler told her in detail about the proposed play. Landry Court was to take part, and she enlisted Laura's influence to get Sheldon Corthell to undertake a role. Page, it appeared, had already promised to help. Laura remembered now that she had heard her speak of it. However, the plan was so immature as yet, that it hardly admitted of very much discussion, and inevitably the conversation came back to its starting-point.

"You know," Laura had remarked in answer to one of Mrs. Cressler's observations upon the capabilities and business ability of "J.," "you know I never heard of him before you spoke of our theatre party. I don't know anything about him."

But Mrs. Cressler promptly supplied the information. Curtis Jadwin was a man about thirty-five, who had begun life without a sou in his pockets. He was a native of Michigan. His people were farmers, nothing more nor less than hardy, honest fellows, who ploughed and sowed for a living. Curtis had only a rudimentary schooling, because he had given up the idea of finishing his studies in the High School in Grand Rapids, on the chance of going into business with a livery stable keeper. Then in time he had bought out the business and had run it for himself. Some one in Chicago owed him money, and in default of payment had offered him a couple of lots on Wabash Avenue. That was how he happened to come to Chicago. Naturally enough as the city grew the Wabash Avenue property—it was near Monroe Street—increased in value. He sold the lots and bought other real estate, sold that and bought somewhere else, and so on, till he owned some of the best business sites in the city. Just his ground rent alone brought him, heaven knew how many thousands a year. He was one of the largest real estate owners in Chicago. But he no longer bought and sold. His property had grown so large that just the management of it alone took up most of his time. He had an office in the Rookery, and perhaps being so close to the Board of Trade Building, had given him a taste for trying a little deal in wheat now and then. As a rule, he deplored speculation. He had no fixed principles about it, like Charlie. Only he was conservative; occasionally he hazarded small operations. Somehow he had never married. There had been affairs. Oh, yes, one or two, of course. Nothing very serious, He just didn't seem to have met the right girl, that was all. He lived on Michigan Avenue, near the corner of Twenty-first Street, in one of those discouraging eternal yellow limestone houses with a basement dining-room. His aunt kept house for him, and his nieces and nephews overran the place. There was always a raft of them there, either coming or going; and the way they exploited him! He supported them all; heaven knew how many there were; such drabs and gawks, all elbows and knees, who soaked themselves with cologne and made companions of the servants. They and the second girls were always squabbling about their things that they found in each other's rooms.

It was growing late. At length Mrs. Cressler rose.

"My goodness, Laura, look at the time; and I've been keeping you up when you must be killed for sleep."

She took herself away, pausing at the doorway long enough to say:

"Do try to manage to take part in the play. J. made me promise that I would get you."

"Well, I think I can," Laura answered. "Only I'll have to see first how our new regime is going to run—the house I mean."

When Mrs. Cressler had gone Laura lost no time in getting to bed. But after she turned out the gas she remembered that she had not "covered" the fire, a custom that she still retained from the daily round of her life at Barrington. She did not light the gas again, but guided by the firelight, spread a shovelful of ashes over the top of the grate. Yet when she had done this, she still knelt there a moment, looking wide-eyed into the glow, thinking over the events of the last twenty-four hours. When all was said and done, she had, after all, found more in Chicago than the clash and trepidation of empire-making, more than the reverberation of the thunder of battle, more than the piping and choiring of sweet music.

First it had been Sheldon Corthell, quiet, persuasive, eloquent. Then Landry Court with his exuberance and extravagance and boyishness, and now—unexpectedly—behold, a new element had appeared—this other one, this man of the world, of affairs, mature, experienced, whom she hardly knew. It was charming she told herself, exciting. Life never had seemed half so delightful.

Romantic, she felt Romance, unseen, intangible, at work all about her. And love, which of all things knowable was dearest to her, came to her unsought.

Her first aversion to the Great Grey City was fast disappearing. She saw it now in a kindlier aspect.

"I think," she said at last, as she still knelt before the fire, looking deep into the coals, absorbed, abstracted, "I think that I am going to be very happy here."

III

On a certain Monday morning, about a month later, Curtis Jadwin descended from his office in the Rookery Building, and turning southward, took his way toward the brokerage and commission office of Gretry, Converse and Co., on the ground floor of the Board of Trade Building, only a few steps away.

It was about nine o'clock; the weather was mild, the sun shone. La Salle Street swarmed with the multitudinous life that seethed about the doors of the innumerable offices of brokers and commission men of the neighbourhood. To the right, in the peristyle of the Illinois Trust Building, groups of clerks, of messengers, of brokers, of clients, and of depositors formed and broke incessantly. To the left, where the facade of the Board of Trade blocked the street, the activity was astonishing, and in and out of the swing doors of its entrance streamed an incessant tide of coming and going. All the life of the neighbourhood seemed to centre at this point—the entrance of the Board of Trade. Two currents that trended swiftly through La Salle and Jackson streets, and that fed, or were fed by, other tributaries that poured in through Fifth Avenue and through Clarke and Dearborn streets, met at this point—one setting in, the other out. The nearer the currents the greater their speed. Men—mere flotsam in the flood—as they turned into La Salle Street from Adams or from Monroe, or even from as far as Madison, seemed to accelerate their pace as they approached. At the Illinois Trust the walk became a stride, at the Rookery the stride was almost a trot. But at the corner of Jackson Street, the Board of Trade now merely the width of the street away, the trot became a run, and young men and boys, under the pretence of escaping the trucks and wagons of the cobbles, dashed across at a veritable gallop, flung themselves panting into the entrance of the Board, were engulfed in the turmoil of the spot, and disappeared with a sudden fillip into the gloom of the interior.

Often Jadwin had noted the scene, and, unimaginative though he was, had long since conceived the notion of some great, some resistless force within the Board of Trade Building that held the tide of the streets within its grip, alternately drawing it in and throwing it forth. Within there, a great whirlpool, a pit of roaring waters spun and thundered, sucking in the life tides of the city, sucking them in as into the mouth of some tremendous cloaca, the maw of some colossal sewer; then vomiting them forth again, spewing them up and out, only to catch them in the return eddy and suck them in afresh.

Thus it went, day after day. Endlessly, ceaselessly the Pit, enormous, thundering, sucked in and spewed out, sending the swirl of its mighty central eddy far out through the city's channels. Terrible at the centre, it was, at the circumference, gentle, insidious and persuasive, the send of the flowing so mild, that to embark upon it, yielding to the influence, was a pleasure that seemed all devoid of risk. But the circumference was not bounded by the city. All through the Northwest, all through the central world of the Wheat the set and whirl of that innermost Pit made itself felt; and it spread and spread and spread till grain in the elevators of Western Iowa moved and stirred and answered to its centripetal force, and men upon the streets of New York felt the mysterious tugging of its undertow engage their feet, embrace their bodies, overwhelm them, and carry them bewildered and unresisting back and downwards to the Pit itself.

Nor was the Pit's centrifugal power any less. Because of some sudden eddy spinning outward from the middle of its turmoil, a dozen bourses of continental Europe clamoured with panic, a dozen Old-World banks, firm as the established hills, trembled and vibrated. Because of an unexpected caprice in the swirling of the inner current, some far-distant channel suddenly dried, and the pinch of famine made itself felt among the vine dressers of Northern Italy, the coal miners of Western Prussia. Or another channel filled, and the starved moujik of the steppes, and the hunger-shrunken coolie of the Ganges' watershed fed suddenly fat and made thank offerings before ikon and idol.

There in the centre of the Nation, midmost of that continent that lay between the oceans of the New World and the Old, in the heart's heart of the affairs of men, roared and rumbled the Pit. It was as if the Wheat, Nourisher of the Nations, as it rolled gigantic and majestic in a vast flood from West to East, here, like a Niagara, finding its flow impeded, burst suddenly into the appalling fury of the Maelstrom, into the chaotic spasm of a world-force, a primeval energy, blood-brother of the earthquake and the glacier, raging and wrathful that its power should be braved by some pinch of human spawn that dared raise barriers across its courses.

Small wonder that Cressler laughed at the thought of cornering wheat, and even now as Jadwin crossed Jackson Street, on his way to his broker's office on the lower floor of the Board of Trade Building, he noted the ebb and flow that issued from its doors, and remembered the huge river of wheat that rolled through this place from the farms of Iowa and ranches of Dakota to the mills and bakeshops of Europe.

"There's something, perhaps, in what Charlie says," he said to himself. "Corner this stuff—my God!"

Gretry, Converse & Co. was the name of the brokerage firm that always handled Jadwin's rare speculative ventures. Converse was dead long since, but the firm still retained its original name. The house was as old and as well established as any on the Board of Trade. It had a reputation for conservatism, and was known more as a Bear than a Bull concern. It was immensely wealthy and immensely important. It discouraged the growth of a clientele of country customers, of small adventurers, knowing well that these were the first to go in a crash, unable to meet margin calls, and leaving to their brokers the responsibility of their disastrous trades. The large, powerful Bears were its friends, the Bears strong of grip, tenacious of jaw, capable of pulling down the strongest Bull. Thus the firm had no consideration for the "outsiders," the "public"—the Lambs. The Lambs! Such a herd, timid, innocent, feeble, as much out of place in La Salle Street as a puppy in a cage of panthers; the Lambs, whom Bull and Bear did not so much as condescend to notice, but who, in their mutual struggle of horn and claw, they crushed to death by the mere rolling of their bodies.

Jadwin did not go directly into Gretry's main office, but instead made his way in at the entrance of the Board of Trade Building, and going on past the stairways that on either hand led up to the "Floor" on the second story, entered the corridor beyond, and thence gained the customers' room of Gretry, Converse & Co. All the more important brokerage firms had offices on the ground floor of the building, offices that had two entrances, one giving upon the street, and one upon the corridor of the Board. Generally the corridor entrance admitted directly to the firm's customers' room. This was the case with the Gretry-Converse house.

Once in the customers' room, Jadwin paused, looking about him.

He could not tell why Gretry had so earnestly desired him to come to his office that morning, but he wanted to know how wheat was selling before talking to the broker. The room was large, and but for the lighted gas, burning crudely without globes, would have been dark. All one wall opposite the door was taken up by a great blackboard covered with chalked figures in columns, and illuminated by a row of overhead gas jets burning under a tin reflector. Before this board files of chairs were placed, and these were occupied by groups of nondescripts, shabbily dressed men, young and old, with tired eyes and unhealthy complexions, who smoked and expectorated, or engaged in interminable conversations.

In front of the blackboard, upon a platform, a young man in shirt-sleeves, his cuffs caught up by metal clamps, walked up and down. Screwed to the blackboard itself was a telegraph instrument, and from time to time, as this buzzed and ticked, the young man chalked up cabalistic, and almost illegible figures under columns headed by initials of certain stocks and bonds, or by the words "Pork," "Oats," or, larger than all the others, "May Wheat." The air of the room was stale, close, and heavy with tobacco fumes. The only noises were the low hum of conversations, the unsteady click of the telegraph key, and the tapping of the chalk in the marker's fingers.

But no one in the room seemed to pay the least attention to the blackboard. One quotation replaced another, and the key and the chalk clicked and tapped incessantly. The occupants of the room, sunk in their chairs, seemed to give no heed; some even turned their backs; one, his handkerchief over his knee, adjusted his spectacles, and opening a newspaper two days old, began to read with peering deliberation, his lips forming each word. These nondescripts gathered there, they knew not why. Every day found them in the same place, always with the same fetid, unlighted cigars, always with the same frayed newspapers two days old. There they sat, inert, stupid, their decaying senses hypnotised and soothed by the sound of the distant rumble of the Pit, that came through the ceiling from the floor of the Board overhead.

One of these figures, that of a very old man, blear-eyed, decrepit, dirty, in a battered top hat and faded frock coat, discoloured and weather-stained at the shoulders, seemed familiar to Jadwin. It recalled some ancient association, he could not say what. But he was unable to see the old man's face distinctly; the light was bad, and he sat with his face turned from him, eating a sandwich, which he held in a trembling hand.

Jadwin, having noted that wheat was selling at 94, went away, glad to be out of the depressing atmosphere of the room.

Gretry was in his office, and Jadwin was admitted at once. He sat down in a chair by the broker's desk, and for the moment the two talked of trivialities. Gretry was a large, placid, smooth-faced man, stolid as an ox; inevitably dressed in blue serge, a quill tooth-pick behind his ear, a Grand Army button in his lapel. He and Jadwin were intimates. The two had come to Chicago almost simultaneously, and had risen together to become the wealthy men they were at the moment. They belonged to the same club, lunched together every day at Kinsley's, and took each other driving behind their respective trotters on alternate Saturday afternoons. In the middle of summer each stole a fortnight from his business, and went fishing at Geneva Lake in Wisconsin.

"I say," Jadwin observed, "I saw an old fellow outside in your customers' room just now that put me in mind of Hargus. You remember that deal of his, the one he tried to swing before he died. Oh—how long ago was that? Bless my soul, that must have been fifteen, yes twenty years ago."

The deal of which Jadwin spoke was the legendary operation of the Board of Trade—a mammoth corner in September wheat, manipulated by this same Hargus, a millionaire, who had tripled his fortune by the corner, and had lost it by some chicanery on the part of his associate before another year. He had run wheat up to nearly two dollars, had been in his day a king all-powerful. Since then all deals had been spoken of in terms of the Hargus affair. Speculators said, "It was almost as bad as the Hargus deal." "It was like the Hargus smash." "It was as big a thing as the Hargus corner." Hargus had become a sort of creature of legends, mythical, heroic, transfigured in the glory of his millions.

"Easily twenty years ago," continued Jadwin. "If Hargus could come to life now, he'd be surprised at the difference in the way we do business these days. Twenty years. Yes, it's all of that. I declare, Sam, we're getting old, aren't we?"

"I guess that was Hargus you saw out there," answered the broker. "He's not dead. Old fellow in a stove-pipe and greasy frock coat? Yes, that's Hargus."

"What!" exclaimed Jadwin. "That Hargus?"

"Of course it was. He comes 'round every day. The clerks give him a dollar every now and then."

"And he's not dead? And that was Hargus, that wretched, broken–whew! I don't want to think of it, Sam!" And Jadwin, taken all aback, sat for a moment speechless.

"Yes, sir," muttered the broker grimly, "that was Hargus."

There was a long silence. Then at last Gretry exclaimed briskly:

"Well, here's what I want to see you about."

He lowered his voice: "You know I've got a correspondent or two at Paris–all the brokers have–and we make no secret as to who they are. But I've had an extra man at work over there for the last six months, very much on the quiet. I don't mind telling you this much–that he's not the least important member of the United States Legation. Well, now and then he is supposed to send me what the reporters call "exclusive news"–that's what I feed him for, and I could run a private steam yacht on what it costs me. But news I get from him is a day or so in advance of everybody else. He hasn't sent me anything very important till this morning. This here just came in."

He picked up a despatch from his desk and read:

"'Utica–headquarters–modification–organic–concomitant–within one month,' which means," he added, "this. I've just deciphered it," and he handed Jadwin a slip of paper on which was written:

"Bill providing for heavy import duties on foreign grains certain to be introduced in French Chamber of Deputies within one month."

"Have you got it?" he demanded of Jadwin, as he took the slip back. "Won't forget it?" He twisted the paper into a roll and burned it carefully in the office cuspidor.

"Now," he remarked, "do you come in? It's just the two of us, J., and I think we can make that Porteous clique look very sick."

"Hum!" murmured Jadwin surprised. "That does give you a twist on the situation. But to tell the truth, Sam, I had sort of made up my mind to keep out of speculation since my last little deal. A man gets into this game, and into it, and into it, and before you know he can't pull out–and he don't want to. Next he gets his nose scratched, and he hits back to make up for it, and just hits into the air and loses his balance–and down he goes. I don't want to make any more money, Sam. I've got my little pile, and before I get too old I want to have some fun out of it."

"But lord love you, J.," objected the other, "this ain't speculation. You can see for yourself how sure it is. I'm not a baby at this business, am I? You'll let me know something of this game, won't you? And I tell you, J., it's found money. The man that sells wheat short on the strength of this has as good as got the money in his vest pocket already. Oh, nonsense, of course you'll come in. I've been laying for that Bull gang since long before the Helmick failure, and now I've got it right where I want it. Look here, J., you aren't the man to throw money away. You'd buy a business block if you knew you could sell it over again at a profit. Now here's the chance to make really a fine Bear deal. Why, as soon as this news gets on the floor there, the price will bust right down, and down, and down. Porteous and his crowd couldn't keep it up to save 'em from the receiver's hand one single minute."

"I know, Sam," answered Jadwin, "and the trouble is, not that I don't want to speculate, but that I do—too much. That's why I said I'd keep out of it. It isn't so much the money as the fun of playing the game. With half a show, I would get in a little more and a little more, till by and by I'd try to throw a big thing, and instead, the big thing would throw me. Why, Sam, when you told me that that wreck out there mumbling a sandwich was Hargus, it made me turn cold."

"Yes, in your feet," retorted Gretry. "I'm not asking you to risk all your money, am I, or a fifth of it, or a twentieth of it? Don't be an ass, J. Are we a conservative house, or aren't we? Do I talk like this when I'm not sure? Look here. Let me sell a million bushels for you. Yes, I know it's a bigger order than I've handled for you before. But this time I want to go right into it, head down and heels up, and get a twist on those Porteous buckoes, and raise 'em right out of their boots. We get a crop report this morning, and if the visible supply is as large as I think it is, the price will go off and unsettle the whole market. I'll sell short for you at the best figures we can get, and you can cover on the slump any time between now and the end of May."

Jadwin hesitated. In spite of himself he felt a Chance had come. Again that strange sixth sense of his, the inexplicable instinct, that only the born speculator knows, warned him. Every now and then during the course of his business career, this intuition came to him, this flair, this intangible, vague premonition, this presentiment that he must seize Opportunity or else Fortune, that so long had stayed at his elbow, would desert him. In the air about him he seemed to feel an influence, a sudden new element, the presence of a new force. It was Luck, the great power, the great goddess, and all at once it had stooped from out the invisible, and just over his head passed swiftly in a rush of glittering wings.

"The thing would have to be handled like glass," observed the broker thoughtfully, his eyes narrowing "A tip like this is public property in twenty-four hours, and it don't give us any too much time. I don't want to break the price by unloading a million or more bushels on 'em all of a sudden. I'll scatter the orders pretty evenly. You see," he added, "here's a big point in our favor. We'll be able to sell on a strong market. The Pit traders have got some crazy war rumour going, and they're as flighty over it as a young ladies' seminary over a great big rat. And even without that, the market is top-heavy. Porteous makes me weary. He and his gang have been bucking it up till we've got an abnormal price. Ninety-four for May wheat! Why, it's ridiculous. Ought to be selling way down in the eighties. The least little jolt would tip her over. Well," he said abruptly, squaring himself at Jadwin, "do we come in? If that same luck of yours is still in working order, here's your chance, J., to make a killing. There's just that gilt-edged, full-morocco chance that a report of big 'visible' would give us."

Jadwin laughed. "Sam," he said, "I'll flip a coin for it."

"Oh, get out," protested the broker; then suddenly—the gambling instinct that a lifetime passed in that place had cultivated in him—exclaimed:

"All right. Flip a coin. But give me your word you'll stay by it. Heads you come in; tails you don't. Will you give me your word?"

"Oh, I don't know about that," replied Jadwin, amused at the foolishness of the whole proceeding. But as he balanced the half-dollar on his thumb-nail, he was all at once absolutely assured that it would fall heads. He flipped it in the air, and even as he watched it spin, said to himself, "It will come heads. It could not possibly be anything else. I know it will be heads."

And as a matter of course the coin fell heads.

"All right," he said, "I'll come in."

"For a million bushels?"

"Yes—for a million. How much in margins will you want?"

Gretry figured a moment on the back of an envelope.

"Fifty thousand dollars," he announced at length.

Jadwin wrote the check on a corner of the broker's desk, and held it a moment before him.

"Good-bye," he said, apostrophising the bit of paper. "Good-bye. I ne'er shall look upon your like again."

Gretry did not laugh.

"Huh!" he grunted. "You'll look upon a hatful of them before the month is out."

That same morning Landry Court found himself in the corridor on the ground floor of the Board of Trade about nine o'clock. He had just come out of the office of Gretry, Converse & Co., where he and the other Pit traders for the house had been receiving their orders for the day.

As he was buying a couple of apples at the news stand at the end of the corridor, Semple and a young Jew named Hirsch, Pit traders for small firms in La Salle Street, joined him.

"Hello, Court, what do you know?"

"Hello, Barry Semple! Hello, Hirsch!" Landry offered the halves of his second apple, and the three stood there a moment, near the foot of the stairs, talking and eating their apples from the points of their penknives.

"I feel sort of seedy this morning," Semple observed between mouthfuls. "Was up late last night at a stag. A friend of mine just got back from Europe, and some of the boys were giving him a little dinner. He was all over the shop, this friend of mine; spent most of his time in Constantinople; had some kind of newspaper business there. It seems that it's a pretty crazy proposition, Turkey and the Sultan and all that. He said that there was nearly a row over the 'Higgins-Pasha' incident, and that the British agent put it pretty straight to the Sultan's secretary. My friend said Constantinople put him in mind of a lot of opera bouffe scenery that had got spilled out in the mud. Say, Court, he said the streets were dirtier than the Chicago streets."

"Oh, come now," said Hirsch.

"Fact! And the dogs! He told us he knows now where all the yellow dogs go to when they die."

"But say," remarked Hirsch, "what is that about the Higgins-Pasha business? I thought that was over long ago."

"Oh, it is," answered Semple easily. He looked at his watch. "I guess it's about time to go up, pretty near half-past nine."

The three mounted the stairs, mingling with the groups of floor traders who, in steadily increasing numbers, had begun to move in the same direction. But on the way Hirsch was stopped by his brother.

"Hey, I got that box of cigars for you."

Hirsch paused. "Oh! All right," he said, then he added: "Say, how about that Higgins-Pasha affair? You remember that row between England and Turkey. They tell me the British agent in Constantinople put it pretty straight to the Sultan the other day."

The other was interested. "He did, hey?" he said. "The market hasn't felt it, though. Guess there's nothing to it. But there's Kelly yonder. He'd know. He's pretty thick with Porteous' men. Might ask him."

"You ask him and let me know. I got to go on the floor. It's nearly time for the gong."

Hirsch's brother found Kelly in the centre of a group of settlement clerks.

"Say, boy," he began, "you ought to know. They tell me there may be trouble between England and Turkey over the Higgins-Pasha incident, and that the British Foreign Office has threatened the Sultan with an ultimatum. I can see the market if that's so."

"Nothing in it," retorted Kelly. "But I'll find out—to make sure, by jingo."

Meanwhile Landry had gained the top of the stairs, and turning to the right, passed through a great doorway, and came out upon the floor of the Board of Trade.

It was a vast enclosure, lighted on either side by great windows of coloured glass, the roof supported by thin iron pillars elaborately decorated. To the left were the bulletin blackboards, and beyond these, in the northwest angle of the floor, a great railed-in space where the Western Union Telegraph was installed. To the right, on the other side of the room, a row of tables, laden with neatly arranged paper bags half full of samples of grains, stretched along the east wall from the doorway of the public room at one end to the telephone room at the other.

The centre of the floor was occupied by the pits. To the left and to the front of Landry the provision pit, to the right the corn pit, while further on at the north extremity of the floor, and nearly under the visitors' gallery, much larger than the other two, and flanked by the wicket of the official recorder, was the wheat pit itself.

Directly opposite the visitors' gallery, high upon the south wall a great dial was affixed, and on the dial a marking hand that indicated the current price of wheat, fluctuating with the changes made in the Pit. Just now it stood at ninety-three and three-eighths, the closing quotation of the preceding day.

As yet all the pits were empty. It was some fifteen minutes after nine. Landry checked his hat and coat at the coat room near the north entrance, and slipped into an old tennis jacket of striped blue flannel. Then, hatless, his hands in his pockets, he leisurely crossed the floor, and sat down in one of the chairs that were ranged in files upon the floor in front of the telegraph enclosure. He scrutinised again the despatches and orders that he held in his hands; then, having fixed them in his memory, tore them into very small bits, looking vaguely about the room, developing his plan of campaign for the morning.

In a sense Landry Court had a double personality. Away from the neighbourhood and influence of La Salle Street, he was "rattle-brained," absent-minded, impractical, and easily excited, the last fellow in the world to be trusted with any business responsibility. But the thunder of the streets around the Board of Trade, and, above all, the movement and atmosphere of the floor itself awoke within him a very different Landry Court; a whole new set of nerves came into being with the tap of the nine-thirty gong, a whole new system of brain machinery began to move with the first figure called in the Pit. And from that instant until the close of the session, no floor trader, no broker's clerk nor scalper was more alert, more shrewd, or kept his head more surely than the same young fellow who confused his social engagements for the evening of the same day. The Landry Court the Dearborn girls knew was a far different young man from him who now leaned his elbows on the arms of the chair upon the floor of the Board, and, his eyes narrowing, his lips tightening, began to speculate upon what was to be the temper of the Pit that morning.

Meanwhile the floor was beginning to fill up. Over in the railed-in space, where the hundreds of telegraph instruments were in place, the operators were arriving in twos and threes. They hung their hats and ulsters upon the pegs in the wall back of them, and in linen coats, or in their shirt-sleeves, went to their seats, or, sitting upon their tables, called back and forth to each other, joshing, cracking jokes. Some few addressed themselves directly to work, and here and there the intermittent clicking of a key began, like a diligent cricket busking himself in advance of its mates.

From the corridors on the ground floor up through the south doors came the pit traders in increasing groups. The noise of footsteps began to echo from the high vaulting of the roof. A messenger boy crossed the floor chanting an unintelligible name.

The groups of traders gradually converged upon the corn and wheat pits, and on the steps of the latter, their arms crossed upon their knees, two men, one wearing a silk skull cap all awry, conversed earnestly in low tones.

Winston, a great, broad-shouldered bass-voiced fellow of some thirty-five years, who was associated with Landry in executing the orders of the Gretry-Converse house, came up to him, and, omitting any salutation, remarked, deliberately, slowly:

"What's all this about this trouble between Turkey and England?"

But before Landry could reply a third trader for the Gretry Company joined the two. This was a young fellow named Rusbridge, lean, black-haired, a constant excitement glinting in his deep-set eyes.

"Say," he exclaimed, "there's something in that, there's something in that!"

"Where did you hear it?" demanded Landry.

"Oh—everywhere." Rusbridge made a vague gesture with one arm. "Hirsch seemed to know all about it. It appears that there's talk of mobilising the Mediterranean squadron. Darned if I know."

"Might ask that 'Inter-Ocean' reporter. He'd be likely to know. I've seen him 'round here this morning, or you might telephone the Associated Press," suggested Landry. "The office never said a word to me."

"Oh, the 'Associated.' They know a lot always, don't they?" jeered Winston. "Yes, I rung 'em up. They 'couldn't confirm the rumour.' That's always the way. You can spend half a million a year in leased wires and special service and subscriptions to news agencies, and you get the first smell of news like this right here on the floor. Remember that time when the Northwestern millers sold a hundred and fifty thousand barrels at one lick? The floor was talking of it three hours before the news slips were sent 'round, or a single wire was in. Suppose we had waited for the Associated people or the Commercial people then?"

"It's that Higgins-Pasha incident, I'll bet," observed Rusbridge, his eyes snapping.

"I heard something about that this morning," returned Landry. "But only that it was—"

"There! What did I tell you?" interrupted Rusbridge. "I said it was everywhere. There's no smoke without some fire. And I wouldn't be a bit surprised if we get cables before noon that the British War Office had sent an ultimatum."

And very naturally a few minutes later Winston, at that time standing on the steps of the corn pit, heard from a certain broker, who had it from a friend who had just received a despatch from some one "in the know," that the British Secretary of State for War had forwarded an ultimatum to the Porte, and that diplomatic relations between Turkey and England were about to be suspended.

All in a moment the entire Floor seemed to be talking of nothing else, and on the outskirts of every group one could overhear the words: "Seizure of custom house," "ultimatum," "Eastern question," "Higgins-Pasha incident." It was the rumour of the day, and before very long the pit traders began to receive a multitude of despatches countermanding selling orders, and directing them not to close out trades under certain very advanced quotations. The brokers began wiring their principals that the market promised to open strong and bullish.

But by now it was near to half-past nine. From the Western Union desks the clicking of the throng of instruments rose into the air in an incessant staccato stridulation. The messenger boys ran back and forth at top speed, dodging in and out among the knots of clerks and traders, colliding with one another, and without interruption intoning the names of those for whom they had despatches. The throng of traders concentrated upon the pits, and at every moment the deep-toned hum of the murmur of many voices swelled like the rising of a tide.

And at this moment, as Landry stood on the rim of the wheat pit, looking towards the telephone booth under the visitors' gallery, he saw the osseous, stoop-shouldered figure of Mr. Cressler—who, though he never speculated, appeared regularly upon the Board every morning—making his way towards one of the windows in the front of the building. His pocket was full of wheat, taken from a bag on one of the sample tables. Opening the window, he scattered the grain upon the sill, and stood for a long moment absorbed and interested in the dazzling flutter of the wings of innumerable pigeons who came to settle upon the ledge, pecking the grain with little, nervous, fastidious taps of their yellow beaks.

Landry cast a glance at the clock beneath the dial on the wall behind him. It was twenty-five minutes after nine. He stood in his accustomed place on the north side of the Wheat Pit, upon the topmost stair. The Pit was full. Below him and on either side of him were the brokers, scalpers, and traders—Hirsch, Semple, Kelly, Winston, and Rusbridge. The redoubtable Leaycraft, who, bidding for himself, was supposed to hold the longest line of May wheat of any one man in the Pit, the insignificant Grossmann, a Jew who wore a flannel shirt, and to whose outcries no one ever paid the least attention. Fairchild, Paterson, and Goodlock, the inseparable trio who represented the Porteous gang, silent men, middle-aged, who had but to speak in order to buy or sell a million bushels on the spot. And others, and still others, veterans of sixty-five, recruits just out of their teens, men who—some of them—in the past had for a moment dominated the entire Pit, but who now were content to play the part of "eighth-chasers," buying and selling on the same day, content with a profit of ten dollars. Others who might at that very moment be nursing plans which in a week's time would make them millionaires; still others who, under a mask of nonchalance, strove to hide the chagrin of yesterday's defeat. And they were there, ready, inordinately alert, ears turned to the faintest sound, eyes searching for the vaguest trace of meaning in those of their rivals, nervous, keyed to the highest tension, ready to thrust deep into the slightest opening, to spring, mercilessly, upon the smallest undefended spot. Grossmann, the little Jew of the grimy flannel shirt, perspired in the stress of the suspense, all but powerless to maintain silence till the signal should be given, drawing trembling fingers across his mouth. Winston, brawny, solid, unperturbed, his hands behind his back, waited immovably planted on his feet with all the gravity of a statue, his eyes preternaturally watchful, keeping Kelly—whom he had divined had some "funny business" on hand—perpetually in sight. The Porteous trio—Fairchild, Paterson, and Goodlock—as if unalarmed, unassailable, all but turned their backs to the Pit, laughing among themselves.

The official reporter climbed to his perch in the little cage on the edge of the Pit, shutting the door after him. By now the chanting of the messenger boys was an uninterrupted chorus. From all sides of the building, and in every direction they crossed and recrossed each other, always running, their hands full of yellow envelopes. From the telephone alcoves came the prolonged, musical rasp of the call bells. In the Western Union booths the keys of the multitude of instruments raged incessantly. Bare-headed young men hurried up to one another, conferred an instant comparing despatches, then separated, darting away at top speed. Men called to each other half-way across the building. Over by the bulletin boards clerks and agents made careful memoranda of primary receipts, and noted down the amount of wheat on passage, the exports and the imports.

And all these sounds, the chatter of the telegraph, the intoning of the messenger boys, the shouts and cries of clerks and traders, the shuffle and trampling of hundreds of feet, the whirring of telephone signals rose into the troubled air, and mingled overhead to form a vast note, prolonged, sustained, that reverberated from vault to vault of the airy roof, and issued from every doorway, every opened window in one long roll of uninterrupted thunder. In the Wheat Pit the bids, no longer obedient of restraint, began one by one to burst out, like the first isolated shots of a skirmish line. Grossmann had flung out an arm crying:

"'Sell twenty-five May at ninety-five and an eighth," while Kelly and Semple had almost simultaneously shouted, "'Give seven-eighths for May!"

The official reporter had been leaning far over to catch the first quotations, one eye upon the clock at the end of the room. The hour and minute hands were at right angles.

Then suddenly, cutting squarely athwart the vague crescendo of the floor came the single incisive stroke of a great gong. Instantly a tumult was unchained. Arms were flung upward in strenuous gestures, and from above the crowding heads in the Wheat Pit a multitude of hands, eager, the fingers extended, leaped into the air. All articulate expression was lost in the single explosion of sound as the traders surged downwards to the centre of the Pit, grabbing each other, struggling towards each other, tramping, stamping, charging through with might and main. Promptly the hand on the great dial above the clock stirred and trembled, and as though driven by the tempest breath of the Pit moved upward through the degrees of its circle. It paused, wavered, stopped at length, and on the instant the hundreds of telegraph keys scattered throughout the building began clicking off the news to the whole country, from the Atlantic to the Pacific and from Mackinac to Mexico, that the Chicago market had made a slight advance and that May wheat, which had closed the day before at ninety-three and three-eighths, had opened that morning at ninety-four and a half.

But the advance brought out no profit-taking sales. The redoubtable Leaycraft and the Porteous trio, Fairchild, Paterson, and Goodlock, shook their heads when the Pit offered ninety-four for parts of their holdings. The price held firm. Goodlock even began to offer ninety-four. At every suspicion of a flurry Grossmann, always with the same gesture as though hurling a javelin, always with the same lamentable wail of distress, cried out:

"'Sell twenty-five May at ninety-five and a fourth."

He held his five fingers spread to indicate the number of "contracts," or lots of five thousand bushels, which he wished to sell, each finger representing one "contract."

And it was at this moment that selling orders began suddenly to pour in upon the Gretry-Converse traders. Even other houses—Teller and West, Burbank & Co., Mattieson and Knight—received their share. The movement was inexplicable, puzzling. With a powerful Bull clique dominating the trading and every prospect of a strong market, who was it who ventured to sell short?

Landry among others found himself commissioned to sell. His orders were to unload three hundred thousand bushels on any advance over and above ninety-four. He kept his eye on Leaycraft, certain that he would force up the figure. But, as it happened, it was not Leaycraft but the Porteous trio who made the advance. Standing in the centre of the Pit, Patterson suddenly flung up his hand and drew it towards him, clutching the air—the conventional gesture of the buyer.

"'Give an eighth for May."

Landry was at him in a second. Twenty voices shouted "sold," and as many traders sprang towards him with outstretched arms. Landry, however, was before them, and his rush carried Paterson half way across the middle space of the Pit.

"Sold, sold."

Paterson nodded, and as Landry noted down the transaction the hand on the dial advanced again, and again held firm.

But after this the activity of the Pit fell away. The trading languished. By degrees the tension of the opening was relaxed. Landry, however, had refrained from selling more than ten "contracts" to Paterson. He had a feeling that another advance would come later on. Rapidly he made his plans. He would sell another fifty thousand bushels if the price went to ninety-four and a half, and would then "feel" the market, letting go small lots here and there, to test its strength, then, the instant he felt the market strong enough, throw a full hundred thousand upon it with a rush before it had time to break. He could feel—almost at his very finger tips—how this market moved, how it strengthened, how it weakened. He knew just when to nurse it, to humor it, to let it settle, and when to crowd it, when to hustle it, when it would stand rough handling.

Grossmann still uttered his plaint from time to time, but no one so much as pretended to listen. The Porteous trio and Leaycraft kept the price steady at ninety-four and an eighth, but showed no inclination to force it higher. For a full five minutes not a trade was recorded. The Pit waited for the Report on the Visible Supply.

And it was during this lull in the morning's business that the idiocy of the English ultimatum to the Porte melted away. As inexplicably and as suddenly as the rumour had started, it now disappeared. Everyone, simultaneously, seemed to ridicule it. England declare war on Turkey! Where was the joke? Who was the damn fool to have started that old, worn-out war scare? But, for all that, there was no reaction from the advance. It seemed to be understood that either Leaycraft or the Porteous crowd stood ready to support the market; and in place of the ultimatum story a feeling began to gain ground that the expected report would indicate a falling off in the "visible," and that it was quite on the cards that the market might even advance another point.

As the interest in the immediate situation declined, the crowd in the Pit grew less dense. Portions of it were deserted; even Grossmann, discouraged, retired to a bench under the visitors' gallery. And a spirit of horse-play, sheer foolishness, strangely inconsistent with the hot-eyed excitement of the few moments after the opening invaded the remaining groups. Leaycraft, the formidable, as well as Paterson of the Porteous gang, and even the solemn Winston, found an apparently inexhaustible diversion in folding their telegrams into pointed javelins and sending them sailing across the room, watching the course of the missiles with profound gravity. A visitor in the gallery—no doubt a Western farmer on a holiday—having put his feet upon the rail, the entire Pit began to groan "boots, boots, boots."

A little later a certain broker came scurrying across the floor from the direction of the telephone room. Panting, he flung himself up the steps of the Pit, forced his way among the traders with vigorous workings of his elbows, and shouted a bid.

"He's sick," shouted Hirsch. "Look out, he's sick. He's going to have a fit." He grabbed the broker by both arms and hustled him into the centre of the Pit. The others caught up the cry, a score of hands pushed the newcomer from man to man. The Pit traders clutched him, pulled his necktie loose, knocked off his hat, vociferating all the while at top voice, "He's sick! He's sick!"

Other brokers and traders came up, and Grossmann, mistaking the commotion for a flurry, ran into the Pit, his eyes wide, waving his arm and wailing:

"'Sell twenty-five May at ninety-five and a quarter."

But the victim, good-natured, readjusted his battered hat, and again repeated his bid.

"Ah, go to bed," protested Hirsch.

"He's the man who struck Billy Paterson."

"Say, a horse bit him. Look out for him, he's going to have a duck-fit."

The incident appeared to be the inspiration for a new "josh" that had a great success, and a group of traders organized themselves into an "anti-cravat committee," and made the rounds of the Pit, twitching the carefully tied scarfs of the unwary out of place. Grossman, indignant at "t'ose monkey-doodle pizeness," withdrew from the centre of the Pit. But while he stood in front of Leaycraft, his back turned, muttering his disgust, the latter, while carrying on a grave conversation with his neighbour, carefully stuck a file of paper javelins all around the Jew's hat band, and then—still without mirth and still continuing to talk—set them on fire.

Landry imagined by now that ninety-four and an eighth was as high a figure as he could reasonably expect that morning, and so began to "work off" his selling orders. Little by little he sold the wheat "short," till all but one large lot was gone.

Then all at once, and for no discoverable immediate reason, wheat, amid an explosion of shouts and vociferations, jumped to ninety-four and a quarter, and before the Pit could take breath, had advanced another eighth, broken to one-quarter, then jumped to the five-eighths mark.

It was the Report on the Visible Supply beyond question, and though it had not yet been posted, this sudden flurry was a sign that it was not only near at hand, but would be bullish.

A few moments later it was bulletined in the gallery beneath the dial, and proved a tremendous surprise to nearly every man upon the floor. No one had imagined the supply was so ample, so all-sufficient to meet the demand. Promptly the Pit responded. Wheat began to pour in heavily. Hirsch, Kelly, Grossmann, Leaycraft, the stolid Winston, and the excitable Rusbridge were hard at it. The price began to give. Suddenly it broke sharply. The hand on the great dial dropped to ninety-three and seven-eighths.

Landry was beside himself. He had not foreseen this break. There was no reckoning on that cursed "visible," and he still had 50,000 bushels to dispose of. There was no telling now how low the price might sink. He must act quickly, radically. He fought his way towards the Porteous crowd, reached over the shoulder of the little Jew Grossmann, who stood in his way, and thrust his hand almost into Paterson's face, shouting:

"'Sell fifty May at seven-eighths."

It was the last one of his unaccountable selling orders of the early morning.

The other shook his head.

"'Sell fifty May at three-quarters."

Suddenly some instinct warned Landry that another break was coming. It was in the very air around him. He could almost physically feel the pressure of renewed avalanches of wheat crowding down the price. Desperate, he grabbed Paterson by the shoulder.

"'Sell fifty May at five-eighths."

"Take it," vociferated the other, as though answering a challenge.

And in the heart of this confusion, in this downward rush of the price, Luck, the golden goddess, passed with the flirt and flash of glittering wings, and hardly before the ticker in Gretry's office had signalled the decline, the memorandum of the trade was down upon Landry's card and Curtis Jadwin stood pledged to deliver, before noon on the last day of May, one million bushels of wheat into the hands of the representatives of the great Bulls of the Board of Trade.

But by now the real business of the morning was over. The Pit knew it. Grossmann, obstinate, hypnotized as it were by one idea, still stood in his accustomed place on the upper edge of the Pit, and from time to time, with the same despairing gesture, emitted his doleful outcry of "'Sell twenty-five May at ninety-five and three-quarters."

Nobody listened. The traders stood around in expectant attitudes, looking into one another's faces, waiting for what they could not exactly say; loath to leave the Pit lest something should "turn up" the moment their backs were turned.

By degrees the clamour died away, ceased, began again irregularly, then abruptly stilled. Here and there a bid was called, an offer made, like the intermittent crack of small arms after the stopping of the cannonade.

"'Sell five May at one-eighth."

"'Sell twenty at one-quarter."

"'Give one-eighth for May."

For an instant the shoutings were renewed. Then suddenly the gong struck. The traders began slowly to leave the Pit. One of the floor officers, an old fellow in uniform and vizored cap, appeared, gently shouldering towards the door the groups wherein the bidding and offering were still languidly going on. His voice full of remonstration, he repeated continually:

"Time's up, gentlemen. Go on now and get your lunch. Lunch time now. Go on now, or I'll have to report you. Time's up."

The tide set toward the doorways. In the gallery the few visitors rose, putting on coats and wraps. Over by the check counter, to the right of the south entrance to the floor, a throng of brokers and traders jostled each other, reaching over one another's shoulders for hats and ulsters. In steadily increasing numbers they poured out of the north and south entrances, on their way to turn in their trading cards to the offices.

Little by little the floor emptied. The provision and grain pits were deserted, and as the clamour of the place lapsed away the telegraph instruments began to make themselves heard once more, together with the chanting of the messenger boys.

Swept clean in the morning, the floor itself, seen now through the thinning groups, was littered from end to end with scattered grain—oats, wheat, corn, and barley, with wisps of hay, peanut shells, apple parings, and orange peel, with torn newspapers, odds and ends of memoranda, crushed paper darts, and above all with a countless multitude of yellow telegraph forms, thousands upon thousands, crumpled and muddied under the trampling of innumerable feet. It was the debris of the battle-field, the abandoned impedimenta and broken weapons of contending armies, the detritus of conflict, torn, broken, and rent, that at the end of each day's combat encumbered the field.

At last even the click of the last of telegraph keys died down. Shouldering themselves into their overcoats, the operators departed, calling back and forth to one another, making "dates," and cracking jokes. Washerwomen appeared with steaming pails, porters pushing great brooms before them began gathering the refuse of the floor into heaps.

Between the wheat and corn pits a band of young fellows, some of them absolute boys, appeared. These were the settlement clerks. They carried long account books. It was their duty to get the trades of the day into a "ring"—to trace the course of a lot of wheat which had changed hands perhaps a score of times during the trading—and their calls of "Wheat sold to Teller and West," "May wheat sold to Burbank & Co.," "May oats sold to Matthewson and Knight," "Wheat sold to Gretry, Converse & Co.," began to echo from wall to wall of the almost deserted room.

A cat, grey and striped, and wearing a dog collar of nickel and red leather, issued from the coat-room and picked her way across the floor. Evidently she was in a mood of the most ingratiating friendliness, and as one after another of the departing traders spoke to her, raised her tail in the air and arched her back against the legs of the empty chairs. The janitor put in an appearance, lowering the tall colored windows with a long rod. A noise of hammering and the scrape of saws began to issue from a corner where a couple of carpenters tinkered about one of the sample tables.

Then at last even the settlement clerks took themselves off. At once there was a great silence, broken only by the harsh rasp of the carpenters' saws and the voice of the janitor exchanging jokes with the washerwomen. The sound of footsteps in distant quarters re-echoed as if in a church.

The washerwomen invaded the floor, spreading soapy and steaming water before them. Over by the sample tables a negro porter in shirt-sleeves swept entire bushels of spilled wheat, crushed, broken, and sodden, into his dust pans.

The day's campaign was over. It was past two o'clock. On the great dial against the eastern wall the indicator stood—sentinel fashion—at ninety-three. Not till the following morning would the whirlpool, the great central force that spun the Niagara of wheat in its grip, thunder and bellow again.

Later on even the washerwomen, even the porter and janitor, departed. An unbroken silence, the peacefulness of an untroubled calm, settled over the place. The rays of the afternoon sun flooded through the west windows in long parallel shafts full of floating golden motes. There was no sound; nothing stirred. The floor of the Board of Trade was deserted. Alone, on the edge of the abandoned Wheat Pit, in a spot where the sunlight fell warmest—an atom of life, lost in the immensity of the empty floor—the grey cat made her toilet, diligently licking the fur on the inside of her thigh, one leg, as if dislocated, thrust into the air above her head.

IV

In the front parlor of the Cresslers' house a little company was gathered—Laura Dearborn and Page, Mrs. Wessels, Mrs. Cressler, and young Miss Gretry, an awkward, plain-faced girl of about nineteen, dressed extravagantly in a decollete gown of blue silk. Curtis Jadwin and Cressler himself stood by the open fireplace smoking. Landry Court fidgeted on the sofa, pretending to listen to the Gretry girl, who told an interminable story of a visit to some wealthy relative who had a country seat in Wisconsin and who raised fancy poultry. She possessed, it appeared, three thousand hens, Brahma, Faverolles, Houdans, Dorkings, even peacocks and tame quails.

Sheldon Corthell, in a dinner coat, an unlighted cigarette between his fingers, discussed the spring exhibit of water-colors with Laura and Mrs. Cressler, Page listening with languid interest. Aunt Wess' turned the leaves of a family album, counting the number of photographs of Mrs. Cressler which it contained.

Black coffee had just been served. It was the occasion of the third rehearsal for the play which was to be given for the benefit of the hospital ward for Jadwin's mission children, and Mrs. Cressler had invited the members of the company for dinner. Just now everyone awaited the arrival of the "coach," Monsieur Gerardy, who was always late.

"To my notion," observed Corthell, "the water-color that pretends to be anything more than a sketch over-steps its intended limits. The elaborated water-color, I contend, must be judged by the same standards as an oil painting. And if that is so, why not have the oil painting at once?"

"And with all that, if you please, not an egg on the place for breakfast," declared the Gretry girl in her thin voice. She was constrained, embarrassed. Of all those present she was the only one to mistake the character of the gathering and appear in formal costume. But one forgave Isabel Gretry such lapses as these. Invariably she did the wrong thing; invariably she was out of place in the matter of inadvertent speech, an awkward accident, the wrong toilet. For all her nineteen years, she yet remained the hoyden, young, undeveloped, and clumsy.

"Never an egg, and three thousand hens in the runs," she continued. "Think of that! The Plymouth Rocks had the pip. And the others, my lands! I don't know. They just didn't lay."

"Ought to tickle the soles of their feet," declared Landry with profound gravity.

"Tickle their feet!"

"Best thing in the world for hens that don't lay. It sort of stirs them up. Oh, every one knows that."

"Fancy now! I'll write to Aunt Alice to-morrow."

Cressler clipped the tip of a fresh cigar, and, turning to Curtis Jadwin, remarked:

"I understand that Leaycraft alone lost nearly fifteen thousand."

He referred to Jadwin's deal in May wheat, the consummation of which had been effected the previous week. Squarely in the midst of the morning session, on the day following the "short" sale of Jadwin's million of bushels, had exploded the news of the intended action of the French chamber. Amid a tremendous clamour the price fell. The Bulls were panic-stricken. Leaycraft the redoubtable was overwhelmed at the very start. The Porteous trio heroically attempted to shoulder the wheat, but the load was too much. They as well gave ground, and, bereft of their support, May wheat, which had opened at ninety-three and five-eighths to ninety-two and a half, broke with the very first attack to ninety-two, hung there a moment, then dropped again to ninety-one and a half, then to ninety-one. Then, in a prolonged shudder of weakness, sank steadily down by quarters to ninety, to eighty-nine, and at last—a final collapse—touched eighty-eight cents. At that figure Jadwin began to cover. There was danger that the buying of so large a lot might bring about a rally in the price. But Gretry, a consummate master of Pit tactics, kept his orders scattered and bought gradually, taking some two or three days to accumulate the grain. Jadwin's luck—the never-failing guardian of the golden wings—seemed to have the affair under immediate supervision, and reports of timely rains in the wheat belt kept the price inert while the trade was being closed. In the end the "deal" was brilliantly successful, and Gretry was still chuckling over the set-back to the Porteous gang. Exactly the amount of his friend's profits Jadwin did not know. As for himself, he had received from Gretry a check for fifty thousand dollars, every cent of which was net profit.

"I'm not going to congratulate you," continued Cressler. "As far as that's concerned, I would rather you had lost than won—if it would have kept you out of the Pit for good. You're cocky now. I know—good Lord, don't I know. I had my share of it. I know how a man gets drawn into this speculating game."

"Charlie, this wasn't speculating," interrupted Jadwin. "It was a certainty. It was found money. If I had known a certain piece of real estate was going to appreciate in value I would have bought it, wouldn't I?"

"All the worse, if it made it seem easy and sure to you. Do you know," he added suddenly. "Do you know that Leaycraft has gone to keep books for a manufacturing concern out in Dubuque?"

Jadwin pulled his mustache. He was looking at Laura Dearborn over the heads of Landry and the Gretry girl.

"I didn't suppose he'd be getting measured for a private yacht," he murmured. Then he continued, pulling his mustache vigorously:

"Charlie, upon my word, what a beautiful—what beautiful hair that girl has!"

Laura was wearing it very high that evening, the shining black coils transfixed by a strange hand-cut ivory comb that had been her grandmother's. She was dressed in black taffeta, with a single great cabbage-rose pinned to her shoulder. She sat very straight in her chair, one hand upon her slender hip, her head a little to one side, listening attentively to Corthell.

By this time the household of the former rectory was running smoothly; everything was in place, the Dearborns were "settled," and a routine had begun. Her first month in her new surroundings had been to Laura an unbroken series of little delights. For formal social distractions she had but little taste. She left those to Page, who, as soon as Lent was over, promptly became involved in a bewildering round of teas, "dancing clubs," dinners, and theatre parties. Mrs. Wessels was her chaperone, and the little middle-aged lady found the satisfaction of a belated youth in conveying her pretty niece to the various functions that occupied her time. Each Friday night saw her in the gallery of a certain smart dancing school of the south side, where she watched Page dance her way from the "first waltz" to the last figure of the german. She counted the couples carefully, and on the way home was always able to say how the attendance of that particular evening compared with that of the former occasion, and also to inform Laura how many times Page had danced with the same young man.

Laura herself was more serious. She had begun a course of reading; no novels, but solemn works full of allusions to "Man" and "Destiny," which she underlined and annotated. Twice a week—on Mondays and Thursdays—she took a French lesson. Corthell managed to enlist the good services of Mrs. Wessels and escorted her to numerous piano and 'cello recitals, to lectures, to concerts. He even succeeded in achieving the consecration of a specified afternoon once a week, spent in his studio in the Fine Arts' Building on the Lake Front, where he read to them "Saint Agnes Eve," "Sordello," "The Light of Asia"—poems which, with their inversions, obscurities, and astonishing arabesques of rhetoric, left Aunt Wess' bewildered, breathless, all but stupefied.

Laura found these readings charming. The studio was beautiful, lofty, the light dim; the sound of Corthell's voice returned from the thick hangings of velvet and tapestry in a subdued murmur. The air was full of the odor of pastilles.

Laura could not fail to be impressed with the artist's tact, his delicacy. In words he never referred to their conversation in the foyer of the Auditorium; only by some unexplained subtlety of attitude he managed to convey to her the distinct impression that he loved her always. That he was patient, waiting for some indefinite, unexpressed development.

Landry Court called upon her as often as she would allow. Once he had prevailed upon her and Page to accompany him to the matinee to see a comic opera. He had pronounced it "bully," unable to see that Laura evinced only a mild interest in the performance. On each propitious occasion he had made love to her extravagantly. He continually protested his profound respect with a volubility and earnestness that was quite uncalled for.

But, meanwhile, the situation had speedily become more complicated by the entrance upon the scene of an unexpected personage. This was Curtis Jadwin. It was impossible to deny the fact that "J." was in love with Mrs. Cressler's protegee. The business man had none of Corthell's talent for significant reticence, none of his tact, and older than she, a man-of-the-world, accustomed to deal with situations with unswerving directness, he, unlike Landry Court, was not in the least afraid of her. From the very first she found herself upon the defensive. Jadwin was aggressive, assertive, and his addresses had all the persistence and vehemence of veritable attack. Landry she could manage with the lifting of a finger, Corthell disturbed her only upon those rare occasions when he made love to her. But Jadwin gave her no time to so much as think of finesse. She was not even allowed to choose her own time and place for fencing, and to parry his invasion upon those intimate personal grounds which she pleased herself to keep secluded called upon her every feminine art of procrastination and strategy.

He contrived to meet her everywhere. He impressed Mrs. Cressler as auxiliary into his campaign, and a series of rencontres followed one another with astonishing rapidity. Now it was another opera party, now a box at McVicker's, now a dinner, or more often a drive through Lincoln Park behind Jadwin's trotters. He even had the Cresslers and Laura over to his mission Sunday-school for the Easter festival, an occasion of which Laura carried away a confused recollection of enormous canvas mottoes, that looked more like campaign banners than texts from the Scriptures, sheaves of calla lilies, imitation bells of tin-foil, revival hymns vociferated with deafening vehemence from seven hundred distended mouths, and through it all the disagreeable smell of poverty, the odor of uncleanliness that mingled strangely with the perfume of the lilies and the aromatic whiffs from the festoons of evergreen.

Thus the first month of her new life had passed Laura did not trouble herself to look very far into the future. She was too much amused with her emancipation from the narrow horizon of her New England environment. She did not concern herself about consequences. Things would go on for themselves, and consequences develop without effort on her part. She never asked herself whether or not she was in love with any of the three men who strove for her favor. She was quite sure she was not ready—yet—to be married. There was even something distasteful in the idea of marriage. She liked Landry Court immensely; she found the afternoons in Corthell's studio delightful; she loved the rides in the park behind Jadwin's horses. She had no desire that any one of these affairs should exclude the other two. She wished nothing to be consummated. As for love, she never let slip an occasion to shock Aunt Wess' by declaring:

"I love—nobody. I shall never marry."

Page, prim, with great parades of her ideas of "good form," declared between her pursed lips that her sister was a flirt. But this was not so. Laura never manoeuvered with her lovers, nor intrigued to keep from any one of them knowledge of her companionship with the other two. So upon such occasions as this, when all three found themselves face to face, she remained unperturbed.

At last, towards half-past eight, Monsieur Gerardy arrived. All through the winter amateur plays had been in great favor, and Gerardy had become, in a sense, a fad. He was in great demand. Consequently, he gave himself airs. His method was that of severity; he posed as a task-master, relentless, never pleased, hustling the amateur actors about without ceremony, scolding and brow-beating. He was a small, excitable man who wore a frock-coat much too small for him, a flowing purple cravatte drawn through a finger ring, and enormous cuffs set off with huge buttons of Mexican onyx. In his lapel was an inevitable carnation, dried, shrunken, and lamentable. He was redolent of perfume and spoke of himself as an artist. He caused it to be understood that in the intervals of "coaching society plays" he gave his attention to the painting of landscapes. Corthell feigned to ignore his very existence.

The play-book in his hand, Monsieur Gerardy clicked his heels in the middle of the floor and punctiliously saluted everyone present, bowing only from his shoulders, his head dropping forward as if propelled by successive dislocations of the vertebrae of his neck.

He explained the cause of his delay. His English was without accent, but at times suddenly entangled itself in curious Gallic constructions.

"Then I propose we begin at once," he announced. "The second act to-night, then, if we have time, the third act—from the book. And I expect the second act to be letter-perfect—let-ter-per-fect. There is nothing there but that." He held up his hand, as if to refuse to consider the least dissention. "There is nothing but that—no other thing."

All but Corthell listened attentively. The artist, however, turning his back, had continued to talk to Laura without lowering his tone, and all through Monsieur Gerardy's exhortation his voice had made itself heard. "Management of light and shade" ... "color scheme" ... "effects of composition."

Monsieur Gerardy's eye glinted in his direction. He struck his play-book sharply into the palm of his hand.

"Come, come!" he cried. "No more nonsense. Now we leave the girls alone and get to work. Here is the scene. Mademoiselle Gretry, if I derange you!" He cleared a space at the end of the parlor, pulling the chairs about. "Be attentive now. Here"—he placed a chair at his right with a flourish, as though planting a banner—"is the porch of Lord Glendale's country house."

"Ah," murmured Landry, winking solemnly at Page, "the chair is the porch of the house."

"And here," shouted Monsieur Gerardy, glaring at him and slamming down another chair, "is a rustic bench and practicable table set for breakfast."

Page began to giggle behind her play-book. Gerardy, his nostrils expanded, gave her his back. The older people, who were not to take part—Jadwin, the Cresslers, and Aunt Wess'—retired to a far corner, Mrs. Cressler declaring that they would constitute the audience.

"On stage," vociferated Monsieur Gerardy, perspiring from his exertions with the furniture. "'Marion enters, timid and hesitating, L. C.' Come, who's Marion? Mademoiselle Gretry, if you please, and for the love of God remember your crossings. Sh! sh!" he cried, waving his arms at the others. "A little silence if you please. Now, Marion."

Isabel Gretry, holding her play-book at her side, one finger marking the place, essayed an entrance with the words:

"'Ah, the old home once more. See the clambering roses have—'"

But Monsieur Gerardy, suddenly compressing his lips as if in a heroic effort to repress his emotion, flung himself into a chair, turning his back and crossing his legs violently. Miss Gretry stopped, very much disturbed, gazing perplexedly at the coach's heaving shoulders.

There was a strained silence, then:

"Isn't—isn't that right?"

As if with the words she had touched a spring, Monsieur Gerardy bounded to his feet.

"Grand God! Is that left-centre where you have made the entrance? In fine, I ask you a little—is that left-centre? You have come in by the rustic bench and practicable table set for breakfast. A fine sight on the night of the performance that. Marion climbs over the rustic breakfast and practicable—over the rustic bench and practicable table, ha, ha, to make the entrance." Still holding the play-book, he clapped hands with elaborate sarcasm. "Ah, yes, good business that. That will bring down the house."

Meanwhile the Gretry girl turned again from left-centre.

"'Ah, the old home again. See—'"

"Stop!" thundered Monsieur Gerardy. "Is that what you call timid and hesitating? Once more, those lines.... No, no. It is not it at all. More of slowness, more of—Here, watch me."

He made the entrance with laborious exaggeration of effect, dragging one foot after another, clutching at the palings of an imaginary fence, while pitching his voice at a feeble falsetto, he quavered:

"'Ah! The old home—ah ... once more. See—' like that," he cried, straightening up. "Now then. We try that entrance again. Don't come on too quick after the curtain. Attention. I clap my hands for the curtain, and count three." He backed away and, tucking the play-book under his arm, struck his palms together. "Now, one—two—three."

But this time Isabel Gretry, in remembering her "business," confused her stage directions once more.

"'Ah, the old home—'"

"Left-centre," interrupted the coach, in a tone of long-suffering patience.

She paused bewildered, and believing that she had spoken her lines too abruptly, began again:

"'See, the clambering—'"

"Left-centre."

"'Ah, the old home—'"

Monsieur Gerardy settled himself deliberately in his chair and resting his head upon one hand closed his eyes. His manner was that of Galileo under torture declaring "still it moves."

"Left-centre."

"Oh—oh, yes. I forgot."

Monsieur Gerardy apostrophized the chandelier with mirthless humour.

"Oh, ha, ha! She forgot."

Still another time Marion tried the entrance, and, as she came on, Monsieur Gerardy made vigorous signals to Page, exclaiming in a hoarse whisper:

"Lady Mary, ready. In a minute you come on. Remember the cue."

Meanwhile Marion had continued:

"'See the clambering vines—'"

"Roses."

"'The clambering rose vines—'"

"Roses, pure and simple."

"'See! The clambering roses, pure and—'"

"Mademoiselle Gretry, will you do me the extreme obligation to bound yourself by the lines of the book?"

"I thought you said—"

"Go on, go on, go on! Is it God-possible to be thus stupid? Lady Mary, ready."

"'See, the clambering roses have wrapped the old stones in a loving embrace. The birds build in the same old nests—'"

"Well, well, Lady Mary, where are you? You enter from the porch."

"I'm waiting for my cue," protested Page. "My cue is: 'Are there none that will remember me.'"

"Say," whispered Landry, coming up behind Page, "it would look bully if you could come out leading a greyhound."

"Ah, so, Mademoiselle Gretry," cried Monsieur Gerardy, "you left out the cue." He became painfully polite. "Give the speech once more, if you please."

"A dog would look bully on the stage," whispered Landry. "And I know where I could get one."

"Where?"

"A friend of mine. He's got a beauty, blue grey—"

They become suddenly aware of a portentous silence The coach, his arms folded, was gazing at Page with tightened lips.

"'None who will remember me,'" he burst out at last. "Three times she gave it."

Page hurried upon the scene with the words:

"'Ah, another glorious morning. The vines are drenched in dew.'" Then, raising her voice and turning toward the "house," "'Arthur.'"

"'Arthur,'" warned the coach. "That's you. Mr. Corthell. Ready. Well then, Mademoiselle Gretry, you have something to say there."

"I can't say it," murmured the Gretry girl, her handkerchief to her face.

"What now? Continue. Your lines are 'I must not be seen here. It would betray all,' then conceal yourself in the arbor. Continue. Speak the line. It is the cue of Arthur."

"I can't," mumbled the girl behind her handkerchief.

"Can't? Why, then?"

"I—I have the nose-bleed."

Upon the instant Monsieur Gerardy quite lost his temper. He turned away, one hand to his head, rolling his eyes as if in mute appeal to heaven, then, whirling about, shook his play-book at the unfortunate Marion, crying out furiously:

"Ah, it lacked but that. You ought to understand at last, that when one rehearses for a play one does not have the nose-bleed. It is not decent."

Miss Gretry retired precipitately, and Laura came forward to say that she would read Marion's lines.

"No, no!" cried Monsieur Gerardy. "You—ah, if they were all like you! You are obliging, but it does not suffice. I am insulted."

The others, astonished, gathered about the "coach." They laboured to explain. Miss

Gretry had intended no slight. In fact she was often taken that way; she was excited, nervous. But Monsieur Gerardy was not to be placated. Ah, no! He knew what was due a gentleman. He closed his eyes and raised his eyebrows to his very hair, murmuring superbly that he was offended. He had but one phrase in answer to all their explanations:

"One does not permit one's self to bleed at the nose during rehearsal."

Laura began to feel a certain resentment. The unfortunate Gretry girl had gone away in tears. What with the embarrassment of the wrong gown, the brow-beating, and the nose-bleed, she was not far from hysterics. She had retired to the dining-room with Mrs. Cressler and from time to time the sounds of her distress made themselves heard. Laura believed it quite time to interfere. After all, who was this Gerardy person, to give himself such airs? Poor Miss Gretry was to blame for nothing. She fixed the little Frenchman with a direct glance, and Page, who caught a glimpse of her face, recognised "the grand manner," and whispered to Landry:

"He'd better look out; he's gone just about as far as Laura will allow."

"It is not convenient," vociferated the "coach." "It is not permissible. I am offended."

"Monsieur Gerardy," said Laura, "we will say nothing more about it, if you please."

There was a silence. Monsieur Gerardy had pretended not to hear. He breathed loud through his nose, and Page hastened to observe that anyhow Marion was not on in the next scenes. Then abruptly, and resuming his normal expression, Monsieur Gerardy said:

"Let us proceed. It advances nothing to lose time. Come. Lady Mary and Arthur, ready."

The rehearsal continued. Laura, who did not come on during the act, went back to her chair in the corner of the room.

But the original group had been broken up. Mrs. Cressler was in the dining-room with the Gretry girl, while Jadwin, Aunt Wess', and Cressler himself were deep in a discussion of mind-reading and spiritualism.

As Laura came up, Jadwin detached himself from the others and met her.

"Poor Miss Gretry!" he observed. "Always the square peg in the round hole. I've sent out for some smelling salts."

It seemed to Laura that the capitalist was especially well-looking on this particular evening. He never dressed with the "smartness" of Sheldon Corthell or Landry Court, but in some way she did not expect that he should. His clothes were not what she was aware were called "stylish," but she had had enough experience with her own tailor-made gowns to know that the material was the very best that money could buy. The apparent absence of any padding in the broad shoulders of the frock coat he wore, to her mind, more than compensated for the "ready-made" scarf, and if the white waistcoat was not fashionably cut, she knew that she had never been able to afford a pique skirt of just that particular grade.

"Suppose we go into the reception-room," he observed abruptly. "Charlie bought a new clock last week that's a marvel. You ought to see it."

"No," she answered. "I am quite comfortable here, and I want to see how Page does in this act."

"I am afraid, Miss Dearborn," he continued, as they found their places, "that you did not have a very good time Sunday afternoon."

He referred to the Easter festival at his mission school. Laura had left rather early, alleging neuralgia and a dinner engagement.

"Why, yes I did," she replied. "Only, to tell the truth, my head ached a little." She was ashamed that she did not altogether delight in her remembrance of Jadwin on that afternoon. He had "addressed" the school, with earnestness it was true, but in a strain decidedly conventional. And the picture he made leading the singing, beating time with the hymn-book, and between the verses declaring that "he wanted to hear everyone's voice in the next verse," did not appeal very forcibly to her imagination. She fancied Sheldon Corthell doing these things, and could not forbear to smile. She had to admit, despite the protests of conscience, that she did prefer the studio to the Sunday-school.

"Oh," remarked Jadwin, "I'm sorry to hear you had a headache. I suppose my little micks" (he invariably spoke of his mission children thus) "do make more noise than music."

"I found them very interesting."

"No, excuse me, but I'm afraid you didn't. My little micks are not interesting—to look at nor to listen to. But I, kind of—well, I don't know," he began pulling his mustache. "It seems to suit me to get down there and get hold of these people. You know Moody put me up to it. He was here about five years ago, and I went to one of his big meetings, and then to all of them. And I met the fellow, too, and I tell you, Miss Dearborn, he stirred me all up. I didn't "get religion." No, nothing like that. But I got a notion it was time to be up and doing, and I figured it out that business principles were as good in religion as they are—well, in La Salle Street, and that if the church people—the men I mean—put as much energy, and shrewdness, and competitive spirit into the saving of souls as they did into the saving of dollars that we might get somewhere. And so I took hold of a half dozen broken-down, bankrupt Sunday-school concerns over here on Archer Avenue that were fighting each other all the time, and amalgamated them all—a regular trust, just as if they were iron foundries—and turned the incompetents out and put my subordinates in, and put the thing on a business basis, and by now, I'll venture to say, there's not a better organised Sunday-school in all Chicago, and I'll bet if D. L. Moody were here to-day he'd say, 'Jadwin, well done, thou good and faithful servant.'"

"I haven't a doubt of it, Mr. Jadwin," Laura hastened to exclaim. "And you must not think that I don't believe you are doing a splendid work."

"Well, it suits me," he repeated. "I like my little micks, and now and then I have a chance to get hold of the kind that it pays to push along. About four months ago I came across a boy in the Bible class; I guess he's about sixteen; name is Bradley—Billy Bradley, father a confirmed drunk, mother takes in washing, sister—we won't speak about; and he seemed to be bright and willing to work, and I gave him a job in my agent's office, just directing envelopes. Well, Miss Dearborn, that boy has a desk of his own now, and the agent tells me he's one of the very best men he's got. He does his work so well that I've been able to discharge two other fellows who sat around and watched the clock for lunch hour, and Bradley does their work now better and quicker than they did, and saves me twenty dollars a week; that's a thousand a year. So much for a business like Sunday-school; so much for taking a good aim when you cast your bread upon the waters. The last time I saw Moody I said, 'Moody, my motto is "not slothful in business, fervent in spirit, praising the Lord."' I remember we were out driving at the time, I took him out behind Lizella—she's almost straight Wilkes' blood and can trot in two-ten, but you can believe he didn't know that—and, as I say, I told him what my motto was, and he said, 'J., good for you; you keep to that. There's no better motto in the world for the American man of business.' He shook my hand when he said it, and I haven't ever forgotten it."

Not a little embarrassed, Laura was at a loss just what to say, and in the end remarked lamely enough:

"I am sure it is the right spirit—the best motto."

"Miss Dearborn," Jadwin began again suddenly, "why don't you take a class down there. The little micks aren't so dreadful when you get to know them."

"I!" exclaimed Laura, rather blankly. She shook her head. "Oh, no, Mr. Jadwin. I should be only an encumbrance. Don't misunderstand me. I approve of the work with all my heart, but I am not fitted—I feel no call. I should be so inapt that I know I should do no good. My training has been so different, you know," she said, smiling. "I am an Episcopalian—'of the straightest sect of the Pharisees.' I should be teaching your little micks all about the meaning of candles, and 'Eastings,' and the absolution and remission of sins."

"I wouldn't care if you did," he answered. "It's the indirect influence I'm thinking of—the indirect influence that a beautiful, pure-hearted, noble-minded woman spreads around her wherever she goes. I know what it has done for me. And I know that not only my little micks, but every teacher and every superintendent in that school would be inspired, and stimulated, and born again so soon as ever you set foot in the building. Men need good women, Miss Dearborn. Men who are doing the work of the world. I believe in women as I believe in Christ. But I don't believe they were made—any more than Christ was—to cultivate—beyond a certain point—their own souls, and refine their own minds, and live in a sort of warmed-over, dilettante, stained-glass world of seclusion and exclusion. No, sir, that won't do for the United States and the men who are making them the greatest nation of the world. The men have got all the get-up-and-get they want, but they need the women to point them straight, and to show them how to lead that other kind of life that isn't all grind. Since I've known you, Miss Dearborn, I've just begun to wake up to the fact that there is that other kind, but I can't lead that life without you. There's no kind of life that's worth anything to me now that don't include you. I don't need to tell you that I want you to marry me. You know that by now, I guess, without any words from me. I love you, and I love you as a man, not as a boy, seriously and earnestly. I can give you no idea how seriously, how earnestly. I want you to be my wife. Laura, my dear girl, I know I could make you happy."

"It isn't," answered Laura slowly, perceiving as he paused that he expected her to say something, "much a question of that."

"What is it, then? I won't make a scene. Don't you love me? Don't you think, my girl, you could ever love me?"

Laura hesitated a long moment. She had taken the rose from her shoulder, and plucking the petals one by one, put them delicately between her teeth. From the other end of the room came the clamorous exhortations of Monsieur Gerardy. Mrs. Cressler and the Gretry girl watched the progress of the rehearsal attentively from the doorway of the dining-room. Aunt Wess' and Mr. Cressler were discussing psychic research and seances, on the sofa on the other side of the room. After a while Laura spoke.

"It isn't that either," she said, choosing her words carefully.

"What is it, then?"

"I don't know—exactly. For one thing, I don't think I want to be married, Mr. Jadwin—to anybody."

"I would wait for you."

"Or to be engaged."

"But the day must come, sooner or later, when you must be both engaged and married. You must ask yourself some time if you love the man who wishes to be your husband. Why not ask yourself now?"

"I do," she answered. "I do ask myself. I have asked myself."

"Well, what do you decide?"

"That I don't know."

"Don't you think you would love me in time? Laura, I am sure you would. I would make you."

"I don't know. I suppose that is a stupid answer. But it is, if I am to be honest, and I am trying very hard to be honest—with you and with myself—the only one I have. I am happy just as I am. I like you and Mr. Cressler and Mr. Corthell—everybody.

But, Mr. Jadwin"—she looked him full in the face, her dark eyes full of gravity—"with a woman it is so serious—to be married. More so than any man ever understood. And, oh, one must be so sure, so sure. And I am not sure now. I am not sure now. Even if I were sure of you, I could not say I was sure of myself. Now and then I tell myself, and even poor, dear Aunt Wess', that I shall never love anybody, that I shall never marry. But I should be bitterly sorry if I thought that was true. It is one of the greatest happinesses to which I look forward, that some day I shall love some one with all my heart and soul, and shall be a true wife, and find my husband's love for me the sweetest thing in my life. But I am sure that that day has not come yet."

"And when it does come," he urged, "may I be the first to know?"

She smiled a little gravely.

"Ah," she answered, "I would not know myself that that day had come until I woke to the fact that I loved the man who had asked me to be his wife, and then it might be too late—for you."

"But now, at least," he persisted, "you love no one."

"Now," she repeated, "I love—no one."

"And I may take such encouragement in that as I can?"

And then, suddenly, capriciously even, Laura, an inexplicable spirit of inconsistency besetting her, was a very different woman from the one who an instant before had spoken so gravely of the seriousness of marriage. She hesitated a moment before answering Jadwin, her head on one side, looking at the rose leaf between her fingers. In a low voice she said at last:

"If you like."

But before Jadwin could reply, Cressler and Aunt Wess' who had been telling each other of their "experiences," of their "premonitions," of the unaccountable things that had happened to them, at length included the others in their conversation.

"J.," remarked Cressler, "did anything funny ever happen to you—warnings, presentiments, that sort of thing? Mrs. Wessels and I have been talking spiritualism. Laura, have you ever had any 'experiences'?"

She shook her head.

"No, no. I am too material, I am afraid."

"How about you, 'J.'?"

"Nothing much, except that I believe in 'luck'—a little. The other day I flipped a coin in Gretry's office. If it fell heads I was to sell wheat short, and somehow I knew all the time that the coin would fall heads—and so it did."

"And you made a great deal of money," said Laura. "I know. Mr. Court was telling me. That was splendid."

"That was deplorable, Laura," said Cressler, gravely. "I hope some day," he continued, "we can all of us get hold of this man and make him solemnly promise never to gamble in wheat again."

Laura stared. To her mind the word "gambling" had always been suspect. It had a bad sound; it seemed to be associated with depravity of the baser sort.

"Gambling!" she murmured.

"They call it buying and selling," he went on, "down there in La Salle Street. But it is simply betting. Betting on the condition of the market weeks, even months, in advance. You bet wheat goes up. I bet it goes down. Those fellows in the Pit don't own the wheat; never even see it. Wou'dn't know what to do with it if they had it. They don't care in the least about the grain. But there are thousands upon thousands of farmers out here in Iowa and Kansas or Dakota who do, and hundreds of thousand of poor devils in Europe who care even more than the farmer. I mean the fellows who raise the grain, and the other fellows who eat it. It's life or death for either of them. And right between these two comes the Chicago speculator, who raises or lowers the price out of all reason, for the benefit of his pocket. You see Laura, here is what I mean." Cressler had suddenly become very earnest. Absorbed, interested, Laura listened intently. "Here is what I mean," pursued Cressler. "It's like this: If we send the price of wheat down too far, the farmer suffers, the fellow who raises it if we send it up too far, the poor man in Europe suffers, the fellow who eats it. And food to the peasant on the continent is bread—not meat or potatoes, as it is with us. The only way to do so that neither the American farmer nor the European peasant suffers, is to keep wheat at an average, legitimate value. The moment you inflate or depress that, somebody suffers right away. And that is just what these gamblers are doing all the time, booming it up or booming it down. Think of it, the food of hundreds and hundreds of thousands of people just at the mercy of a few men down there on the Board of Trade. They make the price. They say just how much the peasant shall pay for his loaf of bread. If he can't pay the price he simply starves. And as for the farmer, why it's ludicrous. If I build a house and offer it for sale, I put my own price on it, and if the price offered don't suit me I don't sell. But if I go out here in Iowa and raise a crop of wheat, I've got to sell it, whether I want to or not at the figure named by some fellows in Chicago. And to make themselves rich, they may make me sell it at a price that bankrupts me."

Laura nodded. She was intensely interested. A whole new order of things was being disclosed, and for the first time in her life she looked into the workings of political economy.

"Oh, that's only one side of it," Cressler went on, heedless of Jadwin's good-humoured protests. "Yes, I know I am a crank on speculating. I'm going to preach a little if you'll let me. I've been a speculator myself, and a ruined one at that, and I know what I am talking about. Here is what I was going to say. These fellows themselves, the gamblers—well, call them speculators, if you like. Oh, the fine, promising manly young men I've seen wrecked—absolutely and hopelessly wrecked and ruined by speculation! It's as easy to get into as going across the street. They make three hundred, five hundred, yes, even a thousand dollars sometimes in a couple of hours, without so much as raising a finger. Think what that means to a boy of twenty-five who's doing clerk work at seventy-five a month. Why, it would take him maybe ten years to save a thousand, and here he's made it in a single morning. Think you can keep him out of speculation then? First thing you know he's thrown up his honest, humdrum position—oh, I've seen it hundreds of times—and takes to hanging round the customers' rooms down there on La Salle Street, and he makes a little, and makes a little more, and finally he is so far in that he can't pull out, and then some billionaire fellow, who has the market in the palm of his hand, tightens one finger, and our young man is ruined, body and mind. He's lost the taste, the very capacity for legitimate business, and he stays on hanging round the Board till he gets to be—all of a sudden—an old man. And then some day some one says, 'Why, where's So-and-so?' and you wake up to the fact that the young fellow has simply disappeared—lost. I tell you the fascination of this Pit gambling is something no one who hasn't experienced it can have the faintest conception of. I believe it's worse than liquor, worse than morphine. Once you get into it, it grips you and draws you and draws you, and the nearer you get to the end the easier it seems to win, till all of a sudden, ah! there's the whirlpool.... 'J.,' keep away from it, my boy."

Jadwin laughed, and leaning over, put his fingers upon Cressler's breast, as though turning off a switch.

"Now, Miss Dearborn," he announced, "we've shut him off. Charlie means all right, but now and then some one brushes against him and opens that switch."

Cressler, good-humouredly laughed with the others, but Laura's smile was perfunctory and her eyes were grave. But there was a diversion. While the others had been talking the rehearsal had proceeded, and now Page beckoned to Laura from the far end of the parlor, calling out:

"Laura—'Beatrice,' it's the third act. You are wanted."

"Oh, I must run," exclaimed Laura, catching up her play-book. "Poor Monsieur Gerardy—we must be a trial to him."

She hurried across the room, where the coach was disposing the furniture for the scene, consulting the stage directions in his book:

"Here the kitchen table, here the old-fashioned writing-desk, here the armoire with practicable doors, here the window. Soh! Who is on? Ah, the young lady of the sick nose, 'Marion.' She is discovered—knitting. And then the duchess—later. That's you Mademoiselle Dearborn. You interrupt—you remember. But then you, ah, you always are right. If they were all like you. Very well, we begin."

Creditably enough the Gretry girl read her part, Monsieur Gerardy interrupting to indicate the crossings and business. Then at her cue, Laura, who was to play the role of the duchess, entered with the words:

"I beg your pardon, but the door stood open. May I come in?"

Monsieur Gerardy murmured:

"Elle est vraiment superbe."

Laura to the very life, to every little trick of carriage and manner was the high-born gentlewoman visiting the home of a dependent. Nothing could have been more dignified, more gracious, more gracefully condescending than her poise. She dramatised not only her role, but the whole of her surroundings. The interior of the little cottage seemed to define itself with almost visible distinctness the moment she set foot upon the scene.

Gerardy tiptoed from group to group, whispering:

"Eh? Very fine, our duchess. She would do well professionally."

But Mrs. Wessels was not altogether convinced. Her eyes following her niece, she said to Corthell:

"It's Laura's 'grand manner.' My word, I know her in that part. That's the way she is when she comes down to the parlor of an evening, and Page introduces her to one of her young men."

"I nearly die," protested Page, beginning to laugh. "Of course it's very natural I should want my friends to like my sister. And Laura comes in as though she were walking on eggs, and gets their names wrong, as though it didn't much matter, and calls them Pinky when their name is Pinckney, and don't listen to what they say, till I want to sink right through the floor with mortification."

In haphazard fashion the rehearsal wore to a close. Monsieur Gerardy stormed and fretted and insisted upon repeating certain scenes over and over again. By ten o'clock the actors were quite worn out. A little supper was served, and very soon afterward Laura made a move toward departing. She was wondering who would see her home, Landry, Jadwin, or Sheldon Corthell.

The day had been sunshiny, warm even, but since nine o'clock the weather had changed for the worse, and by now a heavy rain was falling. Mrs. Cressler begged the two sisters and Mrs. Wessels to stay at her house over night, but Laura refused. Jadwin was suggesting to Cressler the appropriateness of having the coupe brought around to take the sisters home, when Corthell came up to Laura.

"I sent for a couple of hansoms long since," he said. "They are waiting outside now." And that seemed to settle the question.

For all Jadwin's perseverance, the artist seemed—for this time at least—to have the better of the situation.

As the good-bys were being said at the front door Page remarked to Landry:

"You had better go with us as far as the house, so that you can take one of our umbrellas. You can get in with Aunt Wess' and me. There's plenty of room. You can't go home in this storm without an umbrella."

Landry at first refused, haughtily. He might be too poor to parade a lot of hansom cabs around, but he was too proud, to say the least, to ride in 'em when some one else paid.

Page scolded him roundly. What next? The idea. He was not to be so completely silly. She didn't propose to have the responsibility of his catching pneumonia just for the sake of a quibble.

"Some people," she declared, "never seemed to be able to find out that they are grown up."

"Very well," he announced, "I'll go if I can tip the driver a dollar."

Page compressed her lips.

"The man that can afford dollar tips," she said, "can afford to hire the cab in the first place."

"Seventy-five cents, then," he declared resolutely. "Not a cent less. I should feel humiliated with any less."

"Will you please take me down to the cab, Landry Court?" she cried. And without further comment Landry obeyed.

"Now, Miss Dearborn, if you are ready," exclaimed Corthell, as he came up. He held the umbrella over her head, allowing his shoulders to get the drippings.

They cried good-by again all around, and the artist guided her down the slippery steps. He handed her carefully into the hansom, and following, drew down the glasses.

Laura settled herself comfortably far back in her corner, adjusting her skirts and murmuring:

"Such a wet night. Who would have thought it was going to rain? I was afraid you were not coming at first," she added. "At dinner Mrs. Cressler said you had an important committee meeting—something to do with the Art Institute, the award of prizes; was that it?"

"Oh, yes," he answered, indifferently, "something of the sort was on. I suppose it was important—for the Institute. But for me there is only one thing of importance nowadays," he spoke with a studied carelessness, as though announcing a fact that Laura must know already, "and that is, to be near you. It is astonishing. You have no idea of it, how I have ordered my whole life according to that idea."

"As though you expected me to believe that," she answered.

In her other lovers she knew her words would have provoked vehement protestation. But for her it was part of the charm of Corthell's attitude that he never did or said the expected, the ordinary. Just now he seemed more interested in the effect of his love for Laura upon himself than in the manner of her reception of it.

"It is curious," he continued. "I am no longer a boy. I have no enthusiasms. I have known many women, and I have seen enough of what the crowd calls love to know how futile it is, how empty, a vanity of vanities. I had imagined that the poets were wrong, were idealists, seeing the things that should be rather than the things that were. And then," suddenly he drew a deep breath: "this happiness; and to me. And the miracle, the wonderful is there—all at once—in my heart, in my very hand, like a mysterious, beautiful exotic. The poets are wrong," he added. "They have not been idealists enough. I wish—ah, well, never mind."

"What is it that you wish?" she asked, as he broke off suddenly. Laura knew even before she spoke that it would have been better not to have prompted him to continue. Intuitively she had something more than a suspicion that he had led her on to say these very words. And in admitting that she cared to have the conversation proceed upon this footing, she realised that she was sheering towards unequivocal coquetry. She saw the false move now, knew that she had lowered her guard. On all accounts it would have been more dignified to have shown only a mild interest in what Corthell wished. She realised that once more she had acted upon impulse, and she even found time to wonder again how it was that when with this man her impulses, and not her reason prevailed so often. With Landry or with Curtis Jadwin she was always calm, tranquilly self-possessed. But Corthell seemed able to reach all that was impetuous, all that was unreasoned in her nature. To Landry she was more than anything else, an older sister, indulgent, kind-hearted. With Jadwin she found that all the serious, all the sincere, earnest side of her character was apt to come to the front. But Corthell stirred troublous, unknown deeps in her, certain undefined trends of recklessness; and for so long as he held her within his influence, she could not forget her sex a single instant.

It dismayed her to have this strange personality of hers, this other headstrong, impetuous self, discovered to her. She hardly recognised it. It made her a little afraid; and yet, wonder of wonders, she could not altogether dislike it. There was a certain fascination in resigning herself for little instants to the dominion of this daring stranger that was yet herself.

Meanwhile Corthell had answered her:

"I wish," he said, "I wish you could say something—I hardly know what—something to me. So little would be so much."

"But what can I say?" she protested. "I don't know—I—what can I say?"

"It must be yes or no for me," he broke out. "I can't go on this way."

"But why not? Why not?" exclaimed Laura. "Why must we—terminate anything? Why not let things go on just as they are? We are quite happy as we are. There's never been a time of my life when I've been happier than this last three or four months. I don't want to change anything. Ah, here we are."

The hansom drew up in front of the house. Aunt Wess' and Page were already inside. The maid stood in the vestibule in the light that streamed from the half-open front door, an umbrella in her hand. And as Laura alighted, she heard Page's voice calling from the front hall that the others had umbrellas, that the maid was not to wait.

The hansom splashed away, and Corthell and Laura mounted the steps of the house.

"Won't you come in?" she said. "There is a fire in the library."

But he said no, and for a few seconds they stood under the vestibule light, talking. Then Corthell, drawing off his right-hand glove, said:

"I suppose that I have my answer. You do not wish for a change. I understand. You wish to say by that, that you do not love me. If you did love me as I love you, you would wish for just that—a change. You would be as eager as I for that wonderful, wonderful change that makes a new heaven and a new earth."

This time Laura did not answer. There was a moment's silence. Then Corthell said:

"Do you know, I think I shall go away."

"Go away?"

"Yes, to New York. Possibly to Paris. There is a new method of fusing glass that I've promised myself long ago I would look into. I don't know that it interests me much—now. But I think I had better go. At once, within the week. I've not much heart in it; but it seems—under the circumstances—to be appropriate." He held out his bared hand. Laura saw that he was smiling.

"Well, Miss Dearborn—good-by."

"But why should you go?" she cried, distressfully. "How perfectly—ah, don't go," she exclaimed, then in desperate haste added: "It would be absolutely foolish."

"Shall I stay?" he urged. "Do you tell me to stay?"

"Of course I do," she answered. "It would break up the play—your going. It would spoil my part. You play opposite me, you know. Please stay."

"Shall I stay," he asked, "for the sake of your part? There is no one else you would rather have?" He was smiling straight into her eyes, and she guessed what he meant.

She smiled back at him, and the spirit of daring never more awake in her, replied, as she caught his eye:

"There is no one else I would rather have."

Corthell caught her hand of a sudden.

"Laura," he cried, "let us end this fencing and quibbling once and for all. Dear, dear girl, I love you with all the strength of all the good in me. Let me be the best a man can be to the woman he loves."

Laura flashed a smile at him.

"If you can make me love you enough," she answered.

"And you think I can?" he exclaimed.

"You have my permission to try," she said.

She hoped fervently that now, without further words, he would leave her. It seemed to her that it would be the most delicate chivalry on his part—having won this much—to push his advantage no further. She waited anxiously for his next words. She began to fear that she had trusted too much upon her assurance of his tact.

Corthell held out his hand again.

"It is good-night, then, not good-by."

"It is good-night," said Laura.

With the words he was gone, and Laura, entering the house, shut the door behind her with a long breath of satisfaction.

Page and Landry were still in the library. Laura joined them, and for a few moments the three stood before the fireplace talking about the play. Page at length, at the first opportunity, excused herself and went to bed. She made a great show of leaving Landry and Laura alone, and managed to convey the impression that she understood they were anxious to be rid of her.

"Only remember," she remarked to Laura severely, "to lock up and turn out the hall gas. Annie has gone to bed long ago."

"I must dash along, too," declared Landry when Page was gone.

He buttoned his coat about his neck, and Laura followed him out into the hall and found an umbrella for him.

"You were beautiful to-night," he said, as he stood with his hand on the door knob. "Beautiful. I could not keep my eyes off of you, and I could not listen to anybody but you. And now," he declared, solemnly, "I will see your eyes and hear your voice all the rest of the night. I want to explain," he added, "about those hansoms—about coming home with Miss Page and Mrs. Wessels. Mr. Corthell—those were his hansoms, of course. But I wanted an umbrella, and I gave the driver seventy-five cents."

"Why of course, of course," said Laura, not quite divining what he was driving at.

"I don't want you to think that I would be willing to put myself under obligations to anybody."

"Of course, Landry; I understand."

He thrilled at once.

"Ah," he cried, "you don't know what it means to me to look into the eyes of a woman who really understands."

Laura stared, wondering just what she had said.

"Will you turn this hall light out for me, Landry?" she asked. "I never can reach."

He left the front door open and extinguished the jet in its dull red globe. Promptly they were involved in darkness.

"Good-night," she said. "Isn't it dark?"

He stretched out his hand to take hers, but instead his groping fingers touched her waist. Suddenly Laura felt his arm clasp her. Then all at once, before she had time to so much as think of resistance, he had put both arms about her and kissed her squarely on her cheek.

Then the front door closed, and she was left abruptly alone, breathless, stunned, staring wide-eyed into the darkness.

Her first sensation was one merely of amazement. She put her hand quickly to her cheek, first the palm and then the back, murmuring confusedly:

"What? Why?—why?"

Then she whirled about and ran up the stairs, her silks clashing and fluttering about her as she fled, gained her own room, and swung the door violently shut behind her. She turned up the lowered gas and, without knowing why, faced her mirror at once, studying her reflection and watching her hand as it all but scoured the offended cheek.

Then, suddenly, with an upward, uplifting rush, her anger surged within her. She, Laura, Miss Dearborn, who loved no man, who never conceded, never capitulated, whose "grand manner" was a thing proverbial, in all her pitch of pride, in her own home, her own fortress, had been kissed, like a school-girl, like a chambermaid, in the dark, in a corner.

And by—great heavens!—Landry Court. The boy whom she fancied she held in such subjection, such profound respect. Landry Court had dared, had dared to kiss her, to offer her this wretchedly commonplace and petty affront, degrading her to the level of a pretty waitress, making her ridiculous.

She stood rigid, drawn to her full height, in the centre of her bedroom, her fists tense at her sides, her breath short, her eyes flashing, her face aflame. From time to time her words, half smothered, burst from her.

"What does he think I am? How dared he? How dared he?"

All that she could say, any condemnation she could formulate only made her position the more absurd, the more humiliating. It had all been said before by generations of shop-girls, school-girls, and servants, in whose company the affront had ranged her. Landry was to be told in effect that he was never to presume to seek her acquaintance again. Just as the enraged hussy of the street corners and Sunday picnics shouted that the offender should "never dare speak to her again as long as he lived." Never before had she been subjected to this kind of indignity. And simultaneously with the assurance she could hear the shrill voice of the drab of the public balls proclaiming that she had "never been kissed in all her life before."

Of all slights, of all insults, it was the one that robbed her of the very dignity she should assume to rebuke it. The more vehemently she resented it, the more laughable became the whole affair.

But she would resent it, she would resent it, and Landry Court should be driven to acknowledge that the sorriest day of his life was the one on which he had forgotten the respect in which he had pretended to hold her. He had deceived her, then, all along. Because she had—foolishly—relaxed a little towards him, permitted a certain intimacy, this was how he abused it. Ah, well, it would teach her a lesson. Men were like that. She might have known it would come to this. Wilfully they chose to misunderstand, to take advantage of her frankness, her good nature, her good comradeship.

She had been foolish all along, flirting—yes, that was the word for it flirting with Landry and Corthell and Jadwin. No doubt they all compared notes about her. Perhaps they had bet who first should kiss her. Or, at least, there was not one of them who would not kiss her if she gave him a chance.

But if she, in any way, had been to blame for what Landry had done, she would atone for it. She had made herself too cheap, she had found amusement in encouraging these men, in equivocating, in coquetting with them. Now it was time to end the whole business, to send each one of them to the right-about with an unequivocal definite word. She was a good girl, she told herself. She was, in her heart, sincere; she was above the inexpensive diversion of flirting. She had started wrong in her new life, and it was time, high time, to begin over again—with a clean page—to show these men that they dared not presume to take liberties with so much as the tip of her little finger.

So great was her agitation, so eager her desire to act upon her resolve, that she could not wait till morning. It was a physical impossibility for her to remain under what she chose to believe suspicion another hour. If there was any remotest chance that her three lovers had permitted themselves to misunderstand her, they were to be corrected at once, were to be shown their place, and that without mercy.

She called for the maid, Annie, whose husband was the janitor of the house, and who slept in the top story.

"If Henry hasn't gone to bed," said Laura, "tell him to wait up till I call him, or to sleep with his clothes on. There is something I want him to do for me—something important."

It was close upon midnight. Laura turned back into her room, removed her hat and veil, and tossed them, with her coat, upon the bed. She lit another burner of the chandelier, and drew a chair to her writing-desk between the windows.

Her first note was to Landry Court. She wrote it almost with a single spurt of the pen, and dated it carefully, so that he might know it had been written immediately after he had left. Thus it ran:

"Please do not try to see me again at any time or under any circumstances. I want you to understand, very clearly, that I do not wish to continue our acquaintance."

Her letter to Corthell was more difficult, and it was not until she had rewritten it two or three times that it read to her satisfaction.

"My dear Mr. Corthell," so it was worded, "you asked me to-night that our fencing and quibbling be brought to an end. I quite agree with you that it is desirable. I spoke as I did before you left upon an impulse that I shall never cease to regret. I do not wish you to misunderstand me, nor to misinterpret my attitude in any way. You asked me to be your wife, and, very foolishly and wrongly, I gave you—intentionally—an answer which might easily be construed into an encouragement. Understand now that I do not wish you to try to make me love you. I would find it extremely distasteful. And, believe me, it would be quite hopeless. I do not now, and never shall care for you as I should care if I were to be your wife. I beseech you that you will not, in any manner, refer again to this subject. It would only distress and pain me.

"Cordially yours,

"LAURA DEARBORN."

The letter to Curtis Jadwin was almost to the same effect. But she found the writing of it easier than the others. In addressing him she felt herself grow a little more serious, a little more dignified and calm. It ran as follows:

MY DEAR MR. JADWIN:

"When you asked me to become your wife this evening, you deserved a straightforward answer, and instead I replied in a spirit of capriciousness and disingenuousness, which I now earnestly regret, and which ask you to pardon and to ignore.

"I allowed myself to tell you that you might find encouragement in my foolishly spoken words. I am deeply sorry that I should have so forgotten what was due to my own self-respect and to your sincerity.

"If I have permitted myself to convey to you the impression that I would ever be willing to be your wife, let me hasten to correct it. Whatever I said to you this evening, I must answer now—as I should have answered then—truthfully and unhesitatingly, no.

"This, I insist, must be the last word between us upon this unfortunate subject, if we are to continue, as I hope, very good friends.

"Cordially yours,

"LAURA DEARBORN."

She sealed, stamped, and directed the three envelopes, and glanced at the little leather-cased travelling clock that stood on the top of her desk. It was nearly two.

"I could not sleep, I could not sleep," she murmured, "if I did not know they were on the way."

In answer to the bell Henry appeared, and Laura gave him the letters, with orders to mail them at once in the nearest box.

When it was all over she sat down again at her desk, and leaning an elbow upon it, covered her eyes with her hand for a long moment. She felt suddenly very tired, and when at last she lowered her hand, her fingers were wet. But in the end she grew calmer. She felt that, at all events, she had vindicated herself, that her life would begin again to-morrow with a clean page; and when at length she fell asleep, it was to the dreamless unconsciousness of an almost tranquil mind.

She slept late the next morning and breakfasted in bed between ten and eleven. Then, as the last vibrations of last night's commotion died away, a very natural curiosity began to assert itself. She wondered how each of the three men "would take it." In spite of herself she could not keep from wishing that she could be by when they read their dismissals.

Towards the early part of the afternoon, while Laura was in the library reading "Queen's Gardens," the special delivery brought Landry Court's reply. It was one roulade of incoherence, even in places blistered with tears. Landry protested, implored, debased himself to the very dust. His letter bristled with exclamation points, and ended with a prolonged wail of distress and despair.

Quietly, and with a certain merciless sense of pacification, Laura deliberately reduced the letter to strips, burned it upon the hearth, and went back to her Ruskin.

A little later, the afternoon being fine, she determined to ride out to Lincoln Park, not fifteen minutes from her home, to take a little walk there, and to see how many new buds were out.

As she was leaving, Annie gave into her hands a pasteboard box, just brought to the house by a messenger boy.

The box was full of Jacqueminot roses, to the stems of which a note from Corthell was tied. He wrote but a single line:

"So it should have been 'good-by' after all."

Laura had Annie put the roses in Page's room.

"Tell Page she can have them; I don't want them. She can wear them to her dance to-night," she said.

While to herself she added:

"The little buds in the park will be prettier."

She was gone from the house over two hours, for she had elected to walk all the way home. She came back flushed and buoyant from her exercise, her cheeks cool with the Lake breeze, a young maple leaf in one of the revers of her coat. Annie let her in, murmuring:

"A gentleman called just after you went out. I told him you were not at home, but he said he would wait. He is in the library now."

"Who is he? Did he give his name?" demanded Laura.

The maid handed her Curtis Jadwin's card.

V

That year the spring burst over Chicago in a prolonged scintillation of pallid green. For weeks continually the sun shone. The Lake, after persistently cherishing the greys and bitter greens of the winter months, and the rugged white-caps of the northeast gales, mellowed at length, turned to a softened azure blue, and lapsed by degrees to an unruffled calmness, incrusted with innumerable coruscations.

In the parks, first of all, the buds and earliest shoots asserted themselves. The horse-chestnut bourgeons burst their sheaths to spread into trefoils and flame-shaped leaves. The elms, maples, and cottonwoods followed. The sooty, blackened snow upon the grass plats, in the residence quarters, had long since subsided, softening the turf, filling the gutters with rivulets. On all sides one saw men at work laying down the new sod in rectangular patches.

There was a delicious smell of ripening in the air, a smell of sap once more on the move, of humid earths disintegrating from the winter rigidity, of twigs and slender branches stretching themselves under the returning warmth, elastic once more, straining in their bark.

On the North Side, in Washington Square, along the Lake-shore Drive, all up and down the Lincoln Park Boulevard, and all through Erie, Huron, and Superior streets, through North State Street, North Clarke Street, and La Salle Avenue, the minute sparkling of green flashed from tree top to tree top, like the first kindling of dry twigs. One could almost fancy that the click of igniting branch tips was audible as whole beds of yellow-green sparks defined themselves within certain elms and cottonwoods.

Every morning the sun invaded earlier the east windows of Laura Dearborn's bedroom. Every day at noon it stood more nearly overhead above her home. Every afternoon the checkered shadows of the leaves thickened upon the drawn curtains of the library. Within doors the bottle-green flies came out of their lethargy and droned and bumped on the panes. The double windows were removed, screens and awnings took their places; the summer pieces were put into the fireplaces.

All of a sudden vans invaded the streets, piled high with mattresses, rocking-chairs, and bird cages; the inevitable "spring moving" took place. And these furniture vans alternated with great trucks laden with huge elm trees on their way from nursery to lawn. Families and trees alike submitted to the impulse of transplanting, abandoning the winter quarters, migrating with the spring to newer environments, taking root in other soils. Sparrows wrangled on the sidewalks and built ragged nests in the interstices of cornice and coping. In the parks one heard the liquid modulations of robins. The florists' wagons appeared, and from house to house, from lawn to lawn, iron urns and window boxes filled up with pansies, geraniums, fuchsias, and trailing vines. The flower beds, stripped of straw and manure, bloomed again, and at length the great cottonwoods shed their berries, like clusters of tiny grapes, over street and sidewalk.

At length came three days of steady rain, followed by cloudless sunshine and full-bodied, vigorous winds straight from out the south.

Instantly the living embers in tree top and grass plat were fanned to flame. Like veritable fire, the leaves blazed up. Branch after branch caught and crackled; even the dryest, the deadest, were enfolded in the resistless swirl of green. Tree top ignited tree top; the parks and boulevards were one smother of radiance. From end to end and from side to side of the city, fed by the rains, urged by the south winds, spread billowing and surging the superb conflagration of the coming summer.

Then, abruptly, everything hung poised; the leaves, the flowers, the grass, all at fullest stretch, stood motionless, arrested, while the heat, distilled, as it were, from all this seething green, rose like a vast pillar over the city, and stood balanced there in the iridescence of the sky, moveless and immeasurable.

From time to time it appeared as if this pillar broke in the guise of summer storms, and came toppling down upon the city in tremendous detonations of thunder and weltering avalanches of rain. But it broke only to reform, and no sooner had the thunder ceased, the rain intermitted, and the sun again come forth, than one received the vague impression of the swift rebuilding of the vast, invisible column that smothered the city under its bases, towering higher and higher into the rain-washed, crystal-clear atmosphere.

Then the aroma of wet dust, of drenched pavements, musty, acute—the unforgettable exhalation of the city's streets after a shower—pervaded all the air, and the little out-door activities resumed again under the dripping elms and upon the steaming sidewalks.

The evenings were delicious. It was yet too early for the exodus northward to the Wisconsin lakes, but to stay indoors after nightfall was not to be thought of. After six o'clock, all through the streets in the neighbourhood of the Dearborns' home, one could see the family groups "sitting out" upon the front "stoop." Chairs were brought forth, carpets and rugs unrolled upon the steps. From within, through the opened windows of drawing-room and parlour, came the brisk gaiety of pianos. The sidewalks were filled with children clamouring at "tag," "I-spy," or "run-sheep-run." Girls in shirt-waists and young men in flannel suits promenaded to and fro. Visits were exchanged from "stoop" to "stoop," lemonade was served, and claret punch. In their armchairs on the top step, elderly men, householders, capitalists, well-to-do, their large stomachs covered with white waistcoats, their straw hats upon their knees, smoked very fragrant cigars in silent enjoyment, digesting their dinners, taking the air after the grime and hurry of the business districts.

It was on such an evening as this, well on towards the last days of the spring, that Laura Dearborn and Page joined the Cresslers and their party, sitting out like other residents of the neighbourhood on the front steps of their house. Almost every evening nowadays the Dearborn girls came thus to visit with the Cresslers. Sometimes Page brought her mandolin.

Every day of the warm weather seemed only to increase the beauty of the two sisters. Page's brown hair was never more luxuriant, the exquisite colouring of her cheeks never more charming, the boyish outlines of her small, straight figure—immature and a little angular as yet—never more delightful. The seriousness of her straight-browed, grave, grey-blue eyes was still present, but the eyes themselves were, in some indefinable way, deepening, and all the maturity that as yet was withheld from her undeveloped little form looked out from beneath her long lashes.

But Laura was veritably regal. Very slender as yet, no trace of fulness to be seen over hip or breast, the curves all low and flat, she yet carried her extreme height with tranquil confidence, the unperturbed assurance of a chatelaine of the days of feudalism.

Her coal-black hair, high-piled, she wore as if it were a coronet. The warmth of the exuberant spring days had just perceptibly mellowed the even paleness of her face, but to compensate for this all the splendour of coming midsummer nights flashed from her deep-brown eyes.

On this occasion she had put on her coat over her shirt-waist, and a great bunch of violets was tucked into her belt. But no sooner had she exchanged greetings with the others and settled herself in her place than she slipped her coat from her shoulders.

It was while she was doing this that she noted, for the first time, Landry Court standing half in and half out of the shadow of the vestibule behind Mr. Cressler's chair.

"This is the first time he has been here since—since that night," Mrs. Cressler hastened to whisper in Laura's ear. "He told me about—well, he told me what occurred, you know. He came to dinner to-night, and afterwards the poor boy nearly wept in my arms. You never saw such penitence."

Laura put her chin in the air with a little movement of incredulity. But her anger had long since been a thing of the past. Good-tempered, she could not cherish resentment very long. But as yet she had greeted Landry only by the briefest of nods.

"Such a warm night!" she murmured, fanning herself with part of Mr. Cressler's evening paper. "And I never was so thirsty."

"Why, of course," exclaimed Mrs. Cressler. "Isabel," she called, addressing Miss Gretry, who sat on the opposite side of the steps, "isn't the lemonade near you? Fill a couple of glasses for Laura and Page."

Page murmured her thanks, but Laura declined.

"No; just plain water for me," she said. "Isn't there some inside? Mr. Court can get it for me, can't he?" Landry brought the pitcher back, running at top speed and spilling half of it in his eagerness. Laura thanked him with a smile, addressing him, however, by his last name. She somehow managed to convey to him in her manner the information that though his offence was forgotten, their old-time relations were not, for one instant, to be resumed.

Later on, while Page was thrumming her mandolin, Landry whistling a "second," Mrs. Cressler took occasion to remark to Laura:

"I was reading the Paris letter in the 'Inter-Ocean' to-day, and I saw Mr. Corthell's name on the list of American arrivals at the Continental. I guess," she added, "he's going to be gone a long time. I wonder sometimes if he will ever come back. A fellow with his talent, I should imagine would find Chicago—well, less congenial, anyhow, than Paris. But, just the same, I do think it was mean of him to break up our play by going. I'll bet a cookie that he wouldn't take part any more just because you wouldn't. He was just crazy to do that love scene in the fourth act with you. And when you wouldn't play, of course he wouldn't; and then everybody seemed to lose interest with you two out. 'J.' took it all very decently though, don't you think?"

Laura made a murmur of mild assent.

"He was disappointed, too," continued Mrs. Cressler. "I could see that. He thought the play was going to interest a lot of our church people in his Sunday-school. But he never said a word when it fizzled out. Is he coming to-night?"

"Well I declare," said Laura. "How should I know, if you don't?"

Jadwin was an almost regular visitor at the Cresslers' during the first warm evenings. He lived on the South Side, and the distance between his home and that of the Cresslers was very considerable. It was seldom, however, that Jadwin did not drive over. He came in his double-seated buggy, his negro coachman beside him the two coach dogs, "Rex" and "Rox," trotting under the rear axle. His horses were not showy, nor were they made conspicuous by elaborate boots, bandages, and all the other solemn paraphernalia of the stable, yet men upon the sidewalks, amateurs, breeders, and the like—men who understood good stock—never failed to stop to watch the team go by, heads up, the check rein swinging loose, ears all alert, eyes all alight, the breath deep, strong, and slow, and the stride, machine-like, even as the swing of a metronome, thrown out from the shoulder to knee, snapped on from knee to fetlock, from fetlock to pastern, finishing squarely, beautifully, with the thrust of the hoof, planted an instant, then, as it were, flinging the roadway behind it, snatched up again, and again cast forward.

On these occasions Jadwin himself inevitably wore a black "slouch" hat, suggestive of the general of the Civil War, a grey "dust overcoat" with a black velvet collar, and tan gloves, discoloured with the moisture of his palms and all twisted and crumpled with the strain of holding the thoroughbreds to their work.

He always called the time of the trip from the buggy at the Cresslers' horse block, his stop watch in his hand, and, as he joined the groups upon the steps, he was almost sure to remark: "Tugs were loose all the way from the river. They pulled the whole rig by the reins. My hands are about dislocated."

"Page plays very well," murmured Mrs. Cressler as the young girl laid down her mandolin. "I hope J. does come to-night," she added. "I love to have him 'round. He's so hearty and whole-souled."

Laura did not reply. She seemed a little preoccupied this evening, and conversation in the group died away. The night was very beautiful, serene, quiet; and, at this particular hour of the end of the twilight, no one cared to talk much. Cressler lit another cigar, and the filaments of delicate blue smoke hung suspended about his head in the moveless air. Far off, from the direction of the mouth of the river, a lake steamer whistled a prolonged tenor note. Somewhere from an open window in one of the neighbouring houses a violin, accompanied by a piano, began to elaborate the sustained phrases of "Schubert's Serenade." Theatrical as was the theme, the twilight and the muffled hum of the city, lapsing to quiet after the febrile activities of the day, combined to lend it a dignity, a persuasiveness. The children were still playing along the sidewalks, and their staccato gaiety was part of the quiet note to which all sounds of the moment seemed chorded.

After a while Mrs. Cressler began to talk to Laura in a low voice. She and Charlie were going to spend a part of June at Oconomowoc, in Wisconsin. Why could not Laura make up her mind to come with them? She had asked Laura a dozen times already, but couldn't get a yes or no answer from her. What was the reason she could not decide? Didn't she think she would have a good time?

"Page can go," said Laura. "I would like to have you take her. But as for me, I don't know. My plans are so unsettled this summer." She broke off suddenly. "Oh, now, that I think of it, I want to borrow your 'Idylls of the King.' May I take it for a day or two? I'll run in and get it now," she added as she rose. "I know just where to find it. No, please sit still, Mr. Cressler. I'll go."

And with the words she disappeared in doors, leaving Mrs. Cressler to murmur to her husband:

"Strange girl. Sometimes I think I don't know Laura at all. She's so inconsistent. How funny she acts about going to Oconomowoc with us!"

Mr. Cressler permitted himself an amiable grunt of protest.

"Pshaw! Laura's all right. The handsomest girl in Cook County."

"Well, that's not much to do with it, Charlie," sighed Mrs. Cressler. "Oh, dear," she added vaguely. "I don't know."

"Don't know what?"

"I hope Laura's life will be happy."

"Oh, for God's sake, Carrie!"

"There's something about that girl," continued Mrs. Cressler, "that makes my heart bleed for her."

Cressler frowned, puzzled and astonished.

"Hey—what!" he exclaimed. "You're crazy, Carrie!"

"Just the same," persisted Mrs. Cressler, "I just yearn towards her sometimes like a mother. Some people are born to trouble, Charlie; born to trouble, as the sparks fly upward. And you mark my words, Charlie Cressler, Laura is that sort. There's all the pathos in the world in just the way she looks at you from under all that black, black hair, and out of her eyes the saddest eyes sometimes, great, sad, mournful eyes."

"Fiddlesticks!" said Mr. Cressler, resuming his paper.

"I'm positive that Sheldon Corthell asked her to marry him," mused Mrs. Cressler after a moment's silence. "I'm sure that's why he left so suddenly."

Her husband grunted grimly as he turned his paper so as to catch the reflection of the vestibule light.

"Don't you think so, Charlie?"

"Uh! I don't know. I never had much use for that fellow, anyhow."

"He's wonderfully talented," she commented, "and so refined. He always had the most beautiful manners. Did you ever notice his hands?"

"I thought they were like a barber's. Put him in 'J.'s' rig there, behind those horses of his, and how long do you suppose he'd hold those trotters with that pair of hands? Why," he blustered, suddenly, "they'd pull him right over the dashboard."

"Poor little Landry Court!" murmured his wife, lowering her voice. "He's just about heart-broken. He wanted to marry her too. My goodness, she must have brought him up with a round turn. I can see Laura when she is really angry. Poor fellow!"

"If you women would let that boy alone, he might amount to something."

"He told me his life was ruined."

Cressler threw his cigar from him with vast impatience.

"Oh, rot!" he muttered.

"He took it terribly, seriously, Charlie, just the same."

"I'd like to take that young boy in hand and shake some of the nonsense out of him that you women have filled him with. He's got a level head. On the floor every day, and never yet bought a hatful of wheat on his own account. Don't know the meaning of speculation and don't want to. There's a boy with some sense."

"It's just as well," persisted Mrs. Cressler reflectively, "that Laura wouldn't have him. Of course they're not made for each other. But I thought that Corthell would have made her happy. But she won't ever marry 'J.' He asked her to; she didn't tell me, but I know he did. And she's refused him flatly. She won't marry anybody, she says. Said she didn't love anybody, and never would. I'd have loved to have seen her married to 'J.,' but I can see now that they wouldn't have been congenial; and if Laura wouldn't have Sheldon Corthell, who was just made for her, I guess it was no use to expect she'd have 'J.' Laura's got a temperament, and she's artistic, and loves paintings, and poetry, and Shakespeare, and all that, and Curtis don't care for those things at all. They wouldn't have had anything in common. But Corthell—that was different. And Laura did care for him, in a way. He interested her immensely. When he'd get started on art subjects Laura would just hang on every word. My lands, I wouldn't have gone away if I'd been in his boots. You mark my words, Charlie, there was the man for Laura Dearborn, and she'll marry him yet, or I'll miss my guess."

"That's just like you, Carrie—you and the rest of the women," exclaimed Cressler, "always scheming to marry each other off. Why don't you let the girl alone? Laura's all right. She minds her own business, and she's perfectly happy. But you'd go to work and get up a sensation about her, and say that your 'heart bleeds for her,' and that she's born to trouble, and has sad eyes. If she gets into trouble it'll be because some one else makes it for her. You take my advice, and let her paddle her own canoe. She's got the head to do it; don't you worry about that. By the way—" Cressler interrupted himself, seizing the opportunity to change the subject. "By the way, Carrie, Curtis has been speculating again. I'm sure of it."

"Too bad," she murmured.

"So it is," Cressler went on. "He and Gretry are thick as thieves these days. Gretry, I understand, has been selling September wheat for him all last week, and only this morning they closed out another scheme—some corn game. It was all over the Floor just about closing time. They tell me that Curtis landed between eight and ten thousand. Always seems to win. I'd give a lot to keep him out of it; but since his deal in May wheat he's been getting into it more and more."

"Did he sell that property on Washington Street?" she inquired.

"Oh," exclaimed her husband, "I'd forgot. I meant to tell you. No, he didn't sell it. But he did better. He wouldn't sell, and those department store people took a lease. Guess what they pay him. Three hundred thousand a year. 'J.' is getting richer all the time, and why he can't be satisfied with his own business instead of monkeying 'round La Salle Street is a mystery to me."

But, as Mrs. Cressler was about to reply, Laura came to the open window of the parlour.

"Oh, Mrs. Cressler," she called, "I don't seem to find your 'Idylls' after all. I thought they were in the little book-case."

"Wait. I'll find them for you," exclaimed Mrs. Cressler.

"Would you mind?" answered Laura, as Mrs. Cressler rose.

Inside, the gas had not been lighted. The library was dark and cool, and when Mrs. Cressler had found the book for Laura the girl pleaded a headache as an excuse for remaining within. The two sat down by the raised sash of a window at the side of the house, that overlooked the "side yard," where the morning-glories and nasturtiums were in full bloom.

"The house is cooler, isn't it?" observed Mrs. Cressler.

Laura settled herself in her wicker chair, and with a gesture that of late had become habitual with her pushed her heavy coils of hair to one side and patted them softly to place.

"It is getting warmer, I do believe," she said, rather listlessly. "I understand it is to be a very hot summer." Then she added, "I'm to be married in July, Mrs. Cressler."

Mrs. Cressler gasped, and sitting bolt upright stared for one breathless instant at Laura's face, dimly visible in the darkness. Then, stupefied, she managed to vociferate:

"What! Laura! Married? My darling girl!"

"Yes," answered Laura calmly. "In July—or maybe sooner."

"Why, I thought you had rejected Mr. Corthell. I thought that's why he went away."

"Went away? He never went away. I mean it's not Mr. Corthell. It's Mr. Jadwin."

"Thank God!" declared Mrs. Cressler fervently, and with the words kissed Laura on both cheeks. "My dear, dear child, you can't tell how glad I am. From the very first I've said you were made for one another. And I thought all the time that you'd told him you wouldn't have him."

"I did," said Laura. Her manner was quiet. She seemed a little grave. "I told him I did not love him. Only last week I told him so."

"Well, then, why did you promise?"

"My goodness!" exclaimed Laura, with a show of animation. "You don't realize what it's been. Do you suppose you can say 'no' to that man?"

"Of course not, of course not," declared Mrs. Cressler joyfully. "That's 'J.' all over. I might have known he'd have you if he set out to do it."

"Morning, noon, and night," Laura continued. "He seemed willing to wait as long as I wasn't definite; but one day I wrote to him and gave him a square 'No,' so as he couldn't mistake, and just as soon as I'd said that he—he—began. I didn't have any peace until I'd promised him, and the moment I had promised he had a ring on my finger. He'd had it ready in his pocket for weeks it seems. No," she explained, as Mrs. Cressler laid her fingers upon her left hand, "That I would not have—yet."

"Oh, it was like 'J.' to be persistent," repeated Mrs. Cressler.

"Persistent!" murmured Laura. "He simply wouldn't talk of anything else. It was making him sick, he said. And he did have a fever—often. But he would come out to see me just the same. One night, when it was pouring rain—Well, I'll tell you. He had been to dinner with us, and afterwards, in the drawing-room, I told him 'no' for the hundredth time just as plainly as I could, and he went away early—it wasn't eight. I thought that now at last he had given up. But he was back again before ten the same evening. He said he had come back to return a copy of a book I had loaned him—'Jane Eyre' it was. Raining! I never saw it rain as it did that night. He was drenched, and even at dinner he had had a low fever. And then I was sorry for him. I told him he could come to see me again. I didn't propose to have him come down with pneumonia, or typhoid, or something. And so it all began over again."

"But you loved him, Laura?" demanded Mrs. Cressler. "You love him now?"

Laura was silent. Then at length:

"I don't know," she answered.

"Why, of course you love him, Laura," insisted Mrs. Cressler. "You wouldn't have promised him if you hadn't. Of course you love him, don't you?"

"Yes, I—I suppose I must love him, or—as you say—I wouldn't have promised to marry him. He does everything, every little thing I say. He just seems to think of nothing else but to please me from morning until night. And when I finally said I would marry him, why, Mrs. Cressler, he choked all up, and the tears ran down his face, and all he could say was, 'May God bless you! May God bless you!' over and over again, and his hand shook so that—Oh, well," she broke off abruptly. Then added, "Somehow it makes tears come to my eyes to think of it."

"But, Laura," urged Mrs. Cressler, "you love Curtis, don't you? You—you're such a strange girl sometimes. Dear child, talk to me as though I were your mother. There's no one in the world loves you more than I do. You love Curtis, don't you?"

Laura hesitated a long moment.

"Yes," she said, slowly at length. "I think I love him very much—sometimes. And then sometimes I think I don't. I can't tell. There are days when I'm sure of it, and there are others when I wonder if I want to be married, after all. I thought when love came it was to be—oh, uplifting, something glorious like Juliet's love or Marguerite's. Something that would—" Suddenly she struck her hand to her breast, her fingers shut tight, closing to a fist. "Oh, something that would shake me all to pieces. I thought that was the only kind of love there was."

"Oh, that's what you read about in trashy novels," Mrs. Cressler assured her, "or the kind you see at the matinees. I wouldn't let that bother me, Laura. There's no doubt that 'J.' loves you."

Laura brightened a little. "Oh, no," she answered, "there's no doubt about that. It's splendid, that part of it. He seems to think there's nothing in the world too good for me. Just imagine, only yesterday I was saying something about my gloves, I really forget what—something about how hard it was for me to get the kind of gloves I liked. Would you believe it, he got me to give him my measure, and when I saw him in the evening he told me he had cabled to Brussels to some famous glovemaker and had ordered I don't know how many pairs."

"Just like him, just like him!" cried Mrs. Cressler. "I know you will be happy, Laura, dear. You can't help but be with a man who loves you as 'J.' does."

"I think I shall be happy," answered Laura, suddenly grave. "Oh, Mrs. Cressler, I want to be. I hope that I won't come to myself some day, after it is too late, and find that it was all a mistake." Her voice shook a little. "You don't know how nervous I am these days. One minute I am one kind of girl, and the next another kind. I'm so nervous and—oh, I don't know. Oh, I guess it will be all right." She wiped her eyes, and laughed a note. "I don't see why I should cry about it," she murmured.

"Well, Laura," answered Mrs. Cressler, "if you don't love Curtis, don't marry him. That's very simple."

"It's like this, Mrs. Cressler," Laura explained. "I suppose I am very uncharitable and unchristian, but I like the people that like me, and I hate those that don't like me. I can't help it. I know it's wrong, but that's the way I am. And I love to be loved. The man that would love me the most would make me love him. And when Mr. Jadwin seems to care so much, and do so much, and—you know how I mean; it does make a difference of course. I suppose I care as much for Mr. Jadwin as I ever will care for any man. I suppose I must be cold and unemotional."

Mrs. Cressler could not restrain a movement of surprise.

"You unemotional? Why, I thought you just said, Laura, that you had imagined love would be like Juliet and like that girl in 'Faust'—that it was going to shake you all to pieces."

"Did I say that? Well, I told you I was one girl one minute and another another. I don't know myself these days. Oh, hark," she said, abruptly, as the cadence of hoofs began to make itself audible from the end of the side street. "That's the team now. I could recognise those horses' trot as far as I could hear it. Let's go out. I know he would like to have me there when he drives up. And you know"—she put her hand on Mrs. Cressler's arm as the two moved towards the front door—"this is all absolutely a secret as yet."

"Why, of course, Laura dear. But tell me just one thing more," Mrs. Cressler asked, in a whisper, "are you going to have a church wedding?"

"Hey, Carrie," called Mr. Cressler from the stoop, "here's J."

Laura shook her head.

"No, I want it to be very quiet—at our house. We'll go to Geneva Lake for the summer. That's why, you see, I couldn't promise to go to Oconomowoc with you."

They came out upon the front steps, Mrs. Cressler's arm around Laura's waist. It was dark by now, and the air was perceptibly warmer.

The team was swinging down the street close at hand, the hoof beats exactly timed, as if there were but one instead of two horses.

"Well, what's the record to-night J.?" cried Cressler, as Jadwin brought the bays to a stand at the horse block. Jadwin did not respond until he had passed the reins to the coachman, and taking the stop watch from the latter's hand, he drew on his cigar, and held the glowing tip to the dial.

"Eleven minutes and a quarter," he announced, "and we had to wait for the bridge at that."

He came up the steps, fanning himself with his slouch hat, and dropped into the chair that Landry had brought for him.

"Upon my word," he exclaimed, gingerly drawing off his driving gloves, "I've no feeling in my fingers at all. Those fellows will pull my hands clean off some day."

But he was hardly settled in his place before he proposed to send the coachman home, and to take Laura for a drive towards Lincoln Park, and even a little way into the park itself. He promised to have her back within an hour.

"I haven't any hat," objected Laura. "I should love to go, but I ran over here to-night without any hat."

"Well, I wouldn't let that stand in my way, Laura," protested Mrs. Cressler. "It will be simply heavenly in the Park on such a night as this."

In the end Laura borrowed Page's hat, and Jadwin took her away. In the light of the street lamps Mrs. Cressler and the others watched them drive off, sitting side by side behind the fine horses. Jadwin, broad-shouldered, a fresh cigar in his teeth, each rein in a double turn about his large, hard hands; Laura, slim, erect, pale, her black, thick hair throwing a tragic shadow low upon her forehead.

"A fine-looking couple," commented Mr. Cressler as they disappeared.

The hoof beats died away, the team vanished. Landry Court, who stood behind the others, watching, turned to Mrs. Cressler. She thought she detected a little unsteadiness in his voice, but he repeated bravely:

"Yes, yes, that's right. They are a fine, a—a fine-looking couple together, aren't they? A fine-looking couple, to say the least."

A week went by, then two, soon May had passed. On the fifteenth of that month Laura's engagement to Curtis Jadwin was formally announced. The day of the wedding was set for the first week in June.

During this time Laura was never more changeable, more puzzling. Her vivacity seemed suddenly to have been trebled, but it was invaded frequently by strange reactions and perversities that drove her friends and family to distraction.

About a week after her talk with Mrs. Cressler, Laura broke the news to Page. It was a Monday morning. She had spent the time since breakfast in putting her bureau drawers to rights, scattering sachet powders in them, then leaving them open so as to perfume the room. At last she came into the front "upstairs sitting-room," a heap of gloves, stockings, collarettes—the odds and ends of a wildly disordered wardrobe—in her lap. She tumbled all these upon the hearth rug, and sat down upon the floor to sort them carefully. At her little desk near by, Page, in a blue and white shirt waist and golf skirt, her slim little ankles demurely crossed, a cone of foolscap over her forearm to guard against ink spots, was writing in her journal. This was an interminable affair, voluminous, complex, that the young girl had kept ever since she was fifteen. She wrote in it—she hardly knew what—the small doings of the previous day, her comings and goings, accounts of dances, estimates of new acquaintances. But besides this she filled page after page with "impressions," "outpourings," queer little speculations about her soul, quotations from poets, solemn criticisms of new novels, or as often as not mere purposeless meanderings of words, exclamatory, rhapsodic—involved lucubrations quite meaningless and futile, but which at times she re-read with vague thrills of emotion and mystery.

On this occasion Page wrote rapidly and steadily for a few moments after Laura's entrance into the room. Then she paused, her eyes growing wide and thoughtful. She wrote another line and paused again. Seated on the floor, her hands full of gloves,

Laura was murmuring to herself.

"Those are good ... and those, and the black suedes make eight.... And if I could only find the mate to this white one.... Ah, here it is. That makes nine, nine pair."

She put the gloves aside, and turning to the stockings drew one of the silk ones over her arm, and spread out her fingers in the foot.

"Oh, dear," she whispered, "there's a thread started, and now it will simply run the whole length...."

Page's scratching paused again.

"Laura," she asked dreamily, "Laura, how do you spell 'abysmal'?"

"With a y, honey," answered Laura, careful not to smile.

"Oh, Laura," asked Page, "do you ever get very, very sad without knowing why?"

"No, indeed," answered her sister, as she peeled the stocking from her arm. "When I'm sad I know just the reason, you may be sure."

Page sighed again.

"Oh, I don't know," she murmured indefinitely. "I lie awake at night sometimes and wish I were dead."

"You mustn't get morbid, honey," answered her older sister calmly. "It isn't natural for a young healthy little body like you to have such gloomy notions."

"Last night," continued Page, "I got up out of bed and sat by the window a long time. And everything was so still and beautiful, and the moonlight and all—and I said right out loud to myself,

"My breath to Heaven in vapour goes—

You know those lines from Tennyson:

"My breath to Heaven in vapour goes,
May my soul follow soon."

I said it right out loud just like that, and it was just as though something in me had spoken. I got my journal and wrote down, 'Yet in a few days, and thee, the all-beholding sun shall see no more.' It's from Thanatopsis, you know, and I thought how beautiful it would be to leave all this world, and soar and soar, right up to higher planes and be at peace. Laura, dearest, do you think I ever ought to marry?"

"Why not, girlie? Why shouldn't you marry. Of course you'll marry some day, if you find—"

"I should like to be a nun," Page interrupted, shaking her head, mournfully.

"—if you find the man who loves you," continued Laura, "and whom you—you admire and respect—whom you love. What would you say, honey, if—if your sister, if I should be married some of these days?"

Page wheeled about in her chair.

"Oh, Laura, tell me," she cried, "are you joking? Are you going to be married? Who to? I hadn't an idea, but I thought—I suspected."

"Well," observed Laura, slowly, "I might as well tell you—some one will if I don't—Mr. Jadwin wants me to marry him."

"And what did you say? What did you say? Oh, I'll never tell. Oh, Laura, tell me all about it."

"Well, why shouldn't I marry him? Yes—I promised. I said yes. Why shouldn't I? He loves me, and he is rich. Isn't that enough?"

"Oh, no. It isn't. You must love—you do love him?"

"I? Love? Pooh!" cried Laura. "Indeed not. I love nobody."

"Oh, Laura," protested Page earnestly. "Don't, don't talk that way. You mustn't. It's wicked."

Laura put her head in the air.

"I wouldn't give any man that much satisfaction. I think that is the way it ought to be. A man ought to love a woman more than she loves him. It ought to be enough for him if she lets him give her everything she wants in the world. He ought to serve her like the old knights—give up his whole life to satisfy some whim of hers; and it's her part, if she likes, to be cold and distant. That's my idea of love."

"Yes, but they weren't cold and proud to their knights after they'd promised to marry them," urged Page. "They loved them in the end, and married them for love."

"Oh, 'love'!" mocked Laura. "I don't believe in love. You only get your ideas of it from trashy novels and matinees. Girlie," cried Laura, "I am going to have the most beautiful gowns. They're the last things that Miss Dearborn shall buy for herself, and"—she fetched a long breath—"I tell you they are going to be creations."

When at length the lunch bell rang Laura jumped to her feet, adjusting her coiffure with thrusts of her long, white hands, the fingers extended, and ran from the room exclaiming that the whole morning had gone and that half her bureau drawers were still in disarray.

Page, left alone, sat for a long time lost in thought, sighing deeply at intervals, then at last she wrote in her journal:

"A world without Love—oh, what an awful thing that would be. Oh, love is so beautiful—so beautiful, that it makes me sad. When I think of love in all its beauty I am sad, sad like Romola in George Eliot's well-known novel of the same name."

She locked up her journal in the desk drawer, and wiped her pen point until it shone, upon a little square of chamois skin. Her writing-desk was a miracle of neatness, everything in its precise place, the writing-paper in geometrical parallelograms, the pen tray neatly polished.

On the hearth rug, where Laura had sat, Page's searching eye discovered traces of her occupancy—a glove button, a white thread, a hairpin. Page was at great pains to gather them up carefully and drop them into the waste basket.

"Laura is so fly-away," she observed, soberly.

When Laura told the news to Aunt Wess' the little old lady showed no surprise.

"I've been expecting it of late," she remarked. "Well, Laura, Mr. Jadwin is a man of parts. Though, to tell the truth, I thought at first it was to be that Mr. Corthell. He always seemed so distinguished-looking and elegant. I suppose now that that young Mr. Court will have a regular conniption fit."

"Oh, Landry," murmured Laura.

"Where are you going to live, Laura? Here? My word, child, don't be afraid to tell me I must pack. Why, bless you."

"No, no," exclaimed Laura, energetically, "you are to stay right here. We'll talk it all over just as soon as I know more decidedly what our plans are to be. No, we won't live here. Mr. Jadwin is going to buy a new house—on the corner of North Avenue and State Street. It faces Lincoln Park—you know it, the Farnsworth place."

"Why, my word, Laura," cried Aunt Wess' amazed, "why, it's a palace! Of course I know it. Why, it takes in the whole block, child, and there's a conservatory pretty near as big as this house. Well!"

"Yes, I know," answered Laura, shaking her head. "It takes my breath away sometimes. Mr. Jadwin tells me there's an art gallery, too, with an organ in it—a full-sized church organ. Think of it. Isn't it beautiful, beautiful? Isn't it a happiness? And I'll have my own carriage and coupe, and oh, Aunt Wess', a saddle horse if I want to, and a box at the opera, and a country place—that is to be bought day after to-morrow. It's at Geneva Lake. We're to go there after we are married, and Mr. Jadwin has bought the dearest, loveliest, daintiest little steam yacht. He showed the photograph of her yesterday. Oh, honey, honey! It all comes over me sometimes. Think, only a year ago, less than that, I was vegetating there at Barrington, among those wretched old blue-noses, helping Martha with the preserves and all and all; and now"—she threw her arms wide—"I'm just going to live. Think of it, that beautiful house, and servants, and carriages, and paintings, and, oh, honey, how I will dress the part!"

"But I wouldn't think of those things so much, Laura," answered Aunt Wess', rather seriously. "Child, you are not marrying him for carriages and organs and saddle horses and such. You're marrying this Mr. Jadwin because you love him. Aren't you?"

"Oh," cried Laura, "I would marry a ragamuffin if he gave me all these things—gave them to me because he loved me."

Aunt Wess' stared. "I wouldn't talk that way, Laura," she remarked. "Even in fun. At least not before Page."

That same evening Jadwin came to dinner with the two sisters and their aunt. The usual evening drive with Laura was foregone for this occasion. Jadwin had stayed very late at his office, and from there was to come direct to the Dearborns. Besides that, Nip—the trotters were named Nip and Tuck—was lame.

As early as four o'clock in the afternoon Laura, suddenly moved by an unreasoning caprice, began to prepare an elaborate toilet. Not since the opera night had she given so much attention to her appearance. She sent out for an extraordinary quantity of flowers; flowers for the table, flowers for Page and Aunt Wess', great "American beauties" for her corsage, and a huge bunch of violets for the bowl in the library. She insisted that Page should wear her smartest frock, and Mrs. Wessels her grenadine of great occasions. As for herself, she decided upon a dinner gown of black, decollete, with sleeves of lace. Her hair she dressed higher than ever. She resolved upon wearing all her jewelry, and to that end put on all her rings, secured the roses in place with an amethyst brooch, caught up the little locks at the back of her head with a heart-shaped pin of tiny diamonds, and even fastened the ribbon of satin that girdled her waist, with a clasp of flawed turquoises.

Until five in the afternoon she was in the gayest spirits, and went down to the dining-room to supervise the setting of the table, singing to herself.

Then, almost at the very last, when Jadwin might be expected at any moment, her humour changed again, and again, for no discoverable reason.

Page, who came into her sister's room after dressing, to ask how she looked, found her harassed and out of sorts. She was moody, spoke in monosyllables, and suddenly declared that the wearing anxiety of house-keeping was driving her to distraction. Of all days in the week, why had Jadwin chosen this particular one to come to dinner. Men had no sense, could not appreciate a woman's difficulties. Oh, she would be glad when the evening was over.

Then, as an ultimate disaster, she declared that she herself looked "Dutchy." There was no style, no smartness to her dress; her hair was arranged unbecomingly; she was growing thin, peaked. In a word, she looked "Dutchy."

All at once she flung off her roses and dropped into a chair.

"I will not go down to-night," she cried. "You and Aunt Wess' must make out to receive Mr. Jadwin. I simply will not see any one to-night, Mr. Jadwin least of all. Tell him I'm gone to bed sick—which is the truth, I am going to bed, my head is splitting."

All persuasion, entreaty, or cajolery availed nothing. Neither Page nor Aunt Wess' could shake her decision. At last Page hazarded a remonstrance to the effect that if she had known that Laura was not going to be at dinner she would not have taken such pains with her own toilet.

Promptly thereat Laura lost her temper.

"I do declare, Page," she exclaimed, "it seems to me that I get very little thanks for ever taking any interest in your personal appearance. There is not a girl in Chicago—no millionaire's daughter—has any prettier gowns than you. I plan and plan, and go to the most expensive dressmakers so that you will be well dressed, and just as soon as I dare to express the desire to see you appear like a gentlewoman, I get it thrown in my face. And why do I do it? I'm sure I don't know. It's because I'm a poor weak, foolish, indulgent sister. I've given up the idea of ever being loved by you; but I do insist on being respected." Laura rose, stately, severe. It was the "grand manner" now, unequivocally, unmistakably. "I do insist upon being respected," she repeated. "It would be wrong and wicked of me to allow you to ignore and neglect my every wish. I'll not have it, I'll not tolerate it."

Page, aroused, indignant, disdained an answer, but drew in her breath and held it hard, her lips tight pressed.

"It's all very well for you to pose, miss," Laura went on; "to pose as injured innocence. But you understand very well what I mean. If you don't love me, at least I shall not allow you to flout me—deliberately, defiantly. And it does seem strange," she added, her voice beginning to break, "that when we two are all alone in the world, when there's no father or mother—and you are all I have, and when I love you as I do, that there might be on your part—a little consideration—when I only want to be loved for my own sake, and not—and not—when I want to be, oh, loved—loved—loved—"

The two sisters were in each other's arms by now, and Page was crying no less than Laura.

"Oh, little sister," exclaimed Laura, "I know you love me. I know you do. I didn't mean to say that. You must forgive me and be very kind to me these days. I know I'm cross, but sometimes these days I'm so excited and nervous I can't help it, and you must try to bear with me. Hark, there's the bell."

Listening, they heard the servant open the door, and then the sound of Jadwin's voice and the clank of his cane in the porcelain cane rack. But still Laura could not be persuaded to go down. No, she was going to bed; she had neuralgia; she was too nervous to so much as think. Her gown was "Dutchy." And in the end, so unshakable was her resolve, that Page and her aunt had to sit through the dinner with Jadwin and entertain him as best they could.

But as the coffee was being served the three received a genuine surprise. Laura appeared. All her finery was laid off. She wore the simplest, the most veritably monastic, of her dresses, plain to the point of severity. Her hands were bare of rings. Not a single jewel, not even the most modest ornament relieved her sober appearance. She was very quiet, spoke in a low voice and declared she had come down only to drink a glass of mineral water and then to return at once to her room.

As a matter of fact, she did nothing of the kind. The others prevailed upon her to take a cup of coffee. Then the dessert was recalled, and, forgetting herself in an animated discussion with Jadwin as to the name of their steam yacht, she ate two plates of wine jelly before she was aware. She expressed a doubt as to whether a little salad would do her good, and after a vehement exhortation from Jadwin, allowed herself to be persuaded into accepting a sufficiently generous amount.

"I think a classical name would be best for the boat," she declared. "Something like 'Arethusa' or 'The Nereid.'"

They rose from the table and passed into the library. The evening was sultry, threatening a rain-storm, and they preferred not to sit on the "stoop." Jadwin lit a cigar; he still wore his business clothes—the inevitable "cutaway," white waistcoat, and grey trousers of the middle-aged man of affairs.

"Oh, call her the 'Artemis,'" suggested Page.

"Well now, to tell the truth," observed Jadwin, "those names look pretty in print; but somehow I don't fancy them. They're hard to read, and they sound somehow frilled up and fancy. But if you're satisfied, Laura—"

"I knew a young man once," began Aunt Wess', "who had a boat—that was when we lived at Kenwood and Mr. Wessels belonged to the 'Farragut'—and this young man had a boat he called 'Fanchon.' He got tipped over in her one day, he and the three daughters of a lady I knew well, and two days afterward they found them at the bottom of the lake, all holding on to each other; and they fetched them up just like that in one piece. The mother of those girls never smiled once since that day, and her hair turned snow white. That was in 'seventy-nine. I remember it perfectly. The boat's name was 'Fanchon.'"

"But that was a sail boat, Aunt Wess'," objected Laura. "Ours is a steam yacht. There's all the difference in the world."

"I guess they're all pretty risky, those pleasure boats," answered Aunt Wess'. "My word, you couldn't get me to set foot on one."

Jadwin nodded his head at Laura, his eyes twinkling.

"Well, we'll leave 'em all at home, Laura, when we go," he said.

A little later one of Page's "young men" called to see her, and Page took him off into the drawing-room across the hall. Mrs. Wessels seized upon the occasion to slip away unobserved, and Laura and Jadwin were left alone.

"Well, my girl," began Jadwin, "how's the day gone with you?"

She had been seated at the centre table, by the drop light—the only light in the room—turning over the leaves of "The Age of Fable," looking for graceful and appropriate names for the yacht. Jadwin leaned over her and put his hand upon her shoulder.

"Oh, about the same as usual," she answered. "I told Page and Aunt Wess' this morning."

"What did they have to say?" Jadwin laid a soft but clumsy hand upon Laura's head, adding, "Laura, you have the most wonderful hair I ever saw."

"Oh, they were not surprised. Curtis, don't, you are mussing me." She moved her head impatiently; but then smiling, as if to mitigate her abruptness, said, "It always makes me nervous to have my hair touched. No, they were not surprised; unless it was that we were to be married so soon. They were surprised at that. You know I always said it was too soon. Why not put it off, Curtis—until the winter?"

But he scouted this, and then, as she returned to the subject again, interrupted her, drawing some papers from his pocket.

"Oh, by the way," he said, "here are the sketch plans for the alterations of the house at Geneva. The contractor brought them to the office to-day. He's made that change about the dining-room."

"Oh," exclaimed Laura, interested at once, "you mean about building on the conservatory?"

"Hum—no," answered Jadwin a little slowly. "You see, Laura, the difficulty is in getting the thing done this summer. When we go up there we want everything finished, don't we? We don't want a lot of workmen clattering around. I thought maybe we could wait about that conservatory till next year, if you didn't mind."

Laura acquiesced readily enough, but Jadwin could see that she was a little disappointed. Thoughtful, he tugged his mustache in silence for a moment. Perhaps, after all, it could be arranged. Then an idea presented itself to him. Smiling a little awkwardly, he said:

"Laura, I tell you what. I'll make a bargain with you."

She looked up as he hesitated. Jadwin sat down at the table opposite her and leaned forward upon his folded arms.

"Do you know," he began, "I happened to think—Well, here's what I mean," he suddenly declared decisively. "Do you know, Laura, that ever since we've been engaged you've never—Well, you've never—never kissed me of your own accord. It's foolish to talk that way now, isn't it? But, by George! That would be—would be such a wonderful thing for me. I know," he hastened to add, "I know, Laura, you aren't demonstrative. I ought not to expect, maybe, that you— Well, maybe it isn't much. But I was thinking a while ago that there wouldn't be a sweeter thing imaginable for me than if my own girl would come up to me some time—when I wasn't thinking—and of her own accord put her two arms around me and kiss me. And—well, I was thinking about it, and—" He hesitated again, then finished abruptly with, "And it occurred to me that you never had."

Laura made no answer, but smiled rather indefinitely, as she continued to search the pages of the book, her head to one side.

Jadwin continued:

"We'll call it a bargain. Some day—before very long, mind you—you are going to kiss me—that way, understand, of your own accord, when I'm not thinking of it; and I'll get that conservatory in for you. I'll manage it somehow. I'll start those fellows at it to-morrow—twenty of 'em if it's necessary. How about it? Is it a bargain? Some day before long. What do you say?"

Laura hesitated, singularly embarrassed, unable to find the right words.

"Is it a bargain?" persisted Jadwin.

"Oh, if you put it that way," she murmured, "I suppose so—yes."

"You won't forget, because I shan't speak about it again. Promise you won't forget."

"No, I won't forget. Why not call her the 'Thetis'?"

"I was going to suggest the 'Dart,' or the 'Swallow,' or the 'Arrow.' Something like that—to give a notion of speed."

"No. I like the 'Thetis' best."

"That settles it then. She's your steam yacht, Laura."

Later on, when Jadwin was preparing to depart, they stood for a moment in the hallway, while he drew on his gloves and took a fresh cigar from his case.

"I'll call for you here at about ten," he said. "Will that do?"

He spoke of the following morning. He had planned to take Page, Mrs. Wessels, and Laura on a day's excursion to Geneva Lake to see how work was progressing on the country house. Jadwin had set his mind upon passing the summer months after the marriage at the lake, and as the early date of the ceremony made it impossible to erect a new building, he had bought, and was now causing to be remodelled, an old but very well constructed house just outside of the town and once occupied by a local magistrate. The grounds were ample, filled with shade and fruit trees, and fronted upon the lake. Laura had never seen her future country home. But for the past month Jadwin had had a small army of workmen and mechanics busy about the place, and had managed to galvanise the contractors with some of his own energy and persistence. There was every probability that the house and grounds would be finished in time.

"Very well," said Laura, in answer to his question, "at ten we'll be ready. Good-night." She held out her hand. But Jadwin put it quickly aside, and took her swiftly and strongly into his arms, and turning her face to his, kissed her cheek again and again.

Laura submitted, protesting:

"Curtis! Such foolishness. Oh, dear; can't you love me without crumpling me so? Curtis! Please. You are so rough with me, dear."

She pulled away from him, and looked up into his face, surprised to find it suddenly flushed; his eyes were flashing.

"My God," he murmured, with a quick intake of breath, "my God, how I love you, my girl! Just the touch of your hand, the smell of your hair. Oh, sweetheart. It is wonderful! Wonderful!" Then abruptly he was master of himself again.

"Good-night," he said. "Good-night. God bless you," and with the words was gone.

They were married on the last day of June of that summer at eleven o'clock in the morning in the church opposite Laura's house—the Episcopalian church of which she was a member. The wedding was very quiet. Only the Cresslers, Miss Gretry, Page, and Aunt Wess' were present. Immediately afterward the couple were to take the train for Geneva Lake—Jadwin having chartered a car for the occasion.

But the weather on the wedding day was abominable. A warm drizzle, which had set in early in the morning, developed by eleven o'clock into a steady downpour, accompanied by sullen grumblings of very distant thunder.

About an hour before the appointed time Laura insisted that her aunt and sister should leave her. She would allow only Mrs. Cressler to help her. The time passed. The rain continued to fall. At last it wanted but fifteen minutes to eleven.

Page and Aunt Wess', who presented themselves at the church in advance of the others, found the interior cool, dark, and damp. They sat down in a front pew, talking in whispers, looking about them. Druggeting shrouded the reader's stand, the baptismal font, and bishop's chair. Every footfall and every minute sound echoed noisily from the dark vaulting of the nave and chancel. The janitor or sexton, a severe old fellow, who wore a skull cap and loose slippers, was making a great to-do with a pile of pew cushions in a remote corner. The rain drummed with incessant monotony upon the slates overhead, and upon the stained windows on either hand. Page, who attended the church regularly every Sunday morning, now found it all strangely unfamiliar. The saints in the windows looked odd and unecclesiastical; the whole suggestion of the place was uncanonical. In the organ loft a tuner was at work upon the organ, and from time to time the distant mumbling of the thunder was mingled with a sonorous, prolonged note from the pipes.

"My word, how it is raining," whispered Aunt Wess', as the pour upon the roof suddenly swelled in volume.

But Page had taken a prayer book from the rack, and kneeling upon a hassock was repeating the Litany to herself.

It annoyed Aunt Wess'. Excited, aroused, the little old lady was never more in need of a listener. Would Page never be through?

"And Laura's new frock," she whispered, vaguely. "It's going to be ruined."

Page, her lips forming the words, "Good Lord deliver us," fixed her aunt with a reproving glance. To pass the time Aunt Wess' began counting the pews, missing a number here and there, confusing herself, always obliged to begin over again. From the direction of the vestry room came the sound of a closing door. Then all fell silent again. Even the shuffling of the janitor ceased for an instant.

"Isn't it still?" murmured Aunt Wess', her head in the air. "I wonder if that was them. I heard a door slam. They tell me that the rector has been married three times." Page, unheeding and demure, turned a leaf, and began with "All those who travel by land or water." Mr. Cressler and young Miss Gretry appeared. They took their seats behind Page and Aunt Wess', and the party exchanged greetings in low voices. Page reluctantly laid down her prayer book.

"Laura will be over soon," whispered Mr. Cressler. "Carrie is with her. I'm going into the vestry room. J. has just come." He took himself off, walking upon his tiptoes.

Aunt Wess' turned to Page, repeating:

"Do you know they say this rector has been married three times?"

But Page was once more deep in her prayer book, so the little old lady addressed her remark to the Gretry girl.

This other, however, her lips tightly compressed, made a despairing gesture with her hand, and at length managed to say:

"Can't talk."

"Why, heavens, child, whatever is the matter?"

"Makes them worse—when I open my mouth—I've got the hiccoughs."

Aunt Wess' flounced back in her seat, exasperated, out of sorts.

"Well, my word," she murmured to herself, "I never saw such girls."

"Preserve to our use the kindly fruits of the earth," continued Page.

Isabel Gretry's hiccoughs drove Aunt Wess' into "the fidgets." They "got on her nerves." What with them and Page's uninterrupted murmur, she was at length obliged to sit in the far end of the pew, and just as she had settled herself a second time the door of the vestry room opened and the wedding party came out; first Mrs. Cressler, then Laura, then Jadwin and Cressler, and then, robed in billowing white, venerable, his prayer book in his hand, the bishop of the diocese himself. Last of all came the clerk, osseous, perfumed, a gardenia in the lapel of his frock coat, terribly excited, and hurrying about on tiptoe, saying "Sh! Sh!" as a matter of principle.

Jadwin wore a new frock coat and a resplendent Ascot scarf, which Mr. Cressler had bought for him and Page knew at a glance that he was agitated beyond all measure, and was keeping himself in hand only by a tremendous effort. She could guess that his teeth were clenched. He stood by Cressler's side, his head bent forward, his hands—the fingers incessantly twisting and untwisting—clasped behind his back. Never for once did his eyes leave Laura's face.

She herself was absolutely calm, only a little paler perhaps than usual; but never more beautiful, never more charming. Abandoning for this once her accustomed black, she wore a tan travelling dress, tailor made, very smart, a picture hat with heavy plumes set off with a clasp of rhinestones, while into her belt was thrust a great bunch of violets. She drew off her gloves and handed them to Mrs. Cressler. At the same moment Page began to cry softly to herself.

"There's the last of Laura," she whimpered. "There's the last of my dear sister for me."

Aunt Wess' fixed her with a distressful gaze. She sniffed once or twice, and then began fumbling in her reticule for her handkerchief.

"If only her dear father were here," she whispered huskily. "And to think that's the same little girl I used to rap on the head with my thimble for annoying the cat! Oh, if Jonas could be here this day."

"She'll never be the same to me after now," sobbed Page, and as she spoke the Gretry girl, hypnotised with emotion and taken all unawares, gave vent to a shrill hiccough, a veritable yelp, that woke an explosive echo in every corner of the building.

Page could not restrain a giggle, and the giggle strangled with the sobs in her throat, so that the little girl was not far from hysterics.

And just then a sonorous voice, magnificent, orotund, began suddenly from the chancel with the words:

"Dearly beloved, we are gathered together here in the sight of God, and in the face of this company to join together this Man and this Woman in holy matrimony."

Promptly a spirit of reverence, not to say solemnity, pervaded the entire surroundings. The building no longer appeared secular, unecclesiastical. Not in the midst of all the pomp and ceremonial of the Easter service had the chancel and high altar disengaged a more compelling influence. All other intrusive noises died away; the organ was hushed; the fussy janitor was nowhere in sight; the outside clamour of the city seemed dwindling to the faintest, most distant vibration; the whole world was suddenly removed, while the great moment in the lives of the Man and the Woman began.

Page held her breath; the intensity of the situation seemed to her, almost physically, straining tighter and tighter with every passing instant. She was awed, stricken; and Laura appeared to her to be all at once a woman transfigured, semi-angelic, unknowable, exalted. The solemnity of those prolonged, canorous syllables: "I require and charge you both, as ye shall answer at the dreadful day of judgment, when the secrets of all hearts shall be disclosed," weighed down upon her spirits with an almost intolerable majesty. Oh, it was all very well to speak lightly of marriage, to consider it in a vein of mirth. It was a pretty solemn affair, after all; and she herself, Page Dearborn, was a wicked, wicked girl, full of sins, full of deceits and frivolities, meriting of punishment—on "that dreadful day of judgment." Only last week she had deceived Aunt Wess' in the matter of one of her "young men." It was time she stopped. To-day would mark a change. Henceforward, she resolved, she would lead a new life.

"God the Father, God the Son, and God the Holy Ghost ..."

To Page's mind the venerable bishop's voice was filling all the church, as on the day of Pentecost, when the apostles received the Holy Ghost, the building was filled with a "mighty rushing wind."

She knelt down again, but could not bring herself to close her eyes completely. From under her lids she still watched her sister and Jadwin. How Laura must be feeling now! She was, in fact, very pale. There was emotion in Jadwin's eyes. Page could see them plainly. It seemed beautiful that even he, the strong, modern man-of-affairs, should be so moved. How he must love Laura. He was fine, he was noble; and all at once this fineness and nobility of his so affected her that she began to cry again. Then suddenly came the words:

"... That in the world to come ye may have life everlasting. Amen."

There was a moment's silence, then the group about the altar rail broke up.

"Come," said Aunt Wess', getting to her feet, "it's all over, Page. Come, and kiss your sister—Mrs. Jadwin."

In the vestry room Laura stood for a moment, while one after another of the wedding party—even Mr. Cressler—kissed her. When Page's turn came, the two sisters held each other in a close embrace a long moment, but Laura's eyes were always dry. Of all present she was the least excited.

"Here's something," vociferated the ubiquitous clerk, pushing his way forward. "It was on the table when we came out just now. The sexton says a messenger boy brought it. It's for Mrs. Jadwin."

He handed her a large box. Laura opened it. Inside was a great sheaf of Jacqueminot roses and a card, on which was written:

"May that same happiness which you have always inspired in the lives and memories of all who know you be with you always.

"Yrs. S. C."

The party, emerging from the church, hurried across the street to the Dearborns' home, where Laura and Jadwin were to get their valises and hand bags. Jadwin's carriage was already at the door.

They all assembled in the parlor, every one talking at once, while the servants, bare-headed, carried the baggage down to the carriage.

"Oh, wait—wait a minute, I'd forgotten something," cried Laura.

"What is it? Here, I'll get it for you," cried Jadwin and Cressler as she started toward the door. But she waved them off, crying:

"No, no. It's nothing. You wouldn't know where to look."

Alone she ran up the stairs, and gained the second story; then paused a moment on the landing to get her breath and to listen. The rooms near by were quiet, deserted. From below she could hear the voices of the others—their laughter and gaiety. She turned about, and went from room to room, looking long into each; first Aunt Wess's bedroom, then Page's, then the "front sitting-room," then, lastly, her own room. It was still in the disorder caused by that eventful morning; many of the ornaments—her own cherished knick-knacks—were gone, packed and shipped to her new home the day before. Her writing-desk and bureau were bare. On the backs of chairs, and across the footboard of the bed, were the odds and ends of dress she was never to wear again.

For a long time Laura stood looking silently at the empty room. Here she had lived the happiest period of her life; not an object there, however small, that was not hallowed by association. Now she was leaving it forever. Now the new life, the Untried, was to begin. Forever the old days, the old life were gone. Girlhood was gone; the Laura Dearborn that only last night had pressed the pillows of that bed, where was she now? Where was the little black-haired girl of Barrington?

And what was this new life to which she was going forth, under these leaden skies, under this warm mist of rain? The tears—at last—were in her eyes, and the sob in her throat, and she found herself, as she leaned an arm upon the lintel of the door, whispering:

"Good-by. Good-by. Good-by."

Then suddenly Laura, reckless of her wedding finery, forgetful of trivialities, crossed the room and knelt down at the side of the bed. Her head in her folded arms, she prayed—prayed in the little unstudied words of her childhood, prayed that God would take care of her and make her a good girl; prayed that she might be happy; prayed to God to help her in the new life, and that she should be a good and loyal wife.

And then as she knelt there, all at once she felt an arm, strong, heavy even, laid upon her. She raised her head and looked—for the first time—direct into her husband's eyes.

"I knew—" began Jadwin. "I thought—Dear, I understand, I understand."

He said no more than that. But suddenly Laura knew that he, Jadwin, her husband, did "understand," and she discovered, too, in that moment just what it meant to be completely, thoroughly understood—understood without chance of misapprehension, without shadow of doubt; understood to her heart's heart. And with the knowledge a new feeling was born within her. No woman, not her dearest friend; not even Page had ever seemed so close to her as did her husband now. How could she be unhappy henceforward? The future was already brightening.

Suddenly she threw both arms around his neck, and drawing his face down to her, kissed him again and again, and pressed her wet cheek to his—tear-stained like her own.

"It's going to be all right, dear," he said, as she stood from him, though still holding his hand. "It's going to be all right."

"Yes, yes, all right, all right," she assented. "I never seemed to realise it till this minute. From the first I must have loved you without knowing it. And I've been cold and hard to you, and now I'm sorry, sorry. You were wrong, remember that time in the library, when you said I was undemonstrative. I'm not. I love you dearly, dearly, and never for once, for one little moment, am I ever going to allow you to forget it."

Suddenly, as Jadwin recalled the incident of which she spoke, an idea occurred to him.

"Oh, our bargain—remember? You didn't forget after all."

"I did. I did," she cried. "I did forget it. That's the very sweetest thing about it."

VI

The months passed. Soon three years had gone by, and the third winter since the ceremony in St. James' Church drew to its close.

Since that day when—acting upon the foreknowledge of the French import duty—Jadwin had sold his million of bushels short, the price of wheat had been steadily going down. From ninety-three and ninety-four it had dropped to the eighties. Heavy crops the world over had helped the decline. No one was willing to buy wheat. The Bear leaders were strong, unassailable. Lower and lower sagged the price; now it was seventy-five, now seventy-two. From all parts of the country in solid, waveless tides wheat—the mass of it incessantly crushing down the price—came rolling in upon Chicago and the Board of Trade Pit. All over the world the farmers saw season after season of good crops. They were good in the Argentine Republic, and on the Russian steppes. In India, on the little farms of Burmah, of Mysore, and of Sind the grain, year after year, headed out fat, heavy, and well-favoured. In the great San Joaquin valley of California the ranches were one welter of fertility. All over the United States, from the Dakotas, from Nebraska, Iowa, Kansas, and Illinois, from all the wheat belt came steadily the reports of good crops.

But at the same time the low price of grain kept the farmers poor. New mortgages were added to farms already heavily "papered"; even the crops were mortgaged in advance. No new farm implements were bought. Throughout the farming communities of the "Middle West" there were no longer purchases of buggies and parlour organs. Somewhere in other remoter corners of the world the cheap wheat, that meant cheap bread, made living easy and induced prosperity, but in the United States the poverty of the farmer worked upward through the cogs and wheels of the whole great machine of business. It was as though a lubricant had dried up. The cogs and wheels worked slowly and with dislocations. Things were a little out of joint. Wall Street stocks were down. In a word, "times were bad." Thus for three years. It became a proverb on the Chicago Board of Trade that the quickest way to make money was to sell wheat short. One could with almost absolute certainty be sure of buying cheaper than one had sold. And that peculiar, indefinite thing known—among the most unsentimental men in the world—as "sentiment," prevailed more and more strongly in favour of low prices. "The 'sentiment,'" said the market reports, "was bearish"; and the traders, speculators, eighth-chasers, scalpers, brokers, bucket-shop men, and the like—all the world of La Salle Street—had become so accustomed to these "Bear conditions," that it was hard to believe that they would not continue indefinitely.

Jadwin, inevitably, had been again drawn into the troubled waters of the Pit. Always, as from the very first, a Bear, he had once more raided the market, and had once more been successful. Two months after this raid he and Gretry planned still another coup, a deal of greater magnitude than any they had previously hazarded. Laura, who knew very little of her husband's affairs—to which he seldom alluded—saw by the daily papers that at one stage of the affair the "deal" trembled to its base.

But Jadwin was by now "blooded to the game." He no longer needed Gretry's urging to spur him. He had developed into a strategist, bold, of inconceivable effrontery, delighting in the shock of battle, never more jovial, more daring than when under stress of the most merciless attack. On this occasion, when the "other side" resorted to the usual tactics to drive him from the Pit, he led on his enemies to make one single false step. Instantly—disregarding Gretry's entreaties as to caution—Jadwin had brought the vast bulk of his entire fortune to bear, in the manner of a general concentrating his heavy artillery, and crushed the opposition with appalling swiftness.

He issued from the grapple triumphantly, and it was not till long afterward that Laura knew how near, for a few hours, he had been to defeat.

And again the price of wheat declined. In the first week in April, at the end of the third winter of Jadwin's married life, May wheat was selling on the floor of the Chicago Board of Trade at sixty-four, the July option at sixty-five, the September at sixty-six and an eighth. During February of the same year Jadwin had sold short five hundred thousand bushels of May. He believed with Gretry and with the majority of the professional traders that the price would go to sixty.

March passed without any further decline. All through this month and through the first days of April Jadwin was unusually thoughtful. His short wheat gave him no concern. He was now so rich that a mere half-million bushels was not a matter for anxiety. It was the "situation" that arrested his attention.

In some indefinable way, warned by that blessed sixth sense that had made him the successful speculator he was, he felt that somewhere, at some time during the course of the winter, a change had quietly, gradually come about, that it was even then operating. The conditions that had prevailed so consistently for three years, were they now to be shifted a little? He did not know, he could not say. But in the plexus of financial affairs in which he moved and lived he felt—a difference.

For one thing "times" were better, business was better. He could not fail to see that trade was picking up. In dry goods, in hardware, in manufactures there seemed to be a different spirit, and he could imagine that it was a spirit of optimism. There, in that great city where the Heart of the Nation beat, where the diseases of the times, or the times' healthful activities were instantly reflected, Jadwin sensed a more rapid, an easier, more untroubled run of life blood. All through the Body of Things, money, the vital fluid, seemed to be flowing more easily. People seemed richer, the banks were lending more, securities seemed stable, solid. In New York, stocks were booming. Men were making money—were making it, spending it, lending it, exchanging it. Instead of being congested in vaults, safes, and cash boxes, tight, hard, congealed, it was loosening, and, as it were, liquefying, so that it spread and spread and permeated the entire community. The People had money. They were willing to take chances.

So much for the financial conditions.

The spring had been backward, cold, bitter, inhospitable, and Jadwin began to suspect that the wheat crop of his native country, that for so long had been generous, and of excellent quality, was now to prove—it seemed quite possible—scant and of poor condition. He began to watch the weather, and to keep an eye upon the reports from the little county seats and "centres" in the winter wheat States. These, in part, seemed to confirm his suspicions.

From Keokuk, in Iowa, came the news that winter wheat was suffering from want of moisture. Benedict, Yates' Centre, and Douglass, in southeastern Kansas, sent in reports of dry, windy weather that was killing the young grain in every direction, and the same conditions seemed to prevail in the central counties. In Illinois, from Quincy and Waterloo in the west, and from Ridgway in the south, reports came steadily to hand of freezing weather and bitter winds. All through the lower portions of the State the snowfall during the winter had not been heavy enough to protect the seeded grain. But the Ohio crop, it would appear, was promising enough, as was also that of Missouri. In Indiana, however, Jadwin could guess that the hopes of even a moderate yield were fated to be disappointed; persistent cold weather, winter continuing almost up to the first of April, seemed to have definitely settled the question.

But more especially Jadwin watched Nebraska, that State which is one single vast wheat field. How would Nebraska do, Nebraska which alone might feed an entire nation? County seat after county seat began to send in its reports. All over the State the grip of winter held firm even yet. The wheat had been battered by incessant gales, had been nipped and harried by frost; everywhere the young half-grown grain seemed to be perishing. It was a massacre, a veritable slaughter.

But, for all this, nothing could be decided as yet. Other winter wheat States, from which returns were as yet only partial, might easily compensate for the failures elsewhere, and besides all that, the Bears of the Board of Trade might keep the price inert even in face of the news of short yields. As a matter of fact, the more important and stronger Bear traders were already piping their usual strain. Prices were bound to decline, the three years, sagging was not over yet. They, the Bears, were too strong; no Bull news could frighten them. Somehow there was bound to be plenty of wheat. In face of the rumours of a short crop they kept the price inert, weak.

On the tenth of April came the Government report on the condition of winter wheat. It announced an average far below any known for ten years past. On March tenth the same bulletin had shown a moderate supply in farmers' hands, less than one hundred million bushels in fact, and a visible supply of less than forty millions.

The Bear leaders promptly set to work to discount this news. They showed how certain foreign conditions would more than offset the effect of a poor American harvest. They pointed out the fact that the Government report on condition was brought up only to the first of April, and that since that time the weather in the wheat belt had been favorable beyond the wildest hopes.

The April report was made public on the afternoon of the tenth of the month. That same evening Jadwin invited Gretry and his wife to dine at the new house on North Avenue; and after dinner, leaving Mrs. Gretry and Laura in the drawing-room, he brought the broker up to the billiard-room for a game of pool.

But when Gretry had put the balls in the triangle, the two men did not begin to play at once. Jadwin had asked the question that had been uppermost in the minds of each during dinner.

"Well, Sam," he had said, by way of a beginning, "what do you think of this Government report?"

The broker chalked his cue placidly.

"I expect there'll be a bit of reaction on the strength of it, but the market will go off again. I said wheat would go to sixty, and I still say it. It's a long time between now and May."

"I wasn't thinking of crop conditions only," observed Jadwin. "Sam, we're going to have better times and higher prices this summer."

Gretry shook his head and entered into a long argument to show that Jadwin was wrong.

But Jadwin refused to be convinced. All at once he laid the flat of his hand upon the table.

"Sam, we've touched bottom," he declared, "touched bottom all along the line. It's a paper dime to the Sub-Treasury."

"I don't care about the rest of the line," said the broker doggedly, sitting on the edge of the table, "wheat will go to sixty." He indicated the nest of balls with a movement of his chin. "Will you break?"

Jadwin broke and scored, leaving one ball three inches in front of a corner pocket. He called the shot, and as he drew back his cue he said, deliberately:

"Just as sure as I make this pocket wheat will—not go—off—another—cent."

With the last word he drove the ball home and straightened up. Gretry laid down his cue and looked at him quickly. But he did not speak. Jadwin sat down on one of the straight-backed chairs upon the raised platform against the wall and rested his elbows upon his knees.

"Sam," he said, "the time is come for a great big change." He emphasised the word with a tap of his cue upon the floor. "We can't play our game the way we've been playing it the last three years. We've been hammering wheat down and down and down, till we've got it below the cost of production; and now she won't go any further with all the hammering in the world. The other fellows, the rest of this Bear crowd, don't seem to see it, but I see it. Before fall we're going to have higher prices. Wheat is going up, and when it does I mean to be right there."

"We're going to have a dull market right up to the beginning of winter," persisted the other.

"Come and say that to me at the beginning of winter, then," Jadwin retorted. "Look here, Sam, I'm short of May five hundred thousand bushels, and to-morrow morning you are going to send your boys on the floor for me and close that trade."

"You're crazy, J.," protested the broker. "Hold on another month, and I promise you, you'll thank me."

"Not another day, not another hour. This Bear campaign of ours has come to an end. That's said and signed."

"Why, it's just in its prime," protested the broker. "Great heavens, you mustn't get out of the game now, after hanging on for three years."

"I'm not going to get out of it."

"Why, good Lord!" said Gretry, "you don't mean to say that—"

"That I'm going over. That's exactly what I do mean. I'm going to change over so quick to the other side that I'll be there before you can take off your hat. I'm done with a Bear game. It was good while it lasted, but we've worked it for all there was in it. I'm not only going to cover my May shorts and get out of that trade, but"—Jadwin leaned forward and struck his hand upon his knee—"but I'm going to buy. I'm going to buy September wheat, and I'm going to buy it to-morrow, five hundred thousand bushels of it, and if the market goes as I think it will later on, I'm going to buy more. I'm no Bear any longer. I'm going to boost this market right through till the last bell rings; and from now on Curtis Jadwin spells B-u-double l—Bull."

"They'll slaughter you," said Gretry, "slaughter you in cold blood. You're just one man against a gang—a gang of cutthroats. Those Bears have got millions and millions back of them. You don't suppose, do you, that old man Crookes, or Kenniston, or little Sweeny, or all that lot would give you one little bit of a chance for your life if they got a grip on you. Cover your shorts if you want to, but, for God's sake, don't begin to buy in the same breath. You wait a while. If this market has touched bottom, we'll be able to tell in a few days. I'll admit, for the sake of argument, that just now there's a pause. But nobody can tell whether it will turn up or down yet. Now's the time to be conservative, to play it cautious."

"If I was conservative and cautious," answered Jadwin, "I wouldn't be in this game at all. I'd be buying U.S. four percents. That's the big mistake so many of these fellows down here make. They go into a game where the only ones who can possibly win are the ones who take big chances, and then they try to play the thing cautiously. If I wait a while till the market turns up and everybody is buying, how am I any the better off? No, sir, you buy the September option for me to-morrow—five hundred thousand bushels. I deposited the margin to your credit in the Illinois Trust this afternoon."

There was a long silence. Gretry spun a ball between his fingers, top-fashion.

"Well," he said at last, hesitatingly, "well—I don't know, J.—you are either Napoleonic—or—or a colossal idiot."

"Neither one nor the other, Samuel. I'm just using a little common sense.... Is it your shot?"

"I'm blessed if I know."

"Well, we'll start a new game. Sam, I'll give you six balls and beat you in"—he looked at his watch—"beat you before half-past nine."

"For a dollar?"

"I never bet, Sam, and you know it."

Half an hour later Jadwin said:

"Shall we go down and join the ladies? Don't put out your cigar. That's one bargain I made with Laura before we moved in here—that smoking was allowable everywhere."

"Room enough, I guess," observed the broker, as the two stepped into the elevator. "How many rooms have you got here, by the way?"

"Upon my word, I don't know," answered Jadwin. "I discovered a new one yesterday. Fact. I was having a look around, and I came out into a little kind of smoking-room or other that, I swear, I'd never seen before. I had to get Laura to tell me about it."

The elevator sank to the lower floor, and Jadwin and the broker stepped out into the main hallway. From the drawing-room near by came the sound of women's voices.

"Before we go in," said Jadwin, "I want you to see our art gallery and the organ. Last time you were up, remember, the men were still at work in here."

They passed down a broad corridor, and at the end, just before parting the heavy, sombre curtains, Jadwin pressed a couple of electric buttons, and in the open space above the curtain sprang up a lambent, steady glow.

The broker, as he entered, gave a long whistle. The art gallery took in the height of two of the stories of the house. It was shaped like a rotunda, and topped with a vast airy dome of coloured glass. Here and there about the room were glass cabinets full of bibelots, ivory statuettes, old snuff boxes, fans of the sixteenth and seventeenth centuries. The walls themselves were covered with a multitude of pictures, oils, water-colours, with one or two pastels.

But to the left of the entrance, let into the frame of the building, stood a great organ, large enough for a cathedral, and giving to view, in the dulled incandescence of the electrics, its sheaves of mighty pipes.

"Well, this is something like," exclaimed the broker.

"I don't know much about 'em myself," hazarded Jadwin, looking at the pictures, "but Laura can tell you. We bought most of 'em while we were abroad, year before last. Laura says this is the best." He indicated a large "Bougereau" that represented a group of nymphs bathing in a woodland pool.

"H'm!" said the broker, "you wouldn't want some of your Sunday-school superintendents to see this now. This is what the boys down on the Board would call a bar-room picture."

But Jadwin did not laugh.

"It never struck me in just that way," he said, gravely.

"It's a fine piece of work, though," Gretry hastened to add. "Fine, great colouring."

"I like this one pretty well," continued Jadwin, moving to a canvas by Detaille. It was one of the inevitable studies of a cuirassier; in this case a trumpeter, one arm high in the air, the hand clutching the trumpet, the horse, foam-flecked, at a furious gallop. In the rear, through clouds of dust, the rest of the squadron was indicated by a few points of colour.

"Yes, that's pretty neat," concurred Gretry. "He's sure got a gait on. Lord, what a lot of accoutrements those French fellows stick on. Now our boys would chuck about three-fourths of that truck before going into action.... Queer way these artists work," he went on, peering close to the canvas. "Look at it close up and it's just a lot of little daubs, but you get off a distance"—he drew back, cocking his head to one side—"and you see now. Hey—see how the thing bunches up. Pretty neat, isn't it?" He turned from the picture and rolled his eyes about the room.

"Well, well," he murmured. "This certainly is the real thing, J. I suppose, now, it all represents a pretty big pot of money."

"I'm not quite used to it yet myself," said Jadwin. "I was in here last Sunday, thinking it all over, the new house, and the money and all. And it struck me as kind of queer the way things have turned out for me.... Sam, do you know, I can remember the time, up there in Ottawa County, Michigan, on my old dad's farm, when I used to have to get up before day-break to tend the stock, and my sister and I used to run out quick into the stable and stand in the warm cow fodder in the stalls to warm our bare feet.... She up and died when she was about eighteen—galloping consumption. Yes, sir. By George, how I loved that little sister of mine! You remember her, Sam. Remember how you used to come out from Grand Rapids every now and then to go squirrel shooting with me?"

"Sure, sure. Oh, I haven't forgot."

"Well, I was wishing the other day that I could bring Sadie down here, and—oh, I don't know—give her a good time. She never had a good time when she was alive. Work, work, work; morning, noon, and night. I'd like to have made it up to her. I believe in making people happy, Sam. That's the way I take my fun. But it's too late to do it now for my little sister."

"Well," hazarded Gretry, "you got a good wife in yonder to—"

Jadwin interrupted him. He half turned away, thrusting his hands suddenly into his pockets. Partly to himself, partly to his friend he murmured:

"You bet I have, you bet I have. Sam," he exclaimed, then turned away again. "... Oh, well, never mind," he murmured.

Gretry, embarrassed, constrained, put his chin in the air, shutting his eyes in a knowing fashion.

"I understand," he answered. "I understand, J."

"Say, look at this organ here," said Jadwin briskly. "Here's the thing I like to play with."

They crossed to the other side of the room.

"Oh, you've got one of those attachment things," observed the broker.

"Listen now," said Jadwin. He took a perforated roll from the case near at hand and adjusted it, Gretry looking on with the solemn interest that all American business men have in mechanical inventions. Jadwin sat down before it, pulled out a stop or two, and placed his feet on the pedals. A vast preliminary roaring breath soughed through the pipes, with a vibratory rush of power. Then there came a canorous snarl of bass, and then, abruptly, with resistless charm, and with full-bodied, satisfying amplitude of volume the opening movement of the overture of "Carmen."

"Great, great!" shouted Gretry, his voice raised to make himself heard. "That's immense."

The great-lunged harmony was filling the entire gallery, clear cut, each note clearly, sharply treated with a precision that, if mechanical, was yet effective. Jadwin, his eyes now on the stops, now on the sliding strip of paper, played on. Through the sonorous clamour of the pipes Gretry could hear him speaking, but he caught only a word or two.

"Toreador ... horse power ... Madame Calve ... electric motor ... fine song ... storage battery."

The movement thinned out, and dwindled to a strain of delicate lightness, sustained by the smallest pipes and developing a new motive; this was twice repeated, and then ran down to a series of chords and bars that prepared for and prefigured some great effect close at hand. There was a short pause, then with the sudden releasing of a tremendous rush of sound, back surged the melody, with redoubled volume and power, to the original movement.

"That's bully, bully!" shouted Gretry, clapping his hands, and his eye, caught by a movement on the other side of the room, he turned about to see Laura Jadwin standing between the opened curtains at the entrance.

Seen thus unexpectedly, the broker was again overwhelmed with a sense of the beauty of Jadwin's wife. Laura was in evening dress of black lace; her arms and neck were bare. Her black hair was piled high upon her head, a single American Beauty rose nodded against her bare shoulder. She was even yet slim and very tall, her face pale with that unusual paleness of hers that was yet a colour. Around her slender neck was a marvellous collar of pearls many strands deep, set off and held in place by diamond clasps.

With Laura came Mrs. Gretry and Page. The broker's wife was a vivacious, small, rather pretty blonde woman, a little angular, a little faded. She was garrulous, witty, slangy. She wore turquoises in her ears morning, noon, and night.

But three years had made a vast difference in Page Dearborn. All at once she was a young woman. Her straight, hard, little figure had developed, her arms were rounded, her eyes were calmer. She had grown taller, broader. Her former exquisite beauty was perhaps not quite so delicate, so fine, so virginal, so charmingly angular and boyish. There was infinitely more of the woman in it; and perhaps because of this she looked more like Laura than at any time of her life before. But even yet her expression was one of gravity, of seriousness. There was always a certain aloofness about Page. She looked out at the world solemnly, and as if separated from its lighter side. Things humorous interested her only as inexplicable vagaries of the human animal.

"We heard the organ," said Laura, "so we came in. I wanted Mrs. Gretry to listen to it."

The three years that had just passed had been the most important years of Laura Jadwin's life. Since her marriage she had grown intellectually and morally with amazing rapidity. Indeed, so swift had been the change, that it was not so much a growth as a transformation. She was no longer the same half-formed, impulsive girl who had found a delight in the addresses of her three lovers, and who had sat on the floor in the old home on State Street and allowed Landry Court to hold her hand. She looked back upon the Miss Dearborn of those days as though she were another person. How she had grown since then! How she had changed! How different, how infinitely more serious and sweet her life since then had become!

A great fact had entered her world, a great new element, that dwarfed all other thoughts, all other considerations. This was her love for her husband. It was as though until the time of her marriage she had walked in darkness, a darkness that she fancied was day; walked perversely, carelessly, and with a frivolity that was almost wicked. Then, suddenly, she had seen a great light. Love had entered her world. In her new heaven a new light was fixed, and all other things were seen only because of this light; all other things were touched by it, tempered by it, warmed and vivified by it.

It had seemed to date from a certain evening at their country house at Geneva Lake in Wisconsin, where she had spent her honeymoon with her husband. They had been married about ten days. It was a July evening, and they were quite alone on board the little steam yacht the "Thetis." She remembered it all very plainly. It had been so warm that she had not changed her dress after dinner—she recalled that it was of Honiton lace over old-rose silk, and that Curtis had said it was the prettiest he had ever seen. It was an hour before midnight, and the lake was so still as to appear veritably solid. The moon was reflected upon the surface with never a ripple to blur its image. The sky was grey with starlight, and only a vague bar of black between the star shimmer and the pale shield of the water marked the shore line. Never since that night could she hear the call of whip-poor-wills or the piping of night frogs that the scene did not come back to her. The little "Thetis" had throbbed and panted steadily. At the door of the engine room, the engineer—the grey MacKenny, his back discreetly turned—sat smoking a pipe and taking the air. From time to time he would swing himself into the engine room, and the clink and scrape of his shovel made itself heard as he stoked the fire vigorously.

Stretched out in a long wicker deck chair, hatless, a drab coat thrown around her shoulders, Laura had sat near her husband, who had placed himself upon a camp stool, where he could reach the wheel with one hand.

"Well," he had said at last, "are you glad you married me, Miss Dearborn?" And she had caught him about the neck and drawn his face down to hers, and her head thrown back, their lips all but touching, had whispered over and over again:

"I love you—love you—love you!"

That night was final. The marriage ceremony, even that moment in her room, when her husband had taken her in his arms and she had felt the first stirring of love in her heart, all the first week of their married life had been for Laura a whirl, a blur. She had not been able to find herself. Her affection for her husband came and went capriciously. There were moments when she believed herself to be really unhappy. Then, all at once, she seemed to awake. Not the ceremony at St. James' Church, but that awakening had been her marriage. Now it was irrevocable; she was her husband's; she belonged to him indissolubly, forever and forever, and the surrender was a glory. Laura in that moment knew that love, the supreme triumph of a woman's life, was less a victory than a capitulation.

Since then her happiness had been perfect. Literally and truly there was not a cloud, not a mote in her sunshine. She had everything—the love of her husband, great wealth, extraordinary beauty, perfect health, an untroubled mind, friends, position—everything. God had been good to her, beyond all dreams and all deserving. For her had been reserved all the prizes, all the guerdons; for her who had done nothing to merit them.

Her husband she knew was no less happy. In those first three years after their marriage, life was one unending pageant; and their happiness became for them some marvellous, bewildering thing, dazzling, resplendent, a strange, glittering, jewelled Wonder-worker that suddenly had been put into their hands.

As one of the first results of this awakening, Laura reproached herself with having done but little for Page. She told herself that she had not been a good sister, that often she had been unjust, quick tempered, and had made the little girl to suffer because of her caprices. She had not sympathised sufficiently with her small troubles—so she made herself believe—and had found too many occasions to ridicule

Page's intenseness and queer little solemnities. True she had given her a good home, good clothes, and a good education, but she should have given more—more than mere duty-gifts. She should have been more of a companion to the little girl, more of a help; in fine, more of a mother. Laura felt all at once the responsibilities of the elder sister in a family bereft of parents. Page was growing fast, and growing astonishingly beautiful; in a little while she would be a young woman, and over the near horizon, very soon now, must inevitably loom the grave question of her marriage.

But it was only this realisation of certain responsibilities that during the first years of her married life at any time drew away Laura's consideration of her husband. She began to get acquainted with the real man-within-the-man that she knew now revealed himself only after marriage. Jadwin her husband was so different from, so infinitely better than, Jadwin her lover, that Laura sometimes found herself looking back with a kind of retrospective apprehension on the old days and the time when she was simply Miss Dearborn. How little she had known him after all! And how, in the face of this ignorance, this innocence, this absence of any insight into his real character, had she dared to take the irretrievable step that bound her to him for life? The Curtis Jadwin of those early days was so much another man. He might have been a rascal; she could not have known it. As it was, her husband had promptly come to be, for her, the best, the finest man she had ever known. But it might easily have been different.

His attitude towards her was thoughtfulness itself. Hardly ever was he absent from her, even for a day, that he did not bring her some little present, some little keep-sake—or even a bunch of flowers—when he returned in the evening. The anniversaries—Christmas, their wedding day, her birthday—he always observed with great eclat. He took a holiday from his business, surprised her with presents under her pillow, or her dinner-plate, and never failed to take her to the theatre in the evening.

However, it was not only Jadwin's virtues that endeared him to his wife. He was no impeccable hero in her eyes. He was tremendously human. He had his faults, his certain lovable weaknesses, and it was precisely these traits that Laura found so adorable.

For one thing, Jadwin could be magnificently inconsistent. Let him set his mind and heart upon a given pursuit, pleasure, or line of conduct not altogether advisable at the moment, and the ingenuity of the excuses by which he justified himself were monuments of elaborate sophistry. Yet, if later he lost interest, he reversed his arguments with supreme disregard for his former words.

Then, too, he developed a boyish pleasure in certain unessential though cherished objects and occupations, that he indulged extravagantly and to the neglect of things, not to say duties, incontestably of more importance.

One of these objects was the "Thetis." In every conceivable particular the little steam yacht was complete down to the last bolt, the last coat of varnish; but at times during their summer vacations, when Jadwin, in all reason, should have been supervising the laying out of certain unfinished portions of the "grounds"—supervision which could be trusted to no subordinate—he would be found aboard the "Thetis," hatless, in his shirt-sleeves, in solemn debate with the grey MacKenny and—a cleaning rag, or monkey-wrench, or paint brush in his hand—tinkering and pottering about the boat, over and over again. Wealthy as he was, he could have maintained an entire crew on board whose whole duty should have been to screw, and scrub, and scour. But Jadwin would have none of it. "Costs too much," he would declare, with profound gravity. He had the self-made American's handiness with implements and paint brushes, and he would, at high noon and under a murderous sun, make the trip from the house to the dock where the "Thetis" was moored, for the trivial pleasure of tightening a bolt—which did not need tightening; or wake up in the night to tell Laura of some wonderful new idea he had conceived as to the equipment or decoration of the yacht. He had blustered about the extravagance of a "crew," but the sums of money that went to the brightening, refitting, overhauling, repainting, and reballasting of the boat—all absolutely uncalled-for—made even Laura gasp, and would have maintained a dozen sailors an entire year.

This same inconsistency prevailed also in other directions. In the matter of business Jadwin's economy was unimpeachable. He would cavil on a half-dollar's overcharge; he would put himself to downright inconvenience to save the useless expenditure of a dime—and boast of it. But no extravagance was ever too great, no time ever too valuable, when bass were to be caught.

For Jadwin was a fisherman unregenerate. Laura, though an early riser when in the city, was apt to sleep late in the country, and never omitted a two-hours' nap in the heat of the afternoon. Her husband improved these occasions when he was deprived of her society, to indulge in his pastime. Never a morning so forbidding that his lines were not in the water by five o'clock; never a sun so scorching that he was not coaxing a "strike" in the stumps and reeds in the shade under the shores.

It was the one pleasure he could not share with his wife. Laura was unable to bear the monotony of the slow-moving boat, the hours spent without results, the enforced idleness, the cramped positions. Only occasionally could Jadwin prevail upon her to accompany him. And then what preparations! Queen Elizabeth approaching her barge was attended with no less solicitude. MacKenny (who sometimes acted as guide and oarsman) and her husband exhausted their ingenuity to make her comfortable. They held anxious debates: "Do you think she'll like that?" "Wouldn't this make it easier for her?" "Is that the way she liked it last time?" Jadwin himself arranged the cushions, spread the carpet over the bottom of the boat, handed her in, found her old gloves for her, baited her hook, disentangled her line, saw to it that the mineral water in the ice-box was sufficiently cold, and performed an endless series of little attentions looking to her comfort and enjoyment. It was all to no purpose, and at length Laura declared:

"Curtis, dear, it is no use. You just sacrifice every bit of your pleasure to make me comfortable—to make me enjoy it; and I just don't. I'm sorry, I want to share every pleasure with you, but I don't like to fish, and never will. You go alone. I'm just a hindrance to you." And though he blustered at first, Laura had her way.

Once in the period of these three years Laura and her husband had gone abroad. But her experience in England—they did not get to the Continent—had been a disappointment to her. The museums, art galleries, and cathedrals were not of the least interest to Jadwin, and though he followed her from one to another with uncomplaining stoicism, she felt his distress, and had contrived to return home three months ahead of time.

It was during this trip that they had bought so many of the pictures and appointments for the North Avenue house, and Laura's disappointment over her curtailed European travels was mitigated by the anticipation of her pleasure in settling in the new home. This had not been possible immediately after their marriage. For nearly two years the great place had been given over to contractors, architects, decorators, and gardeners, and Laura and her husband had lived, while in Chicago, at a hotel, giving up the one-time rectory on Cass Street to Page and to Aunt Wess'.

But when at last Laura entered upon possession of the North Avenue house, she was not—after the first enthusiasm and excitement over its magnificence had died down—altogether pleased with it, though she told herself the contrary. Outwardly it was all that she could desire. It fronted Lincoln Park, and from all the windows upon that side the most delightful outlooks were obtainable—green woods, open lawns, the parade ground, the Lincoln monument, dells, bushes, smooth drives, flower beds, and fountains. From the great bay window of Laura's own sitting-room she could see far out over Lake Michigan, and watch the procession of great lake steamers, from Milwaukee, far-distant Duluth, and the Sault Sainte Marie—the famous "Soo"—defiling majestically past, making for the mouth of the river, laden to the water's edge with whole harvests of wheat. At night, when the windows were open in the warm weather, she could hear the mournful wash and lapping of the water on the embankments.

The grounds about her home were beautiful. The stable itself was half again as large as her old home opposite St. James's, and the conservatory, in which she took the keenest delight, was a wonderful affair—a vast bubble-like structure of green panes, whence, winter and summer, came a multitude of flowers for the house—violets, lilies of the valley, jonquils, hyacinths, tulips, and her own loved roses.

But the interior of the house was, in parts, less satisfactory. Jadwin, so soon as his marriage was a certainty, had bought the house, and had given over its internal furnishings to a firm of decorators. Innocently enough he had intended to surprise his wife, had told himself that she should not be burdened with the responsibility of selection and planning. Fortunately, however, the decorators were men of taste. There was nothing to offend, and much to delight in the results they obtained in the dining-room, breakfast-room, parlors, drawing-rooms, and suites of bedrooms. But Laura, though the beauty of it all enchanted her, could never rid herself of a feeling that it was not hers. It impressed her with its splendour of natural woods and dull "colour effects," its cunning electrical devices, its mechanical contrivances for comfort, like the ready-made luxury and "convenience" of a Pullman.

However, she had intervened in time to reserve certain of the rooms to herself, and these—the library, her bedroom, and more especially that apartment from whose bay windows she looked out upon the Lake, and which, as if she were still in her old home, she called the "upstairs sitting-room"—she furnished to suit herself.

For very long she found it difficult, even with all her resolution, with all her pleasure in her new-gained wealth, to adapt herself to a manner of living upon so vast a scale. She found herself continually planning the marketing for the next day, forgetting that this now was part of the housekeeper's duties. For months she persisted in "doing her room" after breakfast, just as she had been taught to do in the old days when she was a little girl at Barrington. She was afraid of the elevator, and never really learned how to use the neat little system of telephones that connected the various parts of the house with the servants' quarters. For months her chiefest concern in her wonderful surroundings took the form of a dread of burglars.

Her keenest delights were her stable and the great organ in the art gallery; and these alone more than compensated for her uneasiness in other particulars.

Horses Laura adored—black ones with flowing tails and manes, like certain pictures she had seen. Nowadays, except on the rarest occasions, she never set foot out of doors, except to take her carriage, her coupe, her phaeton, or her dog-cart. Best of all she loved her saddle horses. She had learned to ride, and the morning was inclement indeed that she did not take a long and solitary excursion through the Park, followed by the groom and Jadwin's two spotted coach dogs.

The great organ terrified her at first. But on closer acquaintance she came to regard it as a vast-hearted, sympathetic friend. She already played the piano very well, and she scorned Jadwin's self-playing "attachment." A teacher was engaged to instruct her in the intricacies of stops and of pedals, and in the difficulties of the "echo" organ, "great" organ, "choir," and "swell." So soon as she had mastered these, Laura entered upon a new world of delight. Her taste in music was as yet a little immature—Gounod and even Verdi were its limitations. But to hear, responsive to the lightest pressures of her finger-tips, the mighty instrument go thundering through the cadences of the "Anvil Chorus" gave her a thrilling sense of power that was superb.

The untrained, unguided instinct of the actress in Laura had fostered in her a curious penchant toward melodrama. She had a taste for the magnificent. She revelled in these great musical "effects" upon her organ, the grandiose easily appealed to her, while as for herself, the role of the "grande dame," with this wonderful house for background and environment, came to be for her, quite unconsciously, a sort of game in which she delighted.

It was by this means that, in the end, she succeeded in fitting herself to her new surroundings. Innocently enough, and with a harmless, almost childlike, affectation, she posed a little, and by so doing found the solution of the incongruity between herself—the Laura of moderate means and quiet life—and the massive luxury with which she was now surrounded. Without knowing it, she began to act the part of a great lady—and she acted it well. She assumed the existence of her numerous servants as she assumed the fact of the trees in the park; she gave herself into the hands of her maid, not as Laura Jadwin of herself would have done it, clumsily and with the constraint of inexperience, but as she would have done it if she had been acting the part on the stage, with an air, with all the nonchalance of a marquise, with—in fine—all the superb condescension of her "grand manner."

She knew very well that if she relaxed this hauteur, that her servants would impose on her, would run over her, and in this matter she found new cause for wonder in her husband.

The servants, from the frigid butler to the under groom, adored Jadwin. A half-expressed wish upon his part produced a more immediate effect than Laura's most explicit orders. He never descended to familiarity with them, and, as a matter of fact, ignored them to such an extent that he forgot or confused their names. But where Laura was obeyed with precise formality and chilly deference, Jadwin was served with obsequious alacrity, and with a good humour that even livery and "correct form" could not altogether conceal.

Laura's eyes were first opened to this genuine affection which Jadwin inspired in his servants by an incident which occurred in the first months of their occupancy of the new establishment. One of the gardeners discovered the fact that Jadwin affected gardenias in the lapel of his coat, and thereat was at immense pains to supply him with a fresh bloom from the conservatory each morning. The flower was to be placed at Jadwin's plate, and it was quite the event of the day for the old fellow when the master appeared on the front steps with the flower in his coat. But a feud promptly developed over this matter between the gardener and the maid who took the butler's place at breakfast every morning. Sometimes Jadwin did not get the flower, and the gardener charged the maid with remissness in forgetting to place it at his plate after he had given it into her hands. In the end the affair became so clamourous that

Jadwin himself had to intervene. The gardener was summoned and found to have been in fault only in his eagerness to please.

"Billy," said Jadwin, to the old man at the conclusion of the whole matter, "you're an old fool."

And the gardener thereupon had bridled and stammered as though Jadwin had conferred a gift.

"Now if I had called him 'an old fool,'" observed Laura, "he would have sulked the rest of the week."

The happiest time of the day for Laura was the evening. In the daytime she was variously occupied, but her thoughts continually ran forward to the end of the day, when her husband would be with her. Jadwin breakfasted early, and Laura bore him company no matter how late she had stayed up the night before. By half-past eight he was out of the house, driving down to his office in his buggy behind Nip and Tuck. By nine Laura's own saddle horse was brought to the carriage porch, and until eleven she rode in the park. At twelve she lunched with Page, and in the afternoon—in the "upstairs sitting-room" read her Browning or her Meredith, the latter one of her newest discoveries, till three or four. Sometimes after that she went out in her carriage. If it was to "shop" she drove to the "Rookery," in La Salle Street, after her purchases were made, and sent the footman up to her husband's office to say that she would take him home. Or as often as not she called for Mrs. Cressler or Aunt Wess' or Mrs. Gretry, and carried them off to some exhibit of painting, or flowers, or more rarely—for she had not the least interest in social affairs—to teas or receptions.

But in the evenings, after dinner, she had her husband to herself. Page was almost invariably occupied by one or more of her young men in the drawing-room, but Laura and Jadwin shut themselves in the library, a lofty panelled room—a place of deep leather chairs, tall bookcases, etchings, and sombre brasses—and there, while Jadwin lay stretched out upon the broad sofa, smoking cigars, one hand behind his head, Laura read aloud to him.

His tastes in fiction were very positive. Laura at first had tried to introduce him to her beloved Meredith. But after three chapters, when he had exclaimed, "What's the fool talking about?" she had given over and begun again from another starting-point. Left to himself, his wife sorrowfully admitted that he would have gravitated to the "Mysterious Island" and "Michael Strogoff," or even to "Mr. Potter of Texas" and "Mr. Barnes of New York." But she had set herself to accomplish his literary education, so, Meredith failing, she took up "Treasure Island" and "The Wrecker." Much of these he made her skip.

"Oh, let's get on with the 'story,'" he urged. But Pinkerton for long remained for him an ideal, because he was "smart" and "alive."

"I'm not long very many of art," he announced. "But I believe that any art that don't make the world better and happier is no art at all, and is only fit for the dump heap."

But at last Laura found his abiding affinity in Howells.

"Nothing much happens," he said. "But I know all those people." He never could rid himself of a surreptitious admiration for Bartley Hubbard. He, too, was "smart" and "alive." He had the "get there" to him. "Why," he would say, "I know fifty boys just like him down there in La Salle Street." Lapham he loved as a brother. Never a point in the development of his character that he missed or failed to chuckle over. Bromfield Cory was poohed and boshed quite out of consideration as a "loafer," a "dilletanty," but Lapham had all his sympathy.

"Yes, sir," he would exclaim, interrupting the narrative, "that's just it. That's just what I would have done if I had been in his place. Come, this chap knows what he's writing about—not like that Middleton ass, with his 'Dianas' and 'Amazing Marriages.'"

Occasionally the Jadwins entertained. Laura's husband was proud of his house, and never tired of showing his friends about it. Laura gave Page a "coming-out" dance, and nearly every Sunday the Cresslers came to dinner. But Aunt Wess' could, at first, rarely be induced to pay the household a visit. So much grandeur made the little widow uneasy, even a little suspicious. She would shake her head at Laura, murmuring:

"My word, it's all very fine, but, dear me, Laura, I hope you do pay for everything on the nail, and don't run up any bills. I don't know what your dear father would say to it all, no, I don't." And she would spend hours in counting the electric bulbs, which she insisted were only devices for some new-fangled gas.

"Thirty-three in this one room alone," she would say. "I'd like to see your dear husband's face when he gets his gas bill. And a dressmaker that lives in the house.... Well,—I don't want to say anything."

Thus three years had gone by. The new household settled to a regime. Continually Jadwin grew richer. His real estate appreciated in value; rents went up. Every time he speculated in wheat, it was upon a larger scale, and every time he won. He was a Bear always, and on those rare occasions when he referred to his ventures in Laura's hearing, it was invariably to say that prices were going down. Till at last had come that spring when he believed that the bottom had been touched, had had the talk with Gretry, and had, in secret, "turned Bull," with the suddenness of a strategist.

The matter was yet in Gretry's mind while the party remained in the art gallery; and as they were returning to the drawing-room he detained Jadwin an instant.

"If you are set upon breaking your neck," he said, "you might tell me at what figure you want me to buy for you to-morrow."

"At the market," returned Jadwin. "I want to get into the thing quick."

A little later, when they had all reassembled in the drawing-room, and while Mrs.

Gretry was telling an interminable story of how Isabel had all but asphyxiated herself the night before, a servant announced Landry Court, and the young man entered, spruce and debonair, a bouquet in one hand and a box of candy in the other.

Some days before this Page had lectured him solemnly on the fact that he was over-absorbed in business, and was starving his soul. He should read more, she told him, and she had said that if he would call upon her on this particular night, she would indicate a course of reading for him.

So it came about that, after a few moments, conversation with the older people in the drawing-room, the two adjourned to the library.

There, by way of a beginning, Page asked him what was his favourite character in fiction. She spoke of the beauty of Ruskin's thoughts, of the gracefulness of Charles Lamb's style. The conversation lagged a little. Landry, not to be behind her, declared for the modern novel, and spoke of the "newest book." But Page never read new books; she was not interested, and their talk, unable to establish itself upon a common ground, halted, and was in a fair way to end, until at last, and by insensible degrees, they began to speak of themselves and of each other. Promptly they were all aroused. They listened to one another's words with studious attention, answered with ever-ready promptness, discussed, argued, agreed, and disagreed over and over again.

Landry had said:

"When I was a boy, I always had an ambition to excel all the other boys. I wanted to be the best baseball player on the block—and I was, too. I could pitch three curves when I was fifteen, and I find I am the same now that I am a man grown. When I do a thing, I want to do it better than any one else. From the very first I have always been ambitious. It is my strongest trait. Now," he went on, turning to Page, "your strongest trait is your thoughtfulness. You are what they call introspective."

"Yes, yes," she answered. "Yes, I think so, too."

"You don't need the stimulation of competition. You are at your best when you are with just one person. A crowd doesn't interest you."

"I hate it," she exclaimed.

"Now with me, with a man of my temperament, a crowd is a real inspiration. When every one is talking and shouting around me, or to me, even, my mind works at its best. But," he added, solemnly, "it must be a crowd of men. I can't abide a crowd of women."

"They chatter so," she assented. "I can't either."

"But I find that the companionship of one intelligent, sympathetic woman is as much of a stimulus as a lot of men. It's funny, isn't it, that I should be like that?"

"Yes," she said, "it is funny—strange. But I believe in companionship. I believe that between man and woman that is the great thing—companionship. Love," she added, abruptly, and then broke off with a deep sigh. "Oh, I don't know," she murmured.

"Do you remember those lines:

"Man's love is of his life a thing apart,

'Tis woman's whole existence.

Do you believe that?"

"Well," he asserted, gravely, choosing his words with deliberation, "it might be so, but all depends upon the man and woman. Love," he added, with tremendous gravity, "is the greatest power in the universe."

"I have never been in love," said Page. "Yes, love is a wonderful power."

"I've never been in love, either."

"Never, never been in love?"

"Oh, I've thought I was in love," he said, with a wave of his hand.

"I've never even thought I was," she answered, musing.

"Do you believe in early marriages?" demanded Landry.

"A man should never marry," she said, deliberately, "till he can give his wife a good home, and good clothes and—and that sort of thing. I do not think I shall ever marry."

"You! Why, of course you will. Why not?"

"No, no. It is my disposition. I am morose and taciturn. Laura says so."

Landry protested with vehemence.

"And," she went on, "I have long, brooding fits of melancholy."

"Well, so have I," he threw out recklessly. "At night, sometimes—when I wake up. Then I'm all down in the mouth, and I say, 'What's the use, by jingo?'"

"Do you believe in pessimism? I do. They say Carlyle was a terrible pessimist."

"Well—talking about love. I understand that you can't believe in pessimism and love at the same time. Wouldn't you feel unhappy if you lost your faith in love?"

"Oh, yes, terribly."

There was a moment's silence, and then Landry remarked:

"Now you are the kind of woman that would only love once, but love for that once mighty deep and strong."

Page's eyes grew wide. She murmured:

"'Tis a woman's whole existence—whole existence.' Yes, I think I am like that."

"Do you think Enoch Arden did right in going away after he found them married?"

"Oh, have you read that? Oh, isn't that a beautiful poem? Wasn't he noble? Wasn't he grand? Oh, yes, yes, he did right."

"By George, I wouldn't have gone away. I'd have gone right into that house, and I would have made things hum. I'd have thrown the other fellow out, lock, stock, and barrel."

"That's just like a man, so selfish, only thinking of himself. You don't know the meaning of love—great, true, unselfish love."

"I know the meaning of what's mine. Think I'd give up the woman I loved to another man?"

"Even if she loved the other man best?"

"I'd have my girl first, and find out how she felt about the other man afterwards."

"Oh, but think if you gave her up, how noble it would be. You would have sacrificed all that you held the dearest to an ideal. Oh, if I were in Enoch Arden's place, and my husband thought I was dead, and I knew he was happy with another woman, it would just be a joy to deny myself, sacrifice myself to spare him unhappiness. That would be my idea of love. Then I'd go into a convent."

"Not much. I'd let the other fellow go to the convent. If I loved a woman, I wouldn't let anything in the world stop me from winning her."

"You have so much determination, haven't you?" she said, looking at him.

Landry enlarged his shoulders a little and wagged his head.

"Well," he said, "I don't know, but I'd try pretty hard to get what I wanted, I guess."

"I love to see that characteristic in men," she observed. "Strength, determination."

"Just as a man loves to see a woman womanly," he answered. "Don't you hate strong-minded women?"

"Utterly."

"Now, you are what I would call womanly—the womanliest woman I've ever known."

"Oh, I don't know," she protested, a little confused.

"Yes, you are. You are beautifully womanly—and so high-minded and well read. It's been inspiring to me. I want you should know that. Yes, sir, a real inspiration. It's been inspiring, elevating, to say the least."

"I like to read, if that's what you mean," she hastened to say.

"By Jove, I've got to do some reading, too. It's so hard to find time. But I'll make time. I'll get that 'Stones of Venice' I've heard you speak of, and I'll sit up nights—and keep awake with black coffee—but I'll read that book from cover to cover."

"That's your determination again," Page exclaimed. "Your eyes just flashed when you said it. I believe if you once made up your mind to do a thing, you would do it, no matter how hard it was, wouldn't you?"

"Well, I'd—I'd make things hum, I guess," he admitted.

The next day was Easter Sunday, and Page came down to nine o'clock breakfast a little late, to find Jadwin already finished and deep in the pages of the morning paper. Laura, still at table, was pouring her last cup of coffee.

They were in the breakfast-room, a small, charming apartment, light and airy, and with many windows, one end opening upon the house conservatory. Jadwin was in his frock coat, which later he would wear to church. The famous gardenia was in his lapel. He was freshly shaven, and his fine cigar made a blue haze over his head. Laura was radiant in a white morning gown. A newly cut bunch of violets, large as a cabbage, lay on the table before her.

The whole scene impressed itself sharply upon Page's mind—the fine sunlit room, with its gay open spaces and the glimpse of green leaves from the conservatory, the view of the smooth, trim lawn through the many windows, where an early robin, strayed from the park, was chirruping and feeding; her beautiful sister Laura, with her splendid, overshadowing coiffure, her pale, clear skin, her slender figure; Jadwin, the large, solid man of affairs, with his fine cigar, his gardenia, his well-groomed air. And then the little accessories that meant so much—the smell of violets, of good tobacco, of fragrant coffee; the gleaming damasks, china and silver of the breakfast table; the trim, fresh-looking maid, with her white cap, apron, and cuffs, who came and went; the thoroughbred setter dozing in the sun, and the parrot dozing and chuckling to himself on his perch upon the terrace outside the window.

At the bottom of the lawn was the stable, and upon the concrete in front of its wide-open door the groom was currying one of the carriage horses. While Page addressed herself to her fruit and coffee, Jadwin put down his paper, and, his elbows on the arms of his rattan chair, sat for a long time looking out at the horse. By and by he got up and said:

"That new feed has filled 'em out in good shape. Think I'll go out and tell Jarvis to try it on the buggy team." He pushed open the French windows and went out, the setter sedately following.

Page dug her spoon into her grape-fruit, then suddenly laid it down and turned to Laura, her chin upon her palm.

"Laura," she said, "do you think I ought to marry—a girl of my temperament?"

"Marry?" echoed Laura.

"Sh-h!" whispered Page. "Laura—don't talk so loud. Yes, do you?"

"Well, why not marry, dearie? Why shouldn't you marry when the time comes? Girls as young as you are not supposed to have temperaments."

But instead of answering Page put another question:

"Laura, do you think I am womanly?"

"I think sometimes, Page, that you take your books and your reading too seriously. You've not been out of the house for three days, and I never see you without your note-books and text-books in your hand. You are at it, dear, from morning till night. Studies are all very well—"

"Oh, studies!" exclaimed Page. "I hate them. Laura, what is it to be womanly?"

"To be womanly?" repeated Laura. "Why, I don't know, honey. It's to be kind and well-bred and gentle mostly, and never to be bold or conspicuous—and to love one's home and to take care of it, and to love and believe in one's husband, or parents, or children—or even one's sister—above any one else in the world."

"I think that being womanly is better than being well read," hazarded Page.

"We can be both, Page," Laura told her. "But, honey, I think you had better hurry through your breakfast. If we are going to church this Easter, we want to get an early start. Curtis ordered the carriage half an hour earlier."

"Breakfast!" echoed Page. "I don't want a thing." She drew a deep breath and her eyes grew large. "Laura," she began again presently, "Laura ... Landry Court was here last night, and—oh, I don't know, he's so silly. But he said—well, he said this—well, I said that I understood how he felt about certain things, about 'getting on,' and being clean and fine and all that sort of thing you know; and then he said, 'Oh, you don't know what it means to me to look into the eyes of a woman who really understands.'"

"Did he?" said Laura, lifting her eyebrows.

"Yes, and he seemed so fine and earnest. Laura, wh—" Page adjusted a hairpin at the back of her head, and moved closer to Laura, her eyes on the floor. "Laura—what do you suppose it did mean to him—don't you think it was foolish of him to talk like that?"

"Not at all," Laura said, decisively. "If he said that he meant it—meant that he cared a great deal for you."

"Oh, I didn't mean that!" shrieked Page. "But there's a great deal more to Landry than I think we've suspected. He wants to be more than a mere money-getting machine, he says, and he wants to cultivate his mind and understand art and literature and that. And he wants me to help him, and I said I would. So if you don't mind, he's coming up here certain nights every week, and we're going to—I'm going to read to him. We're going to begin with the 'Ring and the Book.'"

In the later part of May, the weather being unusually hot, the Jadwins, taking Page with them, went up to Geneva Lake for the summer, and the great house fronting Lincoln Park was deserted.

Laura had hoped that now her husband would be able to spend his entire time with her, but in this she was disappointed. At first Jadwin went down to the city but two days a week, but soon this was increased to alternate days. Gretry was a frequent visitor at the country house, and often he and Jadwin, their rocking-chairs side by side in a remote corner of the porch, talked "business" in low tones till far into the night.

"Dear," said Laura, finally, "I'm seeing less and less of you every day, and I had so looked forward to this summer, when we were to be together all the time."

"I hate it as much as you do, Laura," said her husband. "But I do feel as though I ought to be on the spot just for now. I can't get it out of my head that we're going to have livelier times in a few months."

"But even Mr. Gretry says that you don't need to be right in your office every minute of the time. He says you can manage your Board of Trade business from out here just as well, and that you only go into town because you can't keep away from La Salle Street and the sound of the Wheat Pit."

Was this true? Jadwin himself had found it difficult to answer. There had been a time when Gretry had been obliged to urge and coax to get his friend to so much as notice the swirl of the great maelstrom in the Board of Trade Building. But of late Jadwin's eye and ear were forever turned thitherward, and it was he, and no longer Gretry, who took initiatives.

Meanwhile he was making money. As he had predicted, the price of wheat had advanced. May had been a fair-weather month with easy prices, the monthly Government report showing no loss in the condition of the crop. Wheat had gone up from sixty to sixty-six cents, and at a small profit Jadwin had sold some two hundred and fifty thousand bushels. Then had come the hot weather at the end of May. On the floor of the Board of Trade the Pit traders had begun to peel off their coats. It began to look like a hot June, and when cash wheat touched sixty-eight, Jadwin, now more than ever convinced of a coming Bull market, bought another five hundred thousand bushels.

This line he added to in June. Unfavorable weather—excessive heat, followed by flooding rains—had hurt the spring wheat, and in every direction there were complaints of weevils and chinch bugs. Later on other deluges had discoloured and damaged the winter crop. Jadwin was now, by virtue of his recent purchases, "long" one million bushels, and the market held firm at seventy-two cents—a twelve-cent advance in two months.

"She'll react," warned Gretry, "sure. Crookes and Sweeny haven't taken a hand yet. Look out for a heavy French crop. We'll get reports on it soon now. You're playing with a gun, J., that kicks further than it shoots."

"We've not shot her yet," Jadwin said. "We're only just loading her—for Bears," he added, with a wink.

In July came the harvesting returns from all over the country, proving conclusively that for the first time in six years, the United States crop was to be small and poor. The yield was moderate. Only part of it could be graded as "contract." Good wheat would be valuable from now on. Jadwin bought again, and again it was a "lot" of half a million bushels.

Then came the first manifestation of that marvellous golden luck that was to follow Curtis Jadwin through all the coming months. The French wheat crop was announced as poor. In Germany the yield was to be far below the normal. All through Hungary the potato and rye crops were light.

About the middle of the month Jadwin again called the broker to his country house, and took him for a long evening's trip around the lake, aboard the "Thetis." They were alone. MacKenny was at the wheel, and, seated on camp stools in the stern of the little boat, Jadwin outlined his plans for the next few months.

"Sam," he said, "I thought back in April there that we were to touch top prices about the first of this month, but this French and German news has coloured the cat different. I've been figuring that I would get out of this market around the seventies, but she's going higher. I'm going to hold on yet awhile."

"You do it on your own responsibility, then," said the broker. "I warn you the price is top heavy."

"Not much. Seventy-two cents is too cheap. Now I'm going into this hard; and I want to have my own lines out—to be independent of the trade papers that Crookes could buy up any time he wants to. I want you to get me some good, reliable correspondents in Europe; smart, bright fellows that we can depend on. I want one in Liverpool, one in Paris, and one in Odessa, and I want them to cable us about the situation every day."

Gretry thought a while.

"Well," he said, at length, "... yes. I guess I can arrange it. I can get you a good man in Liverpool—Traynard is his name—and there's two or three in Paris we could pick up. Odessa—I don't know. I couldn't say just this minute. But I'll fix it."

These correspondents began to report at the end of July. All over Europe the demand for wheat was active. Grain handlers were not only buying freely, but were contracting for future delivery. In August came the first demands for American wheat, scattered and sporadic at first, then later, a little, a very little more insistent.

Thus the summer wore to its end. The fall "situation" began slowly to define itself, with eastern Europe—densely populated, overcrowded—commencing to show uneasiness as to its supply of food for the winter; and with but a moderate crop in America to meet foreign demands. Russia, the United States, and Argentine would have to feed the world during the next twelve months.

Over the Chicago Wheat Pit the hand of the great indicator stood at seventy-five cents. Jadwin sold out his September wheat at this figure, and then in a single vast clutch bought three million bushels of the December option.

Never before had he ventured so deeply into the Pit. Never before had he committed himself so irrevocably to the send of the current. But something was preparing. Something indefinite and huge. He guessed it, felt it, knew it. On all sides of him he felt a quickening movement. Lethargy, inertia were breaking up. There was buoyancy to the current. In its ever-increasing swiftness there was exhilaration and exuberance.

And he was upon the crest of the wave. Now the forethought, the shrewdness, and the prompt action of those early spring days were beginning to tell. Confident, secure, unassailable, Jadwin plunged in. Every week the swirl of the Pit increased in speed, every week the demands of Europe for American wheat grew more frequent; and at the end of the month the price—which had fluctuated between seventy-five and seventy-eight—in a sudden flurry rushed to seventy-nine, to seventy-nine and a half, and closed, strong, at the even eighty cents.

On the day when the latter figure was reached Jadwin bought a seat upon the Board of Trade.

He was now no longer an "outsider."

VII

One morning in November of the same year Laura joined her husband at breakfast, preoccupied and a little grave, her mind full of a subject about which, she told herself, she could no longer keep from speaking. So soon as an opportunity presented itself, which was when Jadwin laid down his paper and drew his coffee-cup towards him, Laura exclaimed:

"Curtis."

"Well, old girl?"

"Curtis, dear, ... when is it all going to end—your speculating? You never used to be this way. It seems as though, nowadays, I never had you to myself. Even when you are not going over papers and reports and that, or talking by the hour to Mr. Gretry in the library—even when you are not doing all that, your mind seems to be away from me—down there in La Salle Street or the Board of Trade Building. Dearest, you don't know. I don't mean to complain, and I don't want to be exacting or selfish, but—sometimes I—I am lonesome. Don't interrupt," she said, hastily. "I want to say it all at once, and then never speak of it again. Last night, when Mr. Gretry was here, you said, just after dinner, that you would be all through your talk in an hour. And I waited.... I waited till eleven, and then I went to bed. Dear I—I—I was lonesome. The evening was so long. I had put on my very prettiest gown, the one you said you liked so much, and you never seemed to notice. You told me Mr. Gretry was going by nine, and I had it all planned how we would spend the evening together."

But she got no further. Her husband had taken her in his arms, and had interrupted her words with blustering exclamations of self-reproach and self-condemnation. He was a brute, he cried, a senseless, selfish ass, who had no right to such a wife, who was not worth a single one of the tears that by now were trembling on Laura's lashes.

"Now we won't speak of it again," she began. "I suppose I am selfish—"

"Selfish, nothing!" he exclaimed. "Don't talk that way. I'm the one—"

"But," Laura persisted, "some time you will—get out of this speculating for good? Oh, I do look forward to it so! And, Curtis, what is the use? We're so rich now we can't spend our money. What do you want to make more for?"

"Oh, it's not the money," he answered. "It's the fun of the thing; the excitement—"

"That's just it, the 'excitement.' You don't know, Curtis. It is changing you. You are so nervous sometimes, and sometimes you don't listen to me when I talk to you. I can just see what's in your mind. It's wheat—wheat—wheat, wheat—wheat—wheat, all the time. Oh, if you knew how I hated and feared it!"

"Well, old girl, that settles it. I wouldn't make you unhappy a single minute for all the wheat in the world."

"And you will stop speculating?"

"Well, I can't pull out all in a moment, but just as soon as a chance comes I'll get out of the market. At any rate, I won't have any business of mine come between us. I don't like it any more than you do. Why, how long is it since we've read any book together, like we used to when you read aloud to me?"

"Not since we came back from the country."

"By George, that's so, that's so." He shook his head. "I've got to taper off. You're right, Laura. But you don't know, you haven't a guess how this trading in wheat gets a hold of you. And, then, what am I to do? What are we fellows, who have made our money, to do? I've got to be busy. I can't sit down and twiddle my thumbs. And I don't believe in lounging around clubs, or playing with race horses, or murdering game birds, or running some poor, helpless fox to death. Speculating seems to be about the only game, or the only business that's left open to me—that appears to be legitimate. I know I've gone too far into it, and I promise you I'll quit. But it's fine fun. When you know how to swing a deal, and can look ahead, a little further than the other fellows, and can take chances they daren't, and plan and manoeuvre, and then see it all come out just as you had known it would all along—I tell you it's absorbing."

"But you never do tell me," she objected. "I never know what you are doing. I hear through Mr. Court or Mr. Gretry, but never through you. Don't you think you could trust me? I want to enter into your life on its every side, Curtis. Tell me," she suddenly demanded, "what are you doing now?"

"Very well, then," he said, "I'll tell you. Of course you mustn't speak about it. It's nothing very secret, but it's always as well to keep quiet about these things."

She gave her word, and leaned her elbows on the table, prepared to listen intently. Jadwin crushed a lump of sugar against the inside of his coffee cup.

"Well," he began, "I've not been doing anything very exciting, except to buy wheat."

"What for?"

"To sell again. You see, I'm one of those who believe that wheat is going up. I was the very first to see it, I guess, way back last April. Now in August this year, while we were up at the lake, I bought three million bushels."

"Three—million—bushels!" she murmured. "Why, what do you do with it? Where do you put it?"

He tried to explain that he had merely bought the right to call for the grain on a certain date, but she could not understand this very clearly.

"Never mind," she told him, "go on."

"Well, then, at the end of August we found out that the wet weather in England would make a short crop there, and along in September came the news that Siberia would not raise enough to supply the southern provinces of Russia. That left only the United States and the Argentine Republic to feed pretty much the whole world. Of course that would make wheat valuable. Seems to be a short-crop year everywhere. I saw that wheat would go higher and higher, so I bought another million bushels in October, and another early in this month. That's all. You see, I figure that pretty soon those people over in England and Italy and Germany—the people that eat wheat—will be willing to pay us in America big prices for it, because it's so hard to get. They've got to have the wheat—it's bread 'n' butter to them."

"Oh, then why not give it to them?" she cried. "Give it to those poor people—your five million bushels. Why, that would be a godsend to them."

Jadwin stared a moment.

"Oh, that isn't exactly how it works out," he said.

Before he could say more, however, the maid came in and handed to Jadwin three despatches.

"Now those," said Laura, when the servant had gone out, "you get those every morning. Are those part of your business? What do they say?"

"I'll read them to you," he told her as he slit the first envelopes. "They are cablegrams from agents of mine in Europe. Gretry arranged to have them sent to me. Here now, this is from Odessa. It's in cipher, but"—he drew a narrow memorandum-book from his breast pocket—"I'll translate it for you."

He turned the pages of the key book a few moments, jotting down the translation on the back of an envelope with the gold pencil at the end of his watch chain.

"Here's how it reads," he said at last. "'Cash wheat advanced one cent bushel on Liverpool buying, stock light. Shipping to interior. European price not attractive to sellers.'"

"What does that mean?" she asked.

"Well, that Russia will not export wheat, that she has no more than enough for herself, so that Western Europe will have to look to us for her wheat."

"And the others? Read those to me."

Again Jadwin translated.

"This is from Paris:

"'Answer on one million bushels wheat in your market—stocks lighter than expected, and being cleared up.'"

"Which is to say?" she queried.

"They want to know how much I would ask for a million bushels. They find it hard to get the stuff over there—just as I said they would."

"Will you sell it to them?"

"Maybe. I'll talk to Sam about it."

"And now the last one."

"It's from Liverpool, and Liverpool, you must understand, is the great buyer of wheat. It's a tremendously influential place."

He began once more to consult the key book, one finger following the successive code words of the despatch.

Laura, watching him, saw his eyes suddenly contract. "By George," he muttered, all at once, "by George, what's this?"

"What is it?" she demanded. "Is it important?"

But all-absorbed, Jadwin neither heard nor responded. Three times he verified the same word.

"Oh, please tell me," she begged.

Jadwin shook his head impatiently and held up a warning hand.

"Wait, wait," he said. "Wait a minute."

Word for word he wrote out the translation of the cablegram, and then studied it intently.

"That's it," he said, at last. Then he got to his feet. "I guess I've had enough breakfast," he declared. He looked at his watch, touched the call bell, and when the maid appeared said:

"Tell Jarvis to bring the buggy around right away."

"But, dear, what is it?" repeated Laura. "You said you would tell me. You see," she cried, "it's just as I said. You've forgotten my very existence. When it's a question of wheat I count for nothing. And just now, when you read the despatch to yourself, you were all different; such a look came into your face, so cruelly eager, and triumphant and keen."

"You'd be eager, too," he exclaimed, "if you understood. Look; read it for yourself."

He thrust the cable into her hands. Over each code word he had written its translation, and his wife read:

"Large firms here short and in embarrassing position, owing to curtailment in Argentine shipments. Can negotiate for five million wheat if price satisfactory."

"Well?" she asked.

"Well, don't you see what that means? It's the 'European demand' at last. They must have wheat, and I've got it to give 'em—wheat that I bought, oh! at seventy cents, some of it, and they'll pay the market that is, eighty cents, for it. Oh, they'll pay more. They'll pay eighty-two if I want 'em to. France is after the stuff, too. Remember that cable from Paris I just read. They'd bid against each other. Why, if I pull this off, if this goes through—and, by George," he went on, speaking as much to himself as to her, new phases of the affair presenting themselves to him at every moment, "by George, I don't have to throw this wheat into the Pit and break down the price—and Gretry has understandings with the railroads, through the elevator gang, so we get big rebates. Why, this wheat is worth eighty-two cents to them—and then there's this 'curtailment in Argentine shipments.' That's the first word we've had about small crops there. Holy Moses, if the Argentine crop is off, wheat will knock the roof clean off the Board of Trade!" The maid reappeared in the doorway. "The buggy?" queried Jadwin. "All right. I'm off, Laura, and—until it's over keep quiet about all this, you know. Ask me to read you some more cables some day. It brings good luck."

He gathered up his despatches and the mail and was gone. Laura, left alone, sat looking out of the window a long moment. She heard the front door close, and then the sound of the horses' hoofs on the asphalt by the carriage porch. They died down, ceased, and all at once a great silence seemed to settle over the house.

Laura sat thinking. At last she rose.

"It is the first time," she said to herself, "that Curtis ever forgot to kiss me good-by."

The day, for all that the month was December, was fine. The sun shone; under foot the ground was dry and hard. The snow which had fallen ten days before was practically gone. In fine, it was a perfect day for riding. Laura called her maid and got into her habit. The groom with his own horse and "Crusader" were waiting for her when she descended.

That forenoon Laura rode further and longer than usual. Preoccupied at first, her mind burdened with vague anxieties, she nevertheless could not fail to be aroused and stimulated by the sparkle and effervescence of the perfect morning, and the cold, pure glitter of Lake Michigan, green with an intense mineral hue, dotted with whitecaps, and flashing under the morning sky. Lincoln Park was deserted and still; a blue haze shrouded the distant masses of leafless trees, where the gardeners were burning the heaps of leaves. Under her the thoroughbred moved with an ease and a freedom that were superb, throwing back one sharp ear at her lightest word; his rippling mane caressed her hand and forearm, and as she looked down upon his shoulder she could see the long, slender muscles, working smoothly, beneath the satin sheen of the skin. At the water works she turned into the long, straight road that leads to North Lake, and touched Crusader with the crop, checking him slightly at the same time. With a little toss of his head he broke from a trot into a canter, and then, as she leaned forward in the saddle, into his long, even gallop. There was no one to see; she would not be conspicuous, so Laura gave the horse his head, and in another moment he was carrying her with a swiftness that brought the water to her eyes, and that sent her hair flying from her face. She had him completely under control. A touch upon the bit, she knew, would suffice to bring him to a standstill. She knew him to be without fear and without nerves, knew that his every instinct made for her safety, and that this morning's gallop was as much a pleasure to him as to his rider. Beneath her and around her the roadway and landscape flew; the cold air sang in her ears and whipped a faint colour to her pale cheeks; in her deep brown eyes a frosty sparkle came and went, and throughout all her slender figure the blood raced spanking and careering in a full, strong tide of health and gaiety.

She made a circle around North Lake, and came back by way of the Linne monument and the Palm House, Crusader ambling quietly by now, the groom trotting stolidly in the rear. Throughout all her ride she had seen no one but the park gardeners and the single grey-coated, mounted policeman whom she met each time she rode, and who always touched his helmet to her as she cantered past. Possibly she had grown a little careless in looking out for pedestrians at the crossings, for as she turned eastward at the La Salle statue, she all but collided with a gentleman who was traversing the road at the same time.

She brought her horse to a standstill with a little start of apprehension, and started again as she saw that the gentleman was Sheldon Corthell.

"Well," she cried, taken all aback, unable to think of formalities, and relapsing all at once into the young girl of Barrington, Massachusetts, "well, I never—of all the people."

But, no doubt, she had been more in his mind than he in hers, and a meeting with her was for him an eventuality not at all remote. There was more of pleasure than of embarrassment in that first look in which he recognised the wife of Curtis Jadwin.

The artist had changed no whit in the four years since last she had seen him. He seemed as young as ever; there was the same "elegance" to his figure; his hands were just as long and slim as ever; his black beard was no less finely pointed, and the mustaches were brushed away from his lips in the same French style that she remembered he used to affect. He was, as always, carefully dressed. He wore a suit of tweeds of a foreign cut, but no overcoat, a cloth cap of greenish plaid was upon his head, his hands were gloved in dogskin, and under his arm he carried a slender cane of varnished brown bamboo. The only unconventionality in his dress was the cravat, a great bow of black silk that overflowed the lapels of his coat.

But she had no more than time to register a swift impression of the details, when he came quickly forward, one hand extended, the other holding his cap.

"I cannot tell you how glad I am," he exclaimed.

It was the old Corthell beyond doubting or denial. Not a single inflection of his low-pitched, gently modulated voice was wanting; not a single infinitesimal mannerism was changed, even to the little tilting of the chin when he spoke, or the quick winking of the eyelids, or the smile that narrowed the corners of the eyes themselves, or the trick of perfect repose of his whole body. Even his handkerchief, as always, since first she had known him, was tucked into his sleeve at the wrist.

"And so you are back again," she cried. "And when, and how?"

"And so—yes—so I am back again," he repeated, as they shook hands. "Only day before yesterday, and quite surreptitiously. No one knows yet that I am here. I crept in—or my train did—under the cover of night. I have come straight from Tuscany."

"From Tuscany?"

"—and gardens and marble pergolas."

"Now why any one should leave Tuscan gardens and—and all that kind of thing for a winter in Chicago, I cannot see," she said.

"It is a little puzzling," he answered. "But I fancy that my gardens and pergolas and all the rest had come to seem to me a little—as the French would put it—malle. I began to long for a touch of our hard, harsh city again. Harshness has its place, I think, if it is only to cut one's teeth on."

Laura looked down at him, smiling.

"I should have thought you had cut yours long ago," she said.

"Not my wisdom teeth," he urged. "I feel now that I have come to that time of life when it is expedient to have wisdom."

"I have never known that feeling," she confessed, "and I live in the 'hard, harsh' city."

"Oh, that is because you have never known what it meant not to have wisdom," he retorted. "Tell me about everybody," he went on. "Your husband, he is well, of course, and distressfully rich. I heard of him in New York. And Page, our little, solemn Minerva of Dresden china?"

"Oh, yes, Page is well, but you will hardly recognise her; such a young lady nowadays."

"And Mr. Court, 'Landry'? I remember he always impressed me as though he had just had his hair cut; and the Cresslers, and Mrs. Wessels, and—"

"All well. Mrs. Cressler will be delighted to hear you are back. Yes, everybody is well."

"And, last of all, Mrs. Jadwin? But I needn't ask; I can see how well and happy you are."

"And Mr. Corthell," she queried, "is also well and happy?"

"Mr. Corthell," he responded, "is very well, and—tolerably—happy, thank you. One has lost a few illusions, but has managed to keep enough to grow old on. One's latter days are provided for."

"I shouldn't imagine," she told him, "that one lost illusions in Tuscan gardens."

"Quite right," he hastened to reply, smiling cheerfully. "One lost no illusions in Tuscany. One went there to cherish the few that yet remained. But," he added, without change of manner, "one begins to believe that even a lost illusion can be very beautiful sometimes—even in Chicago."

"I want you to dine with us," said Laura. "You've hardly met my husband, and I think you will like some of our pictures. I will have all your old friends there, the Cresslers and Aunt Wess, and all. When can you come?"

"Oh, didn't you get my note?" he asked. "I wrote you yesterday, asking if I might call to-night. You see, I am only in Chicago for a couple of days. I must go on to St.

Louis to-morrow, and shall not be back for a week."

"Note? No, I've had no note from you. Oh, I know what happened. Curtis left in a hurry this morning, and he swooped all the mail into his pocket the last moment. I knew some of my letters were with his. There's where your note went. But, never mind, it makes no difference now that we've met. Yes, by all means, come to-night—to dinner. We're not a bit formal. Curtis won't have it. We dine at six; and I'll try to get the others. Oh, but Page won't be there, I forgot. She and Landry Court are going to have dinner with Aunt Wess', and they are all going to a lecture afterwards."

The artist expressed his appreciation and accepted her invitation.

"Do you know where we live?" she demanded. "You know we've moved since."

"Yes, I know," he told her. "I made up my mind to take a long walk here in the Park this morning, and I passed your house on my way out. You see, I had to look up your address in the directory before writing. Your house awed me, I confess, and the style is surprisingly good."

"But tell me," asked Laura, "you never speak of yourself, what have you been doing since you went away?"

"Nothing. Merely idling, and painting a little, and studying some thirteenth century glass in Avignon and Sienna."

"And shall you go back?"

"Yes, I think so, in about a month. So soon as I have straightened out some little businesses of mine—which puts me in mind," he said, glancing at his watch, "that I have an appointment at eleven, and should be about it."

He said good-by and left her, and Laura cantered homeward in high spirits. She was very glad that Corthell had come back. She had always liked him. He not only talked well himself, but seemed to have the faculty of making her do the same. She remembered that in the old days, before she had met Jadwin, her mind and conversation, for undiscoverable reasons, had never been nimbler, quicker, nor more effective than when in the company of the artist.

Arrived at home, Laura (as soon as she had looked up the definition of "pergola" in the dictionary) lost no time in telephoning to Mrs. Cressler.

"What," this latter cried when she told her the news, "that Sheldon Corthell back again! Well, dear me, if he wasn't the last person in my mind. I do remember the lovely windows he used to paint, and how refined and elegant he always was—and the loveliest hands and voice."

"He's to dine with us to-night, and I want you and Mr. Cressler to come."

"Oh, Laura, child, I just simply can't. Charlie's got a man from Milwaukee coming here to-night, and I've got to feed him. Isn't it too provoking? I've got to sit and listen to those two, clattering commissions and percentages and all, when I might be hearing Sheldon Corthell talk art and poetry and stained glass. I declare, I never have any luck."

At quarter to six that evening Laura sat in the library, before the fireplace, in her black velvet dinner gown, cutting the pages of a new novel, the ivory cutter as it turned and glanced in her hand, appearing to be a mere prolongation of her slender fingers. But she was not interested in the book, and from time to time glanced nervously at the clock upon the mantel-shelf over her head. Jadwin was not home yet, and she was distressed at the thought of keeping dinner waiting. He usually came back from down town at five o'clock, and even earlier. To-day she had expected that quite possibly the business implied in the Liverpool cable of the morning might detain him, but surely he should be home by now; and as the minutes passed she listened more and more anxiously for the sound of hoofs on the driveway at the side of the house.

At five minutes of the hour, when Corthell was announced, there was still no sign of her husband. But as she was crossing the hall on her way to the drawing-room, one of the servants informed her that Mr. Jadwin had just telephoned that he would be home in half an hour.

"Is he on the telephone now?" she asked, quickly. "Where did he telephone from?"

But it appeared that Jadwin had "hung up" without mentioning his whereabouts.

"The buggy came home," said the servant. "Mr. Jadwin told Jarvis not to wait. He said he would come in the street cars."

Laura reflected that she could delay dinner a half hour, and gave orders to that effect.

"We shall have to wait a little," she explained to Corthell as they exchanged greetings in the drawing-room. "Curtis has some special business on hand to-day, and is half an hour late."

They sat down on either side of the fireplace in the lofty apartment, with its sombre hangings of wine-coloured brocade and thick, muffling rugs, and for upwards of three-quarters of an hour Corthell interested her with his description of his life in the cathedral towns of northern Italy. But at the end of that time dinner was announced.

"Has Mr. Jadwin come in yet?" Laura asked of the servant.

"No, madam."

She bit her lip in vexation.

"I can't imagine what can keep Curtis so late," she murmured. "Well," she added, at the end of her resources, "we must make the best of it. I think we will go in, Mr. Corthell, without waiting. Curtis must be here soon now."

But, as a matter of fact, he was not. In the great dining-room, filled with a dull crimson light, the air just touched with the scent of lilies of the valley, Corthell and Mrs. Jadwin dined alone.

"I suppose," observed the artist, "that Mr. Jadwin is a very busy man."

"Oh, no," Laura answered. "His real estate, he says, runs itself, and, as a rule, Mr. Gretry manages most of his Board of Trade business. It is only occasionally that anything keeps him down town late. I scolded him this morning, however, about his speculating, and made him promise not to do so much of it. I hate speculation. It seems to absorb some men so; and I don't believe it's right for a man to allow himself to become absorbed altogether in business."

"Oh, why limit one's absorption to business?" replied Corthell, sipping his wine. "Is it right for one to be absorbed 'altogether' in anything—even in art, even in religion?"

"Oh, religion, I don't know," she protested.

"Isn't that certain contribution," he hazarded, "which we make to the general welfare, over and above our own individual work, isn't that the essential? I suppose, of course, that we must hoe, each of us, his own little row, but it's the stroke or two we give to our neighbour's row—don't you think?—that helps most to cultivate the field."

"But doesn't religion mean more than a stroke or two?" she ventured to reply.

"I'm not so sure," he answered, thoughtfully. "If the stroke or two is taken from one's own work instead of being given in excess of it. One must do one's own hoeing first. That's the foundation of things. A religion that would mean to be 'altogether absorbed' in my neighbour's hoeing would be genuinely pernicious, surely. My row, meanwhile, would lie open to weeds."

"But if your neighbour's row grew flowers?"

"Unfortunately weeds grow faster than the flowers, and the weeds of my row would spread until they choked and killed my neighbour's flowers, I am sure."

"That seems selfish though," she persisted. "Suppose my neighbour were maimed or halt or blind? His poor little row would never be finished. My stroke or two would not help very much."

"Yes, but every row lies between two others, you know. The hoer on the far side of the cripple's row would contribute a stroke or two as well as you. No," he went on, "I am sure one's first duty is to do one's own work. It seems to me that a work accomplished benefits the whole world—the people—pro rata. If we help another at the expense of our work instead of in excess of it, we benefit only the individual, and, pro rata again, rob the people. A little good contributed by everybody to the race is of more, infinitely more, importance than a great deal of good contributed by one individual to another."

"Yes," she admitted, beginning at last to be convinced, "I see what you mean. But one must think very large to see that. It never occurred to me before. The individual—I, Laura Jadwin—counts for nothing. It is the type to which I belong that's important, the mould, the form, the sort of composite photograph of hundreds of thousands of Laura Jadwins. Yes," she continued, her brows bent, her mind hard at work, "what I am, the little things that distinguish me from everybody else, those pass away very quickly, are very ephemeral. But the type Laura Jadwin, that always remains, doesn't it? One must help building up only the permanent things. Then, let's see, the individual may deteriorate, but the type always grows better.... Yes, I think one can say that."

"At least the type never recedes," he prompted.

"Oh, it began good," she cried, as though at a discovery, "and can never go back of that original good. Something keeps it from going below a certain point, and it is left to us to lift it higher and higher. No, the type can't be bad. Of course the type is more important than the individual. And that something that keeps it from going below a certain point is God."

"Or nature."

"So that God and nature," she cried again, "work together? No, no, they are one and the same thing."

"There, don't you see," he remarked, smiling back at her, "how simple it is?"

"Oh-h," exclaimed Laura, with a deep breath, "isn't it beautiful?" She put her hand to her forehead with a little laugh of deprecation. "My," she said, "but those things make you think."

Dinner was over before she was aware of it, and they were still talking animatedly as they rose from the table.

"We will have our coffee in the art gallery," Laura said, "and please smoke."

He lit a cigarette, and the two passed into the great glass-roofed rotunda.

"Here is the one I like best," said Laura, standing before the Bougereau.

"Yes?" he queried, observing the picture thoughtfully. "I suppose," he remarked, "it is because it demands less of you than some others. I see what you mean. It pleases you because it satisfies you so easily. You can grasp it without any effort."

"Oh, I don't know," she ventured.

"Bougereau 'fills a place.' I know it," he answered. "But I cannot persuade myself to admire his art."

"But," she faltered, "I thought that Bougereau was considered the greatest—one of the greatest—his wonderful flesh tints, the drawing, and colouring."

"But I think you will see," he told her, "if you think about it, that for all there is in his picture—back of it—a fine hanging, a beautiful vase would have exactly the same value upon your wall. Now, on the other hand, take this picture." He indicated a small canvas to the right of the bathing nymphs, representing a twilight landscape.

"Oh, that one," said Laura. "We bought that here in America, in New York. It's by a Western artist. I never noticed it much, I'm afraid."

"But now look at it," said Corthell. "Don't you know that the artist saw something more than trees and a pool and afterglow? He had that feeling of night coming on, as he sat there before his sketching easel on the edge of that little pool. He heard the frogs beginning to pipe, I'm sure, and the touch of the night mist was on his hands. And he was very lonely and even a little sad. In those deep shadows under the trees he put something of himself, the gloom and the sadness that he felt at the moment. And that little pool, still and black and sombre—why, the whole thing is the tragedy of a life full of dark, hidden secrets. And the little pool is a heart. No one can say how deep it is, or what dreadful thing one would find at the bottom, or what drowned hopes or what sunken ambitions. That little pool says one word as plain as if it were whispered in the ear—despair. Oh, yes, I prefer it to the nymphs."

"I am very much ashamed," returned Laura, "that I could not see it all before for myself. But I see it now. It is better, of course. I shall come in here often now and study it. Of all the rooms in our house this is the one I like best. But, I am afraid, it has been more because of the organ than of the pictures."

Corthell turned about.

"Oh, the grand, noble organ," he murmured. "I envy you this of all your treasures. May I play for you? Something to compensate for the dreadful, despairing little tarn of the picture."

"I should love to have you," she told him.

He asked permission to lower the lights, and stepping outside the door an instant, pressed the buttons that extinguished all but a very few of them. After he had done this he came back to the organ and detached the self-playing "arrangement" without comment, and seated himself at the console.

Laura lay back in a long chair close at hand. The moment was propitious. The artist's profile silhouetted itself against the shade of a light that burned at the side of the organ, and that gave light to the keyboard. And on this keyboard, full in the reflection, lay his long, slim hands. They were the only things that moved in the room, and the chords and bars of Mendelssohn's "Consolation" seemed, as he played, to flow, not from the instrument, but, like some invisible ether, from his finger-tips themselves.

"You hear," he said to Laura, "the effect of questions and answer in this. The questions are passionate and tumultuous and varied, but the answer is always the same, always calm and soothing and dignified."

She answered with a long breath, speaking just above a whisper:

"Oh, yes, yes, I understand."

He finished and turned towards her a moment. "Possibly not a very high order of art," he said; "a little too 'easy,' perhaps, like the Bougereau, but 'Consolation' should appeal very simply and directly, after all. Do you care for Beethoven?"

"I—I am afraid—" began Laura, but he had continued without waiting for her reply.

"You remember this? The 'Appassionata,' the F minor sonata just the second movement."

But when he had finished Laura begged him to continue.

"Please go on," she said. "Play anything. You can't tell how I love it."

"Here is something I've always liked," he answered, turning back to the keyboard. "It is the 'Mephisto Walzer' of Liszt. He has adapted it himself from his own orchestral score, very ingeniously. It is difficult to render on the organ, but I think you can get the idea of it." As he spoke he began playing, his head very slightly moving to the rhythm of the piece. At the beginning of each new theme, and without interrupting his playing, he offered a word, of explanation:

"Very vivid and arabesque this, don't you think? ... And now this movement; isn't it reckless and capricious, like a woman who hesitates and then takes the leap? Yet there's a certain nobility there, a feeling for ideals. You see it, of course.... And all the while this undercurrent of the sensual, and that feline, eager sentiment ... and here, I think, is the best part of it, the very essence of passion, the voluptuousness that is a veritable anguish.... These long, slow rhythms, tortured, languishing, really dying. It reminds one of 'Phedre'—'Venus toute entiere,' and the rest of it; and Wagner has the same. You find it again in Isolde's motif continually."

Laura was transfixed, all but transported. Here was something better than Gounod and Verdi, something above and beyond the obvious one, two, three, one, two, three of the opera scores as she knew them and played them. Music she understood with an intuitive quickness; and those prolonged chords of Liszt's, heavy and clogged and cloyed with passion, reached some hitherto untouched string within her heart, and with resistless power twanged it so that the vibration of it shook her entire being, and left her quivering and breathless, the tears in her eyes, her hands clasped till the knuckles whitened.

She felt all at once as though a whole new world were opened to her. She stood on Pisgah. And she was ashamed and confused at her ignorance of those things which Corthell tactfully assumed that she knew as a matter of course. What wonderful pleasures she had ignored! How infinitely removed from her had been the real world of art and artists of which Corthell was a part! Ah, but she would make amends now. No more Verdi and Bougereau. She would get rid of the "Bathing Nymphs." Never, never again would she play the "Anvil Chorus." Corthell should select her pictures, and should play to her from Liszt and Beethoven that music which evoked all the turbulent emotion, all the impetuosity and fire and exaltation that she felt was hers.

She wondered at herself. Surely, surely there were two Laura Jadwins. One calm and even and steady, loving the quiet life, loving her home, finding a pleasure in the duties of the housewife. This was the Laura who liked plain, homely, matter-of-fact Mrs. Cressler, who adored her husband, who delighted in Mr. Howells's novels, who abjured society and the formal conventions, who went to church every Sunday, and who was afraid of her own elevator.

But at moments such as this she knew that there was another Laura Jadwin—the Laura Jadwin who might have been a great actress, who had a "temperament," who was impulsive. This was the Laura of the "grand manner," who played the role of the great lady from room to room of her vast house, who read Meredith, who revelled in swift gallops through the park on jet-black, long-tailed horses, who affected black velvet, black jet, and black lace in her gowns, who was conscious and proud of her pale, stately beauty—the Laura Jadwin, in fine, who delighted to recline in a long chair in the dim, beautiful picture gallery and listen with half-shut eyes to the great golden organ thrilling to the passion of Beethoven and Liszt.

The last notes of the organ sank and faded into silence—a silence that left a sense of darkness like that which follows upon the flight of a falling star, and after a long moment Laura sat upright, adjusting the heavy masses of her black hair with thrusts of her long, white fingers. She drew a deep breath.

"Oh," she said, "that was wonderful, wonderful. It is like a new language—no, it is like new thoughts, too fine for language."

"I have always believed so," he answered. "Of all the arts, music, to my notion, is the most intimate. At the other end of the scale you have architecture, which is an expression of and an appeal to the common multitude, a whole people, the mass. Fiction and painting, and even poetry, are affairs of the classes, reaching the groups of the educated. But music—ah, that is different, it is one soul speaking to another soul. The composer meant it for you and himself. No one else has anything to do with it. Because his soul was heavy and broken with grief, or bursting with passion, or tortured with doubt, or searching for some unnamed ideal, he has come to you—you of all the people in the world—with his message, and he tells you of his yearnings and his sadness, knowing that you will sympathise, knowing that your soul has, like his, been acquainted with grief, or with gladness; and in the music his soul speaks to yours, beats with it, blends with it, yes, is even, spiritually, married to it."

And as he spoke the electrics all over the gallery flashed out in a sudden blaze, and Curtis Jadwin entered the room, crying out:

"Are you here, Laura? By George, my girl, we pulled it off, and I've cleaned up five—hundred—thousand—dollars."

Laura and the artist faced quickly about, blinking at the sudden glare, and Laura put her hand over her eyes.

"Oh, I didn't mean to blind you," said her husband, as he came forward. "But I thought it wouldn't be appropriate to tell you the good news in the dark."

Corthell rose, and for the first time Jadwin caught sight of him.

"This is Mr. Corthell, Curtis," Laura said. "You remember him, of course?"

"Why, certainly, certainly," declared Jadwin, shaking Corthell's hand. "Glad to see you again. I hadn't an idea you were here." He was excited, elated, very talkative. "I guess I came in on you abruptly," he observed. "They told me Mrs. Jadwin was in here, and I was full of my good news. By the way, I do remember now. When I came to look over my mail on the way down town this morning, I found a note from you to my wife, saying you would call to-night. Thought it was for me, and opened it before I found the mistake."

"I knew you had gone off with it," said Laura.

"Guess I must have mixed it up with my own mail this morning. I'd have telephoned you about it, Laura, but upon my word I've been so busy all day I clean forgot it. I've let the cat out of the bag already, Mr. Corthell, and I might as well tell the whole thing now. I've been putting through a little deal with some Liverpool fellows to-day, and I had to wait down town to get their cables to-night. You got my telephone, did you, Laura?"

"Yes, but you said then you'd be up in half an hour."

"I know—I know. But those Liverpool cables didn't come till all hours. Well, as I was saying, Mr. Corthell, I had this deal on hand—it was that wheat, Laura, I was telling you about this morning—five million bushels of it, and I found out from my English agent that I could slam it right into a couple of fellows over there, if we could come to terms. We came to terms right enough. Some of that wheat I sold at a profit of fifteen cents on every bushel. My broker and I figured it out just now before I started home, and, as I say, I'm a clean half million to the good. So much for looking ahead a little further than the next man." He dropped into a chair and stretched his arms wide. "Whoo! I'm tired Laura. Seems as though I'd been on my feet all day. Do you suppose Mary, or Martha, or Maggie, or whatever her name is, could rustle me a good strong cup of tea.

"Haven't you dined, Curtis?" cried Laura.

"Oh, I had a stand-up lunch somewhere with Sam. But we were both so excited we might as well have eaten sawdust. Heigho, I sure am tired. It takes it out of you, Mr. Corthell, to make five hundred thousand in about ten hours."

"Indeed I imagine so," assented the artist. Jadwin turned to his wife, and held her glance in his a moment. He was full of triumph, full of the grim humour of the suddenly successful American.

"Hey?" he said. "What do you think of that, Laura," he clapped down his big hand upon his chair arm, "a whole half million—at one grab? Maybe they'll say down there in La Salle Street now that I don't know wheat. Why, Sam—that's Gretry my broker, Mr. Corthell, of Gretry, Converse & Co.—Sam said to me Laura, to-night, he said, 'J.,'—they call me 'J.' down there, Mr. Corthell—'J., I take off my hat to you. I thought you were wrong from the very first, but I guess you know this game better than I do.' Yes, sir, that's what he said, and Sam Gretry has been trading in wheat for pretty nearly thirty years. Oh, I knew it," he cried, with a quick gesture; "I knew wheat was going to go up. I knew it from the first, when all the rest of em laughed at me. I knew this European demand would hit us hard about this time. I knew it was a good thing to buy wheat; I knew it was a good thing to have special agents over in Europe. Oh, they'll all buy now—when I've showed 'em the way. Upon my word, I haven't talked so much in a month of Sundays. You must pardon me, Mr. Corthell. I don't make five hundred thousand every day."

"But this is the last—isn't it?" said Laura.

"Yes," admitted Jadwin, with a quick, deep breath. "I'm done now. No more speculating. Let some one else have a try now. See if they can hold five million bushels till it's wanted. My, my, I am tired—as I've said before. D'that tea come, Laura?"

"What's that in your hand?" she answered, smiling.

Jadwin stared at the cup and saucer he held, whimsically. "Well, well," he exclaimed, "I must be flustered. Corthell," he declared between swallows, "take my advice. Buy May wheat. It'll beat art all hollow."

"Oh, dear, no," returned the artist. "I should lose my senses if I won, and my money if I didn't.

"That's so. Keep out of it. It's a rich man's game. And at that, there's no fun in it unless you risk more than you can afford to lose. Well, let's not talk shop. You're an artist, Mr. Corthell. What do you think of our house?"

Later on when they had said good-by to Corthell, and when Jadwin was making the rounds of the library, art gallery, and drawing-rooms—a nightly task which he never would intrust to the servants—turning down the lights and testing the window fastenings, his wife said:

"And now you are out of it—for good."

"I don't own a grain of wheat," he assured her. "I've got to be out of it."

The next day he went down town for only two or three hours in the afternoon. But he did not go near the Board of Trade building. He talked over a few business matters with the manager of his real estate office, wrote an unimportant letter or two, signed a few orders, was back at home by five o'clock, and in the evening took Laura, Page, and Landry Court to the theatre.

After breakfast the next morning, when he had read his paper, he got up, and, thrusting his hands in his pockets, looked across the table at his wife.

"Well," he said. "Now what'll we do?"

She put down at once the letter she was reading.

"Would you like to drive in the park?" she suggested. "It is a beautiful morning."

"M—m—yes," he answered slowly. "All right. Let's drive in the park."

But she could see that the prospect was not alluring to him.

"No," she said, "no. I don't think you want to do that."

"I don't think I do, either," he admitted. "The fact is, Laura, I just about know that park by heart. Is there anything good in the magazines this month?"

She got them for him, and he installed himself comfortably in the library, with a box of cigars near at hand.

"Ah," he said, fetching a long breath as he settled back in the deep-seated leather chair. "Now this is what I call solid comfort. Better than stewing and fussing about La Salle Street with your mind loaded down with responsibilities and all. This is my idea of life."

But an hour later, when Laura—who had omitted her ride that morning—looked into the room, he was not there. The magazines were helter-skeltered upon the floor and table, where he had tossed each one after turning the leaves. A servant told her that Mr. Jadwin was out in the stables.

She saw him through the window, in a cap and great-coat, talking with the coachman and looking over one of the horses. But he came back to the house in a little while, and she found him in his smoking-room with a novel in his hand.

"Oh, I read that last week," she said, as she caught a glimpse of the title. "Isn't it interesting? Don't you think it is good?"

"Oh—yes—pretty good," he admitted. "Isn't it about time for lunch? Let's go to the matinee this afternoon, Laura. Oh, that's so, it's Thursday; I forgot."

"Let me read that aloud to you," she said, reaching for the book. "I know you'll be interested when you get farther along."

"Honestly, I don't think I would be," he declared. "I've looked ahead in it. It seems terribly dry. Do you know," he said, abruptly, "if the law was off I'd go up to Geneva Lake and fish through the ice. Laura, how would you like to go to Florida?"

"Oh, I tell you," she exclaimed. "Let's go up to Geneva Lake over Christmas. We'll open up the house and take some of the servants along and have a house party."

Eventually this was done. The Cresslers and the Gretrys were invited, together with Sheldon Corthell and Landry Court. Page and Aunt Wess' came as a matter of course. Jadwin brought up some of the horses and a couple of sleighs. On Christmas night they had a great tree, and Corthell composed the words and music for a carol which had a great success.

About a week later, two days after New Year's day, when Landry came down from Chicago on the afternoon train, he was full of the tales of a great day on the Board of Trade. Laura, descending to the sitting-room, just before dinner, found a group in front of the fireplace, where the huge logs were hissing and crackling. Her husband and Cressler were there, and Gretry, who had come down on an earlier train. Page sat near at hand, her chin on her palm, listening intently to Landry, who held the centre of the stage for the moment. In a far corner of the room Sheldon Corthell, in a dinner coat and patent-leather pumps, a cigarette between his fingers, read a volume of Italian verse.

"It was the confirmation of the failure of the Argentine crop that did it," Landry was saying; "that and the tremendous foreign demand. She opened steady enough at eighty-three, but just as soon as the gong tapped we began to get it. Buy, buy, buy. Everybody is in it now. The public are speculating. For one fellow who wants to sell there are a dozen buyers. We had one of the hottest times I ever remember in the Pit this morning."

Laura saw Jadwin's eyes snap.

"I told you we'd get this, Sam," he said, nodding to the broker.

"Oh, there's plenty of wheat," answered Gretry, easily. "Wait till we get dollar wheat—if we do—and see it come out. The farmers haven't sold it all yet. There's always an army of ancient hayseeds who have the stuff tucked away—in old stockings, I guess—and who'll dump it on you all right if you pay enough. There's plenty of wheat. I've seen it happen before. Work the price high enough, and, Lord, how they'll scrape the bins to throw it at you! You'd never guess from what out-of-the-way places it would come."

"I tell you, Sam," retorted Jadwin, "the surplus of wheat is going out of the country—and it's going fast. And some of these shorts will have to hustle lively for it pretty soon."

"The Crookes gang, though," observed Landry, "seem pretty confident the market will break. I'm sure they were selling short this morning."

"The idea," exclaimed Jadwin, incredulously, "the idea of selling short in face of this Argentine collapse, and all this Bull news from Europe!"

"Oh, there are plenty of shorts," urged Gretry. "Plenty of them."

Try as he would, the echoes of the rumbling of the Pit reached Jadwin at every hour of the day and night. The maelstrom there at the foot of La Salle Street was swirling now with a mightier rush than for years past. Thundering, its vortex smoking, it sent its whirling far out over the country, from ocean to ocean, sweeping the wheat into its currents, sucking it in, and spewing it out again in the gigantic pulses of its ebb and flow.

And he, Jadwin, who knew its every eddy, who could foretell its every ripple, was out of it, out of it. Inactive, he sat there idle while the clamour of the Pit swelled daily louder, and while other men, men of little minds, of narrow imaginations, perversely, blindly shut their eyes to the swelling of its waters, neglecting the chances which he would have known how to use with such large, such vast results. That mysterious event which long ago he felt was preparing, was not yet consummated. The great Fact, the great Result which was at last to issue forth from all this turmoil was not yet achieved. Would it refuse to come until a master hand, all powerful, all daring, gripped the levers of the sluice gates that controlled the crashing waters of the Pit? He did not know. Was it the moment for a chief?

Was this upheaval a revolution that called aloud for its Napoleon? Would another, not himself, at last, seeing where so many shut their eyes, step into the place of high command?

Jadwin chafed and fretted in his inaction. As the time when the house party should break up drew to its close, his impatience harried him like a gadfly. He took long drives over the lonely country roads, or tramped the hills or the frozen lake, thoughtful, preoccupied. He still held his seat upon the Board of Trade. He still retained his agents in Europe. Each morning brought him fresh despatches, each evening's paper confirmed his forecasts.

"Oh, I'm out of it for good and all," he assured his wife. "But I know the man who could take up the whole jing-bang of that Crookes crowd in one hand and"—his large fist swiftly knotted as he spoke the words—"scrunch it up like an eggshell, by George."

Landry Court often entertained Page with accounts of the doings on the Board of Trade, and about a fortnight after the Jadwins had returned to their city home he called on her one evening and brought two or three of the morning's papers.

"Have you seen this?" he asked. She shook her head.

"Well," he said, compressing his lips, and narrowing his eyes, "let me tell you, we are having pretty—lively—times—down there on the Board these days. The whole country is talking about it."

He read her certain extracts from the newspapers he had brought. The first article stated that recently a new factor had appeared in the Chicago wheat market. A "Bull" clique had evidently been formed, presumably of New York capitalists, who were ousting the Crookes crowd and were rapidly coming into control of the market. In consequence of this the price of wheat was again mounting.

Another paper spoke of a combine of St. Louis firms who were advancing prices, bulling the market. Still a third said, at the beginning of a half-column article:

"It is now universally conceded that an Unknown Bull has invaded the Chicago wheat market since the beginning of the month, and is now dominating the entire situation. The Bears profess to have no fear of this mysterious enemy, but it is a matter of fact that a multitude of shorts were driven ignominiously to cover on Tuesday last, when the Great Bull gathered in a long line of two million bushels in a single half hour. Scalping and eighth-chasing are almost entirely at an end, the smaller traders dreading to be caught on the horns of the Unknown. The new operator's identity has been carefully concealed, but whoever he is, he is a wonderful trader and is possessed of consummate nerve. It has been rumoured that he hails from New York, and is but one of a large clique who are inaugurating a Bull campaign. But our New York advices are emphatic in denying this report, and we can safely state that the Unknown Bull is a native, and a present inhabitant of the Windy City."

Page looked up at Landry quickly, and he returned her glance without speaking. There was a moment's silence.

"I guess," Landry hazarded, lowering his voice, "I guess we're both thinking of the same thing."

"But I know he told my sister that he was going to stop all that kind of thing. What do you think?"

"I hadn't ought to think anything."

"Say 'shouldn't think,' Landry."

"Shouldn't think, then, anything about it. My business is to execute Mr. Gretry's orders."

"Well, I know this," said Page, "that Mr. Jadwin is down town all day again. You know he stayed away for a while."

"Oh, that may be his real estate business that keeps him down town so much," replied Landry.

"Laura is terribly distressed," Page went on. "I can see that. They used to spend all their evenings together in the library, and Laura would read aloud to him. But now he comes home so tired that sometimes he goes to bed at nine o'clock, and Laura sits there alone reading till eleven and twelve. But she's afraid, too, of the effect upon him. He's getting so absorbed. He don't care for literature now as he did once, or was beginning to when Laura used to read to him; and he never thinks of his Sunday-school. And then, too, if you're to believe Mr. Cressler, there's a chance that he may lose if he is speculating again."

But Landry stoutly protested:

"Well, don't think for one moment that Mr. Curtis Jadwin is going to let any one get the better of him. There's no man—no, nor gang of men—could down him. He's head and shoulders above the biggest of them down there. I tell you he's Napoleonic. Yes, sir, that's what he is, Napoleonic, to say the least. Page," he declared, solemnly, "he's the greatest man I've ever known."

Very soon after this it was no longer a secret to Laura Jadwin that her husband had gone back to the wheat market, and that, too, with such impetuosity, such eagerness, that his rush had carried him to the very heart's heart of the turmoil.

He was now deeply involved; his influence began to be felt. Not an important move on the part of the "Unknown Bull," the nameless mysterious stranger that was not duly noted and discussed by the entire world of La Salle Street.

Almost his very first move, carefully guarded, executed with profoundest secrecy, had been to replace the five million bushels sold to Liverpool by five million more of the May option. This was in January, and all through February and all through the first days of March, while the cry for American wheat rose, insistent and vehement, from fifty cities and centres of eastern Europe; while the jam of men in the Wheat Pit grew ever more frantic, ever more furious, and while the impassive hand on the great dial over the floor of the Board rose, resistless, till it stood at eighty-seven, he bought steadily, gathering in the wheat, calling for it, welcoming it, receiving full in the face and with opened arms the cataract that poured in upon the Pit from Iowa and Nebraska, Minnesota and Dakota, from the dwindling bins of Illinois and the fast-emptying elevators of Kansas and Missouri.

Then, squarely in the midst of the commotion, at a time when Curtis Jadwin owned some ten million bushels of May wheat, fell the Government report on the visible supply.

"Well," said Jadwin, "what do you think of it?"

He and Gretry were in the broker's private room in the offices of Gretry, Converse & Co. They were studying the report of the Government as to the supply of wheat, which had just been published in the editions of the evening papers. It was very late in the afternoon of a lugubrious March day. Long since the gas and electricity had been lighted in the office, while in the streets the lamps at the corners were reflected downward in long shafts of light upon the drenched pavements. From the windows of the room one could see directly up La Salle Street. The cable cars, as they made the turn into or out of the street at the corner of Monroe, threw momentary glares of red and green lights across the mists of rain, and filled the air continually with the jangle of their bells. Further on one caught a glimpse of the Court House rising from the pavement like a rain-washed cliff of black basalt, picked out with winking lights, and beyond that, at the extreme end of the vista, the girders and cables of the La Salle Street bridge.

The sidewalks on either hand were encumbered with the "six o'clock crowd" that poured out incessantly from the street entrances of the office buildings. It was a crowd almost entirely of men, and they moved only in one direction, buttoned to the chin in rain coats, their umbrellas bobbing, their feet scuffling through the little pools of wet in the depressions of the sidewalk. They streamed from out the brokers' offices and commission houses on either side of La Salle Street, continually, unendingly, moving with the dragging sluggishness of the fatigue of a hard day's work. Under that grey sky and blurring veil of rain they lost their individualities, they became conglomerate—a mass, slow-moving, black. All day long the torrent had seethed and thundered through the street—the torrent that swirled out and back from that vast Pit of roaring within the Board of Trade. Now the Pit was stilled, the sluice gates of the torrent locked, and from out the thousands of offices, from out the Board of Trade itself, flowed the black and sluggish lees, the lifeless dregs that filtered back to their level for a few hours, stagnation, till in the morning, the whirlpool revolving once more, should again suck them back into its vortex.

The rain fell uninterruptedly. There was no wind. The cable cars jolted and jostled over the tracks with a strident whir of vibrating window glass. In the street, immediately in front of the entrance to the Board of Trade, a group of pigeons, garnet-eyed, trim, with coral-coloured feet and iridescent breasts, strutted and fluttered, pecking at the handfuls of wheat that a porter threw them from the windows of the floor of the Board.

"Well," repeated Jadwin, shifting with a movement of his lips his unlit cigar to the other corner of his mouth, "well, what do you think of it?"

The broker, intent upon the figures and statistics, replied only by an indefinite movement of the head.

"Why, Sam," observed Jadwin, looking up from the paper, "there's less than a hundred million bushels in the farmers' hands.... That's awfully small. Sam, that's awfully small."

"It ain't, as you might say, colossal," admitted Gretry.

There was a long silence while the two men studied the report still further. Gretry took a pamphlet of statistics from a pigeon-hole of his desk, and compared certain figures with those mentioned in the report.

Outside the rain swept against the windows with the subdued rustle of silk. A newsboy raised a Gregorian chant as he went down the street.

"By George, Sam," Jadwin said again, "do you know that a whole pile of that wheat has got to go to Europe before July? How have the shipments been?"

"About five millions a week."

"Why, think of that, twenty millions a month, and it's—let's see, April, May, June, July—four months before a new crop. Eighty million bushels will go out of the country in the next four months—eighty million out of less than a hundred millions."

"Looks that way," answered Gretry.

"Here," said Jadwin, "let's get some figures. Let's get a squint on the whole situation. Got a 'Price Current' here? Let's find out what the stocks are in Chicago. I don't believe the elevators are exactly bursting, and, say," he called after the broker, who had started for the front office, "say, find out about the primary receipts, and the Paris and Liverpool stocks. Bet you what you like that Paris and Liverpool together couldn't show ten million to save their necks."

In a few moments Gretry was back again, his hands full of pamphlets and "trade" journals.

By now the offices were quite deserted. The last clerk had gone home. Without, the neighbourhood was emptying rapidly. Only a few stragglers hurried over the glistening sidewalks; only a few lights yet remained in the facades of the tall, grey office buildings. And in the widening silence the cooing of the pigeons on the ledges and window-sills of the Board of Trade Building made itself heard with increasing distinctness.

Before Gretry's desk the two men leaned over the litter of papers. The broker's pencil was in his hand and from time to time he figured rapidly on a sheet of note paper.

"And," observed Jadwin after a while, "and you see how the millers up here in the Northwest have been grinding up all the grain in sight. Do you see that?"

"Yes," said Gretry, then he added, "navigation will be open in another month up there in the straits."

"That's so, too," exclaimed Jadwin, "and what wheat there is here will be moving out. I'd forgotten that point. Ain't you glad you aren't short of wheat these days?"

"There's plenty of fellows that are, though," returned Gretry. "I've got a lot of short wheat on my books—a lot of it."

All at once as Gretry spoke Jadwin started, and looked at him with a curious glance.

"You have, hey?" he said. "There are a lot of fellows who have sold short?"

"Oh, yes, some of Crookes' followers—yes, quite a lot of them."

Jadwin was silent a moment, tugging at his mustache. Then suddenly he leaned forward, his finger almost in Gretry's face.

"Why, look here," he cried. "Don't you see? Don't you see?"

"See what?" demanded the broker, puzzled at the other's vehemence.

Jadwin loosened his collar with a forefinger.

"Great Scott! I'll choke in a minute. See what? Why, I own ten million bushels of this wheat already, and Europe will take eighty million out of the country. Why, there ain't going to be any wheat left in Chicago by May! If I get in now and buy a long line of cash wheat, where are all these fellows who've sold short going to get it to deliver to me? Say, where are they going to get it? Come on now, tell me, where are they going to get it?"

Gretry laid down his pencil and stared at Jadwin, looked long at the papers on his desk, consulted his pencilled memoranda, then thrust his hands deep into his pockets, with a long breath. Bewildered, and as if stupefied, he gazed again into Jadwin's face.

"My God!" he murmured at last.

"Well, where are they going to get it?" Jadwin cried once more, his face suddenly scarlet.

"J.," faltered the broker, "J., I—I'm damned if I know."

And then, all in the same moment, the two men were on their feet. The event which all those past eleven months had been preparing was suddenly consummated, suddenly stood revealed, as though a veil had been ripped asunder, as though an explosion had crashed through the air upon them, deafening, blinding.

Jadwin sprang forward, gripping the broker by the shoulder.

"Sam," he shouted, "do you know—great God!—do you know what this means? Sam, we can corner the market!"

VIII

On that particular morning in April, the trading around the Wheat Pit on the floor of the Chicago Board of Trade began practically a full five minutes ahead of the stroke of the gong; and the throng of brokers and clerks that surged in and about the Pit itself was so great that it overflowed and spread out over the floor between the wheat and corn pits, ousting the traders in oats from their traditional ground. The market had closed the day before with May wheat at ninety-eight and five-eighths, and the Bulls had prophesied and promised that the magic legend "Dollar wheat" would be on the Western Union wires before another twenty-four hours.

The indications pointed to a lively morning's work. Never for an instant during the past six weeks had the trading sagged or languished. The air of the Pit was surcharged with a veritable electricity; it had the effervescence of champagne, or of a mountain-top at sunrise. It was buoyant, thrilling.

The "Unknown Bull" was to all appearance still in control; the whole market hung upon his horns; and from time to time, one felt the sudden upward thrust, powerful, tremendous, as he flung the wheat up another notch. The "tailers"—the little Bulls—were radiant. In the dark, they hung hard by their unseen and mysterious friend who daily, weekly, was making them richer. The Bears were scarcely visible. The Great Bull in a single superb rush had driven them nearly out of the Pit. Growling, grumbling they had retreated, and only at distance dared so much as to bare a claw. Just the formidable lowering of the Great Bull's frontlet sufficed, so it seemed, to check their every move of aggression or resistance. And all the while, Liverpool, Paris, Odessa, and Buda-Pesth clamoured ever louder and louder for the grain that meant food to the crowded streets and barren farms of Europe.

A few moments before the opening Charles Cressler was in the public room, in the southeast corner of the building, where smoking was allowed, finishing his morning's cigar. But as he heard the distant striking of the gong, and the roar of the Pit as it began to get under way, with a prolonged rumbling trepidation like the advancing of a great flood, he threw his cigar away and stepped out from the public room to the main floor, going on towards the front windows. At the sample tables he filled his pockets with wheat, and once at the windows raised the sash and spread the pigeons' breakfast on the granite ledge.

While he was watching the confused fluttering of flashing wings, that on the instant filled the air in front of the window, he was all at once surprised to hear a voice at his elbow, wishing him good morning.

"Seem to know you, don't they?"

Cressler turned about.

"Oh," he said. "Hullo, hullo—yes, they know me all right. Especially that red and white hen. She's got a lame wing since yesterday, and if I don't watch, the others would drive her off. The pouter brute yonder, for instance. He's a regular pirate. Wants all the wheat himself. Don't ever seem to get enough."

"Well," observed the newcomer, laconically, "there are others."

The man who spoke was about forty years of age. His name was Calvin Hardy Crookes. He was very small and very slim. His hair was yet dark, and his face—smooth-shaven and triangulated in shape, like a cat's—was dark as well. The eyebrows were thin and black, and the lips too were thin and were puckered a little, like the mouth of a tight-shut sack. The face was secretive, impassive, and cold.

The man himself was dressed like a dandy. His coat and trousers were of the very newest fashion. He wore a white waistcoat, drab gaiters, a gold watch and chain, a jewelled scarf pin, and a seal ring. From the top pocket of his coat protruded the finger tips of a pair of unworn red gloves.

"Yes," continued Crookes, unfolding a brand-new pocket handkerchief as he spoke. "There are others—who never know when they've got enough wheat."

"Oh, you mean the 'Unknown Bull.'"

"I mean the unknown damned fool," returned Crookes placidly.

There was not a trace of the snob about Charles Cressler. No one could be more democratic. But at the same time, as this interview proceeded, he could not fight down nor altogether ignore a certain qualm of gratified vanity. Had the matter risen to the realm of his consciousness, he would have hated himself for this. But it went no further than a vaguely felt increase of self-esteem. He seemed to feel more important in his own eyes; he would have liked to have his friends see him just now talking with this man. "Crookes was saying to-day—" he would observe when next he met an acquaintance. For C. H. Crookes was conceded to be the "biggest man" in La Salle Street. Not even the growing importance of the new and mysterious Bull could quite make the market forget the Great Bear. Inactive during all this trampling and goring in the Pit, there were yet those who, even as they strove against the Bull, cast uneasy glances over their shoulders, wondering why the Bear did not come to the help of his own.

"Well, yes," admitted Cressler, combing his short beard, "yes, he is a fool."

The contrast between the two men was extreme. Each was precisely what the other was not. The one, long, angular, loose-jointed; the other, tight, trim, small, and compact. The one osseous, the other sleek; the one stoop-shouldered, the other erect as a corporal of infantry.

But as Cressler was about to continue Crookes put his chin in the air.

"Hark!" he said. "What's that?"

For from the direction of the Wheat Pit had come a sudden and vehement renewal of tumult. The traders as one man were roaring in chorus. There were cheers; hats went up into the air. On the floor by the lowest step two brokers, their hands trumpet-wise to their mouths, shouted at top voice to certain friends at a distance, while above them, on the topmost step of the Pit, a half-dozen others, their arms at fullest stretch, threw the hand signals that interpreted the fluctuations in the price, to their associates in the various parts of the building. Again and again the cheers rose, violent hip-hip-hurrahs and tigers, while from all corners and parts of the floor men and boys came scurrying up. Visitors in the gallery leaned eagerly upon the railing. Over in the provision pit, trading ceased for the moment, and all heads were turned towards the commotion of the wheat traders.

"Ah," commented Crookes, "they did get it there at last."

For the hand on the dial had suddenly jumped another degree, and not a messenger boy, not a porter not a janitor, none whose work or life brought him in touch with the Board of Trade, that did not feel the thrill. The news flashed out to the world on a hundred telegraph wires; it was called to a hundred offices across the telephone lines. From every doorway, even, as it seemed, from every window of the building, spreading thence all over the city, the State, the Northwest, the entire nation, sped the magic words, "Dollar wheat."

Crookes turned to Cressler.

"Can you lunch with me to-day—at Kinsley's? I'd like to have a talk with you."

And as soon as Cressler had accepted the invitation, Crookes, with a succinct nod, turned upon his heel and walked away.

At Kinsley's that day, in a private room on the second floor, Cressler met not only Crookes, but his associate Sweeny, and another gentleman by the name of Freye, the latter one of his oldest and best-liked friends.

Sweeny was an Irishman, florid, flamboyant, talkative, who spoke with a faint brogue, and who tagged every observation, argument, or remark with the phrase, "Do you understand me, gen'lemen?" Freye, a German-American, was a quiet fellow, very handsome, with black side whiskers and a humourous, twinkling eye. The three were members of the Board of Trade, and were always associated with the Bear forces. Indeed, they could be said to be its leaders. Between them, as Cressler afterwards was accustomed to say, "They could have bought pretty much all of the West Side."

And during the course of the luncheon these three, with a simplicity and a directness that for the moment left Cressler breathless, announced that they were preparing to drive the Unknown Bull out of the Pit, and asked him to become one of the clique.

Crookes, whom Cressler intuitively singled out as the leader, did not so much as open his mouth till Sweeny had talked himself breathless, and all the preliminaries were out of the way. Then he remarked, his eye as lifeless as the eye of a fish, his voice as expressionless as the voice of Fate itself:

"I don't know who the big Bull is, and I don't care a curse. But he don't suit my book. I want him out of the market. We've let him have his way now for three or four months. We figured we'd let him run to the dollar mark. The May option closed this morning at a dollar and an eighth.... Now we take hold.

"But," Cressler hastened to object, "you forget—I'm not a speculator."

Freye smiled, and tapped his friend on the arm.

"I guess, Charlie," he said, "that there won't be much speculating about this."

"Why, gen'lemen," cried Sweeny, brandishing a fork, "we're going to sell him right out o' the market, so we are. Simply flood out the son-of-a-gun—you understand me, gen'lemen?"

Cressler shook his head.

"No," he answered. "No, you must count me out. I quit speculating years ago. And, besides, to sell short on this kind of market—I don't need to tell you what you risk."

"Risk hell!" muttered Crookes.

"Well, now, I'll explain to you, Charlie," began Freye.

The other two withdrew a little from the conversation. Crookes, as ever monosyllabic, took himself on in a little while, and Sweeny, his chair tipped back against the wall, his hands clasped behind his head, listened to Freye explaining to Cressler the plans of the proposed clique and the lines of their attack.

He talked for nearly an hour and a half, at the end of which time the lunch table was one litter of papers—letters, contracts, warehouse receipts, tabulated statistics, and the like.

"Well," said Freye, at length, "well, Charlie, do you see the game? What do you think of it?"

"It's about as ingenious a scheme as I ever heard of, Billy," answered Cressler. "You can't lose, with Crookes back of it."

"Well, then, we can count you in, hey?"

"Count nothing," declared Cressler, stoutly. "I don't speculate."

"But have you thought of this?" urged Freye, and went over the entire proposition, from a fresh point of view, winding up with the exclamation: "Why, Charlie, we're going to make our everlasting fortunes."

"I don't want any everlasting fortune, Billy Freye," protested Cressler. "Look here, Billy. You must remember I'm a pretty old cock. You boys are all youngsters. I've got a little money left and a little business, and I want to grow old quiet-like. I had my fling, you know, when you boys were in knickerbockers. Now you let me keep out of all this. You get some one else."

"No, we'll be jiggered if we do," exclaimed Sweeny. "Say, are ye scared we can't buy that trade journal? Why, we have it in our pocket, so we have. D'ye think Crookes, now, couldn't make Bear sentiment with the public, with just the lift o' one forefinger? Why, he owns most of the commercial columns of the dailies already. D'ye think he couldn't swamp that market with sellin' orders in the shorter end o' two days? D'ye think we won't all hold together, now? Is that the bug in the butter? Sure, now, listen. Let me tell you—"

"You can't tell me anything about this scheme that you've not told me before," declared Cressler. "You'll win, of course. Crookes & Co. are like Rothschild—earthquakes couldn't budge 'em. But I promised myself years ago to keep out of the speculative market, and I mean to stick by it."

"Oh, get on with you, Charlie," said Freye, good-humouredly, "you're scared."

"Of what," asked Cressler, "speculating? You bet I am, and when you're as old as I am, and have been through three panics, and have known what it meant to have a corner bust under you, you'll be scared of speculating too."

"But suppose we can prove to you," said Sweeny, all at once, "that we're not speculating—that the other fellow, this fool Bull is doing the speculating?"

"I'll go into anything in the way of legitimate trading," answered Cressler, getting up from the table. "You convince me that your clique is not a speculative clique, and I'll come in. But I don't see how your deal can be anything else."

"Will you meet us here to-morrow?" asked Sweeny, as they got into their overcoats.

"It won't do you any good," persisted Cressler.

"Well, will you meet us just the same?" the other insisted. And in the end Cressler accepted.

On the steps of the restaurant they parted, and the two leaders watched Cressler's broad, stooped shoulders disappear down the street.

"He's as good as in already," Sweeny declared. "I'll fix him to-morrow. Once a speculator, always a speculator. He was the cock of the cow-yard in his day, and the thing is in the blood. He gave himself clean, clean away when he let out he was afraid o' speculating. You can't be afraid of anything that ain't got a hold on you. Y' understand me now?"

"Well," observed Freye, "we've got to get him in."

"Talk to me about that now," Sweeny answered. "I'm new to some parts o' this scheme o' yours yet. Why is Crookes so keen on having him in? I'm not so keen. We could get along without him. He ain't so god-awful rich, y' know."

"No, but he's a solid, conservative cash grain man," answered Freye, "who hasn't been associated with speculating for years. Crookes has got to have that element in the clique before we can approach Stires & Co. We may have to get a pile of money from them, and they're apt to be scary and cautious. Cressler being in, do you see, gives the clique a substantial, conservative character. You let Crookes manage it. He knows his business."

"Say," exclaimed Sweeny, an idea occurring to him, "I thought Crookes was going to put us wise to-day. He must know by now who the Big Bull is."

"No doubt he does know," answered the other. "He'll tell us when he's ready. But I think I could copper the individual. There was a great big jag of wheat sold to Liverpool a little while ago through Gretry, Converse & Co., who've been acting for Curtis Jadwin for a good many years."

"Oh, Jadwin, hey? Hi! we're after big game now, I'm thinking."

"But look here," warned Freye. "Here's a point. Cressler is not to know by the longest kind of chalk; anyhow not until he's so far in, he can't pull out. He and Jadwin are good friends, I'm told. Hello, it's raining a little. Well, I've got to be moving. See you at lunch to-morrow."

As Cressler turned into La Salle Street the light sprinkle of rain suddenly swelled to a deluge, and he had barely time to dodge into the portico of the Illinois Trust to escape a drenching. All the passers-by close at hand were making for the same shelter, and among these Cressler was surprised to see Curtis Jadwin, who came running up the narrow lane from the cafe entrance of the Grand Pacific Hotel.

"Hello! Hello, J.," he cried, when his friend came panting up the steps, "as the whale said to Jonah, 'Come in out of the wet.'"

The two friends stood a moment under the portico, their coat collars turned up, watching the scurrying in the street.

"Well," said Cressler, at last, "I see we got 'dollar wheat' this morning."

"Yes," answered Jadwin, nodding, "'dollar wheat.'"

"I suppose," went on Cressler, "I suppose you are sorry, now that you're not in it any more."

"Oh, no," replied Jadwin, nibbling off the end of a cigar. "No, I'm—I'm just as well out of it."

"And it's for good and all this time, eh?"

"For good and all."

"Well," commented Cressler, "some one else has begun where you left off, I guess. This Unknown Bull, I mean. All the boys are trying to find out who he is. Crookes, though, was saying to me—Cal Crookes, you know—he was saying he didn't care who he was. Crookes is out of the market, too, I understand—and means to keep out, he says, till the Big Bull gets tired. Wonder who the Big Bull is."

"Oh, there isn't any Big Bull," blustered Jadwin. "There's simply a lot of heavy buying, or maybe there might be a ring of New York men operating through Gretry. I don't know; and I guess I'm like Crookes, I don't care—now that I'm out of the game. Real estate is too lively now to think of anything else; keeps me on the keen jump early and late. I tell you what, Charlie, this city isn't half grown yet. And do you know, I've noticed another thing—cities grow to the westward. I've got a building and loan association going, out in the suburbs on the West Side, that's a dandy. Well, looks as though the rain had stopped. Remember me to madam. So long, Charlie."

On leaving Cressler Jadwin went on to his offices in The Rookery, close at hand. But he had no more than settled himself at his desk, when he was called up on his telephone.

"Hello!" said a small, dry transformation of Gretry's voice. "Hello, is that you, J.? Well, in the matter of that cash wheat in Duluth, I've bought that for you."

"All right," answered Jadwin, then he added, "I guess we had better have a long talk now."

"I was going to propose that," answered the broker. "Meet me this evening at seven at the Grand Pacific. It's just as well that we're not seen together nowadays. Don't ask for me. Go right into the smoking-room. I'll be there. And, by the way, I shall expect a reply from Minneapolis about half-past five this afternoon. I would like to be able to get at you at once when that comes in. Can you wait down for that?"

"Well, I was going home," objected Jadwin. "I wasn't home to dinner last night, and Mrs. Jadwin—"

"This is pretty important, you know," warned the broker. "And if I call you up on your residence telephone, there's always the chance of somebody cutting in and overhearing us."

"Oh, very well, then," assented Jadwin. "I'll call it a day. I'll get home for luncheon to-morrow. It can't be helped. By the way, I met Cressler this afternoon, Sam, and he seemed sort of suspicious of things, to me—as though he had an inkling."

"Better hang up," came back the broker's voice. "Better hang up, J. There's big risk telephoning like this. I'll see you to-night. Good-by."

And so it was that about half an hour later Laura was called to the telephone in the library.

"Oh, not coming home at all to-night?" she cried blankly in response to Jadwin's message.

"It's just impossible, old girl," he answered.

"But why?" she insisted.

"Oh, business; this building and loan association of mine."

"Oh, I know it can't be that. Why don't you let Mr. Gretry manage your—"

But at this point Jadwin, the warning of Gretry still fresh in his mind, interrupted quickly:

"I must hang up now, Laura. Good-by. I'll see you to-morrow noon and explain it all to you. Good-by.... Laura.... Hello! ... Are you there yet? ... Hello, hello!"

But Jadwin had heard in the receiver the rattle and click as of a tiny door closing. The receiver was silent and dead; and he knew that his wife, disappointed and angry, had "hung up" without saying good-by.

The days passed. Soon another week had gone by. The wheat market steadied down after the dollar mark was reached, and for a few days a calmer period intervened. Down beneath the surface, below the ebb and flow of the currents, the great forces were silently at work reshaping the "situation." Millions of dollars were beginning to be set in motion to govern the millions of bushels of wheat. At the end of the third week of the month Freye reported to Crookes that Cressler was "in," and promptly negotiations were opened between the clique and the great banking house of the Stires. But meanwhile Jadwin and Gretry, foreseeing no opposition, realising the incalculable advantage that their knowledge of the possibility of a "corner" gave them, were, quietly enough, gathering in the grain. As early as the end of March Jadwin, as incidental to his contemplated corner of May wheat, had bought up a full half of the small supply of cash wheat in Duluth, Chicago, Liverpool and Paris—some twenty million bushels; and against this had sold short an equal amount of the July option. Having the actual wheat in hand he could not lose. If wheat went up, his twenty million bushels were all the more valuable; if it went down, he covered his short sales at a profit. And all the while, steadily, persistently, he bought May wheat, till Gretry's book showed him to be possessed of over twenty million bushels of the grain deliverable for that month.

But all this took not only his every minute of time, but his every thought, his every consideration. He who had only so short a while before considered the amount of five million bushels burdensome, demanding careful attention, was now called upon to watch, govern, and control the tremendous forces latent in a line of forty million. At times he remembered the Curtis Jadwin of the spring before his marriage, the Curtis Jadwin who had sold a pitiful million on the strength of the news of the French import duty, and had considered the deal "big." Well, he was a different man since that time. Then he had been suspicious of speculation, had feared it even. Now he had discovered that there were in him powers, capabilities, and a breadth of grasp hitherto unsuspected. He could control the Chicago wheat market, and the man who could do that might well call himself "great," without presumption. He knew that he overtopped them all—Gretry, the Crookes gang, the arrogant, sneering Bears, all the men of the world of the Board of Trade. He was stronger, bigger, shrewder than them all. A few days now would show, when they would all wake to the fact that wheat, which they had promised to deliver before they had it in hand, was not to be got except from him—and at whatever price he chose to impose. He could exact from them a hundred dollars a bushel if he chose, and they must pay him the price or become bankrupts.

By now his mind was upon this one great fact—May Wheat—continually. It was with him the instant he woke in the morning. It kept him company during his hasty breakfast; in the rhythm of his horses' hoofs, as the team carried him down town he heard, "Wheat—wheat—wheat, wheat—wheat—wheat." No sooner did he enter La Salle Street, than the roar of traffic came to his ears as the roar of the torrent of wheat which drove through Chicago from the Western farms to the mills and bakeshops of Europe. There at the foot of the street the torrent swirled once upon itself, forty million strong, in the eddy which he told himself he mastered. The afternoon waned, night came on. The day's business was to be gone over; the morrow's campaign was to be planned; little, unexpected side issues, a score of them, a hundred of them, cropped out from hour to hour; new decisions had to be taken each minute. At dinner time he left the office, and his horses carried him home again, while again their hoofs upon the asphalt beat out unceasingly the monotone of the one refrain, "Wheat—wheat—wheat, wheat—wheat—wheat." At dinner table he could not eat. Between each course he found himself going over the day's work, testing it, questioning himself, "Was this rightly done?" "Was that particular decision sound?" "Is there a loophole here?" "Just what was the meaning of that despatch?" After the meal the papers, contracts, statistics and reports which he had brought with him in his Gladstone bag were to be studied. As often as not Gretry called, and the two, shut in the library, talked, discussed, and planned till long after midnight.

Then at last, when he had shut the front door upon his lieutenant and turned to face the empty, silent house, came the moment's reaction. The tired brain flagged and drooped; exhaustion, like a weight of lead, hung upon his heels. But somewhere a hall clock struck, a single, booming note, like a gong—like the signal that would unchain the tempest in the Pit to-morrow morning. Wheat—wheat—wheat, wheat—wheat—wheat! Instantly the jaded senses braced again, instantly the wearied mind sprang to its post. He turned out the lights, he locked the front door. Long since the great house was asleep. In the cold, dim silence of the earliest dawn Curtis Jadwin went to bed, only to lie awake, staring up into the darkness, planning, devising new measures, reviewing the day's doings, while the faint tides of blood behind the eardrums murmured ceaselessly to the overdriven brain, "Wheat—wheat—wheat, wheat—wheat—wheat. Forty million bushels, forty million, forty million."

Whole days now went by when he saw his wife only at breakfast and at dinner. At times she was angry, hurt, and grieved that he should leave her so much alone. But there were moments when she was sorry for him. She seemed to divine that he was not all to blame.

What Laura thought he could only guess. She no longer spoke of his absorption in business. At times he thought he saw reproach and appeal in her dark eyes, at times anger and a pride cruelly wounded. A few months ago this would have touched him. But now he all at once broke out vehemently:

"You think I am wilfully doing this! You don't know, you haven't a guess. I corner the wheat! Great heavens, it is the wheat that has cornered me! The corner made itself. I happened to stand between two sets of circumstances, and they made me do what I've done. I couldn't get out of it now, with all the good will in the world. Go to the theatre to-night with you and the Cresslers? Why, old girl, you might as well ask me to go to Jericho. Let that Mr. Corthell take my place."

And very naturally this is what was done. The artist sent a great bunch of roses to Mrs. Jadwin upon the receipt of her invitation, and after the play had the party to supper in his apartments, that overlooked the Lake Front. Supper over, he escorted her, Mrs. Cressler, and Page back to their respective homes.

By a coincidence that struck them all as very amusing, he was the only man of the party. At the last moment Page had received a telegram from Landry. He was, it appeared, sick, and in bed. The day's work on the Board of Trade had quite used him up for the moment, and his doctor forbade him to stir out of doors. Mrs. Cressler explained that Charlie had something on his mind these days, that was making an old man of him.

"He don't ever talk shop with me," she said. "I'm sure he hasn't been speculating, but he's worried and fidgety to beat all I ever saw, this last week; and now this evening he had to take himself off to meet some customer or other at the Palmer House."

They dropped Mrs. Cressler at the door of her home and then went on to the Jadwins'.

"I remember," said Laura to Corthell, "that once before the three of us came home this way. Remember? It was the night of the opera. That was the night I first met Mr. Jadwin."

"It was the night of the Helmick failure," said Page, seriously, "and the office buildings were all lit up. See," she added, as they drove up to the house, "there's a light in the library, and it must be nearly one o'clock. Mr. Jadwin is up yet."

Laura fell suddenly silent. When was it all going to end, and how? Night after night her husband shut himself thus in the library, and toiled on till early dawn. She enjoyed no companionship with him. Her evenings were long, her time hung with insupportable heaviness upon her hands.

"Shall you be at home?" inquired Corthell, as he held her hand a moment at the door. "Shall you be at home to-morrow evening? May I come and play to you again?"

"Yes, yes," she answered. "Yes, I shall be home. Yes, do come."

Laura's carriage drove the artist back to his apartments. All the way he sat motionless in his place, looking out of the window with unseeing eyes. His cigarette went out. He drew another from his case, but forgot to light it.

Thoughtful and abstracted he slowly mounted the stairway—the elevator having stopped for the night—to his studio, let himself in, and, throwing aside his hat and coat, sat down without lighting the gas in front of the fireplace, where (the weather being even yet sharp) an armful of logs smouldered on the flagstones.

His man, Evans, came from out an inner room to ask if he wanted anything. Corthell got out of his evening coat, and Evans brought him his smoking-jacket and set the little table with its long tin box of cigarettes and ash trays at his elbow. Then he lit the tall lamp of corroded bronze, with its heavy silk shade, that stood on a table in the angle of the room, drew the curtains, put a fresh log upon the fire, held the tiny silver alcohol burner to Corthell while the latter lighted a fresh cigarette, and then with a murmured "Good-night, sir," went out, closing the door with the precaution of a depredator.

This suite of rooms, facing the Lake Front, was what Corthell called "home," Whenever he went away, he left it exactly as it was, in the charge of the faithful Evans; and no mater how long he was absent, he never returned thither without a sense of welcome and relief. Even now, perplexed as he was, he was conscious of a feeling of comfort and pleasure as he settled himself in his chair.

The lamp threw a dull illumination about the room. It was a picturesque apartment, carefully planned. Not an object that had not been chosen with care and the utmost discrimination. The walls had been treated with copper leaf till they produced a sombre, iridescent effect of green and faint gold, that suggested the depth of a forest glade shot through with the sunset. Shelves bearing eighteenth-century books in seal brown tree calf—Addison, the "Spectator," Junius and Racine, Rochefoucauld and Pascal hung against it here and there. On every hand the eye rested upon some small masterpiece of art or workmanship. Now it was an antique portrait bust of the days of decadent Rome, black marble with a bronze tiara; now a framed page of a fourteenth-century version of "Li Quatres Filz d'Aymon," with an illuminated letter of miraculous workmanship; or a Renaissance gonfalon of silk once white but now brown with age, yet in the centre blazing with the escutcheon and quarterings of a dead queen. Between the windows stood an ivory statuette of the "Venus of the Heel," done in the days of the magnificent Lorenzo. An original Cazin, and a chalk drawing by Baudry hung against the wall close by together with a bronze tablet by Saint Gaudens; while across the entire end of the room opposite the fireplace, worked in the tapestry of the best period of the northern French school, Halcyone, her arms already blossoming into wings, hovered over the dead body of Ceyx, his long hair streaming like seaweed in the blue waters of the AEgean.

For a long time Corthell sat motionless, looking into the fire. In an adjoining room a clock chimed the half hour of one, and the artist stirred, passing his long fingers across his eyes.

After a long while he rose, and going to the fireplace, leaned an arm against the overhanging shelf, and resting his forehead against it, remained in that position, looking down at the smouldering logs.

"She is unhappy," he murmured at length. "It is not difficult to see that.... Unhappy and lonely. Oh, fool, fool to have left her when you might have stayed! Oh, fool, fool, not to find the strength to leave her now when you should not remain!"

The following evening Corthell called upon Mrs. Jadwin. She was alone, as he usually found her. He had brought a book of poems with him, and instead of passing the evening in the art gallery, as they had planned, he read aloud to her from Rossetti. Nothing could have been more conventional than their conversation, nothing more impersonal. But on his way home one feature of their talk suddenly occurred to him. It struck him as significant; but of what he did not care to put into words. Neither he nor Laura had once spoken of Jadwin throughout the entire evening.

Little by little the companionship grew. Corthell shut his eyes, his ears. The thought of Laura, the recollection of their last evening together, the anticipation of the next meeting filled all his waking hours. He refused to think; he resigned himself to the drift of the current. Jadwin he rarely saw. But on those few occasions when he and Laura's husband met, he could detect no lack of cordiality in the other's greeting. Once even Jadwin had remarked:

"I'm very glad you have come to see Mrs. Jadwin, Corthell. I have to be away so much these days, I'm afraid she would be lonesome if it wasn't for some one like you to drop in now and then and talk art to her."

By slow degrees the companionship trended toward intimacy. At the various theatres and concerts he was her escort. He called upon her two or three times each week. At his studio entertainments Laura was always present. How—Corthell asked himself—did she regard the affair? She gave him no sign; she never intimated that his presence was otherwise than agreeable. Was this tacit acquiescence of hers an encouragement? Was she willing to afficher herself, as a married woman, with a cavalier? Her married life was intolerable, he was sure of that; her husband uncongenial. He told himself that she detested him.

Once, however, this belief was rather shocked by an unexpected and (to him) an inconsistent reaction on Laura's part. She had made an engagement with him to spend an afternoon in the Art Institute, looking over certain newly acquired canvases. But upon calling for her an hour after luncheon he was informed that Mrs. Jadwin was not at home. When next she saw him she told him that she had spent the entire day with her husband. They had taken an early train and had gone up to Geneva Lake to look over their country house, and to prepare for its opening, later on in the spring. They had taken the decision so unexpectedly that she had no time to tell him of the change in her plans. Corthell wondered if she had—as a matter of fact—forgotten all about her appointment with him. He never quite understood the incident, and afterwards asked himself whether or no he could be so sure, after all, of the estrangement between the husband and wife. He guessed it to be possible that on this occasion Jadwin had suddenly decided to give himself a holiday, and that Laura had been quick to take advantage of it. Was it true, then, that Jadwin had but to speak the word to have Laura forget all else? Was it true that the mere nod of his head was enough to call her back to him? Corthell was puzzled. He would not admit this to be true. She was, he was persuaded, a woman of more spirit, of more pride than this would seem to indicate. Corthell ended by believing that Jadwin had, in some way, coerced her; though he fancied that for the few days immediately following the excursion Laura had never been gayer, more alert, more radiant.

But the days went on, and it was easy to see that his business kept Jadwin more and more from his wife. Often now, Corthell knew, he passed the night down town, and upon those occasions when he managed to get home after the day's work, he was exhausted, worn out, and went to bed almost immediately after dinner. More than ever now the artist and Mrs. Jadwin were thrown together.

On a certain Sunday evening, the first really hot day of the year, Laura and Page went over to spend an hour with the Cresslers, and—as they were all wont to do in the old days before Laura's marriage—the party "sat out on the front stoop." For a wonder, Jadwin was able to be present. Laura had prevailed upon him to give her this evening and the evening of the following Wednesday—on which latter occasion she had planned that they were to take a long drive in the park in the buggy, just the two of them, as it had been in the days of their courtship.

Corthell came to the Cresslers quite as a matter of course. He had dined with the Jadwins at the great North Avenue house and afterwards the three, preferring to walk, had come down to the Cresslers on foot.

But evidently the artist was to see but little of Laura Jadwin that evening. She contrived to keep by her husband continually. She even managed to get him away from the others, and the two, leaving the rest upon the steps, sat in the parlour of the Cresslers' house, talking.

By and by Laura, full of her projects, exclaimed:

"Where shall we go? I thought, perhaps, we would not have dinner at home, but you could come back to the house just a little—a little bit—early, and you could drive me out to the restaurant there in the park, and we could have dinner there, just as though we weren't married just as though we were sweethearts again. Oh, I do hope the weather will be fine."

"Oh," answered Jadwin, "you mean Wednesday evening. Dear old girl, honestly, I—I don't believe I can make it after all. You see, Wednesday—"

Laura sat suddenly erect.

"But you said," she began, her voice faltering a little, "you said—"

"Honey, I know I did, but you must let me off this time again."

She did not answer. It was too dark for him to see her face; but, uneasy at her silence, he began an elaborate explanation. Laura, however, interrupted. Calmly enough, she said:

"Oh, that's all right. No, no, I don't mind. Of course, if you are busy."

"Well, you see, don't you, old girl?"

"Oh, yes, yes, I see," she answered. She rose.

"I think," she said, "we had better be going home. Don't you?"

"Yes, I do," he assented. "I'm pretty tired myself. I've had a hard day's work. I'm thirsty, too," he added, as he got up. "Would you like to have a drink of water, too?"

She shook her head, and while he disappeared in the direction of the Cresslers' dining-room, she stood alone a moment in the darkened room looking out into the street. She felt that her cheeks were hot. Her hands, hanging at her sides, shut themselves into tight fists.

"What, you are all alone?" said Corthell's voice, behind her.

She turned about quickly.

"I must be going," he said. "I came to say good night." He held out his hand.

"Good night," she answered, as she gave him hers. Then all at once she added:

"Come to see me again—soon, will you? Come Wednesday night."

And then, his heart leaping to his throat, Corthell felt her hand, as it lay in his, close for an instant firmly about his fingers.

"I shall expect you Wednesday then?" she repeated.

He crushed her hand in his grip, and suddenly bent and kissed it.

"Good night," she said, quietly. Jadwin's step sounded at the doorway.

"Good night," he whispered, and in another moment was gone.

During these days Laura no longer knew herself. At every hour she changed; her moods came and went with a rapidity that bewildered all those who were around her. At times her gaiety filled the whole of her beautiful house; at times she shut herself in her apartments, denying herself to every one, and, her head bowed upon her folded arms, wept as though her heart was breaking, without knowing why.

For a few days a veritable seizure of religious enthusiasm held sway over her. She spoke of endowing a hospital, of doing church work among the "slums" of the city. But no sooner had her friends readjusted their points of view to suit this new development than she was off upon another tangent, and was one afternoon seen at the races, with Mrs. Gretry, in her showiest victoria, wearing a great flaring hat and a bouquet of crimson flowers.

She never repeated this performance, however, for a new fad took possession of her the very next day. She memorised the role of Lady Macbeth, built a stage in the ballroom at the top of the house, and, locking herself in, rehearsed the part, for three days uninterruptedly, dressed in elaborate costume, declaiming in chest tones to the empty room:

"'The raven himself is hoarse that croaks the entrance of Duncan under my battlements.'"

Then, tiring of Lady Macbeth, she took up Juliet, Portia, and Ophelia; each with appropriate costumes, studying with tireless avidity, and frightening Aunt Wess' with her declaration that "she might go on the stage after all." She even entertained the notion of having Sheldon Corthell paint her portrait as Lady Macbeth.

As often as the thought of the artist presented itself to her she fought to put it from her. Yes, yes, he came to see her often, very often. Perhaps he loved her yet. Well, suppose he did? He had always loved her. It was not wrong to have him love her, to have him with her. Without his company, great heavens, her life would be lonely beyond words and beyond endurance. Besides, was it to be thought, for an instant, that she, she, Laura Jadwin, in her pitch of pride, with all her beauty, with her quick, keen mind, was to pine, to droop to fade in oblivion and neglect? Was she to blame? Let those who neglected her look to it. Her youth was all with her yet, and all her power to attract, to compel admiration.

When Corthell came to see her on the Wednesday evening in question, Laura said to him, after a few moments, conversation in the drawing-room:

"Oh, you remember the picture you taught me to appreciate—the picture of the little pool in the art gallery, the one you called 'Despair'? I have hung it in my own particular room upstairs—my sitting-room—so as to have it where I can see it always. I love it now. But," she added, "I am not sure about the light. I think it could be hung to better advantage." She hesitated a moment, then, with a sudden, impulsive movement, she turned to him.

"Won't you come up with me, and tell me where to hang it?"

They took the little elevator to the floor above, and Laura led the artist to the room in question—her "sitting-room," a wide, airy place, the polished floor covered with deep skins, the walls wainscotted half way to the ceiling, in dull woods. Shelves of books were everywhere, together with potted plants and tall brass lamps. A long "Madeira" chair stood at the window which overlooked the park and lake, and near to it a great round table of San Domingo mahogany, with tea things and almost diaphanous china.

"What a beautiful room," murmured Corthell, as she touched the button in the wall that opened the current, "and how much you have impressed your individuality upon it. I should have known that you lived here. If you were thousands of miles away and I had entered here, I should have known it was yours—and loved it for such."

"Here is the picture," she said, indicating where it hung. "Doesn't it seem to you that the light is bad?"

But he explained to her that it was not so, and that she had but to incline the canvas a little more from the wall to get a good effect.

"Of course, of course," she assented, as he held the picture in place. "Of course. I shall have it hung over again to-morrow."

For some moments they remained standing in the centre of the room, looking at the picture and talking of it. And then, without remembering just how it had happened, Laura found herself leaning back in the Madeira chair, Corthell seated near at hand by the round table.

"I am glad you like my room," she said. "It is here that I spend most of my time. Often lately I have had my dinner here. Page goes out a great deal now, and so I am left alone occasionally. Last night I sat here in the dark for a long time. The house was so still, everybody was out—even some of the servants. It was so warm, I raised the windows and I sat here for hours looking out over the lake. I could hear it lapping and washing against the shore—almost like a sea. And it was so still, so still; and I was thinking of the time when I was a little girl back at Barrington, years and years ago, picking whortle-berries down in the 'water lot,' and how I got lost once in the corn—the stalks were away above my head—and how happy I was when my father would take me up on the hay wagon. Ah, I was happy in those days—just a freckled, black-haired slip of a little girl, with my frock torn and my hands all scratched with the berry bushes."

She had begun by dramatising, but by now she was acting—acting with all her histrionic power at fullest stretch, acting the part of a woman unhappy amid luxuries, who looked back with regret and with longing towards a joyous, simple childhood. She was sincere and she was not sincere. Part of her—one of those two Laura Jadwins who at different times, but with equal right called themselves "I," knew just what effect her words, her pose, would have upon a man who sympathised with her, who loved her. But the other Laura Jadwin would have resented as petty, as even wrong, the insinuation that she was not wholly, thoroughly sincere. All that she was saying was true. No one, so she believed, ever was placed before as she was placed now. No one had ever spoken as now she spoke. Her chin upon one slender finger, she went on, her eyes growing wide:

"If I had only known then that those days were to be, the happiest of my life.... This great house, all the beauty of it, and all this wealth, what does it amount to?" Her voice was the voice of Phedre, and the gesture of lassitude with which she let her arms fall into her lap was precisely that which only the day before she had used to accompany Portia's plaint of

—my little body is a-weary of this great world.

Yet, at the same time, Laura knew that her heart was genuinely aching with real sadness, and that the tears which stood in her eyes were as sincere as any she had ever shed.

"All this wealth," she continued, her head dropping back upon the cushion of the chair as she spoke, "what does it matter; for what does it compensate? Oh, I would give it all gladly, gladly, to be that little black-haired girl again, back in Squire Dearborn's water lot; with my hands stained with the whortle-berries and the nettles in my fingers—and my little lover, who called me his beau-heart and bought me a blue hair ribbon, and kissed me behind the pump house."

"Ah," said Corthell, quickly and earnestly, "that is the secret. It was love—even the foolish boy and girl love—love that after all made your life sweet then."

She let her hands fall into her lap, and, musing, turned the rings back and forth upon her fingers.

"Don't you think so?" he asked, in a low voice.

She bent her head slowly, without replying. Then for a long moment neither spoke. Laura played with her rings. The artist, leaning forward in his chair, looked with vague eyes across the room. And no interval of time since his return, no words that had ever passed between them, had been so fraught with significance, so potent in drawing them together as this brief, wordless moment.

At last Corthell turned towards her.

"You must not think," he murmured, "that your life is without love now. I will not have you believe that."

But she made no answer.

"If you would only see," he went on. "If you would only condescend to look, you would know that there is a love which has enfolded your life for years. You have shut it out from you always. But it has been yours, just the same; it has lain at your door, it has looked—oh, God knows with what longing!—through your windows. You have never stirred abroad that it has not followed you. Not a footprint of yours that it does not know and cherish. Do you think that your life is without love? Why, it is all around you—all around you but voiceless. It has no right to speak, it only has the right to suffer."

Still Laura said no word. Her head turned from him, she looked out of the window, and once more the seconds passed while neither spoke. The clock on the table ticked steadily. In the distance, through the open window, came the incessant, mournful wash of the lake. All around them the house was still. At length Laura sat upright in her chair.

"I think I will have this room done over while we are away this summer," she said. "Don't you think it would be effective if the wainscotting went almost to the ceiling?"

He glanced critically about the room.

"Very," he answered, briskly. "There is no background so beautiful as wood."

"And I might finish it off at the top with a narrow shelf."

"Provided you promised not to put brass 'plaques' or pewter kitchen ware upon it."

"Do smoke," she urged him. "I know you want to. You will find matches on the table."

But Corthell, as he lit his cigarette, produced his own match box. It was a curious bit of antique silver, which he had bought in a Viennese pawnshop, heart-shaped and topped with a small ducal coronet of worn gold. On one side he had caused his name to be engraved in small script. Now, as Laura admired it, he held it towards her.

"An old pouncet-box, I believe," he informed her, "or possibly it held an ointment for her finger nails." He spilled the matches into his hand. "You see the red stain still on the inside; and—smell," he added, as she took it from him. "Even the odour of the sulphur matches cannot smother the quaint old perfume, distilled perhaps three centuries ago."

An hour later Corthell left her. She did not follow him further than the threshold of the room, but let him find his way to the front door alone.

When he had gone she returned to the room, and for a little while sat in her accustomed place by the window overlooking the park and the lake. Very soon after Corthell's departure she heard Page, Landry Court, and Mrs. Wessels come in; then at length rousing from her reverie she prepared for bed. But, as she passed the round mahogany table, on her way to her bedroom, she was aware of a little object lying upon it, near to where she had sat.

"Oh, he forgot it," she murmured, as she picked up Corthell's heart-shaped match box. She glanced at it a moment, indifferently; but her mind was full of other things.

She laid it down again upon the table, and going on to her own room, went to bed.

Jadwin did not come home that night, and in the morning Laura presided at breakfast table in his place. Landry Court, Page, and Aunt Wess' were there; for occasionally nowadays, when the trio went to one of their interminable concerts or lectures, Landry stayed over night at the house.

"Any message for your husband, Mrs. Jadwin?" inquired Landry, as he prepared to go down town after breakfast. "I always see him in Mr. Gretry's office the first thing. Any message for him?"

"No," answered Laura, simply.

"Oh, by the way," spoke up Aunt Wess', "we met that Mr. Corthell on the corner last night, just as he was leaving. I was real sorry not to get home here before he left. I've never heard him play on that big organ, and I've been wanting to for ever so long. I hurried home last night, hoping I might have caught him before he left. I was regularly disappointed."

"That's too bad," murmured Laura, and then, for obscure reasons, she had the stupidity to add: "And we were in the art gallery the whole evening. He played beautifully."

Towards eleven o'clock that morning Laura took her usual ride, but she had not been away from the house quite an hour before she turned back.

All at once she had remembered something. She returned homeward, now urging Crusader to a flying gallop, now curbing him to his slowest ambling walk. That which had so abruptly presented itself to her mind was the fact that Corthell's match box—his name engraved across its front—still lay in plain sight upon the table in her sitting-room—the peculiar and particular place of her privacy.

It was so much her own, this room, that she had given orders that the servants were to ignore it in their day's routine. She looked after its order herself. Yet, for all that, the maids or the housekeeper often passed through it, on their way to the suite beyond, and occasionally Page or Aunt Wess' came there to read, in her absence. The family spoke of the place sometimes as the "upstairs sitting-room," sometimes simply as "Laura's room."

Now, as she cantered homeward, Laura had it vividly in her mind that she had not so much as glanced at the room before leaving the house that morning. The servants would not touch the place. But it was quite possible that Aunt Wess' or Page—

Laura, the blood mounting to her forehead, struck the horse sharply with her crop. The pettiness of the predicament, the small meanness of her situation struck across her face like the flagellations of tiny whips. That she should stoop to this! She who had held her head so high.

Abruptly she reined in the horse again. No, she would not hurry. Exercising all her self-control, she went on her way with deliberate slowness, so that it was past twelve o'clock when she dismounted under the carriage porch.

Her fingers clutched tightly about her crop, she mounted to her sitting-room and entered, closing the door behind her.

She went directly to the table, and then, catching her breath, with a quick, apprehensive sinking of the heart, stopped short. The little heart-shaped match box was gone, and on the couch in the corner of the room Page, her book fallen to the floor beside her, lay curled up and asleep.

A loop of her riding-habit over her arm, the toe of her boot tapping the floor nervously, Laura stood motionless in the centre of the room, her lips tight pressed, the fingers of one gloved hand drumming rapidly upon her riding-crop. She was bewildered, and an anxiety cruelly poignant, a dread of something she could not name, gripped suddenly at her throat.

Could she have been mistaken? Was it upon the table that she had seen the match box after all? If it lay elsewhere about the room, she must find it at once. Never had she felt so degraded as now, when, moving with such softness and swiftness as she could in her agitation command, she went here and there about the room, peering into the corners of her desk, searching upon the floor, upon the chairs, everywhere, anywhere; her face crimson, her breath failing her, her hands opening and shutting.

But the silver heart with its crown of worn gold was not to be found. Laura, at the end of half an hour, was obliged to give over searching. She was certain the match box lay upon the mahogany table when last she left the room. It had not been mislaid; of that she was now persuaded.

But while she sat at the desk, still in habit and hat, rummaging for the fourth time among the drawers and shelves, she was all at once aware, even without turning around, that Page was awake and watching her. Laura cleared her throat.

"Have you seen my blue note paper, Page?" she asked. "I want to drop a note to Mrs. Cressler, right away."

"No," said Page, as she rose from the couch. "No, I haven't seen it." She came towards her sister across the room. "I thought, maybe," she added, gravely, as she drew the heart-shaped match box from her pocket, "that you might be looking for this. I took it. I knew you wouldn't care to have Mr. Jadwin find it here."

Laura struck the little silver heart from Page's hand, with a violence that sent it spinning across the room, and sprang to her feet.

"You took it!" she cried. "You took it! How dare you! What do you mean? What do I care if Curtis should find it here? What's it to me that he should know that Mr. Corthell came up here? Of course he was here."

But Page, though very pale, was perfectly calm under her sister's outburst.

"If you didn't care whether any one knew that Mr. Corthell came up here," she said, quietly, "why did you tell us this morning at breakfast that you and he were in the art gallery the whole evening? I thought," she added, with elaborate blandness, "I thought I would be doing you a service in hiding the match box."

"A service! You! What have I to hide?" cried Laura, almost inarticulate. "Of course I said we were in the art gallery the whole evening. So we were. We did—I do remember now—we did come up here for an instant, to see how my picture hung. We went downstairs again at once. We did not so much as sit down. He was not in the room two minutes."

"He was here," returned Page, "long enough to smoke half a dozen times." She pointed to a silver pen tray on the mahogany table, hidden behind a book rack and littered with the ashes and charred stumps of some five or six cigarettes.

"Really, Laura," Page remarked. "Really, you manage very awkwardly, it seems to me."

Laura caught her riding-crop in her right hand

"Don't you—don't you make me forget myself;" she cried, breathlessly.

"It seems to me," observed Page, quietly, "that you've done that long since, yourself."

Laura flung the crop down and folded her arms.

"Now," she cried, her eyes blazing and rivetted upon Page's. "Now, just what do you mean? Sit down," she commanded, flinging a hand towards a chair, "sit down, and tell me just what you mean by all this."

But Page remained standing. She met her sister's gaze without wavering.

"Do you want me to believe," she answered, "that it made no difference to you that Mr. Corthell's match safe was here?"

"Not the least," exclaimed Laura. "Not the least."

"Then why did you search for it so when you came in? I was not asleep all of the time. I saw you."

"Because," answered Laura, "because—I—because—" Then all at once she burst out afresh: "Have I got to answer to you for what I do? Have I got to explain? All your life long you've pretended to judge your sister. Now you've gone too far. Now I forbid it—from this day on. What I do is my affair; I'll ask nobody's advice. I'll do as I please, do you understand?" The tears sprang to her eyes, the sobs strangled in her throat. "I'll do as I please, as I please," and with the words she sank down in the chair by her desk and struck her bare knuckles again and again upon the open lid, crying out through her tears and her sobs, and from between her tight-shut teeth: "I'll do as I please, do you understand? As I please, as I please! I will be happy. I will, I will, I will!"

"Oh, darling, dearest—" cried Page, running forward. But Laura, on her feet once more, thrust her back.

"Don't touch me," she cried. "I hate you!" She put her fists to her temples and, her eyes closed, rocked herself to and fro. "Don't you touch me. Go away from me; go away from me. I hate you; I hate you all. I hate this house, I hate this life. You are all killing me. Oh, my God, if I could only die!"

She flung herself full length upon the couch, face downward. Her sobs shook her from head to foot.

Page knelt at her side, an arm about her shoulder, but to all her sister's consolations Laura, her voice muffled in her folded arms, only cried:

"Let me alone, let me alone. Don't touch me."

For a time Page tried to make herself heard; then, after a moment's reflection, she got up and drew out the pin in Laura's hat. She took off the hat, loosened the scarf around Laura's neck, and then deftly, silently, while her sister lay inert and sobbing beneath her hands, removed the stiff, tight riding-habit. She brought a towel dipped in cold water from the adjoining room and bathed Laura's face and hands.

But her sister would not be comforted, would not respond to her entreaties or caresses. The better part of an hour went by; Page, knowing her sister's nature, in the end held her peace, waiting for the paroxysm to wear itself out.

After a while Laura's weeping resolved itself into long, shuddering breaths, and at length she managed to say, in a faint, choked voice:

"Will you bring me the cologne from my dressing-table, honey? My head aches so."

And, as Page ran towards the door, she added: "And my hand mirror, too. Are my eyes all swollen?"

And that was the last word upon the subject between the two sisters.

But the evening of the same day, between eight and nine o'clock, while Laura was searching the shelves of the library for a book with which to while away the long evening that she knew impended, Corthell's card was brought to her.

"I am not at home," she told the servant. "Or—wait," she added. Then, after a moment's thought, she said: "Very well. Show him in here."

Laura received the artist, standing very erect and pale upon the great white rug before the empty fireplace. Her hands were behind her back when he came in, and as he crossed the room she did not move.

"I was not going to see you at first," she said. "I told the servant I was not at home. But I changed my mind—I wanted to say something to you."

He stood at the other end of the fireplace, an elbow upon an angle of the massive mantel, and as she spoke the last words he looked at her quickly. As usual, they were quite alone. The heavy, muffling curtain of the doorway shut them in effectually.

"I have something to say to you," continued Laura. Then, quietly enough, she said: "You must not come to see me any more."

He turned abruptly away from her, and for a moment did not speak. Then at last, his voice low, he faced her again and asked:

"Have I offended?"

She shook her head.

"No," he said, quietly. "No, I knew it was not that." There was a long silence. The artist looked at the floor his hand slowly stroking the back of one of the big leather chairs.

"I knew it must come," he answered, at length, "sooner or later. You are right—of course. I should not have come back to America. I should not have believed that I was strong enough to trust myself. Then"—he looked at her steadily. His words came from his lips one by one, very slowly. His voice was hardly more than a whisper. "Then, I am—never to see you—again... Is that it?"

"Yes."

"Do you know what that means for me?" he cried. "Do you realise—" he drew in his breath sharply. "Never to see you again! To lose even the little that is left to me now. I—I—" He turned away quickly and walked to a window and stood a moment, his back turned, looking out, his hands clasped behind him. Then, after a long moment, he faced about. His manner was quiet again, his voice very low.

"But before I go," he said, "will you answer me, at least, this—it can do no harm now that I am to leave you—answer me, and I know you will speak the truth: Are you happy, Laura?"

She closed her eyes.

"You have not the right to know."

"You are not happy," he declared. "I can see it, I know it. If you were, you would have told me so.... If I promise you," he went on. "If I promise you to go away now, and never to try to see you again, may I come once more—to say good-by?"

She shook her head.

"It is so little for you to grant," he pleaded, "and it is so incalculably much for me to look forward to in the little time that yet remains. I do not even ask to see you alone. I will not harass you with any heroics."

"Oh, what good will it do," she cried, wearily, "for you to see me again? Why will you make me more unhappy than I am? Why did you come back?"

"Because," he answered, steadily, "because I love you more than"—he partly raised a clenched fist and let it fall slowly upon the back of the chair, "more than any other consideration in the world."

"Don't!" she cried. "You must not. Never, never say that to me again. Will you go—please?"

"Oh, if I had not gone from you four years ago!" he cried. "If I had only stayed then! Not a day of my life since that I have not regretted it. You could have loved me then. I know it, I know it, and, God forgive me, but I know you could love me now—"

"Will you go?" she cried.

"I dare you to say you could not," he flashed out

Laura shut her eyes and put her hands over her ears. "I could not, I could not," she murmured, monotonously, over and over again. "I could not, I could not."

She heard him start suddenly, and opened her eyes in time to see him come quickly towards her. She threw out a defensive hand, but he caught the arm itself to him and, before she could resist, had kissed it again and again through the interstices of the lace sleeve. Upon her bare shoulder she felt the sudden passion of his lips.

A quick, sharp gasp, a sudden qualm of breathlessness wrenched through her, to her very finger tips, with a fierce leap of the blood, a wild bound of the heart.

She tore back from him with a violence that rent away the lace upon her arm, and stood off from him, erect and rigid, a fine, delicate, trembling vibrating through all her being. On her pale cheeks the colour suddenly flamed.

"Go, go," was all she had voice to utter.

"And may I see you once more—only once?"

"Yes, yes, anything, only go, go—if you love me!"

He left the room. In another moment she heard the front door close.

"Curtis," said Laura, when next she saw her husband, "Curtis, you could not—stay with me, that last time. Remember? When we were to go for a drive. Can you spend this evening with me? Just us two, here at home—or I'll go out with you. I'll do anything you say." She looked at him steadily an instant. "It is not—not easy for a woman to ask—for me to ask favours like this. Each time I tell myself it will be the last. I am—you must remember this, Curtis, I am—perhaps I am a little proud. Don't you see?"

They were at breakfast table again. It was the morning after Laura had given Corthell his dismissal. As she spoke Jadwin brought his hand down upon the table with a bang.

"You bet I will," he exclaimed; "you bet I'll stay with you to-night. Business can go to the devil! And we won't go out either; we'll stay right here. You get something to read to me, and we'll have one of our old evenings again. We—"

All at once Jadwin paused, laid down his knife and fork, and looked strangely to and fro about the room.

"We'll have one of our old evenings again," he repeated, slowly.

"What is it, Curtis?" demanded his wife. "What is the matter?"

"Oh—nothing," he answered.

"Why, yes there was. Tell me."

"No, no. I'm all right now," he returned, briskly enough.

"No," she insisted. "You must tell me. Are you sick?"

He hesitated a moment. Then:

"Sick?" he queried. "No, indeed. But—I'll tell you. Since a few days I've had," he put his fingers to his forehead between his eyes, "I've had a queer sensation right there. It comes and goes."

"A headache?"

"N-no. It's hard to describe. A sort of numbness. Sometimes it's as though there was a heavy iron cap—a helmet on my head. And sometimes it—I don't know it seems as if there were fog, or something or other, inside. I'll take a good long rest this summer, as soon as we can get away. Another month or six weeks, and I'll have things ship-shape and so as I can leave them. Then we'll go up to Geneva, and, by Jingo, I'll loaf." He was silent for a moment, frowning, passing his hand across his forehead and winking his eyes. Then, with a return of his usual alertness, he looked at his watch.

"Hi!" he exclaimed. "I must be off. I won't be home to dinner to-night. But you can expect me by eight o'clock, sure. I promise I'll be here on the minute."

But, as he kissed his wife good-by, Laura put her arms about his neck.

"Oh, I don't want you to leave me at all, ever, ever! Curtis, love me, love me always, dear. And be thoughtful of me and kind to me. And remember that you are all I have in the world; you are father and mother to me, and my dear husband as well. I know you do love me; but there are times—Oh," she cried, suddenly "if I thought you did not love me—love me better than anything, anything—I could not love you; Curtis, I could not, I could not. No, no," she cried, "don't interrupt. Hear me out. Maybe it is wrong of me to feel that way, but I'm only a woman, dear. I love you but I love Love too. Women are like that; right or wrong, weak or strong, they must be—must be loved above everything else in the world. Now go, go to your business; you mustn't be late. Hark, there is Jarvis with the team. Go now. Good-by, good-by, and I'll expect you at eight."

True to his word, Jadwin reached his home that evening promptly at the promised hour. As he came into the house, however, the door-man met him in the hall, and, as he took his master's hat and stick, explained that Mrs. Jadwin was in the art gallery, and that she had said he was to come there at once.

Laura had planned a little surprise. The art gallery was darkened. Here and there behind the dull-blue shades a light burned low. But one of the movable reflectors that were used to throw a light upon the pictures in the topmost rows was burning brilliantly. It was turned from Jadwin as he entered, and its broad cone of intense white light was thrown full upon Laura, who stood over against the organ in the full costume of "Theodora."

For an instant Jadwin was taken all aback.

"What the devil!" he ejaculated, stopping short in the doorway.

Laura ran forward to him, the chains, ornaments, and swinging pendants chiming furiously as she moved.

"I did surprise you, I did surprise you," she laughed. "Isn't it gorgeous?" She turned about before him, her arms raised. "Isn't it superb? Do you remember Bernhardt—and that scene in the Emperor Justinian's box at the amphitheatre? Say now that your wife isn't beautiful. I am, am I not?" she exclaimed defiantly, her head raised. "Say it, say it."

"Well, what for a girl!" gasped Jadwin, "to get herself up—"

"Say that I am beautiful," commanded Laura.

"Well, I just about guess you are," he cried.

"The most beautiful woman you have ever known?" she insisted. Then on the instant added: "Oh, I may be really as plain as a kitchen-maid, but you must believe that I am not. I would rather be ugly and have you think me beautiful, than to be the most beautiful woman in the world and have you think me plain. Tell me—am I not the most beautiful woman you ever saw?"

"The most beautiful I ever saw," he repeated, fervently. "But—Lord, what will you do next? Whatever put it into your head to get into this rig?"

"Oh, I don't know. I just took the notion. You've seen me in every one of my gowns. I sent down for this, this morning, just after you left. Curtis, if you hadn't made me love you enough to be your wife, Laura Dearborn would have been a great actress. I feel it in my finger tips. Ah!" she cried, suddenly flinging up her head till the pendants of the crown clashed again. "I could have been magnificent. You don't believe it. Listen. This is Athalia—the queen in the Old Testament, you remember."

"Hold on," he protested. "I thought you were this Theodora person."

"I know—but never mind. I am anything I choose. Sit down; listen. It's from Racine's 'Athalie,' and the wicked queen has had this terrible dream of her mother Jezabel. It's French, but I'll make you see."

And "taking stage," as it were, in the centre of the room, Laura began:

"Son ombre vers mon lit a paru se baisser Et moi, je lui tendais les mains pour l'embrasser; Mais je n'ai plus trouve q'un horrible melange D'os et de chair meurtris et traines dans la fange, Des lambeaux pleins de sang, et des membres affreux Que les chiens d'evorants se disputaient entre eux."

"Great God!" exclaimed Jadwin, ignorant of the words yet, in spite of himself, carried away by the fury and passion of her rendering.

Laura struck her palms together.

"Just what 'Abner' says," she cried. "The very words."

"Abner?"

"In the play. I knew I could make you feel it."

"Well, well," murmured her husband, shaking his head, bewildered even yet. "Well, it's a strange wife I've got here."

"When you've realised that," returned Laura, "you've just begun to understand me."

Never had he seen her gayer. Her vivacity was bewildering.

"I wish," she cried, all at once, "I wish I had dressed as 'Carmen,' and I would have danced for you. Oh, and you could have played the air for me on the organ. I have the costume upstairs now. Wait! I will, I will! Sit right where you are—no, fix the attachment to the organ while I'm gone. Oh, be gay with me to-night," she cried, throwing her arms around him. "This is my night, isn't it? And I am to be just as foolish as I please."

With the words she ran from the room, but was back in an incredibly short time, gowned as Bizet's cigarette girl, a red rose in her black hair, castanets upon her fingers.

Jadwin began the bolero.

"Can you see me dance, and play at the same time?"

"Yes, yes. Go on. How do you know anything about a Spanish dance?"

"I learned it long ago. I know everything about anything I choose, to-night. Play, play it fast."

She danced as though she would never tire, with the same force of passion that she had thrown into Athalie. Her yellow skirt was a flash of flame spurting from the floor, and her whole body seemed to move with the same wild, untamed spirit as a tongue of fire. The castanets snapped like the crackling of sparks; her black mantilla was a hovering cloud of smoke. She was incarnate flame, capricious and riotous, elusive and dazzling.

Then suddenly she tossed the castanets far across the room and dropped upon the couch, panting and laughing.

"There," she cried, "now I feel better. That had to come out. Come over here and sit by me. Now, maybe you'll admit that I can dance too."

"You sure can," answered Jadwin, as she made a place for him among the cushions. "That was wonderful. But, at the same time, old girl, I wouldn't—wouldn't—"

"Wouldn't what?"

"Well, do too much of that. It's sort of over-wrought—a little, and unnatural. I like you best when you are your old self, quiet, and calm, and dignified. It's when you are quiet that you are at your best. I didn't know you had this streak in you. You are that excitable to-night!"

"Let me be so then. It's myself, for the moment whatever it is. But now I'll be quiet. Now we'll talk. Have you had a hard day? Oh, and did your head bother you again?"

"No, things were a little easier down town to-day. But that queer feeling in my head did come back as I was coming home—and my head aches a little now, besides."

"Your head aches!" she exclaimed. "Let me do something for it. And I've been making it worse with all my foolishness."

"No, no; that's all right," he assured her. "I tell you what we'll do. I'll lie down here a bit, and you play something for me. Something quiet. I get so tired down there in La Salle Street, Laura, you don't know."

And while he stretched out at full length upon the couch, his wife, at the organ, played the music she knew he liked best—old songs, "Daisy Dean," "Lord Lovell," "When Stars Are in the Quiet Sky," and "Open Thy Lattice to Me."

When at length she paused, he nodded his head with pleasure.

"That's pretty," he said. "Ah, that is blame pretty. Honey, it's just like medicine to me," he continued, "to lie here, quiet like this, with the lights low, and have my dear girl play those old, old tunes. My old governor, Laura, used to play that 'Open the Lattice to me,' that and 'Father, oh, Father, Come Home with me Now'—used to play 'em on his fiddle." His arm under his head, he went on, looking vaguely at the opposite wall. "Lord love me, I can see that kitchen in the old farmhouse as plain! The walls were just logs and plaster, and there were upright supports in each corner, where we used to measure our heights—we children. And the fireplace was there," he added, gesturing with his arm, "and there was the wood box, and over here was an old kind of dresser with drawers, and the torty-shell cat always had her kittens under there. Honey, I was happy then. Of course I've got you now, and that's all the difference in the world. But you're the only thing that does make a difference. We've got a fine place and a mint of money I suppose—and I'm proud of it. But I don't know.... If they'd let me be and put us two—just you and me—back in the old house with the bare floors and the rawhide chairs and the shuck beds, I guess we'd manage. If you're happy, you're happy; that's about the size of it. And sometimes I think that we'd be happier—you and I—chumming along shoulder to shoulder, poor an' working hard, than making big money an' spending big money, why—oh, I don't know ... if you're happy, that's the thing that counts, and if all this stuff," he kicked out a careless foot at the pictures, the heavy hangings, the glass cabinets of bibelots, "if all this stuff stood in the way of it—well—it could go to the devil! That's not poetry maybe, but it's the truth."

Laura came over to where her husband lay, and sat by him, and took his head in her lap, smoothing his forehead with her long white hands.

"Oh, if I could only keep you like this always," she murmured. "Keep you untroubled, and kind, and true. This is my husband again. Oh, you are a man, Curtis; a great, strong, kind-hearted man, with no little graces, nor petty culture, nor trivial fine speeches, nor false sham, imitation polish. I love you. Ah, I love you, love you, dear!"

"Old girl!" said Jadwin, stroking her hand.

"Do you want me to read to you now?" she asked.

"Just this is pretty good, it seems to me."

As he spoke, there came a step in the hall and a knock.

Laura sat up, frowning.

"I told them I was not to be disturbed," she exclaimed under her breath. Then, "Come in," she called.

"Mr. Gretry, sir," announced the servant. "Said he wished to see you at once, sir."

"Tell him," cried Laura, turning quickly to Jadwin, "tell him you're not at home—that you can't see him."

"I've got to see him," answered Jadwin, sitting up. "He wouldn't come here himself unless it was for something important."

"Can I come in, J.?" spoke the broker, from the hall. And even through the thick curtains they could hear how his voice rang with excitement and anxiety.

"Can I come in? I followed the servant right up, you see. I know—"

"Yes, yes. Come in," answered Jadwin. Laura, her face flushing, threw a fold of the couch cover over her costume as Gretry, his hat still on his head, stepped quickly into the room.

Jadwin met him half way, and Laura from her place on the couch heard the rapidly spoken words between the general and his lieutenant.

"Now we're in for it!" Gretry exclaimed.

"Yes—well?" Jadwin's voice was as incisive and quick as the fall of an axe.

"I've just found out," said Gretry, "that Crookes and his crowd are going to take hold to-morrow. There'll be hell to pay in the morning. They are going to attack us the minute the gong goes."

"Who's with them?"

"I don't know; nobody does. Sweeny, of course. But he has a gang back of him—besides, he's got good credit with the banks. I told you you'd have to fight him sooner or later."

"Well, we'll fight him then. Don't get scared. Crookes ain't the Great Mogul."

"Holy Moses, I'd like to know who is, then."

"I am. And he's got to know it. There's not room for Crookes and me in this game. One of us two has got to control this market. If he gets in my way, by God, I'll smash him!"

"Well, then, J., you and I have got to do some tall talking to-night. You'd better come down to the Grand Pacific Hotel right away. Court is there already. It was him, nervy little cuss, that found out about Crookes. Can you come now, at once? Good evening, Mrs. Jadwin. I'm sorry to take him from you, but business is business."

No, it was not. To the wife of the great manipulator, listening with a sinking heart to this courier from the front, it was battle. The Battle of the Streets was again in array. Again the trumpet sounded, again the rush of thousands of feet filled all the air. Even here, here in her home, her husband's head upon her lap, in the quiet and stillness of her hour, the distant rumble came to her ears. Somewhere, far off there in the darkness of the night, the great forces were manoeuvring for position once more. To-morrow would come the grapple, and one or the other must fall—her husband or the enemy. How keep him to herself when the great conflict impended? She knew how the thunder of the captains and the shoutings appealed to him. She had seen him almost leap to his arms out of her embrace. He was all the man she had called him, and less strong, less eager, less brave, she would have loved him less.

Yet she had lost him again, lost him at the very moment she believed she had won him back.

"Don't go, don't go," she whispered to him, as he kissed her good-by. "Oh, dearest, don't go! This was my evening."

"I must, I must, Laura. Good-by, old girl. Don't keep me—see, Sam is waiting."

He kissed her hastily twice.

"Now, Sam," he said, turning toward the broker.

"Good night, Mrs. Jadwin."

"Good-by, old girl."

They turned toward the door.

"You see, young Court was down there at the bank, and he noticed that checks—"

The voices died away as the hangings of the entrance fell to place. The front door clashed and closed.

Laura sat upright in her place, listening, one fist pressed against her lips.

There was no more noise. The silence of the vast empty house widened around her at the shutting of the door as the ripples widen on a pool with the falling of the stone. She crushed her knuckles tighter and tighter over her lips, she pressed her fingers to her eyes, she slowly clasped and reclasped her hands, listening for what she did not know. She thought of her husband hurrying away from her, ignoring her, and her love for him in the haste and heat of battle. She thought of Corthell, whom she had sent from her, forever, shutting his love from out her life.

Crushed, broken, Laura laid herself down among the cushions, her face buried in her arm. Above her and around her rose the dimly lit gallery, lowering with luminous shadows. Only a point or two of light illuminated the place. The gold frames of the pictures reflected it dully; the massive organ pipes, just outlined in faint blurs of light, towered far into the gloom above. The whole place, with its half-seen gorgeous hangings, its darkened magnificence, was like a huge, dim interior of Byzantium.

Lost, beneath the great height of the dome, and in the wide reach of the floor space, in her foolish finery of bangles, silks, high comb, and little rosetted slippers, Laura Jadwin lay half hidden among the cushions of the couch. If she wept, she wept in silence, and the muffling stillness of the lofty gallery was broken but once, when a cry, half whisper, half sob, rose to the deaf, blind darkness:

"Oh, now I am alone, alone, alone!"

IX

"Well, that's about all then, I guess," said Gretry at last, as he pushed back his chair and rose from the table.

He and Jadwin were in a room on the third floor of the Grand Pacific Hotel, facing Jackson Street. It was three o'clock in the morning. Both men were in their shirt-sleeves; the table at which they had been sitting was scattered over with papers, telegraph blanks, and at Jadwin's elbow stood a lacquer tray filled with the stumps of cigars and burnt matches, together with one of the hotel pitchers of ice water.

"Yes," assented Jadwin, absently, running through a sheaf of telegrams, "that's all we can do—until we see what kind of a game Crookes means to play. I'll be at your office by eight."

"Well," said the broker, getting into his coat, "I guess I'll go to my room and try to get a little sleep. I wish I could see how we'll be to-morrow night at this time."

Jadwin made a sharp movement of impatience.

"Damnation, Sam, aren't you ever going to let up croaking? If you're afraid of this thing, get out of it. Haven't I got enough to bother me?"

"Oh, say! Say, hold on, hold on, old man," remonstrated the broker, in an injured voice. "You're terrible touchy sometimes, J., of late. I was only trying to look ahead a little. Don't think I want to back out. You ought to know me by this time, J."

"There, there, I'm sorry, Sam," Jadwin hastened to answer, getting up and shaking the other by the shoulder. "I am touchy these days. There's so many things to think of, and all at the same time. I do get nervous. I never slept one little wink last night—and you know the night before I didn't turn in till two in the morning."

"Lord, you go swearing and damning 'round here like a pirate sometimes, J.," Gretry went on. "I haven't heard you cuss before in twenty years. Look out, now, that I don't tell on you to your Sunday-school superintendents."

"I guess they'd cuss, too," observed Jadwin, "if they were long forty million wheat, and had to know just where every hatful of it was every second of the time. It was all very well for us to whoop about swinging a corner that afternoon in your office. But the real thing—well, you don't have any trouble keeping awake. Do you suppose we can keep the fact of our corner dark much longer?"

"I fancy not," answered the broker, putting on his hat and thrusting his papers into his breast pocket. "If we bust Crookes, it'll come out—and it won't matter then. I think we've got all the shorts there are."

"I'm laying particularly for Dave Scannel," remarked Jadwin. "I hope he's in up to his neck, and if he is, by the Great Horn Spoon, I'll bankrupt him, or my name is not Jadwin! I'll wring him bone-dry. If I once get a twist of that rat, I won't leave him hide nor hair to cover the wart he calls his heart."

"Why, what all has Scannel ever done to you?" demanded the other, amazed.

"Nothing, but I found out the other day that old Hargus—poor old, broken-backed, half-starved Hargus—I found out that it was Scannel that ruined him. Hargus and he had a big deal on, you know—oh, ages ago—and Scannel sold out on him. Great God, it was the dirtiest, damnedest treachery I ever heard of! Scannel made his pile, and what's Hargus now? Why, he's a scarecrow. And he has a little niece that he supports, heaven only knows how. I've seen her, and she's pretty as a picture. Well, that's all right; I'm going to carry fifty thousand wheat for Hargus, and

I've got another scheme for him, too. By God, the poor old boy won't go hungry again if I know it! But if I lay my hands on Scannel—if we catch him in the corner—holy, suffering Moses, but I'll make him squeal!"

Gretry nodded, to say he understood and approved.

"I guess you've got him," he remarked. "Well, I must get to bed. Good night, J."

"Good night, Sam. See you in the morning."

And before the door of the room was closed, Jadwin was back at the table again. Once more, painfully, toilfully, he went over his plans, retesting, altering, recombining, his hands full of lists, of despatches, and of endless columns of memoranda. Occasionally he murmured fragments of sentences to himself. "H'm ... I must look out for that.... They can't touch us there.... The annex of that Nickel Plate elevator will hold—let's see ... half a million.... If I buy the grain within five days after arrival I've got to pay storage, which is, let's see—three-quarters of a cent times eighty thousand...."

An hour passed. At length Jadwin pushed back from the table, drank a glass of ice water, and rose, stretching.

"Lord, I must get some sleep," he muttered.

He threw off his clothes and went to bed, but even as he composed himself to sleep, the noises of the street in the awakening city invaded the room through the chink of the window he had left open. The noises were vague. They blended easily into a far-off murmur; they came nearer; they developed into a cadence:

"Wheat-wheat-wheat, wheat-wheat-wheat."

Jadwin roused up. He had just been dropping off to sleep. He rose and shut the window, and again threw himself down. He was weary to death; not a nerve of his body that did not droop and flag. His eyes closed slowly. Then, all at once, his whole body twitched sharply in a sudden spasm, a simultaneous recoil of every muscle. His heart began to beat rapidly, his breath failed him. Broad awake, he sat up in bed.

"H'm!" he muttered. "That was a start—must have been dreaming, surely."

Then he paused, frowning, his eyes narrowing; he looked to and fro about the room, lit by the subdued glow that came in through the transom from a globe in the hall outside. Slowly his hand went to his forehead.

With almost the abruptness of a blow, that strange, indescribable sensation had returned to his head. It was as though he were struggling with a fog in the interior of his brain; or again it was a numbness, a weight, or sometimes it had more of the feeling of a heavy, tight-drawn band across his temples.

"Smoking too much, I guess," murmured Jadwin. But he knew this was not the reason, and as he spoke, there smote across his face the first indefinite sensation of an unnamed fear.

He gave a quick, short breath, and straightened himself, passing his hands over his face.

"What the deuce," he muttered, "does this mean?"

For a long moment he remained sitting upright in bed, looking from wall to wall of the room. He felt a little calmer. He shrugged his shoulders impatiently.

"Look here," he said to the opposite wall, "I guess I'm not a schoolgirl, to have nerves at this late date. High time to get to sleep, if I'm to mix things with Crookes to-morrow."

But he could not sleep. While the city woke to its multitudinous life below his windows, while the grey light of morning drowned the yellow haze from the gas jet that came through the transom, while the "early call" alarms rang in neighbouring rooms, Curtis Jadwin lay awake, staring at the ceiling, now concentrating his thoughts upon the vast operation in which he found himself engaged, following out again all its complexities, its inconceivable ramifications, or now puzzling over the inexplicable numbness, the queer, dull weight that descended upon his brain so soon as he allowed its activity to relax.

By five o'clock he found it intolerable to remain longer in bed; he rose, bathed, dressed, ordered his breakfast, and, descending to the office of the hotel, read the earliest editions of the morning papers for half an hour.

Then, at last, as he sat in the corner of the office deep in an armchair, the tired shoulders began to droop, the wearied head to nod. The paper slipped from his fingers, his chin sank upon his collar.

To his ears the early clamour of the street, the cries of newsboys, the rattle of drays came in a dull murmur. It seemed to him that very far off a great throng was forming. It was menacing, shouting. It stirred, it moved, it was advancing. It came galloping down the street, shouting with insensate fury; now it was at the corner, now it burst into the entrance of the hotel. Its clamour was deafening, but intelligible. For a thousand, a million, forty million voices were shouting in cadence:

"Wheat-wheat-wheat, wheat-wheat-wheat."

Jadwin woke abruptly, half starting from his chair. The morning sun was coming in through the windows; the clock above the hotel desk was striking seven, and a waiter stood at his elbow, saying:

"Your breakfast is served, Mr. Jadwin."

He had no appetite. He could eat nothing but a few mouthfuls of toast, and long before the appointed hour he sat in Gretry's office, waiting for the broker to appear, drumming on the arm of his chair, plucking at the buttons of his coat, and wondering why it was that every now and then all the objects in his range of vision seemed to move slowly back and stand upon the same plane.

By degrees he lapsed into a sort of lethargy, a wretched counterfeit of sleep, his eyes half closed, his breath irregular. But, such as it was, it was infinitely grateful. The little, over-driven cogs and wheels of the mind, at least, moved more slowly. Perhaps by and by this might actually develop into genuine, blessed oblivion.

But there was a quick step outside the door. Gretry came in.

"Oh, J.! Here already, are you? Well, Crookes will begin to sell at the very tap of the bell."

"He will, hey?" Jadwin was on his feet. Instantly the jaded nerves braced taut again; instantly the tiny machinery of the brain spun again at its fullest limit. "He's going to try to sell us out, is he? All right. We'll sell, too. We'll see who can sell the most—Crookes or Jadwin."

"Sell! You mean buy, of course."

"No, I don't. I've been thinking it over since you left last night. Wheat is worth exactly what it is selling for this blessed day. I've not inflated it up one single eighth yet; Crookes thinks I have. Good Lord, I can read him like a book! He thinks I've boosted the stuff above what it's worth, and that a little shove will send it down. He can send it down to ten cents if he likes, but it'll jump back like a rubber ball. I'll sell bushel for bushel with him as long as he wants to keep it up."

"Heavens and earth, J.," exclaimed Gretry, with a long breath, "the risk is about as big as holding up the Bank of England. You are depreciating the value of about forty million dollars' worth of your property with every cent she breaks."

"You do as I tell you—you'll see I'm right," answered Jadwin. "Get your boys in here, and we'll give 'em the day's orders."

The "Crookes affair"—as among themselves the group of men who centred about Jadwin spoke of it—was one of the sharpest fights known on the Board of Trade for many a long day. It developed with amazing unexpectedness and was watched with breathless interest from every produce exchange between the oceans.

It occupied every moment of each morning's session of the Board of Trade for four furious, never-to-be-forgotten days. Promptly at half-past nine o'clock on Tuesday morning Crookes began to sell May wheat short, and instantly, to the surprise of every Pit trader on the floor, the price broke with his very first attack. In twenty minutes it was down half a cent. Then came the really big surprise of the day. Landry Court, the known representative of the firm which all along had fostered and encouraged the rise in the price, appeared in the Pit, and instead of buying, upset all precedent and all calculation by selling as freely as the Crookes men themselves. For three days the battle went on. But to the outside world—even to the Pit itself—it seemed less a battle than a rout. The "Unknown Bull" was down, was beaten at last. He had inflated the price of the wheat, he had backed a false, an artificial, and unwarrantable boom, and now he was being broken. Ah Crookes knew when to strike. Here was the great general—the real leader who so long had held back.

By the end of the Friday session, Crookes and his clique had sold five million bushels, "going short," promising to deliver wheat that they did not own, but expected to buy at low prices. The market that day closed at ninety-five.

Friday night, in Jadwin's room in the Grand Pacific, a conference was held between

Gretry, Landry Court, two of Gretry's most trusted lieutenants, and Jadwin himself. Two results issued from this conference. One took the form of a cipher cable to Jadwin's Liverpool agent, which, translated, read: "Buy all wheat that is offered till market advances one penny." The other was the general order issued to Landry Court and the four other Pit traders for the Gretry-Converse house, to the effect that in the morning they were to go into the Pit and, making no demonstration, begin to buy back the wheat they had been selling all the week. Each of them was to buy one million bushels. Jadwin had, as Gretry put it, "timed Crookes to a split second," foreseeing the exact moment when he would make his supreme effort. Sure enough, on that very Saturday Crookes was selling more freely than ever, confident of breaking the Bull ere the closing gong should ring.

But before the end of the morning wheat was up two cents. Buying orders had poured in upon the market. The price had stiffened almost of itself. Above the indicator upon the great dial there seemed to be an invisible, inexplicable magnet that lifted it higher and higher, for all the strenuous efforts of the Bears to drag it down.

A feeling of nervousness began to prevail. The small traders, who had been wild to sell short during the first days of the movement, began on Monday to cover a little here and there.

"Now," declared Jadwin that night, "now's the time to open up all along the line hard. If we start her with a rush to-morrow morning, she'll go to a dollar all by herself."

Tuesday morning, therefore, the Gretry-Converse traders bought another five million bushels. The price under this stimulus went up with the buoyancy of a feather. The little shorts, more and more uneasy, and beginning to cover by the scores, forced it up even higher.

The nervousness of the "crowd" increased. Perhaps, after all, Crookes was not so omnipotent. Perhaps, after all, the Unknown Bull had another fight in him. Then the "outsiders" came into the market. All in a moment all the traders were talking "higher prices." Everybody now was as eager to buy as, a week before, they had been eager to sell. The price went up by convulsive bounds. Crookes dared not buy, dared not purchase the wheat to make good his promises of delivery, for fear of putting up the price on himself higher still. Dismayed, chagrined, and humiliated, he and his clique sat back inert, watching the tremendous reaction, hoping against hope that the market would break again.

But now it became difficult to get wheat at all. All of a sudden nobody was selling. The buyers in the Pit commenced to bid against each other, offering a dollar and two cents. The wheat did not "come out." They bid a dollar two and a half, a dollar two and five-eighths; still no wheat. Frantic, they shook their fingers in the very faces of Landry Court and the Gretry traders, shouting: "A dollar, two and seven-eighths! A dollar, three! Three and an eighth! A quarter! Three-eighths! A half!" But the others shook their heads. Except on extraordinary advances of a whole cent at a time, there was no wheat for sale.

At the last-named price Crookes acknowledged defeat. Somewhere in his big machine a screw had been loose. Somehow he had miscalculated. So long as he and his associates sold and sold and sold, the price would go down. The instant they tried to cover there was no wheat for sale, and the price leaped up again with an elasticity that no power could control.

He saw now that he and his followers had to face a loss of several cents a bushel on each one of the five million they had sold. They had not been able to cover one single sale, and the situation was back again exactly as before his onslaught, the Unknown Bull in securer control than ever before.

But Crookes had, at last, begun to suspect the true condition of affairs, and now that the market was hourly growing tighter and more congested, his suspicion was confirmed. Alone, locked in his private office, he thought it out, and at last remarked to himself:

"Somebody has a great big line of wheat that is not on the market at all. Somebody has got all the wheat there is. I guess I know his name. I guess the visible supply of May wheat in the Chicago market is cornered."

This was at a time when the price stood at a dollar and one cent. Crookes—who from the first had managed and handled the operations of his confederates—knew very well that if he now bought in all the wheat his clique had sold short, the price would go up long before he could complete the deal. He said nothing to the others, further than that they should "hold on a little longer, in the hopes of a turn," but very quietly he began to cover his own personal sales—his share of the five million sold by his clique. Foreseeing the collapse of his scheme, he got out of the market; at a loss, it was true, but still no more than he could stand. If he "held on a little longer, in the hopes of a turn," there was no telling how deep the Bull would gore him. This was no time to think much about "obligations." It had got to be "every man for himself" by now.

A few days after this Crookes sat in his office in the building in La Salle Street that bore his name. It was about eleven o'clock in the morning. His dry, small, beardless face creased a little at the corners of the mouth as he heard the ticker chattering behind him. He knew how the tape read. There had been another flurry on the Board that morning, not half an hour since, and wheat was up again. In the last thirty-six hours it had advanced three cents, and he knew very well that at that very minute the "boys" on the floor were offering nine cents over the dollar for the May option—and not getting it. The market was in a tumult. He fancied he could almost hear the thunder of the Pit as it swirled. All La Salle Street was listening and watching, all Chicago, all the nation, all the world. Not a "factor" on the London

'Change who did not turn an ear down the wind to catch the echo of this turmoil, not an agent de change in the peristyle of the Paris Bourse, who did not strain to note the every modulation of its mighty diapason.

"Well," said the little voice of the man-within-the-man, who in the person of Calvin Hardy Crookes sat listening to the ticker in his office, "well, let it roar. It sure can't hurt C. H. C."

"Can you see Mr. Cressler?" said the clerk at the door.

He came in with a hurried, unsteady step. The long, stooping figure was unkempt; was, in a sense, unjointed, as though some support had been withdrawn. The eyes were deep-sunk, the bones of the face were gaunt and bare; and from moment to moment the man swallowed quickly and moistened his lips.

Crookes nodded as his ally came up, and one finger raised, pointed to a chair. He himself was impassive, calm. He did not move. Taciturn as ever, he waited for the other to speak.

"I want to talk with you, Mr. Crookes," began Cressler, hurriedly. "I—I made up my mind to it day before yesterday, but I put it off. I had hoped that things would come our way. But I can't delay now.... Mr. Crookes, I can't stand this any longer. I must get out of the clique. I haven't the ready money to stand this pace."

There was a silence. Crookes neither moved nor changed expression. His small eyes fixed upon the other, he waited for Cressler to go on.

"I might remind you," Cressler continued, "that when I joined your party I expressly stipulated that our operations should not be speculative."

"You knew—" began Crookes.

"Oh, I have nothing to say," Cressler interrupted. "I did know. I knew from the first it was to be speculation. I tried to deceive myself. I—well, this don't interest you. The point is I must get out of the market. I don't like to go back on you others"—Cressler's fingers were fiddling with his watch chain—"I don't like to—I mean to say you must let me out. You must let me cover—at once. I am—very nearly bankrupt now. Another half-cent rise, and I'm done for. It will take as it is—my—my—all my ready money—all my savings for the last ten years to buy in my wheat."

"Let's see. How much did I sell for you?" demanded Crookes. "Five hundred thousand?"

"Yes, five hundred thousand at ninety-eight—and we're at a dollar nine now. It's an eleven-cent jump. I—I can't stand another eighth. I must cover at once."

Crookes, without answering, drew his desk telephone to him.

"Hello!" he said after a moment. "Hello! ... Buy five hundred May, at the market, right away."

He hung up the receiver and leaned back in his chair.

"They'll report the trade in a minute," he said. "Better wait and see."

Cressler stood at the window, his hands clasped behind his back, looking down into the street. He did not answer. The seconds passed, then the minutes. Crookes turned to his desk and signed a few letters, the scrape of his pen the only noise to break the silence of the room. Then at last he observed:

"Pretty bum weather for this time of the year."

Cressler nodded. He took off his hat, and pushed the hair back from his forehead with a slow, persistent gesture; then as the ticker began to click again, he faced around quickly, and crossing the room, ran the tape through his fingers.

"God," he muttered, between his teeth, "I hope your men didn't lose any time. It's up again."

There was a step at the door, and as Crookes called to come in, the office messenger entered and put a slip of paper into his hands. Crookes looked at it, and pushed it across his desk towards Cressler.

"Here you are," he observed. "That's your trade. Five hundred May, at a dollar ten. You were lucky to get it at that—or at any price."

"Ten!" cried the other, as he took the paper.

Crookes turned away again, and glanced indifferently over his letters. Cressler laid the slip carefully down upon the ledge of the desk, and though Crookes did not look up, he could almost feel how the man braced himself, got a grip of himself, put all his resources to the stretch to meet this blow squarely in the front.

"And I said another eighth would bust me," Cressler remarked, with a short laugh. "Well," he added, grimly, "it looks as though I were busted. I suppose, though, we must all expect to get the knife once in a while—mustn't we? Well, there goes fifty thousand dollars of my good money."

"I can tell you who's got it, if you care to know," answered Crookes. "It's a pewter quarter to Government bonds that Gretry, Converse & Co. sold that wheat to you. They've got about all the wheat there is."

"I know, of course, they've been heavy buyers—for this Unknown Bull they talk so much about."

"Well, he ain't Unknown to me," declared Crookes. "I know him. It's Curtis Jadwin. He's the man we've been fighting all along, and all hell's going to break loose down here in three or four days. He's cornered the market."

"Jadwin! You mean J.—Curtis—my friend?"

Crookes grunted an affirmative.

"But—why, he told me he was out of the market—for good."

Crookes did not seem to consider that the remark called for any useless words. He put his hands in his pockets and looked at Cressler.

"Does he know?" faltered Cressler. "Do you suppose he could have heard that I was in this clique of yours?"

"Not unless you told him yourself."

Cressler stood up, clearing his throat.

"I have not told him, Mr. Crookes," he said. "You would do me an especial favor if you would keep it from the public, from everybody, from Mr. Jadwin, that I was a member of this ring."

Crookes swung his chair around and faced his desk.

"Hell! You don't suppose I'm going to talk, do you?"

"Well.... Good-morning, Mr. Crookes."

"Good-morning."

Left alone, Crookes took a turn the length of the room. Then he paused in the middle of the floor, looking down thoughtfully at his trim, small feet.

"Jadwin!" he muttered. "Hm! ... Think you're boss of the boat now, don't you? Think I'm done with you, hey? Oh, yes, you'll run a corner in wheat, will you? Well, here's a point for your consideration Mr. Curtis Jadwin, 'Don't get so big that all the other fellows can see you—they throw bricks.'"

He sat down in his chair, and passed a thin and delicate hand across his lean mouth.

"No," he muttered, "I won't try to kill you any more. You've cornered wheat, have you? All right.... Your own wheat, my smart Aleck, will do all the killing I want."

Then at last the news of the great corner, authoritative, definite, went out over all the country, and promptly the figure and name of Curtis Jadwin loomed suddenly huge and formidable in the eye of the public. There was no wheat on the Chicago market. He, the great man, the "Napoleon of La Salle Street," had it all. He sold it or hoarded it, as suited his pleasure. He dictated the price to those men who must buy it of him to fill their contracts. His hand was upon the indicator of the wheat dial of the Board of Trade, and he moved it through as many or as few of the degrees of the circle as he chose.

The newspapers, not only of Chicago, but of every city in the Union, exploited him for "stories." The history of his corner, how he had effected it, its chronology, its results, were told and retold, till his name was familiar in the homes and at the firesides of uncounted thousands. "Anecdotes" were circulated concerning him, interviews—concocted for the most part in the editorial rooms—were printed. His picture appeared. He was described as a cool, calm man of steel, with a cold and calculating grey eye, "piercing as an eagle's"; as a desperate gambler, bold as a buccaneer, his eye black and fiery—a veritable pirate; as a mild, small man with a weak chin and a deprecatory demeanour; as a jolly and roistering "high roller," addicted to actresses, suppers, and to bathing in champagne.

In the Democratic press he was assailed as little better than a thief, vituperated as an oppressor of the people, who ground the faces of the poor, and battened in the luxury wrung from the toiling millions. The Republican papers spoke solemnly of the new era of prosperity upon which the country was entering, referred to the stimulating effect of the higher prices upon capitalised industry, and distorted the situation to an augury of a sweeping Republican victory in the next Presidential campaign.

Day in and day out Gretry's office, where Jadwin now fixed his headquarters, was besieged. Reporters waited in the anteroom for whole half days to get but a nod and a word from the great man. Promoters, inventors, small financiers, agents, manufacturers, even "crayon artists" and horse dealers, even tailors and yacht builders rubbed shoulders with one another outside the door marked "Private."

Farmers from Iowa or Kansas come to town to sell their little quotas of wheat at the prices they once had deemed impossible, shook his hand on the street, and urged him to come out and see "God's own country."

But once, however, an entire deputation of these wheat growers found their way into the sanctum. They came bearing a presentation cup of silver, and their spokesman, stammering and horribly embarrassed in unwonted broadcloth and varnished boots, delivered a short address. He explained that all through the Middle West, all through the wheat belts, a great wave of prosperity was rolling because of Jadwin's corner. Mortgages were being paid off, new and improved farming implements were being bought, new areas seeded new live stock acquired. The men were buying buggies again, the women parlor melodeons, houses and homes were going up; in short, the entire farming population of the Middle West was being daily enriched. In a letter that Jadwin received about this time from an old fellow living in "Bates Corners," Kansas, occurred the words:

"—and, sir, you must know that not a night passes that my little girl, now going on seven, sir, and the brightest of her class in the county seat grammar school, does not pray to have God bless Mister Jadwin, who helped papa save the farm."

If there was another side, if the brilliancy of his triumph yet threw a shadow behind it, Jadwin could ignore it. It was far from him, he could not see it. Yet for all this a story came to him about this time that for long would not be quite forgotten. It came through Corthell, but very indirectly, passed on by a dozen mouths before it reached his ears.

It told of an American, an art student, who at the moment was on a tramping tour through the north of Italy. It was an ugly story. Jadwin pished and pshawed, refusing to believe it, condemning it as ridiculous exaggeration, but somehow it appealed to an uncompromising sense of the probable; it rang true.

"And I met this boy," the student had said, "on the high road, about a kilometre outside of Arezzo. He was a fine fellow of twenty or twenty-two. He knew nothing of the world. England he supposed to be part of the mainland of Europe. For him Cavour and Mazzini were still alive. But when I announced myself American, he roused at once.

"'Ah, American,' he said. 'We know of your compatriot, then, here in Italy—this

Jadwin of Chicago, who has bought all the wheat. We have no more bread. The loaf is small as the fist, and costly. We cannot buy it, we have no money. For myself, I do not care. I am young. I can eat lentils and cress. But' and here his voice was a whisper—'but my mother—my mother!'"

"It's a lie!" Jadwin cried. "Of course it's a lie. Good God, if I were to believe every damned story the papers print about me these days I'd go insane."

Yet when he put up the price of wheat to a dollar and twenty cents, the great flour mills of Minnesota and Wisconsin stopped grinding, and finding a greater profit in selling the grain than in milling it, threw their stores upon the market. Though the bakers did not increase the price of their bread as a consequence of this, the loaf—even in Chicago, even in the centre of that great Middle West that weltered in the luxury of production—was smaller, and from all the poorer districts of the city came complaints, protests, and vague grumblings of discontent.

On a certain Monday, about the middle of May, Jadwin sat at Gretry's desk (long since given over to his use), in the office on the ground floor of the Board of Trade, swinging nervously back and forth in the swivel chair, drumming his fingers upon the arms, and glancing continually at the clock that hung against the opposite wall. It was about eleven in the morning. The Board of Trade vibrated with the vast trepidation of the Pit, that for two hours had spun and sucked, and guttered and disgorged just overhead. The waiting-room of the office was more than usually crowded. Parasites of every description polished the walls with shoulder and elbow. Millionaires and beggars jostled one another about the doorway. The vice-president of a bank watched the door of the private office covertly; the traffic manager of a railroad exchanged yarns with a group of reporters while awaiting his turn.

As Gretry, the great man's lieutenant, hurried through the anteroom, conversation suddenly ceased, and half a dozen of the more impatient sprang forward. But the broker pushed his way through the crowd, shaking his head, excusing himself as best he might, and entering the office, closed the door behind him.

At the clash of the lock Jadwin started half-way from his chair, then recognising the broker, sank back with a quick breath.

"Why don't you knock, or something, Sam?" he exclaimed. "Might as well kill a man as scare him to death. Well, how goes it?"

"All right. I've fixed the warehouse crowd—and we just about 'own' the editorial and news sheets of these papers." He threw a memorandum down upon the desk. "I'm off again now. Got an appointment with the Northwestern crowd in ten minutes. Has Hargus or Scannel shown up yet?"

"Hargus is always out in your customers' room," answered Jadwin. "I can get him whenever I want him. But Scannel has not shown up yet. I thought when we put up the price again Friday we'd bring him in. I thought you'd figured out that he couldn't stand that rise."

"He can't stand it," answered Gretry. "He'll be in to see you to-morrow or next day."

"To-morrow or next day won't do," answered Jadwin. "I want to put the knife into him to-day. You go up there on the floor and put the price up another cent. That will bring him, or I'll miss my guess."

Gretry nodded. "All right," he said, "it's your game. Shall I see you at lunch?"

"Lunch! I can't eat. But I'll drop around and hear what the Northwestern people had to say to you."

A few moments after Gretry had gone Jadwin heard the ticker on the other side of the room begin to chatter furiously; and at the same time he could fancy that the distant thunder of the Pit grew suddenly more violent, taking on a sharper, shriller note. He looked at the tape. The one-cent rise had been effected.

"You will hold out, will you, you brute?" muttered Jadwin. "See how you like that now." He took out his watch. "You'll be running in to me in just about ten minutes' time."

He turned about, and calling a clerk, gave orders to have Hargus found and brought to him.

When the old fellow appeared Jadwin jumped up and gave him his hand as he came slowly forward.

His rusty top hat was in his hand; from the breast pocket of his faded and dirty frock coat a bundle of ancient newspapers protruded. His shoestring tie straggled over his frayed shirt front, while at his wrist one of his crumpled cuffs, detached from the sleeve, showed the bare, thin wrist between cloth and linen, and encumbered the fingers in which he held the unlit stump of a fetid cigar.

Evidently bewildered as to the cause of this summons, he looked up perplexed at Jadwin as he came up, out of his dim, red-lidded eyes.

"Sit down, Hargus. Glad to see you," called Jadwin.

"Hey?"

The voice was faint and a little querulous.

"I say, sit down. Have a chair. I want to have a talk with you. You ran a corner in wheat once yourself."

"Oh.... Wheat."

"Yes, your corner. You remember?"

"Yes. Oh, that was long ago. In seventy-eight it was—the September option. And the Board made wheat in the cars 'regular.'"

His voice trailed off into silence, and he looked vaguely about on the floor of the room, sucking in his cheeks, and passing the edge of one large, osseous hand across his lips.

"Well, you lost all your money that time, I believe. Scannel, your partner, sold out on you."

"Hey? It was in seventy-eight.... The secretary of the Board announced our suspension at ten in the morning. If the Board had not voted to make wheat in the cars 'regular'—"

He went on and on, in an impassive monotone, repeating, word for word, the same phrases he had used for so long that they had lost all significance.

"Well," broke in Jadwin, at last, "it was Scannel your partner, did for you. Scannel, I say. You know, Dave Scannel."

The old man looked at him confusedly. Then, as the name forced itself upon the atrophied brain, there flashed, for one instant, into the pale, blurred eye, a light, a glint, a brief, quick spark of an old, long-forgotten fire. It gleamed there an instant, but the next sank again.

Plaintively, querulously he repeated:

"It was in seventy-eight.... I lost three hundred thousand dollars."

"How's your little niece getting on?" at last demanded Jadwin.

"My little niece—you mean Lizzie? ... Well and happy, well and happy. I—I got"—he drew a thick bundle of dirty papers from his pocket, envelopes, newspapers, circulars, and the like—"I—I—I got, I got her picture here somewheres."

"Yes, yes, I know, I know," cried Jadwin. "I've seen it. You showed it to me yesterday, you remember."

"I—I got it here somewheres ... somewheres," persisted the old man, fumbling and peering, and as he spoke the clerk from the doorway announced:

"Mr. Scannel."

This latter was a large, thick man, red-faced, with white, short whiskers of an almost wiry texture. He had a small, gimlet-like eye, enormous, hairy ears, wore a "sack" suit, a highly polished top hat, and entered the office with a great flourish of manner and a defiant trumpeting "Well, how do, Captain?"

Jadwin nodded, glancing up under his scowl.

"Hello!" he said.

The other subsided into a chair, and returned scowl for scowl.

"Oh, well," he muttered, "if that's your style."

He had observed Hargus sitting by the other side of the desk, still fumbling and mumbling in his dirty memoranda, but he gave no sign of recognition. There was a moment's silence, then in a voice from which all the first bluffness was studiously excluded, Scannel said:

"Well, you've rung the bell on me. I'm a sucker. I know it. I'm one of the few hundred other God-damned fools that you've managed to catch out shooting snipe. Now what I want to know is, how much is it going to cost me to get out of your corner? What's the figure? What do you say?"

"I got a good deal to say," remarked Jadwin, scowling again.

But Hargus had at last thrust a photograph into his hands.

"There it is," he said. "That's it. That's Lizzie."

Jadwin took the picture without looking at it, and as he continued to speak, held it in his fingers, and occasionally tapped it upon the desk.

"I know. I know, Hargus," he answered. "I got a good deal to say, Mr. David Scannel. Do you see this old man here?"

"Oh-h, cut it out!" growled the other.

"It's Hargus. You know him very well. You used to know him better. You and he together tried to swing a great big deal in September wheat once upon a time. Hargus! I say, Hargus!"

The old man looked up.

"Here's the man we were talking about, Scannel, you remember. Remember Dave Scannel, who was your partner in seventy-eight? Look at him. This is him now. He's a rich man now. Remember Scannel?"

Hargus, his bleared old eyes blinking and watering, looked across the desk at the other.

"Oh, what's the game?" exclaimed Scannel. "I ain't here on exhibition, I guess. I—"

But he was interrupted by a sharp, quick gasp that all at once issued from Hargus's trembling lips. The old man said no word, but he leaned far forward in his chair, his eyes fixed upon Scannel, his breath coming short, his fingers dancing against his chin.

"Yes, that's him, Hargus," said Jadwin. "You and he had a big deal on your hands a long time ago," he continued, turning suddenly upon Scannel, a pulse in his temple beginning to beat. "A big deal, and you sold him out."

"It's a lie!" cried the other.

Jadwin beat his fist upon the arm of his chair. His voice was almost a shout as he answered:

"You—sold—him—out. I know you. I know the kind of bug you are. You ruined him to save your own dirty hide, and all his life since poor old Hargus has been living off the charity of the boys down here, pinched and hungry and neglected, and getting on, God knows how; yes, and supporting his little niece, too, while you, you have been loafing about your clubs, and sprawling on your steam yachts, and dangling round after your kept women—on the money you stole from him."

Scannel squared himself in his chair, his little eyes twinkling.

"Look here," he cried, furiously, "I don't take that kind of talk from the best man that ever wore shoe-leather. Cut it out, understand? Cut it out."

Jadwin's lower jaw set with a menacing click; aggressive, masterful, he leaned forward.

"You interrupt me again," he declared, "and you'll go out of that door a bankrupt. You listen to me and take my orders. That's what you're here to-day for. If you think you can get your wheat somewheres else, suppose you try."

Scannel sullenly settled himself in his place. He did not answer. Hargus, his eye wandering again, looked distressfully from one to the other. Then Jadwin, after shuffling among the papers of his desk, fixed a certain memorandum with his glance. All at once, whirling about and facing the other, he said quickly:

"You are short to our firm two million bushels at a dollar a bushel."

"Nothing of the sort," cried the other. "It's a million and a half."

Jadwin could not forbear a twinkle of grim humour as he saw how easily Scannel had fallen into the trap.

"You're short a million and a half, then," he repeated. "I'll let you have six hundred thousand of it at a dollar and a half a bushel."

"A dollar and a half! Why, my God, man! Oh well"—Scannel spread out his hands nonchalantly—"I shall simply go into bankruptcy—just as you said."

"Oh, no, you won't," replied Jadwin, pushing back and crossing his legs. "I've had your financial standing computed very carefully, Mr. Scannel. You've got the ready money. I know what you can stand without busting, to the fraction of a cent."

"Why, it's ridiculous. That handful of wheat will cost me three hundred thousand dollars."

"Pre-cisely."

And then all at once Scannel surrendered. Stony, imperturbable, he drew his check book from his pocket.

"Make it payable to bearer," said Jadwin.

The other complied, and Jadwin took the check and looked it over carefully.

"Now," he said, "watch here, Dave Scannel. You see this check? And now," he added, thrusting it into Hargus's hands, "you see where it goes. There's the principal of your debt paid off."

"The principal?"

"You haven't forgotten the interest, have you? won't compound it, because that might bust you. But six per cent interest on three hundred thousand since 1878, comes to—let's see—three hundred and sixty thousand dollars. And you still owe me nine hundred thousand bushels of wheat." He ciphered a moment on a sheet of note paper. "If I charge you a dollar and forty a bushel for that wheat, it will come to that sum exactly.... Yes, that's correct. I'll let you have the balance of that wheat at a dollar forty. Make the check payable to bearer as before."

For a second Scannel hesitated, his face purple, his teeth grinding together, then muttering his rage beneath his breath, opened his check book again.

"Thank you," said Jadwin as he took the check.

He touched his call bell.

"Kinzie," he said to the clerk who answered it, "after the close of the market to-day send delivery slips for a million and a half wheat to Mr. Scannel. His account with us has been settled."

Jadwin turned to the old man, reaching out the second check to him.

"Here you are, Hargus. Put it away carefully. You see what it is, don't you? Buy your Lizzie a little gold watch with a hundred of it, and tell her it's from Curtis Jadwin, with his compliments.... What, going, Scannel? Well, good-by to you, sir, and hey!" he called after him, "please don't slam the door as you go out."

But he dodged with a defensive gesture as the pane of glass almost leaped from its casing, as Scannel stormed across the threshold.

Jadwin turned to Hargus, with a solemn wink.

"He did slam it after all, didn't he?"

The old fellow, however, sat fingering the two checks in silence. Then he looked up at Jadwin, scared and trembling.

"I—I don't know," he murmured, feebly. "I am a very old man. This—this is a great deal of money, sir. I—I can't say; I—I don't know. I'm an old man ... an old man."

"You won't lose 'em, now?"

"No, no. I'll deposit them at once in the Illinois Trust. I shall ask—I should like."

"I'll send a clerk with you."

"Yes, yes, that is about what—what I—what I was about to suggest. But I must say, Mr. Jadwin—"

He began to stammer his thanks. But Jadwin cut him off. Rising, he guided Hargus to the door, one hand on his shoulder, and at the entrance to the outer office called a clerk.

"Take Mr. Hargus over to the Illinois Trust, Kinzie, and introduce him. He wants to open an account."

The old man started off with the clerk, but before Jadwin had reseated himself at his desk was back again. He was suddenly all excitement, as if a great idea had abruptly taken possession of him. Stealthy, furtive, he glanced continually over his shoulder as he spoke, talking in whispers, a trembling hand shielding his lips.

"You—you are in—you are in control now," he said. "You could give—hey? You could give me—just a little—just one word. A word would be enough, hey? hey? Just a little tip. My God, I could make fifty dollars by noon."

"Why, man, I've just given you about half a million."

"Half a million? I don't know. But"—he plucked Jadwin tremulously by the sleeve—"just a word," he begged. "Hey, just yes or no."

"Haven't you enough with those two checks?"

"Those checks? Oh, I know, I know, I know I'll salt 'em down. Yes, in the Illinois Trust. I won't touch 'em—not those. But just a little tip now, hey?"

"Not a word. Not a word. Take him along, Kinzie."

One week after this Jadwin sold, through his agents in Paris, a tremendous line of "cash" wheat at a dollar and sixty cents the bushel. By now the foreign demand was a thing almost insensate. There was no question as to the price. It was, "Give us the wheat, at whatever cost, at whatever figure, at whatever expense; only that it be rushed to our markets with all the swiftness of steam and steel." At home, upon the Chicago Board of Trade, Jadwin was as completely master of the market as of his own right hand. Everything stopped when he raised a finger; everything leaped to life with the fury of obsession when he nodded his head. His wealth increased with such stupefying rapidity, that at no time was he able to even approximate the gains that accrued to him because of his corner. It was more than twenty million, and less than fifty million. That was all he knew. Nor were the everlasting hills more secure than he from the attack of any human enemy. Out of the ranks of the conquered there issued not so much as a whisper of hostility. Within his own sphere no Czar, no satrap, no Caesar ever wielded power more resistless.

"Sam," said Curtis Jadwin, at length to the broker, "Sam, nothing in the world can stop me now. They think I've been doing something big, don't they, with this corner. Why, I've only just begun. This is just a feeler. Now I'm going to let 'em know just how big a gun C. J. really is. I'm going to swing this deal right over into July. I'm going to buy in my July shorts."

The two men were in Gretry's office as usual, and as Jadwin spoke, the broker glanced up incredulously.

"Now you are for sure crazy."

Jadwin jumped to his feet.

"Crazy!" he vociferated. "Crazy! What do you mean? Crazy! For God's sake, Sam, what—Look here, don't use that word to me. I—it don't suit. What I've done isn't exactly the work of—of—takes brains, let me tell you. And look here, look here, I say, I'm going to swing this deal right over into July. Think I'm going to let go now, when I've just begun to get a real grip on things? A pretty fool I'd look like to get out now—even if I could. Get out? How are we going to unload our big line of wheat without breaking the price on us? No, sir, not much. This market is going up to two dollars." He smote a knee with his clinched fist, his face going abruptly crimson. "I say two dollars," he cried. "Two dollars, do you hear? It will go there, you'll see, you'll see."

"Reports on the new crop will begin to come in in June." Gretry's warning was almost a cry. "The price of wheat is so high now, that God knows how many farmers will plant it this spring. You may have to take care of a record harvest."

"I know better," retorted Jadwin. "I'm watching this thing. You can't tell me anything about it. I've got it all figured out, your 'new crop.'"

"Well, then you're the Lord Almighty himself."

"I don't like that kind of joke. I don't like that kind of joke. It's blasphemous," exclaimed Jadwin. "Go, get it off on Crookes. He'd appreciate it, but I don't. But this new crop now—look here."

And for upwards of two hours Jadwin argued and figured, and showed to Gretry endless tables of statistics to prove that he was right.

But at the end Gretry shook his head. Calmly and deliberately he spoke his mind.

"J., listen to me. You've done a big thing. I know it, and I know, too, that there've been lots of times in the last year or so when I've been wrong and you've been right. But now, J., so help me God, we've reached our limit. Wheat is worth a dollar and a half to-day, and not one cent more. Every eighth over that figure is inflation. If you run it up to two dollars—"

"It will go there of itself, I tell you."

"—if you run it up to two dollars, it will be that top-heavy, that the littlest kick in the world will knock it over. Be satisfied now with what you got. J., it's common sense. Close out your long line of May, and then stop. Suppose the price does break a little, you'd still make your pile. But swing this deal over into July, and it's ruin, ruin. I may have been mistaken before, but I know I'm right now. And do you realise, J., that yesterday in the Pit there were some short sales? There's some of them dared to go short of wheat against you—even at the very top of your corner—and there was more selling this morning. You've always got to buy, you know. If they all began to sell to you at once they'd bust you. It's only because you've got 'em so scared—I believe—that keeps 'em from it. But it looks to me as though this selling proved that they were picking up heart. They think they can get the wheat from the farmers when harvesting begins. And I tell you, J., you've put the price of wheat so high, that the wheat areas are extending all over the country."

"You're scared," cried Jadwin. "That's the trouble with you, Sam. You've been scared from the start. Can't you see, man, can't you see that this market is a regular tornado?"

"I see that the farmers all over the country are planting wheat as they've never planted it before. Great Scott, J., you're fighting against the earth itself."

"Well, we'll fight it, then. I'll stop those hayseeds. What do I own all these newspapers and trade journals for? We'll begin sending out reports to-morrow that'll discourage any big wheat planting."

"And then, too," went on Gretry, "here's another point. Do you know, you ought to be in bed this very minute. You haven't got any nerves left at all. You acknowledge yourself that you don't sleep any more. And, good Lord, the moment any one of us contradicts you, or opposes you, you go off the handle to beat the Dutch. I know it's a strain, old man, but you want to keep yourself in hand if you go on with this thing. If you should break down now—well, I don't like to think of what would happen. You ought to see a doctor."

"Oh-h, fiddlesticks," exclaimed Jadwin, "I'm all right. I don't need a doctor, haven't time to see one anyhow. Don't you bother about me. I'm all right."

Was he? That same night, the first he had spent under his own roof for four days, Jadwin lay awake till the clocks struck four, asking himself the same question. No, he was not all right. Something was very wrong with him, and whatever it might be, it was growing worse. The sensation of the iron clamp about his head was almost permanent by now, and just the walk between his room at the Grand Pacific and Gretry's office left him panting and exhausted. Then had come vertigoes and strange, inexplicable qualms, as if he were in an elevator that sank under him with terrifying rapidity.

Going to and fro in La Salle Street, or sitting in Gretry's office, where the roar of the Pit dinned forever in his ears, he could forget these strange symptoms. It was the night he dreaded—the long hours he must spend alone. The instant the strain was relaxed, the gallop of hoofs, or as the beat of ungovernable torrents began in his brain. Always the beat dropped to the same cadence, always the pulse spelled out the same words:

"Wheat-wheat-wheat, wheat-wheat-wheat."

And of late, during the long and still watches of the night, while he stared at the ceiling, or counted the hours that must pass before his next dose of bromide of potassium, a new turn had been given to the screw.

This was a sensation, the like of which he found it difficult to describe. But it seemed to be a slow, tense crisping of every tiniest nerve in his body. It would begin as he lay in bed—counting interminably to get himself to sleep—between his knees and ankles, and thence slowly spread to every part of him, creeping upward, from loin to shoulder, in a gradual wave of torture that was not pain, yet infinitely worse. A dry, pringling aura as of billions of minute electric shocks crept upward over his flesh, till it reached his head, where it seemed to culminate in a white flash, which he felt rather than saw.

His body felt strange and unfamiliar to him. It seemed to have no weight, and at times his hands would appear to swell swiftly to the size of mammoth boxing-gloves, so that he must rub them together to feel that they were his own.

He put off consulting a doctor from day to day, alleging that he had not the time. But the real reason, though he never admitted it, was the fear that the doctor might tell him what he guessed to be the truth.

Were his wits leaving him? The horror of the question smote through him like the drive of a javelin. What was to happen? What nameless calamity impended?

"Wheat-wheat-wheat, wheat-wheat-wheat."

His watch under his pillow took up the refrain. How to grasp the morrow's business, how control the sluice gates of that torrent he had unchained, with this unspeakable crumbling and disintegrating of his faculties going on?

Jaded, feeble, he rose to meet another day. He drove down town, trying not to hear the beat of his horses' hoofs. Dizzy and stupefied, he gained Gretry's office, and alone with his terrors sat in the chair before his desk, waiting, waiting.

Then far away the great gong struck. Just over his head, penetrating wood and iron, he heard the mighty throe of the Pit once more beginning, moving. And then, once again, the limp and ravelled fibres of being grew tight with a wrench. Under the stimulus of the roar of the maelstrom, the flagging, wavering brain righted itself once more, and—how, he himself could not say—the business of the day was despatched, the battle was once more urged. Often he acted upon what he knew to be blind, unreasoned instinct. Judgment, clear reasoning, at times, he felt, forsook him. Decisions that involved what seemed to be the very stronghold of his situation, had to be taken without a moment's warning. He decided for or against without knowing why. Under his feet fissures opened. He must take the leap without seeing the other edge. Somehow he always landed upon his feet; somehow his great, cumbersome engine, lurching, swaying, in spite of loosened joints, always kept the track.

Luck, his golden goddess, the genius of glittering wings, was with him yet. Sorely tried, flouted even she yet remained faithful, lending a helping hand to lost and wandering judgment.

So the month of May drew to its close. Between the twenty-fifth and the thirtieth Jadwin covered his July shortage, despite Gretry's protests and warnings. To him they seemed idle enough. He was too rich, too strong now to fear any issue. Daily the profits of the corner increased. The unfortunate shorts were wrung dry and drier. In Gretry's office they heard their sentences, and as time went on, and Jadwin beheld more and more of these broken speculators, a vast contempt for human nature grew within him.

Some few of his beaten enemies were resolute enough, accepting defeat with grim carelessness, or with sphinx-like indifference, or even with airy jocularity. But for the most part their alert, eager deference, their tame subservience, the abject humility and debasement of their bent shoulders drove Jadwin to the verge of self-control. He grew to detest the business; he regretted even the defiant brutality of Scannel, a rascal, but none the less keeping his head high. The more the fellows cringed to him, the tighter he wrenched the screw. In a few cases he found a pleasure in relenting entirely, selling his wheat to the unfortunates at a price that left them without loss; but in the end the business hardened his heart to any distress his mercilessness might entail. He took his profits as a Bourbon took his taxes, as if by right of birth. Somewhere, in a long-forgotten history of his brief school days, he had come across a phrase that he remembered now, by some devious and distant process of association, and when he heard of the calamities that his campaign had wrought, of the shipwrecked fortunes and careers that were sucked down by the Pit, he found it possible to say, with a short laugh, and a lift of one shoulder:

"Vae victis."

His wife he saw but seldom. Occasionally they breakfasted together; more often they met at dinner. But that was all. Jadwin's life by now had come to be so irregular, and his few hours of sleep so precious and so easily disturbed, that he had long since occupied a separate apartment.

What Laura's life was at this time he no longer knew. She never spoke of it to him; never nowadays complained of loneliness. When he saw her she appeared to be cheerful. But this very cheerfulness made him uneasy, and at times, through the murk of the chaff of wheat, through the bellow of the Pit, and the crash of collapsing fortunes there reached him a suspicion that all was not well with Laura.

Once he had made an abortive attempt to break from the turmoil of La Salle Street and the Board of Trade, and, for a time at least, to get back to the old life they both had loved—to get back, in a word, to her. But the consequences had been all but disastrous. Now he could not keep away.

"Corner wheat!" he had exclaimed to her, the following day. "Corner wheat! It's the wheat that has cornered me. It's like holding a wolf by the ears, bad to hold on, but worse to let go."

But absorbed, blinded, deafened by the whirl of things, Curtis Jadwin could not see how perilously well grounded had been his faint suspicion as to Laura's distress.

On the day after her evening with her husband in the art gallery, the evening when Gretry had broken in upon them like a courier from the front, Laura had risen from her bed to look out upon a world suddenly empty.

Corthell she had sent from her forever. Jadwin was once more snatched from her side. Where, now, was she to turn? Jadwin had urged her to go to the country—to their place at Geneva Lake—but she refused. She saw the change that had of late come over her husband, saw his lean face, the hot, tired eyes, the trembling fingers and nervous gestures. Vaguely she imagined approaching disaster. If anything happened to Curtis, her place was at his side.

During the days that Jadwin and Crookes were at grapples Laura found means to occupy her mind with all manner of small activities. She overhauled her wardrobe, planned her summer gowns, paid daily visits to her dressmakers, rode and drove in the park, till every turn of the roads, every tree, every bush was familiar, to the point of wearisome contempt.

Then suddenly she began to indulge in a mania for old books and first editions. She haunted the stationers and second-hand bookstores, studied the authorities, followed the auctions, and bought right and left, with reckless extravagance. But the taste soon palled upon her. With so much money at her command there was none of the spice of the hunt in the affair. She had but to express a desire for a certain treasure, and forthwith it was put into her hand.

She found it so in all other things. Her desires were gratified with an abruptness that killed the zest of them. She felt none of the joy of possession; the little personal relation between her and her belongings vanished away. Her gowns, beautiful beyond all she had ever imagined, were of no more interest to her than a drawerful of outworn gloves. She bought horses till she could no longer tell them apart; her carriages crowded three supplementary stables in the neighbourhood. Her flowers, miracles of laborious cultivation, filled the whole house with their fragrance. Wherever she went deference moved before her like a guard; her beauty, her enormous wealth, her wonderful horses, her exquisite gowns made of her a cynosure, a veritable queen.

And hardly a day passed that Laura Jadwin, in the solitude of her own boudoir, did not fling her arms wide in a gesture of lassitude and infinite weariness, crying out:

"Oh, the ennui and stupidity of all this wretched life!"

She could look forward to nothing. One day was like the next. No one came to see her. For all her great house and for all her money, she had made but few friends. Her "grand manner" had never helped her popularity. She passed her evenings alone in her "upstairs sitting-room," reading, reading till far into the night, or, the lights extinguished, sat at her open window listening to the monotonous lap and wash of the lake.

At such moments she thought of the men who had come into her life—of the love she had known almost from her girlhood. She remembered her first serious affair. It had been with the impecunious theological student who was her tutor. He had worn glasses and little black side whiskers, and had implored her to marry him and come to China, where he was to be a missionary. Every time that he came he had brought her a new book to read, and he had taken her for long walks up towards the hills where the old powder mill stood. Then it was the young lawyer—the "brightest man in Worcester County"—who took her driving in a hired buggy, sent her a multitude of paper novels (which she never read), with every love passage carefully underscored, and wrote very bad verse to her eyes and hair, whose "velvet blackness was the shadow of a crown." Or, again, it was the youthful cavalry officer met in a flying visit to her Boston aunt, who loved her on first sight, gave her his photograph in uniform and a bead belt of Apache workmanship. He was forever singing to her—to a guitar accompaniment—an old love song:

"At midnight hour Beneath the tower He murmured soft, 'Oh nothing fearing With thine own true soldier fly.'"

Then she had come to Chicago, and Landry Court, with his bright enthusiasms and fine exaltations had loved her. She had never taken him very seriously but none the less it had been very sweet to know his whole universe depended upon the nod of her head, and that her influence over him had been so potent, had kept him clean and loyal and honest.

And after this Corthell and Jadwin had come into her life, the artist and the man of affairs. She remembered Corthell's quiet, patient, earnest devotion of those days before her marriage. He rarely spoke to her of his love, but by some ingenious subtlety he had filled her whole life with it. His little attentions, his undemonstrative solicitudes came precisely when and where they were most appropriate. He had never failed her. Whenever she had needed him, or even, when through caprice or impulse she had turned to him, it always had been to find that long since he had carefully prepared for that very contingency. His thoughtfulness of her had been a thing to wonder at. He remembered for months, years even, her most trivial fancies, her unexpressed dislikes. He knew her tastes, as if by instinct; he prepared little surprises for her, and placed them in her way without ostentation, and quite as matters of course. He never permitted her to be embarrassed; the little annoying situations of the day's life he had smoothed away long before they had ensnared her. He never was off his guard, never disturbed, never excited.

And he amused her, he entertained her without seeming to do so. He made her talk; he made her think. He stimulated and aroused her, so that she herself talked and thought with a brilliancy that surprised herself. In fine, he had so contrived that she associated him with everything that was agreeable.

She had sent him away the first time, and he had gone without a murmur; only to come back loyal as ever, silent, watchful, sympathetic, his love for her deeper, stronger than before, and—as always timely—bringing to her a companionship at the moment of all others when she was most alone.

Now she had driven him from her again, and this time, she very well knew, it was to be forever. She had shut the door upon this great love.

Laura stirred abruptly in her place, adjusting her hair with nervous fingers.

And, last of all, it had been Jadwin, her husband. She rose and went to the window, and stood there a long moment, looking off into the night over the park. It was warm and very still. A few carriage lamps glimpsed among the trees like fireflies. Along the walks and upon the benches she could see the glow of white dresses and could catch the sound of laughter. Far off somewhere in the shrubbery, she thought she heard a band playing. To the northeast lay the lake, shimmering under the moon, dotted here and there with the coloured lights of steamers.

She turned back into the room. The great house was still. From all its suites of rooms, its corridors, galleries, and hallways there came no sound. There was no one upon the same floor as herself. She had read all her books. It was too late to go out—and there was no one to go with. To go to bed was ridiculous. She was never more wakeful, never more alive, never more ready to be amused, diverted, entertained.

She thought of the organ, and descending to the art gallery, played Bach, Palestrina, and Stainer for an hour; then suddenly she started from the console, with a sharp, impatient movement of her head.

"Why do I play this stupid music?" she exclaimed. She called a servant and asked:

"Has Mr. Jadwin come in yet?"

"Mr. Gretry just this minute telephoned that Mr. Jadwin would not be home to-night."

When the servant had gone out Laura, her lips compressed, flung up her head. Her hands shut to hard fists, her eye flashed. Rigid, erect in the middle of the floor, her arms folded, she uttered a smothered exclamation over and over again under her breath.

All at once anger mastered her—anger and a certain defiant recklessness, an abrupt spirit of revolt. She straightened herself suddenly, as one who takes a decision. Then, swiftly, she went out of the art gallery, and, crossing the hallway, entered the library and opened a great writing-desk that stood in a recess under a small stained window.

She pulled the sheets of note paper towards her and wrote a short letter, directing the envelope to Sheldon Corthell, The Fine Arts Building, Michigan Avenue.

"Call a messenger," she said to the servant who answered her ring, "and have him take—or send him in here when he comes."

She rested the letter against the inkstand, and leaned back in her chair, looking at it, her fingers plucking swiftly at the lace of her dress. Her head was in a whirl. A confusion of thoughts, impulses, desires, half-formed resolves, half-named regrets, swarmed and spun about her. She felt as though she had all at once taken a leap—a leap which had landed her in a place whence she could see a new and terrible country, an unfamiliar place—terrible, yet beautiful—unexplored, and for that reason all the more inviting, a place of shadows.

Laura rose and paced the floor, her hands pressed together over her heart. She was excited, her cheeks flushed, a certain breathless exhilaration came and went within her breast, and in place of the intolerable ennui of the last days, there came over her a sudden, an almost wild animation, and from out her black eyes there shot a kind of furious gaiety.

But she was aroused by a step at the door. The messenger stood there, a figure ridiculously inadequate for the intensity of all that was involved in the issue of the hour—a weazened, stunted boy, in a uniform many sizes too large.

Laura, seated at her desk, held the note towards him resolutely. Now was no time to hesitate, to temporise. If she did not hold to her resolve now, what was there to look forward to? Could one's life be emptier than hers—emptier, more intolerable, more humiliating?

"Take this note to that address," she said, putting the envelope and a coin in the boy's hand. "Wait for an answer."

The boy shut the letter in his book, which he thrust into his breast pocket, buttoning his coat over it. He nodded and turned away.

Still seated, Laura watched him moving towards the door. Well, it was over now. She had chosen. She had taken the leap. What new life was to begin for her to-morrow? What did it all mean? With an inconceivable rapidity her thoughts began racing through, her brain.

She did not move. Her hands, gripped tight together, rested upon the desk before her. Without turning her head, she watched the retreating messenger, from under her lashes. He passed out of the door, the curtain fell behind him.

And only then, when the irrevocableness of the step was all but an accomplished fact, came the reaction.

"Stop!" she cried, springing up. "Stop! Come back here. Wait a moment."

What had happened? She could neither understand nor explain. Somehow an instant of clear vision had come, and in that instant a power within her that was herself and not herself, and laid hold upon her will. No, no, she could not, she could not, after all. She took the note back.

"I have changed my mind," she said, abruptly. "You may keep the money. There is no message to be sent."

As soon as the boy had gone she opened the envelope and read what she had written. But now the words seemed the work of another mind than her own. They were unfamiliar; they were not the words of the Laura Jadwin she knew. Why was it that from the very first hours of her acquaintance with this man, and in every circumstance of their intimacy, she had always acted upon impulse? What was there in him that called into being all that was reckless in her?

And for how long was she to be able to control these impulses? This time she had prevailed once more against that other impetuous self of hers. Would she prevail the next time? And in these struggles, was she growing stronger as she overcame, or weaker? She did not know. She tore the note into fragments, and making a heap of them in the pen tray, burned them carefully.

During the week following upon this, Laura found her trouble more than ever keen. She was burdened with a new distress. The incident of the note to Corthell, recalled at the last moment, had opened her eyes to possibilities of the situation hitherto unguessed. She saw now what she might be capable of doing in a moment of headstrong caprice, she saw depths in her nature she had not plumbed. Whether these hidden pitfalls were peculiarly hers, or whether they were common to all women placed as she now found herself, she did not pause to inquire. She thought only of results, and she was afraid.

But for the matter of that, Laura had long since passed the point of deliberate consideration or reasoned calculation. The reaction had been as powerful as the original purpose, and she was even yet struggling blindly, intuitively.

For what she was now about to do she could give no reason, and the motives for this final and supreme effort to conquer the league of circumstances which hemmed her in were obscure. She did not even ask what they were. She knew only that she was in trouble, and yet it was to the cause of her distress that she addressed herself. Blindly she turned to her husband; and all the woman in her roused itself, girded itself, called up its every resource in one last test, in one ultimate trial of strength between her and the terrible growing power of that blind, soulless force that roared and guttered and sucked, down there in the midst of the city.

She alone, one unaided woman, her only auxiliaries her beauty, her wit, and the frayed, strained bands of a sorely tried love, stood forth like a challenger, against Charybdis, joined battle with the Cloaca, held back with her slim, white hands against the power of the maelstrom that swung the Nations in its grip.

In the solitude of her room she took the resolve. Her troubles were multiplying; she, too, was in the current, the end of which was a pit—a pit black and without bottom. Once already its grip had seized her, once already she had yielded to the insidious drift. Now suddenly aware of a danger, she fought back, and her hands beating the air for help, turned towards the greatest strength she knew.

"I want my husband," she cried, aloud, to the empty darkness of the night. "I want my husband. I will have him; he is mine, he is mine. There shall nothing take me from him; there shall nothing take him from me."

Her first opportunity came upon a Sunday soon afterward. Jadwin, wakeful all the Saturday night, slept a little in the forenoon, and after dinner Laura came to him in his smoking-room, as he lay on the leather lounge trying to read. His wife seated herself at a writing-table in a corner of the room, and by and by began turning the slips of a calendar that stood at her elbow. At last she tore off one of the slips and held it up.

"Curtis."

"Well, old girl?"

"Do you see that date?"

He looked over to her.

"Do you see that date? Do you know of anything that makes that day different—a little—from other days? It's June thirteenth. Do you remember what June thirteenth is?"

Puzzled, he shook his head.

"No—no."

Laura took up a pen and wrote a few words in the space above the printed figures reserved for memoranda. Then she handed the slip to her husband, who read aloud what she had written.

"'Laura Jadwin's birthday.' Why, upon my word," he declared, sitting upright. "So it is, so it is. June thirteenth, of course. And I was beast enough not to realise it. Honey, I can't remember anything these days, it seems."

"But you are going to remember this time?" she said. "You are not going to forget it now. That evening is going to mark the beginning of—oh, Curtis, it is going to be a new beginning of everything. You'll see. I'm going to manage it. I don't know how, but you are going to love me so that nothing, no business, no money, no wheat will ever keep you from me. I will make you. And that evening, that evening of June thirteenth is mine. The day your business can have you, but from six o'clock on you are mine." She crossed the room quickly and took both his hands in hers and knelt beside him. "It is mine," she said, "if you love me. Do you understand, dear? You will come home at six o'clock, and whatever happens—oh, if all La Salle Street should burn to the ground, and all your millions of bushels of wheat with it—whatever happens, you—will—not—leave—me—nor think of anything else but just me, me. That evening is mine, and you will give it to me, just as I have said. I won't remind you of it again. I won't speak of it again. I will leave it to you. But—you will give me that evening if you love me. Dear, do you see just what I mean? ... If you love me.... No—no don't say a word, we won't talk about it at all. No, no, please. Not another word. I don't want you to promise, or pledge yourself, or anything like that. You've heard what I said—and that's all there is about it. We'll talk of something else. By the way, have you seen Mr. Cressler lately?"

"No," he said, falling into her mood. "No haven't seen Charlie in over a month. Wonder what's become of him?"

"I understand he's been sick," she told him. "I met Mrs. Cressler the other day, and she said she was bothered about him."

"Well, what's the matter with old Charlie?"

"She doesn't know, herself. He's not sick enough to go to bed, but he doesn't or won't go down town to his business. She says she can see him growing thinner every day. He keeps telling her he's all right, but for all that, she says, she's afraid he's going to come down with some kind of sickness pretty soon."

"Say," said Jadwin, "suppose we drop around to see them this afternoon? Wouldn't you like to? I haven't seen him in over a month, as I say. Or telephone them to come up and have dinner. Charlie's about as old a friend as I have. We used to be together about every hour of the day when we first came to Chicago. Let's go over to see him this afternoon and cheer him up."

"No," said Laura, decisively. "Curtis, you must have one day of rest out of the week. You are going to lie down all the rest of the afternoon, and sleep if you can. I'll call on them to-morrow."

"Well, all right," he assented. "I suppose I ought to sleep if I can. And then Sam is coming up here, by five. He's going to bring some railroad men with him. We've got a lot to do. Yes, I guess, old girl, I'll try to get forty winks before they get here. And, Laura," he added, taking her hand as she rose to go, "Laura, this is the last lap. In just another month now—oh, at the outside, six weeks—I'll have closed the corner, and then, old girl, you and I will go somewheres, anywhere you like, and then we'll have a good time together all the rest of our lives—all the rest of our lives, honey. Good-by. Now I think I can go to sleep."

She arranged the cushions under his head and drew the curtains close over the windows, and went out, softly closing the door behind her. And a half hour later, when she stole in to look at him, she found him asleep at last, the tired eyes closed, and the arm, with its broad, strong hand, resting under his head. She stood a long moment in the middle of the room, looking down at him; and then slipped out as noiselessly as she had come, the tears trembling on her eyelashes.

Laura Jadwin did not call on the Cresslers the next day, nor even the next after that. For three days she kept indoors, held prisoner by a series of petty incidents; now the delay in the finishing of her new gowns, now by the excessive heat, now by a spell of rain. By Thursday, however, at the beginning of the second week of the month, the storm was gone, and the sun once more shone. Early in the afternoon Laura telephoned to Mrs. Cressler.

"How are you and Mr. Cressler?" she asked. "I'm coming over to take luncheon with you and your husband, if you will let me."

"Oh, Charlie is about the same, Laura," answered Mrs. Cressler's voice. "I guess the dear man has been working too hard, that's all. Do come over and cheer him up. If I'm not here when you come, you just make yourself at home. I've got to go down town to see about railroad tickets and all. I'm going to pack my old man right off to Oconomowoc before I'm another day older. Made up my mind to it last night, and I don't want him to be bothered with tickets or time cards, or baggage or anything. I'll run down and do it all myself. You come right up whenever you're ready and keep Charlie company. How's your husband, Laura child?"

"Oh, Curtis is well," she answered. "He gets very tired at times."

"Well, I can understand it. Lands alive, child whatever are you going to do with all your money? They tell me that J. has made millions in the last three or four months. A man I was talking to last week said his corner was the greatest thing ever known on the Chicago Board of Trade. Well, good-by, Laura, come up whenever you're ready. I'll see you at lunch. Charlie is right here. He says to give you his love." An hour later Laura's victoria stopped in front of the Cressler's house, and the little footman descended with the agility of a monkey, to stand, soldier-like, at the steps, the lap robe over his arm.

Laura gave orders to have the victoria call for her at three, and ran quickly up the front steps. The front entrance was open, the screen door on the latch, and she entered without ceremony.

"Mrs. Cressler!" she called, as she stood in the hallway drawing off her gloves. "Mrs. Cressler! Carrie, have you gone yet?"

But the maid, Annie, appeared at the head of the stairs, on the landing of the second floor, a towel bound about her head, her duster in her hand.

"Mrs. Cressler has gone out, Mrs. Jadwin," she said. "She said you was to make yourself at home, and she'd be back by noon."

Laura nodded, and standing before the hatrack in the hall, took off her hat and gloves, and folded her veil into her purse. The house was old-fashioned, very homelike and spacious, cool, with broad halls and wide windows. In the "front library," where Laura entered first, were steel engravings of the style of the seventies, "whatnots" crowded with shells, Chinese coins, lacquer boxes, and the inevitable sawfish bill. The mantel was mottled white marble, and its shelf bore the usual bronze and gilt clock, decorated by a female figure in classic draperies, reclining against a globe. An oil painting of a mountain landscape hung against one wall; and on a table of black walnut, with a red marble slab, that stood between the front windows, were a stereoscope and a rosewood music box.

The piano, an old style Chickering, stood diagonally across the far corner of the room, by the closed sliding doors, and Laura sat down here and began to play the "Mephisto Walzer," which she had been at pains to learn since the night Corthell had rendered it on her great organ in the art gallery.

But when she had played as much as she could remember of the music, she rose and closed the piano, and pushed back the folding doors between the room she was in and the "back library," a small room where Mrs. Cressler kept her books of poetry.

As Laura entered the room she was surprised to see Mr. Cressler there, seated in his armchair, his back turned toward her.

"Why, I didn't know you were here, Mr. Cressler," she said, as she came up to him.

She laid her hand upon his arm. But Cressler was dead; and as Laura touched him the head dropped upon the shoulder and showed the bullet hole in the temple, just in front of the ear.

X

The suicide of Charles Cressler had occurred on the tenth of June, and the report of it, together with the wretched story of his friend's final surrender to a temptation he had never outlived, reached Curtis Jadwin early on the morning of the eleventh.

He and Gretry were at their accustomed places in the latter's office, and the news seemed to shut out all the sunshine that had been flooding in through the broad plate-glass windows. After their first incoherent horror, the two sat staring at each other, speechless.

"My God, my God," groaned Jadwin, as if in the throes of a deadly sickness. "He was in the Crookes' ring, and we never knew it—I've killed him, Sam. I might as well have held that pistol myself." He stamped his foot, striking his fist across his forehead, "Great God—my best friend—Charlie—Charlie Cressler! Sam, I shall go mad if this—if this—"

"Steady, steady does it, J.," warned the broker, his hand upon his shoulder, "we got to keep a grip on ourselves to-day. We've got a lot to think of. We'll think about Charlie, later. Just now ... well it's business now. Mathewson & Knight have called on us for margins—twenty thousand dollars."

He laid the slip down in front of Jadwin, as he sat at his desk.

"Oh, this can wait?" exclaimed Jadwin. "Let it go till this afternoon. I can't talk business now. Think of Carrie—Mrs. Cressler, I—"

"No," answered Gretry, reflectively and slowly, looking anywhere but in Jadwin's face. "N—no, I don't think we'd better wait. I think we'd better meet these margin calls promptly. It's always better to keep our trades margined up."

Jadwin faced around.

"Why," he cried, "one would think, to hear you talk, as though there was danger of me busting here at any hour."

Gretry did not answer. There was a moment's silence Then the broker caught his principal's eye and held it a second.

"Well," he answered, "you saw how freely they sold to us in the Pit yesterday. We've got to buy, and buy and buy, to keep our price up; and look here, look at these reports from our correspondents—everything points to a banner crop. There's been an increase of acreage everywhere, because of our high prices. See this from Travers"—he picked up a despatch and read: "'Preliminary returns of spring wheat in two Dakotas, subject to revision, indicate a total area seeded of sixteen million acres, which added to area in winter wheat states, makes total of forty-three million, or nearly four million acres greater than last year.'"

"Lot of damned sentiment," cried Jadwin, refusing to be convinced. "Two-thirds of that wheat won't grade, and Europe will take nearly all of it. What we ought to do is to send our men into the Pit and buy another million, buy more than these fools can offer. Buy 'em to a standstill."

"That takes a big pile of money then," said the broker. "More than we can lay our hands on this morning. The best we can do is to take all the Bears are offering, and support the market. The moment they offer us wheat and we don't buy it, that moment—as you know, yourself—they'll throw wheat at you by the train load, and the price will break, and we with it."

"Think we'll get rid of much wheat to-day?" demanded Jadwin.

By now it had became vitally necessary for Jadwin to sell out his holdings. His "long line" was a fearful expense, insurance and storage charges were eating rapidly into the profits. He must get rid of the load he was carrying, little by little. To do this at a profit, he had adopted the expedient of flooding the Pit with buying orders just before the close of the session, and then as the price rose under this stimulus, selling quickly, before it had time to break. At first this had succeeded. But of late he must buy more and more to keep the price up, while the moment that he began to sell, the price began to drop; so that now, in order to sell one bushel, he must buy two.

"Think we can unload much on 'em to-day?" repeated Jadwin.

"I don't know," answered Gretry, slowly and thoughtfully. "Perhaps—there's a chance—. Frankly, J., I don't think we can. The Pit is taking heart, that's the truth of it. Those fellows are not so scared of us as they were a while ago. It's the new crop, as I've said over and over again. We've put wheat so high, that all the farmers have planted it, and are getting ready to dump it on us. The Pit knows that, of course. Why, just think, they are harvesting in some places. These fellows we've caught in the corner will be able to buy all the wheat they want from the farmers if they can hold out a little longer. And that Government report yesterday showed that the growing wheat is in good condition."

"Nothing of the sort. It was a little over eighty-six."

"Good enough," declared Gretry, "good enough so that it broke the price down to a dollar and twenty. Just think, we were at a dollar and a half a little while ago."

"And we'll be at two dollars in another ten days, I tell you."

"Do you know how we stand, J.?" said the broker gravely. "Do you know how we stand—financially? It's taken pretty nearly every cent of our ready money to support this July market. Oh, we can figure out our paper profits into the millions. We've got thirty, forty, fifty million bushels of wheat that's worth over a dollar a bushel, but if we can't sell it, we're none the better off—and that wheat is costing us six thousand dollars a day. Hell, old man, where's the money going to come from? You don't seem to realise that we are in a precarious condition." He raised an arm, and pointed above him in the direction of the floor of the Board of Trade.

"The moment we can't give our boys—Landry Court, and the rest of 'em—the moment we can't give them buying orders, that Pit will suck us down like a chip. The moment we admit that we can't buy all the wheat that's offered, there's the moment we bust."

"Well, we'll buy it," cried Jadwin, through his set teeth. "I'll show those brutes. Look here, is it money we want? You cable to Paris and offer two million, at—oh, at eight cents below the market; and to Liverpool, and let 'em have twopence off on the same amount. They'll snap it up as quick as look at it. That will bring in one lot of money, and as for the rest, I guess I've got some real estate in this town that's pretty good security."

"What—you going to mortgage part of that?"

"No," cried Jadwin, jumping up with a quick impatient gesture, "no, I'm going to mortgage all of it, and I'm going to do it to-day—this morning. If you say we're in a precarious condition, it's no time for half measures. I'll have more money than you'll know what to do with in the Illinois Trust by three o'clock this afternoon, and when the Board opens to-morrow morning, I'm going to light into those cattle in the Pit there, so as they'll think a locomotive has struck 'em. They'd stand me off, would they? They'd try to sell me down; they won't cover when I turn the screw! I'll show 'em, Sam Gretry. I'll run wheat up so high before the next two days, that the Bank of England can't pull it down, and before the Pit can catch its breath, I'll sell our long line, and with the profits of that, by God! I'll run it up again. Two dollars! Why, it will be two fifty here so quick you won't know how it's happened. I've just been fooling with this crowd until now. Now, I'm really going to get down to business."

Gretry did not answer. He twirled his pencil between his fingers, and stared down at the papers on his desk. Once he started to speak, but checked himself. Then at last he turned about.

"All right," he said, briskly. "We'll see what that will do."

"I'm going over to the Illinois Trust now," said Jadwin, putting on his hat. "When your boys come in for their orders, tell them for to-day just to support the market. If there's much wheat offered they'd better buy it. Tell them not to let the market go below a dollar twenty. When I come back we'll make out those cables."

That day Jadwin carried out his programme so vehemently announced to his broker. Upon every piece of real estate that he owned he placed as heavy a mortgage as the property would stand. Even his old house on Michigan Avenue, even the "homestead" on North State Street were encumbered. The time was come, he felt, for the grand coup, the last huge strategical move, the concentration of every piece of heavy artillery. Never in all his multitude of operations on the Chicago Board of Trade had he failed. He knew he would not fail now; Luck, the golden goddess, still staid at his shoulder. He did more than mortgage his property; he floated a number of promissory notes. His credit, always unimpeachable, he taxed to its farthest stretch; from every source he gathered in the sinews of the war he was waging. No sum was too great to daunt him, none too small to be overlooked. Reserves, van and rear, battle line and skirmish outposts he summoned together to form one single vast column of attack.

It was on this same day while Jadwin, pressed for money, was leaving no stone unturned to secure ready cash, that he came across old Hargus in his usual place in Gretry's customers' room, reading a two days old newspaper. Of a sudden an idea occurred to Jadwin. He took the old man aside. "Hargus," he said, "do you want a good investment for your money, that money I turned over to you? I can give you a better rate than the bank, and pretty good security. Let me have about a hundred thousand at—oh, ten per cent."

"Hey—what?" asked the old fellow querulously. Jadwin repeated his request.

But Hargus cast a suspicious glance at him and drew away.

"I—I don't lend my money," he observed.

"Why—you old fool," exclaimed Jadwin. "Here, is it more interest you want? Why, we'll say fifteen per cent., if you like."

"I don't lend my money," exclaimed Hargus, shaking his head. "I ain't got any to lend," and with the words took himself off.

One source of help alone Jadwin left untried. Sorely tempted, he nevertheless kept himself from involving his wife's money in the hazard. Laura, in her own name, was possessed of a little fortune; sure as he was of winning, Jadwin none the less hesitated from seeking an auxiliary here. He felt it was a matter of pride. He could not bring himself to make use of a woman's succour.

But his entire personal fortune now swung in the balance. It was the last fight, the supreme attempt—the final consummate assault, and the thrill of a victory more brilliant, more conclusive, more decisive than any he had ever known, vibrated in Jadwin's breast, as he went to and fro in Jackson, Adams, and La Salle streets all through that day of the eleventh.

But he knew the danger—knew just how terrible was to be the grapple. Once that same day a certain detail of business took him near to the entrance of the Floor. Though he did not so much as look inside the doors, he could not but hear the thunder of the Pit; and even in that moment of confidence, his great triumph only a few hours distant, Jadwin, for the instant, stood daunted. The roar was appalling, the whirlpool was again unchained, the maelstrom was again unleashed. And during the briefest of seconds he could fancy that the familiar bellow of its swirling, had taken on another pitch. Out of that hideous turmoil, he imagined, there issued a strange unwonted note; as it were, the first rasp and grind of a new avalanche just beginning to stir, a diapason more profound than any he had yet known, a hollow distant bourdon as of the slipping and sliding of some almighty and chaotic power.

It was the Wheat, the Wheat! It was on the move again. From the farms of Illinois and Iowa, from the ranches of Kansas and Nebraska, from all the reaches of the Middle West, the Wheat, like a tidal wave, was rising, rising. Almighty, blood-brother to the earthquake, coeval with the volcano and the whirlwind, that gigantic world-force, that colossal billow, Nourisher of the Nations, was swelling and advancing.

There in the Pit its first premonitory eddies already swirled and spun. If even the first ripples of the tide smote terribly upon the heart, what was it to be when the ocean itself burst through, on its eternal way from west to east? For an instant came clear vision. What were these shouting, gesticulating men of the Board of Trade, these brokers, traders, and speculators? It was not these he fought, it was that fatal New Harvest; it was the Wheat; it was—as Gretry had said—the very Earth itself. What were those scattered hundreds of farmers of the Middle West, who because he had put the price so high had planted the grain as never before? What had they to do with it? Why the Wheat had grown itself; demand and supply, these were the two great laws the Wheat obeyed. Almost blasphemous in his effrontery, he had tampered with these laws, and had roused a Titan. He had laid his puny human grasp upon Creation and the very earth herself, the great mother, feeling the touch of the cobweb that the human insect had spun, had stirred at last in her sleep and sent her omnipotence moving through the grooves of the world, to find and crush the disturber of her appointed courses.

The new harvest was coming in; the new harvest of wheat, huge beyond possibility of control; so vast that no money could buy it, so swift that no strategy could turn it. But Jadwin hurried away from the sound of the near roaring of the Pit. No, no. Luck was with him; he had mastered the current of the Pit many times before—he would master it again. The day passed and the night, and at nine o'clock the following morning, he and Gretry once more met in the broker's office.

Gretry turned a pale face upon his principal.

"I've just received," he said, "the answers to our cables to Liverpool and Paris. I offered wheat at both places, as you know, cheaper than we've ever offered it there before."

"Yes—well?"

"Well," answered Gretry, looking gravely into Jadwin's eyes, "well—they won't take it."

On the morning of her birthday—the thirteenth of the month—when Laura descended to the breakfast room, she found Page already there. Though it was barely half-past seven, her sister was dressed for the street. She wore a smart red hat, and as she stood by the French windows, looking out, she drew her gloves back and forth between her fingers, with a nervous, impatient gesture.

"Why," said Laura, as she sat down at her place, "why, Pagie, what is in the wind to-day?"

"Landry is coming," Page explained, facing about and glancing at the watch pinned to her waist. "He is going to take me down to see the Board of Trade—from the visitor's gallery, you know. He said this would probably be a great day. Did Mr. Jadwin come home last night?"

Laura shook her head, without speech. She did not choose to put into words the fact that for three days—with the exception of an hour or two, on the evening after that horrible day of her visit to the Cresslers' house—she had seen nothing of her husband.

"Landry says," continued Page, "that it is awful—down there, these days. He says that it is the greatest fight in the history of La Salle Street. Has Mr. Jadwin, said anything to you? Is he going to win?"

"I don't know," answered Laura, in a low voice; "I don't know anything about it, Page."

She was wondering if even Page had forgotten. When she had come into the room, her first glance had been towards her place at table. But there was nothing there, not even so much as an envelope; and no one had so much as wished her joy of the little anniversary. She had thought Page might have remembered, but her sister's next words showed that she had more on her mind than birthdays.

"Laura," she began, sitting down opposite to her, and unfolding her napkin, with laborious precision. "Laura—Landry and I—Well ... we're going to be married in the fall."

"Why, Pagie," cried Laura, "I'm just as glad as I can be for you. He's a fine, clean fellow, and I know he will make you a good husband."

Page drew a deep breath.

"Well," she said, "I'm glad you think so, too. Before you and Mr. Jadwin were married, I wasn't sure about having him care for me, because at that time—well—" Page looked up with a queer little smile, "I guess you could have had him—if you had wanted to."

"Oh, that," cried Laura. "Why, Landry never really cared for me. It was all the silliest kind of flirtation. The moment he knew you better, I stood no chance at all."

"We're going to take an apartment on Michigan Avenue, near the Auditorium," said Page, "and keep house. We've talked it all over, and know just how much it will cost to live and keep one servant. I'm going to serve the loveliest little dinners; I've learned the kind of cooking he likes already. Oh, I guess there he is now," she cried, as they heard the front door close.

Landry came in, carrying a great bunch of cut flowers, and a box of candy. He was as spruce as though he were already the bridegroom, his cheeks pink, his blonde hair radiant. But he was thin and a little worn, a dull feverish glitter came and went in his eyes, and his nervousness, the strain and excitement which beset him were in his every gesture, in every word of his rapid speech.

"We'll have to hurry," he told Page. "I must be down there hours ahead of time this morning."

"How is Curtis?" demanded Laura. "Have you seen him lately? How is he getting on with—with his speculating?"

Landry made a sharp gesture of resignation.

"I don't know," he answered. "I guess nobody knows. We had a fearful day yesterday, but I think we controlled the situation at the end. We ran the price up and up and up till I thought it would never stop. If the Pit thought Mr. Jadwin was beaten, I guess they found out how they were mistaken. For a time there, we were just driving them. But then Mr. Gretry sent word to us in the Pit to sell, and we couldn't hold them. They came back at us like wolves; they beat the price down five cents, in as many minutes. We had to quit selling, and buy again. But then Mr. Jadwin went at them with a rush. Oh, it was grand! We steadied the price at a dollar and fifteen, stiffened it up to eighteen and a half, and then sent it up again, three cents at a time, till we'd hammered it back to a dollar and a quarter."

"But Curtis himself," inquired Laura, "is he all right, is he well?"

"I only saw him once," answered Landry. "He was in Mr. Gretry's office. Yes, he looked all right. He's nervous, of course. But Mr. Gretry looks like the sick man. He looks all frazzled out."

"I guess, we'd better be going," said Page, getting up from the table. "Have you had your breakfast, Landry? Won't you have some coffee?"

"Oh, I breakfasted hours ago," he answered. "But you are right. We had better be moving. If you are going to get a seat in the gallery, you must be there half an hour ahead of time, to say the least. Shall I take any word to your husband from you, Mrs. Jadwin?"

"Tell him that I wish him good luck," she answered, "and—yes, ask him, if he remembers what day of the month this is—or no, don't ask him that. Say nothing about it. Just tell him I send him my very best love, and that I wish him all the success in the world."

It was about nine o'clock, when Landry and Page reached the foot of La Salle Street. The morning was fine and cool. The sky over the Board of Trade sparkled with sunlight, and the air was full of fluttering wings of the multitude of pigeons that lived upon the leakage of grain around the Board of Trade building.

"Mr. Cressler used to feed them regularly," said Landry, as they paused on the street corner opposite the Board. "Poor—poor Mr. Cressler—the funeral is to-morrow, you know."

Page shut her eyes.

"Oh," she murmured, "think, think of Laura finding him there like that. Oh, it would have killed me, it would have killed me."

"Somehow," observed Landry, a puzzled expression in his eyes, "somehow, by George! she don't seem to mind very much. You'd have thought a shock like that would have made her sick."

"Oh! Laura," cried Page. "I don't know her any more these days, she is just like stone—just as though she were crowding down every emotion or any feeling she ever had. She seems to be holding herself in with all her strength—for something—and afraid to let go a finger, for fear she would give way altogether. When she told me about that morning at the Cresslers' house, her voice was just like ice; she said, 'Mr. Cressler has shot himself. I found him dead in his library.' She never shed a tear, and she spoke, oh, in such a terrible monotone. Oh! dear," cried Page, "I wish all this was over, and we could all get away from Chicago, and take Mr. Jadwin with us, and get him back to be as he used to be, always so light-hearted, and thoughtful and kindly. He used to be making jokes from morning till night. Oh, I loved him just as if he were my father."

They crossed the street, and Landry, taking her by the arm, ushered her into the corridor on the ground floor of the Board.

"Now, keep close to me," he said, "and see if we can get through somewhere here."

The stairs leading up to the main floor were already crowded with visitors, some standing in line close to the wall, others aimlessly wandering up and down, looking and listening, their heads in the air. One of these, a gentleman with a tall white hat, shook his head at Landry and Page, as they pressed by him.

"You can't get up there," he said, "even if they let you in. They're packed in like sardines already."

But Landry reassured Page with a knowing nod of his head.

"I told the guide up in the gallery to reserve a seat for you. I guess we'll manage."

But when they reached the staircase that connected the main floor with the visitors' gallery, it became a question as to whether or not they could even get to the seat. The crowd was packed solidly upon the stairs, between the wall and the balustrades. There were men in top hats, and women in silks; rough fellows of the poorer streets, and gaudily dressed queens of obscure neighborhoods, while mixed with these one saw the faded and shabby wrecks that perennially drifted about the Board of Trade, the failures who sat on the chairs of the customers' rooms day in and day out, reading old newspapers, smoking vile cigars. And there were young men of the type of clerks and bookkeepers, young men with drawn, worn faces, and hot, tired eyes, who pressed upward, silent, their lips compressed, listening intently to the indefinite echoing murmur that was filling the building.

For on this morning of the thirteenth of June, the Board of Trade, its halls, corridors, offices, and stairways were already thrilling with a vague and terrible sound. It was only a little after nine o'clock. The trading would not begin for another half hour, but, even now, the mutter of the whirlpool, the growl of the Pit was making itself felt. The eddies were gathering; the thousands of subsidiary torrents that fed the cloaca were moving. From all over the immediate neighborhood they came, from the offices of hundreds of commission houses, from brokers' offices, from banks, from the tall, grey buildings of La Salle Street, from the street itself. And even from greater distances they came; auxiliary currents set in from all the reach of the Great Northwest, from Minneapolis, Duluth, and Milwaukee. From the Southwest, St. Louis, Omaha, and Kansas City contributed to the volume. The Atlantic Seaboard, New York, and Boston and Philadelphia sent out their tributary streams; London, Liverpool, Paris, and Odessa merged their influences with the vast world-wide flowing that bore down upon Chicago, and that now began slowly, slowly to centre and circle about the Wheat Pit of the Board of Trade.

Small wonder that the building to Page's ears vibrated to a strange and ominous humming. She heard it in the distant clicking of telegraph keys, in the echo of hurried whispered conversations held in dark corners, in the noise of rapid footsteps, in the trilling of telephone bells. These sounds came from all around her; they issued from the offices of the building below her, above her and on either side. She was surrounded with them, and they mingled together to form one prolonged and muffled roar, that from moment to moment increased in volume.

The Pit was getting under way; the whirlpool was forming, and the sound of its courses was like the sound of the ocean in storm, heard at a distance.

Page and Landry were still halfway up the last stairway. Above and below, the throng was packed dense and immobilised. But, little by little, Landry wormed a way for them, winning one step at a time. But he was very anxious; again and again he looked at his watch. At last he said:

"I've got to go. It's just madness for me to stay another minute. I'll give you my card."

"Well, leave me here," Page urged. "It can't be helped. I'm all right. Give me your card. I'll tell the guide in the gallery that you kept the seat for me—if I ever can get there. You must go. Don't stay another minute. If you can, come for me here in the gallery, when it's over. I'll wait for you. But if you can't come, all right. I can take care of myself."

He could but assent to this. This was no time to think of small things. He left her and bore back with all his might through the crowd, gained the landing at the turn of the balustrade, waved his hat to her and disappeared.

A quarter of an hour went by. Page, caught in the crowd, could neither advance nor retreat. Ahead of her, some twenty steps away, she could see the back rows of seats in the gallery. But they were already occupied. It seemed hopeless to expect to see anything of the floor that day. But she could no longer extricate herself from the press; there was nothing to do but stay where she was.

On every side of her she caught odds and ends of dialogues and scraps of discussions, and while she waited she found an interest in listening to these, as they reached her from time to time.

"Well," observed the man in the tall white hat, who had discouraged Landry from attempting to reach the gallery, "well, he's shaken 'em up pretty well. Whether he downs 'em or they down him, he's made a good fight."

His companion, a young man with eyeglasses, who wore a wonderful white waistcoat with queer glass buttons, assented, and Page heard him add:

"Big operator, that Jadwin."

"They're doing for him now, though."

"I ain't so sure. He's got another fight in him. You'll see."

"Ever see him?"

"No, no, he don't come into the Pit—these big men never do."

Directly in front of Page two women kept up an interminable discourse.

"Well," said the one, "that's all very well, but Mr. Jadwin made my sister-in-law—she lives in Dubuque, you know—a rich woman. She bought some wheat, just for fun, you know, a long time ago, and held on till Mr. Jadwin put the price up to four times what she paid for it. Then she sold out. My, you ought to see the lovely house she's building, and her son's gone to Europe, to study art, if you please, and a year ago, my dear, they didn't have a cent, not a cent, but her husband's salary."

"There's the other side, too, though," answered her companion, adding in a hoarse whisper: "If Mr. Jadwin fails to-day—well, honestly, Julia, I don't know what Philip will do."

But, from another group at Page's elbow, a man's bass voice cut across the subdued chatter of the two women.

"'Guess we'll pull through, somehow. Burbank & Co., though—by George! I'm not sure about them. They are pretty well involved in this thing, and there's two or three smaller firms that are dependent on them. If Gretry-Converse & Co. should suspend, Burbank would go with a crash sure. And there's that bank in Keokuk; they can't stand much more. Their depositors would run 'em quick as how-do-you-do, if there was a smash here in Chicago."

"Oh, Jadwin will pull through."

"Well, I hope so—by Jingo! I hope so. Say, by the way, how did you come out?"

"Me! Hoh! Say my boy, the next time I get into a wheat trade you'll know it. I was one of the merry paretics who believed that Crookes was the Great Lum-tum. I tailed on to his clique. Lord love you! Jadwin put the knife into me to the tune of twelve thousand dollars. But, say, look here; aren't we ever going to get up to that blame gallery? We ain't going to see any of this, and I—hark!—by God! there goes the gong. They've begun. Say, say, hear 'em, will you! Holy Moses! say—listen to that! Did you ever hear—Lord! I wish we could see—could get somewhere where we could see something."

His friend turned to him and spoke a sentence that was drowned in the sudden vast volume of sound that all at once shook the building.

"Hey—what?"

The other shouted into his ear. But even then his friend could not hear. Nor did he listen. The crowd upon the staircases had surged irresistibly forward and upward. There was a sudden outburst of cries. Women's voices were raised in expostulation, and even fear.

"Oh, oh—don't push so!"

"My arm! oh!—oh, I shall faint ... please."

But the men, their escorts, held back furiously; their faces purple, they shouted imprecations over their shoulders.

"Here, here, you damn fools, what you doing?"

"Don't crowd so!"

"Get back, back!"

"There's a lady fainted here. Get back you! We'll all have a chance to see. Good Lord! ain't there a policeman anywheres?"

"Say, say! It's going down—the price. It broke three cents, just then, at the opening, they say."

"This is the worst I ever saw or heard of."

"My God! if Jadwin can only hold 'em.

"You bet he'll hold 'em."

"Hold nothing!—Oh! say my friend, it don't do you any good to crowd like that."

"It's the people behind: I'm not doing it. Say, do you know where they're at on the floor? The wheat, I mean, is it going up or down?"

"Up, they tell me. There was a rally; I don't know. How can we tell here? We—Hi! there they go again. Lord! that must have been a smash. I guess the Board of Trade won't forget this day in a hurry. Heavens, you can't hear yourself think!

"Glad I ain't down there in the Pit."

But, at last, a group of policemen appeared. By main strength they shouldered their way to the top of the stairs, and then began pushing the crowd back. At every instant they shouted:

"Move on now, clear the stairway. No seats left!"

But at this Page, who, by the rush of the crowd had been carried almost to the top of the stairs, managed to extricate an arm from the press, and hold Landry's card in the air. She even hazarded a little deception:

"I have a pass. Will you let me through, please?"

Luckily one of the officers heard her. He bore down heavily with all the mass of his two hundred pounds and the majesty of the law he represented, to the rescue and succour of this very pretty girl.

"Let the lady through," he roared, forcing a passage with both elbows. "Come right along, Miss. Stand back you, now. Can't you see the lady has a pass? Now then, Miss, and be quick about it, I can't keep 'em back forever."

Jostled and hustled, her dress crumpled, her hat awry, Page made her way forward, till the officer caught her by the arm, and pulled her out of the press. With a long breath she gained the landing of the gallery.

The guide, an old fellow in a uniform of blue, with brass buttons and a visored cap, stood near by, and to him she presented Landry's card.

"Oh, yes, oh, yes," he shouted in her ear, after he had glanced it over. "You were the party Mr. Court spoke about. You just came in time. I wouldn't 'a dared hold your seat a minute longer."

He led her down the crowded aisle between rows of theatre chairs, all of which were occupied, to one vacant seat in the very front row.

"You can see everything, now," he cried, making a trumpet of his palm. "You're Mister Jadwin's niece. I know, I know. Ah, it's a wild day, Miss. They ain't done much yet, and Mr. Jadwin's holding his own, just now. But I thought for a moment they had him on the run. You see that—my, my, there was a sharp rally. But he's holding on strong yet."

Page took her seat, and leaning forward looked down into the Wheat Pit.

Once free of the crowd after leaving Page, Landry ran with all the swiftness of his long legs down the stair, and through the corridors till, all out of breath, he gained Gretry's private office. The other Pit traders for the house, some eight or ten men, were already assembled, and just as Landry entered by one door, the broker himself came in from the customers' room. Jadwin was nowhere to be seen.

"What are the orders for to-day, sir?"

Gretry was very pale. Despite his long experience on the Board of Trade, Landry could see anxiety in every change of his expression, in every motion of his hands. The broker before answering the question crossed the room to the water cooler and drank a brief swallow. Then emptying the glass he refilled it, moistened his lips again, and again emptied and filled the goblet. He put it down, caught it up once more, filled it, emptied it, drinking now in long draughts, now in little sips. He was quite unconscious of his actions, and Landry as he watched, felt his heart sink. Things must, indeed, be at a desperate pass when Gretry, the calm, the clear-headed, the placid, was thus upset.

"Your orders?" said the broker, at last. "The same as yesterday; keep the market up—that's all. It must not go below a dollar fifteen. But act on the defensive. Don't be aggressive, unless I send word. There will probably be very heavy selling the first few moments. You can buy, each of you, up to half a million bushels apiece. If that don't keep the price up, if they still are selling after that ... well"; Gretry paused a moment, irresolutely, "well," he added suddenly, "if they are still selling freely after you've each bought half a million, I'll let you know what to do. And, look here," he continued, facing the group, "look here—keep your heads cool ... I guess to-day will decide things. Watch the Crookes crowd pretty closely. I understand they're up to something again. That's all, I guess."

Landry and the other Gretry traders hurried from the office up to the floor. Landry's heart was beating thick and slow and hard, his teeth were shut tight. Every nerve, every fibre of him braced itself with the rigidity of drawn wire, to meet the issue of the impending hours. Now, was to come the last grapple. He had never lived through a crisis such as this before. Would he prevail, would he keep his head? Would he avoid or balk the thousand and one little subterfuges, tricks, and traps that the hostile traders would prepare for him—prepare with a quickness, a suddenness that all but defied the sharpest, keenest watchfulness?

Was the gong never going to strike? He found himself, all at once, on the edge of the Wheat Pit. It was jammed tight with the crowd of traders and the excitement that disengaged itself from that tense, vehement crowd of white faces and glittering eyes was veritably sickening, veritably weakening. Men on either side of him were shouting mere incoherencies, to which nobody, not even themselves, were listening. Others silent, gnawed their nails to the quick, breathing rapidly, audibly even, their nostrils expanding and contracting. All around roared the vague thunder that since early morning had shaken the building. In the Pit the bids leaped to and fro, though the time of opening had not yet come; the very planks under foot seemed spinning about in the first huge warning swirl of the Pit's centripetal convulsion. There was dizziness in the air. Something, some infinite immeasurable power, onrushing in its eternal courses, shook the Pit in its grasp. Something deafened the ears, blinded the eyes, dulled and numbed the mind, with its roar, with the chaff and dust of its whirlwind passage, with the stupefying sense of its power, coeval with the earthquake and glacier, merciless, all-powerful, a primal basic throe of creation itself, unassailable, inviolate, and untamed.

Had the trading begun? Had the gong struck? Landry never knew, never so much as heard the clang of the great bell. All at once he was fighting; all at once he was caught, as it were, from off the stable earth, and flung headlong into the heart and centre of the Pit. What he did, he could not say; what went on about him, he could not distinguish. He only knew that roar was succeeding roar, that there was crashing through his ears, through his very brain, the combined bellow of a hundred Niagaras. Hands clutched and tore at him, his own tore and clutched in turn. The Pit was mad, was drunk and frenzied; not a man of all those who fought and scrambled and shouted who knew what he or his neighbour did. They only knew that a support long thought to be secure was giving way; not gradually, not evenly, but by horrible collapses, and equally horrible upward leaps. Now it held, now it broke, now it reformed again, rose again, then again in hideous cataclysms fell from beneath their feet to lower depths than before. The official reporter leaned back in his place, helpless. On the wall overhead, the indicator on the dial was rocking back and forth, like the mast of a ship caught in a monsoon. The price of July wheat no man could so much as approximate. The fluctuations were no longer by fractions of a cent, but by ten cents, fifteen cents twenty-five cents at a time. On one side of the Pit wheat sold at ninety cents, on the other at a dollar and a quarter.

And all the while above the din upon the floor, above the tramplings and the shoutings in the Pit, there seemed to thrill and swell that appalling roar of the Wheat itself coming in, coming on like a tidal wave, bursting through, dashing barriers aside, rolling like a measureless, almighty river, from the farms of Iowa and the ranches of California, on to the East—to the bakeshops and hungry mouths of Europe.

Landry caught one of the Gretry traders by the arm.

"What shall we do?" he shouted. "I've bought up to my limit. No more orders have come in. The market has gone from under us. What's to be done?"

"I don't know," the other shouted back, "I don't know. We're all gone to hell; looks like the last smash. There are no more supporting orders—something's gone wrong. Gretry hasn't sent any word."

Then, Landry, beside himself with excitement and with actual terror, hardly knowing even yet what he did, turned sharply about. He fought his way out of the Pit; he ran hatless and panting across the floor, in and out between the groups of spectators, down the stairs to the corridor below, and into the Gretry-Converse offices.

In the outer office a group of reporters and the representatives of a great commercial agency were besieging one of the heads of the firm. They assaulted him with questions.

"Just tell us where you are at—that's all we want to know."

"Just what is the price of July wheat?"

"Is Jadwin winning or losing?"

But the other threw out an arm in a wild gesture of helplessness.

"We don't know, ourselves," he cried. "The market has run clean away from everybody. You know as much about it as I do. It's simply hell broken loose, that's all. We can't tell where we are at for days to come."

Landry rushed on. He swung open the door of the private office and entered, slamming it behind him and crying out:

"Mr. Gretry, what are we to do? We've had no orders."

But no one listened to him. Of the group that gathered around Gretry's desk, no one so much as turned a head.

Jadwin stood there in the centre of the others, hatless, his face pale, his eyes congested with blood. Gretry fronted him, one hand upon his arm. In the remainder of the group Landry recognised the senior clerk of the office, one of the heads of a great banking house, and a couple of other men—confidential agents, who had helped to manipulate the great corner.

"But you can't," Gretry was exclaiming. "You can't; don't you see we can't meet our margin calls? It's the end of the game. You've got no more money."

"It's a lie!" Never so long as he lived did Landry forget the voice in which Jadwin cried the words: "It's a lie! Keep on buying, I tell you. Take all they'll offer. I tell you we'll touch the two dollar mark before noon."

"Not another order goes up to that floor," retorted Gretry. "Why, J., ask any of these gentlemen here. They'll tell you."

"It's useless, Mr. Jadwin," said the banker, quietly. "You were practically beaten two days ago."

"Mr. Jadwin," pleaded the senior clerk, "for God's sake listen to reason. Our firm—"

But Jadwin was beyond all appeal. He threw off Gretry's hand.

"Your firm, your firm—you've been cowards from the start. I know you, I know you. You have sold me out. Crookes has bought you. Get out of my way!" he shouted. "Get out of my way! Do you hear? I'll play my hand alone from now on."

"J., old man—why—see here, man," Gretry implored, still holding him by the arm; "here, where are you going?"

Jadwin's voice rang like a trumpet call:

"Into the Pit."

"Look here—wait—here. Hold him back, gentlemen. He don't know what he's about."

"If you won't execute my orders, I'll act myself. I'm going into the Pit, I tell you."

"J., you're mad, old fellow. You're ruined—don't you understand?—you're ruined."

"Then God curse you, Sam Gretry, for the man who failed me in a crisis." And as he spoke Curtis Jadwin struck the broker full in the face.

Gretry staggered back from the blow, catching at the edge of his desk. His pale face flashed to crimson for an instant, his fists clinched; then his hands fell to his sides.

"No," he said, "let him go, let him go. The man is merely mad."

But, Jadwin, struggling for a second in the midst of the group that tried to hold him, suddenly flung off the restraining clasps, thrust the men to one side, and rushed from the room.

Gretry dropped into his chair before his desk.

"It's the end," he said, simply.

He drew a sheet of note paper to him, and in a shaking hand wrote a couple of lines.

"Take that," he said, handing the note to the senior clerk, "take that to the secretary of the Board at once."

And straight into the turmoil and confusion of the Pit, to the scene of so many of his victories, the battle ground whereon again and again, his enemies routed, he had remained the victor undisputed, undismayed came the "Great Bull." No sooner had he set foot within the entrance to the Floor, than the news went flashing and flying from lip to lip. The galleries knew it, the public room, and the Western Union knew it, the telephone booths knew it, and lastly even the Wheat Pit, torn and tossed and rent asunder by the force this man himself had unchained, knew it, and knowing stood dismayed.

For even then, so great had been his power, so complete his dominion, and so well-rooted the fear which he had inspired, that this last move in the great game he had been playing, this unexpected, direct, personal assumption of control struck a sense of consternation into the heart of the hardiest of his enemies.

Jadwin himself, the great man, the "Great Bull" in the Pit! What was about to happen? Had they been too premature in their hope of his defeat? Had he been preparing some secret, unexpected manoeuvre? For a second they hesitated, then moved by a common impulse, feeling the push of the wonderful new harvest behind them, they gathered themselves together for the final assault, and again offered the wheat for sale; offered it by thousands upon thousands of bushels; poured, as it were, the reapings of entire principalities out upon the floor of the Board of Trade.

Jadwin was in the thick of the confusion by now. And the avalanche, the undiked Ocean of the Wheat, leaping to the lash of the hurricane, struck him fairly in the face.

He heard it now, he heard nothing else. The Wheat had broken from his control. For months, he had, by the might of his single arm, held it back; but now it rose like the upbuilding of a colossal billow. It towered, towered, hung poised for an instant, and then, with a thunder as of the grind and crash of chaotic worlds, broke upon him, burst through the Pit and raced past him, on and on to the eastward and to the hungry nations.

And then, under the stress and violence of the hour, something snapped in his brain. The murk behind his eyes had been suddenly pierced by a white flash. The strange qualms and tiny nervous paroxysms of the last few months all at once culminated in some indefinite, indefinable crisis, and the wheels and cogs of all activities save one lapsed away and ceased. Only one function of the complicated machine persisted; but it moved with a rapidity of vibration that seemed to be tearing the tissues of being to shreds, while its rhythm beat out the old and terrible cadence:

"Wheat—wheat—wheat, wheat—wheat—wheat."

Blind and insensate, Jadwin strove against the torrent of the Wheat. There in the middle of the Pit, surrounded and assaulted by herd after herd of wolves yelping for his destruction, he stood braced, rigid upon his feet, his head up, his hand, the great bony hand that once had held the whole Pit in its grip, flung high in the air, in a gesture of defiance, while his voice like the clangour of bugles sounding to the charge of the forlorn hope, rang out again and again, over the din of his enemies:

"Give a dollar for July—give a dollar for July!"

With one accord they leaped upon him. The little group of his traders was swept aside. Landry alone, Landry who had never left his side since his rush from out Gretry's office, Landry Court, loyal to the last, his one remaining soldier, white, shaking, the sobs strangling in his throat, clung to him desperately. Another billow of wheat was preparing. They two—the beaten general and his young armour bearer—heard it coming; hissing, raging, bellowing, it swept down upon them. Landry uttered a cry. Flesh and blood could not stand this strain. He cowered at his chief's side, his shoulders bent, one arm above his head, as if to ward off an actual physical force.

But Jadwin, iron to the end, stood erect. All unknowing what he did, he had taken Landry's hand in his and the boy felt the grip on his fingers like the contracting of a vise of steel. The other hand, as though holding up a standard, was still in the air, and his great deep-toned voice went out across the tumult, proclaiming to the end his battle cry:

"Give a dollar for July—give a dollar for July!"

But, little by little, Landry became aware that the tumult of the Pit was intermitting. There were sudden lapses in the shouting, and in these lapses he could hear from somewhere out upon the floor voices that were crying: "Order—order, order, gentlemen."

But, again and again the clamour broke out. It would die down for an instant, in response to these appeals, only to burst out afresh as certain groups of traders started the pandemonium again, by the wild outcrying of their offers. At last, however, the older men in the Pit, regaining some measure of self-control, took up the word, going to and fro in the press, repeating "Order, order."

And then, all at once, the Pit, the entire floor of the Board of Trade was struck dumb. All at once the tension was relaxed, the furious struggling and stamping was stilled. Landry, bewildered, still holding his chief by the hand, looked about him. On the floor, near at hand, stood the president of the Board of Trade himself, and with him the vice-president and a group of the directors. Evidently it had been these who had called the traders to order. But it was not toward them now that the hundreds of men in the Pit and on the floor were looking.

In the little balcony on the south wall opposite the visitors' gallery a figure had appeared, a tall grave man, in a long black coat—the secretary of the Board of Trade. Landry with the others saw him, saw him advance to the edge of the railing, and fix his glance upon the Wheat Pit. In his hand he carried a slip of paper.

And then in the midst of that profound silence the secretary announced:

"All trades with Gretry, Converse & Co. must be closed at once."

The words had not ceased to echo in the high vaultings of the roof before they were greeted with a wild, shrill yell of exultation and triumph, that burst from the crowding masses in the Wheat Pit.

Beaten; beaten at last, the Great Bull! Smashed! The great corner smashed! Jadwin busted! They themselves saved, saved, saved! Cheer followed upon cheer, yell after yell. Hats went into the air. In a frenzy of delight men danced and leaped and capered upon the edge of the Pit, clasping their arms about each other, shaking each others' hands, cheering and hurrahing till their strained voices became hoarse and faint.

Some few of the older men protested. There were cries of:

"Shame, shame!"

"Order—let him alone."

"Let him be; he's down now. Shame, shame!"

But the jubilee was irrepressible, they had been too cruelly pressed, these others; they had felt the weight of the Bull's hoof, the rip of his horn. Now they had beaten him, had pulled him down.

"Yah-h-h, whoop, yi, yi, yi. Busted, busted, busted. Hip, hip, hip, and a tiger!"

"Come away, sir. For God's sake, Mr. Jadwin, come away."

Landry was pleading with Jadwin, clutching his arm in both his hands, his lips to his chief's ear to make himself heard above the yelping of the mob.

Jadwin was silent now. He seemed no longer to see or hear; heavily, painfully he leaned upon the young man's shoulder.

"Come away, sir—for God's sake!"

The group of traders parted before them, cheering even while they gave place, cheering with eyes averted, unwilling to see the ruin that meant for them salvation.

"Yah-h-h. Yah-h-h, busted, busted!"

Landry had put his arm about Jadwin, and gripped him close as he led him from the Pit. The sobs were in his throat again, and tears of excitement, of grief, of anger and impotence were running down his face.

"Yah-h-h. Yah-h-h, he's done for, busted, busted!"

"Damn you all," cried Landry, throwing out a furious fist, "damn you all; you brutes, you beasts! If he'd so much as raised a finger a week ago, you'd have run for your lives."

But the cheering drowned his voice; and as the two passed out of the Pit upon the floor, the gong that closed the trading struck and, as it seemed, put a period, definite and final to the conclusion of Curtis Jadwin's career as speculator.

Across the floor towards the doorway Landry led his defeated captain. Jadwin was in a daze, he saw nothing, heard nothing. Quietly he submitted to Landry's guiding arm. The visitors in the galleries bent far over to see him pass, and from all over the floor, spectators, hangers-on, corn-and-provision traders, messenger boys, clerks and reporters came hurrying to watch the final exit of the Great Bull, from the scene of his many victories and his one overwhelming defeat.

In silence they watched him go by. Only in the distance from the direction of the Pit itself came the sound of dying cheers. But at the doorway stood a figure that Landry recognised at once—a small man, lean-faced, trimly dressed, his clean-shaven lips pursed like the mouth of a shut money bag, imperturbable as ever, cold, unexcited—Calvin Crookes himself.

And as Jadwin passed, Landry heard the Bear leader say:

"They can cheer now, all they want. They didn't do it. It was the wheat itself that beat him; no combination of men could have done it—go on, cheer, you damn fools! He was a bigger man than the best of us."

With the striking of the gong, and the general movement of the crowd in the galleries towards the exits, Page rose, drawing a long breath, pressing her hands an instant to her burning cheeks. She had seen all that had happened, but she had not understood. The whole morning had been a whirl and a blur. She had looked down upon a jam of men, who for three hours had done nothing but shout and struggle. She had seen Jadwin come into the Pit, and almost at once the shouts had turned to cheers. That must have meant, she thought, that Jadwin had done something to please those excited men. They were all his friends, no doubt. They were cheering him—cheering his success. He had won then! And yet that announcement from the opposite balcony, to the effect that business with Mr. Gretry must be stopped, immediately! That had an ominous ring. Or, perhaps, that meant only a momentary check.

As she descended the stairways, with the departing spectators, she distinctly heard a man's voice behind her exclaim:

"Well, that does for him!"

Possibly, after all, Mr. Jadwin had lost some money that morning. She was desperately anxious to find Landry, and to learn the truth of what had happened, and for a long moment after the last visitors had disappeared she remained at the foot of the gallery stairway, hoping that he would come for her. But she saw nothing of him, and soon remembered she had told him to come for her, only in case he was able to get away. No doubt he was too busy now. Even if Mr. Jadwin had won, the morning's work had evidently been of tremendous importance. This had been a great day for the wheat speculators. It was not surprising that Landry should be detained. She would wait till she saw him the next day to find out all that had taken place.

Page returned home. It was long past the hour for luncheon when she came into the dining-room of the North Avenue house.

"Where is my sister?" she asked of the maid, as she sat down to the table; "has she lunched yet?"

But it appeared that Mrs. Jadwin had sent down word to say that she wanted no lunch, that she had a headache and would remain in her room.

Page hurried through with her chocolate and salad, and ordering a cup of strong tea, carried it up to Laura's "sitting-room" herself.

Laura, in a long tea-gown lay back in the Madeira chair, her hands clasped behind her head, doing nothing apparently but looking out of the window. She was paler even than usual, and to Page's mind seemed preoccupied, and in a certain indefinite way tense and hard. Page, as she had told Landry that morning, had remarked this tenseness, this rigidity on the part of her sister, of late. But to-day it was more pronounced than ever. Something surely was the matter with Laura. She seemed like one who had staked everything upon a hazard and, blind to all else, was keeping back emotion with all her strength, while she watched and waited for the issue. Page guessed that her sister's trouble had to do with Jadwin's complete absorption in business, but she preferred to hold her peace. By nature the young girl "minded her own business," and Laura was not a woman who confided her troubles to anybody. Only once had Page presumed to meddle in her sister's affairs, and the result had not encouraged a repetition of the intervention. Since the affair of the silver match box she had kept her distance.

Laura on this occasion declined to drink the tea Page had brought. She wanted nothing, she said; her head ached a little, she only wished to lie down and be quiet.

"I've been down to the Board of Trade all the morning," Page remarked.

Laura fixed her with a swift glance; she demanded quickly:

"Did you see Curtis?"

"No—or, yes, once; he came out on the floor. Oh, Laura, it was so exciting there this morning. Something important happened, I know. I can't believe it's that way all the time. I'm afraid Mr. Jadwin lost a great deal of money. I heard some one behind me say so, but I couldn't understand what was going on. For months I've been trying to get a clear idea of wheat trading, just because it was Landry's business, but to-day I couldn't make anything of it at all."

"Did Curtis say he was coming home this evening?"

"No. Don't you understand, I didn't see him to talk to."

"Well, why didn't you, Page?"

"Why, Laura, honey, don't be cross. You don't know how rushed everything was. I didn't even try to see Landry."

"Did he seem very busy?"

"Who, Landry? I—"

"No, no, no, Curtis."

"Oh, I should say so. Why, Laura, I think, honestly, I think wheat went down to—oh, way down. They say that means so much to Mr. Jadwin, and it went down, down, down. It looked that way to me. Don't that mean that he'll lose a great deal of money? And Landry seemed so brave and courageous through it all. Oh, I felt for him so; I just wanted to go right into the Pit with him and stand by his shoulder."

Laura started up with a sharp gesture of impatience and exasperation, crying:

"Oh, what do I care about wheat—about this wretched scrambling for money. Curtis was busy, you say? He looked that way?"

Page nodded: "Everybody was," she said. Then she hazarded:

"I wouldn't worry, Laura. Of course, a man must give a great deal of time to his business. I didn't mind when Landry couldn't come home with me."

"Oh—Landry," murmured Laura.

On the instant Page bridled, her eyes snapping.

"I think that was very uncalled for," she exclaimed, sitting bolt upright, "and I can tell you this, Laura Jadwin, if you did care a little more about wheat—about your husband's business—if you had taken more of an interest in his work, if you had tried to enter more into his life, and be a help to him—and—and sympathise—and—" Page caught her breath, a little bewildered at her own vehemence and audacity. But she had committed herself now; recklessly she plunged on. "Just think; he may be fighting the battle of his life down there in La Salle Street, and you don't know anything about it—no, nor want to know. 'What do you care about wheat,' that's what you said. Well, I don't care either, just for the wheat itself, but it's Landry's business, his work; and right or wrong—" Page jumped to her feet, her fists tight shut, her face scarlet, her head upraised, "right or wrong, good or bad, I'd put my two hands into the fire to help him."

"What business—" began Laura; but Page was not to be interrupted. "And if he did leave me alone sometimes," she said; "do you think I would draw a long face, and think only of my own troubles. I guess he's got his own troubles too. If my husband had a battle to fight, do you think I'd mope and pine because he left me at home; no I wouldn't. I'd help him buckle his sword on, and when he came back to me I wouldn't tell him how lonesome I'd been, but I'd take care of him and cry over his wounds, and tell him to be brave–and–and–and I'd help him."

And with the words, Page, the tears in her eyes and the sobs in her throat, flung out of the room, shutting the door violently behind her.

Laura's first sensation was one of anger only. As always, her younger sister had presumed again to judge her, had chosen this day of all others, to annoy her. She gazed an instant at the closed door, then rose and put her chin in the air. She was right, and Page her husband, everybody, were wrong. She had been flouted, ignored. She paced the length of the room a couple of times, then threw herself down upon the couch, her chin supported on her palm.

As she crossed the room, however, her eye had been caught by an opened note from Mrs. Cressler, received the day before, and apprising her of the date of the funeral. At the sight, all the tragedy leaped up again in her mind and recollection, and in fancy she stood again in the back parlour of the Cressler home; her fingers pressed over her mouth to shut back the cries, horror and the terror of sudden death rending her heart, shaking the brain itself. Again and again since that dreadful moment had the fear come back, mingled with grief, with compassion, and the bitter sorrow of a kind friend gone forever from her side. And then, her resolution girding itself, her will power at fullest stretch, she had put the tragedy from her. Other and–for her–more momentous events impended. Everything in life, even death itself, must stand aside while her love was put to the test. Life and death were little things. Love only existed; let her husband's career fail; what did it import so only love stood the strain and issued from the struggle triumphant? And now, as she lay upon her couch, she crushed down all compunction for the pitiful calamity whose last scene she had discovered, her thoughts once more upon her husband and herself. Had the shock of that spectacle in the Cresslers' house, and the wearing suspense in which she had lived of late, so torn and disordered the delicate feminine nerves that a kind of hysteria animated and directed her impulses, her words, and actions? Laura did not know. She only knew that the day was going and that her husband neither came near her nor sent her word.

Even if he had been very busy, this was her birthday,–though he had lost millions! Could he not have sent even the foolishest little present to her, even a line–three words on a scrap of paper? But she checked herself. The day was not over yet; perhaps, perhaps he would remember her, after all, before the afternoon was over. He was managing a little surprise for her, no doubt. He knew what day this was. After their talk that Sunday in his smoking-room he would not forget. And, besides, it was the evening that he had promised should be hers. "If he loved her," she had said, he would give that evening to her. Never, never would Curtis fail her when conjured by that spell.

Laura had planned a little dinner for that night. It was to be served at eight. Page would have dined earlier; only herself and her husband were to be present. It was to be her birthday dinner. All the noisy, clamourous world should be excluded; no faintest rumble of the Pit would intrude. She would have him all to herself. He would, so she determined, forget everything else in his love for her. She would be beautiful as never before—brilliant, resistless, and dazzling. She would have him at her feet, her own, her own again, as much her own as her very hands. And before she would let him go he would forever and forever have abjured the Battle of the Street that had so often caught him from her. The Pit should not have him; the sweep of that great whirlpool should never again prevail against the power of love.

Yes, she had suffered, she had known the humiliation of a woman neglected. But it was to end now; her pride would never again be lowered, her love never again be ignored.

But the afternoon passed and evening drew on without any word from him. In spite of her anxiety, she yet murmured over and over again as she paced the floor of her room, listening for the ringing of the door bell:

"He will send word, he will send word. I know he will."

By four o'clock she had begun to dress. Never had she made a toilet more superb, more careful. She disdained a "costume" on this great evening. It was not to be "Theodora" now, nor "Juliet," nor "Carmen." It was to be only Laura Jadwin—just herself, unaided by theatricals, unadorned by tinsel. But it seemed consistent none the less to choose her most beautiful gown for the occasion, to panoply herself in every charm that was her own. Her dress, that closely sheathed the low, flat curves of her body and that left her slender arms and neck bare, was one shimmer of black scales, iridescent, undulating with light to her every movement. In the coils and masses of her black hair she fixed her two great cabochons of pearls, and clasped about her neck her palm-broad collaret of pearls and diamonds. Against one shoulder nodded a bunch of Jacqueminots, royal red, imperial.

It was hard upon six o'clock when at last she dismissed her maid. Left alone, she stood for a moment in front of her long mirror that reflected her image from head to foot, and at the sight she could not forbear a smile and a sudden proud lifting of her head. All the woman in her preened and plumed herself in the consciousness of the power of her beauty. Let the Battle of the Street clamour never so loudly now, let the suction of the Pit be never so strong, Eve triumphed. Venus toute entiere s'attachait a sa proie.

These women of America, these others who allowed business to draw their husbands from them more and more, who submitted to those cruel conditions that forced them to be content with the wreckage left after the storm and stress of the day's work—the jaded mind, the exhausted body, the faculties dulled by overwork—she was sorry for them. They, less radiant than herself, less potent to charm, could not call their husbands back. But she, Laura, was beautiful; she knew it; she gloried in her beauty. It was her strength. She felt the same pride in it as the warrior in a finely tempered weapon.

And to-night her beauty was brighter than ever. It was a veritable aureole that crowned her. She knew herself to be invincible. So only that he saw her thus, she knew that she would conquer. And he would come. "If he loved her," she had said. By his love for her he had promised; by his love she knew she would prevail.

And then at last, somewhere out of the twilight, somewhere out of those lowest, unplumbed depths of her own heart, came the first tremor of doubt, come the tardy vibration of the silver cord which Page had struck so sharply. Was it—after all—Love, that she cherished and strove for—love, or self-love? Ever since Page had spoken she seemed to have fought against the intrusion of this idea. But, little by little, it rose to the surface. At last, for an instant, it seemed to confront her.

Was this, after all, the right way to win her husband back to her—this display of her beauty, this parade of dress, this exploitation of self?

Self, self. Had she been selfish from the very first? What real interest had she taken in her husband's work? "Right or wrong, good or bad, I would put my two hands into the fire to help him." Was this the way? Was not this the only way? Win him back to her? What if there were more need for her to win back to him? Oh, once she had been able to say that love, the supreme triumph of a woman's life, was less a victory than a capitulation. Had she ordered her life upon that ideal? Did she even believe in the ideal at this day? Whither had this cruel cult of self led her?

Dimly Laura Jadwin began to see and to understand a whole new conception of her little world. The birth of a new being within her was not for that night. It was conception only—the sensation of a new element, a new force that was not herself, somewhere in the inner chambers of her being.

The woman in her was too complex, the fibres of character too intricate and mature to be wrenched into new shapes by any sudden revolution. But just so surely as the day was going, just so surely as the New Day would follow upon the night, conception had taken place within her. Whatever she did that evening, whatever came to her, through whatever crises she should hurry, she would not now be quite the same. She had been accustomed to tell herself that there were two Lauras. Now suddenly, behold, she seemed to recognise a third—a third that rose above and forgot the other two, that in some beautiful, mysterious way was identity ignoring self.

But the change was not to be abrupt. Very, very vaguely the thoughts came to her. The change would be slow, slow—would be evolution, not revolution. The consummation was to be achieved in the coming years. For to-night she was—what was she? Only a woman, weak, torn by emotion, driven by impulse, and entering upon what she imagined was a great crisis in her life.

But meanwhile the time was passing. Laura descended to the library and, picking up a book, composed herself to read. When six o'clock struck, she made haste to assure herself that of course she could not expect him exactly on the hour. No, she must make allowances; the day—as Page had suspected—had probably been an important one. He would be a little late, but he would come soon. "If you love me, you will come," she had said.

But an hour later Laura paced the room with tight-shut lips and burning cheeks. She was still alone; her day, her hour, was passing, and he had not so much as sent word. For a moment the thought occurred to her that he might perhaps be in great trouble, in great straits, that there was an excuse. But instantly she repudiated the notion.

"No, no," she cried, beneath her breath. "He should come, no matter what has happened. Or even, at the very least, he could send word."

The minutes dragged by. No roll of wheels echoed under the carriage porch; no step sounded at the outer door. The house was still, the street without was still, the silence of the midsummer evening widened, unbroken around her, like a vast calm pool. Only the musical Gregorians of the newsboys chanting the evening's extras from corner to corner of the streets rose into the air from time to time. She was once more alone. Was she to fail again? Was she to be set aside once more, as so often heretofore—set aside, flouted, ignored, forgotten? "If you love me," she had said.

And this was to be the supreme test. This evening was to decide which was the great influence of his life—was to prove whether or not love was paramount. This was the crucial hour. "And he knows it," cried Laura. "He knows it. He did not forget, could not have forgotten."

The half hour passed, then the hour, and as eight o'clock chimed from the clock over the mantelshelf Laura stopped, suddenly rigid, in the midst of the floor.

Her anger leaped like fire within her. All the passion of the woman scorned shook her from head to foot. At the very moment of her triumph she had been flouted, in the pitch of her pride! And this was not the only time. All at once the past disappointments, slights, and humiliations came again to her memory. She had pleaded, and had been rebuffed again and again; she had given all and had received neglect—she, Laura, beautiful beyond other women, who had known love, devoted service, and the most thoughtful consideration from her earliest girlhood, had been cast aside.

Suddenly she bent her head quickly, listening intently. Then she drew a deep breath, murmuring "At last, at last!"

For the sound of a footstep in the vestibule was unmistakable. He had come after all. But so late, so late! No, she could not be gracious at once; he must be made to feel how deeply he had offended; he must sue humbly, very humbly, for pardon. The servant's step sounded in the hall on the way towards the front door.

"I am in here, Matthew," she called. "In the library. Tell him I am in here."

She cast a quick glance at herself in the mirror close at hand, touched her hair with rapid fingers, smoothed the agitation from her forehead, and sat down in a deep chair near the fireplace, opening a book, turning her back towards the door.

She heard him come in, but did not move. Even as he crossed the floor she kept her head turned away. The footsteps paused near at hand. There was a moment's silence. Then slowly Laura, laying down her book, turned and faced him.

"With many very, very happy returns of the day," said Sheldon Corthell, as he held towards her a cluster of deep-blue violets.

Laura sprang to her feet, a hand upon her cheek, her eyes wide and flashing.

"You?" was all she had breath to utter. "You?"

The artist smiled as he laid the flowers upon the table. "I am going away again to-morrow," he said, "for always, I think. Have I startled you? I only came to say good-by—and to wish you a happy birthday."

"Oh you remembered!" she cried. "You remembered! I might have known you would."

But the revulsion had been too great. She had been wrong after all. Jadwin had forgotten. Emotions to which she could put no name swelled in her heart and rose in a quick, gasping sob to her throat. The tears sprang to her eyes. Old impulses, forgotten impetuosities whipped her on.

"Oh, you remembered, you remembered!" she cried again, holding out both her hands.

He caught them in his own.

"Remembered!" he echoed. "I have never forgotten."

"No, no," she replied, shaking her head, winking back the tears. "You don't understand. I spoke before I thought. You don't understand."

"I do, believe me, I do," he exclaimed. "I understand you better than you understand yourself."

Laura's answer was a cry.

"Oh, then, why did you ever leave me—you who did understand me? Why did you leave me only because I told you to go? Why didn't you make me love you then? Why didn't you make me understand myself?" She clasped her hands tight together upon her breast; her words, torn by her sobs, came all but incoherent from behind her shut teeth. "No, no!" she exclaimed, as he made towards her. "Don't touch me, don't touch me! It is too late."

"It is not too late. Listen—listen to me."

"Oh, why weren't you a man, strong enough to know a woman's weakness? You can only torture me now. Ah, I hate you! I hate you!"

"You love me! I tell you, you love me!" he cried, passionately, and before she was aware of it she was in his arms, his lips were against her lips, were on her shoulders, her neck.

"You love me!" he cried. "You love me! I defy you to say you do not."

"Oh, make me love you, then," she answered. "Make me believe that you do love me."

"Don't you know," he cried, "don't you know how I have loved you? Oh, from the very first! My love has been my life, has been my death, my one joy, and my one bitterness. It has always been you, dearest, year after year, hour after hour. And now I've found you again. And now I shall never, never let you go."

"No, no! Ah, don't, don't!" she begged. "I implore you. I am weak, weak. Just a word, and I would forget everything."

"And I do speak that word, and your own heart answers me in spite of you, and you will forget—forget everything of unhappiness in your life—"

"Please, please," she entreated, breathlessly. Then, taking the leap: "Ah, I love you, I love you!"

"—Forget all your unhappiness," he went on, holding her close to him. "Forget the one great mistake we both made. Forget everything, everything, everything but that we love each other."

"Don't let me think, then," she cried. "Don't let me think. Make me forget everything, every little hour, every little moment that has passed before this day. Oh, if I remembered once, I would kill you, kill you with my hands! I don't know what I am saying," she moaned, "I don't know what I am saying. I am mad, I think. Yes—I—it must be that." She pulled back from him, looking into his face with wide-opened eyes.

"What have I said, what have we done, what are you here for?"

"To take you away," he answered, gently, holding her in his arms, looking down into her eyes. "To take you far away with me. To give my whole life to making you forget that you were ever unhappy."

"And you will never leave me alone—never once?"

"Never, never once."

She drew back from him, looking about the room with unseeing eyes, her fingers plucking and tearing at the lace of her dress; her voice was faint and small, like the voice of a little child.

"I—I am afraid to be alone. Oh, I must never be alone again so long as I shall live. I think I should die."

"And you never shall be; never again. Ah, this is my birthday, too, sweetheart. I am born again to-night."

Laura clung to his arm; it was as though she were in the dark, surrounded by the vague terrors of her girlhood. "And you will always love me, love me, love me?" she whispered. "Sheldon, Sheldon, love me always, always, with all your heart and soul and strength."

Tears stood in Corthell's eyes as he answered:

"God forgive whoever—whatever has brought you to this pass," he said.

And, as if it were a realisation of his thought, there suddenly came to the ears of both the roll of wheels upon the asphalt under the carriage porch and the trampling of iron-shod hoofs.

"Is that your husband?" Corthell's quick eye took in Laura's disarranged coiffure, one black lock low upon her neck, the roses at her shoulder crushed and broken, and the bright spot on either cheek.

"Is that your husband?"

"My husband—I don't know." She looked up at him with unseeing eyes. "Where is my husband? I have no husband. You are letting me remember," she cried, in terror. "You are letting me remember. Ah, no, no, you don't love me! I hate you!"

Quickly he bent and kissed her.

"I will come for you to-morrow evening," he said. "You will be ready then to go with me?"

"Ready then? Yes, yes, to go with you anywhere."

He stood still a moment, listening. Somewhere a door closed. He heard the hoofs upon the asphalt again.

"Good-by," he whispered. "God bless you! Good-by till to-morrow night." And with the words he was gone. The front door of the house closed quietly.

Had he come back again? Laura turned in her place on the long divan at the sound of a heavy tread by the door of the library.

Then an uncertain hand drew the heavy curtain aside. Jadwin, her husband, stood before her, his eyes sunken deep in his head, his face dead white, his hand shaking. He stood for a long instant in the middle of the room, looking at her. Then at last his lips moved:

"Old girl.... Honey."

Laura rose, and all but groped her way towards him, her heart beating, the tears streaming down her face.

"My husband, my husband!"

Together they made their way to the divan, and sank down upon it side by side, holding to each other, trembling and fearful, like children in the night.

"Honey," whispered Jadwin, after a while. "Honey, it's dark, it's dark. Something happened.... I don't remember," he put his hand uncertainly to his head, "I can't remember very well; but it's dark—a little."

"It's dark," she repeated, in a low whisper. "It's dark, dark. Something happened. Yes. I must not remember."

They spoke no further. A long time passed. Pressed close together, Curtis Jadwin and his wife sat there in the vast, gorgeous room, silent and trembling, ridden with unnamed fears, groping in the darkness.

And while they remained thus, holding close by one another, a prolonged and wailing cry rose suddenly from the street, and passed on through the city under the stars and the wide canopy of the darkness.

"Extra, oh-h-h, extra! All about the Smash of the Great Wheat Corner! All about the Failure of Curtis Jadwin!"

CONCLUSION

The evening had closed in wet and misty. All day long a chill wind had blown across the city from off the lake, and by eight o'clock, when Laura and Jadwin came down to the dismantled library, a heavy rain was falling.

Laura gave Jadwin her arm as they made their way across the room—their footsteps echoing strangely from the uncarpeted boards.

"There, dear," she said. "Give me the valise. Now sit down on the packing box there. Are you tired? You had better put your hat on. It is full of draughts here, now that all the furniture and curtains are out."

"No, no. I'm all right, old girl. Is the hack there yet?"

"Not yet. You're sure you're not tired?" she insisted. "You had a pretty bad siege of it, you know, and this is only the first week you've been up. You remember how the doctor—"

"I've had too good a nurse," he answered, stroking her hand, "not to be fine as a fiddle by now. You must be tired yourself, Laura. Why, for whole days there—and nights, too, they tell me—you never left the room."

She shook her head, as though dismissing the subject.

"I wonder," she said, sitting down upon a smaller packing-box and clasping a knee in her hands, "I wonder what the West will be like. Do you know I think I am going to like it, Curtis?"

"It will be starting in all over again, old girl," he said, with a warning shake of his head. "Pretty hard at first, I'm afraid."

She laughed an almost contemptuous note.

"Hard! Now?" She took his hand and laid it to her cheek.

"By all the rules you ought to hate me," he began. "What have I done for you but hurt you and, at last, bring you to—"

But she shut her gloved hand over his mouth.

"Stop!" she cried. "Hush, dear. You have brought me the greatest happiness of my life."

Then under her breath, her eyes wide and thoughtful, she murmured:

"A capitulation and not a triumph, and I have won a victory by surrendering."

"Hey—what?" demanded Jadwin. "I didn't hear."

"Never mind," she answered. "It was nothing. 'The world is all before us where to choose,' now, isn't it? And this big house and all the life we have led in it was just an incident in our lives—an incident that is closed."

"Looks like it, to look around this room," he said, grimly. "Nothing left but the wall paper. What do you suppose are in these boxes?"

"They're labelled 'books and portieres.'"

"Who bought 'em I wonder? I'd have thought the party who bought the house would have taken them. Well, it was a wrench to see the place and all go so dirt cheap, and the 'Thetis', too, by George! But I'm glad now. It's as though we had lightened ship." He looked at his watch. "That hack ought to be here pretty soon. I'm glad we checked the trunks from the house; gives us more time."

"Oh, by the way," exclaimed Laura, all at once opening her satchel. "I had a long letter from Page this morning, from New York. Do you want to hear what she has to say? I've only had time to read part of it myself. It's the first one I've had from her since their marriage."

He lit a cigar.

"Go ahead," he said, settling himself on the box. "What does Mrs. Court have to say?"

"'My dearest sister,'" began Laura. "'Here we are, Landry and I, in New York at last. Very tired and mussed after the ride on the cars, but in a darling little hotel where the proprietor is head cook and everybody speaks French. I know my accent is improving, and Landry has learned any quantity of phrases already. We are reading George Sand out loud, and are making up the longest vocabulary. To-night we are going to a concert, and I've found out that there's a really fine course of lectures to be given soon on "Literary Tendencies," or something like that. Quel chance. Landry is intensely interested. You've no idea what a deep mind he has, Laura—a real thinker.

"'But here's really a big piece of news. We may not have to give up our old home where we lived when we first came to Chicago. Aunt Wess' wrote the other day to say that, if you were willing, she would rent it, and then sublet all the lower floor to Landry and me, so we could have a real house over our heads and not the under side of the floor of the flat overhead. And she is such an old dear, I know we could all get along beautifully. Write me about this as soon as you can. I know you'll be willing, and Aunt Wess, said she'd agree to whatever rent you suggested.

"'We went to call on Mrs. Cressler day before yesterday. She's been here nearly a fortnight by now, and is living with a maiden sister of hers in a very beautiful house fronting Central Park (not so beautiful as our palace on North Avenue. Never, never will I forget that house). She will probably stay here now always. She says the very sight of the old neighbourhoods in Chicago would be more than she could bear. Poor Mrs. Cressler! How fortunate for her that her sister'—and so on, and so on," broke in Laura, hastily.

"Read it, read it," said Jadwin, turning sharply away. "Don't skip a line. I want to hear every word."

"That's all there is to it," Laura returned. "'We'll be back,'" she went on, turning a page of the letter, "'in about three weeks, and Landry will take up his work in that railroad office. No more speculating for him, he says. He talks of Mr. Jadwin continually. You never saw or heard of such devotion. He says that Mr. Jadwin is a genius, the greatest financier in the country, and that he knows he could have won if they all hadn't turned against him that day. He never gets tired telling me that Mr. Jadwin has been a father to him—the kindest, biggest-hearted man he ever knew—'"

Jadwin pulled his mustache rapidly.

"Pshaw, pish, nonsense—little fool!" he blustered.

"He simply worshipped you from the first, Curtis," commented Laura. "Even after he knew I was to marry you. He never once was jealous, never once would listen to a word against you from any one."

"Well—well, what else does Mrs. Court say?"

"'I am glad to hear,'" read Laura, "'that Mr. Gretry did not fail, though Landry tells me he must have lost a great deal of money. Landry tells me that eighteen brokers' houses failed in Chicago the day after Mr. Gretry suspended. Isabel sent us a wedding present—a lovely medicine chest full of homoeopathic medicines, little pills and things, you know. But, as Landry and I are never sick and both laugh at homoeopathy, I declare I don't know just what we will do with it. Landry is as careful of me as though I were a wax doll. But I do wish he would think more of his own health. He never will wear his mackintosh in rainy weather. I've been studying his tastes so carefully. He likes French light opera better than English, and bright colours in his cravats, and he simply adores stuffed tomatoes.

"'We both send our love, and Landry especially wants to be remembered to Mr. Jadwin. I hope this letter will come in time for us to wish you both bon voyage and bon succes. How splendid of Mr. Jadwin to have started his new business even while he was convalescent! Landry says he knows he will make two or three more fortunes in the next few years.

"'Good-by, Laura, dear. Ever your loving sister,

"'PAGE COURT.

"'P.S.—I open this letter again to tell you that we met Mr. Corthell on the street yesterday. He sails for Europe to-day.'"

"Oh," said Jadwin, as Laura put the letter quickly down, "Corthell—that artist chap. By the way, whatever became of him?"

Laura settled a comb in the back of her hair.

"He went away," she said. "You remember—I told you—told you all about it."

She would have turned away her head, but he laid a hand upon her shoulder.

"I remember," he answered, looking squarely into her eyes, "I remember nothing—only that I have been to blame for everything. I told you once—long ago—that I understood. And I understand now, old girl, understand as I never did before. I fancy we both have been living according to a wrong notion of things. We started right when we were first married, but I worked away from it somehow and pulled you along with me. But we've both been through a great big change, honey, a great big change, and we're starting all over again.... Well, there's the carriage, I guess."

They rose, gathering up their valises.

"Hoh!" said Jadwin. "No servants now, Laura, to carry our things down for us and open the door, and it's a hack, old girl, instead of the victoria or coupe."

"What if it is?" she cried. "What do 'things,' servants, money, and all amount to now?"

As Jadwin laid his hand upon the knob of the front door, he all at once put down his valise and put his arm about his wife. She caught him about the neck and looked deep into his eyes a long moment. And then, without speaking, they kissed each other.

In the outer vestibule, he raised the umbrella and held it over her head.

"Hold it a minute, will you, Laura?" he said.

He gave it into her hand and swung the door of the house shut behind him. The noise woke a hollow echo throughout all the series of empty, denuded rooms. Jadwin slipped the key in his pocket.

"Come," he said.

They stepped out from the vestibule. It was already dark. The rain was falling in gentle slants through the odorous, cool air. Across the street in the park the first leaves were beginning to fall; the lake lapped and washed quietly against the stone embankments and a belated bicyclist stole past across the asphalt, with the silent flitting of a bat, his lamp throwing a fan of orange-coloured haze into the mist of rain.

In the street in front of the house the driver, descending from the box, held open the door of the hack. Jadwin handed Laura in, gave an address to the driver, and got in himself, slamming the door after. They heard the driver mount to his seat and speak to his horses.

"Well," said Jadwin, rubbing the fog from the window pane of the door, "look your last at the old place, Laura. You'll never see it again."

But she would not look.

"No, no," she said. "I'll look at you, dearest, at you, and our future, which is to be happier than any years we have ever known."

Jadwin did not answer other than by taking her hand in his, and in silence they drove through the city towards the train that was to carry them to the new life. A phase of the existences of each was closed definitely. The great corner was a thing of the past; the great corner with the long train of disasters its collapse had started. The great failure had precipitated smaller failures, and the aggregate of smaller failures had pulled down one business house after another. For weeks afterward, the successive crashes were like the shock and reverberation of undermined buildings toppling to their ruin. An important bank had suspended payment, and hundreds of depositors had found their little fortunes swept away. The ramifications of the catastrophe were unbelievable. The whole tone of financial affairs seemed changed. Money was "tight" again, credit was withdrawn. The business world began to speak of hard times, once more.

But Laura would not admit her husband was in any way to blame. He had suffered, too. She repeated to herself his words, again and again:

"The wheat cornered itself. I simply stood between two sets of circumstances. The wheat cornered me, not I the wheat."

And all those millions and millions of bushels of Wheat were gone now. The Wheat that had killed Cressler, that had ingulfed Jadwin's fortune and all but unseated reason itself; the Wheat that had intervened like a great torrent to drag her husband from her side and drown him in the roaring vortices of the Pit, had passed on, resistless, along its ordered and predetermined courses from West to East? like a vast Titanic flood, had passed, leaving Death and Ruin in its wake, but bearing Life and Prosperity to the crowded cities and centres of Europe.

For a moment, vague, dark perplexities assailed her, questionings as to the elemental forces, the forces of demand and supply that ruled the world. This huge resistless Nourisher of the Nations—why was it that it could not reach the People, could not fulfil its destiny, unmarred by all this suffering, unattended by all this misery?

She did not know. But as she searched, troubled and disturbed for an answer, she was aware of a certain familiarity in the neighbourhood the carriage was traversing. The strange sense of having lived through this scene, these circumstances, once before, took hold upon her.

She looked out quickly, on either hand, through the blurred glasses of the carriage doors. Surely, surely, this locality had once before impressed itself upon her imagination. She turned to her husband, an exclamation upon her lips; but Jadwin, by the dim light of the carriage lanterns, was studying a railroad folder.

All at once, intuitively, Laura turned in her place, and raising the flap that covered the little window at the back of the carriage, looked behind. On either side of the vista in converging lines stretched the tall office buildings, lights burning in a few of their windows, even yet. Over the end of the street the lead-coloured sky was broken by a pale faint haze of light, and silhouetted against this rose a sombre mass, unbroken by any glimmer, rearing a black and formidable facade against the blur of the sky behind it.

And this was the last impression of the part of her life that that day brought to a close; the tall gray office buildings, the murk of rain, the haze of light in the heavens, and raised against it, the pile of the Board of Trade building, black, monolithic, crouching on its foundations like a monstrous sphinx with blind eyes, silent, grave—crouching there without a sound, without sign of life, under the night and the drifting veil of rain.

CPSIA information can be obtained
at www.ICGtesting.com
Printed in the USA
BVHW030938300119
538840BV00039B/267/P